TURNER'S AWAKENING

JAMES SEYMOUR

To find out more about this book
including the paperback edition, please visit:
www.vividpublishing.com.au/turnersawakening

ISBN: 978-1-922565-81-5 (second revised edition)
Published by Vivid Publishing
A division of Fontaine Publishing Group
P.O. Box 948, Fremantle
Western Australia 6959
www.vividpublishing.com.au

Disclaimer

In this publication, all characters – other than the obvious historical figures – are fictitious, and any resemblance to real persons, living or dead, is purely coincidental.

This novel is set primarily in the Guildford area of the UK and spanning some cities and outlying settlements of Scotland, some towns and suburbs of Ireland, Kingston, Jamacia and some references to South Africa. The combination of historical information and fictional detail has been attempted, and the author has provided explanatory footnotes where possible. Some place names and sites are fictitious, and any resemblance of these fictitious names and sites to actual places is purely coincidental.

Books by James Seymour

Turner's Rage, Vivid Publishing 2020
Turner's Awakening, Vivid Publishing 2022

. . . .

Keep an eye out for the release date
for book three of the Turner series.

Published by Vivid Publishing
www.vividpublishing.com.au

Many thanks to

Faye and Trev
Without your inspiration, this series would never have been possible

Judith
For being our guide and friend in England

Errol
Your splendid book[1] helped immensely in cross-checking research

David
For your wonderful help in editing and continual encouragement

Julieanne
For putting up with me while I ventured into another time

Jason and Nicola-Jane
For putting up with my requests and many changes

[1] 'The Boy Who Told Stories' by Errol Seymour, Vivid Publishing, 2019, an intriguing account of a pioneering family in Western Australia. If you're a history buff you must read this splendid book. Recommended by James Seymour.

Foreword

The language used in this story is modern English, with a few hints of the Georgian and Regency eras. The purpose here is purely making the novel easy to read – helping everyone with their time management.

The novel is the second in the Turner series and follows the adventures of the Turner family, particularly William, in a time of rapid change. While writing the first novel, I found the characters so interesting that I decided to expand the series, allowing more opportunity for developing the character of other members of the Turner family. 'Turner's Awakening' is a continually growing plot filled with deep emotions, amazing adventures, and surprising outcomes.

The list of characters reveals a large cast. Some economy was necessary to ensure the novel was manageable, particularly minimising the number of pages has been challenging. Everyone has their favourite characters, so my apologies to those whose favourites play a lesser role this time.

The benefit of these long novels is that the reader receives so much more for their money. It also allows more interaction with the characters, so they become your friends as you read along.

The focus in this book sees Anne Turner take centre stage in Part 1 and Part 2, with Jonathan Turner and William becoming more prominent in Part 3. As in real-life situations, the issues are complex and challenging, developing our understanding of human nature. Readers who have finished 'Turner's Rage' will be immediately at home in this novel. For those who start with 'Turner's Awakening', I have added a 'Prologue' that provides sufficient coverage of events in the previous book.

The extensive 'List of Characters' will help the reader check back on family lines and relationships.

This second novel has a wealth of experiences for the avid reader to explore. Locked away while writing during Covid on cold winter nights, I drifted back into the history and stories of my ancestors. Much of the inspiration for this series comes from their exploits. I hope I have captured both the English and the Irish character in the following chapters.

Now it is time for the beginning of the adventure. Hold on tight as the plot accelerates until the novel's last page.

Find a quiet, comfy place with a hot coffee and an Irish liqueur and start thumbing through the pages. I hope you enjoy the second book in this series as much as I loved writing it.

James Seymour, October 2021

Prologue

Sunday 18 November 1826

We join the Turner family at 'Huntley', their rented lodgings at Greenwich, on the day following the wedding of Mr Thomas Turner, son of Jonathan and Eleanora, and Miss Marion Steele, daughter of Alexander and Jennifer Steele and niece of Marjorie McPherson, Hamish McPherson's wife.

The successful wedding was the second for the Turner Family in 1826. Bethany Turner, Jonathan and Eleanora's eldest daughter, married Doctor Neville Bassington in October, with Thomas and Marion following in November. Anne's engagement to Sir Robert South has been announced, and Lady Emma South, devotedly in love with young Doctor David Sopwith, waits for a proposal. There seems no end to marital activity changing the family dynamics.

Young William Turner hopes that relations between himself and his father are improving. However, despite encouragement from his mother and others, he still mistrusts his father. Jonathan Turner's dislike for his youngest son continues simmering under the surface while Neville Bassington keeps a close watch on Jonathan ensuring William's safety.

The Turner businesses prosper along with Hamish McPherson's pub network. The size of the company and the new steam-powered flour mill require significant operational change, and Anne and Jonathan struggle with the pressures of development. Meanwhile, in Guildford, England, the industrial revolution is changing everything rapidly, often resulting in violent reactions from the displaced workers. The class system is under attack as industrialists accumulate colossal wealth and shake Britain loose from the rural lifestyle.

Anne faces the challenge of navigating her entry into the upper class and managing a business in a man's world. Clementine commences work in her father's business office and must carve out a place for herself outside her home. Madeline, almost through childhood, stays close to her mother and encourages Eleanora through bouts of ill health.

Robert is disappointed in his brother, Sir Hugh, when he discovers the estate has been mismanaged and its financial position perilous. Robert and Anne have no choice and commence enquiries about where the lost money has gone. Meanwhile, Sir Hugh decides on a sudden departure for Jamaica, where he will inspect the family plantations.

In Ireland, the Republicans are recovering from the loss of the captured Royal Navy frigate *Providence*. We meet some new characters in Chapter 1 of 'Turner's Awakening' who will lead us deep into the Irish heartland. Anne is unaware her fiancée will soon be at battle again but on far more dangerous grounds. The Turner family have caught the eye of Mrs Janet Stubbington, a mysterious government operative.

In Greenwich, William, unaware of the changing world around him, plays with dogs and makes mischief as all seven-year-old boys do!

Turner's Rage

List of Characters

November 1826 – April 1827

Note: The same character may be shown in two or more places depending on changes in their status as the story continues. A character introduced in this book may not be displayed depending on the dramatic impact.

SURREY, ENGLAND
GUILDFORD

The Jonathan Turner Family of Guildford

Jonathan Turner	Father of William	Baker and Business Owner
Eleanora Turner	Mother of William	Wife of Jonathan Turner
Thomas Jonathan Turner	Son of Jonathan & Eleanora	Baker
Bethany Bassington (nee Turner)	Daughter of Jonathan & Eleanora	Wife of Dr Bassington
Anne Jessica Turner	Daughter of Jonathan & Eleanora	Accountant & Home help
Clementine Felicity Turner	Daughter of Jonathan & Eleanora	Home help
Madeline Amber Turner	Daughter of Jonathan & Eleanora	Child
Simeon Henry Turner	Son of Jonathan & Eleanora	Child
William Earnest Turner	Son of Jonathan & Eleanora	Child
Marcia Angela Turner	Daughter of Jonathan & Eleanora	Child

Service Staff of the Turner Family

Mrs Jennings	Cook
Miss Ivy Grey	Assistant Cook
Miss Jessica (Jess) Swamp	Scullery Maid

Miss Aggie Peters	Maid
Mrs Ethel Nibley	Mrs Turner's Maid
Miss Rosalind Nibley	Mrs Nibley's daughter
Joseph Hinge	Stable Hand
Nanny Smithers	Jeremy's nanny.

The Thomas Turner Family of Guildford

Thomas Jonathan Turner	Son of Jonathan & Eleanora Brewer
Mrs Marion Turner (nee Steele)	Wife of Thomas and Daughter of Alexander & Jennifer Steele

Turner Business Offices, Guildford

Miss Daisy Eltham	Receptionist

Turner Family Dogs

Nosey

Family Doctors and Medical Staff

Dr Neville Bassington	Doctor
Dr David Sopwith	Doctor
Mrs Gertrude Plumridge	Midwife

The Bassington Family of Guildford

Doctor Neville Bassington	Doctor – Guildford Medical Practice
Mrs Bethany Bassington (nee Turner)	Wife of Neville and first daughter of Jonathan Turner

Service Staff:

Mrs Ivy Goodhew	Housekeeper and Cook

The South Family of Guildford Residence Name: 'Porting'

Captain Sir Robert Douglas South	Second Son of the Earl of Fintelton, Sir David South
Lady Anne Jessica South (nee Turner)	Wife of Sir Robert

Service Staff:

Mrs Norma Kirby	Housekeeper and Cook
Miss Mary Hedge	Lady's Maid to Lady South
Mr James Pocket	Carriage Driver, Footman and Stable Hand

The Local Church, Guildford

The Reverend Andrew Taggart	Rector
Mrs Laura Taggart	The Rector's wife and church worker
Mrs Glossip	Church worker
Mr Jonathan Turner	Chairman, Parish Council
Mr Rupert Smith	Parish Council
Mr Blake Wood	Parish Council & Council Secretary & Solicitor
Miss Ruby Bowers	Student – Church School
Miss Dawn Luckett	Student – Church School
Master Edward Wood	Student – Church School
Master Samuel Birch	Student – Church School

The Turner Bakery

Mr Jeb Hiscock	Bakery Manager
Mr Peter Hammer	Senior Foreman
Mr Aaron Hall	Baker
Miss Rose Bell	Baker
Miss Sophia Stanton	Pastry Baker
Miss Heather Gant	Bakers Assistant
Mr Ralph Fenn	Bakery Cart Driver
Miss Audrey Stern	Senior Accounts Clerk
Mr Robert Baxter	Stable Manager
Judd Hedge	Stable Man

Hurst's Tailors and Seamstresses

Mrs Fiona Smith	Seamstress and Guildford Shop Manager
Mr Lionel Wall	Taylor and Manager Woking, and Manager of the Store chain

The Steam-Powered Flour Mill

Mr Terence Spencer	Mill Manager
Mrs Lydia Spencer	Wife of Terence
Master Levi Spencer	Son of Terence and Lydia
Miss Andrea Spencer	Daughter of Terence and Lydia

The Sopwith Family, Guildford, Surrey

Dr David Sopwith	Local Doctor	Guildford Medical Practice
Miss Victoria Sopwith	David's Sister	

Service Staff for the Sopwith Family

Mrs Molly Lane	Housekeeper
Miss Judith Malone	Victoria Sopwith's Maid
Mr Stuart Winks	Carriage Driver and Footman

The Watson Family of Guildford

Dr Bryan Watson	Local Doctor, formerly General Practitioner, Killarow, Isle of Islay, Scotland
Mrs Jessica Watson	Wife of Dr Watson
Master Archie Watson	Son of Doctor Watson
Miss Sophie Watson	Daughter of Doctor Watson

The Petherton Family, Cloverdale Chase, Guildford

Mr Benjamin Petherton	Resident of Guildford
Mrs Miriam Petherton	Wife of Benjamin (Deceased)
Miss Clare Petherton	Daughter of Mr Petherton
Mrs Irene Preston	Miss Clare Petherton's Governess
Butler	Mr John Steadman
Mr Samuel Grey	Head Gardener
'Ralph'	Petherton Family Dog

The Wood Family of Guildford

Mr Blake Wood	Attorney
Mrs Mary Wood	Wife of Blake
Miss Cloe Wood	Daughter of Blake and Mary
Master Edward Wood	Son of Blake and Mary

The Guilford Community

Mr Rupert Smith	Mayor & Parish Council Member
Mrs Marjorie Smith	Wife of Rupert
Mr Blake Wood	Solicitor
Mr Isaiah Linton	Blacksmith
Mr Ian Robinson	Robinson's Builders
Doctor Wilfred Chenning	Medical Practitioner, Woodbridge

Guildford Constabulary

Mr Michael Rawlins	Parish Constable

The Guildford Institute

Mr Henry Sharples	Institute Volunteer Officer

The Guildford Medical Practice

Dr Neville Bassington	Founding Partner
Dr David Sopwith	Founding Partner
Miss Jenny Swift	Nurse and Receptionist

Lions Bank of Guildford

Mr Thomas Meyhew	Founder and Owner
Mr Lawrence Appleby	High Street Branch Manager
Mr John Short	Bank Teller and Clerk
Miss Stella Morton	Mr Meyhew's, Secretary

WOKING

The Local Church at Woking

Rev Charles Upton

Mrs Wendy Upton

EPSOM and EWELL

The Turner Family of Ewell

Richard Turner	Uncle of William, Brother of Jonathon, Pub Owner 'The Black Swan'
Sarah Turner	Aunt of William, wife of Richard

Oliver Turner	Son of Richard & Sarah	Pub Manager, Epsom
Harry Turner	Son of Richard & Sarah	Pub Manager, Ewell
Katherine Turner	Daughter of Richard & Sarah	Child

The Racing Horse Pub, Epson

| Mr Oliver Turner | Manager, Racing Horse Pub and son of Richard Turner |
| Mr Thomas Baxter | Stable Manager |

WEST SUSSEX, ENGLAND

The South Family of Fintelton Manor

Earl Sir David South	Earl of Fintelton and Lord of the Manor
Countess Lady Jane South	Wife of Sir David
Sir Hugh David South	Son and Entailed Heir of Sir David
Sir Robert Douglas South RN	Son of Sir David
Lady Emma Felicity South	Daughter of Sir David

Service Staff of the South Family

Mr Malcolm Stem	'Fintelton' Estate Manager
Mr Thomas Pike	Butler
Mrs Cora Walsh	Housekeeper
Mr Henry Barrett	Earls Valet
Mrs Judy Wapples	Cook
Miss Margaret Lane	Lady Jane's personal maid
Miss Jane Winston	Lady Emma's maid
Miss Sally Johnson	Maid
Miss Hope Smith	Maid

In-Laws of the Souths, Wimbleton, London

| Sir John Philps | Brother of Lady Jane South |
| Lady Angela Philps | Sir John's wife |

Tenant Farmers of Fintelton

| Mr Michael Merton | Tenant Farmer |
| Mrs Jenny Merton | Wife of Michael |

The Rows Untied Bank, Portsmouth

Mr Francis Hadley	Branch Manager
Mr Charles Stillsen	Head Teller
Mr Dudley Hankerton	Supervisor, Ledger Department

HAMPSHIRE, ENGLAND

The Black Whale Pub, Portsmouth

Michael McGinty	Proprietor, The Black Whale Pub
Mrs Biddie Quinn	Manager, The Black Whale Pub

The Johnstone Family of Basking Manor, Hampshire

Lady Lily Johnstone	Daughter of the Earl of Baskin

BEDFORDSHIRE, ENGLAND

The Green Family Bedfordshire

Sir Harrold Green	Deceased
Lady Fiona Green (nee Furness)	Widow of Sir Harrold and daughter of the Earl of Calsand

The Wendarm Family Bedfordshire

Sir Peter Wendarm	Deceased
Lady Clarissa Wendarm	Daughter of Viscount Martinhoof

LONDON, ENGLAND

Huntley House, Greenwich Rented during the Steele Turner Wedding

Mr Charles Boot	Butler
Miss Mary Troath	Lady's Maid
Miss Annabelle Black	Maid

"Harting" House, St James Square London Residence of the Earl and Countess of Fintelton

Mr Matthew Staines	Butler
Mrs Cora Walsh	Housekeeper
Mrs Trudy Falconer	Assistant Housekeeper
Mr Henry Barrett	Earls Valet

Miss Judy Wapples	Cook
Miss Margaret Lane	Lady Jane's maid
Miss Jane Winston	Lady Emma's maid

Manifold & Stout Attorneys

| Mr Michael Manifold | Senior Partner, Manifold & Stout (Deceased) |
| Mr Evan Finchley | Senior Partner, Manifold & Stout |

The Bassington Family of London

Mr David Bassington	Newspaper Owner and Bookseller
Mrs Jennifer Bassington	Wife of David
Doctor Neville Winston Bassington	Son of David & Jennifer , RN
Miss Megan Bassington	Daughter of David & Jennifer

The McPherson Family of Greenwich

Mr Hamish McPherson	Brewer and Business Manager	
Mrs Marjorie McPherson	Spouse of Hamish	
Mr Douglas McPherson	Son of Hamish	Brewery Manager Glasgow
Mr Archie McPherson	Son of Hamish	Brewery Manager Edinburgh
Mr Lachlan McPherson	Son of Hamish	Brewery Manager Edinburgh
Mrs Taye McPherson	Wife of Lachlan	
Mr James McPherson	Son of Hamish	Brewery Manager & Business Man, Glasgow
Miss Isla O'Connor	Partner of James	

Service Staff – McPherson Family

Jenkins	Butler
Babcock	Coach Driver
Miss Jones	Nanny

The Steele Family of Woolwich

| Mr Alexander Steele | Engineer & Founder of Woods Artillery Foundry |
| Mrs Jennifer Steele | Wife of Alexander - Deceased |

Mrs Marion Turner (nee Steele)	Daughter of Alexander & Jennifer

Local Church, Greenwich

Archdeacon Rufus Handle	Rector and Rural Dean
Mrs Felicity Handle	Wife of Archdeacon Handle

Royal Academy

Sir Bertram Penting, Marquess of Questlow	Member and Supporter of the Royal Academy
Lady Sarah Penting, Marchioness Of Questlow	Wife of Sir Bertram
Mr Edmond Fortescue	Master of Ceremonies, Irish Benefit Ball and Chair of the Irish Benefit Charity, and Member of the Royal Academy
Mrs Dorothy Fortescue	Wife of Mr Fortescue

Polkinghorne Home, Mayfair, London

Mr Stephen Polkinghorne	Importer, Polkinghorne Imports Plc.
Miss Eliza Best	Nurse
Mr Timothy Nottle	Butler
Miss Sadie Fullham	Maid
Doctor John Arrowsmith	Family Doctor

BRITISH NAVY

The Crew of HMS Shadow Under the Command of Captain Robert South

Captain Sir Robert South	Captain
Sargent Michael Swanton	Captain's Servant
Lieutenant Stewart Fenton	First Lieutenant
Lieutenant Adrian Miles	Second Lieutenant
Lieutenant Samuel Peters	Third Lieutenant
Lieutenant Richard Hemming	Lieutenant Quartermaster
Lieutenant Wallace Kennedy	Lieutenant
Lieutenant Richard Hemsworth	Lieutenant
Lieutenant Reginald Smith	Surgeon

Mr William Collins	Midshipman
Mr Albert Kent	Midshipman
Mr Kevin Trotters	Master (Sailing Master)
Mr John Fulcher	Master at Arms
Major Horace Coombes	Marine Commander
Lieutenant Stanley White	2IC to Major Coombes
Sergeant Philip Wait	Marines Sergeant

The Crew of HMS Restless Under the Command of Lieutenant Frederick Ham

Commander Frederick Ham	Commander

Admiralty

Admiral Sir Franklin Crouch	First Naval Lord
Lady Katherine Crouch	Wife of Admiral Crouch
Sir Cecil Fowey, Earl of Dawlting	Advisor to the Board of Navy
Lady Hannah Fowey Countess of Dawlting	Wife of the Earl of Dawlting
Admiral Walter Bird, Viscount of Stantstead and Killarney	Member Admiralty Board
Lady Patricia Bird, Viscountess of Stantstead and Killupan	Wife of Admiral Bird
Colonel Jonathan Scott	Admiralty Security Chief of Staff
Captain Russell Hastings	Deputy to Colonel Scott

Flagship, Commander in Chief, Blue Fleet, Portsmouth

Admiral Sir Tristan Sutherland	Commander in Chief, Portsmouth Blue Fleet
Lady Amanda Sutherland	Wife of Sir Tristan
Commodore Richard Jacobs	Secretary to Admiral Sutherland
Captain Rosco Graham	Captain of the Flagship

Royal Navy Offices, Portsmouth

Lieutenant Martin Russell   Administration Officer

United Kingdom Investments

Mrs Janet Stubbington   Wife of Frank Stubbington – Deceased

Mr Charles Stubbington   Son of Janet

Mr Ross Stubbington   Son of Janet

JAMAICA
Stephenson's Attorneys Kingston Jamaica

Mr William Stephenson   Senior Partner

Mis Jill Hall   Receptionist and Clerk

Kingston, Jamaica, Community

Dr Ronald Cowper   General Practitioner, Kingston City

Nurse Cynthia Jackson   General Practice, Kingston City

Mr Stephen Polkinghorne   Plantation Owner and Businessman

Grand Hotel, Kingston, Jamaica

Miss Sandy White   Maid

Governor's Office, Kingston, Jamaica

The Right Hon. General Sir William Wade   Governor of Jamaica

The Right Hon Lady Cynthia Wade   Governor's wife

Major Walter Ponsonby   Aide-de-Camp

The Barque, Frogmore, Sailing Vessel, to the Indies

Captain Verner Eriksen   Captain of the SS Frogmore

Sir Hugh South   First Class Passenger

Lady Clarissa Wendarm   First Class Passenger

Mrs Fiona Green   First Class Passenger, Lady Clarissa's Companion

IRELAND

Cobh, Community, Ireland

Doctor Smythe	Local Doctor
Mrs Mary Reid	Resident

Irish Nationalists, Cobh

Mr Aiden Reid	Port Charlotte Camp Commander and Brothers member
Mr Sean Reid	Aiden Reid's younger brother and Brothers member
Mr Daniel Magee	Brothers member
Mr Dylan Reagan	Brothers member
Mr Brendan Callaghan	Brothers member
Mr Connor Smith	Brothers member
Mr Michael Walsh	Brothers organiser, and Cobh Commander
Mr Dan O'Leary	Brothers organiser, and Cobh Intelligence Officer
Miss Ruby O'Leary	Brothers member and sister of Dan O'Leary
Miss Ruth Walsh	Brothers member and sister of Michael Walsh

Hannigan's Pub, Cobh

Mr Lester Sloan	Staff Manager

Walsh Family, Cobh, Ireland

Mrs Madge Walsh	Wife of Seamus's brother

Walsh Family, Garranes, Ireland

Mr Seamus Walsh	Farmer, Tenant of Lord Kellwick
Mrs Flann Walsh	Wife of Seamus
Mr Michael Walsh	Eldest son of Seamus, Brothers' organiser, and Cobh Brothers' Commander
Miss Ruth Walsh	Eldest daughter of Seamus, and Brothers' member
Miss Orla Walsh	Daughter of Seamus and Flann
Miss Tara Walsh	Daughter of Seamus and Flann

Irish Nationalists, Dublin

Mr Braydon Kelly	Brothers Intelligence Officer, Dublin
Mr Iain Murphy	Brothers organiser, Dublin

Dublin Community

Mrs Máire (pronounced 'Moira') Reid	Aiden Reid's Aunt

Lord Kellwick's Estate, Outside Cork, Ireland

Sir Mason Ferguson, Earl of Kellwick	Member of the British Mission to Ireland
Lady Susan Ferguson, Countess Of Kellwick	Wife of the Earl of Kellwick
Mr Samuel Higgins	Chief Land Agent, Kellwick Estate
Mr William O'Neill	Butler
Mrs Maeve Carroll	Housekeeper

SCOTLAND

Killarow Doctor's Surgery, Isle of Islay

Dr Bryan Watson	Town Doctor
Mrs Jessica Watson	Wife of Dr Watson
Master Archie Watson	Son of Doctor Watson
Miss Sophie Watson	Daughter of Doctor Watson

Port Ellen Safe House, Isle of Islay

Mr Callum Ferguson	Brothers member, Scotland
Mrs Ruth Ferguson (Walsh)	Brothers member, Scotland

Irish Nationalists, Glasgow

Mr Iain Hughes	Brothers member and recruiter
Mr Robert Murray	Brothers member and recruiter
Mr Ian Doyle	Brothers member and recruiter
Mr Angus Faulkner	Brothers Organiser and Safehouse Manager Glasgow
Mr Fergus Taylor	Brothers member

PART 1

'Death is always Inconvenient!'

Anonymous Anglican Bishop

Chapter 1

November 1826

William ran as hard as he could. His father was gaining on him, and he was unsure how long he could keep this up. Rushing up the High Street, his legs were tiring as he dodged people and disappeared amongst the crowd.

Bystanders quickly moved aside for the yelling man chasing William, "Stop that, boy! Stop Him!"

The small boy scampered up a laneway and around the back of the church. Resting, William peered around the masonry fence and saw his father rapidly following. Hidden by the wall, he was off past the church, down the town path and racing across the High Street, nearly knocking over a lady in the process. Picking up her parcel, he said, "Sorry, Ma'am!" then sprinted towards Abbot's Hospital, through the corridors and out the back, along the fences until he reached his back gate.

Exhausted and breathing heavily, William quietly walked past the woodshed and gently stepped onto the kitchen verandah, always listening for any noise from his father. The seven-year-old was like a cat with his senses alert for any sign of danger. It was quiet! He opened the mudroom door, removed his shoes, and quietly opened the scullery door. A strong hand grabbed the scruff of his neck and held him fast despite his struggle.

Jonathan Turner growled, 'William, I will beat you, boy!'

He saw his father's raging face over his shoulder. The man was mad – there was no other explanation. His father dragged him backwards and locked the mudroom door. Releasing him, he grasped a whip from its place on the back wall. William's eyes enlarged as he saw what was coming. He screamed, "No, No, Please, No……!"

"Will! Will, you are dreaming again!" Simeon gently shook his shoulder. "Quiet, man, or father will be on us for making noise!"

William opened his eyes, taking a deep breath, almost screaming again. He quickly realised they were in Greenwich and not home in Guildford. Seeing the concerned face of his elder brother Simeon close by, he let out his breath and lay there silently, blinking.

"At a boy, calm down. You are safe! It was a dream. Relax there for a while; it is nearly morning!"

There was no way William could relax; the dream felt so real he was terrified.

"Too many blankets, brother! Let me take one off."

William clutched the safety of his blankets and smiled up at Simeon with wide-open eyes. Gently his older brother released his grip, knowing that William was fully awake. Smiling at Will, Simeon pulled his bedclothes over him and kept a watch from his pillow.

The bedroom door opened, and one of Simeon and William's older sisters, Clementine, peeked in and entered.

"It is fine, Clemmie. Will was dreaming again. Probably about Father!"

She came over and felt William's forehead. He was hot. She quietly released his grip and removed one of the blankets. Clementine brushed his hair back over his face and sat down on the bed beside him. She covered herself with the blanket and stroked his hair as he slowly relaxed and closed his eyes. He rolled towards her and moved his arm across her legs, taking her hand. She gently squeezed it.

Comforted by his sister's presence, William was now calm and relaxed, and Clemmie could hear his gentle breathing. She leaned back against the wall and, through the window, could see a few early morning lights appearing from the neighbouring kitchens. She thought, 'Why was it that father disliked William so much? The other children all received his affection. But not Will. Yet Will was the sweetest brother you could wish for.' She could not understand it.

Sitting quietly, she prayed that their parents downstairs had not heard him crying out. Her father was a troubled man, and the last thing they wanted was his sleep disturbed. She sighed and listened as the cold northerly wind gently moved the windowpane backwards and forwards.

At 'Huntley', the morning in Greenwich …

The Greenwich wedding and reception of Mr Thomas Turner and Miss Marion Steele was a great success, and it was well after midnight before the Turner family and their guests retired at 'Huntley'. Mr Charles Boot, the butler, rose early and checked the breakfast preparations. Every room in the house was full, and Charles presumed there would be no guests before eight in the morning, with the reception finishing late last night.

He enjoyed the Turner family as they were not pretentious, and the additional guests were well-mannered. As this would probably be the busiest day of the Turner's visit, he was keen that the breakfast was perfect. Charles noted on his timepiece that it was six-thirty, then smiled as he admired the well-set-out breakfast room. Thomas Turner surprised him when he entered and inspected each empty serving tray on the sideboard.

"Why, Mr Turner, I did not expect you down till later in the morning!"

"Sorry, Mr Boot, but I was feeling a bit peckish! What time do the staff serve breakfast?"

"After a late night, Sir, we normally start serving at eight o'clock. The staff are still at breakfast. May I arrange a cup of tea for you? Perhaps also a cup for your lady, Sir?"

"Yes, please. Some toast would also be good. I think Miss Steel, ah, I mean Mrs Turner, will come down later. I would say around ten!"

"Very Good, Sir. By the way, Sir, may I congratulate you and Mrs Turner on your marriage."

"Thank you, Mr Boot. Please excuse my mistake. I will probably make a few tongue slips in the coming weeks."

"I'm sure you will adjust quickly, Sir!"

The butler left the room on his errand. As he descended the servants' stairwell, he sighed, 'There is always an early riser! Why not stay in bed with your new bride? Oh well.'

Eleanora Turner opened her eyes from a peaceful sleep. Disturbed by the maid making up the fire in her room, she noticed the faint light and soft rain tapping on the window.

"Thank you, Annabelle."

"My pleasure, Mrs Turner."

"Is that rain that I hear?"

"Yes, Mrs Turner. A slight shower but not constant. I think we will be scarce of sunshine today."

As Annabelle Black collected her implements and exited the room, Eleanora Turner lay in her comfortable bed, enjoying the fire's warmth. She contemplated yesterday's wedding for her son and the family's pending return home. Marion and Thomas would leave after lunch for their honeymoon. Thomas now had his own family – she would miss her firstborn but welcomed his new wife.

Strangely she felt some energy this morning, a good sign given her poor health this year. Eleanora rose and peeked into her husband's adjoining room, finding Jonathan fast asleep. He had struggled with his sleep over the past few days. She was glad he was resting peacefully. The respite would be refreshing, strengthening him for their commitments in London before setting off for

Guildford. Despite the joy of this trip, Eleanora longed for home and fresh country air. Greenwich and London were far too busy.

Quietly pulling the cord for the maid, she thought, 'Some tea and buttered rolls shared with Jonathan would be nice before rising!'

Anne and Emma were still asleep in their room upstairs. However, down the hallway, Doctor David Sopwith, dressed in athletic gear, prepared for some exercise before breakfast. Robert South, who shared the room with David, also felt the need for some training. Rushing downstairs, they sought out the butler in the staff kitchen.

"Mr Boot, we are off for a run. We need some exercise. Which direction is best for Shooters Hill?"

"Doctor Sopwith and Sir Robert, Good morning! If you depart via this side door and down past the stables, you will see the gate in the back fence, which opens onto a meadow adjoining the army shooting range. They will not be using the range on a Sunday. Shooters Hill will appear in the distance if you run along the side of the range."

"Thank you. We shall be back in an hour or so."

"An hour or so! Surely not that long, David?" Robert was becoming reluctant on hearing the time required for this exercise.

"Breakfast will be ready when you return, gentlemen."

David nodded with a slight smile and moved off. Robert frowned and followed.

As Charles Boot sent off a footman with the newly married couple's trays upstairs, he noticed Mrs Turner's bell ringing.

"Mrs Nibley! Is anyone attending Mrs Turner?"

"Yes, I asked Annabelle. She will be back presently."

Nanny Jones yawned as she raised her head off the pillow. Seeing the time and realising she had overslept, she leapt out of bed, freshened herself up, dressed, and raced upstairs to check the children's rooms. The girls were all sleeping, and Simeon was fast asleep in the boys' room, but William's bed was empty. Where was he? His bedclothes were on the floor, so William had dressed. She rushed downstairs.

"Mr Boot, have you seen William Turner this morning?"

"Yes, Nanny Jones, he is out in the backyard, playing with the dog."

Through the window, she spied William throwing a stick for a Great Dane. She smiled in relief and put on her coat as she ventured out.

"William, if you are going outside, you should tell me!"

"I tried, Nanny, but you were asleep!"

"Thank you, but next time wake me! Only stay out here for another ten minutes as the rain is coming again. It would be best if you cleaned yourself before breakfast. They will serve it soon!"

William kept playing with the large hound, who was now enjoying a pat and rub. Nanny Jones returned inside and found Ethel Nibley's daughter, Rosalind, eating toast at the kitchen table.

"Rosalind, would you keep an eye on William, please? You will find him outside the kitchen playing with 'Herman' the hound. I do not want him running off. I must prepare the other children for breakfast."

Rosalind nodded in agreement. She positioned herself on the back steps eating some toast and watching William. Still waking up, Rosalind rubbed her eyes and yawned. When she looked again, William and the dog were gone.

North of Port Charlotte, Isle of Islay, Scotland ...

The freezing early morning wind whipped around the long stable building, which overlooked Loch Indaal. Aiden Reid, deep in thought, stood quietly, unaware of the biting cold and the flapping thatch roof behind him. His mind angrily flashed back and relived the night of the battle and the consequences. His attempts at repressing the despair welling up inside him were useless as he recalled his screaming brother resisting the doctor who amputated Sean's left foot and arm. The British gunboat's grapeshot was relentlessly accurate, killing and injuring the men. He shuddered at the thought of so many cold, lifeless bodies along the shoreline.

Spitting on the ground in disgust, he thought, 'A traitor must have given our position away. How else could the British have found us? Whoever it was would pay, and so would the British. I will have my revenge!'

The sun would soon break over the eastern horizon revealing the outline of three large fishing vessels moored not fifty yards out in the choppy water of the loch. Late the previous night, two luggers[1] stowed with their camp equipment, departed under darkness and disappeared through Laggan Bay towards Ireland. There was also room for the injured and some womenfolk who cared for them. He was thankful Sean was in good hands and would now be heading down the Irish east coast, reaching Cobh in a few days. The remaining members of the brothers' party would leave on the fishing boats today.

'Damn the British!' Aiden clenched his teeth in anger. The captured frigate was ready for its mission, with piles of wood stacked higher than the gunwales. The blazing fire ship would have created havoc in Portsmouth harbour – a devastating blow for the British and a great victory for the Republicans. Achieving their objective was so near, and now it was in ruins. Aiden sighed,

---

[1] A lugger is a sailing vessel defined by its rig, using the lug sail on all or one of its several masts. They were widely used as working craft, particularly of the coasts of France, England, Ireland and Scotland. Luggers varied extensively in size and design. Some were undecked open craft and others fully decked. Wikipedia.

turned, and entered the barn. Two men stood up as they saw him.

"Daniel, Is he ready?"

"Yes!"

"Put him in the back of the cart! Dylan, make sure everything is loaded on board before I return. We must leave by midday. The British will be back, so nothing must remain intact. Light that bonfire as soon as you can. I should be back at half-past ten. Now get a move on!"

Doing up the buttons of his coat Aiden walked outside and mounted the back of the cart. He checked that the shaking youth was blindfolded, gagged, and his ankles and wrists were securely tied. Satisfied, he covered the lad with a blanket, clambered onto the seat, and whipped the horse, setting off at a cantering pace. The frosty late November air was bitter as the cart travelled north towards Bridgend.

'How did they find us so quickly?' The brothers' committee was sure the British would search Ireland for months before turning towards Scotland. The stakes were higher now as the enemy, knowing their position, would soon return with reinforcements. They must be out of here, fade into the Irish community, and set new plans. But this would not bring back the thirty-seven men dead from the English grapeshot. Perhaps more if the injured lost their fight for recovery.

Aiden was a hard man, having suffered under British rule during his forty-one years. The sorrow from Sean's injuries was a growing rage inside him made worse by the frigate's unexpected loss. They both understood the risks ahead when they made the commitments required by the brothers. For a free Ireland, no sacrifice was too great. But how would his mother understand Sean being disabled from his injuries? This rebellion suddenly became personal for Aiden. It was more than he could stand. Why not kill this Scottish lad lying in the back of the cart? He could dump him somewhere noteworthy as a public protest. No! He understood the sorrow his mother would feel for Sean. Why should another mother suffer the same because of the British?

Short of Bridgend by five hundred yards, he slowed the cart down, turning it towards Port Charlotte. Jumping down, he lifted the lad out. They had held the surgeon's son hostage, ensuring the village doctor would tend the Irish wounded. Several brothers had died, but the doctor worked continuously for three days and ensured many survived. He kept his end of the bargain. Now his son should be returned unharmed.

"Archie! I will untie your ankles in a minute but do not run. If you do, I will shoot you in the head. Do you hear me? Nod, and tell me you understand?"

The boy was trembling but nodded as instructed.

"Once I untie your ankles, I will then untie your hands. Please do not remove the blindfold, or I will shoot you. I have a letter here for your father.

You are five hundred yards short of the intersection at Bridgend. When your father arrives, give him the letter. He should be here at twelve. Do you understand?"

The boy nodded.

Aiden untied the boy and placed the letter in the lad's trembling hands.

"Count aloud slowly until you reach one hundred. Only then remove your blindfold. The intersection is a short walk, and you can wait there. Start counting aloud now!"

The boy hesitated but quietly said in a scratchy voice, "One, two, three………."

Aiden mounted the cart and whipped the horse into a canter as he raced back toward Port Charlotte.

As the miles passed, he thought again about how the British discovered them. 'Someone must have given them away. It was the only explanation. Perhaps a brother was caught and tortured. Perhaps some stupid drunk spilled some information. Who knows? We must find out and stop the leaking. Whoever did it was responsible for the lives of thirty-seven good men. Mother Mary! How long till we rid ourselves of these British autocrats who take our lands and homes, rape our sisters, and murder our brothers?'

Aiden was all too aware of the criminal conditions the British forced upon the Irish people. Their land was stolen, had no vote and no say in justice as their poverty deepened. All he knew was corruption, misery, and repression. Now Sean had suffered crippling injuries and would face a life of begging! He would find out who broke the silence and gave them away. Then he would deliver some justice of his own for Sean. These British autocrats would pay for this dearly.

At 'Huntley', Greenwich …

Rosalind checked through the stable building, but there was no sign of William or the dog. Now worried, she rushed around behind the stables. In the long meadow grass, she saw William calling the dog with a rabbit in its mouth. The tiny creature struggled for freedom as the dog ran back, answering the call.

Sitting down slightly out of William's reach, the Great Dane dared him with wide-open big brown eyes. The dog's senses were bristling, and he sat tensed, ready for the slightest movement from William. The boy turned his back and walked away, approaching Rosalind at the gate.

"Come on, Herman. Here boy!"

The dog followed but kept its distance. As William came near the gate where Rosalind stood, he asked, "Is he following me?"

Rosalind, gaining interest, nodded in affirmation. She quickly moved back from the gate, keeping out of the way.

William whispered, "How many steps behind me?"

Rosalind put up three fingers. William smiled, opened the gate, and stood aside for the dog.

The dog trustfully continued walking through, holding the squirming rabbit in its mouth.

In a flash, William tackled the dog, pushing it over on a startled and frozen Rosalind. As he quickly grabbed the rabbit out of the great Dane's mouth, the large dog clumsily knocked Rosalind flat on the muddy ground. As Herman clambered over her, regaining his footing, the dog searched for the rabbit.

Sitting up, Rosalind found mud all over her new dress, worn for the first time this morning. William stood above her, holding the squirming rabbit high in the air. He smiled, "Got it!" The dog then lurched at him, jumping for the rabbit. She pushed the dog away as they were squeezed against the gate, with mud splashing everywhere.

"Look what you have done, William? My dress is covered in mud. Mother will kill me for this. Oh, No, No, No!"

William stopped and looked down, "You are alright; it is only mud!"

"That is the point. It is mud all over my dress for church, and all my other dresses are in the wash. Boys, you are idiots!"

William thought about this. Perhaps rushing for the rabbit was a mistake. He enjoyed the fun, but seeing how dirty and angry Rosalind was, he sensed repercussions. Fearing the consequences of his father finding out, he suggested an alternative.

"My sister Clementine will have another dress. She is your size. Come on, we will find her."

He pulled Rosalind up as she wiped the mud off her face. He noticed her sobbing and the tears running down her cheeks. How would he keep her out of view and find Clemmie? As he pulled her towards the back door, a hand came down on his shoulder and stopped him in his tracks.

With a squirming rabbit in one hand and a tearful Rosalind in the other, William turned, finding the inquiring eyes of Doctor Sopwith focused on him.

"Well, William and Rosalind, what is going on here?"

The dog saw his opportunity, snatched the rabbit out of William's hand and ran off with its catch.

"Rosalind fell over, and we thought Clementine might have a clean, spare dress!"

"I think we will all visit the kitchen as Mrs Nibley will require an explanation. Then, William, you may accompany Sir Robert as he finds Clementine and fetches the clean dress. It is not so bad, Rosalind. Let us clean you up. I'm sure Clementine will be down quickly."

The three of them entered the kitchen via the back door, and Ethel Nibley looked up with an open mouth as she saw her daughter covered in mud and William looking uncomfortable.

An exhausted Robert South appeared and limped in.

"Did I hear my name mentioned, David?"

Doctor Sopwith then explained the situation and asked if Robert might escort William off in search of Clementine. He then carefully talked with Rosalind, ensuring she was not injured.

Later In the Breakfast Room at 'Huntley' …

Anne Turner entered, discovering David Sopwith chatting with her fiancée, Robert South. The two men stood as Anne joined them.

"Good morning, Anne." Robert said, "We were discussing injuries at sea. David is most interested!"

Anne smiled, "David, thank you for solving that problem with William and Rosalind this morning. Clementine's cousin Katherine is the same size and supplied a dress. They are changing Rosalind now. She has recovered and will be fine. Thank you for your assistance. You may have saved my youngest brother from an unpleasant situation!"

David smiled, "It was nothing, just a coincidence. We finished our run and found them at the back gate with the dog. Mud was everywhere, and William was becoming desperate. I am sure he learnt a lesson this morning."

Anne's eyes opened wide, "You both went running?"

"Yes. We went through the meadow and up Shooters Hill around Severndroog Castle and back. Great views from up there!"

"Oh, Severndroog Castle, remember the wonderful picnic we had there, Robert! How I would love to see it again."

Robert recalling the weather outside and his struggle up the hill, said, "Believe me, it is not quite the weather for the castle now, Anne. It has been raining and is a bit cold for the ladies."

Anne became disappointed and revealed a downcast face to her fiancée, "You are probably correct, but someday, Robert, might we visit there again?"

Robert realising his mistake, said immediately, "And so we shall! I am sure the owner would happily give his permission. Admiral Sutherland introduced me."

"Thank you, Robert – I have fond memories of the castle. But we must talk in confidence while we are alone here."

Robert looked up from his breakfast with interest. David, focusing with a questioning face, asked, "This would not involve Robert's sister, would it?"

"Yes, David, it would. Emma and I are now close friends. I spent the last week with her, and I have some insights. If not for your confiding in me previously, I would not dare raise this matter."

David nodded in agreement, and Robert uncomfortably asked, "Anne, should I be included? I would not be interfering?"

David and Anne both agreed that Robert should remain.

With a serious face, Anne announced, "David, the time for action has come!"

David looked up at Anne and said, "Really!"

Robert enquired, "What exactly do you mean, Anne?"

Anne moaned a little and said, "Now, you two, please take me seriously here!"

Robert smiled at David, who was a bit lost for words. They both put their cutlery down and listened.

"David, Emma told me confidently that you have declared your love for her and that she loves you."

David swallowed and then said. "Yes, that is true!"

"Well, Emma wonders why you do not propose. She is most eager for your proposal! A lady may not openly declare her love unless the gentleman proposes first."

Both boys then said, "Really!"

"Of course. Do you think a woman enjoys being dangled on a line waiting for the …… whatever it is? David, she is waiting for you! Manners demand that you propose first, and then she may accept and openly discuss it. She is confused about why you have not proposed!"

David Sopwith looked with wide-open eyes at Anne as if something had clicked inside him, "Well, I was considering when I should do that! I think I was building up enough courage. Perhaps, Robert, you could help me with this?"

Robert looked up in alarm, "Well …. "

Anne became frustrated with both David and Robert, "No, David, this is something you and Emma must do alone. She deserves it. It will be one of her life's most important and happiest moments."

"A special day for you as well!" Robert happily added.

David stood and moved away from the table. At the window, he turned and walked back with his hands clasped together. Then he said, "You see, Robert, my parents and brother are dead. I only have my sister, and she is in Ireland. So, having met Anne on a few occasions and respecting her wisdom, I confided in her. I hope you can forgive me for that?"

"Of course, David. Of course. Now treat me as a friend like Anne. Ask me what you should do?"

David said, "I would appreciate your advice, Robert. What should I do?"

"Propose as soon as you find the opportunity!" A friendly smile grew on Robert's face, and he was patting David on the back as Emma entered the room.

"What are you three all so happy about?"

Anne blushed and then sweetly said, "David will explain!"

David started turning white until Robert put his arm around him, explaining, "David and I have been discussing war injuries. It has alarmed him a little. Perhaps, Emma, you and David might take a turn in the garden. Calm him down with some sunshine and fresh air. You understand?" Robert raised his eyebrows.

Emma wondered why a doctor would lose his colour over injuries, but Anne grasped control of the situation, "Look, the sun is out in the garden again. What a wonderful opportunity, David?"

David regaining some colour, said, "Yes, Emma, I would appreciate you taking a short walk with me. We will return quickly for breakfast."

Emma looked a little surprised but obliged, and David took her hand and moved out through the breakfast room doors across the balcony leading into the garden.

Robert and Anne peeped carefully through a side window as the couple strolled along the garden path and paused talking. Robert held Anne in his arms and kissed her on the back of her neck. Enjoying the feeling and giggling, she squirmed around and faced him, "I thought for a moment, we must say the words for him. He is petrified, isn't he?"

"He will succeed. Look, he is down on one knee!"

Anne was beside herself, "Oh, this is wonderful!"

Neville and Bethany arrived for breakfast, and Neville inquired, "What's so wonderful, Anne?"

"Shush, Neville! Come and see, but just peek around the corner."

Neville and Bethany joined them and saw David down on one knee, and Emma was crying with joy and saying, "Yes, David, yes!"

The butler, who watched the whole affair, stood in the corner of the breakfast room, ready for Neville and Bethany when he noticed Herman galloping towards the young couple in the garden. He quickly rushed after the dog, thinking, 'Oh No!'

The Great Dane, who met David earlier and enjoyed his scent, ran and jumped up, one paw on David's chest and the other on Emma's shoulder, the dead rabbit still in his mouth, and joined their conversation. Emma and David stood in a trance for a moment as Emma's joy turned into fright with the dead rabbit waving in her face. She lurched away and fell over backwards, leaving David holding the dog.

David looked hopefully at the breakfast room and spied Charles running, "I say, Mr Boot! Would you please call the dog off? Thank you."

Charles Boot was already running across the porch, desperately calling, "Herman, Herman here. Here boy!"

The butler pulled the large dog away. Emma began smiling again as David assisted her up.

The others came out and swarmed around David and Emma giving them congratulations, big hugs, and slaps on the back.

David stood there with a great smile, saying, "Well, Well!"

Anne whispered in his ear, "David, after lunch, you must take Emma and meet with her father. The carriage will be ready for you both. We will expect you back for dinner, and you may tell us all about it."

Having thought his ordeal was over, the smile disappeared off David's face. Then he said again, "Well, well. Come, Emma, shall we have breakfast before heading for church?"

As they moved into the breakfast room, the sun hid behind a large cloud, and a light rain commenced falling again.

The Barque², Frogmore, Heading for Ireland …

Sir Hugh South, the Earl of Fintelton's heir, felt a disturbance in his stomach as the barque *Frogmore* rounded Land's End and headed for Cobh, the first port of call before the long trip across the Atlantic and then the Indies.

"Surely, I'm not seasick! Must be something I ate!"

Sir Hugh's ticket was for a first-class cabin with the services of a steward. Finding his accommodation wet and cramped and now struggling with seasickness, he was somewhat dissatisfied. However, the steward informed him that his cabin was the best onboard, and no better options were available. The provision of a good bottle of scotch occupied him during the first day of the voyage, and at mid-morning, on the second day, with some fire in his belly, he decided to tackle the elements.

As the waves rolled the ship, climbing the narrow stairs proved difficult. Crawling onto the deck, Sir Hugh was rewarded with sunshine and a fresh breeze, a relief from the stale air below. He stood and gulped in a large refreshing breath before a cloud of sea spray hit his face. Sir Hugh turned quickly from the wind, bending over and shook the water away. Gasping and opening his eyes, he beheld the vision of a very handsome lady and her companion.

"I'm sorry, I must appear as a drunken man. The movement of this ship has affected me. My first time!"

The shorter lady said nothing and looked away, but the taller, more handsome lady smiled, "It can be quite a challenge the first time!"

She was around Sir Hugh's age, refined and did not appear phased.

"My apologies, ladies, for the lack of an introduction. Perhaps I might correct this at dinner! I have some business in the Indies with my plantations."

---

² The Barque is a sailing vessel with a particular sail plan. This comprises three (or more) masts, for-and-aft sails on the aftermost mast and square sails on all other masts. Wikipedia.

"Why, yes, Sir. My companion Mrs Green and I also visit Kingston!"

"I say this air is refreshing. I felt quite uncomfortable in my cabin, but this time on deck has considerably cleared my head. I hope I have the pleasure of joining you and your husband at dinner?"

"You will have the pleasure of myself and Mrs Green. Unfortunately, my husband passed away in February of this year. I will also be inspecting plantations in Jamaica. So, we shall enjoy your company for at least a month unless the captain finds a shorter route."

"My condolences, Madam. I shall arrange an introduction for dinner!"

Sir Hugh excused himself with a shallow bow and took a few turns around the main deck. He enjoyed his time, and the prospect of some female company among the passengers stirred his interest, diverting his thoughts from seasickness.

The *Frogmore* sped on towards Cobh, the port for Cork.

Bowmore, Isle of Islay, Scotland ...

Doctor Bryan Watson sat with his wife, Jessica, in the small surgery room at the front of their Bowmore house. Bryan, a good Presbyterian, was convinced by a canny church friend about establishing a practice in Islay some five years ago. The island was short of a doctor, and Bryan, with a missionary calling in his heart, decided on the wilds of Islay. Since first arriving in Killarow, he joined with his wife for morning tea each day, attempting compensation for losing her Glasgow friends. Despite the island's small population, restricting the number of residents suitable for friendships, his wife was now increasing her circle of acquaintants.

"Jessica, this letter is of some concern!" She noticed how Bryan's left-hand shook as he placed a letter on the desk and then lifted his cup of tea, taking a sip.

"We must leave Islay soon! The letter from these republicans contains a threat of violence against us if we provide any information about their activities. They may return, and who knows what they will do next time. Praise God that we have Archie back unharmed."

"But Bryan, they are gone now. We are all safe. Surely now they are discovered, they would not return?"

"The Irish think of this as a war, Jessica! I treated most of their men and know their faces and names. I was sure they would kill me before they left. When they freed me, I was astonished! You understand they murdered some of that poor crew from the frigate and buried them somewhere near Port Charlotte in a mass grave. We will never be safe here again!"

"But Bryan, this is our home now! Where would we go? Perhaps you would find work again in Glasgow!"

"No, they have men there and Scottish support! I heard them talking. We must find somewhere as far away from here as possible! A place the Irish would not find us. This morning I have been doing some research. When I was young, my parents often took us on holidays in London and the towns around that area. I remember one such town with a lovely river running through a little valley. The place was small but busy, and I am sure it has grown since then. Pass me that atlas, please. I will see if I can find it."

"It is quite temperate in summer down near London, Bryan. I'm not sure if I would like the heat!"

"Jessica, if the Irish return, they will require my services again and kill me. There are two options! Either you become a widow and remain here, or we leave for the south, and you continue as a comfortable English Doctor's wife. Which would you prefer? Do not forget we nearly lost Archie. I was not sure they would keep their word. Thank the Lord they did!"

Jessica Watson was beside herself with fear while the Irish detained Archie and Bryan. On her husband's return without her son, she found sleep impossible until they reunited. Now they were all back together, and the crisis was over; she had convinced herself their family was safe. Bryan's comments about reprisals brought back all the fear. As she viewed the surrounding country from the surgery door, she considered the decision they must make. She loved their comfortable home here, the wide-open spaces, and the peacefulness of the countryside. She would miss it immensely and the families who were now their close friends. But in her heart, she knew the sacrifice was for her family's safety.

"I think you are right, Bryan. We must protect Archie and Sophie. Have you found it?"

"I think so. It was on the River Wey. The town is called Guildford. It is around thirty miles southwest of London, so in the country. I think we would be safe there. I'm sure such a country town would need many a good doctor!"

The Turner Bakery, Guildford …

Jeb Hiscock, the Turner Bakery manager, stood beside Anne Turner's desk mid-morning in the general office area. Audrey Stern sat there perplexed with the figures in front of her, "It does not balance, Jeb, and I have tried everything I know, but I don't understand why not. I need Miss Turner's direction! She would know what I have done wrong."

In his deep voice, Jeb softly encouraged Audrey, "Perhaps you have not done anything wrong!"

Audrey smiled, "Thank you for your kind thought, but it must balance; otherwise, I know there is a problem."

"Audrey, are tomorrow's orders ready yet? I need them so Peter can commence the preparations for the morning."

"Sorry, Jeb! This ledger has taken far longer than I thought. I was distracted and have not started them yet. I'll start now!"

Jeb realised that Audrey was unfamiliar with the bakery order process, given Anne only gave her one training session before leaving for the wedding. He knew it would take some time, and they must have them by lunch.

Jeb hesitated but knew there was no alternative, "I will go down and speak with Peter and Aaron, and then I will be back. We can do them together, so they are ready straight after lunch. Today will be a long day. I will be late home tonight."

Audrey was grateful for his help; she also knew Jeb lived at Batton Place. It was an hour's fast walk. An idea popped into her mind, "You will miss dinner! My parents have a spare room – why not stay in Guildford? Mother will be only too pleased; that way, you will have dinner."

"Are you sure? It certainly would save me the travel time."

Audrey was pleased that Jeb would accept the offer, "I'm quite sure. She will welcome the company. Father can be a bit boring. I will let her know you are coming."

As Jeb discussed some issues with Peter and Aaron, Terrence Spencer, the mill manager, came looking for him.

"Jeb, when will you be free to talk?"

"I must be back in the office and quickly finish tomorrow's orders, but I would be free straight after lunch, say two o'clock. Can it wait till then, Terry?"

"Yes. Come as soon as you can and bring Peter with you. You both need to hear this!"

"Peter must work with the other bakers on tomorrow's preparations, so it will only be me. Sorry, but the prep is essential."

"I see. Well, I will expect you at two."

The mill manager rushed off, nodding his head. Jeb was surprised at Terry's urgency; it was unusual that he would be in such a state. 'No time now. The orders are waiting.' He rushed back up the stairs and sat at the desk beside Audrey, where they split the papers between them.

'Harting', St James's Square, London ...

Mrs Laura Taggart, the Reverend Andrew Taggart's wife, sat with Lady Emma South and Miss Anne Turner, enjoying the warmth of the raging fire, having dined for a second evening at Harting. Laura's husband, Andrew, talked with Lady Jane South and the Earl at the other end of the room.

The previous night Laura and Andrew felt privileged as they joined the

South family at a large dinner where the Earl announced the engagement of Anne Turner and the Earl's second son, Sir Robert. In addition, the Earl made a surprise announcement of his daughter's engagement, Lady Emma, and young Doctor David Sopwith. Laura Taggart enjoyed the chat and was interested in hearing the story of David and Emma's romance.

"My dear Lady Emma, I am so glad that David has proposed, and you can now declare your engagement."

"Thank you, Mrs Taggart. The days since last Sunday have been so exciting."

"Well, we have known David for around two years since he took residence in Guildford. He is our family doctor. David has always appeared somewhat shy despite his excellent manners. I am now impressed that he found the courage for a proposal."

"It was quite a task for him, Mrs Taggart, but he found some good support from my friend Anne and Robert. Anne, as you relate it so well, please tell Mrs Taggart the story! She will enjoy the details as she is a close friend and will keep it in confidence."

Laura Taggart smiled in agreement, and Anne took a deep breath.

"Well, Mrs Taggart, you will recall that David and Robert stayed with us at 'Huntley' after the wedding. The party planned breakfast together on Sunday before attending Greenwich church. I found Robert and David deep in conversation when I entered the breakfast room. Noticing no one else present, I decided this was the opportunity to encourage David. So, I said, "While we three are alone here, we must talk in confidence!"

Anne's recollection of the story entertained Laura Taggart, especially the episode with the dog's antics.

"Lady Emma, you will never forget that proposal."

"No, Mrs Taggart or the dead rabbit!" They all laughed again.

"You and Anne must be very close, Lady Emma?"

"Oh yes, Mrs Taggart, we have become best friends. Anne has shown me a different world from the Estate. Living in Guildford will be a refreshing change, and we shall attend your church."

"Have you set a date for the wedding – not yet, but once we know Robert and Anne's date, it will be soon afterwards. The next thing will be finding a house – while I love David's present home, we might require a slightly larger one in the future."

"I have heard the Prestons are moving for family reasons. Perhaps when the house comes on the market, you and David should inspect it. The house is large and has plenty of room for servants. It might be just the thing."

"Thank you, Mrs Taggart. I will keep it in mind. Once we are settled, I hope you and Reverend Taggart will often visit?"

Further along the room, Lady Jane and the Reverend Andrew watched as the Earl gently nodded off in his comfortable chair beside them. Lady Jane placed a small throw on Sir David and settled back into her comfy chair.

"I shall miss all the young people when they leave tomorrow and return home."

"You stay on here, Lady Jane?"

"Yes, we have some engagements before we return, but I long for Fintelton. London is exciting, but I prefer the country, especially at Christmas."

Andrew Taggart was surprised by the kind mention Lord Fintelton made of him in his dinner speech the previous night. The Reverend Taggart's ministry was mainly in Guildford, and the Souths attended the local church in Petersfield, so he was curious about the praise.

Lady Jane noticed the thoughtful expression on Andrew's face.

"Reverend Taggart, you may wonder why His Lordship and I place such a high value on our acquaintance with you?"

"Yes, my Lady, the issue has crossed my mind."

"While we are out of earshot from the others, let me talk frankly with you. Reverend, every new minister that the bishop sends our way has always followed the same thought pattern, which is what the Earl and I can do for them! Please do not misunderstand what I am saying. Normally the complaints are about money or their comfort and so on."

As she talked, Lady Jane kept a close watch on her husband.

"With you, Andrew, if I might be bold and use your Christian name, it has always been the reverse. Your approach has always been, 'What may I do for you?' Since we made your acquaintance some twenty-five years ago, you have never requested anything of us, but you have provided your friendship and service often and freely. That friendship we value very highly."

Lady Jane paused for a moment. Andrew, somewhat embarrassed, said, "That is very kind of you, Lady Jane."

"I understand you are acquainted with our son, Sir Hugh?"

"Yes, my Lady."

"Hugh has had a troubled life. He started well as a fine young boy, but his interests led him astray as he came of age. That has continued for many years, unfortunately, with consequences."

Andrew Taggart was now unsure of what he should say.

"Before he departed overseas and a few weeks after Neville Bassington and Bethany Turner's wedding, we talked one night, and he apologised for the mess he has made of his life. Our conversation was long and detailed, and I must admit we both shed many tears. He felt he could not speak with his father as my husband now finds great difficulty addressing delicate questions. So, he confided in me.

I noticed a difference in Sir Hugh soon after the wedding in Guildford.

When we talked before we left for London, he was resolute that he would change his life for the better. I felt a new spirit in the boy I had not seen in him since he was young."

Andrew Taggart remembered the several discussions between Sir Hugh and himself as they had wrestled together through his problems and their final farewell. He felt he could not share this with Lady Jane as he must not break Sir Hugh's confidence.

"Andrew, I might never use your Christian name again as I do tonight, but I must thank you for what you have done for my boy. It may be a turning point in his life. Please accept my heartfelt thanks."

"Thank you, Lady Jane. We should both keep him in our prayers."

The countess gave Andrew a warm smile and then gently woke her husband, "Come, my dear! It is time you were in bed."

During their coach journey that night, Andrew Taggart astonished his wife by suddenly bursting into uncontrolled sobbing and clutched his handkerchief against his eyes. Knowing the gentle soul Andrew was, Laura understood it was enough to put her arm around him and rest her head on his shoulder.

A stray cat rushed across the dark wet street ahead of the coach, startling the horses. The coachman gently flicked the reins, "Steady girls, just a cat. Steady."

Later that evening, after the guests departed, Robert, Emma and Anne sat beside the fireplace discussing the estate's issues. A soft knock on the door distracted Robert, and he answered the call.

"A message for you, Sir Robert from the Admiralty."

"Thank you, Staines."

Robert took the message and quickly opened it, "The Admiralty requires me for a meeting on Thursday! I must remain in London rather than journeying with you, Anne, as far as Guildford."

Anne smiled with some disappointment but then realised there might be some benefit in this delay.

"Robert, perhaps this delay is a blessing in disguise. There will be additional time with your family. Also, as I am staying overnight, perhaps in the morning, we could see a bit of London together, on the condition you drop me back at Greenwich tomorrow evening. I hope either Aggie or Ethel has packed my things, but I must be back in time for dinner. Perhaps David and Emma would join us for lunch tomorrow."

Emma was thrilled with the plan, "Yes, Anne! Why, depending on where we go, Mother and Father might join us."

They all agreed with Anne's suggestion.

"Given what we now know about the estate, I suggest that on Thursday morning, you arrange a meeting with your father and mother and discuss the issues. I think you will find your mother supportive."

Robert knew he was due at the Admiralty by eleven, so it would be tight, "I think that will work. I will encourage father on an early rise that day."

"Make it straight after breakfast, Robert. They must be made aware of the difficulties!"

Cobh, Ireland ...

The three men pulled their coats tight against the cold rain as they made their way up the dark, deserted street towards Hannigan's pub. Keeping in the shadows, they darted down an alley to the rear of the building, climbed several flights of stairs, then knocked three times on a darkened door. Waiting silently, they took care remaining in the shadows of a wide overhanging lintel.

At the end of two minutes, two knocks came from the other side. Aiden gave four more knocks, and the door opened into a completely dark room. Once inside, a young lady closed the door and lit a candle. Ruby O'Leary gave each of the men a kiss on the cheek.

"I have been waiting for you! The others are back with the injured, hidden in different homes on the farms. Doctor Smythe is doing the best he can. What happened?"

"The British discovered us. Someone must have given us away!"

Ruby frowned, "The others are waiting across the hall."

The Brothers' committee members sat around the small half-lit room in various places. No one welcomed the men as they came in. An older man sitting at the rear took a long suck on his pipe, stubbed it, and then stood. He came forward and first shook Aiden's hand, then the hands of Brendan Callaghan and Connor Smith. He poured each a drink and quietly asked, "Well, boys, we have heard from the others. Now you tell us your version of what happened."

Brendan and Connor agreed that Aiden should speak for them.

Aiden stood and explained, "We were taken completely by surprise. Someone must have tipped them off. How else would they have found us? We covered every possibility at Port Charlotte. It must have come from within the brothers[3] somehow!"

"Surely not, me lad! We all know tis punishable by death!"

"Iain, they were on the ship before anyone heard them. They knew where the ship was and eliminated our guards with crossbow fire. It was well-planned,

---

[3] There were various groups of Irish Republicans over the two hundred years prior to Irish independence. I have termed the name 'Brothers' in this book as a fictional group working towards Irish independence from the British. Any likeness or similarity of the group with any historical group is purely coincidental. Author's comment.

and they executed it perfectly. We stood no chance. For a mission requiring that amount of planning, they knew well in advance and made damn sure there was no warning."

"Surely, lad, it must have been someone from Port Charlotte?"

"Couldn't have been. Most of the locals were locked up, and we took hostages for those around town. The cooperating crew members were taken ashore and locked in a stable. We shot any crew who tried escaping. The villagers were too scared for anything foolhardy. Anyway, we were not there that long. There is no other explanation. It must have come from within the brothers!"

Iain Murphy rubbed his hand across a whiskered chin. He was an organiser for the brothers long before the Emmet uprising[4] and knew the risks in agitating for Irish freedom. He would die for his country if it were needed. But this exercise was now a disaster, with thirty-seven of his men dead and many more recovering in hidden-away places. The British recapturing the frigate would now put their plans back months, perhaps a year. It was a cruel blow, and if it was the fault of some loose talk by a brother, then he must find that brother and ………. stop him!

Sitting down and lighting his pipe again, he looked up at Aiden, "Well, if it was someone inside the brothers, then who was it?"

"Iain, we have a clue! I am positive the ship that came was the same one we tried boarding near Portsmouth. We could not see the markings from the shore, but they were the same shape. They were searching for us. Somehow, they found out where we were. We need the details of that ship's movements over the last month. Then we trace back against which brothers were in the ports they visited."

"You think they have a brother who is their contact?"

"Perhaps it may be as simple as someone shouting drinks, getting our man drunk, and the brother spilling the beans. But we now know whoever that Royal Navy Captain was – he was smart! They did their undercover work and found us, and far too quickly. They found someone who knew where the frigate was hidden."

Iain put his pipe down, "That is possible, lad. Dan O'Leary, could you find out who knew about the camp and where they travelled for the previous month? Dan, you should visit Dublin for a few days and talk with the committee. Give Aiden the information when you return."

"Iain, I am not sure Aiden is right. What you want will be a lot of work for

---

[4] Robert Emmet (4 March 1778 – 20 September 1803) was an Irish Republican, an Irish nationalist patriot, orator, and rebel leader. After leading an abortive rebellion against British rule in 1803 he was captured and then tried and executed for high treason against the British King George III of Great Britain and Ireland. He is highly honoured by Irish communities throughout the world with statues in various countries, one such example is in Washington DC on Embassy Row. Wikipedia.

a hunch. No one in the brothers would be that stupid. Asking them for that information may also put their contacts at risk!"

"Dan, do you have a better suggestion?"

Dan O'Leary was a deep thinker in his mid-thirties and understood the members' commitment. If the British caught them, the charge would be hanging, and their families persecuted by association. They would never mention anything confidential to a non- brother's member. He was not convinced but stood there and said nothing.

"Good, now, Aiden; seeing this is your suggestion, you can follow the trail once we have the information. You know the penalty that a brother must pay. But find out what you can before you take him for a walk. Bring your report back here."

Aiden nodded in agreement. Iain Murphy resumed his seat as Michael Walsh continued chairing the meeting.

"Brothers, I think Aiden may be right. The British possibly know more about us than we would like. They may have even traced us here. It is time we disappeared for at least a month or two. For the next few months, we all must lie low and go farming. Spread the word in your groups. Once this settles down, I will send a message when the next gathering is required. Off home now, boys!"

As the others left, Aiden remained still. Michael approached him, "I'm sorry about your brother! Sean is a fine lad. I will visit and provide some support." He put his arm around Aiden and hugged him. Aiden stood there, motionless, with a hollow expression on his face.

"Now, Aiden, remember this is a war. Sean did his duty the same as the fellas on the other side. We will do what we can for him. There is no need for pent-up thoughts of revenge."

"Who told you I was thinking that?"

"Nobody did! I can see it in your eyes."

Aiden Reid looked away and said, "I cannot deny the thought was in my mind."

Dan O'Leary came over and quietly said, "Take care of Sean and your mother, Aiden. You have earned some time off. We do not need you lost on some senseless mission of revenge. Now tell me the name of that ship you saw?"

"*Restless*! HMS *Restless*."

Chapter 2

The Turner Bakery, Guildford …

Early Wednesday morning Terrance Spencer appeared out of the dark from the mill and tapped Jeb on the shoulder. It was three in the morning as the bakery staff arrived, stamping the ground and hugging their coats, eager to warm themselves inside. Jeb Hiscock held his long coat tight as he opened the front doors and ushered the staff in, out of the cold.

On seeing Terry, Jeb remembered missing the meeting on Monday, "Sorry, Terry, the meeting completely slipped my mind."

"No harm was done! Other things came up for me, and Tuesday was the same. But yesterday afternoon, I received a tip-off. I have been here all-night keeping watch!"

"Whatever for?"

"For the same reason as Monday! Some men attempted a break-in of the mill last night. We can talk now before you start. It will only take five minutes. We should discuss this privately."

Jeb was alarmed and walked with Terry across the wharf towards the mill.

"As you know, I like a pint before I go home and usually frequent the Kings Arms. On Saturday, I talked with some friends, and one of them took me aside and said there was trouble stirring from the outlying mills. My friend explained that a mill employee's father lost his job at the Albion Mills[5] in London. The father moved the family and found work in a nearby country mill."

Jeb scratched his head, recalling the story, "That's right, Thomas told me about that. Someone burnt the place down. They thought the sacked mill

---

[5] The Albion Mills, Southwark, London was completed in 1786 and was one of the first steam powered flour mills in England. It was highly efficient for the time, with local mills closing, unable to match its productivity and costs. It was gutted by fire in 1791. The cause of the fire was unknown. However, resentment against the changes being created by the advent of steam power, low wages, and the social effects of the industrial revolution in large cities such as London may have influenced the culprits. Wikipedia.

workers were responsible but could never prove it."

"You are correct. It was big news at the time. This chap's son finds it is happening again. A story is being spread that our mill will take away all the local mills' business. My friend informed me that this fellow is stirring up trouble by telling them about future job losses. Now workers in other mills are becoming worried.

At first, I thought nothing of it and enjoyed my Sunday off, attending church, seeing you there and spending time with the family that afternoon. On Tuesday, I met my friend again. It was not by chance as he heard that some mill workers were thinking of copying the Albion Mill fire before the builders completed our mill. He was not sure when but said it would be soon."

"Terry, when I heard about the Albion Mills, I asked Thomas about having guards. He said there was no need as they would only slowly bring the mill into production and not disturb the existing mills. But with this man spreading rumours, the workers' timing is not ours. They are afraid for their jobs, and I don't blame them. But it is not right what they are planning."

Terry was impatient, "Jeb, by last night, I was anxious and returned after dinner and kept watch. I locked up everything solid and set up camp on the mill's first floor. There is a good view from there. At around two in the morning, I heard noise along the wharf, and three men came into view. They walked up and started trying the locks. So, I called out, 'Hey! Get away from those locks, you men! That must have scared them as they ran off. No one came back."

"My goodness, that was only an hour ago! It would have been better if you had told me yesterday. I could have stayed!"

"Jeb, by the time I returned, you were long gone. From now on, we need at least two security guards a night. I think these mill workers will return but in larger numbers!"

"I am sure Mr Turner would agree. Let me get the bakery working this morning, and then I will call on Michael Rawlins, the Parish Constable. He has watchmen who we might call in. Mr Turner is not due back until Friday afternoon. I'm sure he will put on more men after that."

"But what if they come back tonight in strength? There may be ten or twenty of these men. We need a plan, Jeb and fast."

"Let me find the constable and discuss it with him. We need more information on who these men are and what they intend. Michael will still be in bed, but I will visit him for breakfast. We will join you after that. Thank you for last night, Terry. I am glad you were not hurt."

Anne, arriving at Huntley on late Wednesday afternoon, quickly sought out Neville Bassington.

"Neville, please may I ask a favour!" Anne stood there with a pleading smile on her face.

"What is it, Anne?"

"Forgive me for asking this, but I know you are hiring your coach for the return journey tomorrow and will travel straight through in a day. Would I be imposing if I came with you and Bethany? I have lost so much time over the last ten days, and I must catch up. Please?"

Neville considered the request and smiled, "It would be a pleasure. After all, you are my sister-in-law. What would Bethany say if I turned you down?"

"Thank you so much, Neville. I will send a rider and alert Ivy, so she has some food and the beds ready for us."

Neville became suspicious, "Us, Anne?"

Anne blushed and appeared embarrassed, "I am sorry, Neville. I did not mention that father asked if William might also travel with me. Would that be satisfactory?"

Neville frowned and gave the question some consideration. He realised merit in the request as Jonathan would be more comfortable without William and the boy more relaxed away from his father.

"Certainly, Anne. But it will be a late arrival so that William may fall asleep. We will drop you off first when we reach Guildford. Also, I will need you both ready for an early start tomorrow morning by seven-thirty."

"Thank you, Neville. We will be ready."

'Harting', St James's Square, London …

On Thursday morning, entering the drawing room where his mother and father were seated, Robert announced, "Father, I must discuss the estate with you. Mother, would you join the conversation as well, please? I have been talking with Mr Stem, who advises that the finances are not what they should be!"

Sir David sat in his armchair and replied, "Robert, you must not worry about the estate. Hugh is on top of things, and I keep in contact with Mr Manifold at the Attorneys. He takes care of all the investments and the plantations in the Indies. It is all under control."

Lady Jane found herself confused and asked, "Robert, what do you mean that things are not what they should be?"

"Let me explain, Mother. I am afraid things are not under control. Father, when did you last speak directly with Mr Manifold?"

"Well, I receive a letter from him every month. I expect there will be a letter waiting on my return."

"Father, things might not be the way you think they are. Mr Manifold has been dead for over three years! The letters that come are from the senior partner, Mr Finchley. He tells us that he has received no response from any letters sent in the last five years. There are urgent matters not addressed, and the staff wages are often overdue."

Lady Jane was caught entirely by surprise, "Well, David, what do you say about that?"

The Earl took another sip of his morning tea, "Don't worry, my dear, Mr Manifold is taking care of it all."

Lady Jane looked away from Lord Fintelton, somewhat frustrated, "Robert, shall we take a quick walk in the square?"

At the front doorway, Staines assisted them with their coats and saw them out. They walked across into the square and talked as they followed the path.

"Robert, I have felt that your father has had selective hearing for some years. But it appears that there is a more serious problem. He censors out anything he will not address. That is why he could speak so well at the dinner Tuesday night but made no sense at all on the subject today. Tell me, Robert, what are the problems?"

Robert quickly ran through his discoveries so far. Lady Jane looked down and kept walking.

"You say the investments have done well, but the estate is in terrible shape!"

"Yes, and Hugh may be walking into an unfriendly situation in the Indies. Emma wrote advising him, but it may be too late."

"So, Hugh might be in danger, and Emma is aware of all you tell us?"

"Yes, she helped me with the research. It all started with a discreet discussion with Pike. He revealed that money appeared tight as the servants often were paid late. Mr Stem confirmed the shortages of money. I asked if Emma would call on our attorneys and write a letter in advance. Mr Finchley, the new senior partner, fully confirmed what I was slowly uncovering. Mother, the intent here is to secure your future and estates."

"I understand, Robert, and I am very thankful for what you have done. I am so glad I have such caring children."

They walked on in silence until they faced 'Harting'. Lady Jane stopped and looked at the beautiful building.

"How bad is it, Robert? We could always sell 'Harting', which would provide a pretty sum. Surely that would pay all the debts."

Robert admired the building and resisted the suggestion. Who knows? He may become an Admiral one day, and 'Harting' may become a convenient residence. What better than his traditional family home?

"Mother, we have examined Mr Stem's books, and although Father and Hugh have not managed the estate well, it is not beyond recovery. But Hugh must be more constrained in his expenditure, the tenant farmers' rents recovered, and we must find some productivity increases."

"Robert, when you say 'we', who has looked at the books with you?"

"Well, Emma, of course, and I wanted someone who was an expert on books, so I involved Anne."

"Without consulting your father, Hugh or myself?"

"Anne was uncomfortable with my request and asked if she might be excused, but I insisted on her remaining for two reasons, no, for three reasons! First, I required assistance understanding the books; secondly, she understood finances and was a tremendous help in explaining the financial situation; thirdly, she is the woman I shall marry, and I trust her completely."

"I cannot argue with that, Robert. The family has gained a valuable addition."

Lady Jane South, upset that the Earl could no longer manage the estate affairs, had suspected there might be difficulties for some time. Equally disappointing was that Hugh avoided discussing the issues with her. Lady Jane was practical and agreed with Robert's proposal that they find a solution. She agreed that Anne's assistance would assist them in sorting out the mismanagement of the estate. She hoped Hugh was changing his ways but feared his past interests in womanising and drinking might consume him and result in their downfall.

"Mother, you understand I will be away for long periods in the navy. Hugh is also away and may not return for some time so Emma will work with you. I would encourage Anne's involvement as she is an intelligent young lady and understands how large businesses run. She has the skills we need currently and in the future. We can fix this problem if we work as a team."

Lady Jane gazed across St James's Square at the family's London home 'Harting'. She sighed. "It would be a pity selling the townhouse". The countess knew Sir David would continue happily at Fintelton, not caring what anyone did. She smiled. She was very thankful for her son Robert.

"Robert, I agree. We will work as a team. I will write a letter this afternoon and invite Anne for a stay at Fintelton. If you are not there, it will be a team of girls. Oh, what fun we will have!"

"That is the spirit, Mother. Now I must away, the Admiralty calls!"

"Robert?" Lady Jane stood there in silence for a moment. "Thank you!"

Robert smiled. He appreciated what she meant. Gently kissing his mother, Robert turned and rushed for his carriage. He was running late!

On the Guildford Road …

As the coach made its way out of London early Thursday morning, Bethany noticed how the passing suburbs entranced William.

"He is in a world of his own, Anne!" She indicated at the young lad glued beside the window.

"He has seen London but once before, Beth! He is fascinated by the crowds of people and the factory smoke." Anne smiled, content that William would be no bother on this trip.

The conversation as they set off was rapid, with much-excited comments about Thomas's wedding and the dinner at St. James's Square. As the suburbs passed and the coach entered the country, they became content in a quiet lull. The evening before was late, and with the early start, Anne was becoming drowsy. With William consumed at the carriage window, she sat back, closed her eyes and relaxed.

Soon she found herself with Robert entering a large ballroom lit by magnificently gleaming gold chandeliers and rose bloom decorations of red and pink surrounding candelabras. Men in evening dress and ladies in dazzling costumes crowded the room. She and Robert were soon dancing among a host of other couples enjoying the magical orchestra music. Anne felt as light as a feather as Robert twirled her around and around the dance floor as if she were gliding in his arms. At an interval, Robert spied some friends and introduced Anne, "Lady Beauchamp! May I introduce my fiancée, Miss Anne Turner?"

Lady Beauchamp turned and greeted Robert with a smile and inspected Anne through her spectacles. Anne was keen on meeting some of Robert's acquaintances and gave a polite curtsey with a gleaming smile. Robert continued, "Anne, this is Lady Beauchamp's daughter, Evelyn."

After fluttering her fan, Evelyn directed her gaze at Anne, giving her a half-smile, "A pleasure Miss Anne. I do recall hearing of your engagement; you must find this company far different from the country. I understand you are the daughter of a country baker!" She snickered a laugh behind her fan.

Before Anne could reply, Evelyn cut off Anne and spoke again, "Why Mother, there are the Glassons, and Jennifer is with them. We must see them. Come, Mother!" With that, she led her mother away without even nodding goodbye.

Anne stood there with her mouth open, amazed at the rudeness of the slight.

"Anne!" Someone was calling – Anne opened her eyes.

"Anne, are you alright?" Anne rubbed her eyes and then saw the friendly concern of her sister.

"Oh, Bethany, I must have dozed off! I was dreaming."

"It must have been a frightening dream, as your expression appeared most disturbed!"

"It was nothing, Bethany – just a dream!"

William turned from the window, "Like my dream Anne when I thought father was beating mother?"

"Yes, it probably was William. Perhaps we should consider a happier subject?"

Bethany, concerned for Anne, reached out and held her hands, "Think about all the good things we enjoyed in London, Anne. So much has happened since July! Why I am married, Thomas and Marion are wed, and now you and Robert are engaged. Who knows what will happen next?" Bethany turned away as Neville pointed out a landmark.

Anne relaxed, drifting back and recalling their ten days in London. Besides the wedding, the event most pleasing was the dinner at 'Harting', St James's Square, where Robert's father, the Earl, announced Robert and her engagement. She smiled as she remembered the lavish dinner, rehearing Lord Fintelton's kind words and the wonderful hug Robert gave her as everyone cheered and clapped.

Sir David stood and smiled at the large gathering of guests at 'Harting' that night.

"Good evening, friends. I will make this as short as possible as I am not known as the world's most famous orator."

Sir John Philps, Lady Jane's younger brother, chipped in, saying, "Here, Here, David, but you can tell a good tale! Ha, Ha."

"Thank you, Sir John, no more champagne for you tonight!"

Everyone laughed, including Sir John.

"As you all know, our youngest son Robert and the lovely Miss Anne Turner have announced their engagement."

There was wild applause as the young couple stood up, taking a bow and waving at various friends.

The Earl continued, "Tonight, I have pleasure in welcoming Mr Jonathan Turner and Mrs Eleanora Turner, Anne's father and mother from Guildford. Also, Doctor Neville and Mrs Bethany Bassington visit as well. Bethany, of course, is Anne's sister.

Now, this story is interesting. Robert and Neville have served for years in the navy. It is not unknown that Lady Jane has pined for Robert to marry, but there has never been a mention of a woman in either boy's life. Then suddenly, Neville meets a beautiful young Bethany Turner, and they are married, and then Robert arrives home and tells me he will marry Bethany's sister Anne. It appears Neville and Bethany commenced a rush of romances. We were pleased for Neville, and there was a beautiful wedding in Guildford, celebrated by Reverend Andrew Taggart, a good friend of the family who joins us tonight."

Lord Fintelton kindly pointed towards Reverend Taggart, and there was some applause for Andrew as he stood and waved.

"Now I was wondering who this young Anne girl was! But my wife assured me she was admirably suitable. You will all know that I am getting on and focusing more on the roses in the garden than keeping track of where Robert lives or works. It appears that he has been spending quite a lot of time in Guildford. So, I was curious about this young lady who will become my daughter-in-law!

My first opportunity to meet Anne was when she joined our family on a London trip. We sat together in the coach, sharing each other's company during an enjoyable journey. Well, ladies and gentlemen, I must advise you that her beauty, charm, and grace overcame me from the first moment I met this young lady. But friends, I find she is highly intelligent and would be an asset to any of our country's most significant families." Sir David turned and looked directly at Anne. "Lady Jane and I could not have wished for a more wonderful daughter-in-law than Anne."

There was an uproar of cheers and well-wishes from the assembled company.

A large bump shaking the carriage suddenly interrupted her present thoughts. She wiped away a tiny tear and regained her seat.

"You were miles away, Anne. What were you thinking about?"

"I was doing what you asked and remembering the happy things. The dinner at 'Harting', Bethany! Robert and I are engaged. Six months ago, I could never have imagined such a thing. It is like a fairy tale. It is so wonderful, and we shall be so happy."

"Anne, we share your happiness! You and Robert are made for each other. I am sure your life with him will be perfect. Lots of children and very peaceful."

Neville was surprised by Bethany's comment, "I'm not sure it will be peaceful with him being in the navy, but exciting, yes!"

They all laughed, and Anne pushed her fear of moving into the aristocratic circles as far into the background as it would fit. She considered, 'If that were the worst life could throw at her, then why worry?'

In the Servants Coach leaving Greenwich ...
Aggie, holding some knitting, sat back as the coach rattled along towards Blackheath Hill. It was a busy start ensuring they packed everything for the return home. The plan was for an early morning tea for Mrs Turner and then heading through London and out into the country at ten in the morning. The staff happily rested in the carriage for the day's journey before overnighting at the Epsom pub half-owned by Mr Turner.

"Time for some knitting before the next round starts! Will you join me, Mrs Jennings?"

The two ladies sat together and enjoyed each other's company as they shared comments on their different patterns. Across from them, Ethel Nibley quietly read a book.

"Mr Turner was angry after the wedding when he finally found William with me in the carriage! I thought he would have realised that is where the boy would be."

Mrs Jennings advised, "Aggie, perhaps you should have told either Nanny or Mrs Turner that he was with you!"

"Perhaps I should have, but he was safe. Do you think Mr Turner is still angry with me?"

"Mrs Turner will settle him down. For some reason, he is irritated whenever William is involved. Don't worry, Aggie; I am sure it is all forgotten!"

"Have you noticed how badly he treats the boy? None of the other children is chastised like William. I feel so sorry for the little man."

"Stay clear of that, Aggie. It is a dangerous place. Best not interfere."

"Why is that Mrs Jennings?"

"Best left unsaid! Things happened before your time here. Better left forgot now."

Aggie heeded the warning but found it hard to reconcile William's harsh treatment by his father.

Ethel Nibley looked up, "I hope Rosalind is on her best behaviour. She is travelling with Clemmie in the Turner's carriage. Rosalind and Clementine have become good friends. Now for the coach ride! This time in the coach will be a luxury, having some time for reading!"

Mrs Jennings and Aggie smiled back at Ethel. Aggie continued knitting, "Your daughter is such a sweet little thing, Ethel! She will do well in life. Mrs Turner is not worried at all by class distinction. She sees the real value in people and is very generous. Pity Mr Turner is not more like that!"

"Now, Aggie! Be careful what you say. You never know who is listening!"

The Racing Horse Pub, Epson, Surrey ...

The Spowith's coach made good time and was well ahead of the Turner's coaches when entering Epsom. After lunch at the Racing Horse Pub, David suggested a walk may be in order before they were cooped up in the coach again for hours ahead. Andrew Taggart readily agreed as they loved walking and would return in a half-hour, meeting at the coach. Emma and David followed at a more sedate pace.

"Emma, this is the first time we have been alone today. I do love you so much! May I kiss you again?"

"I see no reason why not! A little kiss would be appreciated, David. After all, we are engaged!"

Being the perfect gentleman, David found his attraction for Emma, suddenly overcame his manners and, standing close, kissed her gently and then continued the kiss for some minutes. Those passing by lifted their eyebrows but carefully avoided the young lovers, not disturbing them.

"I have so much I must confide in you, Emma! It is hard deciding on where I should start. But there are some important issues we must agree on before we reach Guildford."

Emma rearranging herself after finally being released from his arms, found herself much aroused, "David, why not dine with me tonight at the Fox and Hound?"

"Nothing would please me more, but knowing you were staying with Anne, I accepted an invitation from Neville and Bethany. Perhaps they would join us at the hotel. We shall visit them and ask once we are in Guildford before dropping you at the Turner house."

"No, David, I forgot William! Anne will not leave him on his own. Perhaps we must decide once we are there."

David nodded in agreement and then became somewhat serious. As they walked along the quiet footpath, he was anxious that Emma understood his financial situation.

"Emma, I have always been concerned that it must be for love and not for any other reason when I marry. My greatest fear was that you would reject me as my standing in society was far below yours, and I have only a country doctor's living for your support. I know this has been a hard decision for you, and now I am sure our love is true. You cannot imagine how glad I am about this!"

Emma leaned against David and kissed him softly, "David, I will love you till I die, and if anything prevents us, we will run away together and find our own life elsewhere. I am determined now that we marry."

David Sopwith could not have loved her more as he was now sure she would be the love of his life.

"There are two issues I must explain before we continue in the coach."

"I am all ears, David!"

"Well, I have been discrete since making my home in Guildford. I completely trust Neville Bassington and have shared my true life situation with him. He is the only person I have told, and I feel it only right to share this with you and your family. You see, I have seen many unhappy marriages because of money. My mother, bless her loving heart, always advised me that I should marry for love. She was a wonderful person, and I miss her greatly, but my financial situation is not quite as desperate as you might think!"

Emma's interest was now entirely focused on what David was saying.

"My parent's financial situation was one of great wealth. When my parents and elder brother died, I inherited their assets and property in Ireland and London. Also, my sister gained a large inheritance and is quite financially independent."

Emma blushed and, with wide-open eyes, questioned, "Then the statement you made of no interest in your parent's estates meant you are not concerned about this inheritance. But you did inherit from your parents?"

"Yes, that is how I have always explained it, and I would like it kept that way. I have always desired the position of a country doctor and felt no need for a large manor or country estate. My patients' care has always been my first concern, but I understand this must change in the future. Now you are my first concern Emma, and I will manage my patients differently."

For Emma, the prospect of living in a house in Guildford seemed romantic, and she was keen that they spend their first years there. They may require a larger home in time, but there was no rush. She desired further clarification on what he was saying.

"David, I will enjoy our first years in your house in Guildford but remember, I will be mistress of the house and may make some changes or ask for a larger house that will benefit both of us. But when you speak of wealth, might you be more specific?"

"Yes, the two estates in Ireland are huge and have estate managers, and each brings in a handsome income. My parents were both from wealthy families and built up a family fortune in addition to the estates before their sad demise. It is huge wealth, and I have avoided disclosing the fact while living in Guildford. You and I must think long and carefully about how we deal with this together. However, I am pleased that your circumstances will not be as restricted as you may have thought."

Emma sat there, taking in what David now disclosed.

"I am pleasantly surprised, David, and I hope I may assist you in this dilemma. But what is the second issue we must discuss?"

"You will recall that I mentioned I have a sister."

"Yes, what is her name?"

"Victoria. She is now eighteen and lives with a guardian on the Coleraine estate in Ireland. Her greatest wish is to join me here and make Guildford her home. I am the only family she has, and she wishes for proximity. I am proposing a house purchase as she will want her independence, but I hope you will be her friend. She will arrive in late December and stay with me until we settle the accommodation requirements."

"Victoria will be most welcome, David, and she must join us at Fintelton for Christmas."

"That we shall do!"

David was far more relaxed now he had revealed his actual situation in life. The news overcame Emma, and she stood there thinking about how she should handle this. She would tread very carefully, given his desire that his wealth remains undisclosed. They would enjoy the adventure together.

"There is one other slight issue, Emma!"

"What can that be, David?"

"I have promised Simeon and William that we shall finish the model boat soon. The boat will require more of my attention than you may feel necessary. But I must honour my commitment to this."

"So, you should, David." She gave him a mischievous smile and said, "I intend on spending some more time with Anne in Guildford as well."

He gently took her hand, "We shall be so happy, Emma. You have made me the happiest man in England."

The Barque, Frogmore, Mid Atlantic Ocean ...

Sir Hugh South suddenly woke with a lurch of the ship as it weathered the high seas running in the Atlantic for the past week. A dim light appeared, seeping through the cabin door, and Hugh realised the steward would soon bring his morning tea.

He looked down at the outline of the naked woman lying under the bedding beside him. He thought, 'Clarissa must be the most beautiful woman I have ever bedded!' She rested there gently breathing, shining long dark hair across her face, almost purring as she slept. When he first met her, he knew they would enjoy each other's company. Slowly but surely, he won her trust and finally lured her into his bed. Her lovemaking was exceptional, and he found himself exhausted after the second time last night. Hugh now sensed a growing feeling of attachment for her.

He puffed up his pillows and moved his body back so he could watch her beside him. She opened her eyes and smiled.

"Good morning, Lady Clarissa. Morning is near upon us!"

Clarissa covered her mouth as she yawned, sitting up with the sheet across her chest. The beautiful lines of her body aroused Hugh.

"I must return before Fiona finds me missing. Where is my nightgown!" She pulled the sheet and blankets close, shuddering from the cold.

Hugh leaned down and kissed her. Moving down beside her, he pulled her close against his chest.

"There's time for a quickie!"

She giggled and kissed him back, enjoying the warmth of his body against hers.

"Perhaps. It depends on how gentle you are!"

They started kissing each other madly as a soft knock came on the door.

"Clarissa, it is Fiona. It is time to dress! You should come now before it is light!"

Clarissa Wendarm looked up and answered, "Coming, Fiona!"

Hugh sighed, "Where did you find Fiona? She can be a terrible nuisance!"

"She is a family relation. Her husband died of some sickness. It took me ages convincing her to be my chaperone. I will tell you more later. Must be off now!"

Clarissa pulled herself out of Hugh's bed, covering herself with a dressing gown, then bent down and kissed him, "Till breakfast, Darling."

Hugh watched as she lightly closed the door and slipped away. Her departing words calmed him, 'That's nice. No woman has ever called me Darling before.' He found Clarissa good company and was becoming fond of her.

Fiona Green was not pleased and warned her companion, "You should not have been with him last night. Who knows where this may lead!"

"On the contrary, my Dear Fiona. I know exactly where this is leading!"

The Turner House, Guildford, Surrey ...

After a speedy trip from London, Neville's coach pulled up outside Anne's family home on the High Street.

"The roads are becoming far better, Anne. A few months ago, I would not have believed how quickly we managed this trip today. My bed will be comfortable tonight rather than staying overnight in a hotel. Now you and William will be safe? I should imagine David, Emma, and the Taggarts will arrive soon. Will you join us for dinner?"

"Thank you, Neville, but I think I shall remain at home with William tonight. Ivy will have a meal waiting for us. William will be in bed early after this long day in the coach. Thank you for the offer, but perhaps you might invite Emma. It may be her last chance of being with David for a while."

"I shall leave a note with David's housekeeper and invite them. I'm sure David will escort Emma home at a reasonable time."

"Thank you, Neville, for a safe trip. I, too, long for my bed tonight. Come, William! We must find Ivy and organise dinner. Bye."

Ivy packed William's lunch in the morning and had Jess escort him to school. Then she provided a beautiful breakfast, served in the dining room, for Anne and Emma.

"I don't remember Ivy being here when I last visited, Anne?"

"No, she was not here then, but father hired her before the wedding in Greenwich. She house-sat for us while we were away and now assists Mrs Jennings in the kitchen. He also hired Jessica Swamp as a scullery maid. Mother used the same agency Aggie came from."

"I must say that Ivy is a beautiful cook. These small omelettes are delicious!" Anne noticed how Emma was enjoying the meal.

"Emma, what are your plans for today? We should discuss the Estate finances this morning if possible. You will recall our discussions with Robert on Tuesday night. If money is missing, the sooner we solve this situation, the better. Now that your mother is helping us, we should develop a plan."

With years of bookkeeping experience, Anne knew there would be various ways someone could easily manipulate the Estate's books. Especially if few people were involved and the bookkeeping system operated on trust. She wondered if all estates managed their financial affairs the same way.

As Ivy passed Anne a cup of tea, she refocused on breakfast. Emma took a sip of tea and then smiled.

"I thought I might visit Hursts today before dining with David tonight. If I might bother you for another night's accommodation, I will set off for Fintelton tomorrow. Why don't you join me, Anne, and I will show you Petersfield?"

"Thank you, Emma, but I must catch up on my work. You will be no bother here tonight, but I warn you the main party will arrive later today, and the house will be busy. Thank goodness for that new bedroom beside the boys upstairs. Father will house my sisters there, and we can hide in my room and avoid the chaos once they all arrive." They both laughed, knowing how full the house would be.

"Now, while we have some quiet, we should quickly discuss the estate's finances."

The Barque, Frogmore, off Newfoundland ...
Captain Verner Eriksen dined with the first-class passengers and enjoyed a relaxed meal, the first in some time after the ship cleared the Atlantic gale. The sea was calm, and all the passengers were considerably relieved, having a dining room where the floor was stable.

The captain addressed the passengers, "Ladies and Gentlemen, my apologies for the past eight days of rough weather. I will find your company most refreshing tonight now the gale is over.

The weather ahead appears calm. Hopefully, this will continue as we head towards the American coast and then onto New York."

Hugh wanted more information, "Captain, in terms of the trip, where exactly are we now and how long before we reach Jamaica?"

"Sir Hugh, at present, we are passing St John's, Newfoundland and are heading down past Nova Scotia, around Nantucket and into New York. We should berth in New York in about a week. There we stay for three days taking on supplies and some further passengers. The next stop will be Jamaica. If the wind holds from the north, then I expect a voyage of a week or two before reaching Kingston."

"Thank you, Captain."

Hugh looked at Clarissa, and she smiled back at him. Having finished his dinner, he must commence two letters before they reached New York. After that, Hugh had plans for some more intimate time with Lady Wendarm. Moving towards her, he found she was in deep conversation with the captain.

"Excuse me, Captain, if I might have a quick word with Lady Wendarm? It will take but a minute!"

"Why, of course, Sir Hugh!"

The captain politely excused himself. Hugh sat alongside Clarissa and quietly said, "I must finish some letters in my cabin, but I should be finished by ten. Would you join me for drinks, say after ten tonight?"

"There is nothing I would enjoy more, Sir Hugh. However, I must decline tonight due to a minor health issue. Please forgive me, but perhaps tomorrow!" Clarissa said this with a pleading smile.

Hugh was disappointed as she looked ravishing tonight. Now being totally under her spell, he would agree with any excuse.

"Perhaps I might convince Fiona! She would enjoy a game of cards. I will ask her, and she will call on you."

"Certainly, Clarissa! I hope you are soon well."

He smiled, stood up and beckoned the steward, "I require two bottles of scotch and a glass in my cabin. As soon as you can, please! I am going there directly."

"Yes, Sir! One glass or two?"

Not wanting the steward to doubt his form, he smiled and replied, "Yes, of course, two!"

Hugh slipped the steward a half-crown and winked. He then turned and made for his cabin.

Sitting at his desk, he pulled out a quill, ink and paper and drafted a letter.

'Frogmore', New York

Lady Fintelton
Countess of Fintelton
Harting House
St James's Square
St James's
London

Dear Mother

I am writing about a private matter and would ask for your discretion for the time being.

After boarding the ship in Southampton, I spent the first day in my cabin as I found seasickness had taken hold of me. However, this soon passed, and I gained courage and ventured on deck. There I first met Lady Clarissa Wendarm. Since then, we have formed a close friendship, and I find her a reliable companion on this long voyage.

I appreciate your advice on close attachments, so I am writing for your assistance and the provision of some information. Lady Wendarm has informed me that she is a widow. Her husband was a large land-holder in the midlands with a title of which I am unaware. He died some twelve months ago, and Lady Clarissa was the beneficiary of his estate. The lady travels with a similar reason for visiting Jamaica, familiarising herself with the plantations she inherited.

While I have become quite fond of Clarissa, I would not commit myself until I know her background. With that in mind and your previous advice on marriage partners, I wonder if you would make specific enquiries verifying Lady Clarissa Wendarm's background.

Thank you, mother, for this. I am sure the lady is genuine, and I hope you confirm this for me.

I shall post this letter from New York. Perhaps I might receive a reply in Kingston some weeks after I arrive.

The sea crossing has been uneventful, and I welcome discovering New York's delights as we port there for three days.

Your loving son
Hugh.

Hearing a knock, Hugh stood and opened the cabin door. It was Fiona Green.

"Sir Hugh, Lady Wendarm advised you would enjoy a hand or two of cards tonight. In the saloon, of course!"

Hugh, assuring Fiona he would soon be there, packed up his letters and writing equipment and set off directly. While dreading the card game, he must observe good manners as Clarissa, in her sickbed, would be expecting a report.

As the night went on, he found Fiona, an engaging conversationalist with a good knowledge of wheat farming and agriculture, which were his pet interests outside the use of women.

At the end of the game, Fiona hesitated but said, "Sir Hugh, I enjoyed the cards. Thank you!"

"It was my pleasure, Fiona."

"Sir Hugh, may I be bold and speak confidently with you?"

Hugh wondered where this request was leading. However, he detected that Fiona was unsure whether she should trust him, "Fiona, if this concerns Lady Wendarm, then perhaps you should not mention it."

Fiona looked away and could see that they were the last passengers remaining in the saloon except for the wait staff.

She leaned over and whispered but loud enough, so Hugh heard, "Then I will risk my confidence in you, Sir. Take care, Sir! What you see may not be what it seems! Take care!"

Fiona stood, said goodnight, and walked off to her cabin. Hugh sat there, wondering what she meant. Of course, he must maintain her confidence, but perhaps he thought she was paranoid about her companion, Clarissa or jealous of her. That must be it. You never knew what these women were thinking. Better left alone. Hugh put it out of his mind and decided on a bottle of scotch before bed.

The Turner's Return Home ...

Jonathan was far happier now that Eleanora was resting in her room. The London wedding and appointments were demanding, and he was encouraged by how well her health stood the test. He decided on a shortcut from Greenwich that would reduce the travel time for his wife. Unfortunately, the roads were in a deteriorated condition, and the coach broke a wheel outside Croydon. Eleanora slipped from her seat, injuring her back, so they stayed overnight in a pleasant hotel while the stable men arranged the wheel repairs. A local doctor supplied some potions that eased Eleanora's pain, allowing a resumption of their journey home on Friday.

Early Saturday morning, Jonathan checked that Eleanora was comfortable, then left in a rush for the bakery and mill, eager to catch up on events while they were away. Before entering the bakery, he crossed the road and inspected the offices that Robinson's men were fitting out. Finding Anne there, deep in discussion with the builders, he left and sought out Terry.

"Terry, fill me in on the mill's startup program. How has it gone?"

"Before that, Mr Turner, we should find Jeb as there is a more urgent problem!"

Jonathan was surprised by this, nodded, and they set off for the bakery.

"Jeb! Would you join us for a few minutes?"

"Certainly, Mr Turner. Is this about the guards?"

Still unaware of the problem, Jonathan blurted out, "Where can we talk?"

"On the wharf – there is no one over there at present."

Jeb explained Terry's story about the outlying mill workers creating trouble and the guards protecting the Turner mill. Johnathan became anxious as he recalled the fire at the Albion Mills some thirty-five years ago.

"Right, I will talk with Constable Rawlins straight after this and then the Mayor. We need this stopped quickly. In the meantime, Jeb, please double the guard. Terry, now the mill issues?"

Terry was worried about the boiler's pressure capacity, as he had witnessed previous explosions after pressure exceeded tolerance levels. He insisted that the engineers install a pressure gauge[6] with an override valve in case of an emergency. Jonathan reluctantly agreed with Terry and hoped the process would not take too long.

Now most concerned about rioting mill workers invading Guildford, Jonathan made straight for the Parish Constable's house and collected him before meeting Rupert Smith, the Mayor.

"Rupert, I need watchmen there every night until we can settle this issue. The mill is good for the future of Guildford. We must protect it!"

"I agree, Jonathan, but I don't have enough watchmen. Perhaps a fence around the mill would make it more secure?"

"Yes, yes, why not? The builders are working in my new offices now. I will go directly there and reassign them. In the interim, will you provide watchmen, Rupert?"

"Constable Rawlins will rally as many as he can find. But the cost of their wages must be your expense, Jonathan, as the council budget will not afford this."

"Agreed. That is fair!"

Leaving the parish constable with the Mayor, Jonathan quickly jogged down High Street and entered the new offices where Robinson's men had almost finished the alterations. He found Ian Robinson and explained the immediate need for a fence around his mill and storehouse. The builder wasted no time accepting the new job and inspected the site with Jonathan.

"Mr Turner, we can do the job, and it will take some weeks, but first, we will need the materials – that will slow us down! I will place the order today, and delivery should start by next Tuesday. Until we complete the fence, you will need another way of protecting your mill! In the meantime, my men will finish your new offices."

Jonathan could see the logic in what Robinson said: "I understand. Let us hope we can save the mill from this mob! I must go now."

At his bakery desk, he sat slumped over, head in his hands, struggling to decide on his next move.

"Father?" He looked up and found Anne standing beside him. "Come

---

[6] In 1790 James Watt invented the pressure gauge for steam engines. This was a huge step forward for safety.

with me, Father?"

While gathering his thoughts, Jonathan found this interruption unwelcome, but before he could complain, Anne said, "I have a solution, Father. Follow me!"

Jonathan, his face turning red, lifted his eyes and saw something he was missing, a calm approach in a desperate situation. He checked himself and followed Anne. She led him across the road and climbed the stairs to the first floor of the new offices.

"Father, this end of the office building is finished. We can set up a command post here." Jonathan opened his mouth again, but Anne raised her hand, silencing him.

"If you look out this window, you will see we have an excellent view of the mill, the wharf, and the bulk store. But at night it will be dark. If we place lanterns at appropriate places, there will be no darkness where the trespassing men may hide. We place other lookouts at either end of the buildings so they can warn us of anyone approaching. We keep our main supply of men protecting the mill in these offices where they may sleep until needed."

Jonathan's rage subsided as he saw that his daughter was managing the problem and a solution was developing. He should have consulted her earlier.

"Anne, that is a fine plan, but where do we find a supply of men? Who will help us?"

"Jeb will visit Batton Place! He feels plenty of men there will support us, especially with your open support for catholic emancipation."

"God bless them! Thank you, Anne. I am amazed."

"No rest for you yet, Father. We set up our command centre here, and we first put together a council of war and make plans. We must be ready for the attack!" Anne smiled and said, "It is a bit like playing pirates with William!"

Jonathan broke out into a nervous laugh.

Chapter 3

The Turner Household, Guildford …

Clementine and Rosalind, now good friends, chatted merrily with Mrs Turner in her bedroom. The happy banter relieved her boredom as Eleanor rested her back.

"Are they annoying you, Mrs Turner? If they are, I will have them in the kitchen in an instant."

"No, not at all, Ethel. I enjoy the company and their young thoughts. Now Ethel, please tell me what colour ribbon best suits the hat Rosalind is sewing?"

"Well, I always consult my mother about matching materials. She is good with colours. But I must say I do like the light blue colour. It is beautiful!"

"Yes, it is, but it depends on what you are wearing with it. A colour that matches your wardrobe is probably the best choice."

"Oh, Mrs Turner, before we discuss colours further, I should advise that Doctor Sopwith sent a message saying he would call at two, and it is nearly that time now."

"Certainly, Ethel, please show him in when he arrives."

"Let me put this wrap around you and straighten the bedclothes. Here girls, give me a hand, please."

The girls put down their sewing and assisted Ethel in straightening the sheets and blankets.

Ethel asked again, "Should the girls come with me while you see the Doctor, Ma'am?"

"No, Ethel, they may stay. I am sure it is a social call."

"Thank you, Ma'am."

"Rosalind, tell me about the colours of your dresses!"

Shortly after two, Rosalind, deep into the details of colour, was disturbed by a knock at the door as it slowly opened.

"Ah, David. Thank you for calling."

"Good day, Mrs Turner. I finished early today and thought I might work with Simeon and William on the boat."

"That is kind of you, David."

The girls smiled at each other.

"Tell me, Mrs Turner, how are you recovering from that nasty bump in the carriage?"

"Moving around is still quite difficult. I do a little bit each day!"

"I know Neville is managing your recovery, but I suggest you try walking each morning and afternoon. Extend the walking daily, and you will recover by the end of the week. I would also suggest that Ethel keeps the fire lit. It is quite cold in here, Mrs Turner."

"Yes, we noticed that. Perhaps before you go, you would summon Simeon and William. They will make it up."

"I understand Mr Turner and Anne are at the bakery?"

"Yes, there is a lot of work they must catch up on after the wedding in Greenwich."

"Has Mr Turner mentioned that I would commence swimming lessons with Simeon and William before we launch the boat?"

Both girls looked enviously towards Eleanora Turner.

"The boys and I must attend the Institute and check the boat plan. Mr Sharples will be helpful with certain woodworking tools. After that, we may attend the men's club and have the first swimming lesson. If Mr Turner is unavailable, I'm sure Doctor Bassington will join us."

"David, you will not see Mr Turner until tomorrow, so please go ahead. I must warn you that the girls are envious of the boys."

"My apologies for this, girls! As far as I know, the only pool big enough in Guildford is at the men's club. But if you convinced your mother and family to join the Souths and Sopwiths next July at the Isle of Wight, we could arrange many swimming lessons."

Clementine blurted out, "Oh, Mother, I have never seen the sea. Please, may we all go? It would be wonderful."

"I will discuss it with your father, Clementine." Eleanora could see Rosalind was very eager as well.

"Thank you for your kind suggestion, David. It sounds most interesting. Let us know more at a closer time, and we will consider it. Now, girls, we must …… Oh!"

Eleanora bent over, holding her stomach. The pain was sharp and sudden, and she gave a loud moan. David Sopwith immediately reverted into medical mode.

"Rosalind, please find Ethel! Sorry, I meant your mother! Please call her. Clementine, a wet washer, please and a dry towel." The two girls sprinted off.

"Has the pain subsided, Mrs Turner?"

"Yes, it is subsiding. It is nothing. Please do not worry."

"I'm not sure about that."

David gave Eleanora a quick examination and informed her, "I think this little one will be coming a bit before everyone expected it!"

Eleanora looked up in fear, "Please, David! Do not tell Jonathan. I am sure it is only a passing pain."

David was sure it was not.

"Would you mind if Neville made another examination soon? I would value his opinion. Also, perhaps it would be best to forget about exercise and remain in bed for the next two days. Given your back problems from the trip, I would ask that you rest now."

As Doctor Sopwith left, he spoke with Ethel, "If anything else occurs, call Neville or me immediately. I will be at the Institute with the boys."

Eleanora called the girls back in for company. Clementine, at thirteen years, seeing her mother was downcast, possessed the same gift of perception as William. She had suspected for some time that her mother was seriously ill and made every effort to cheer her up.

"Mother, may we look at your hats in the cupboard?"

"Yes, dear, please do."

The girls opened the wardrobe door. There was an assortment of hats on the top shelf, and Clementine selected one. Rosalind spied a hat case on the bottom of the wardrobe and pulled it out. Opening the case, she found a beautiful light hat with feathers and a white veil.

"That was the hat I wore as part of my going away outfit when I was married. I have kept it as I was so fond of it all these years."

"It is a beautiful hat, Mrs Turner. It suits your colours."

With a clatter of shoes, Simeon and William entered the room and made up the fire.

The Guildford Institute ...

Mr Henry Sharples looked up from his desk as the doctor, followed by the two boys, entered the Institute. Doctor Sopwith smiled and approached Mr Sharples.

"Good day, Mr Sharples. We enquire about books on woodworking instruments. I have several at home, but I need an instrument I recall from boatbuilding books. Would you have a specific book on this subject?"

Mr Sharples considered the request, "Perhaps if I perused the plan and the part you wish shaped."

"We can do better than that. Pass the wood, please, William. Here, come over, and I will lay out the plan, and you may inspect our piece of wood."

Doctor Sopwith approached a large table where Mr Linton, one of the town's blacksmiths, was reading.

"Excuse me, Mr Linton, might we set this plan out at this end of the table? We shall not disturb you."

"Certainly, Doctor."

With that, David laid out the plan and pointed out the part. Mr Linton, who enjoyed woodwork, could not resist standing and glancing at the plan.

Henry Sharples always helped those who asked for assistance. He studied the plan with interest and then inspected the piece of wood, "I think we have a book on tools for that kind of work. Follow me, Doctor."

Mr Sharples and Doctor Sopwith set off in search of the books. Mr Linton raised his eyebrows as he sat beside William, who was now holding the piece of wood.

"Well, William Turner, building boat, are ye?"

"Yes, Mr Linton. A model boat! This piece of wood is for the keel."

"Right. Mind I lookun?"

William considered Mr Linton, who sat beside him and seemed like his head touched the ceiling. He checked with Simeon, who shrugged, so William smiling, passed Mr Linton the piece of wood.

With a frown, the blacksmith tested the wood with his thumbnail, "Ah! This wood be un ash! No good! If you want build boat keel, you need oak!"

"Why!"

"Because it strong and good wood for working. It be shaped. Give plan here ……….. please un!"

As Simeon pushed the plan closer, Mr Linton leaned over, and William pointed out the keel.

"Thank Yee, William, I see un. Let me see now, need piece oak three feet long. That do it!"

Doctor Sopwith and Mr Sharples came back with two large books. William spoke first.

"Mr Linton thinks we should use oak!"

David Sopwith looked at Mr Linton and said, "I'm sorry, Mr Linton. I hope the boys have not bothered you?"

"No, no, I start un conversation. I must apologise, Doctor! I like work with wood, and I hear you talking. Look at piece of wood you using. No good! It ash! Use oak for keel. It easier work with an stronger. My Oath! Come down workshop now; I have piece you can have. Also, have tools. I show you how! Come on, youngins?"

"Well, thank you, Mr Linton. Why not! Let us be off. Thank you, Mr Sharples, for your help. Perhaps you could set those books aside for me till tomorrow. We will go with Mr Linton and take advantage of his kind offer now."

The boys did not argue, as visiting the blacksmith's shop was like inviting bees to the honeypot!

Leaving London for Portsmouth …

It was late afternoon at 'Harting' as Robert boarded his carriage, coat in hand.

"Right, Staines, I have everything. Thank you for your service during my stay. I know you will look after my parents until they return. Make sure they do not stay any longer than next Friday. The weather worsens, and the roads may become impassable at Christmas."

"I will do my best, Sir."

"Please remember the London Gazette tomorrow. I shall read it at Fintelton once it arrives."

"I shall take care of that, Sir Robert."

With that, Robert nodded and boarded his coach. Taping the ceiling, the coach sped off for Wimbledon, where he would stay the night with his mother's brother, Sir John, and Lady Angela Philps. Robert felt that with an early start on Saturday morning, he would easily reach Guildford before mid-afternoon.

As the coach moved slowly through the London traffic, Robert sat back and recalled the great honour he had received at the Admiralty. On reaching the Admiralty on Thursday, the reception clerk handed him a message advising him of a delay until Friday at two pm. Robert quickly decided he would use the extra time purchasing Christmas presents.

On Friday, he arrived at the Admiralty five minutes late. In a rush, he dashed around several carriages, walked across the footpath and into the reception. There he found a line of thirty officers waiting for access and impatiently milling in the foyer. He sighed, realising he would now be well and truly late. Then, spying a familiar face on the balcony above, he waved. Their eyes met, and Robert was thankful that the officer acknowledged. Colonel Jonathan Scott was quickly down the stairs and arranged Robert's entry.

"We meet again, Commander South!"

Robert saluted, "Thank you for the assistance, Colonel. I am running a bit late."

"We were expecting you! Come upstairs, please." Robert welcomed the assistance.

On entering the First Lord's waiting room, he saluted and introduced himself.

"Commander Sir Robert South, reporting for Admiral Crouch, Sir."

The Commodore lifted his eyes and said, "Sir Robert, you are five minutes late!"

"Yes, Sir. The traffic!"

It was an embarrassing moment for Robert; however, the Commodore broke into a great smile and said, "No matter, they are running ten minutes late, so you are lucky. Take a seat, Commander South."

The office was empty besides himself, Colonel Scott sitting on the other side of the room, and the Commodore at the reception desk. The Commodore steadily worked on a pile of papers that Robert could only assume dealt with the Board of Admiralty matters.

Robert ventured a comment, "Sir, any idea what this appointment is about?"

The Commodore looked up, smiled, and then continued working.

Colonel Scott stood and moved beside him, "Sir Robert, I recall our meeting last time. It was outside Admiral Crouch's house in Mayfair. I understand you have seen action since then?"

Robert was unsure why this army man was here, but he must respect the rank, "Yes, Colonel. That is correct."

"By the way, I met your fiancée some weeks ago before they entered Admiral Crouch's house for dinner. She was with the Earl and Countess of Fintelton and their daughter. Miss Anne is a fine young lady. May I congratulate you on your engagement, Sir?"

"Thank you, Colonel! It is kind of you. May I be so bold and enquire how an army man finds himself at the Admiralty?"

"Ah! You must have missed all the coaches parked downstairs in your hurry. The Earl of Dawlting, Sir Cecil Fowey, is here! I lead the personal security team for the government and protect the Earl. Given he attends here today with the other Admirals, we are keeping a close watch. As I knew your face, it made the processing downstairs a little faster."

"Thank you for advising me, Colonel. Much obliged. By the way, do you know what this meeting is about?"

The Colonel smiled and took a seat. Robert swallowed and leaned back against his chair, realising these men kept their secrets well!

Admiral Sutherland opened the door ten minutes later, "Are Robert, sorry about the delay, but we are running a little late. Please come in."

As Robert walked past, the Commodore gave him a wink.

Sir Franklin Crouch, First Lord of the Admiralty, rushed over, "Well done, Robert, I knew you could do it. Congratulations on a magnificent mission."

"Thank you, Admiral." Robert was honoured as he and Admiral Couch shook hands. Several other Admirals came over and introduced themselves, offering their congratulations. Sir Cecil Fowey came across and shook his hand.

"Well done, South. You have provided us with the most valuable information at your own risk. I am glad you are looking so well."

Admiral Sutherland interrupted the proceedings, "Have a seat here, Robert. We have some good news for you."

The other Admirals all took their seats, with Sir Cecil Fowey seated at the end of the table.

Admiral Sutherland stood up.

"Gentlemen. May I present Commander Sir Robert South, Commander of HMS *Restless*."

Robert immediately stood at attention, given the introduction. The high-ranking group gave gentle applause, and then Admiral Sutherland indicated that Robert should be seated again.

"Gentlemen. You have all read Commander South's report. For us, it is inspired reading, if I say so myself. I am fortunate that Commander South serves under the flag of the Blue Fleet. The Admiralty appreciates his successful mission, which resulted in the recapture and return of HMS *Providence*."

Admiral Sutherland introduced Admiral Crouch, "I have great pleasure now introducing Admiral Sir Franklin Crouch, First Sea Lord of the British Navy, who will make this presentation."

Admiral Crouch stood with a broad smile, walked around the table and faced Robert, who immediately rose.

"Commander South, on behalf of our King, His Most Excellent King George the Fourth. It is a great honour to read and present this citation. "

CITATION

'Let it be known:

That during the early hours of Friday morning, the third of November in the year of our Lord eighteen hundred and twenty-six that Commander Sir Robert Douglas South of His Majesty's Ship Restless located and recovered His Majesty's Ship Providence, returning home the ship, captain and the remaining members of the crew.

HMS Providence was boarded, captured, and hidden by traitors plotting against the British Crown. The Admiralty issued orders that Commander South should search and recover HMS Providence. He infiltrated the enemy at great personal risk and gathered vital intelligence revealing the captured vessel's location. Two days later, Commander South led and successfully carried out a mission by stealth where members of the HMS Restless crew approached, boarded, and overcame the sentries on HMS Providence. Under shore fire from musket and cannon, Commander South retook HMS Providence and safely returned the frigate to Portsmouth.

In recognition of his bravery and skills, Commander South shall henceforth hold the rank of Captain in His Majesty's Navy.

God Save the King.'

"Commander South! I have great pleasure in presenting this citation and advising you of your promotion.

Congratulations Captain South."

Robert stood there, dumbfounded for a moment, with a silly smile as if it were a dream. Then he snapped out of it, shaking the Admiral's hand, followed by congratulation from the other board members.

"Come, Robert, let us drink your health and celebrate your promotion." Admiral Crouch indicated an entertaining area at the end of the meeting room.

Robert joined the Board in light refreshments, where the King and the new captain were toasted.

Admiral Sutherland then approached and said quietly, "Congratulations, Robert. This ceremony has been one of the most rewarding moments in my time as Admiral."

"I am thankful, Sir Tristan. I hope we have many more moments together."

"Well said, Robert. I have something in mind for you. Captain Winsgate, who suffers from both old war injuries and bad health, has surrendered his commission of HMS *Shadow*. She is a twenty-eight-gun frigate and in reasonable condition. The First Lord believes the Admiralty will overlook seniority in this case. I am appointing you as the captain. Congratulations as the new Captain of HMS *Shadow*."

Robert took a step backwards and was overcome again by the Admiral's gesture.

"Thank you, Sir. This appointment is far earlier than I expected. I am honoured indeed! Tell me, please, what does the future hold for Captain Foster?"

"We will find him a shore posting. He will have a long recovery and must be near his family. Once recovered, we will keep him busy, Robert."

"I am much relieved that he is recovering, Sir. He is a fine man and has been my great mentor."

"You and many others hold him in high esteem. You will find him at the navy hospital at Gosport. Perhaps you might pay him a visit on your return. I will expect you back by Tuesday week, please. We have a mission for you, and your orders will be ready. Captain."

"Admiral."

Admiral Crouch then approached Robert. The Admiral's smile was gone, and Robert recognised that the festivities were over.

"Sir Robert, Admiral Sutherland has a short mission for you once you return. But keep this in mind. There are troubles brewing in the East Mediterranean. This new Tsar, Nicholas[7], is intent on expanding his empire. Our policy is intervention and limiting Russian expansion. Once you have finished Admiral Sutherland's business, I will be calling upon you again. You will join the British flotilla in the east Mediterranean. You have time for Sutherland's mission before you join the main action. By the way, Robert, some advice. You are one of our youngest Captains. Might I suggest when making decisions, you think carefully? In most situations, there is no harm in taking your time. You will do well, Robert. Congratulations, young man! Now off you go. I understand you have other things on your mind."

"Thank you, Admiral Crouch. I am greatly honoured by what has happened here today. I will serve His Majesty with honour, Sir. Thank you."

"By the way, Robert, your appointment will be in the London Gazette [8]tomorrow. You should purchase a copy."

Robert quickly left the room and faced a smiling Colonel Scott and Commodore Crawford, who stood at attention and saluted the new Captain. Robert saluted back, and they shook hands.

Colonel Scott said with a hearty voice, "Congratulation, Captain South. A worthy promotion, indeed. I think we will be meeting again soon!"

Robert had not considered all the words Colonel Scott said. As the coach bumped along towards Wimbledon, he wondered what the Colonel meant about meeting again soon.

Turner Household, Guildford ...

Anne peeped into her mother's bedroom and found her reading. Eleanora looked up as she entered, "Anne, I was thinking about you before. I am glad you are here."

"I, too, about you, Mother! How are you this evening?"

"Feeling quite well, Darling. Now I must thank you for introducing the attorneys in London, Manifold and Stout. I felt Mr Finchley's advice made perfect sense, and I believe your father has written and retained their services. I want the company business, and the inheritances settled before .... Well, you will understand what I mean, Anne!"

---

[7] In December 1825, the diplomatic landscape changed with the death of Tsar Alexander and the succession of his younger brother Nicholas I to the Russian throne. Nicholas was a more decisive and risk-taking character than his brother, as well as being far more nationalistic. Wikipedia.

[8] The London Gazette is one of the official journals of records or Government gazettes of the Government of the United Kingdom, and the most important among such official journals in the United Kingdom, in which certain statutory notices are required to be published. The London Gazette claims to be the oldest surviving English newspaper and the oldest continuously published newspaper in the UK, having been first published on 7 November 1665 as the Oxford Gazette. Wikipedia.

"You are courageous, Mother! Let us hope these events may not happen for some time."

"I hope so, too, Anne, but I am becoming so tired, and I worry about the baby's birth. If I should not survive, these things must be in place before anything happens."

They looked at each other in silence, both understanding the inconvenient truth. Eleanora saw a tear coming from her daughter's eye. She opened her arms, and they hugged each other.

Anne, recovering, softly said, "I shall be there for you, Mother, till the end, but I do not know how I will cope without you!"

"Of all my children, bar William, you are the strongest, Anne. You will cope, Darling, and you shall excel with Robert by your side."

Anne, always encouraging her mother, sat up and smiled back, "I'm glad you have that confidence in me, Mother. I am unsure if I am worthy of it, but I hope I emulate your wonderful example."

Eleanora smiled, "Anne, I have thought long and hard about the inheritance, and your father and I have discussed and agreed upon this. You are an integral part of the Turner bakery and mill management. So, the company will now pay you the correct manager's salary, compensating you for your effort. All the children shall inherit equal portions in this new company your father has established. On my demise, my share will be split equally between the children. Of course, your father will have the controlling interest and, on his death, will leave his interest equally divided among the children.

But as you know, I am the sole owner of Hurst's, for which your father has provided stewardship for the last ten years. I find your father has little interest in the venture, and the business has not grown since I inherited it.

So, I am leaving you the controlling interest in Hursts. I know you have a flair for fashion and the skills for business development. I think you are ready for this challenge. I am sure that with your insight, you will create a healthy future for Hursts."

Anne was stunned at this decision and sat there in silence with a surprised expression.

"Mother, thank you so much. I am speechless about this. I am so thankful, but we must hope it never eventuates."

Eleanora shed a tear and said, "Anne, Darling! It will eventuate and probably well before we expect it."

As they sat there in silence, comforting each other, a soft knocking on the door gained Anne's attention.

"Miss Anne, a message from Sir Robert has arrived!"

Michael Walsh had kept a low profile in case the watchmen started a search in Cobh for those involved in the battle for the frigate. He was satisfied that the injured were carefully hidden and should not raise suspicion. In any case, many watchmen in the south of Ireland were sympathetic and would turn a blind eye.

Michael took a break from the work they had been doing in the garden with his mother and father.

"Why are you planting potatoes under the flower bed?"

Seamus Walsh, Michael's father, stood as tall as his son at five foot eleven with streaks of grey appearing in his thinning hair. He was lean from a life of manual labour and continued staple food shortages. "If they grow, it will help feed the children, and we keep it hidden from the harvest. We have been doing it yearly, and the land agents never suspect a thing."

"If you put them right behind the back of the daisy plant with the shoots facing up, they are hidden completely. These little fellows might be very popular one night when no other food is on the table." His mother smiled as she demonstrated planting a potato behind a large garden plant.

"The trouble, Flann, is if the plant dies, we must search for the potato."

"Seamus, we always find them. You worry too much."

Michael's father sat beside his wife and brushed the thin hair across his forehead, "I am sick of worrying. With Ruth away and you, Michael, being so involved in the struggle. I wonder when they will catch you. Is it all worth it? I have been thinking that we should emigrate. The more I think about it, the more convinced I am that our future lies in Boston."

With a strong but whispering voice, Flann reprimanded him, "Not until our little Ruth is back from Islay, Seamus. I will not leave until my daughter is back in my arms."

Breathing out in despair, Seamus leaned towards his son and asked, "When will she return, Michael?"

"Ruthy is doing a good job up there and saves all her money. I hear nothing but good reports about her. She has settled well and become an important part of the Glasgow route. Perhaps three months, maybe six."

Seamus shook his head, "Flann, I am not sure we can wait that long. Even without Michael and Ruth, feeding the four children is a struggle. The tenancy is so small it will never generate any savings for us. When we go, the brothers must give us support. Would you enquire on our behalf, Michael? When will you speak with them?"

"I will give it a few weeks. While here, I must visit Sean Reid and his mother and check Sean's recovery. That way, I can tell the folks down in Cobh."

Seamus spat on the ground, "Why did they take that frigate in the first place? The mission was ill-fated from the start. I am no strategist, but I could see that many young Irish boys would be lost for no reason. What were they thinking, Michael?"

Michael sat there and had no answer. He, too, wondered why the brothers launched the mission. But he must focus on the future.

"Once I am in Cobh, I will ask about Ruth."

"Well, son! It is getting on. We need these potatoes planted before dark. Mind you carefully cover them behind each plant."

Flann stood up, "Thank you for the bread, Michael. It will be a treat tonight. We have not had real bread for months. How I long for the Irish summer."

The Turner Bakery, Guildford ...

Early Saturday morning Jonathan Turner assembled the staff he needed around a table in the nearly completed Turner business offices. Anne took the minutes as they discussed the flour mill's defences. As the discussion continued, Anne was thinking more proactively.

"Father, now the men are aware of the failure of the first attempt; perhaps they are having second thoughts. The consequences of being caught may now be on their mind. It is time that we spread some positive information among the surrounding mills.

Tell them our new flour mill will concentrate on other markets rather than the local ones. We could say it may be many years before the local mills are affected by ours."

Jonathan Turner liked the idea, "I understand your suggestion, Anne. It might put their minds at rest, but is it the truth? We will not purchase flour from the local mills anymore!"

"Yes, Father, that is true, but London and Reading will soon receive our products. So, the local markets will not be affected in the short term. Surely, we cannot guarantee what will happen in the long term as technology changes everything, and other competitors, perhaps from London, might enter the market."

Jeb agreed with Anne, "What Anne says is correct, Mr Turner. We could send men out spreading the word. The feedback from the mill owners might also be helpful. Better talking with them than guessing when a riot will come!"

Jonathan scratched his head, "What do you think, Terry?"

Terence Spencer still had a worried look, "I like the idea, but I will keep my ears open at the pub. This trouble is just beginning and will increase as mills along the river Wey fail. But I like Miss Anne's suggestion and would support it."

After the meeting, Anne checked the progress of each of her staff against their weekly timetable. Satisfied, she pulled out the McPherson contracts and spent the next hour pouring through the many clauses, finding several of concern. One clause was so ridiculous she was amazed her father had agreed. She must speak with him promptly. She had never really trusted the McPhersons, and this clause was consistent with her fears. The issue required a private conversation.

Anne took the contracts with her on her way home for lunch. As she walked up the High Street, Doctor Sopwith appeared coming in the other direction.

He stopped and nodded, "Good day, Anne."

Anne noticed that David seemed concerned. He explained, "Emma and I are both aware of your kind invitation for Christmas that my sister Victoria and I have accepted. However, my engagement and the Souths expecting us at Fintelton over Christmas leaves me in a difficult position!"

"Oh, I understand, David. We were concerned that you would be on your own. The circumstances are quite changed now. Please enjoy your time at Fintelton with Emma and your sister. Mother and father will be quite understanding."

"Thank you, Anne. Tell the boys we will finish the boat before or soon after Christmas. We might discuss this more at dinner tonight. I will enjoy catching up with Robert again. Now, I must be on my way. My next appointment is in five minutes. Good day, Anne."

Anne rushed on towards home, appreciating the lovely group of friends she enjoyed here in Guildford. Slowing down, she recalled the conversation with Emma and Robert about the estate's finances. There had been no tenant farmer payments since eighteen twenty-three. How could that happen with Sir Hugh negotiating the grain contracts? Surely, he would check on their tenant payments each harvest.

Anne was uncomfortable with the situation. She knew Sir Hugh left unusually quickly without advising anyone until after he sailed. Perhaps Hugh was somehow involved, but why? Tonight, she would discuss it with Emma and Robert, but she would not mention Hugh until more information was available.

Anne was still pondering the estate's finances as she walked into the kitchen. There she found her father finishing lunch and Emma opposite him with Marcia on her lap.

"Welcome, back, Emma!" Anne hugged Emma and kissed Marcia.

Jonathan smiled, "Lady Emma is early, Anne and will have the entire afternoon with you. Perhaps a bit of shopping, and you both may meet Robert when he arrives for his fitting?"

"Yes, Father, but before that, we must discuss an urgent matter. First, some lunch and then Lady Emma might allow us half an hour."

Jonathan and Emma looked at Anne as if this were an unusual request, given that her guest was here.

"It is important, Father, and there is a need for action!"

Emma said, "Mr Turner, I would be quite happy reading for half an hour. Perhaps Marcia and I might read a book. Would you like that, Marcia?"

"Yes, and Buster would like it too. I will find him."

Marcia hopped off her lap and raced out the door, searching for her favourite toy bear.

"Emma, you are looking so well. I apologise for the delay, but we have been working hard to catch up, and there are a few issues. But I assure you we will go shopping as soon as I meet with Father."

As Jonathan left, the two girls fell into conversation. Anne explained her meeting with David and that Christmas was all sorted.

Emma replied, "Thank you, Anne – that is a relief."

"Emma, I was thinking about our last conversation on Tuesday. The Estate finances. Have you any further information?"

"No, but we can discuss it with Robert later this afternoon after his fitting at Hursts. What was it that you were concerned about?"

"Well, who controls the estate at the moment?"

"My father! But since Robert's discussion with father and mother, I think mother will play a far more active role."

"Good. We shall talk this afternoon. I have some ideas."

They commenced on hot bowls of soup and toast that Mrs Jennings provided.

After lunch, Anne excused herself and entered her father's study.

"Come in, Anne. Now, what is it?"

Anne sat down and pulled the financial reports out of her bag and the contracts. She placed them on his desk.

"First, we should discuss the McPherson contracts for the two pubs. I understand that we have invested twenty-five thousand pounds in each pub. Is that correct?"

"Yes, Anne and a good investment it is. You have seen the returns!"

"Father, did you read the contracts before signing them?"

Jonathan Turner became uncomfortable, "I quickly perused them, and Hamish pointed out a few clauses. I was satisfied. I trusted in what Hamish was telling me."

Anne was disappointed with her father, "I thought you told me the attorneys reviewed the contracts?"

"Well, I thought about it but decided to save money!"

"Father, there is a clause in each contract that says if any of our business ventures, Turner business ventures, becomes unfinancial, then the investments we made in the pubs revert to Hamish McPherson's brewing company, in full, without compensation."

Jonathan looked at Anne in disbelief, "Hamish did not explain this. That is unfair! There must be compensation, or we could lose fifty thousand pounds in investment. Show me the clause."

Anne opened the relevant page in each contract and pointed out each clause. Jonathan was now nervous and was shaking his head. He muttered as he read the clause over and over. It was the same in both contracts.

"I must visit Greenwich and talk with him. These clauses must be changed quickly. Hamish will comply. It may have been put there by mistake. I will leave tomorrow."

"Thank you, father. Now the second issue! As I expected, our cash flow will be quite low this month. There must be no additional projects or expenses until after Christmas."

Jonathan looked up from the contracts, "What does the November report show? I expected surplus cash this month."

"Yes, there is a slight surplus, but there are also several large debtors, including the government, which we are waiting on for payments. We must be prudent for December."

"There is a problem with the mill boiler! There will be extra on that."

"Then pay them a small deposit, with the remainder of the bill due in January. We must conserve our cash in December. Next year will also be difficult, but we will manage. But please tell me if anything extra comes up!"

Jonathan was rereading the contracts as he listened.

"I trusted him," Jonathan murmured. "Something like this can destroy trust!"

"Father, I will come with you. We will work as a team and see him together. I must hear his explanation for this. Send him a note and request a meeting in Greenwich next Tuesday, late morning."

Jonathan looked at Anne and then smiled, "Have you no trust in me, daughter?'

"Yes, I do, Father, especially after mother advised me of your discussions about my future. Thank you, Father."

"It is what should be. I depend greatly on you, Anne, and with Thomas entering the brewing game, if I should be incapacitated, you will be the replacement, General Manager."

"From now on, negotiating agreements is something we should do together, Father. There are over two hundred and fifty thousand pounds invested and many people employed in our business. I think it is the right time for these changes. With Thomas gone, how would I find the information and solve any problems if your health failed?"

Jonathan could not argue with that, "We shall negotiate with Hamish together!"

"I will ask Emma if we may stay at 'Harting'. She will send a message, and Lady Jane will expect us. Perhaps mentioning 'Harting' and Mr McPherson's knowledge of his wife's desire for recognition in society may persuade Hamish that the contracts require adjustment."

Jonathan looked at Anne with a wry smile and said, "You are a clever lady, Anne Turner!"

"Thank you, Father. We must make the most of our society contacts!"

Dinner at the Turner's household ...

The Turners enjoyed a delicious dinner with David Sopwith, Emma, and Robert South as the honoured guests that night. There was much merriment about both couples' engagement, and Neville and Bethany were thrilled they had started a rush of marriages.

Jonathan Turner took the opportunity of asking David Sopwith about progress on the model boat with the boys.

David reported, "We had some good luck at the Institute."

Eleanora said, "Henry Sharples is a helpful man. So many people have benefitted from his mentoring."

David continued, "We were looking for books on tools when Mr Linton, the Blacksmith, appeared and offered help. He supplied a piece of oak for the keel and helped us carve it into shape. We are now working on the framework and making good progress."

David took a bite of food, "We missed you at the swimming lesson Mr Turner."

"Ah, I have been busy, David. My apologies. Perhaps I might attend the next lesson."

Neville added, "Think nothing of it, Jonathan! I became David's assistant and survived the water."

"You can both swim then?"

Neville chuckled, "It was quite helpful in the Navy, Sir!"

"Of course!"

Eleanora was curious, "How did the boys perform, David?"

"Very well. Both picked up the basic strokes quite easily. William seems better coordinated than Simeon, but we will have them swimming in a few weeks. The water is heated, so they found it like a warm bath and relaxing. It is designed like an old Roman bath but only three feet deep. The first lessons were floating exercises. It is important not to be afraid of submerging in the water. Once they mastered that, they were into learning strokes."

"And the men's club had no objections?"

"Certainly not, but the pool was a bit busy. The Warden advised that Monday afternoon would be the best time. So next Monday we are into it again. Mr Turner, are you free?"

"Unfortunately, not. Anne and I must be in London on business. It is a pressing matter that we cannot set aside. Perhaps the Monday following?"

David nodded in agreement, and a surprised Eleanora said, "Jonathan, you had not told me of this trip. How long will you be gone?"

"We should be back by Friday evening, Dear. We hope, Emma, that your parents might provide us with accommodation."

"Yes, Anne told me before dinner. They will be delighted with some company. I sent a rider this afternoon notifying them you will arrive on Monday."

Jonathan smiled. He was tense as his thoughts were elsewhere. He knew Jeb would send a message if any disturbance occurred at the mill.

The Turner Company Offices, Guildford ...

After dinner, Jonathan excused himself and visited the offices. He knew the guards were in place, but he decided to check anyway. As the late hours of Saturday night passed by, Jonathan found himself becoming drowsy. This guard duty was a young man's game, and he decided to return home. As he left, he noticed Jeb and Rob Baxter, the stable manager, approaching.

"Mr Turner, while it is quiet, might we talk?"

"Certainly!"

Rob spoke first, "Mr Turner, the trial of the London fast carts went well, but on arrival, the McPherson Breweries' office manager advised they require twice as much bread and pastries as we delivered!"

"We can increase production as soon as we move into the newly available space." Jeb nodded in agreement, wondering how long it would take to demolish the offices and install new ovens.

"Will the carts carry twice the load?"

"No, Sir. We will need bigger carts. For the time being, we can tie on an extra tray. That will help. But doubling it will require either an additional or a new larger cart. We probably need at least three new carts that are far bigger."

"I'll speak with Anne. She will arrange it with Fulcher's blacksmiths. They made our existing carts. Would you do a design for exactly what you need and have it ready, say, in two or three days?"

"Yes, Sir. In the meantime, might I send two carts until the new ones are available?"

"I agree it appears the only solution at present."

Jeb, looking concerned, spoke, "Mr Turner, I know we are guarding the mill and store here, but what about your home? Remember the burglary! What if these men know where you live?"

"It is well secured now, Jeb. I doubt they would try anything there. But thank you for your concern. I will ask Constable Rawlins if he might keep a regular watch. I hope you have a quiet night here. Good night."

The Guildford General Medical Practice ...

On Monday morning, Neville Bassington was at his desk when David Sopwith arrived, having visited a patient's home, "How was Mr Hall, David?"

"Still suffering from gout, I'm afraid. It will be a few weeks before the patient recovers. At his age, it may be longer. We will see! While you are without patients, Neville, we should discuss Mrs Turner."

Neville looked up with interest.

"I was visiting late Saturday morning when she had an unexpected pain. I examined her quickly, and the baby appeared more advanced than we thought. I think it will arrive sometime in the next few weeks."

"That would be premature, David. My initial thoughts were of a late February delivery."

"Might I ask that you make another examination, Neville? I think you may revise your opinion. The unexpected pain was a warning contraction. When I examined her, I found ..."

The conversation continued for some time as the two doctors discussed the patient. Neville was convinced and agreed to another examination within days.

"Of course, this may impact her underlying condition quite severely. I'm not sure if she will live through the delivery."

"You mean the tumours in her breasts?"

"Yes. I believe it is cancer[9], but I am not sure. It would account for the continual tiredness. Of course, the pregnancy would also add to this. But not for such a long time."

David thought about Neville's comment, "How will Mr Turner cope if she does not survive?"

"Not well! Not well at all!"

Turner Bakery, Guildford ...

On Monday evening, Terry and Jeb sat at a desk in the new offices watching over the mill.

"My friend tells me there is still unrest despite that incident the other night where we scared them away. You take the first watch, Jeb. I am tired and need some sleep. Wake me at eleven, and I will take over."

---

[9] The earliest known descriptions of cancer appear in several papyri from ancient Egypt. The Edwin Smith Papyrus was written around 1600 BC (possibly a fragmentary copy of a text from 2500 BC) and contains a description of cancer, as well as a procedure to remove breast tumours by cauterization, wryly stating that the disease has no treatment. Wikipedia.

Terry found a spot at the back of the office, lay down on several straw mats piled as a mattress, and pulled a blanket over himself. Jeb took a sip of the hot tea that he was slowly drinking. All was quiet out on the pier. Hopefully, it would be a peaceful night. Sitting there, he watched the calm water running downstream towards Dapdune wharf. His thoughts wandered towards Audrey and what she was doing. Since spending the night at her mother's house saving him the hour-long walk home, he had noticed her more. She was an attractive girl with a lovely personality.

Jeb's thoughts were disturbed as the water on the river saw some splashing in front of the pier. Suddenly he was vigilant. He sat up and screwed his eyes, focusing on the water. Perhaps the mill workers were coming by the river this time. Then he heard a duck's quack, and two ducks paddled across the river, climbing out on the far bank.

Relaxing, pleasant thoughts of Audrey returned, 'I wonder ...!'

Jeb's day was long, and he should have found a replacement for his watch that night. After adjusting the new ovens, he decided to remain for his shift. The bakery manager had underestimated how tired he was, and his eyelids slowly closed, his head gently slipping onto folded arms. He was soon fast asleep.

He stirred some hours later, knocking over his cold cup of tea. His eyes opened, and in his drowsiness, he wondered where he was. Raising his head and rubbing his eyes, he looked around and heard the gentle snoring of Terry at the rear of the office. The fire was out, and the room was freezing. Jeb stood and stretched before making up the fire. As he returned to his post, he noticed a movement in the corner of his eye.

Turning, he stared out across the road towards the bulk store. Nothing moved, but he was sure he had noticed something. Listening hard through the slightly open window, Jeb heard Terry roll over, and his intense snoring stopped. Jeb, thinking he was mistaken, smiled as he pushed himself up. As Jeb relaxed and was about to make a fresh cup of tea, he saw it again. This time he saw a man darting across the open space between the shadows carrying a large bundle of sticks. Suddenly Jeb was fully alert. He rushed back across the office and shook Terry, "Wake up! They are back."

Terry was soon by his side at the window, whispering, "What is it?"

"There, look!" Another figure with a large bundle of sticks dashed across the road towards the mill, hiding in the shadows.

"I see them. You pull the cord and alert the others. I am busting! I must go out and take a leak. I'll join you over there."

Jeb was not pleased about Terry disappearing but knew he must follow the agreed process. They decided on a system where the guards could alert the other watchmen sleeping in the mill. A rope pulled would make sufficient noise warning the others who had bedded down on the first floor. Jeb gave it a few more tugs making sure the men were awake.

He peered out the window again and saw another man running from the bulk store to the mill with a larger bundle of sticks. There must be at least three of them, perhaps more, and it appeared they would burn the mill down. He could wait no longer. He sped off towards an unseen mill entrance covered in hessian, allowing him a quick and silent entry.

Climbing up a ladder, he reached the first landing and quietly moved into a position where he could see the Parish Constable. He thought it strange that constable Rawlins was standing as he crept towards him. It was the last thing Jeb remembered as a man with a heavy baton knocked him out cold. He fell on the floor unconscious as Constable Michael Rawlins gagged and bound to a pillar watched in terror. His other two watchmen had suffered the same fate.

"Peter, we got their lookout. All clear – get the fire going!" The group leader monitored his men on the ground floor as they built their pile of combustible material beside a wooden wall that separated the hopper area from the mill's supplies store. There was plenty of fuel, and if the fire took hold, it would engulf the entire mill.

The intruder on the landing appeared the group's leader and quietly informed the captives, "Sorry, mates, but you will go up with the mill. It is not worth my life having you identify me. The mill will be ashes in thirty minutes – serves you right for putting honest men out of a job!" With that, he turned and moved towards a ladder that connected with the ground floor. He laughed as he saw the fire crackling.

Terry appeared from nowhere and smashed him across the back of the head with the butt of his pistol. The intruder fell stunned on the floor, knocked partially unconscious. Terry quickly pulled out some thin twine and tied the man's hands and feet against a ladder. Quietly, he moved back and commenced untying Constable Rawlins and his men.

A call from below came, "Henry, hurry up; the fire is well alight. We must get out of here. Henry?"

Constable Rawlins stretched his hands and legs and rubbed them, getting the circulation moving after the restrictions of the tight ropes. He asked Terry, "What next?"

"I'll go downstairs with my pistol. You shout a warning at the trespassers. Say we will fire if they move. Got it! Then get down there as quick as you can."

"Right!"

Terry was off instantly, crawling past the secured intruder and scuttling down the ladder. The men fanning the fire assumed the descending man was Henry. As soon as Terry was on the ground floor, the constable had his men follow. From the rail, he bellowed in his loudest voice, "You men are under arrest. Raise your hands, or we will fire."

The men panicked, realising the mill owners had discovered them. One said, "Damn this, I'm not going to the gallows!" and fled towards the central doorway. Another cried, "Wait, Sam, I'm with you!" Terry rushed the second man, bashing him across the forehead. Now facing the other three men, he said, "Who's next?" The men raised their hands as the watchmen approached and tied them up.

Sam was over the doorway and outside. He disappeared into the night. Constable Rawlins said as he approached Terry, "Never mind, we will get him tomorrow once we find out where these men are from."

"Forget him, Michael! We must put out the fire!"

Constable Rawlins suddenly focused on the blazing wall remembering the mill was on fire. "Right," he said, rushing for the sand buckets at the side of the mill. The fire burned brightly, with yellow-orange flames reaching ten feet from the bonfire. The wooden wall above had ignited and was now well alight. The Constable's watchmen rapidly attacked the bonfire base, putting it out, but the wall was out of their reach. Terry then remembered that Jeb and the man Henry were upstairs. He rushed up the ladder and found Jeb sitting up and holding his head.

"Jeb, quick, we must get out of here!" Terry attempted but could not raise Jeb to his feet.

Suddenly smelling the smoke, Jeb realised the danger and called out, "Terry, the cistern, open the cistern!"

Terry's mind flashed back to the cistern they had installed for water pressure. It had an outlet valve and a suspended moveable gutter attached. You could direct the water, and it would reach the wall. He rushed towards the cistern platform and unwound the outlet valve. The gutter was long and heavy, but as he strained, it slowly moved until it was above the burning wall. Water poured down the wall, and the fire was extinguished within minutes. Breathing a sigh of relief, he closed the outlet.

Walking back, he found Jeb standing but with blood still seeping down the side of his head.

"Come on, Jeb, let me bandage that blow for you."

Jeb smiled, "We did it, Terry. We got them. We did it!"

"Don't get too excited, Jeb. We are probably only at the beginning. But, well done, the plan worked – but we may refine it before the next time." They both laughed.

"Mr Turner will have no pity for these lads! We should get them out of here."

They ensured the leader's hands remained tied as they unwound him from the ladder. Terry pushed the struggling man over the landing edge, the constable half catching him as he came down.

"Take that, you bugger!" Terry was angry, showing no pity towards the men who would destroy their livelihood and burn them alive.

Chapter 4

'Harting', St James's Square, London …

Anne and her father, Jonathan, arrived in London at St James's Square at about four in the afternoon. Matthew Staines, the butler, answered the door.

"Sir David and Lady Jane are expecting you, Mr Turner. Welcome back and welcome, Miss Turner."

"Thank you, Staines. We did not expect our return would be so soon!"

"On business, Sir?"

"Yes, Miss Anne has urgent business with the McPhersons tomorrow, and I will be there assisting her. She is heavily involved in running the company now. Would you have someone bring in the luggage, please?"

"Certainly, Sir."

Anne smiled as she came in.

Staines requested, "Please follow me. I will have the footmen bring your luggage. Dinner will be at seven."

"Thank you, Staines. The news is good about Sir Robert! A captain now. Well, done!"

"Yes, Sir. Good news, indeed! Lord Fintelton is impressed with his progress. I'm sure he will raise the subject during dinner tonight."

They walked up the main stairs together.

Anne was entering her room when Staines said, "Miss Turner, there is a note on the dressing table from Lady Fintelton. She asked if you would read it before dinner, please."

Anne, noticing the letter, went over and picked it up. She wondered why Lady Jane would not come and talk with her in private.

"Thank you, Staines."

She closed the door and opened the note.

"My Dearest Anne,
How glad I am that you and Robert are engaged. I think the two of you

will be happy, and you will provide the understanding and support he will require as a navy captain.

Emma and Robert have confided in me of your assistance with some of the estate's financial problems. I am embarrassed that Lord Fintelton and Sir Hugh have not managed the estate well in the last few years, resulting in our current issues. Robert has advised me that he may be away for long periods at sea. He recommends that you, Emma, and I work as a team and solve the problems.

I am so glad that you have agreed. We will work well together, and I will learn much from this process. Since meeting you, I have the highest regard for your wisdom and friendship. It would be wonderful if you and Robert were married now; however, I understand this must wait until you both set a time for the wedding. Let us hope we can solve the estate's problems long before then.

Please, there is some need for caution. His Lordship is in denial about the estate matters. He will not discuss issues he cannot control anymore. I am unsure if this results from a physiological or mental disorder. It would be preferable if we did not discuss the actions we are considering in the Earl's presence. We have no idea what his reaction might be.

Once again, let me say how happy I am that you will visit and be my future daughter-in-law. Emma, you and I will have a wonderful time sorting these problems together. I will set aside some time tomorrow when we might meet and catch up. Your company at dinner tonight will be a delight.

Your loving future mother-in-law

Lady Jane South
Countess of Fintelton

Anne reread the note and smiled as she saw Lady Jane was open about her family's problems and accepting Anne's involvement. It was clear that Lady Jane was declaring her full support no matter what Anne's challenges with the aristocracy might be.

Unsure of her reception on this visit, she now felt relieved. Perhaps her involvement in assisting David Sopwith and Emma's engagement may have influenced Lady Jane's approval.

At dinner that night, the four of them had a lively conversation. Lord Fintelton talked about his estate and grain production while Jonathan explained his new mill strategy and a broader market opportunity. The two men seemed very relaxed in each other's company, which allowed some discussion between Anne and Lady Jane.

"Anne, I understand you are here on business. I was unaware you were so involved in your father's company."

"Well, I have worked with Father since I was thirteen, commencing after I left the local church school. Father is a marvellous mentor, and I have been a keen reader of business and finance at the Guildford Institute."

"Your father indicated that you would be leading the negotiations?"

"Yes, I am more familiar with the contractual and legal side of the issues and will handle those discussions. I hope we solve them quickly and then we might come back and spend a pleasant afternoon with you. Perhaps I could bring Mrs Marjorie McPherson along for afternoon tea. Would that be possible?"

Lady Jane at first hesitated, then said, "Certainly, Dear. I will be glad of the company. The Earl usually sleeps in the afternoon, so he is alert at night. It can sometimes become dull here, although London provides many opportunities for my attention if I can find the energy. Being out and about in excess at my age can become tedious. Yes, bring her back with you, and we shall enjoy her company and have tea, say, at four pm."

"That is kind of you, Milady. I am sure Mrs McPherson will be most appreciative."

Lady Jane smiled and said, "I am sure she will!"

Anne noticed the slight smile and thought, 'Lady Jane is knowledgeable indeed. She understands what is happening here.'

"Now, Anne, you must join us at Fintelton this coming Saturday and Sunday. We will travel through Guildford on Friday and stop at your home to pick you up. Robert will be attending, and David Sopwith. He will probably give Lord Fintelton a check-up on Saturday. I shall invite Neville and Bethany also. We shall have a lovely party and catch up before Christmas. Sadly, Hugh will miss the occasion with us this year."

"It will be near Christmas, but if Robert is present, I will be there. That timing should work as I am away most of this week, so another day will not hurt. I will catch up on my work when I return. Have you heard from Sir Hugh?"

"No letters from Hugh so far, but I expect one soon. At Fintelton, you and Robert might discuss when the wedding will be! We must coordinate with Emma and David; your suggestions will influence David! Perhaps you might mention a wedding date if the opportunity arises. I pray my husband's continuing good health is maintained. It would be a shame if he could not walk Emma down the aisle."

They both agreed on that.

"Lady Jane, the date will depend on the navy, but we will prioritise it at Fintelton. Might I ask, do you visit the tenant farmers before Christmas?"

"Sometimes, I do. It depends on whether Lord Fintelton has already made the visits."

"I assume the tenants all attend church on a Sunday morning in Petersfield?"

"Some do! Sir David enjoys talking with them after the service."

'Perhaps I could join your visiting on Sunday afternoon. Would that be appropriate?"

"Anne, it would be a treat, and I will introduce you around. Pike should have the Christmas packages ready, but I will send a message reminding him. I understand your intention. You desire an observation at the coalface. A good way of finding out what we are dealing with?"

"Yes."

"You are a most clever young lady, Anne. You keep surprising me. Now while you are at Fintelton, we must discuss how I might introduce you into society next year."

Anne's eyes opened wide, nodding in reply. She was terrified of the thought!

The Turner Household, Guildford ...

"Ethel?" Mrs Turner called for her maid.

There was no response. Eleanora knew they would be in the kitchen, and she must either ring her bell or find someone upstairs. She stood up and walked towards the bedroom door but then suffered the full force of a severe contraction. She doubled over in pain and fell on the floor.

Madeline and Marcia, who were in the bedroom further down the hallway, were playing together. Madeline heard someone grunt as they fell. She looked up, listening, but there was no other noise.

"I thought I heard someone fall!"

Marcia stood up and peered out the bedroom door, "No one out there!"

Madeline decided on a further investigation and walked along the hall, followed by Marcia. As she passed her mother's bedroom, she noticed the door was slightly ajar, and she peeked in. Her mother was lying on the floor, softly moaning with a small pool of water beside her.

Kneeling by her mother's side, she asked, "Mother, are you injured?"

Eleanora moaned, "No, Darling, fetch Ethel, please!"

Madeline stood up and rushed down the stairs. Bursting through the kitchen door, she called, "Ethel! Mother is on the floor groaning! She is calling for you."

Ethel immediately rushed for Mrs Turner's room, finding a crying Marcia hugging her mother on the floor.

"Mrs Turner, what is it?"

"The baby is coming. My waters have broken. Please call the doctor and the midwife."

"Are you sure?"

"Yes, yes, that was a strong contraction, and another is coming now." She cried in pain for a moment and then recovered.

"This baby is coming, whether we are ready or not, and it is coming fast!"

Aggie lifted Marcia into her arms as Ethel helped raise Mrs Turner onto her feet. Mrs Jennings arrived and assisted Eleanora as she struggled onto the bed.

"Aggie! Call the Doctor, please and then the midwife."

"Yes, Mrs Nibley, I will be back as soon as I can." She squeezed Eleanora's hand and placed Marcia beside a concerned Madeline. Eleanora smiled at Aggie as she felt another contraction coming.

"Oh, no!" Eleanora turned very pale and moaned in agony as the contraction took hold.

Ethel and Mrs Jennings made her as comfortable as they could. However, this was not an easy task for a woman having contractions. Ethel thought, 'It always happens when the men are away. Mr Turner would be petrified if he were here. Perhaps it is a good thing he is away!'

"Mrs Turner, I think we need you in your nightgown. After the next contraction, we will stand you up and change you. The nightgown is here, so let me start undoing some of this before the next one."

Ethel checked the clock. It was ten in the morning. What was keeping the doctor? Eleanora started moaning again as another contraction started.

The lady's maid wiped Eleanora's face with a washer, and then as the contraction eased, Ethel asked, "Was the last baby fast? I mean, did it come quickly?"

"Yes, after seven babies, Marcia came quickly. I think it only took an hour. But I think this one is coming quicker."

Just as the ladies changed Eleanora into her nightdress, Mrs Gertrude Plumridge burst into the room, throwing her wet coat on the floor, and said, "I'm here, Eleanora. No worrying now! Everything will be fine!"

Gertrude had presided over Eleanora's last five births. She was a big capable woman with a round red face, sandy brown hair tied in a bun, and a constant smile that reassured the mothers. Ethel understood from village chatter that Mrs Plumridge had delivered half the children in Guildford. Gertrude's happy smiling face put Eleanora at ease immediately, and she held Gertie's hands with all her might which was not a strong grip in her weak condition.

'Now, don't worry, this' un will be out before you know it. All will be better then. I bet you are sick of this young'un being stuck inside there. Now let me have a look."

Eleanora screamed as a contraction became stronger.

As Gertrude examined her patient, her eyes opened wide, and she said, "Well, I just got here in the nick of time, didn't I!"

Doctor Bassington was having a cup of morning tea before his next patient arrived as Aggie burst into the surgery reception, screaming, "'Octor, 'Octor, a baby is coming!'

Neville heard the commotion and walked out with a cup of tea in his hand, finding a drenched and breathless Aggie facing him.

"Don't just stand there, 'Octor, Mrs Eleanora is having the baby!"

Neville said, "I'll be there in five minutes! Aggie, go back and help, please! Jenny, transfer my patients to Doctor Sopwith. He should return within the hour. Thanks! Please would you also let my wife know?" Neville rushed back into his surgery and checked his bag. He was confident that the baby would be born healthy, but what would be the effect on Eleanora? She was frail, and he was concerned about her other illnesses."

Neville pulled on his coat and rushed out into the miserable weather.

Greenwich …

The Turners arrived at the McPherson house ten minutes late for their meeting. They left early, allowing plenty of time, knowing that London's traffic would be slow, particularly with the rain. But there was a collision between a coach and a cart spilling wares all over the wet road. Both drivers were frantically protecting their property from various scavengers creating minor chaos. Many coaches continued lining up with impatient passengers, annoyed at the delay. Finally, after their driver decided on an alternative route, they arrived in Greenwich.

Jonathan buttoned his coat before jumping out, holding an umbrella over Anne as she alighted. She reached back into the coach and picked up the bundle of contracts and other papers they would discuss with Hamish.

Jonathan said, "Do you have everything you need, Anne?"

"Yes, I think so. Let me recheck the carriage."

She looked back into the carriage and noticed one sheaf of paper below the seat. One of the footmen retrieved it for her.

"Thank you. All set now, Father!"

Jenkins, the butler, was at the top of the stairs and welcomed them. Jonathan thought the butler looked remarkably well and commented, "Hello Jenkins, you are looking well!"

"Thank you, Mr Turner and Miss Turner. Please, come in out of this terrible weather. Mr McPherson expects you and will be with you in a minute or two. Let me take your coats."

"Thank you, Jenkins."

Marjorie McPherson rushed into the room, hugging Anne and then greeting Jonathan.

"Oh, it is so good you are here, Jonathan and Anne. Now, how is Eleanora? We were worried about her the last time we met. The baby is due mid-February! Is it not?"

"Yes, thank you, Marjorie. She is well, and a pleasant Christmas will be very welcome before the little screamer arrives."

"Good. Now let us know as soon as anything happens on the baby front. We are most anxious for her. I understand you are staying at St James's Square. How wonderful. We have just received a honeymoon postcard from Marion in Paris. She posted it a week ago, so it has made good time. It says she and Thomas are enjoying their visit there. We shall meet with them in Glasgow and spend Christmas with the boys. James has a large house so there will be no problems with accommodation. Hamish will use the time reviewing brewery operations, and I will visit the grandchildren, so I expect we will be back around the end of January."

"I'm sure it will be a fine visit, Marjorie." Jonathan was quickly adding a comment as Marjorie took a breath.

"Jonathan and Anne, welcome." Hamish appeared, "I insist on you both staying for lunch. Now we should start work, shall we? Marjorie, would you please ask Jenkins for a light lunch served at about twelve-thirty? That would be wonderful."

Hamish showed Jonathan and Anne into his office. As he shut the door, he said, "I think Marjorie is missing Marion very much. Probably far more than Marion misses Marjorie!"

Anne spoke up, "Oh, that is sad. Well, she will have my company for lunch, and I will cheer her up."

"Wonderful, Anne. You always bless us when you visit!"

"Thank you, Mr McPherson. However, you may not say that after our discussion, but the compliment is welcome."

Hamish was confused and enquired, "So what are the issues?"

Jonathan focused on his host and explained, "Hamish, I am taking your advice and delegating more. I have asked Anne if she would lead the discussion."

Anne was eager for a solution and immediately said, "Mr McPherson, there are two pressing issues. Firstly, the quantities of bread required by the London pubs and some clauses we need clarification on in the pub contracts."

"Let us get the order quantities out of the way first." Hamish could see that Anne was quite sure of her facts, and he would not argue any of the points. The best solution here, he surmised, was that he placated the young lady. Let her have the first-round win.

Anne carefully explained how the existing fast carts' capacity was too small, given the product ordered. She outlined the extra cost of building larger carts and the temporary charge for sending an additional cart per night. She suggested a fee structure that covered the added cost.

Hamish sat back in his chair and thought about this. Dipping his pen in ink, he scribbled some quick calculations. Then he looked up and smiled.

"That's fair. That is agreed! Might I suggest not bothering with building new carts? Continue sending the two carts until you establish the London bakery. The following year the carts may service Reading. I already have three sites locked in there and another under consideration. It will be a growth centre and will require far more of your product."

Anne smiled, "Thank you. We shall do that and thank you for the increased orders. Now the other issue is the contracts for the pubs. I reviewed them and found most items very satisfactory. However, on clause fifty-two, I was a bit surprised."

Hamish opened a drawer in his desk and pulled out a box of contracts. He leafed through them and pulled out the two for the Turners. He opened the first contract and read the clause.

"Yes, I have read it. Now, what is the problem?" He looked at Anne with a passive face as if he were at a loss understanding her point.

"Well, Mr McPherson, we have invested twenty-five thousand pounds in each pub. It appears from reading the contracts that if any of our businesses become unfinancial, we will forfeit the full fifty thousand pounds. The penalty seems unfair, given you would receive the total of our investment, and the contract would leave us nothing!"

"Anne, the reason for that clause is that I take a high risk on each investor invited into the partnership. My investment in the pool is far larger. If one investor has financial difficulties, I do not want attorneys chasing me for money supporting a failed investor. It is a cleaner and better method using a forfeit mechanism."

"But if investors buy shares in a company, they all take the same risk. If the share value falls, say, by ten per cent, they all lose ten per cent. Indeed, we should similarly word the contract. It is too severe that one hundred per cent of the investment be forfeited on the contract's condition. There must be a provision allowing recovery! If an investor leaves the partnership, there should be a formula outlining what equity they take with them. If it were us, we would agree that there must be some leaving costs, but not one hundred per cent. The penalty is far too excessive.

For the pub at Epsom, there are only two partners, yourself and my father. Let us say our tailor shop became unfinancial. Our other businesses would provide funds allowing for such a situation. So how would the clause ever be practical."

Hamish sat back and reread the contract. He looked at Jonathan and then back at Anne.

"Anne, your father and I have signed the contract. It is a contract signed in good faith. We have an agreement. Isn't that right, Jonathan?"

Before Jonathan could respond, Anne suddenly said, "Oh, I forgot earlier! I should invite Mrs McPherson for afternoon tea this afternoon with Lady Jane South at 'Harting'! Lady Jane so enjoyed her company at dinner when we gathered there. Please do not let me forget over lunch about the invitation. Mrs McPherson will be so pleased!"

Anne gave a beautiful smile, and Jonathan nodded in agreement.

Hamish McPherson considered Anne and then Jonathan. He looked out the study window, not seeing the view as he appreciated that an intimate invitation for afternoon tea at 'Harting' would be a priceless gift for his wife, especially when she was missing Marion so much. He took a long deep breath and then smiled.

'Let us change these contracts, shall we? Now Anne, what would be an appropriate wording for clause fifty-two?"

Jonathan Turner sat up in his chair and was amazed at how Anne out-manoeuvred possibly the most brilliant businessman he knew. He smiled; Hamish may not be appreciating this new delegation.

The meeting continued with several clauses being crossed out and rewritten, then signed and dated by Hamish and Jonathan.

At the end of the meeting, Hamish said, "These written copies, signed and initialled by us both, are legal, but I will have my attorneys draw up new contracts with the amended wording sent soon for your signature. I am thinking Anne Turner that I should offer you a job here. You are a brilliant negotiator. Now let us join Marjorie for lunch, and you may extend the invitation for afternoon tea!"

Hamish raised his eyebrows as he emphasised his wife's pending St James's Square invitation.

"Thank you, Mr McPherson. It will be a pleasure."

They shook hands, and Hamish put his arm around Jonathan's shoulders as they walked from Hamish's office. He said, "I will consult with Anne in the future, Jonathan. She made a lot of sense today. I think we have far better contracts as a result now!"

Turner Household, Guildford …
Doctor Neville Bassington climbed the staircase, hearing the loud cries of a newborn baby from above. He thought, 'I am a bit late for this one!'

As he entered the room, Gertrude, with a belligerent glare, said, "No need, Doctor! All taken care of here." This midwife believed that a doctor was an unnecessary hindrance during a birth.

Neville, smiling and ignoring the rude comment, said, "Better late than never!"

In front of him, he saw a smiling Eleanora Turner holding an unwashed new baby in her arms.

"Congratulations, Eleanora. Is it a boy or a girl?"

"Thank you, Neville. It is a boy, and he has a good voice."

"Yes, I heard him as I was coming up. Sounds very healthy."

Bethany burst into the room, "Mother, the baby is here! I came as soon as I heard."

"Here, come and hold him. He is a lovely little boy."

Bethany picked up the little man and cooed over him, delighting Eleanor. Neville asked the midwife about the details of the birth, readying himself before he examined Mrs Turner. The midwife was reluctant, but the doctor soon persuaded her. Neville was not happy with what she told him. He then explained that he would make his examination, and it may be best if the midwife took the baby for a few minutes, cleaned him up, and cleared the room of guests.

"How are you coping, Eleanora?"

"I am so tired, Neville. I cannot do that ever again. I am amazed I got through the delivery."

"You are looking better than I expected, Eleanora. A wet nurse may be in order at least until your strength returns."

"No, Neville, I will feed him, so his mother's milk brings him into this world. He needs that now more than anything else. But I am exhausted."

Neville quietly started examining her and was disturbed by what he found. Then he looked up and saw that Eleanora was fast asleep. She was not even registering for the examination.

He covered her up and opened the bedroom door.

"Gertrude, would you come in, please?"

Portsmouth, England …

Robert sat across the desk from Admiral Sutherland in Fleet Headquarters at Portsmouth. The day outside was grey and overcast with a cold, westerly blowing and intermittent heavy rain. It was clear there were many issues on the Admiral's mind as he fingered through the papers on his desk.

"You're a lucky fellow, Robert. Captain of a ship at such a young age. Make the most of it! I fear the age of sail will end earlier than we thought. These steam engines are changing the world. Not my cup of tea at all. But it may provide new opportunities for young fellas like you.

Now here are your orders. I expect you are curious about your new destination. From your last mission, we know the location of the traitor's base. It will take the rebels time to dismantle a large campsite like that. We suspect some rebels will still be posing as community members upon your return. It appears the locals did not question them, and I would say that money rather than loyalty was the influence. Now they must pay the price.

I have two barques coming into port early next week. These will transport two companies of soldiers, and a packet will transport horses and camp equipment. I have also assigned an additional company of marines that will be divided between *Shadow* and *Restless*.

Major Coombes will control the land operation. You will escort and protect this convoy and support the landing at Port Charlotte.

The army will search and destroy the area of all enemy activities. They will also interview local townspeople asking why they supported the traitors and what became of *Providence*'s crew. We must find out the fate of the crew members taken ashore. The information they provide will be invaluable. This operation may become a dirty business, Robert, and you should let the army handle it. They will destroy anything left of the enemy camp. I expect most of them are long gone, but who knows what they will find."

"Admiral, you mention Major Coombes. Has he been promoted?"

"Yes. Coombes performed well on your recent operation. A worthy promotion!"

"Will Major Coombes be sailing with me on Shadow?"

"Yes, he will need quarters. I expect he will want his command post on *Shadow* until they set up ashore in Port Charlotte. Lieutenant Ham will support you in *Restless*. The aim is to complete the mission within a month. Unfortunately, you will be away for Christmas, but we cannot avoid that. The traitors will not expect a follow-up action in late December if they are still there. It will be cold, so prepare well for this one. I want you away by Tuesday the twelfth of December, Robert. The Troops will be here on the Saturday before. I will expect you back by late January."

"That suits me fine, Sir. This Saturday, I am expected at Fintelton, and the timeline should allow for adequate preparations if we work hard this week. However, I do need three extra officers, Sir. I would have taken Ham, but he has earned his command of Restless. But a good first officer would be handy. For now, I will take on that role as well."

"I have Jacobs working on it, Robert. Leave it with me as there are a couple of good men available. With some luck, you will have a first officer by early next week. Jacobs has his staff resupplying your ship. He assures me the port quartermaster has properly victualed *Shadow*, and the masts and rigging are sound. You have the standard allowance of powder, and as this is a short mission, it should be sufficient."

"Well, I am thankful, Sir. If you excuse me, I shall board *Shadow* and take command."

"Robert, remain vigilant. You have a new crew but keep on guard. There are thousands of Irish men in the navy. This disturbance is far from over. Keep a good watch! On your way then, Captain South."

'Harting', St James's Square, London …
Matthew Staines, the butler at 'Harting', sorted the mail and distributed it into the various boxes for delivery. Noting the time, Lady Jane's maid, Margaret Lane, took her mistress's mail with her as she climbed the servants' stairs towards the countess's room. She entered quietly, placing the mail on the dressing table and opened the curtains letting in the greyish morning light.

"What time is it, Margaret?'

"Good morning, my Lady. It is just past eight on Wednesday morning. Would you be coming down for breakfast this morning or having it in your room, Ma'am?"

"I will be coming down, Margaret! I must talk with Anne before she leaves."

"Certainly, My Lady. Is there anything I can assist with before going down?"

"Yes, my clothes for today. Quickly please, I must not miss them."

"I have laid your clothes out on the settee, Milady. I will attend the Turners and request a delay. They have finished breakfast and will soon depart. Would you like your mail here, Milady?"

"No, Margaret, if you would pop it down on the breakfast table, please, and yes, please ask if they would wait. Then return here and assist me!"

Margaret rushed off downstairs and advised Staines of the delay. The lady's maid found Anne reading in the drawing room.

"Miss Anne, Lady Jane apologises that she is not up yet but asks if you could delay your departure until she comes down. She has something urgent she must discuss with you."

Anne, having said their goodbyes last night, was not expecting this. She wondered if it involved Marjorie McPherson. Lady Jane may regret the new friendship. For Marjorie, her visit was a major social success, but at times became somewhat embarrassing for Lady Jane and Anne. Perhaps she may be of some assistance here.

"That will be fine, Margaret. I will advise my father."

Soon after that, Lady Jane appeared and seemed a little flustered.

"I'm sorry, Dear. Your departure slipped my mind this morning. I forgot there were guests here. My apologies. Now, where can we talk? Come through here! My writing table will do. We can sit there."

Lady Jane led Anne into a small, delicately furnished room that appeared to be a study.

"This is where I write my letters. I write far more often now as it saves on travel time."

Anne smiled, "My mother does the same! Lady Jane, thank you again for hosting Mrs McPherson yesterday afternoon. I realise her acquaintance was unexpected, but she is new to London and hardly knows anyone. She is most appreciative of the introduction."

"Well, she has been here twice, so that should please her. I must say we do not have much in common, but perhaps it is because she has different interests. Her life is full of her husband's accomplishments, and she talks a lot about her sons. I know nothing really of them except they run pubs and breweries. I found myself lost for words at times."

"She would not have noticed. She is more interested in her own stories!"

Lady Jane smiled and, with her hand, shielded a little laugh, "Oh yes, you have her to a tee. Well done, Anne. Be careful who you share this with, but I understand you speak with me in confidence. Thank you for waiting, as I have a question. Now the acquaintance is made, Mrs McPherson will wish the relationship to develop. I'm not sure I want that!"

Anne saw the reservation in Lady Jane's look. Understanding the countess's discomfort, Anne had thought long and hard last night about how Lady Jane might manage Marjorie McPherson.

"Lady Jane, might I suggest a strategy?"

"Anne, I thought you might advise me on this, and I was right. Let me hear this strategy as it will be well received."

They both lowered their heads and leaned forward like thieves discussing how they would go about a burglary. Five minutes later, Lady Jane sat back and gave a polite snicker as Anne sat with a beaming smile, looking quite smug.

"Oh Anne, that is good! You are a clever young thing. I can see why you keep Robert on his toes. You are always one step ahead. I like the strategy, and I will use it. Thank you so much, having you here has been a pleasure. I think our weekend at Fintelton will be most enjoyable."

"I too."

They stood up, and Lady Jane hugged Anne. It was time the Turners departed.

As they walked out, the countess asked, "Did the meeting end well yesterday?"

"It ended in a very satisfying result!"

Lady Jane nodded as if she understood, "Good! We leave here tomorrow morning and change horses in Epsom before reaching Guildford. We shall collect you around ten in the morning on Friday, Dear!"

As the coach sped towards Whitehall, Anne sat back and thought, "Lady Jane is far more intelligent than anyone realises. She will be a wonderful mother-in-law."

During breakfast, the countess thumbed through her mail. The letter that attracted her interest was from Sir Hugh. She noted the New York postmark.

She searched for the letter opener but could not find it, so she carefully broke the seal and opened the envelope, ensuring she did not slice a finger. Taking out the letter, she read it in full.

Lady Jane was amazed. Hugh suggested a future attachment with this Lady. The news was unexpected, but her son demonstrated good sense in asking for assistance. Checking the claims of Lady Wendarm before the relationship developed was most necessary. Today being her last day in London, she must make a start on this. Having finished breakfast, she dashed into her writing room and checked her diary. The day was free. She knew the exact person who would provide the information needed. 'I shall call on Lady Angela Philps this morning!'

Lady Jane rang her bell, and soon after that, Margaret appeared.

"Margaret, order my carriage for ten, please. I will visit Lady Angela Philps as soon as I have dressed. Now I will meet you upstairs."

"Yes, Milady. I will have Staines arrange the carriage."

"Thank you."

The Turner Coach, Travelling towards Guildford ...

As the Turner coach sped across Westminster bridge, Jonathan placed a handkerchief across his face guarding against the Thames' unpleasant smell. Jonathon Turner thought about how easily Anne managed the negotiations yesterday. He was amazed by her skills and gentility. He could not decide who was the most determined in life, either Anne or his son, William.

One question crossed his mind: the depth of knowledge she possessed about investments, investors, and company structures. He could not recall previous discussions with her on these subjects. Anne's schooling would not have covered these disciplines, so where had she acquired this knowledge?

He raised his eyes and noticed her contentedly watching the London suburbs pass by.

"Anne, what are you thinking about?"

"I long for the country, the fresh air and the beauty of nature. I enjoy living in Guildford far more than the city. I like the peace of country life."

Jonathon considered this, "I am afraid with your business interests, you will have little time for the country."

"Depends on how we develop the business, Father." She smiled.

"Very true. Now I have been thinking, and I am curious about something."

She smiled, waiting for the question.

"When you were negotiating with Hamish yesterday about companies and investors and the need for an equitable solution, I was impressed. But I wondered how you have become educated about these issues."

"Father, I have worked mornings for you in the bakery since I was thirteen. This employment kindled my interest in commercial activities. After a few years, I stumbled across the Institute one afternoon and met Mr Sharples. I told him of my interests, and he found some books for me. Since then, I have taught myself accounting, and I have read as much business history as I could find.

Mr Sharples arranged my attendance at free courses by the Institute. So, I gained an education in finance, and it is now helping me with our situation."

Jonathon sat back, thought briefly, and said, "That is an amazing story, Anne. You have done far more than I have ever imagined. I see a very bright future for you."

"Thank you, father. While we have the opportunity, may we discuss the bakery's growth strategy? With the increased flour production, we must consider the timing of our new bakery in London."

"I would enjoy that, Anne."

Anne, encouraged by her father's undivided attention, explained how various financial structures might assist their development. He, in turn, felt as if a whole new range of opportunities were emerging before him. They enjoyed the conversation for several hours as the coach rattled through the countryside.

The Turner Household, Guildford ...

Neville came out of the bedroom and requested Bethany and Ethel's company in the parlour.

As he waited, he poured himself a half scotch and drank it. The day outside was cold, and he noticed the parlour fire was not lit. He thought, 'This fire should be well alight! The heat was essential for the floors above.' He was far more worried today that Eleanora could deteriorate at any time.

Coming into the parlour, Bethany and Ethel joined him, Beth giving him a look of concern.

"It is a beautiful baby, Neville, and mother rested so well last night! Father will be so pleased."

Neville smiled and said, "I think he will be more pleased that your mother lived through the delivery and is with us today."

The smile disappeared off Beth's face, "Is there something wrong, Neville?"

"I'm not sure. From my discussions with Gertrude, the baby came quickly, and there were other issues. She again drifted into a deep sleep as we talked during the examination. That is not usual for a mother on the day after birth. They usually are so excited, cooing over the baby and wanting it in their arms. I am worried she is declining rather than improving.

All I can say is that your mother must have a will of iron, as other women would not have survived what she has gone through!".

Beth grinned, "We come from good stock, we Turners!"

They all smiled.

"I might stay here tonight, and you should join me. It would be easier if I were on hand in any emergency. Your father's room is free. Ethel! Mrs Turner needs a deep sleep, so perhaps you would ask Mrs Jennings if she might watch over the little one tonight. The baby might become hungry today, and I am not sure Eleanora will cope. If she feeds him at night, we must abide by her decision, but someone must be with her.

Beth, we should return for dinner here, and we will talk again."

Ethel taking note of the arrangements, said, "Very well, Sir. I will arrange the guest room for you both."

"Ethel. Why is the fire not lit in here?"

"The boys forgot their chores last night. So, I was waiting until they came home this afternoon from school. They will bring the wood in then."

"I see! How about I fetch the wood and make it up, but someone must feed it and keep it going? The house must remain warm; it is critical for Eleanora and the baby."

"Thank you, Sir."

Ethel quickly rushed off. Bethany could see that Ethel was upset as everything was usually totally under control, "Neville, I think that was a bit harsh. Ethel is trying to cope with all of this. Your comment was unnecessary. You should have made the fire up without the criticism!"

"Your father is so tight with his money that he has no boy making up the fires. I think he needs that butler he was considering. A butler would sort it out. The house is large, requiring at least one or two men, boys, whatever, to keep up with the maintenance. Otherwise, things will become …. well, you know what I mean, Beth?"

"I understand, but please – just for me, Neville? Please find a time with Ethel and explain you were not criticising her. It was not her fault!"

"Yes. I will. I was too harsh! Sorry."

Bethany moved closer and quietly said, "Do you think something is wrong? Mother looked so happy and relieved."

"That is the problem, Beth. I am not sure. She appears well, but without warning, she collapses as if unconscious. I would blame the birth, but it may not be the cause. Perhaps it relates more to her long-term issues. But if that were the case, she would not look well. It is strange. But let us see what eventuates tonight. Hopefully, all will be fine."

Neville thought about the situation and said, "What about your father and Anne? Should we send a message?"

"It is Wednesday now, so they should be in Ewell tonight. They will be home tomorrow in the late afternoon. I do not want them travelling on the roads at night. Best let them come as planned."

Royal Navy Hospital, Gosport …
The coach pulled up at the hospital's front entrance in the pouring rain. The coachman jumped down with an umbrella and escorted Robert up the steps.

"Thank you. I will be about half an hour if you would park and wait, please."

"Aye, Sir."

Robert nodded and then entered the hospital. At the reception desk, he asked, "I am looking for my friend, Captain Mark Foster. Would you direct me, please?"

"Sorry, Sir, visiting hours commence at three in the afternoon and finish at four-thirty. If you would return, then please?"

"I am sorry, nurse, but this is a matter of national security. I am Sir Robert South, Captain of HMS *Shadow*. I come straight from Admiral Sutherland's office. Please show me the way! Captain Foster will vouch for me!"

The nurse carefully looked at Robert and decided that, against her better judgement, she should let this young-looking captain through. Calling an orderly, she instructed that Captain Foster confirm Captain South's identity before the attendant left.

Robert followed the orderly up some stairs, along a corridor, and into what seemed a recreation area for officers. At the window sitting alone, was Captain Foster.

"Excuse me, Captain Foster. You have a visitor! Would you please identify this man before I leave?"

Foster turned around and smiled when he saw it was Robert. "Certainly. This is my friend, Captain Sir Robert South. Thank you for escorting him up here."

The orderly nodded and, satisfied with the recognition, left.

"Welcome, Robert! It has been too long since we last met."

"Captain Foster, it is a pleasure, and I am glad you are recovering so well."

The two friends chatted for some time before Robert knew it was nearing his leaving time.

Robert leaned closer and lowered his voice, "Captain, there is a question that perplexes me. I understand orders are private between you and the Admiralty, and please do not answer if that is your wish. But would you tell me the specific orders for your west coast of Ireland mission?"

Foster regarded South and smiled. "You cannot understand what happened! I have been going over the events endlessly myself. The committee of inquiry has not sat yet, and I wonder how I will come out of it. But it is all in my report, Robert."

"Unfortunately, your report is restricted, Sir."

"I see. Well, my orders directed that I sail for Donegal and enter at night. There would be navy contacts expecting me there. It was quite clear that this should be my first port of call. Following that, my orders gave me full control of how I should carry out the patrolling. But, of course, we never got further than the Donegal approach up the river. The Irish had a chain across the channel. As you know, the channel there is narrow, so we were trapped. At least six cutters of armed men were waiting for us. I can't prove this, but I am sure the Irish somehow knew we were coming."

Robert considered his account and asked, "Did you go into port somewhere between Portsmouth and Donegal?"

"No, my orders specifically noted Donegal as the first port of call. I cannot understand how they knew we were coming!"

Mark Foster and Robert South continued talking for another ten minutes, and then Robert bid him farewell.

"Sir, I must thank you for your mentoring over the years. It will stand me in good stead as I take command of HMS *Shadow*. Your assistance here today has helped with my understanding of this Irish situation. I will visit again after our next voyage, which approaches."

"Robert, one word of advice. Be careful. Trust no one and keep your orders under lock and key. I am sure someone was a traitor on board and discovered our orders. It is the only explanation."

"Thank you, Sir. I will take your advice."

HMS Shadow, Portsmouth ...

The Third Lieutenant, Mr Samuel Peters, stood on the quarter-deck wondering when the captain would arrive at his new command. Peters came only three days ago and joined three other lieutenants, all junior and with minimal experience on a man of war. At least Peters was from a frigate recently returned from Gibraltar and was familiar with this type of ship.

Also, there were three midshipmen, with another two expected tomorrow. The numbers were short by sixty-three of the two hundred and fifty crew needed for the ship's company. Peters was concerned the frigate was undermanned, and there was no way they could embark unless they found more crew. At present, he was the senior officer on board. He must talk with the captain about the crew's situation.

The young lieutenant was aware of the capture of *Providence* and its recapture by Captain South. Anxious about meeting this captain whose reputation was growing, he was keen on pleasing his new commander. However, he must tread carefully as the captain might not appreciate his suggestions. Time would tell!

Lieutenant Richard Hemsworth walked forward and reported, "Sir! A message from the Admiral. Captain South is on his way."

"Thank you, Mr Hemsworth. We officers will pipe him aboard. Round up the few we have and the young gentlemen, please. Let the captain's servant know also. Have the Yeoman check that all correct flags are up and prepare the crew. Also, the watch should have the lanterns lit as the daylight is fading."

"Aye, Sir."

Peters could not see any movement from the quay yet, but there were twenty, possibly thirty men with ditty bags milling around, obviously waiting for something. Then he saw three cutters pull against the quay, and the men climbed on board. Following that, two officers joined the first cutter, and it immediately headed for the frigate.

As Peters watched, the other two boats full of men followed the first cutter. He thought, 'At last! The captain has been busy finding us some more crew!'

"Lieutenant Hemsworth! Please clear away the private craft from the starboard side of the ship. Put them on the port side. They may move back once the captain's cutter is gone."

Then Peters saw more movement on the quayside as some marines arrived and waited for transport.

Hemsworth was looking out from the quarter-deck rail, "Sir, looks like the marines have arrived as well."

"Yes, Mr Hemsworth, it appears things are finally happening."

Brotherhood Meeting Place, Dublin …

Dan O'Leary sat with two other Brother's members at a small table in a pub at the Dublin docks.

"You say they suspect some brother gave away the position by mistake during a hard night of drinking?"

"That is the theory; who knows whether it is right or not? Now, do you have that information on the ship, Braydon?"

"Yes, I have it here ……. somewhere, I do!" Braydon Kelly scrambled through a pile of papers he pulled from his ditty bag. Dara Walsh said nothing but continually watched who came into the pub. It was near closing time, so the pub was empty except for two tables beside the entrance.

"Here it is." He passed it across, and Dan quickly checked down the lists. After a good five minutes, Dan looked into the eyes of Braydon and smiled, "So you are telling me that *Restless* was in Glasgow for two nights in the week before the attack?"

"Yes, me, lad!"

"I thought Aiden was dreaming when he suggested an informer, but this cannot be a coincidence! Can it, Braydon?"

"It appears not!"

"So, who was in Glasgow on those nights?"

"Well, that will take a bit longer – give me a few weeks. But I do have some other information on *Restless*. One of our men loading some cargo on the first night she was in dock noticed a navy gig quietly moored at the end of the pier, and two men looking like sailors walked past through the shadows. Our man could not identify them as it was dark, but he did notice one of the men was very tall and muscular. The gig returned downriver towards the navy dock."

"What about the other man?"

"He was of normal size."

"Anything else?"

"Yes, the officer who reported at the harbour master's office was a Lieutenant Ham. But we know from our friends in Portsmouth that the captain of *Restless* was a Commander South. Perhaps he delegated the job, but it seems a bit odd. Also, have you ever heard of a Commander in charge of a sloop?"

Dan looked hard at Braydon. The pieces of the puzzle were coming together quicker than he expected. Yet, they needed more information on the brothers in Glasgow that night.

"This is not a coincidence! As soon as you find further information, send a rider with the message. I will bring Aiden next time."

Dara softly nudged Braydon and pointed out two strangers standing at the front of the pub.

"Do your stuff, Dara!"

Braydon and Dan sat still as they sipped their beers. Dara got up and went through the front door and off down the street. By the time Dara was five paces out of the pub, the table where the three were sitting was empty.

The Turner Household, Guildford …

Late Wednesday night Jonathan Turner entered his wife's bedroom and stood there with a wide-open smile, "Eleanora, you look so well! I am so pleased for you. Now, let me see my new son?"

Jonathan picked up the baby and cradled him in his arms.

"Jonathan, you are back. I did not expect you till tomorrow. I am so relieved you have returned. The baby came unexpectedly, and there was no stopping him. But he is a beautiful, healthy little boy and a hungry one."

"Anne and I decided we should travel straight through. We changed horses at Epsom. Fortunately, the roads were improving, and our trip was fast. We both longed for home."

Following Jonathan, Anne came into the room, rushed over, and kissed her mother, "May I hold him, Father?"

"Let me have him a little while yet, Anne. I can see your mother's eyes and nose in him. And look at those tiny little fingers. Oh, he has a good grip. He will need a name! Eleanora, have you given it any thought?"

"Jonathan, I was keen we made the decision together. Neville and David have given me such wonderful care, and we must not forget Jeremy Stephens. So, I thought that perhaps you would agree with Jeremy Neville David Turner?"

Jonathan thought about this briefly and smiled, "I agree! It is a fine choice, and we should agree on that. Here Anne, have a hold of your brother, Jeremy."

Anne took him willingly while waiting anxiously for a cuddle, "Oh, Jeremy, you are so beautiful. Perhaps you will become a doctor!" She kissed him on the forehead and said, "I hope my babies will be all like this one."

Eleanora was overjoyed that Jonathan agreed with the name and that Anne was so fond of the little man. She watched the doting father and daughter talking at the baby as he occasionally opened his eyes and made a smile, probably caused by wind. However, it created the right effect.

"Oh, look, he is smiling!" Anne exclaimed as she gently rocked him.

Sitting beside Eleanora, Jonathan asked, "How are you, my love?"

She sat up a little more, "I am fine, Jonathan, just very tired."

"Good, good. Now Neville tells me he has organised a wet nurse so you may rest and regain your strength. I think this is a good decision, Eleanora."

"Well, at first, I resisted what he said, but now I see that there may be some use in this. I prefer feeding Jeremy myself, but perhaps I could share with a wet nurse. I will welcome the rest."

"Good. I will confirm the arrangements."

"Tell me, Jonathan, was your trip successful?"

"I delegated, and Anne carried out the negotiations. She did a splendid job, and we have new contracts that are fairer, and even Hamish was pleased with the outcome. Especially for Marjorie!"

"For Marjorie?"

"Yes, I will let Anne tell you about that. Now I must unpack and visit the mill. Mrs Jennings may still give us a late dinner before I go there. Is there any news from Terry?"

"As far as I know, no word at all! It must be quiet at the mill."

As Anne explained how Marjorie's desire for introductions helped with the negotiations, Jonathan walked out. He heard Anne and Eleanora laughing loudly as the story unfolded. He smiled, relieved that Eleanora had survived the birth and looked so well. It was a blessing for Christmas, having a new child in the house.

Chapter 5

Port Charlotte, Isle of Islay, Scotland …

In the early morning hours, the stiff wind whistled through the rigging of the boats anchored at Port Charlotte. Carefully a fishing vessel with only a flapping jib edged in through the choppy water nudging against the quay, where a single figure jumped out and ran sheltering from the pouring rain. A crewman pushed the fishing vessel out, and it edged away and quickly disappeared into the foggy darkness and swirling mist. Carrying a ditty bag, he sheltered beside a building near the quay, carefully looking around before making his way up the slight incline into the settlement.

Callum Ferguson heard a light knocking on his bedroom window.

"Who be knocking here at this time of night, Callum?"

'Not sure, Ruth. Let me see."

Callum opened the indoor shutters and held a candle against the window. He saw Braydon Kelly smiling at him and pointing towards the back door before disappearing. Shivering, Callum pulled on a coat and darted from the bedroom, lighting a candle and unlocking the door bolt. The wet and shivering man rushed out of the rain.

"Braydon! Take off your coat and hang it here. I will put a few blankets in front of the fire. You can dry out and rest. We will talk in the morning."

"Thank you, Callum. Let Ruth know I am here, so I don't surprise her."

"Perhaps it is I who should take fright?"

"No, man! Just passing through and catching the Port Ellen ferry for Glasgow. Talk in the morning about a cart ride! Now you jump back into bed, lad, with that warm little lass!"

'Harting', St James's Square, London …

On Thursday morning, the winds dropped below a gentle breeze rustling the leaves and spreading them over the Square. The leafless trees seemed like starving people as the wind slightly moved them, mimicking waving hands in the breeze.

Lady Jane South, seated in the carriage, rugged up and warm, waited for the Earl. She considered the cold season outside and remembered that Christmas was now only three weeks away. The countess had always enjoyed the cold winter weather, knowing plenty of fires would keep the manor warm. Then she considered the cold's effect on the poor and decided on a generous donation for the poor box this Christmas.

Once the footmen had settled the Earl and rugged him up, she looked down at the book that Lady Angela loaned her, listing various noble English families and the page that mentioned the Wendarms. Lady Clarissa Wendarm was genuine. However, it appeared from what Angela told her that Hugh's description was not entirely correct.

The book mentioning the Wendarm family contained most of the family history until Sir Geoffrey Wendarm, Clarissa's husband. The family went back generations and, over the years, accumulated extensive land holdings in the north. Lady Clarissa's husband, Sir Geoffrey Wendarm, inherited the estate some years ago when his father died. It was here that Lady Angela added the recent details.

Sir Geoffrey married Clarissa soon after receiving the inheritance. They then moved to the Wendarm estate in the country, living in luxury and entertaining on a grand scale. Rumours spread that Sir Geoffrey was off in London having an affair six months after the marriage, and she remained on the estate with various men entertaining her over the years.

Sir Geoffrey was a keen gambler and loved playing cards despite having little skill at the game. Unfortunately, he built up significant debts, and the only solution was the sale of his estate. They kept some of the plantations in the Indies as their remaining assets. These were of dubious worth but provided the couple with some income.

After settling his debts and with little money available, they rented a house in Hammersmith, which afforded them some luxury at an affordable price. Sir Geoffrey became a recluse, mostly remaining at home drinking. Lady Clarissa sought friends who would still recognise her and maintained a reduced social life.

Seven months later, the police found Sir Geoffrey's body washed up on the shore of the Thames. The coroner determined the cause of death as drowning. Of course, Lady Clarissa was bereft, but stories circulated that she celebrated Sir Geoffrey's end some days later with a large party at some gentleman's cottage in the country. Fortunately, there were no children from the marriage. Lady Clarissa inherited the plantations in the Indies.

The countess carefully considered what she should write in her reply. It would be best to confirm that Lady Clarissa was genuine; however, Lady Jane decided that a warning of this lady's reputation for wandering interests, free attachments, and dubious character would not go astray. It would be some time before Hugh received this reply, and who knows what would happen by then. Her one hope was that Sir Hugh was not keen on marriage, and his usual antics of using women for his satisfaction would continue. She sighed, wishing for a faster way of making contact.

Then she smiled as she thought about picking up Anne on Friday morning on their way home. Lady Jane was unsure precisely what it was about this girl, but a warm feeling in her heart always accompanied thoughts of Anne. It was a blessing that Robert had found her.

The Turner Bakery, Guildford, late morning…

Anne spent time with Audrey on Thursday morning, checking the office work before reviewing the sales trends. The books were in far better shape this time, and only a few areas needed attention. The banking was complete, and the balances matched those on the note the bank clerk delivered that morning without reconciliations. She was pleased with what she found and made a point of encouraging Audrey. The time spent training was paying off, and she was now confident Audrey would take over her old role.

Terry Spencer discussed the pressure release valve and the new mill fence with Anne's father. Since the attempted arson, the community felt tense, with much speculation about the Magistrate's verdict when the court convened the next week.

"Terry, now that the emergency valve is in, may we commence full production again?"

"Yes, Mr Turner, thank you for acting on this so quickly, as it may save lives in the future."

Terry walked off, greeting Anne with a nod and a smile as he passed. Anne took her opportunity, "Father, everything here is where it should be. The sales figures are on your desk with the cash flow. I will have lunch at home and pack for the weekend. You remember that I leave for Fintelton tomorrow morning with the Souths?"

Jonathan raised his eyes from his work, "Yes, that's right! I will talk with you at dinner, Anne. Jeb and I must discuss the biscuit production line and next week's office shift across the road. Then there are further issues in the bakery. Please let your mother know I will have lunch here today."

Jonathan refocused on his work. As Anne stood and gathered her things, Jeb came in and sat down with her father.

"I'll leave you two at it then!"

They both smiled and continued their conversation about the production line.

As Anne walked up the High Street, she decided to visit Hursts. She was short of a scarf that would match her dress for tomorrow. On entering the tailor and dressmaker's shop, Anne noticed Mrs Smith serving a young lady admiring the scarves. She was well dressed, about the same height as Anne, perhaps slightly shorter, and wore her brown hair in a bun under a pretty hat. Anne made a friendly comment, "My, that is a pretty scarf! I need a similar one but with a speck of blue in it rather than the red."

The young lady looked up and smiled politely but modestly backed away. Anne assumed this lady was either somewhat timid or felt that a reply might prove embarrassing without a proper introduction.

Anne apologised, "I'm sorry, I did not intend any rudeness! Please, continue your conversation with Mrs Smith. Excuse me." Anne moved away as Mrs Smith looked up and said, "Please join us, Miss Anne. I am sure this young lady will not mind. She has arrived in town this morning!"

At the mention of Anne's name, the young woman looked hard at her and then said in a beautiful soft Irish voice, "You would not be Miss Anne Turner, would you?"

Anne realised from the young lady's speech she was of the upper class, and her accent was distinctly Irish, "Yes, I am. Forgive my lack of manners as we are not introduced, but may I enquire who you are?"

The young lady gave a smile of relief, "Indeed, you may. I am Victoria Sopwith, and I arrived at eleven o'clock on the coach from Basingstoke. There was some time before lunch, so I thought I might browse the shops looking for clothing. It is wonderful meeting you here. What a coincidence. My brother has written so much about you!"

"Miss Sopwith, you have taken me quite by surprise. David has told me much about you too. I am so pleased to make your acquaintance."

They both politely bowed to each other.

"Now, I must insist you call me Anne. Where are you staying?"

"Please, Miss Turner, I mean Anne, you must call me Victoria. My maid went with some porters, and my luggage should be at David's residence by now. The housekeeper will have received them. The ship from Ireland was early, and the coach journey was faster than expected. David thought I would not arrive until Monday. So, I am early. I took a cup of coffee at the hotel over there. The Fox and something!"

"The Fox and Hound!"

"Yes, that is it. I decided to do some shopping and then hire a carriage. David wrote about Hursts, so I thought I should start here."

Mrs Smith said, "Well, as you know, the owner!" She indicated towards Anne. "You will receive special attention, Miss Sopwith."

Victoria smiled.

"David is not with you?"

"No, I checked at the medical practice, and they advised that he left early this morning and is away until Monday. I shall see him late Monday afternoon. I was keen on exercise and using my time well, so I thought I might go shopping."

Anne enquired, "You have a chaperone with you?"

"Yes, I have a maid, but I sent her with my luggage. David told me Guildford is a very safe place, and I would enjoy the shops."

"Well, Victoria, I am joining Emma and David tomorrow at Fintelton Estate. I think you must join our party. There will be plenty of room for you in the carriage. Shall we have lunch and discuss this? I am not leaving you here in town on your own!"

Victoria stood back, smiled and said, "That is most kind of you, Anne. But will David be annoyed?"

"Not at all! I will not have that! We will arrive tomorrow with the Earl and Countess, which will be a pleasant surprise for him. Lady Emma would insist you attend. She would be embarrassed if she found that you were here, alone. David does not think of these things!"

"Yes, David can be a bit absent-minded at times. I must admit I would be glad of the company."

"What do you say then, Victoria? Will you join us tomorrow for the weekend at Fintelton? We will return on Monday. Lady Jane has arranged the carriage, so you shall have the Earl, the Countess and myself as escorts."

"I think I will come, Anne. It will certainly be a surprise for David."

"It will be good company for me as well, Victoria. This visit will be my first, and I am unsure what we should expect; however, it will be far grander than what you find here in Guildford. Come, let's have some lunch. Oh, we should purchase these scarves before we go!"

The Barque, Frogmore, off the Virgin Islands ...

Sir Hugh and Lady Clarissa stood on the quarterdeck towards the stern, enjoying the warmer weather in the Caribbean.

"What land is that over there, Hugh?"

"The Virgin Islands[10]. The captain advised that merchant vessels keep clear of Cuba and route this way for safety. The Spanish have quite an influence in the Caribbean, and British ships avoid the foreign-controlled islands."

"Then we should be in Kingston within a day or two?"

"Yes. At Kingston, where are you staying?"

"Well, we have bookings for several nights at the Grand Hotel, and then,

---

[10] The British Virgin Islands, officially simply the Virgin Islands, were a British overseas territory in the Caribbean, to the east of Puerto Rico and the US Virgin Islands and northwest of Anguilla. Wikipedia.

hopefully, we find transport and set up residence at the largest plantation."

"Sugar Cane?"

"Yes! I understand the sugar trade is quite lucrative. And You?"

"Sugar, indigo, coffee, and cotton. I expect the inspection process will be lengthy. I may be in Kingston for some time. How long will you stay, Clarissa?"

"A similar time, but my main purpose is selling the plantations. I fear I must return home as soon as I can complete my business here."

"Well, the Grand sounds attractive. I will accompany you and then check in myself. Then I must present my credentials to the Governor, probably on Monday. Once that is done, I will visit my largest plantation first."

Lady Clarissa moved closer and rubbed her hip against his, "The Grand will not be as convenient as the ship. Will it?"

"No, it will not!"

"Then, Darling, we should make the best of the next few nights!"

Sir Hugh grinned, pulled her close, and kissed her on the back of the ear.

The Turner Household, Guildford ...

The students were delighted to hear that the Reverend Taggart had cancelled school for the day. He was attending a rural deanery meeting and returning well after lunch. William and Simeon worked together chopping firewood in the backyard. Despite the day being cold, the boys were hot and sweaty and enjoyed a cool drink as they took a break.

Both said, "Thanks, Mrs Jennings, that was good!"

Mrs Jennings became concerned as she noticed half the woodpile was yet untouched.

"Your father may be home soon for lunch, so a bit more chopping before then might please him. William, please stack all this chopped firewood in the woodshed."

The boys nodded in agreement and continued with their job. Mrs Jennings was impressed at how readily they continued working without any complaint. They were both good boys, and she felt their father treated them unfairly.

Simeon made significant progress in another hour, with the pile behind the shed visibly decreasing in size. He put down the axe and felt his sore hands. William stacked the chopped wood in a dry area in the woodshed.

Pondering the pile of uncut wood, Simeon considered that his father had not specified the progress required. Now there was plenty of chopped wood for the next week, so why cut anymore? Before sharing this with Will, he would watch him have a turn at chopping. His brother needed the practice.

William stood axe in hands and feet together and took a mighty swing at the wood on the block. He missed, and the axe dug into the chopping block.

"Will, you're not standing correctly!"

"Yes, I am! I was just unlucky. Watch this!"

William swung the axe again, missing the chopping block completely.

As William wrestled the axe free, Simeon said, "You must put your left foot out in front of the right foot. The feet should be in line with the wood on the block. That way, you swing the axe softer but chop more wood!"

William looked up at Simeon, taking a deep breath as he pulled the axe free again, "Show me?"

Simeon walked over and took the axe. He faced the chopping block and positioned his feet as he had explained. Balancing himself correctly, he swung the axe using far less energy and struck the piece of wood on target, the wood splintering into fireplace-sized chunks.

"Did you see that?"

Walking forward and nodding, William said, "Yeah, I got it!"

"Do not swing the axe so hard. Accuracy is the thing. Position your feet as mine were and then hit the wood in the middle."

William carefully positioned his feet and then looked at the piece of wood resting on the chopping block. He placed the edge of the axe blade on the wood piece, confirming his aim.

"That's right!" Simeon called.

William swung the axe in a beautiful arc, the blade descending precisely on target. The piece of wood split into pieces.

"Wow!" screamed William. "Did you see that!"

"Good Will! Try swinging it softer. Now see if you can do it again?"

"Of course, I can."

William quickly placed another block of wood on the chopping block and took up his old position without thinking, taking a mighty swing at the block. This time he completely missed the chopping block, and the axe head disappeared into the ground.

Simeon began laughing, pointing at the axe. Going red in the face at being laughed at, William walked around angry with himself, then picked up the axe again and positioned his feet correctly. He gently swung the axe and hit the wood, splintering it into fire-sized bits.

Anne and Victoria stood on the back verandah and clapped as William looked up.

"That was an excellent chop, William. You will soon be as good as Simeon at chopping the firewood."

The boys walked over and wondered who Anne's new friend was.

"Simeon and William, let me introduce Miss Victoria Sopwith. She is Doctor Sopwith's sister."

With a big smile, William said, "Hello, Miss Sopwith. I am William Turner.

Did you see me chop the wood? I did all that!" Pointing at the pile of chopped wood.

Simeon frowning at Will's comment, said, "Hello!"

Victoria smiled, "You are both very clever chopping so much!"

Simeon spoke up, "We both did it. I chopped, and William stacked it up."

William was surprised by Victoria's accent, "You speak in a funny way. Where do you come from?"

"I come from Ireland. Do I sound funny?"

William looked at her and said, "Yes, but I like it."

"So do I," Simeon said.

"Well, I'll try talking the way you do. It may take me a while!"

"Come on, boys and have some lunch."

William tugged Victoria's sleeve and said, "Doctor Sopwith is helping us build a boat. It is over here under some cloth."

Victoria nodded in agreement and followed both boys along the verandah where the boat frame was stored.

William could not contain his excitement about the boat, "It is nearly finished, and now it is time for the boat's skin. We will be doing some more next Saturday. You can watch if you like!"

"He built a boat in Ireland just like this one. It would be fun seeing it finished."

Anne watched William and saw that he was taken with Victoria. She felt a bit jealous but quickly brushed it aside. She led the way back into the kitchen, where Mrs Jennings placed bowls of hot soup and freshly baked bread on the table. Each bowl was quickly accounted for, warming them on such a cold day. During lunch, Victoria talked about where she lived north of Belfast in Ireland.

"It sounds beautiful, Victoria. It must be lovely living there?"

"You would think so, but I found it quite lonely. My only companion was Miss O'Brien, my permanent chaperone and, before that, a governess. David was at medical school when my parents and brother died. Fortunately, he was of an age allowing him the legal right as one of my trustees. He visited often, but there were long times when I had no company." Then she said with a smile in her voice, "As a result, I am very well-read!"

They all laughed.

"So, you are happy now you are in Guildford?"

"Yes, I love being with David; he is my only family. There are no aunts or uncles. He is it, and I am excited to be with him again tomorrow. I have not seen him since last Christmas. I am also curious about his fiancée, Lady Emma."

"Well, you will meet her and my fiancée Robert and the rest of the guests tomorrow. Perhaps there will be too many people?"

"No, I like meeting as many people as I can. I find travel is a great adventure and a release from my seclusion in Ireland. Meeting so many people in Guildford is wonderful."

Anne suddenly realised they were eating in the kitchen and not the dining room, "Oh Victoria, I must apologise for not asking you into the dining room. You must think of me as so rude and common. I am so sorry!"

Victoria chuckled, "Anne, it was lovely sharing with you here and with the boys. I felt treated as one of the family. Please be at ease as I enjoyed it."

"Anne, Anne?" William asked.

"Yes, William."

"May we all walk down to the river after lunch?"

"William, I am sure mother will wish an introduction with Victoria first, but after that, if we all rug up with jumpers and coats, then I cannot see why not. The weather looks clear. But we cannot stay too long as we must pack for tomorrow."

"We can show Victoria where the pirate fights take place!"

With a gleam in her eye, Victoria said, "Oh, that sounds exciting, William!"

The Turner Household, Guildford ...

Sir David and Lady Jane's coach arrived at eight am sharp. The previous evening Anne sent a message explaining the situation with Victoria Sopwith's arrival in Guildford.

"Thank you for including Victoria today, Lady Jane."

"Nonsense, my dear girl. It will be a pleasant surprise for David and Emma. I agree we must not leave her alone in Guildford until David returns. She must accompany us as I am keen for an introduction."

The carriage proceeded down High Street, turning at the market square and up the hill past the castle where a coach stood outside the Sopwith house.

"This is it!" Anne was excited as their coach stopped.

The Front door opened, and Victoria, dressed in a beautiful travelling suit, came out and approached.

"Lord Fintelton and Lady Fintelton, please may I introduce Miss Victoria Sopwith!"

Victoria curtseyed. The Earl, who had stepped out of the carriage, kissed her hand.

"Delighted, My Dear. I am so glad you could join us. Now, this is Lady Fintelton."

Victoria curtsied again, saying, "It is an honour meeting you, Lady Fintelton. My brother has written and told me so much about your beautiful daughter."

"I am delighted, Victoria. Now please come aboard and David if you would arrange the footmen. They must stow Victoria's luggage, please."

"Thank you, Lady Jane, but there is no need. My maid, Judith, has arranged a coach and will follow with my luggage if that is acceptable?"

"Certainly, Victoria. I am impressed with your organisation." As Victoria moved into the coach, Lady Jane looked at Anne and raised her eyebrows. Anne smiled, understanding how impressed Lady Jane must be. Victoria noticed the looks of approval and commented, "Judith has been with me since I was fourteen. She is most capable and takes care of many of my arrangements."

With that, the coach moved off towards Petersfield. From there, they sped on through Harting and onto the Fintelton Estate.

As the carriage steadily progressed along the estate driveway, Lady Jane spoke, "I do hope Pike has all the fires going. It is becoming colder as we near sunset. I would not be surprised if there were a frost tonight."

The Earl nodded in agreement, but Lady Jane, aware of his poor hearing, was unsure if he heard what she was saying.

As the coach pulled up, Pike and several servants rushed out with wraps ready for transferring the Earl and Countess inside. Sir David and Lady Jane made a quick exit. Anne would have introduced Victoria, but the butler took her hand and led her up the stairs and through the front entrance. From nowhere, Robert appeared, put his arms around Anne, and gave her a big kiss.

"Welcome, Anne. We are together at Fintelton earlier than we had planned! I am so glad you are here!"

"Oh, Robert, I am freezing!" she shivered, and Robert felt it.

"Come quickly out of this cold. It is wonderfully warm inside."

Anne needed no further encouragement and bolted up the stairs laughing with Robert chasing her. As they rushed through the front door and into the warm entrance foyer, they found an overjoyed David Sopwith hugging his little sister.

Port Ellen, Isle of Islay, Scotland ...

As the cart descended the slight hill into Port Ellen, Braydon Kelly continued giving Callum Ferguson instructions.

"Now, when the British come, identify all the officers, particularly the navy ones. I need their names, ranks and the names of their ships. Also, I must know how they treat the residents here. Take note of anyone the British do not harass. It might indicate a possible link with them, someone who gave our position away. As soon as they leave, send me the information."

"Will you return here or straight home?"

"Home. Within a week or two at the most! The British will have arrived by then. Keep a low profile but watch what they do. Perhaps use Ruth on the cart – she can pay visits back and forth, keeping an eye on them. Even strike up a friendship. You know what I mean. Make her available at the pub a few nights."

Callum frowned, "I am not sure about that. I do not want Ruth in danger!"

"I hope you're not falling for Ruth, Callum. Remember, she is a brother's member and volunteered for this role. No time for sentiment here, Callum. We are fighting a war. Get the information for me!"

Callum dropped Braydon off at the pier, then turned and parked his cart behind the pub. He tied up the horse, went inside and ordered a pint. Sitting near the window, Callum kept watch, taking note of who was boarding the ferry and making sure Braydon left. He was unsure of Braydon's role with the brothers, but he surmised it might be gathering intelligence given the questions he asked. Despite his loyalty towards the Irish cause, he questioned whether he supported the right side. The Irish had suffered a total defeat here. He was aware of the penalty the brothers handed out for even suspected treachery. Callum had always suspected his Irish brothers might be untrustworthy, so he decided to stay one step ahead of them. Perhaps the British could offer some insurance.

Nearly twenty minutes later, a family hurried past the pub carrying much luggage, indicating a long trip. Callum recognised Doctor Watson, his wife and children as he led them onto the pier. He served the brothers well, caring for the injured after the battle. He was kind and offered care for the prisoners, but the Irish stopped him quickly. Where was the Watson family going? Callum finished his third beer, left the pub, and remained out of sight while watching them board the ferry.

As the boat departed, he racked his brains, recalling where the doctor's surgery was. He mounted his cart, drove along the shorefront, and then gave the reigns a flick as he encouraged the horse up the hill and onto the Bowmore road. Callum was sure the surgery was behind the village with a view of Port Charlotte across Loch Indaal. Why would the doctor and his family leave such a pleasant spot?

Within the hour, he pulled his cart up outside the surgery, where a man was gardening in the front yard. Hopping down, he approached the man and asked, "Excuse me, Sir! Is the surgery open?"

"Are ye blind, man? The doctor's gone, and he will not be back! The town council are looking for a new one."

"That was quick! Why did he leave?"

"Said he got a better offer in England."

"Well, thank you, friend!"

"If you want a doctor, lad, you be out of luck, but there is a nurse who comes in the mornings. Otherwise, you should be on that Glasgow ferry, lad!"

Callum tipped his hat acknowledging the man's help, remounted the cart, and drove off. As he slowly steered the carriage horse down into the village, he considered why the doctor would take his family away so quickly. It appeared the Doctor might have had his feathers ruffled!

The Barque, Frogmore, Kingston Harbour, Jamaica ...

The ship glided past Port Royal and anchored in Kingston harbour well before dawn. As the pier was fully occupied with other ships, a tender carried the passengers and their luggage ashore. It was a long process made worse by the humidity, which increased as they reached the wharf. The breeze was light, and the morning sun burned, increasing the temperature as the passengers searched for shade.

Sir Hugh ensured Lady Clarissa and Mrs Green's bookings were correct at the Grand Hotel and arranged a dinner table for eight o'clock that night. He booked himself in and followed the porter upstairs. It was a two-storied wooden building with large verandahs along the hotel's front with views across the bay. While probably the best hotel in town, he felt it was a bit run down and needed a thorough whitewash and sprucing up with some lime paint. The rooms were large, airy, and comfortable, with four-poster beds and mosquito nets. He hoped the nets worked as he scratched his wrists, having already been bitten by the hungry insects several times.

Leaving the hotel in a carriage, he ventured out seeking his attorneys. Following the directions given by the desk clerk, he gazed around as the carriage moved deeper into the town area. The road was wide and dusty, and the heat increased as the coachman stopped under a tree. Pointing along the street, the driver seemed impatient. Sir Hugh hopped down, thanked the driver, and walked towards the corner. To Hugh's surprise, the driver cracked his whip, and the coach rushed away in the direction of the Grand Hotel.

Hugh watched it disappear down the street and wondered how he would find his way back. As he turned and walked up a slightly rising incline, he felt the sweat running down his back. Feeling most uncomfortable, he thought, 'This was a horrible climate! How could people live here?' Turning the corner, he discovered a collection of buildings made of both wood and stone. He walked along the street and finally found a newly whitewashed shop with a sign indicating Stephenson's Attorneys.

On trying the door, he found it locked, but a young lady was inside at the reception desk. He knocked on the glass, and she smiled and came across with some keys. Before opening the door, she carefully surveyed the street and then unlocked and opened the entrance.

"May I be of assistance, Sir?"

"Yes, I am Sir Hugh South from Fintelton Manor Estate in England. I represent the Earl of Fintelton. I arrived on the ship *Frogmore* this morning! I was wondering if Mr Stephenson was in?"

The young lady ushered Sir Hugh in and relocked the door, "I'm sorry, Sir Hugh, we only open on Saturday mornings for tenant payments. Mr Stephenson will not be back till Monday morning. Perhaps I could book you an appointment for Monday?"

"Yes, that would be good. What time would that be?"

"Around eleven in the morning."

"Nothing earlier?"

"I'm afraid not. Mr Stephenson does not start until ten each day; he already has an appointment at ten. Eleven is the best we have."

"I'll take that, thanks. Good day, Miss ....?"

"Miss Jill Hall, Sir Hugh."

"Thank you, Miss Hall. I shall return on Monday morning. Good day."

"Sir Hugh. Are you travelling without a coach?"

"Strange that you should ask, as the coach I hired disappeared as soon as they let me down here."

"It is understandable. There has been some unrest, and there are several gangs creating trouble. Saturday morning is not a good time. I suggest we send for a coach."

"Thank you, Miss Hall. I was unaware of the situation."

Taking a deep breath, Jill Hall opened the door and called a boy. Placing a halfpenny in his hand, the lad rushed off.

While he waited, Sir Hugh considered his next objective. He must find the address of the Governor's residence. Sir Hugh fixed his attention again on the receptionist.

"Excuse me again, Miss Hall. By any chance, could you give me the Governor's address?"

"Certainly. I will write it out for you. Sir Hugh, I suggest you check with the concierge about safety before leaving the hotel. Also, demand a reliable coach. A small tip will ensure your safety. Unfortunately, we do not have the peacefulness here; you enjoy in England."

The Turner Household, Guildford ...

Eleanora, holding the baby, realised how tired she was becoming. She was now questioning her determination not to have a wet nurse. Ethel and Mrs Jennings came in at times during the night and helped, but they were now sound asleep downstairs. Perhaps Jonathan was right; a wet nurse would give her the needed rest time.

The fireplace was showing only a weak glow in the darkness, and the room was becoming colder. Eleanora shivered as she nursed Jeremy, her beautiful little one.

A soft noise outside caught her attention, and William came into her room, approaching her bed.

"I can't sleep, mother. May I come in with you?"

"Yes, you can, William, but first, would you make up the fire? Then, we will both be warm!"

William turned and looked at the fire.

"It is nearly out!"

He went across and found some kindling and placed it on the glowing embers. It soon started crackling with flames. He then put some large pieces of wood on the fire and stood back as he watched the fire grow. Then he placed the grill around the fire and walked across, hopping into the bed.

"Thank you, William. You did that well!"

Sitting beside his mother, he blurted out, "I chopped some wood yesterday! Simeon is better at it than me, but I am getting better."

"Well, you are as tall as Simeon now. You will be particularly good at chopping wood as you grow stronger."

William nodded and then peeked at the baby, curled up in his mother's arms, fast asleep. William put his little finger into Jeremy's hand, and the baby grasped it.

"He has a strong grip for a baby!"

"Yes, he does. He is beautiful! Would you like a nurse for a while?"

"Yes, but what if he wakes up?"

"Jeremy has just been fed and burped. He is tired out. He will sleep for an hour now."

Eleanora put the baby into William's arms, ensuring he was secure. Then she sat back, relieved, closing her eyes as the room became warm. William sat looking down at the baby, "Mother, you will not die, will you?"

"I hope not, William. Why do you ask?"

"Well, lots of mothers die after having a baby. My friends at school have told me. I had a bad dream about it, and Father belted me hard because of it. I was so afraid, and then I woke up."

"No, William, I will not die at present. I love you too much for that!"

William thought about that as Eleanora yawned again. How would 'love' keep his mother alive? People died when someone spilled blood, so she would perhaps die if his mother had lost blood. He was about to ask her if she had lost much blood but noticed that her eyes were closed, and she was breathing softly.

William whispered, "Mother, are you asleep?"

There was no answer. The boy realised that his mother was exhausted. So, he quietly sat there with the baby. It was twenty minutes before someone came into the room. Both mother and baby had not stirred, and William maintained watch, ensuring they were both safe.

Mrs Jennings first checked that the fire was burning well and noticed William with the baby cradled in his arms. She lit some more candles and then addressed him with a hushed voice, "Well, what a good boy you are, William. How long have you been here?"

"I could not sleep, so I came down. Mother fell asleep and left me with the baby! You know this baby makes a lot of noise while he sleeps. He grunts and groans and has little stretches. He is quite funny."

"You have done a good job then, haven't you? I'll take him now."

Mrs Jennings picked up the baby, enjoying the cuddle. Then she said, "Off now, back upstairs, William. You can have another hour, then come for breakfast before putting on your church clothes."

William quietly hopped out of bed and made his way out. At the door, he found himself face to face with his father. William took a step backwards. Jonathan Turner said nothing but scowled down at the boy.

Mrs Jennings explained, "William did a good job minding the baby while Mrs Turner slept!"

Jonathan said, "I am going downstairs and will fetch her a cup of tea."

William crept past as his father talked with Mrs Jennings.

"She is asleep now and probably needs more. We were up several times during the night with the baby."

Jonathan nodded in agreement and then looked down. The boy was gone.

"The kettle is boiled if you would enjoy some tea yourself, Mr Turner."

"Thank you. I will do that."

Fintelton Manor, Outside Petersfield, Sussex …
Anne awoke, hearing the maid opening the curtains. The early morning light barely lit the room, and Jane lit some candles. Anne noticed the manor house had easterly views, and as the sun peaked over the horizon, she could make out the pastures running away down a slight valley.

"Good morning, Miss Anne."

"Morning, Jane. What time is it, please?"

"About seven-thirty, Miss. The countess has requested breakfast for eight-thirty, and the coaches will leave for church at nine-thirty. I understand the family is attending the ten-thirty service in Petersfield this morning."

"Thank you, Jane."

"I have left a tray with tea and some toast. Will you require help with dressing or your hair, Ma'am?"

"A little help with my hair would be appreciated, Jane, but please give me forty-five minutes. Then, I shall need you."

"Yes, Milady, I will be back then."

The maid left the room, and Anne sat in bed, sipping tea and taking a bite of toast. With a smile, she felt she could tolerate this lifestyle if Robert could afford it. The dinner last night was relaxed and friendly. It was a great family occasion for Lord Fintelton and the Countess, with Emma, Robert, and their prospective partners attending. The lively conversation involved many stories about old times and past events with humorous anecdotes. Neville and Bethany fitted in well, and Lady Jane made no secret of what good friends Neville and Robert were and how much she appreciated that over the years.

Sir David and Lady Jane retired around ten-thirty. Victoria, after a long day, soon followed them. That left the young adults talking, playing cards and enjoying the warmth of the fireplace while drinking some imported French red wine. It was a wonderful night for Anne, sitting beside Robert and snuggling up in front of the fire.

Today would be different for her with their church commitments, Robert leaving after lunch and visiting the tenant farmers with the countess in the afternoon. She hoped Lady Jane was ready and organised for this as it was her one chance at understanding the tenant farmer payments. But more of this later. She hopped out of bed and readied herself for breakfast.

After Church, at Guildford ...

Jonathan Turner deeply conversed with the Reverend Andrew Taggart, pleased with their temporary Parish Council appointment. After Jeremy Stephens' death, the attorney, Mr Blake Wood, replaced him as council secretary.

"The records are now all up to date, and the minutes are available well before the meetings, Jonathan. We are in a far better situation than when Jeremy, bless his heart, was doing the job of Council Secretary. We must vote Blake in at the annual vestry meeting."

"Should not be a problem, Andrew. I think everyone agrees. I enjoy his conversation! Do you have any business with him?"

As Jonathan talked, he saw a well-presented lady who appeared familiar across the courtyard. She spoke with two young gentlemen, who were smartly dressed and seemed in a hurry. He recalled seeing one of the men before but could not remember where. The two men courteously said their goodbyes and walked down the High Street.

"No, Jonathan. Why do you ask?"

"I have him representing my business when the Magistrates meet next Tuesday for the trial of the arsonists." Jonathan could not recall who this familiar lady was.

"Andrew, who is that lady over there? She was talking with two young gentlemen, but they have now walked off."

"Yes, I met them as they exited the church. She is Mrs Janet Stubbington from London. She and her two sons have visited friends for the last two days. They broke their journey here before travelling on to Bristol. Why? Are you acquainted with her?"

Jonathan's memory was working hard. He was sure they had met. Then he remembered Hamish McPherson had introduced her as one of the other Reading Pub investors. At that moment, Mrs Stubbington walked across in their direction.

"Good morning, Jonathan. What a delightful coincidence. My sons and I are on a fact-finding trip and will hopefully reach Bristol by Thursday. We have been investors now since the unfortunate demise of my husband. But, of course, you are aware of this!"

"Yes, welcome, Janet. You attended Marion and Thomas' wedding in Greenwich. I apologise for not having more opportunities for social activities, but a lot happened to our family during that time. Will you be staying in Guildford long?"

Andrew Taggart excused himself at this point as other parishioners were waiting for his attention. Eleanora Turner noticed Jonathan conversing with an unknown woman and was curious about who she might be. Walking across with Jeremy in her arms, she inquired, "Well, Jonathan, perhaps you might introduce me?"

"Of course, Dear. May I introduce Mrs Janet Stubbington, a fellow investor with me in the pub at Reading? The project the McPhersons are establishing. I met Janet there at a meeting with Hamish McPherson. We toured the pub together and then had dinner with Hamish."

"Delighted, Mrs Stubbington."

"Please, Mrs Turner, call me Janet. I must congratulate you on your new arrival. You look very well, having just delivered, and that is a delightful outfit you are wearing."

"We are fortunate as we own a chain of Tailors and Dressmakers. Mrs Smith at Hursts, our shop in Guildford, takes special care of the family."

"You are fortunate, indeed. I am always on the lookout for good dressmakers! Now, where is the shop situated?"

"Well, it is one hundred yards down the High Street on your left. It is called 'Hursts – Tailors and Dressmakers'. Are you staying in town long? I only ask because, as you are an acquaintance of Jonathan, I thought you and your sons might join us for luncheon?"

"Eleanora, that is a most generous offer, indeed, at such short notice. Unfortunately, we have commitments for the remainder of the day. However,

Jonathan, there are some business issues about the pub in Reading that I would value discussing with you tomorrow, if possible. Would, say, eleven in the morning be convenient? We leave on the early afternoon coach for Reading, so as I will first visit Hursts in the morning, late morning is the only time left."

Before Jonathan could answer, Clemmie knocked into him as she chased William, "Sorry, Father! William, bring that back here!" She rushed off after William, who had disappeared into the crowd. Eleanora smiled as Jonathan glared after Clemmie before answering Mrs Stubbington.

"Excuse my children, Janet. I shall be at my office in the bakery. I will expect you at eleven."

"Thank you, Jonathan. Good day Eleanora."

"Good day Janet."

Eleanora watched as Janet Stubbington walked down the stairs and into the street. She then briskly headed towards the river along the High Street, waving as she passed.

"What a business-like woman Jonathan. Was she like that in Reading?"

"Oh, yes. Even more so. Mrs Stubbington is very forthright!"

"I hope Anne never becomes like that!"

"I am sure she will not. Marrying Robert will be the best thing in the world for her. As for Clemmie and William, I will deal with them at home."

Jonathan watched as Janet Stubbington walked steadily away towards the Fox and Hound. He worried, 'What on earth did she require from him?'

Petersfield ...

Returning from the church at Petersfield, Lady Emma sat beside Victoria and spoke with her. They found their large party was too great a number at church for the family pew. As the Dartmund family, who owned the next pew, were away in Portsmouth, the verger quickly assisted, knowing the Dartmunds were friends of the Earl. He unlocked the pew and ushered them in.

Emma noticed that Victoria nodded off a couple of times during the service, particularly during the sermon. She contemplated that Victoria's interest in religion might not match her brother, David.

In the coach, she inquired, "I hope you don't mind me asking Victoria, but I noticed you seemed a little sleepy during the service?"

"Oh, it has been a long week of travel from Ireland, and I am still recovering from disturbed sleep. I am a person who needs her sleep. Yes! David is interested in theology, but I struggle with the difficult concepts. I am a much less sophisticated believer, but I support the church and believe in God! I enjoy attending and assist where I can."

"I agree. At times, I struggle to understand what the preacher is dwelling on. Quite often, when you ask for an explanation, it becomes even more confusing. The only exception I found is the Reverend Andrew Taggart in Guildford. His sermons are interesting, and he makes perfect sense every time he mounts the pulpit."

"Then I should prefer him. I lose interest if I cannot understand."

"Might I ask how old you are, Victoria?"

"I am seventeen…. and a half. And you?"

"A little older. I am now twenty."

Victoria nodded as if this was what she expected.

"And how do you find Fintelton compared to where you live in Ireland."

"Very nice indeed – it is a lot warmer here, and I have made many friends. I am afraid I may be dull as my conversation is limited. In Ireland, we have two estates, one at Cookstown in Ulster and the other near Coleraine on the Bann River. Coleraine is about fifty miles northwest of Belfast. Both estates breed livestock and produce flax. I have never visited Cookstown, but David has many times, and he can tell you about that. But I would say Ireland is far greener than here."

"Thank you, but I meant the house where you live."

Victoria breathed in, "Sorry, I thought you meant the countryside. The house is large indeed, larger than Fintelton but is empty as the family is all gone. I lived in a cottage adjoining the main house. It is around the size of the Guildford home of the Turners."

Emma was quite amazed by this description.

Victoria said, "I'm sure David will take you there once you are married."

Emma found Victoria's manners perfect, and she shared David's quest for knowledge, perhaps in a more relaxed way. Her Trustees had protected her life from the world, and she was a gentle and content soul.

"So, I understand you will remain here in Guildford."

"David has told you! It is a huge move for me as I have spent most of my life in Ireland. I often feel that I am Irish, but I was born in England, and in the coming years, I hope to discover much about my beginnings and the country here. The main attraction is being near my brother, as having lost my mother, father, and brother, I crave family relationships. Having you as my sister-in-law will be wonderful as well."

"It shall indeed. It seems I am gaining two sisters-in-law."

Victoria inquired with interest, "Who is the other?"

"Anne, she and my brother Robert are engaged!"

"Emma, forgive me. I forgot!"

They both giggled and enjoyed each other's company.

Anne and Robert took a stroll hand in hand by themselves before lunch. He was keen on pointing out areas of interest on the estate, including the direction towards the sea.

"When we are married, I insist you are at Portsmouth each time I sail and return from a voyage. That way, you will become familiar with the sea."

"Robert, I will be sad when you leave. It is hard enough when you depart from Guildford. I want us together every day and not separated, but I understand the demands of your career and will do the best I can."

"Well, let us enjoy our time together here. This lane leads towards the threshing room where Hugh and I would watch the men separating the wheat husks and bundling the chaff. We never became bored at harvest time. There was always something interesting happening."

"You and Hugh were close when you were young?"

"We were brothers! The three of us, including Emma, were more like a mutual support group. Upper-class members were above everyone else and only talked with select people. Without each other, we would have become very lonely."

"What happened with your relationship with Hugh then?"

"As we grew up, he had his tastes, and I had mine. We were separated when I was thirteen and joined the navy. Being five years older than me, he was already interested in his other pursuits. I had not yet started my education, but I quickly learnt once I was in the navy. I think it is fair to say we wanted different things in life. I will always honour him as my brother, but that does not mean I must agree with his pursuits."

"Of course!"

"Are you enjoying Fintelton, Anne?"

"Yes, it is a very romantic place. Whoever designed it was clever with the large balcony overlooking the valley. It is a beautiful outlook. The rooms are spacious and warm, and I find it has a character of its own that grows on you. I am sure you enjoyed your childhood here."

"It had its advantages. When we are married, and I am abroad, will you live here with my parents?"

Anne was taken aback by this suggestion. She thought Robert knew she must be near her work in Guildford.

"Robert, we have discussed this and agreed on having a house in Guildford. You know I must be near the Turner businesses."

"Yes, I understand that, but I would not like you living alone while I am away. What if you were with child?"

"Robert, I shall have a housekeeper. With the money my father now pays me, I can easily afford this. I will cope well in Guildford as there will be family and good medical attention close. But I would regularly spend time with your parents when you are away, particularly when the children arrive, as they should enjoy their grandchildren. I would never deprive them of that joy!"

Robert smiled and was encouraged by this answer, "I have thought about the wedding. There is an opportunity after my next mission."

"This mission, Robert." Anne was concerned, "Does it involve your last mission?"

Robert paused as he thought about security, "Anne, I am bound by the need for security, but I am sure you will keep it confidential. The Irish Republicans are becoming increasingly violent. They captured HMS *Providence* in the Irish Sea and butchered many of the crew, including Captain Foster. I visited him last Wednesday at the naval hospital in Gosport. The British government and the Admiral were hell-bent on recovering *Providence*, which we accomplished. In that battle, the Irish and we lost lives and suffered many injuries."

Robert explained the action and the outcomes it prevented. Anne listened in silence.

"The enemy will have disappeared by now, but this next mission involves a small British army force which will ensure the enemy is gone and interview the townsfolk for information. I will have a far lower profile transporting the army and standing by and assisting if anything flares up, which it will not. Now you must keep all this confidential, Anne. Given that these Irish consider this a war, any information leakage might endanger our lives."

"Our lives?"

"Yes, the Irish are everywhere in Britain. They have left their homeland for jobs and to escape the atrocious conditions the landowners keep them in. But their aim is for a free Ireland, and they have a significant network in England."

Anne shuddered and took a step backwards as she thought about what Robert had said.

"Are we safe here, Robert?"

"Very safe! It is the well-known people and events they target. The republicans stir up an anti-British fever in their population, hoping for increased support. We must not let this happen!"

"I was unaware of how dangerous the situation has become."

"It is a developing problem but one we, the British, have created. It is my opinion that Irish independence is inevitable. It will come one day, but many men on both sides will unnecessarily die before it comes. But keep that confidential as well, as it is not a view my masters would appreciate."

"So once again, you are going into danger?"

"No, the army will do most of the work. Horace will be commanding over three hundred and fifty troops. The navy must deliver the troops and bring them back. The mission should be straightforward and short."

"But if the locals supported the Irish, it may be tricky. They may also hold some grudges against the English?"

"They might, but Horace will deal with that. He is in command this time. My role will be a support role."

"England, Scotland, and Ireland are not that far apart, Robert. They would not take any revenge here, would they? I have heard stories of the uprisings and the things they do."

"No, nothing will happen here. The Rebels have suffered a critical blow. It may be the end of their uprisings for some time. They will be reorganising for months."

"I hope so!"

"I will be back the third week in January, and the fleet leaves for the Mediterranean in mid-March. If we chose a date in one of the first two weeks of February, we could have two weeks together, say on the Isle of Wight. I know it is soon, but it is the only option."

Anne considered this, "If we don't marry then, when will be the next opportunity?"

"When the fleet returns from the eastern Mediterranean. That might be between six and twelve months away."

"Then, the second Saturday in February is the date. Oh, Robert, your mother will be so pleased! She is eager that your father sees you married and assists Emma in her planning."

"I am more concerned that you are happy, Anne. I want you certain before we set the date."

They stopped walking and faced each other.

Looking up into his smiling face, she wanted his arms around her forever, "Robert, hold me please and never let me go!"

Her tears freely flowed as he held and kissed her.

Sniffling, Anne said, "I have never been more certain of anything in my life."

He wiped her eyes with his handkerchief, still holding her close, and kissed her again.

"Without you, Anne, I should never be happy again. I will never let you go and will always return."

Half crying and half laughing, she cried, "Make sure you do, Captain South! Come, we must tell your parents about the date, and I must let my mother and father know."

Chapter 6

Fintelton Estate, Outside Petersfield, Sussex …

With a pleasant smile, Lady Jane South sat beside her husband, The Earl of Fintelton, at the Sunday luncheon with family and friends. The only family member missing was Sir Hugh, and she would advise him by letter.

Sir David rose and clinked his glass. As this was a family occasion, including the Souths and Bassingtons, Lord Fintelton quickly said, "Family and friends, there is an important issue that my wife and I must announce while we are all at lunch. I am sure the Countess will handle this far better than me, so Lady Jane will make the announcement."

Suddenly there was a hush in the room, and everyone fixed their eyes on the countess.

"Everyone will be happy knowing that Robert and Anne have set a date for their wedding. It will be on Saturday, the tenth of February 1827, in Guildford. Is not that wonderful?" There were wild shouts of excitement and applause. "I'm sure David and Emma will set a date soon after this!"

David Sopwith concurred with Lady Jane, "Here, here!"

Emma took his hand and quietly suggested, "Anne and Robert will holiday on the Isle of Wight for two weeks. Why not have our wedding soon after they return and before Robert leaves for the Mediterranean." She squeezed his hand and gave him a gentle kiss on the cheek.

David, enjoying the scent of her perfume and followed by a light kiss, was easily persuaded.

"Why not, Emma! I would marry you tomorrow if it were possible."

"It is Darling, but it might not be arranged that quickly! I think Saturday the tenth of March may be best. Are you in agreement?" David turned, took Emma in his arms, and kissed her with much vigour. He gently said, "I am not sure how I will wait that long, but I will try."

Silence descended over the company as they witnessed this unexpected outflow of passion from a usually well-contained gentleman. Emma grasping the situation, announced politely, "Mother, David and I have decided on a wedding date as Saturday the tenth of March 1827, at Petersfield, and we will be very cross if anyone here today does not attend!"

Once again, the luncheon erupted into cheering and applause, and many conversations took place, including Emma, Anne and Lady Jane immediately putting their heads together and commencing the planning.

Tenant Farmer Home, Petersfield …

Anne, recovering from a tearful farewell with Robert, joined Lady Jane in the drawing room, where the countess checked the tenant's Christmas packages. As Anne watched, Lady Jane checked each box for a note with the name and address.

The countess noticing Anne's arrival, said, "Ah, there you are, Anne. I expect you are upset with Robert leaving but be of good cheer as you will soon see him again. With the wedding approaching, the time will fly by. Then you and Robert will be away on your honeymoon."

Anne was a bit teary as she knew the new mission held dangers for Robert, and this time she was far more aware of the risks involved.

"I always wonder if he will return. He always tells me that it will be a simple mission, but when he comes home, I find he has been in the thick of battle. Surely, he has had enough adventure and could return and live a normal life?"

Lady Jane noticed the worry on her face, "Anne, being in the navy is normal for Robert. He has no other profession. He was exceptionally fortunate to become a Captain at this early age. I'm afraid that's how it must be!"

"Yes, you are right, but I worry about him!"

"That is perfectly natural, my Dear. Now come and help me check these packages. I think there are notes on all of them?"

Anne quickly checked them and agreed with Lady Jane.

"Most tenant farmers live in East Harting, so we will start there."

They called the footmen, who loaded the packages into the coach. Lady Jane checked the list of tenant farmers and said, "We shall start with Mr Merton. He is the closest to here. Now I know you seek some information from these visits, so how might we gather this?"

Anne shook herself. She must rise above the sorrow of Robert leaving. She would see him again soon enough. Her concentration on the task at hand was more important. She switched focus and answered Lady Jane.

"Once you have given your normal message, please introduce me. I will make a quick conversation with the tenant. From what happens with Mr Merton, we will discuss refinements once back in the carriage."

As they approached the first tenant farmer's house, Lady Jane said, "Here we are!"

Anne hopped down with the help of a footman and followed with the package in hand. She was surprised at the drab little cottage where the tenant lived.

A wiry older man in working clothes came out, followed by his wife.

"Ah, Mr Michael Merton, Good day! We have brought your Christmas package and wish you a Merry Christmas."

Lady Jane took the package from Anne and then passed it over into Mr Merton's shaking hands. He, in turn, placed it in Mrs Merton's arms and then thanked Lady Jane.

Mr Merton said, "That is so kind of you, Lady Jane. Please, thank His Lordship for us."

"I will. Now, this is Miss Anne Turner. She will marry my son, Sir Robert, in February next. I was keen that you met her as she will be helping me in the future and is learning about life here on the estate."

Mrs Merton then said, "Good afternoon, Miss Anne. It is very nice of you to come today." She gave her a courtesy, and Mr Merton gave a slight bow. Anne was not expecting this treatment but accepted it with a smile.

Anne said, "It is lovely meeting you both as well. Please, tell me about the farm. How long have you lived here? I expect the farm is close by somewhere. Is that correct?"

Mrs Merton said, "Yes, the Estate provides the cottages. We have lived here all our lives. The farm is about a mile down the road, and Michael walks there every day. May we offer you some tea?"

"Thank you, but we have a lot of packages here and must deliver them this afternoon, so perhaps next time. Tell me, Mr Merton, how has the harvest been this year? I understand it is hard finding workers?"

Mr Merton seemed reluctant but then blurted out, "Well, it was fine while the children were still home. But now they are gone, the cost of labour is high. The harvest has been good this year, so we are slightly ahead!"

Lady Jane said, "Sir David sends his thanks for your contributions this year. He apologises for not being with me, but he is unwell."

"We like seeing him and that fellow, Malcolm Stem. That Malcolm now gives us paper receipt for every payment we make. Jenny here keeps the records and does the money. I am out on the farm all day. She does the money! She pays Mr Malcolm, she does. She does it well, mind you! I would be lost without her."

Jenny Merton smiled but was embarrassed and looked down at the ground.

Anne said, "I hope Mr Stem treats you well, Mrs Merton?"

"Oh, yes. Mr Stem is a real gentleman and helps us wherever he can."

Lady Jane smiled at Mr Merton and said, "I'm sure Jenny is a great help, Mr Merton."

Mr Merton nodded in agreement.

Lady Jane was keen on moving on. "Now we must be off. Lots more visits this afternoon."

Anne, keen on more information, quickly asked another question, "Mr Merton, I am sure you don't mind me asking, but at harvest time, how is the grain collected for the market?"

Mr Merton looked at her and wondered why she would ask such a question, "Why the merchants come and collect the bags, Miss. We have a store on the farm, near the threshing room. The merchants collect from there and give us a receipt. Jenny makes sure they pay us the right amount. It changes next year. Some bakery in Guildford is buying all the grain. We do not know how that will work. Probably the same!"

"Thank you, Mr Merton. I have never been on a farm before. It has been interesting hearing about it."

Jenny Merton said, "You be welcome here for a cup of tea sometime, Miss Anne. We can talk some more."

"Thank you, Jenny. I may do that. Well, good day and have a pleasant Christmas."

The Mertons thanked them again, and the countess and Anne pressed on towards the next farmer's cottage. Anne found that each tenant told a consistent story agreeing with the Mertons. It appeared that there was a basic system in place that should be capable of reconciliation. Now she needed more information from the Estate.

The Estate Office Fintelton Manor ...

Anne planned a meeting with Mr Stem at the Estate Office early on Monday morning. Before she left for Guildford, she was keen on fully understanding the transactions between the Estate and the tenants. After much encouragement, Emma agreed she would accompany Anne on the condition they returned by breakfast, as this would be Emma's last few hours with David before he set off.

"If that is the only problem, Emma, you must visit me soon."

Emma smiled, "I can assure you I will do that!"

Anne took a deep breath and blew out some steam from her mouth, revelling in the pristine country air, "I love the early morning! It is the most beautiful time of the day for a stroll."

Emma found Anne most persistent for her company and wondered what the meeting's importance was with Mr Stem.

The Estate Office was around two hundred yards from the Manor house, with several outbuildings and two small residences nearby. It was still dark as the girls set off, with the beginnings of light glimmering on the horizon. A light, misty fog was developing in the valley and moving their way.

Emma tightened her coat against the cold, "I have not been up this early in years, Anne. Why is this meeting so important?"

"I think the Estate Manager may have information that may give us some direction in this investigation. I will explain after we meet with him."

Emma suddenly jumped in fright as some small animals dashed across the laneway. Grasping Anne's arm tightly, she cried out, "Ooh! What is that, Anne?"

"Just some rabbits, Emma!" Then Anne said with a smile, "I thought you were the farmer among us?"

"I am in the daytime!"

They both giggled as they made their way along the foggy lane. Soon a dull light in the estate office window came into view.

"There it is!" Emma was keen on being inside again.

"Let me ask the questions, Emma. I expect Mr Stem will be helpful, and this won't take long at all."

"Why did we rise so early then?"

"Because I am not sure exactly what he will say. We may need far more time if the answers are not what I expect!"

Emma shivered, "Oh, I hope he has the fire going!"

On reaching the Estate Office, Anne gently knocked on the door. Emma was amazed as she noticed the number of farmhands already at their work.

"Welcome, Miss Anne and Lady Emma. It is an honour having you visit my office. Please come in, out of the cold!"

"With pleasure Mr Stem. May I sit beside the fire?" Emma rushed in and warmed her hands near the fireplace. Anne followed and found the rich aroma of brewed coffee somewhat tempting.

"Now, ladies, may I provide you with a warm cup of coffee?"

The girls readily agreed and sipped the coffee as soon as Malcolm Stem passed across the full cups. Emma felt the tension leaving her body as she reclined, enjoying the warmth of the fireplace and the hot coffee. Anne refocused on the business, hoping Emma would hear the conversation and not fall asleep in her newfound comfort.

"Mr Stem, thank you for seeing us. We are leaving for Guildford later this morning, and I was keen on discussing certain matters with you before we left. Sir Robert has informed me of the cash flow shortage of the estate, and I am working with Lady Jane and Lady Emma on gathering information so we may solve the situation."

Malcolm Stem smiled, "I thought your visit might involve the issues Sir Robert raised with me. I am glad that you are making enquiries."

"I am afraid we are only in the early stages, Mr Stem. Some information from you would be most helpful." Emma smiled in agreement with Anne's comments.

"I will assist where I can and hope I am of some help. The books are here, ready for you."

Anne was relieved by the Estate Manager's friendly and open manner. Given their previous positive dealings, she held a high opinion of Mr Stem. She assumed beforehand that any signs of resistance would certainly indicate some involvement. But Mr Stem was keen on helping without any hesitation.

"Lady Jane and I visited the tenants yesterday with their Christmas packages. I took the opportunity to talk with each tenant and enquired how they paid their dues. The first tenant, Mr Michael Merton and his wife, Jenny, explained how you issue receipts for their payments. Do you record these receipts in a journal Mr Stem?"

"Yes, Miss Anne. Here, in this journal." Malcolm Stem passed across a large bound book of foolscap size, which Anne had not seen before. She opened it and traced through the various receipts entered down the column. A puzzled look spread across her face.

"Mr Stem, this journal is far different from the Tenant Payments Journal that Sir Robert provided me with."

"Yes, Miss Anne. I keep this journal regularly updated as the tenants pay their dues. The other journal is the one Sir Hugh keeps. It normally resides in the Manor with him, but he left it with me while he is in the Indies for safekeeping."

"I see. Mr Stem, are the tenants making their payments on time?"

"Yes, Miss Anne, all are except for Mr Park and Mr Crimmins. The Parks have had some sickness, and Mr Park has indicated he will relinquish his tenancy in January next year. Half Mr Crimmins's crop was short this year, and he has pledged the dues by the next harvest."

"Then are you saying the tenant income should be around the same amount as the previous year?"

"Oh yes, Miss Anne. The receipts are consistent with other years except, of course, for Mr Park and Mr Crimmins. Each year for the last twenty years is listed there. There is little variation. Sir Hugh sent our men along, helping the tenants this year because of the high labour cost. The additional help did the trick, and the harvest was consistent with other years."

"May I sit at your desk Mr Stem with pen and paper and this journal? I should complete some quick calculations, please, using these figures."

"Certainly, Milady!"

Mr Stem sat down with Emma in front of the fire, and they talked as Anne busily transcribed figures and looked at trends. Once half an hour passed, Emma grew impatient and asked, "Anne, we must return for breakfast soon?"

"Just five minutes more, Emma!"

Emma asked Mr Stem, "Now tell me, Mr Stem, how is the cash flow holding up?"

Mr Stem sighed, "We have less than five hundred pounds in the working account, Milady. I hoped Sir Hugh would have left instructions, but it appears not. I must ask His Lordship for an additional deposit soon."

Emma frowned, unaware that her father had transferred money from somewhere else. She now realised she was unaware of the source of the estate's monies. Thank goodness for Robert and Anne!

"I think I have the information I wanted now! Thank you, Mr Stem. Just two other questions, please, before we go. At what time of the year do the tenants make their payments?"

"Well, after the winter harvest in April and then the summer harvest in October. Why do you ask?"

"I am mapping out the estate's cash flows."

Malcolm Stem nodded but seemed confused by what a cash flow map was. Before he could ask, Anne spoke, "Mr Stem, who does the banking for the estate?"

"Well, I do, Miss Anne. Sir Hugh prepares the banking, and I take it into Lions Bank, Petersfield, and deposit it. While he is away, he has left precise instructions for me."

Malcolm Stem passed over the written instructions, and Anne quickly read them.

"Has this always been the system?"

"For the last seven years, Miss. Before that, His Lordship would prepare the banking. Lord Fintelton's eyes gave him trouble, so Sir Hugh took over the role."

Anne suddenly knew she had found one of the missing links. Sir Hugh was involved, but was it a cash shortage or was the money banked elsewhere? Without more detail, revealing any conclusions would be inappropriate, as Emma might misinterpret them. Anne needed more information before she introduced Emma's brother into the equation.

"Sorry, Mr Stem, may I see the most recent receipts."

"Yes, Miss, they are here." The Estate Manager passed them over.

"Thank you."

Anne checked the top three or four receipts and found three accounts, not one! One was the Estate's working account, an investment account, and the other an Estate Sundry account. Anne quickly jotted down the account numbers.

"Thank you, Mr Stem, this has been most helpful."

Emma put down her cup, hopped up, and thanked Mr Stem. Outside, the sun was sneaking up above the low clouds in the east, and the girls enjoyed the beautiful view, with the sun slowly clearing away the early morning foggy mists.

As they walked together, Emma turned and mentioned, "Thank you, Anne!"

"What for?"

"Being out early with you has reminded me of the real world while enjoying luxury in the Manor House. I take the benefits I enjoy for granted and should not!"

"I, too, have discovered something! But I am not sure I welcome my discovery or what it might mean."

"Whatever do you mean, Anne?"

"Let us have breakfast, Emma. We have a big day ahead of us!"

The Turner Bakery, Guildford ...

Mrs Stubbington arrived at the bakery on Monday morning at eleven o'clock sharp. Jeb brought her through and found Jonathan packing some boxes in the office.

"Ah, Mrs Stubbington, welcome."

"Thank you, Jonathan. I must say this is a rather large bakery, Sir!"

"My father commenced the business some thirty years ago, and we have expanded over time. With the help of Hamish McPherson, we will start another bakery in London late next year."

"How exciting, Jonathan. It appears business is going well for you?"

"Well, Janet, we have a good team here and always manage our business ambitions within our financial capabilities."

"A good principle. I like that."

"Now, would you like a seat?" Jonathan offered a chair. "Then, we may discuss the issues with the Reading investment?"

Mrs Stubbington remained standing, "Thank you, Jonathan, but I think it may be preferable if we go for a walk along the river!"

Jonathan looked at Janet for a few seconds before realising she wanted somewhere for a private talk. He stood and nodded, following as she walked out of the bakery and towards the riverbank. Once they were alone, Janet explained her business and the need for privacy.

"Jonathan, you must improve your office situation. It is not a place where clients may confide in you."

"Yes, we are moving our office this week, across the road, into a new building. We will demolish the present office and expand the bakery. Next time you visit, I will welcome you there."

Janet looked at him knowingly and then cast her eyes down the river. The Wey flowed past gently, with ducks and swans gliding in and out of the weeping willows that dipped in the water. It was not a warm day, but the sun was out, and there was no breeze. The activity that was going on at the wharf nearby was like a brightly painted portrait.

"This is quite a pretty place, Jonathan. I am sure you enjoy living here. When you open the new bakery in London, will you move there?"

"No. We plan on staying here forever. Guildford is our home."

"Good. Let me familiarise you with some of my business activities. Hamish has told you my story but only some of it. There is much that Hamish is unaware of."

Jonathan looked up as he was surprised by this. He suspected a relationship between Hamish and Janet but was unsure of its nature.

"That night in Reading, you hesitated rather than knocking on Hamish's hotel door. I am sure you remember! Well, I will clarify why I was in his room. It was for business purposes only. I am one of several partners involved in an investment company. The senior partners wish their identities to remain private; however, they come with the highest credentials. When you heard our voices that night, I discussed information that Hamish had collected. One of those pieces of information was about you!"

"How did you know I was listening at the door? I was after a word with Hamish and considered knocking but heard someone talking with him, so I went away."

"Yes, but only after listening for a while, Jonathan!"

"I heard it was you and would have knocked, but I thought better of it."

"Well, in my line of business, Jonathan, I require some assistance with security. One of my men was watching and was ready, but there was no need as you retired soon after that. By the way, Hamish has only the highest opinion of your integrity."

Jonathan was astonished. He remembered now. The man who passed in the hallway was one of the young gentlemen with Janet on Sunday morning at church.

"That man was …!"

"Yes, he works with me on security!"

Now Jonathan was becoming worried. He was unaware of being watched in the hotel. Who was this woman, and what did she want?

"Jonathan, my senior partner, has provided me with instructions. We take pleasure in offering you a proposal. Of course, you will require time to consider the document. It is a challenging proposal, but we feel you have the connections and resources we require."

Jonathan noticed a couple of people walking along the river bank towards them and signalled Janet. She nodded, and they walked upstream towards the footbridge.

As they walked, she said, "You work closely with Hamish McPherson. Thomas's marriage connects you with his family. You have a lot of money invested in some of his projects, so you have made inquiries about his activities. Well, our company, too, has invested money in Hamish's projects. Let us say that we have provided financial assistance for his companies. However, we have now decided that as a precaution, we require some assistance in ensuring he is only helping us."

"What do you mean by helping us?"

Janet looked at him and sighed, "Jonathan, there are some things better left unsaid!"

"Janet, I struggle with where this is coming from?"

"You will recall someone breaking into your house while you were away."

"Yes."

"Well, Hamish shared this information with us quite quickly. It was no accident that one of the burglars was found in the lock along the river here."

Jonathan stopped walking and stood back from her. She knew far more about him than he thought. He remembered Hamish recounting the threat on his life.

She noticed his caution and reassured him, "Jonathan, I am here as a friend. You are completely safe!"

"How can I help you? I am only a baker!"

"You are far more than a baker now, Jonathan. You have various businesses that are all expanding, and with our help, that will continue. We desire your business success and building a relationship with the McPhersons. Find out as much as you can about them. I will visit regularly and discuss this information with you. At times we may ask for more specific details. That is all. I will pass your collected information to our senior partners for assessment."

"Would this not be spying on Hamish? I would be going behind my partner's back."

"No, you are sharing information with a trusted friend. It will be kept confidential. You understand that we must ensure the safety of our investment, which is far larger than yours. Also, remember he is providing us with information on you."

"How do I know you are genuine in this, Janet?"

"I was sure you would ask this question, Jonathan. You have provided the Admiralty with a large trial order of biscuits! I understand the invoice remains unpaid. As soon as I have your signed agreement, the navy will make the payment, and you will secure the long-term contract."

Jonathan looked at her and thought there was only one place where they could gain this power.

Janet smiled, "Convinced?"

Jonathan nodded in agreement. She was a woman with whom he would not disagree. He would assist where he could.

Janet said, "A gentleman named Mr Smith will visit your home tomorrow with some documents. Please ask him if he would wait on the porch while you read and sign the contract. Once signed, please give Mr Smith the package. He will then pass you another package that will be the initial investment set out in the agreement. I will be in contact with you in early March."

Jonathan nodded in agreement, wondering if he had any choice in this at all.

"There is one item of information you might advise me on now. Are you aware if Hamish has any connection with the Irish?"

"Not that I am aware. Hamish has never mentioned them. However, I do know he brings in wheat from France."

"Yes, we know that and how you are partaking in the advantages. We will ensure there is no problem with this. Please inform me immediately if you hear of any relationship with the Irish. Your copy of the contract will have my contact details on it. Send the information by a rider, so we waste no time."

Jonathan, swallowing, said nothing further.

"Oh, by the way, Jonathan, you should have a far more secure house. My men paid an unnoticed visit there yesterday, checking your security. Here are the desk keys from the study. I suggest you find a more secure and larger house matching your position in society! There is no substitute for alert and trustful servants. Good day!"

Jonathan stood there with his mouth open as she walked away. He would have called after her, but he thought better of it. In this game, he was a beginner and must proceed carefully. Perhaps Hamish could advise him, or should he keep this private? He would read the agreement tomorrow and decide.

The Guildford Medical Practice ...

On arriving at his Guildford home on Monday afternoon, Doctor David Sopwith first settled his sister and then rushed off in the direction of his medical practice. Victoria was quite content reading until dinner as she was exhausted after the weekend at Fintelton.

Doctor Sopwith sent a message advising the Turner household that if Mr Turner were available, he would arrange a swimming lesson for Simeon and William late Tuesday afternoon. Walking around into Neville's office, he sat down, ready for their daily discussion of the patient list for tomorrow.

"Neville, some patients are waiting! Should I see them first, or will the patient list not take long?"

"It won't take long, but first, have a read of this letter!" Neville passed it over and raised his eyebrows.

David was interested in the letter.

Doctor Bryan Watson
The Chimes
High Street
Wimbledon, London

The Doctor in Charge
Guildford Medical Practice
Quarry Street
Guildford, Surrey

Dear Sir,

I am writing in search of employment as a Doctor/Surgeon in Guilford.

Recently my family and I have arrived in London and remain with relatives at the above address. We desire a country life and have selected Guildford as an ideal situation where we might settle.

I graduated as a Surgeon from the University of Glasgow and have practised at a general hospital for two years and then at the Isle of Islay for five years as a country doctor. My family and I have agreed that there will be opportunities in England unavailable for our family in Scotland. I am interested in further study and would welcome a full-time position where I might work with a peer group interested in surgery and fracture repair.

I have written several letters inquiring about doctors in the Guildford area and will visit the town in the second week of the new year, when I will make calls offering my services. I would be available for part-time work but would prefer a full-time position.

Thank you for your time.

Your servant
Doctor Bryan Watson

"Sounds interesting, Neville. What do you think?"

"I think I need a larger client list before we hire another team member. There has been no invitation from Harley Street yet. Since I applied, it has been so long that I might discard my hopes of entering the Sloan Practice. But I will keep Doctor Watson's letter on file."

"Give it until the new year Neville and then decide. Who knows, the specialists in London may send you a Christmas present! But let me reply and advise him we would welcome interviewing him. Who knows, there may be a sudden increase of patients?"

They both laughed.

"Are you set for a swimming lesson with the boys late tomorrow afternoon? I am hoping Jonathan might join us."

"Yes, I will attend, but I fear Jonathan will be busy. The Magistrate's court will require him – the arson case – you remember?"

"Of course! Of course!"

The Lions Bank of Guildford …

Anne sat in the waiting room outside the manager's office. She would discuss the Turner businesses' current financial position and borrowing capacity.

Mr Thomas Meyhew, the bank's founder and long-term friend of the family, was consistently obliging in their dealings. Still, as with all bankers, he was concerned that the Turners guard against overextending themselves. Guildford had experienced solid commercial growth, and with this growth, the Lions Bank had also seen a steady increase in customers and deposits. The Turners were now a large customer with a substantial cash turnover. With the new initiatives in the bakery, the construction of a flour mill and her father's investments in McPherson's Breweries, their reserves had depleted quickly, arousing the bank's concern.

Anne's aim was that the Turner businesses remained debt-free, but she realised that this might not be possible for the Christmas period given the last few months' high expenditures. They would need bank support with a small temporary overdraft. She would question Mr Meyhew if the new company structure would assist their prospect of short-term borrowing.

The manager's door opened, and Mr Meyhew emerged, inviting in Anne.

Indicating a seat, he asked, "Anne, how may I assist you today?"

"Thank you for your time, Mr Meyhew. If I could confirm our current cash position and explain our cash needs over the next three months. Christmas is a busy time for the bakery, so I put forward our meeting, giving us plenty of time for a further meeting if required."

"Certainly, Anne. Now, I see you have the journals there. We can work through them together."

After about twenty minutes, Mr Meyhew sat back and sighed. He explained, "The business is growing quickly, and the returns on the investment in Epson are impressive, but I am concerned that the reserves are decreasing. The investment in the Reading brewery required a transfer of twenty-five thousand pounds from the reserve account, but there will be no income from that investment until the end of next year. Your cash forecast indicates that by mid-next year, you will have depleted the cash reserves to a dangerous level without an offsetting growth in revenue."

"Mr Meyhew, as you know, cash is always short during the two weeks before Christmas, but following that in January, we have an excess as debtors pay up. I also have a new analysis of our future cash projections. Our cash situation should be strong again by the end of next year. Would the bank allow us some credit from today till the end of the first week in January rather than drawing on our reserve account?"

"The bank will cover the business's needs, Anne, but please ensure the following."

Mr Meyhew explained the requirements.

Anne was relieved, nodding her understanding. She decided it would be prudent not to discuss these matters at present. Still, she must ask a question about the Fintelton Estate.

"Thank you, Mr Meyhew. There was just one other question if I might ask?"

"Yes, Anne."

"This, of course, is quite confidential, so I will carefully brief you. As you know, Sir Robert South and I have announced our engagement. Robert has confided in me that the cash holdings of the Fintelton Estate have eroded over the last few years. Lady Jane, Lady Emma and I have examined the Estate's cash flow trail, tracing its sources and understanding how the banking is prepared. I understand that the Souths use the Lions bank branch in Petersfield. Would that be correct?"

"Anne, I would usually not disclose such details, but as you will soon be one of their family, I see no harm in it, especially if you are working with Lady Fintelton. Yes, they are a client of ours."

"Thank you. At the end of the day or the week, are the deposits transferred to Guildford?"

"Partially! The branch keeps a standard balance based on forecasts to meet our customers' daily needs. If larger amounts are required, the Petersfield manager must obtain a draft from Guildford. Once this process is complete, we transfer the money by coach. It is uncommon but may happen occasionally."

"So, the Petersfield branch has its accounting records independent of this office?"

"Yes, it must ensure the proper stewardship of the money."

"Does this office audit the work done in the Petersfield branch?"

"Yes. We have senior tellers who regularly travel between branches and internally audit the records."

"So, there is no possibility of money disappearing?"

Mr Meyhew was becoming agitated, "Tell me why you ask these questions, Anne. Perhaps I may be of more assistance if you give me more information?"

"I have done the books of the Estate, approximately, and it appears around seventy thousand pounds is missing over the last few years. I would ask for your confidentiality Mr Meyhew until our examination is complete. But somehow, the money disappears, and the person responsible is covering their trail cleverly."

"And you suspect someone in the bank?"

"I'm not sure at this stage, but I require more information on the systems!"

"I can assure you the bank would not have lost it. However, it does deserve a check, as you are talking about a huge sum of money. I will personally look at the figures for the estate myself. Perhaps we could talk again in the new year. And Anne, given you are not part of the family yet, it may be prudent that the Earl or the Countess accompanies you. May I also suggest we have a separate meeting so that Mr Turner's business is not discussed and remains private?"

As he said this, he raised his eyebrows.

"Thank you, Mr Meyhew. I knew you would be understanding and helpful. Thank you again, and a Merry Christmas, Sir."

"Merry Christmas, Miss Anne."

Before Anne left, she turned and asked, "Mr Meyhew, just one other question, please. Has there been staff turnover in the branch at Petersfield during the last six months?"

Mr Meyhew taking in a deep breath and not disguising his frustration, replied, "Miss Anne, I can assure you of the accurate systems we use to check bank balances. There will be no problems there with accounting and security."

"Sorry, Mr Meyhew, I was asking as I have a friend who may be interested in a job there?"

"Oh, I see. Yes, we have had the resignation of a teller, a Mrs Constance. She resigned in October this year. She was with us for many years, and we were sad she left."

"That is strange, Mr Meyhew. I thought only men were tellers in banks?"

"You are correct! Mrs Constance came with high recommendations. Normally we would not have considered a woman but recruiting competent staff in Petersfield proved difficult. We decided on an exception, given her skills and references."

"How many years was she with your bank?"

"About five years."

"Thank you, Mr Meyhew. Good day."

Cobh, Ireland ...

Michael Walsh and his mother stood outside the three-room cottage as a light snow started falling. Frann shivered as she gently knocked on the door of the safe house. The message came about an hour ago that Sean Reid's health was deteriorating quickly. Doctor Smythe did all he could, but a recovery now seemed unlikely.

The door opened, and Aiden Reid faced them, the strain on his face showing, "Sean is nearly gone. Doctor Smythe feels it will be within the hour."

Mrs Walsh wrapped her arms around Aiden and hugged him, shedding some tears on his shoulder.

Michael grunted, "It must have been the Scottish doctor – didn't treat him, right?"

"No, Michael, Doctor Smythe said the Scottish doctor's work was good. No one can guarantee against infection in the wounds. He was surprised Sean lasted so long and made it home. It was several weeks before the infection set in. Nothing much they can do now."

"Sounds like you appreciated this Scotsman, Aiden?"

"He worked non-stop for three days, Michael. No sleep at all. Could not ask any more of him!"

Michael carefully watched the expression on Aiden's face.

"We brought you some bread and potatoes, man. Also, a bottle of gin for your mother. How is she coping?"

"My mother says little now. She has accepted we will lose Sean. Who knows how she will cope once he is gone?"

They stood there saying nothing for a few minutes. Michael passed the basket across.

"Thank you, Michael. Christmas will be sad this year, but the food is most welcome. Once Sean is gone, I will let you all know."

Michael nodded, and Mrs Walsh hugged and kissed him, saying, "Be strong for your family, Aiden. Sean will soon be in a better place."

Aiden sniffled and rubbed his nose, "Thank you, Mrs Walsh." Then looking at Michael, he asked, "Any more news from Dan yet?"

"No, the man from Dublin is not back. They expect him soon!"

Aiden nodded and returned inside the cottage, closing the door.

As they walked away, Frann quietly shared, "Michael, Aiden has changed. There is no life in him anymore. This crisis has sucked the life out of him."

"It is a terrible time for Aiden and his mother. We will be there for them. He will recover in time."

Michael Walsh said no more, but he knew his mother was right. Aiden was like a dormant volcano that might awaken at any minute. Michael knew once the grieving was over, the anger would erupt. The problem was when would the eruption come and how he could keep Aiden under control.

The butler announced dinner. Hamish and Marjorie McPherson enjoyed being with family in Scotland and meeting Isla, who he assumed was James's wife. Marion and Thomas Turner decided to enjoy a meal out, giving James some private time with his parents.

Marion had collapsed in grief on the previous day at the tragic news of her mother's passing away. At first, she was most distressed, but later in the day, she reconciled that her mother's condition made the outcome inevitable, and perhaps she was now in a better place. Even so, it was a sad day. The arrangements were complete for their return home, but they would stay at the McPherson's house in Greenwich. Thomas thought a dinner out might be helpful.

Marion was calmer today, and Hamish and Marjorie were proud of how she pulled herself together. They were also glad for Thomas, who was a great comfort, reinforcing their belief that the match between Thomas and Marion was strong and boded well for the future.

As they walked into dinner, Hamish escorted Isla and asked her, "Now, where in Scotland were you born, Isla? I should also ask where that beautiful Irish accent came from?"

"Mr McPherson, I must explain. I was not born in Scotland but in Cork, Ireland. I come from a good Catholic family in Cork, southern Ireland. My father owns a pub there, where James and I met. His ship docked in Cobh for a few days, and while the crew worked hard, James visited Cork and wandered into the pub."

Hamish was astounded. He concealed his surprise but wondered why one of his ships was in Cobh.

"I'm sure it is a beautiful place. I have heard a bit about it, but you might share some of its highlights with me over dinner."

"A pleasure Mr McPherson. It is my home, and I am a proud Irish woman."

James made sure that his parents' dinner would be perfect. He employed an excellent cook with a good grasp of the local culinary traditions. Later, as they were having coffee, James thought the time was right for the good news as the footmen served dessert.

"Mother and Father, I think it is time I announced some good news about myself and Isla. We met over a year ago in Cork, and Isla then joined me here in Glasgow. We have lived together since then, and Isla is expecting our first child."

It took a few seconds as Hamish took in the enormity of the message while Marjorie said straight away, "How wonderful, James. When is the baby due? Hamish, isn't this wonderful?"

"Yes, dear, wonderful!" Hamish, hiding his emotions well, maintained a pleasant smile as he congratulated the couple. He immediately suspected there might be more but realised this was a situation he should carefully navigate. James was now thirty and should have been more careful in his choice. But surely, he would understand that!

Marjorie said, "Oh, James, you are a secret one, aren't you? You never told us you were married?"

"We are not married, Mother!"

Marjorie was unsure if she heard correctly and would have asked again, but James cut her off.

"I know what you are thinking, Father. There may be some problems here. However, love is a strange thing. It crosses boundaries. We are both sure that there is no need for marriage!"

James's father, who was preparing for the next round, was shocked and completely surprised. Hamish called on all his strength and remained calm, "Well, congratulations, Isla and James, and may I say you have chosen an alternative lifestyle that the mainstream may not appreciate. But we will support you as best we can, and please forgive us as this comes as a complete surprise. Might I have a scotch, James?"

Isla jumped up and poured Hamish a large scotch from the drink's cabinet.

"Thank you, Isla. Tell me, are you a practising Catholic?"

"No, Mr McPherson, but I honour their beliefs."

"But not marriage?"

"Well, James is a protestant! So, if we married, the child would become protestant. The child will be a catholic, and we will remain unmarried."

Hamish smiled – he would not inflame the situation and be as accommodating as possible, "I see. What you both must be sure of is that now you have crossed the boundary, you may still return without injury?"

James straightened his back and replied, "We have no wish to return across the boundary."

Hamish was finding this conversation most confronting, "Thankfully, Catholic emancipation is coming, and that will help, but the ingrained attitudes of our society may not. Surely for the child's good, Isla, you would marry and become a protestant. You say you are not a practising catholic, so what does it matter?"

"No, Mr McPherson, I am a Catholic, and that's what I will stay! There is no shame in being a catholic in Ireland, and our country will be a republic one day."

"I see. But you are living in Scotland?"

There was a silence at the table until Marjorie could not hold back, "Well, Catholic or not, I am not concerned. Now Isla, when is the child due?"

"In early May, Mrs McPherson. I am through the early stages, thank goodness. I had a lot of morning sickness, but that is over now."

"Oh, I'm glad for you. We will be back in May for the birth."

"Well, that is if James and Isla are still here! I think James will advise us of the details."

"You are correct, Father! Isla would prefer if we were near her mother at the birth, so we shall be in Ireland. You would be welcome in Cork, but it may be better if we notify you once the baby is born."

"Oh, that is lovely, Isla, so you should be. Why I would love to spend some time in Cork, Hamish!"

Hamish suggested, "Perhaps, James, you might consider, for the well-being of the child, becoming a Catholic, and in that way, you could marry?"

"No, Father, I am content being a member of the Church of Scotland."

For the first time in his life, Hamish McPherson was completely short of words. He sat there with a dull, confused grin in total disbelief.

Commander in Chief's Office, Blue Fleet, Portsmouth ...

Captain Sir Robert South entered the reception area of Admiral Sutherland's office and asked for Commodore Jacobs.

Within a few minutes, Jacobs entered the room. "Sir Robert! What brings you here? The Admiral will not return until tomorrow."

"I was hoping that you, Commodore, might assist me with an issue. We sail tomorrow, and I hope twenty more sailors will arrive today. The Admiral has reassigned some of the crew of a frigate in refit. Once they are on board, we will have a full compliment."

Jacobs was aware of the transfer and smiled, "I can assure you they will arrive today, Captain."

"Commodore, I have been considering the previous mission of *Restless* when Captain Hughes was attacked and boarded. I am mindful that this situation is far from over."

"Sir Robert, after your gallant last mission, it will be some time before the republicans can regather and mount any challenges. I'm sure this mission will be uneventful."

"I agree with you, Sir. However, did Hughes write a report on the incident? Also, would you have a copy of the orders I might see?"

"Yes, there is a report, and the orders will be on file. Tell me, Sir Robert, what are you seeking?"

"There may be similarities with the events I experienced on my mission. It may be of some help."

Commodore Jacobs thought about Robert's suggestion, "I have read the report, and I am familiar with the orders. As far as I know, there is nothing of significance."

Robert pressed the matter, "Might I see the report and the orders, please? I will read them here."

Given that Robert would soon embark on his mission, Jacobs could see no harm in reviewing the documents. "Certainly, Captain. I doubt it will be of great help." The Commodore frowned, "I think you will be wasting your time as the Admiral, and I have reviewed them several times." The Commodore walked off and reappeared some minutes later with the documents. "You may use the Admiral's office as he will not return until tomorrow."

"Thank you, Commander Jacobs."

Robert took the report, entered the Admiral's office, and sat at a conference table, eager to read the papers. It took more than half an hour before he had carefully completed reading Hughes' report and orders. As Robert reread certain parts of the document, he realised that similarities with his mission existed. Raising his eyes, he gazed out a window at the foul weather now making Portsmouth conditions unpleasant. The pattern of the assignments was the same. But was it a coincidence, or was there something sinister here? He needed more time to consider this new information. Raising anything with Jacobs would be useless, given how dismissively he had treated Robert's request. Now was not the time for any further discussion.

Robert gathered the documents and left the office, placing the report and orders on Commodore Jacob's desk.

"Find anything, Sir Robert?"

"No, it was as you said. All very straightforward."

"Well, good luck with the mission. Should be much quieter this time."

"I hope so. Thank you, Commodore, for allowing me access. I will see you in four or five weeks."

Commodore Jacobs watched as Captain South left the reception area. Looking down at the reports, Jacobs decided he would reread the documents in detail. He was not sure whether South had found something or not.

The Turner Household, Guildford ...

Richard, Sarah, and their daughter Katherine arrived on the Saturday afternoon before Christmas and took up the few spare bedrooms. Eleanora was glad Neville and Beth were not staying, as this would have been impossible.

Eleanora allocated Katherine to the spare bed in Anne's room and promised that once Anne was married in February, Clementine could move in there as well. This understanding placated a wistful Clemmie, keen on moving in with Anne and Katherine.

At dinner that night, Richard explained his plans for the property in South Africa. He had purchased much timber and other building materials, now on a ship already embarked for South Africa. It would be delivered on his land by their arrival so he could commence construction of a large comfortable house. The cattle and sheep purchased would follow soon after their departure and be driven overland from Port Elizabeth.

As dinner ended, Mrs Jennings announced, "It is snowing!" Temperatures that day were unseasonably low, and there was almost no traffic on the High Street late in the afternoon. During their journey, Sarah commented on how cold she was. There was an expectation that perhaps it might snow.

Simeon and William jumped from their chairs and peered out from the front door. As they watched, the snow became heavier and heavier. The rest of the family joined them on the front portico, and there was much excitement.

Jonathan Turner hung behind as he worried about what transpired between himself and Mrs Stubbington. The agreement was signed and exchanged for the package Mr Smith passed over. Jonathan left the package unopened on his desk, unsure he had made the right decision. On Wednesday, two days after Jonathan signed the contract, Anne approached him at work with a smile, advising that a rider arrived with a draft from the Admiralty paying in full the invoice for the first trial shipment of biscuits.

Eleanora wandered over, finding Jonathan deep in thought. He stood beside Richard, who seemed as excited as the children about the snow.

She shone with happiness, whispering, "This is wonderful, Jonathan. We are all together as a family, and it is nearly Christmas. Now there is snow. Such a perfect ending for eighteen twenty-six. I wonder if it will snow all night?'

"I am not sure, Eleanora!"

"Well, we shall wait and see."

"Yes, we will!"

Eleanora pointed at the children, "Look at Simeon and William. They are throwing snowballs. You better stand back!"

Jonathan stepped back as a snowball flew past him and hit Richard in the face. Richard wiped his face and powered into action, calling, "I will teach you a lesson, young William!"

"It is good that you did not step forward, Jonathan!"

"Perhaps, I should not have!"

Eleanora looked hard at Jonathan and smiled, "This year has been hectic, but the next few days will be a happy time. I am sure eighteen twenty-seven will be a better year?"

Jonathan Turner re-joined the present, amazed his wife was so happy and full of life. The frown left and was replaced by a loving smile, "I'm glad you are enjoying this festive season, Eleanora. Your happiness is my desire!"

"Thank you, Jon! This Christmas is already the happiest I have ever known."

Chapter 7

Turner Household, Guildford, England ...

As Christmas and New Year were well over, Anne commenced a fourth letter to Robert. The other three written before Christmas remained unanswered, but she understood that mail for the navy travelled slowly. 'So much news I must tell him! I will write again today, but it may be a week or two before I can expect a reply.' She continued writing but then heard the boys clattering up the stairs making far too much noise. She rushed out and called, "Simeon and William come here!"

The noise immediately stopped as they turned and faced her. Clemmie was with them and asked, "Why, Anne?"

Anne mouthed, "Come here!" pointing at the floor straight in front of her feet with an expression of determination on her face.

The three children understood this was important and would not test Anne's goodwill. They stepped down and walked across.

"Come into my room!" They followed Anne without question.

"You know that mother is not well at all, and she always sleeps at this time in the afternoon. Why were you making such a clatter? You know she needs rest, and the baby must not be disturbed."

"Sorry, Anne, we forgot!" Simeon spoke softly, not wishing to wake his mother.

Clemmie pleaded, "Anne, the boys will launch their boat this afternoon. Victoria and Dr Sopwith will be there. We must change clothes and take the boat. Will you join us at the river?"

"Yes, Anne, please come. The boat is finally ready!"

Anne could see the wild excitement in William's eyes. His pent-up energy was infectious, and Anne decided Robert's letter could wait.

"I must see this – now be quiet as you go up and change, and we shall all walk together. I will tell Mrs Nibley where we are going."

The children rushed off but on tiptoe, careful that their mother and baby brother were not disturbed.

The procession grew as they neared the River Wey. Neville and Bethany joined the children surrounding Simeon as he carefully carried the little boat.

David Sopwith and Victoria were waiting at the riverbank. Anne ran across and held Victoria's hands.

"Victoria, how are you? We have not met since Sunday. How has your week been?"

"Anne, I have been busy considering real estate. I must not remain at David's house once he is married. I am sure he and Emma will require their privacy. I was thinking about consulting your father – he has knowledge of Guildford and appropriate houses that might be available."

"I am sure the request would be well received. Let me know if I may be of help."

"I would not think of bothering you, Anne. I know how busy you must be with the wedding. It is I who should be offering my assistance. Less than six weeks until the date – you must be excited?"

"Yes, I am. Victoria, I have a fitting for the wedding dress at two-thirty tomorrow afternoon, and I would be honoured if you attended. I am sure you can provide some advice. Mother should be there if her health allows."

"How is she, Anne?"

"She mostly sleeps, and thankfully we have a wet nurse for the baby. I hope her energy increases soon! But enough of that, I shall expect you at Hursts tomorrow. My brother, Thomas, and his wife, Marion, are coming. I am not sure if you have met them yet?"

As the group of friends grew along the riverbank, Mrs Ethel Nibley darted into the Turner business offices, up the stairs and knocked on Jonathan Turner's office door.

"Come!"

Ethel opened the door and entered.

"Why, Ethel! What brings you here? I thought you were minding Mrs Turner?"

"I was, Sir, but I left Aggie and the wet nurse with her. Mr Turner, the boys, your sons, will launch their new sailboat on the river in a few minutes. I felt I should remind you. You should not miss an occasion such as this!"

"Thank you, Ethel, but I am not interested in toy boats."

Ethel could see that Jonathan was reluctant to become involved with his sons' interests. Since she commenced service with the family, she knew the detachment was becoming more apparent. The other staff sometimes discussed it with her. He favoured his elder son, Thomas, and the girls but strangely not the younger boys.

"Mr Turner, you should join the gathering of friends and family beside the riverbank. The celebration is important for your sons, who would greatly welcome your presence. The boat launching is an opportunity for building that relationship with them. There will be fewer and fewer opportunities as they grow. You should celebrate the launch with them."

Jonathan Turner put down his pen and looked at Ethel, "Ethel! Are you convinced it is that important?"

"I know it is, Sir! Please encourage them."

Jonathan stood and looked out the window along the riverbank. He could see the growing crowd and various people talking with Simeon and William as the boys displayed the boat.

"What would I say?"

Ethel was amazed at how thoughtless Jonathon could be at times. In frustration, she breathed deeply and said, "Tell them it is a beautiful boat and how clever they were building it. Thank Doctor Sopwith for his help. He has given his time freely and taught them much – perhaps time a father should have made for his sons!"

Jonathan glared at Ethel, "Mind what you say, Ethel! I do not have the skills of Doctor Sopwith." He turned his back on her and watched the gathering by the river from his window in silence.

"No, Sir! I apologise. I must return now as Mrs Turner will need me. Do not miss this chance with them, Mr Turner!"

"Thank you, Ethel."

Ethel made her way downstairs and out the front door of the offices. Still talking with Victoria and glancing across Thomas's shoulder, Anne noticed Ethel coming out and rushing along the footpath and then up High Street towards their home. Anne wondered why Ethel would be there. Perhaps it was a message from home. Anne re-joined her conversation.

As the guests edged towards the riverbank for the launching, David Sopwith looked up and was surprised to see Jonathan Turner approaching. Jonathan patted each of the boys on the head.

"Well done, boys. What will you call your boat then?"

They both looked up, amazed their father was bothering to attend. William cried out with excitement and pride, "Father, we will name her after mother, as she convinced you about using the wood. We shall call her Ellena!"

Johnathan was quite moved that they would honour their mother in this way. He found it hard speaking as the emotion welled up inside him, "She ….. she will be greatly honoured by your noble thoughts, boys!"

David Sopwith took the boat gently off the boys and held it up high so everyone could see. As Thomas uncorked a bottle of champagne, Jonathan started catching the spirit of the occasion.

David held up his hand as the group gathered closer, "Ladies and Gentlemen, welcome to the Guildford Shipyards." There was a murmur of laughter.

"This afternoon, the honourable Mrs Marion Turner will name this wonderful boat. If you would, please come forward, Marion."

There was a hush as Marion moved beside the boat. She called Simeon and William over and ensured Thomas had the champagne bottle open. Gathering her thoughts, she decided on what she would say.

Marion placed her hands on the shoulders of William and Simeon, "Ladies and Gentlemen, I am honoured that the builders of this boat selected me for the naming and launching. It gives me great pleasure to name this boat the sailing boat 'Ellena'! May all who sail her do so in safety!" Marion dampened the boat's bow with some champagne and, laughing, flicked some into both boys' eyes.

A few cheers and clapping occurred as David Sopwith placed the boat into the water tethered by a long fishing pole. The shining little boat turned across the wind and started making its way across the river under full sail. A chant of 'Hurrah, Hurrah!' rose among the spectators. There were many words of congratulations as the crowd admired the pretty little boat named 'Ellena'.

Simeon, standing beside the water, was rubbing his eyes free of the champagne when he stepped backward, and the bank gave way. He fell into the water and came up splashing. Seeing his son in difficulty, Jonathan quickly rushed into the water and pulled him out. They both clambered back onto the bank.

"Thank you, Father! I missed my footing."

Helping Jonathan up, Neville noticed him looking down at his wet shoes, socks and trousers. A red tinge was appearing on his brow. Neville quietly reminded Jonathan, "Proverbs! Proverbs, Jonathan!" Jonathan looked directly at Neville and remembered how he should control his anger.

Taking a breath, he asked, "Are you all right, Simeon?"

"Yes, Father. Just a bit damp."

As the gathering dispersed, Neville whispered in Bethany's ear, "Thank goodness, it was not William!"

Kingston, Jamaica …

Lady Clarissa Wendarm and Mrs Fiona Green's eyes met in the upstairs hallway after lunch.

"I missed you at lunch, Fiona! Where have you been?"

"Finalising our transport! We leave for England next week. The carriage will arrive on Monday morning at ten, and we will set off for the port at last. We must finish our packing over the next few days and be ready early Monday morning."

"Thank you, Fiona, that is good of you. Would you start on mine, Darling? I will be rather busy tonight!"

"Sorry Clarissa, remember I am not your maid! I am the one paying your way. So, perhaps given the dinner appointment tonight, you might start this afternoon or hire a maid out of your own money. Now, where is Sir Hugh? He promised that we would make up a foursome for cards tonight."

Upset about Fiona's rebuff, Clarissa spat out, "No, he was not at lunch. Perhaps you might mount a search! I have not seen him now for two days." With that, she walked off.

Fiona watched as she strutted down the stairs towards the lounge. Clarissa would recover soon, probably as soon as she required more money. Walking along the corridor until she reached Sir Hugh's door, Fiona gently knocked. There was a cough but nothing else. Gently, she tried the door and found it unlocked. Entering, she called, "Sir Hugh! It is Fiona. Are you alright?"

There was no answer. Fiona carefully moved through the sitting area and into the bedroom. There she found a prostrate Sir Hugh on his bed, sweating profusely.

"My goodness, Sir Hugh!"

She carefully pulled the mosquito net aside and knelt beside him. His head faced her, and through his dry, cracked lips, he whispered, "Water, please, water!"

"Yes, at once."

In a slight panic, Fiona found an empty water jug and dirty glass on a nearby table.

"Sir Hugh. I shall return quickly with a full jug and clean glass. Please, see if you can turn over onto your back."

Fiona rushed out of the room and downstairs. The receptionist raised her head as the lady asked, "Please call a doctor. Sir Hugh South, in room fifteen, is most unwell." She rushed into the bar and collected a jug of water and a clean glass. Thanking the barman, she hurried back upstairs with her precious cargo.

Sir Hugh was still on his side and breathing weakly. Fiona filled the glass with water but saw he could not sip. "We must get you on your back, Hugh, and sitting up a bit."

He nodded and slowly rolled onto his back. Fiona found some cushions and, with some help from the patient, gently sat him slightly up on the pillows. She then held the glass as he sipped slowly.

Once his thirst was satisfied, Hugh lay back and closed his eyes, drifting into a deep sleep. Fiona wiped his brow with a damp cloth and then walked over, opening the French doors letting in some fresh air. The hot air slowly moved the mosquito net, but Fiona realised it would not provide any relief.

She moved a chair over, sat beside the bed and used a wet washer, sponging his forehead again. Hugh was burning up with a fever. Sitting back, she noticed some jars on the table beside her. Fiona picked one up and saw it was unopened, but the labelling read 'Mercury Ointment'.

"Oh, No!"

Fiona immediately thought of her late husband, who used the same ointment but died from the disease. She was familiar with the cream, which was not a cure but gave some relief. Fiona gasped as she saw Hugh, weak and miserable, in his bed. It brought back all the memories of nursing her husband, Harrold, through that terrible sickness. She had found Sir Hugh a kind gentleman during the voyage, but she now realised his relations with women were extensive if he needed this ointment.

A knock on the door announced the doctor. A young English man, around thirty, entered carrying his medical bag. He had a pleasant but concerned smile and was well-dressed for Kingston.

"Hello, are you the Doctor?"

"Yes, Milady, I am Doctor Ronald Cowper. Whom am I addressing, please?"

"I am Mrs Fiona Green, from Bedfordshire in England, Doctor. I find my friend Sir Hugh South has been taken ill. Would you please examine him and advise me of the required treatment?"

"Please forgive me for asking Mrs Green, but will Sir Hugh be paying the bill?"

Fiona took a sharp breath but pleasantly said, "No. I will take care of the bill, Doctor Cowper. Now, if you would examine him, please."

Doctor Cowper raised his eyebrows and proceeded with the examination. He also took note of the ointment on the bedside table. Fiona stood out on the balcony giving the doctor some privacy. After around thirty minutes, Doctor Cowper joined her.

"Mrs Green, how long have you and Sir Hugh been in Kingston?"

"Doctor, if I might explain the situation!" Fiona was anxious that Doctor Cowper understood her relationship with Sir Hugh. It was enough that she should tolerate Clarissa, but she would not have her name dragged through the mud.

"I am travelling with Lady Clarissa Wendarm, and we first became acquainted with Sir Hugh several days out of Southampton. Since arriving in Kingston, we have all kept company. However, Sir Hugh spent the last week visiting his plantations and returned here on Sunday night. I believe the accommodation on the plantations was somewhat lacking. Our party dined with him on Sunday, but he has been uncharacteristically missing since then. It now being Wednesday, I sought him out today, checking on his welfare, and found him unwell."

"I assume you would be his closest friend here in Jamaica?"

"Well, Lady Clarissa and myself."

"Then, I will not mince my words, Mrs Green. It is not the 'marsh fever'[11]. He has a high fever, the symptoms of influenza and a nasty rash. My diagnosis is that Sir Hugh has the French Pox[12], and the condition is well advanced. I cannot find any severe lesions or deformities, but the typical sores are present. Given the stage of the disease, he is fortunate there are no obvious physical symptoms.

The two jars of mercury ointment on the table confirm my diagnosis. I presume he brought these with him but has not been using them?"

"I'm not sure, Doctor! We only met him on the ship and knew little of his background. However, I am familiar with the disease! My late husband contracted it."

"My condolences, Mrs Green. Would you please check his luggage for any letters of introduction or Doctor's instructions that might give us more detail? Assuming Sir Hugh survives the next week, he should use the mercury ointment each morning and night. It may help, and it may not. If he recovers from this bout, which is quite serious, he must convalesce for some time. Of course, travel is out of the question for the next few months, and after that, I would advise that he return home if possible. However, you and Lady Clarissa must prepare yourself for the worst – I have seen this disease many times here, and it shows no mercy. I fear Sir Hugh will not last the week."

Doctor Cowper stood there, considering Sir Hugh's treatment, gazing at the view across the bay.

"Mrs Green, someone must apply the ointment. If you feel it is not your place, I will arrange for a nurse to visit and deal with it day and night. But he will need someone caring for him for the next few weeks. As I said, he will either recover or die this week. Let us hope he recovers!"

"Amen, Doctor. Yes, I would appreciate the nurse, thank you."

"There is one other issue Mrs Green, which is a rather delicate matter, so I will do my best at being discrete. Anyone having sexual relations with Sir Hugh is at a high risk of contracting the disease. If this has occurred, then I would suggest an urgent examination."

Fiona Green immediately thought of her husband, Harrold. She shuddered, remembering the terrible agony before his death. It was a miracle her husband did not infect her. She looked up at Doctor Cowper.

"My husband died of this dreadful pox, Sir, and I am most fortunate in avoiding the disease. I can assure you that there is no need for an examination

---

[11] Malaria was commonly known as marsh fever. The term 'malaria' first appeared in English literature about 1829. Wikipedia.

[12] Syphilis.

of myself. I cannot speak for Lady Clarissa, but I will advise her of your recommendation. I understand that she and Sir Hugh were intimate on the ship."

"I see. Then why would Lady Clarissa not be here?"

"I'm afraid she has a wandering interest, Doctor!"

The Doctor looked out over the bay again, considering her answer.

"You are a kind woman Mrs Green, and you suffer much. I wish you well on your new mission. I will call tomorrow afternoon if that is convenient. Please call if Sir Hugh's condition deteriorates."

"Thank you, Doctor Cowper."

"The nurse will be here around five o'clock."

The doctor excused himself and left Sir Hugh in her care. She wandered back beside the bed and sat down. As Sir Hugh slept, she bent over, putting her face in her hands, and cried as all the pain returned, remembering how her Harrold had suffered.

The River Wey, Guildford ...

Simeon and William found a safe spot on the river to sail the SS *Ellena* back and forth. After each journey, they adjusted the sail, hoping it would increase her speed through the water.

They noticed an older lad sitting along the bank admiring the boat. He looked friendly enough, so William called out. "Would you like a go? It is our new boat!"

"Aye, Lad!"

Simeon and William sat up, wondering about this boy's strange accent.

"You talk funny – where are you from?"

"Scotland!"

William was puzzled, "Where is Scotland?"

Simeon chipped in, "It is north of England, William. I will show you the globe when we go home."

"My name is Archie! Archie Watson. What is yours?"

"I'm Simeon, Simeon Turner! And this is my brother, William."

Archie nodded and admired the boat, "She's a beauty. Where did you get her?"

"We made it!"

"With a little help from our friend, Doctor Sopwith!" Simeon thought they should not take all the credit.

"How did you make the wood bend?"

"You soak it in water overnight. Then when you put it on, it bends easily." Simeon was proud of the knowledge he had learned from Doctor Sopwith.

"Those people who are watching further along the bank. Do they know you?"

"Aye! That is my mother and my sister, Sophie. We are staying here for a few days. My parents have decided to live here, and I will attend the Free School."

Simeon was keen on impressing Archie, "We attend the Church School. I think father will enrol me at the Free School, but not for a few years yet."

The boys enjoyed Archie's friendly company until his mother called him, and their family walked towards the High Street.

The Guildford Medical Practice ...

Neville found an envelope marked Sloan Specialist Practice, Harley Street, London, on his desk. It was the expected letter that would advise if his application was successful. Carefully he broke the seal and opened the letter.

Sloan Specialist Practice
Harley Street
London

Dr Neville Bassington
Guildford Medical Practice
Quarry Street
Guildford, Surrey

Dear Doctor, Bassington
I am pleased to advise that your application for membership in this specialist practice is successful. The practice partners offer a warm welcome and look forward with excitement, given the experience you will bring and share with us.

Attached, you will find the terms and conditions of your joining the practice. These should be no different from what we discussed at the interview.

The practice partners have allocated you a room for either part-time or full-time work. We kindly ask that you advise us of your starting date at your earliest convenience.

Please sign and return the attached contract.
Congratulations on your joining the practice.

Yours faithfully

Dr Mark Sloan   *Dr Reginald Fisher*   *Dr Edward Maynard*

A smile came across Neville's face, and he darted down the corridor, knocking on David South's door. He found David busy with a patient, so he apologised and excused himself. Neville was so excited that he grabbed his coat and dashed off home, searching for Bethany.

McPherson's Residence, Greenwich ...

Janet Stubbington sat in Hamish's study, sipping scotch whiskey, and finding the details Hamish revealed intriguing. He explained, "I knew nothing of this until James sprang it on me at dinner. As you can imagine, I was somewhat stunned. James is unaware of our arrangements, but finding he has links with the Irish immediately worried me. I used the excuse of Jennifer Steele's memorial service next week, cutting our stay there short. We left soon after Christmas and made a dash home."

"I am sure your wife appreciated that?"

"It was difficult, but I convinced Marjorie that Marion would need support at the memorial service. I also promised a return trip in March, allowing myself time to consider what action I must take. Marjorie was most annoyed at returning so soon, but she was a great comfort for Marion on arriving back in Greenwich."

"So, what are you proposing, Hamish."

"I don't know. The girl Isla is pregnant, my wife is already doting on another grandchild, and James seems unmovable on this radical lifestyle. If not for our agreement, I would have given him his notice. He cannot remain as a manager in Glasgow! However, I delayed so we could discuss before any action was taken."

"Thank you, Hamish, for being so open about the situation. You mentioned one of the ships was in Cobh, and he met her in Cork. What was one of the company ships doing in Cobh?"

"Not sure! I have asked for the manifest and why we were doing business there. It should come in the mail next week."

"I understand that James knows about our enforcers in Guildford, but is he aware of our agreement?"

"No, no one does. The family thinks I am a successful businessman funding all the operations out of my resources."

"Good! Keep it that way. I must discuss this with my partners at the office. This change in James's life choices might work well for us. Perhaps James, unknowingly, will help with our enquiries?"

"I don't want my son in danger, Janet! Especially if he is unaware."

"Hamish, he is thirty years of age. He has chosen his way. What we must do is find out what path he is following. The details of why your ship was in Cobh may answer this for us. I will return next week, and we will talk further.

In the meantime, relax, Hamish. You have been open with us, and we will do our best for you. Good day."

Janet put down her unfinished glass of scotch and left the room. The butler saw her out.

Hamish sat there thinking, 'Stupid James. He seems unaware of the trouble he is causing. I pray he is not tinkering with the Irish republicans.'

Hursts, Tailors and Dressmakers, Guildford ...

Victoria Sopwith found her way through and entered the lady's fitting area. Bethany Bassington, standing in for an indisposed Mrs Eleanor Turner, greeted her.

"Victoria, my mother, is worn out, so I volunteered my assistance. I'm so glad you are here, as two sets of eyes are better than one."

"Thank you, Bethany. I will do my best, but I must warn you this will be my first experience with wedding dresses, so you may find me somewhat lacking!"

"We will muddle through together."

"I heard the good news about Neville joining a Harley Street practice. Why even in Ireland, we have heard of Harley Street. Please pass on my congratulations. I'm sure he is most excited."

"Yes! He is chafing at the bit, planning our departure already. The problem is that I enjoy our life here in Guildford but am also keen on exploring London. I think I will travel with him as we are still only in our first year of marriage, and I would enjoy some time in London."

"I, too, am fascinated by that large city, perhaps I might join you, and we could explore it together. Anne might also come and Emma. While Neville works, we will have fun."

"That is a super idea, Victoria. Are you familiar with London?"

"No, I have never been there before, and I am sure David will allow me if I am with you and Anne."

"We will do this, Victoria. You have opened a new opportunity for me. Thank you."

Victoria smiled and appreciated Bethany's warm friendship. Since her mother died six years ago, companionship has been a rare experience. Guildford felt more like home as the days passed.

"Well, ladies, here is the bride!" Mrs Smith stood back and ushered in Anne.

The beautiful long white robe and the long train following transfixed Bethany and Victoria. Anne appeared more beautiful than an angel, even without her hair being set and any makeup. The dress sparkled from tiny sequins throughout the fabric and would dazzle as she walked down the aisle.

Bethany found her voice first, "Anne! That is beautiful. What can I say?"

Anne stood there with a gleaming smile, appreciating the words of praise, "Well, there are lots of small items we must discuss. Should I have sequins on the train, or should it be plain?"

Victoria considered the train and then commented, "I think plain as if you have sparklers in the train, it will draw attention away from you and onto the train. On the day, you must be the centre of attention, Anne, so the dress, not the train, must be the focal point."

Anne suddenly realised that Victoria had an eye for detail and understood the aims of design and the response it would produce from onlookers. As the conversation proceeded, Mrs Smith, Bethany and Anne were astounded at Victoria's fashion knowledge.

Mrs Smith asked, "Have you studied fashion, Victoria?"

"I spent years by myself on the estate and often entertained myself with every bit of literature I could find. I speak fluent French, so I also learnt from any available French books. There was no shortage of money, so I purchased whatever I wanted, including materials and patterns, on Belfast visits. It passed the time well, and I enjoyed creating dresses. It is fun!" She smiled and turned back, gently feeling the material. She made several welcome suggestions during the fitting session that impressed the ladies.

The dressmaker lifted her eyebrows at Anne, who broke out in a lovely smile in return. At last, Anne had discovered Victoria's interest, and it was not unwelcome.

As they left Hursts, Anne mentioned her coming visit this Saturday and Sunday at Fintelton.

"Would you join me, Victoria? Emma and Lady Jane will be thrilled if you come, and it will give us time for a fashion discussion. You might also assist us with the wedding plans. I think you have a gift for decorations as well. There are still many bits and pieces needing a decision."

"That is so kind of you, Anne. I would love that. What are the arrangements?"

"We leave before lunch on Friday and should arrive just after dark for dinner. We return on Monday, leaving mid-morning and arriving at Guildford late afternoon."

"That sounds very sensible. I will have my maid arrange her transport requirements. Do you have a maid, as she is welcome in my maid's carriage?"

Anne was amused. Victoria's lifestyle was one Anne could only dream of, "No, I have no maid, Victoria. My mother's maid, Mrs Nibley or Aggie, often assist me."

"One of them would be welcome travelling with my maid."

"I think Emma will share her maid, Jane, with me. That will be more than sufficient. But thank you so much for the offer."

The Turner Household, Guildford …

Eleanora found her strength returning that night at dinner and sat at the table feeling some energy, "Jonathan, you have not told us what transpired at the Magistrates' Court on Tuesday?"

"My apologies, Dear! It was my intention, but you retired early last night. The Magistrate heard the initial pleadings and decided that the arson charges would stand, but only the leader would be charged with attempted murder. The Magistrate scheduled the next hearing for London. My guess is they will be transported rather than executed. The execution would create too much angst in the surrounding areas, whereas transportation[13] means a possible release after seven years and starting a new life in New South Wales. The Magistrate set the trial date for late March."

"Father, will you attend?" Anne felt he should be there as this was a serious case, and the court would call Jeb, Terry and Constable Rawlins as witnesses.

"I have not decided yet! Jeb and Terry must go, so I should remain here and manage the operations. We are not sure of the timing yet, and the court may meet in late February. The trial may coincide with your Uncle Richard and family departing for South Africa. We have agreed I will be with them at Southampton and return here with Katherine."

"Father, if you do not attend, then I must. I feel it is important that someone from the family represents us. I think Jeb and Terry would feel more secure with some support."

"I see no harm in that!"

Bethany and Neville had joined them for dinner. Neville could no longer keep his news, "I have good news, Jonathan and Eleanora! My application for the specialist practice in Harley Street is accepted."

Eleanora was surprised, "Congratulations, Neville, this is wonderful news. But what exactly does this mean?"

As Neville shook Jonathan's hand, he said, "It means I will be practising in London quite soon. I am only proposing two days every second week, and the partners at the practice have endorsed this as sensible until my client base builds up. Over the next few years, it may become alternate full weeks in London and here."

Jonathan was intrigued, "How do you attract clients?"

"I will visit Doctors and explain my specialty of treating major injuries. In time I hope they will refer patients. I will also consult with hospital resident doctors, as many workplace injuries require immediate treatment. My time

---

[13] The British government ended transportation of convicts to the American colonies at the start of the American Revolution. An alternative site was needed to relieve further overcrowding of British prisons and hulks. Britain chose Australia as the site of a penal colony, and in 1787, the First Fleet of eleven convict ships set sail for Botany Bay, arriving on 20 January 1788, and founded Sydney, New South Wales, the first European settlement on the continent. Wikipedia.

will be busy, and my patient list will soon build up."

"This calls for some champagne! We must toast our new specialist." Jonathan called for Mrs Jennings and asked for a bottle.

Anne, thinking about the move, asked, "Bethany, what about you? Will you travel with Neville?"

"Yes, Anne, he has promised me a tour of London, and we have only begun our adventures there. I want some more sightseeing before any children arrive." Bethany looked lovingly into Neville's deep brown eyes, "Do you recall your promise?"

"I will never forget. It was one of the most significant turning points in my life." With that, he kissed her lightly, and everyone smiled.

"How is David taking the news, Neville?"

"He is pleased for me, Anne, but I think he is concerned about how he will cope while I am away. The practice cannot financially fund another doctor, so we must solve this issue. He managed it previously before we joined practices. We will make it work!"

"Will you stay with your parents in London or rent?"

"At first, yes, but once the specialist practice builds up, we will rent."

Anne was excited about that, "Bethany, may I stay with you in September when we start the new bakery in London? We could visit Piccadilly and all the arcades. I went there with Emma, and it was so special. You will love it."

"Why wait for September, Anne? Let us do it sooner. After all, I won't see much of Neville during the day!"

Port Charlotte, Isle of Islay, Scotland …
Robert surveyed the freshly piled mound of dirt, extending twenty yards from him. With some enforced help from the locals, the marines discovered the site of a mass grave. Strangely the rebels used a burial site that was easily located as if they wanted it found!

Gritting his teeth, Robert continued with the grim task of identifying the crew members he would recognise from *Providence*. Having served on the frigate for several years, he knew the crew members well. They had uncovered fifty-five men from the grave; despite some decomposition, Robert was already sure of eighteen.

"These other corpses must be the Irish casualties. The bodies I have identified are all officers and midshipmen from *Providence*. There are no sailors! Perhaps all the crew that came ashore took the side of the Irish. The question is, where were they taken or hidden?"

Horace rubbed the stubble on his chin, "How many men were in the crew, Robert?"

"Well, a full complement would have been around two hundred and twenty sailors. That's not including the officers –twelve officers and six midshipmen."

"So, we found forty-three sailors and Captain Foster on the ship alive and seven dead sailors when we reclaimed her. That means one hundred and seventy men are missing."

They both stood there as they watched the marines refill the grave.

"Where are the one hundred and seventy men? Perhaps there is another grave, or the Irish are holding them somewhere." Robert could not understand how one hundred and seventy men could disappear.

Horace scratched his chin, "We need some way of breaking this silence that the locals are keeping. Some building of relationships is necessary."

A small group of locals watched from further up the hill. They stood silently, paying their respects as the marines refilled the grave.

"There is much we don't know about this situation, Horace. Besides the grave, the Irish have left nothing. They will be in hiding now. We foiled their plan, but I am sure this is a temporary lull. They will be back."

"That is what the locals are afraid of, Robert. I do not blame them for not speaking. The Scottish do not have much respect for the English. We could try some pitchcapping[14], but that may not inspire friendship."

"What about the way we found *Providence* first, Horace? Do you think you can outdrink a Scotsman tonight!"

Horace smiled, "If it is necessary, yes! But perhaps we can delegate. It is time some of the younger officers demonstrated their prowess. You pick one of yours, and I will choose a marine. It will be a navy-army joint manoeuvre!"

"Fair enough. Lieutenant Peters is my man. Who is yours?"

"Lieutenant White will do. I think it is time we returned and briefed them."

The Grand Hotel, Kingston, Jamaica ...

"Fiona, it is Clarissa! Are you in there?"

Clarissa knocked as she entered Sir Hugh's bedroom. She found Fiona sleeping in a chair in the late afternoon heat on the verandah.

"Oh, Clarissa, you took me by surprise." She yawned and rubbed her eyes before looking at a happy Lady Clarissa Wendarm.

"Fiona, I have found a replacement for Sir Hugh at cards tonight. Mr Stephen Polkinghorne is on business with his plantations and has given me some advice. I think you will find him charming. Now how is our dear Sir Hugh?"

Fiona Green found her companion's lack of concern for anyone except herself irritating. Clarissa would do anything to avoid responsibility. She

---

[14] Pitchcapping was a form of torture used by the British military against suspected Irish rebels during the period of the 1798 rebellion, most famously on Anthony Perry, one of the leaders of the Wexford rebels. Wikipedia.

must have a party whenever possible, affairs with new men, and never considering the consequences. Fiona could not understand a woman who purely lived for pleasure.

"The Doctor called and examined Sir Hugh. I am afraid the news is not good. He has the French Pox and is severely affected. The Doctor feels he may die this week. It is serious, Clarissa, but there is not a great deal we can do except keep an eye on him."

"Well, in that case, Fiona, you will be free tonight for dinner and cards."

"Clarissa, I thought you might watch over Sir Hugh, considering your relationship with him. The doctor wants a close eye kept on him."

"Oh, no. That is not my job, Fiona. Perhaps you should hire someone!"

"Clarissa, I have been with him all day. Would you stay with him for a little while until I change and freshen up?"

Clarissa looked alarmed but realised she owed her travelling companion some liberty, "Of course, Fiona. Now do not be too long. As Mr Polkinghorne will be joining us for dinner at seven."

"Thank you, Clarissa. I will be quick as I am expecting the nurse."

Fiona, relishing the opportunity, rushed off. Lady Clarissa sat at a desk near the open verandah doors and looked around. She enjoyed the light breeze drifting in, slightly relieving the oppressive heat. Clarissa quickly became impatient and searched for something to entertain her. She noticed a pile of mail on Sir Hugh's desk. Lady Wendarm could not restrain herself and flipped through the letters finding an unopened one from Lady Fintelton. Given Hugh's state of health, she was sure he would not be aware of its delivery. Clarissa quickly deposited the letter into her handbag. She also noticed a letter for Lady Emma South ready for the post. Clarissa thought, 'Why, that could be useful as well.'

Lady Wendarm was quietly wondering about the letters' content when the door opened, and a tall Jamaican lady in a nurse's uniform entered.

"Excuse me, Ma'am, but I am Nurse Jackson. The nurse for Sir Hugh South."

"Please come in. I am Lady Clarissa Wendarm. I have been looking after Sir Hugh all day. He is so sick, the poor little fellow! Thank you for coming. Now I will leave you with him as I must dress for dinner. I shall return in a little while. Do not be concerned if you finish before I return, as I shall return promptly. Mrs Green and I are entertaining tonight and wonder if you might watch over Sir Hugh. Or perhaps you would arrange for someone. Mrs Green, of course, will be paying."

The nurse smiled, "Certainly, Milady. I will arrange this as soon as I have dealt with Sir Hugh's medication. Now, if you would excuse me."

Lady Clarissa exited rather quickly, thinking, 'My, Sir Hugh, we have looked after you so well today!'

The Local Pub, Port Charlotte, Isle of Islay, Scotland …

The two officers, not dressed in uniform, had enjoyed a good meal and were now slowly making friends in the local pub at Port Charlotte. Lieutenant White was excitedly discussing the best fishing spots with some locals. At the same time, Lieutenant Samuel Peters had struck up a conversation with a pretty, young lass called Ruth, cleaning the tables.

"Now tell me, Ruth, why do you live here in Port Charlotte?"

"There is not much work in Belfast. My parents had a contact here and arranged the job."

"How long have you been here?"

"Round three years now working in the distillery and a few nights in the pub here. It is tedious work, but the nights are fun meeting folks in the pub."

"What kind of fun do you have, then?"

She raised her eyebrows and smiled, "Well, if you buy me a few drinks after work, I might show you."

Samuel Peters already understood the local mistrust of the English on this Scottish Island. He found Ruth's friendly nature welcome. She was attractive, had a good sense of humour, was talkative, and different from the other islanders. He welcomed the chance of some female company.

"Which ship are you from, Samuel Peters?"

"Call me Sam, please, Ruth. I am on HMS *Shadow*. I was posted on a few months ago. Were you here when the navy retook the frigate?"

Ruth looked hard at him and said, "I was! The Irish locked us away like prisoners. We needed food, clothes, and playtime for children, so they let us out in twos and threes, but not for more than three hours. They told us they would shoot one of the men if we escaped. So, we always came back. It was terrifying! I shiver just thinking about it."

"You are safe now that the Navy and Army are here."

"What about when you are gone? I fear the Irish will return."

"They won't be returning here; now we have discovered their camp."

Ruth looked at Samuel Peters and smiled, "Have you a room here, Samuel?"

"Should I get one?"

"Well, if you want a drink with me after work Sam, then you best get one." She gave him a wink.

Samuel Peters sat up and suggested, "Perhaps not here. What about the other pub down the road? Might be a bit more private!"

"In about half an hour."

The High Street, Guildford …

Madeline, Simeon, and William met Archie Watson, his sister, and his mother in the street, walking home from school. The boys were rushing, pulling Madeline along as they were keen on sailing the *Ellena* this afternoon. Simeon spotted Archie first.

"Archie! Archie, we are sailing the boat again this afternoon. Can you come? We will meet you there. Same place."

Archie looked up at his mother and asked, "May I, Mother?"

"First, you should introduce us, Archie, and then we will know who these fine youngsters are?"

"Sorry, Mother. Simeon, William and I presume this is your older sister. May I present my mother, Mrs Watson? Sorry, I forgot your surname, Simeon."

Madeline was interested in Archie's sister and spoke quickly, "It is Simeon and William Turner, Mrs Watson, and I am Madeline Turner. We all attend Reverend Taggart's school at the church."

"Hello, Madeline. How did you know my name?"

"Simeon and William told my parents at dinner last night about meeting Archie."

"I see, Madeline. Well, thank you for the introduction. Let me introduce my daughter, Sophie. It appears she is about your age."

"Hello, Sophie! Are you interested in watching the sailing boat this afternoon?"

"Only if my mother comes. I am a bit afraid of Guildford yet. We have not been here that long. Mother, will you come?"

"Certainly, Dear. Archie must change out of his school uniform first. We will meet you at the river later, boys. And you too, Madeline."

The boys cheered and rushed off, leaving Madeline with the Watsons.

"I'm sorry, Mrs Watson, but they are always excited after school, especially when they sail their new boat. I must go home now and change. We will be back near the riverbank soon."

Jessica Watson was impressed with Madeline's kind manners, "I understand, Madeline. We shall meet you by the riverbank."

The Turner Household, Guildford …

Anne assisted Mrs Jennings and Aggie in the kitchen with the dinner preparations as an excited William and Simeon came through holding the good ship, *Ellena*.

"We are meeting Archie at the riverbank and sailing."

Anne was confused, "Who is Archie?"

"The boy we met by the river the other day. We told Mother and Father at dinner - remember?"

Anne racked her mind, unfamiliar with this name.

Simeon added more description, "He is the one with the Scottish accent."

Then Anne remembered. "Well, it will be later, as you boys have not chopped the wood yet! Father will be annoyed if he finds you missed the chopping."

"But Anne, that will take an hour, and Archie will be gone."

"I am sorry, but you should remember you have chores."

Simeon looked forlorn, and William stamped his foot.

"The sooner you start, the sooner you will reach the river."

The boys took their sailing boat back onto the verandah and gently placed it down. Simeon grabbed the axe, and William set up some wood.

Madeline approached Anne, who was now concentrating on the dinner preparations.

"Anne, it is more complicated than what the boys told you. We met Mrs Watson, Sophie and Archie in the High Street and asked if they would join us at the riverbank. They are all coming. We should be there soon, and I was keen on meeting Sophie. They will think we have misled them if we do not arrive."

"I see!" Anne considered what Madeline had said and realised the truth in her comments. It would be best if she escorted Maddie there and explained the boy's delay. "Mrs Jennings, I must go with Madeline on an errand. I am sorry, but Ivy or Jess must fill in for me. Come, Madeline, let us sort this out!"

Anne and Madeline found Mrs Watson, Archie and Sophie waiting for the boys at the riverside.

"Mrs Watson. Please forgive my manners, as an introduction has not been possible. I am Miss Anne Turner, one of William and Simeon's sisters."

"It is a pleasure, Miss Turner. We were waiting for the boys and their boat."

"Yes, Mrs Watson. I understand this. The boys forgot some of their chores which they must complete before they return. They are hard at it at present. I must apologise on their behalf as they have inconvenienced you, and I am so sorry. They will be here later, perhaps in three-quarters of an hour."

"What a pity, but I will ask them about their chores next time. But boys become excited about these events." Jessica Watson smiled and did not seem upset at all. "This is a beautiful place! We have only been here briefly, and hope Guildford will be our home."

"I am spoilt – I have lived here all my life and only recently visited London for the first time. Pray, where have you come from?"

"We moved from one of the outlying islands in Scotland. Our circumstances changed, and we decided a move was the right decision. Bryan decided we should find a growing country town rather than a city. We like open spaces."

"Might I ask what your husband does, Mrs Watson?"

"Bryan is a doctor, and he is looking for work in Guildford. There is some work with Doctor Chenning out at Woodbridge, but nothing regular yet. It will increase over time, I am sure!"

"I'm sure it will, and I am glad you are enjoying Guildford. I understand Archie attends the Free School, but what of Sophie?"

Anne and Jessica Watson took note of the two girls chatting happily a few paces away.

"We have not found a school for her yet. She is eleven and has no friends here. A school would solve that problem, but we are still looking."

"Madeline turned eleven last October and attends Reverend Taggart's school. There is a slight charge, but it is a good school. I was a student there myself and enjoyed it immensely. If I can be of help, please call on me. I will be only too happy if you require more information."

"Thank you, Miss Turner, that is most kind of you. Now we must be off as I must start preparing dinner. Tell the boys that Archie will join them another time. Come on, children, it is time we were going."

Madeline was sad and waved as Sophie followed her mother. Sophie looked back and waved as they went towards the High Street.

Anne was impressed with the Watsons and decided to tell Neville about Doctor Bryan Watson.

HMS Shadow, Port Charlotte …

It was three o'clock in the morning and bitterly cold. The wind was only a mild breeze, and a light fog was forming across the bay. A small rowing boat bumped alongside the hull of *Shadow* in the darkness. Callum Ferguson softly called out, "Ahoy, there!" Surprised by the man's sudden appearance, the marines trained several muskets on him as he stood in the boat. Using the light of a lantern, Midshipman William Collins peered down over the side and yelled, "What is your business here, man?"

"Quiet, Officer! I have some information for the Captain. Can I come aboard?"

"Stay where you are, man! Remain there for a minute or two until I return."

"Aye, Laddie, take five if you need them. I will still be here then!"

"Marines, keep your guns on him! I will fetch the First Lieutenant."

Collins dashed off for Lieutenant Fenton's cabin and knocked urgently.

Fenton was soon on deck and called down, "What's your name, and what is this information about?"

"Well, Officer, Sir. I hear you are asking about what happened when the Irish were here. I think I can help. My name is Mr John Smith. A good Scottish name if you understand my meaning."

"Come up, Mr Smith, and we can talk. But remember, I have four marines with loaded muskets aimed at you, so don't try anything stupid."

Fenton watched as Mr Smith attached his dingy and climbed over the ship's rail. He stood on the deck and faced them.

"Mr Smith, I am Lieutenant Fenton. Firstly, Mr Smith, please remove your balaclava."

"I'd rather not, lad, as the Irish have threatened anyone here who reveals information with death. There are still Irish here, and they will carry out the threat. I must talk with your Captain."

"We will see about that, Mr Smith, after we have searched you. You may keep your balaclava on but remain calm as we search you. We would not want you shot, would we?"

"Aye, Laddie."

Two marines put down their muskets, moved forward, and carefully searched Smith.

"Clean, Sir."

"All right, Mr Smith. Now, what do you want?"

"Protection, Mr Officer. I will trade the information you need for my protection. I want out of Port Charlotte. Protection in England where I will be safe."

Fenton stood there and thought about it. Then he asked, "And what information have you for the captain?"

"Have you found the hundred and seventy crew missing from 'Providence?"

Fenton knew from discussions with his Captain that this was one of the confusing issues confronting them. None of the locals would talk, and the officers were baffled by the crew's disappearance.

Callum could see he had played the right card. The Officer was now in two minds.

"I know where they are, Lieutenant Fenton, me lad. Wake the Captain, please!"

Chapter 8

The Turner House, Guildford …

Ethel Nibley found Mrs Turner collapsed in the drawing room. Eleanora had been reading there half an hour ago, but the lady's maid was unsure how long she had been on the floor. Quickly feeling for a pulse, Ethel found one, but it was weak.

"Mrs Turner? Mrs Turner, can you hear me?"

There was no response. Eleanora was unconscious, and her body temperature was dropping. Ethel wrapped a blanket around her and then sought help from the kitchen staff. Gathering around the prostrate lady, they lifted and carried her up the stairs and gently placed her on the bed.

Aggie noticed that during this whole transfer, Mrs Turner never regained consciousness.

"She is well under, Ethel! We need a doctor straight away!"

"Yes, send someone. I heard Doctor Bassington is doing country visits today, so it will be Doctor Sopwith. Let us hope he is in town. Clementine, would you send Simeon quickly, please."

William, Simeon, and Madeline, who recently returned from school, ate afternoon tea at the kitchen table. Aggie quickly dispatched Simeon with an urgent message for the doctor. William and Madeline bolted upstairs, finding their mother on her bed.

"Mother, are you alright?" William looked at his mother, hoping for a reply. As far as he could see, she was deeply asleep. He gently nudged her shoulder, but there was no response. She remained asleep.

"Be very gentle, William", Ethel said. "We think she is unconscious. Now that may be because she hit her head when she fell, or it may have been because she is being affected by something else."

William sat beside his mother's bed and held her hand. Madeline was given a face cloth by Ethel and told that she could keep her mother cool by gently touching it with the wet material every so often. The children pressed in beside the bed, and Ethel was content, allowing them there. She felt it was better if they knew what was happening.

Simeon returned and said the doctor had two more urgent appointments before he could come. He would be there as soon as he could. It was about four in the afternoon, and the sun was setting quickly. As the late afternoon light faded over Guildford, Ethel and Clementine lit several candles.

William said in alarm, "Her hands are becoming colder!".

"Give them a gentle rub, William. Whisper in your mother's ear and tell her how much you love her."

Ethel had seen this all before. When her husband died some years ago, the doctor gently explained the sequence of events. As the body fails, some systems shut down first and then others until the body cannot survive. She could see it happening here. Whatever had happened in that room while Mrs Turner was reading had been quite significant—possibly a stroke, a fall, and a knock on the head. But Ethel knew her mistress was dying, and it would not be long now.

William looked at his mother and back at Ethel. He saw that Ethel was holding back from saying too much. Suddenly he realised this was far more serious than he had thought. What was wrong here? Was Mother dying? A chill came through his body, and he shook a little – he had seen Olivia dead. Despite the ash-encrusted body, her colour became entirely white, as if the blood was not in the body anymore. Mother's colour was changing, and her breath was becoming a faint rasp as if she was gasping for breath.

"Mother, please wake up. I love you so much. I need you here with me. I need you, Mother!" As William whispered in her ear, he smelt her beautiful scent. William saw her golden hair falling over her chest. She looked so relaxed with her eyes closed and a low rasp in her breathing.

"Why doesn't she wake up, Ethel? I want her to wake up!"

Clementine, fearing this day, moved behind William placing her hands on his shoulders and gently squeezing them.

Softly she said, "I'm sure she can hear you, William. Just keep talking in her ear. It will help her and you. Madeline, you talk gently in the other ear. You both know she loves you so much. Now you must tell her how much you love her. She can hear you even if she can't answer back."

Madeline watched Clementine from the other side of the bed. Under-standing that her big sister was comforting William, the tears began coming. She stood, wiping her eyes, and asked, "Is she dying, Ethel?"

"I'm not sure, Madeline, but would you do something for me, please?"

"Yes!"

"Would you tell Aggie that Marcia should remain in the kitchen with her? Ask Jessica if she will fetch Mr Turner, Thomas and Marion. Also, ask Ivy if she would find Bethany, Anne, and Reverend Taggart. Then come back, please."

"Yes!"

"Off you go while we look after your mother."

Madeline went off with a brave face. Soon she returned and stood with the others gathered around their mother. Clementine sat down on the chair beside the bed and placed Madeline on her knee, holding her tightly. Madeline held her mother's hand, gently saying sweet things in her ear. Then they stopped talking and waited.

They stood there for nearly fifteen minutes in silence. Ethel lightly felt Eleanora's forehead; despite the blankets they had piled on her, the forehead was cold. Eleanora's breathing continued struggling. Then she stopped breathing, and her mouth fell open.

Doctor Sopwith came into the room and moved quickly between the children. He felt her pulse, which was no longer there. He looked down on Eleanora Turner and saw a stunning woman at peace. Even in death, she looked beautiful. The sight amazed him.

"I am afraid she is gone, children. She is now with Jesus."

There was a chilled silence, and the girls, overcome by the mention of their mother's death, started sobbing. Ethel and Mrs Jennings gave hugs where they could.

William sat there, holding his mother's hand. For him, she had been the one constant in his life. She had been his protector from Father. Now she was gone. He buried his head in the sheets beside his mother and cried. Simeon put his arms around him and also shed a tear.

Doctor Sopwith stood back and watched the family grieve their mother. He moved out onto the balcony and gave them some time. The sobbing sounds were all too familiar, having seen them many times before. It brought back the memory of his father, mother, and brother's death from that tragic accident in Ireland. He would never recover from the day he received the news and comforted Victoria for weeks afterwards. But in time, he and Victoria had accepted the reality.

Quietly walking back into the room, Doctor Sopwith said, "Ethel, would you take everyone out now? I must complete a final examination."

"Yes, Doctor, just give me a minute or two as I talk with each of them."

Ethel went around the children picking them up and hugging them. Then she explained that their mother was gone, and the staff must tidy up the body so they could come back later and say their final goodbyes. Strangely each of them understood and slowly moved out of the room.

The process took time, and finally, the room emptied, leaving the doctor with Mrs Turner and Ethel. A distraught Mrs Jennings hugged each of them and ensured they had a job keeping their minds busy. It was the first time she had seen everyone helping in silence. There were no complaints, no fights, just a silence among them that was broken only by the clatter of kitchen utensils.

Reverend Andrew Taggart, a close family friend, arrived, rushed upstairs and entered the bedroom.

"David, I understand she is gone. Did she feel any pain?"

"No, Reverend, it was peaceful, and the children were with her."

"What about Jonathan?"

Ethel looked up and said, "He will be here soon."

Andrew looked fondly down at Eleanora, said a silent prayer, and then backed out of the room and went downstairs, where he would wait for Mr Turner.

Jonathan Turner ran along the street with a pained expression on his face. He rushed up the stairs and through the front door straight into Reverend Andrew Taggart.

"Andrew! Is it true?"

Andrew did not smile but kept a sorrowful face. Jonathon immediately knew his wife was dead.

"I'm sorry, Jonathan, but Eleanora died this afternoon at about four-thirty. I have only now arrived myself ....!"

Jonathan could wait no longer. He rushed up the stairs and into his wife's bedroom. There he found Ethel putting some powder on Eleanora's face and Doctor Sopwith keeping an eye on the procedure.

"What has happened, David? What has happened?"

"I'm afraid she collapsed this afternoon at about three-thirty in the drawing room. I got here as fast as I could, but she died before I arrived. There was nothing I could do, Jonathan. Eleanora's death was natural – there were no remedies available. I am sorry, Jonathan. I am truly very, very sorry."

Jonathan approached the bed, and Ethel stood aside. He looked down at his wife, who Ethel had beautifully prepared. She looked alive, beaming life, but she was dead.

"Please give me a few minutes with her, and then the family can come in, and the Reverend can say some prayers."

David and Ethel withdrew. Jonathan stood beside the bed, and as he held his wife's hand, he leant over and kissed her forehead. The tears streamed down his cheeks as he viewed her lifeless body and said his last goodbyes. Then the family came in and knelt with him as Andrew Taggart led them in prayer.

After this, Jonathan Turner stood up and silently went down the stairs, along the hall and entered his study, closing the door.

Doctor Sopwith, who had been treating Jonathan, came into the study without knocking and sat beside him.

"Jonathan, you must take this draft, please. It will help you sleep tonight."

"I do not want any of your drafts, Doctor. I want my wife back!"

"I know that Jonathan, but I cannot bring her back! Now I understand more about you than most people, and I know the grief will soon turn into rage. I know your rage might turn violent. I must be sure that you are under control tonight. Otherwise, I must remove the family from here and ensure you do not harm them."

"Do you believe that I would hurt my family?"

"I know what happens with your rage, Jonathan. You lose all focus. You may not be aware of what you are doing. Drink this, so we are all safe tonight. Eleanora would agree with this, and I, as your friend, would encourage you. Please!"

Jonathan looked up with glaring eyes, knowing that David was right. Deep within Jonathan, his stress levels were stirring, and the rage was slowly growing. Doctor Sopwith could see it as well and was becoming slightly alarmed. Once again, David wished Neville was here.

David Sopwith's display of friendship touched Jonathan. Initially, Jonathan could not stand this fellow as he considered him arrogant. But Jonathan now realised this was his misapprehension. David Sopwith, on closer acquaintance, had displayed his family such kindness that Jonathan was ashamed of his initial judgement. He had been wrong about a fine man.

Slowly Jonathan found he could suppress the rage that was growing.

"Thank you, David, for your friendship. I have always misjudged you, and I am sorry for that. Give it here, Doctor."

Jonathan drank the draft down. Then he looked at David.

"Thank you for your care. I am feeling calmer now."

"Thank you, Jonathan. I will call again in the morning. Do you mind if the Reverend Taggart summons the undertaker? It would be better if they took Eleanora's body now."

Jonathan yawned, "Thank you, David. I appreciate all you have done for us. I think that the draft you gave me must be strong. So, you think the body should go now? You want my wife taken away?"

"She is dead, Jonathan. The undertaker will prepare her body for the funeral. The body cannot remain here!"

"Why not – this is where she belongs. At home!"

Jonathan gritted his teeth. He could not stand the undertaker taking his wife away less than an hour after he had come home. "Surely, she can lie there overnight. I need time with her before saying goodbye."

"It would be better for the family now if she went with the undertaker, Jonathan. It is not only you who is grieving. If I were you, I would go upstairs and curl up in bed. We can talk in the morning."

Jonathan rubbed his eyes as he looked at David. Then he stood up and walked upstairs into his bedroom.

David Sopwith had no intention of calling in the morning. He would sleep in the boys' room tonight in case this man went wild again. He would never forgive himself if he left the children unprotected from the grieving father. He stood and walked out, closing the door of the study.

Lions Bank of Guildford ...

Anne sat in the manager's office of the Lions Bank in Guildford, waiting for Mr Meyhew's return. Now she had further information and possessed a letter of authority from Lady Jane South, the Countess of Fintelton. She was keen on some progress.

The Bank Manager returned, "Miss Anne, I am sorry for the delay, but I always verify Lady Fintelton's signature before I honour a letter of authority. It is correct, so may I ask what information you require."

"Thank you, Mr Meyhew. The Fintelton Estate Manager, Mr Stem, has provided me with the details of three accounts. Here are the account numbers. Would you please confirm this for me and the accounts' balances?"

"Certainly. I have only today received last Friday's balances from Petersfield."

Mr Meyhew jotted down the account numbers and the balances and passed them over. Anne quickly checked them and asked, "Does the Estate hold any other accounts with your bank?"

"Not directly. The Earl, the Countess and Lady Emma use the Estate accounts, but Sir Hugh has two personal accounts of his own."

"Might I have the details for those, Mr Meyhew?"

"I am afraid not, Miss Anne, as you would need authority from Sir Hugh to release that information."

"I see. Mr Meyhew, perhaps we might access the information in another way. We have authority for the Fintelton Estate accounts. Would the bank prepare a listing of every transfer from the Fintelton accounts into Sir Hugh's accounts for the last three years? This period would provide a good sample."

Mr Meyhew took a deep breath. "Miss Anne, you are stretching the friendship here, but we can compile this for you. There would be a slight charge. Leave it with me until next week. I only have so many staff, so we will free up someone as they have spare time."

"Thank you, Mr Meyhew. I appreciate this. Also, at our last meeting, you indicated you would check the Petersfield systems to ensure there was no missing money."

"Yes, Miss Anne. From our systems, it appears nothing is missing. However, we will investigate the problem if you find any evidence!"

Anne sat there thinking and then asked, "Mr Meyhew, you recall you mentioned a Mrs Constance who left your employ recently?"

Mr Meyhew smiled, "Miss Anne, I suspected at the time that your enquiry was a bit deeper than looking for work for another person."

Anne blushed, "Well, it was, and it wasn't. I inquired about Clementine, but she is now working in our accounting office at the bakery. However, I have thought long and hard about Mrs Constance, and I was wondering if you could tell me something about her, such as her references and her family life."

"Miss Anne, you are very suspicious; however, given the situation, I will oblige. We hold all the staff files for the Petersfield branch at Guildford. I have Mrs Constance's file here." Mr Meyhew smiled and lifted his eyebrows.

They both laughed.

"I think, Miss Anne, you would make a good banker if you were ever inclined."

Anne nodded in agreement.

"Now, Mrs Constance. She had a husband in the army and a son. The husband, unfortunately, lost his life in a battle in India. I believe he held the rank of sergeant. Mrs Constance lived in Portsmouth before joining the Petersfield branch. She worked in the Portsmouth Cooperative Bank, now one of our associated banks. Her references were very sound—two from the Portsmouth Cooperative Bank and one from a local minister. There was also an excellent character reference from Sir Hugh South that swayed the debate about appointing a female teller. Sir Hugh must have known Mrs Constance in some way."

"Sir Hugh South! Sir Robert's brother?"

"Yes, Miss Anne. Sir Hugh's recommendation carried such weight that the Petersfield Manager and our Head Teller in Guildford did not check the other references. When you asked about employees at our previous meeting and mentioned Mrs Constance's name, I took the liberty of reviewing her file. This is one instance where the bank's system failed."

There was a silence between Anne and Mr Meyhew. Anne now knew that a relationship existed between Sir Hugh and Mrs Constance. But what could it be? She must find the referees and discuss this with them.

"Mr Meyhew, might I have the names and addresses of the referees from the Portsmouth Cooperative Bank and the local minister, please."

"Miss Anne, I assume you will contact these people. Is that correct?"

"It is possible, Mr Meyhew."

Mr Meyhew looked down at the file on his desk. A slight look of worry appeared on his face for the first time.

"Miss Anne. As a result of your inquiries, I discovered that our interview staff failed to complete their reference checks for Mrs Constance. Now, this was some six years ago. Given the time passed, it is not worth my disciplining staff; however, I am concerned that Sir Hugh was one of the referees, and his family is a large client of our bank. I am worried that these issues might create a difficult situation for the bank and the South family.

As I said earlier, as far as the bank is concerned, no money is missing. However, you believe that money is missing, so your review of the estate books must isolate the lost funds specifically. The bank will assist as best we can.

I will provide you with the names and addresses of the referees on two conditions. The conditions are that the Lions bank's name and my name must not be mentioned during your enquiries. Secondly, you would keep me informed of any search outcomes, as it may be that the bank has missed something. I know not what! But as I previously said, I welcome any questions you may have."

"Mr Meyhew, I agree! We have an agreement."

With that, Mr Meyhew passed across an envelope, "The information of the referees is enclosed."

"Thank you for your help today, Mr Meyhew. I will call again once I have the information I require from the referees. Perhaps two heads are better than one."

Anne exited the bank and found Ivy outside, searching for her.

"Miss Anne! Miss Anne, you are required at home urgently, please." Ivy began sobbing.

Taking the young maid in her arms, Anne asked, "Why, Ivy! Whatever is the matter?"

HMS Shadow, Port Charlotte ...

Robert rubbed his eyes as he sat up in his bunk. Swanton was standing there waiting for him with his coat.

"Sir, you are needed on deck. Mr Fenton requires your assistance."

Quickly, he cleared his mind of sleep and focused on the task at hand. Robert pulled on his uniform and boots, took the coat from his servant, and scrambled out onto the quarter deck. There he found a scruffy man sitting on a stool with four marines guarding him. The first Lieutenant turned as Robert approached.

"Captain, this man claims he has information for us and is proposing a trade for his safety. He was using the alias John Smith and came alongside in a dinghy. Said he would not show his face because of fear of reprisals ashore."

Robert had a good look at the man who sat there watching him.

"Bring me a stool, Mr Fenton."

"Yes, Sir."

Robert walked within hearing distance of the man and addressed him.

"Well, Mr Smith, let me hear your proposition."

Callum Ferguson was surprised by the captain's youth and concluded this was becoming a trap. The officer addressing him was far too young for a captain, let alone a commander.

"I must speak with whoever is in charge. A young man such as you could not be the captain. What do you take me for?"

"I can assure you, Mr Smith, I am the captain! On this ship, I have total authority! If I feel you might jeopardise our mission, then the power rests with me deciding your punishment. Now please tell me your proposition. You have five minutes before I execute you."

Callum looked up, thinking it was a bluff. He spat on the deck and stood. "You are no captain!"

"Mr Swanton, you may convince our friend here who is the captain of this ship."

Swanton appeared from behind Callum grasping his hair and yanking his head back into an arm lock. Holding a knife against Callum's throat, Swanton drew a slight amount of blood.

"He is the captain, my son! Now you either agree with me, or your life will end."

"I will agree. You are the captain, Sir. Might I ask your name, please?"

"Captain Sir Robert South."

Swanton loosened his grip. Callum took a deep breath and shook himself free.

"Now, Mr Smith, tell me your proposition."

"The Irish rebels were here for some time before HMS *Providence* was taken and hidden in the loch. The other residents of Port Charlotte and I were threatened with death if we spoke out against them. Irish are still in the town, but you will never find them. The townsfolk fear retribution if anyone reveals what went on. If I talk with you, you must promise safety for my lass and me when you leave."

"Mr Smith, it will depend on what information you provide."

"You have been searching for the crew of *Providence*?"

"Yes."

"Well, you may stop searching as they are not here. The nationalists were smart. The crew of *Providence* feared the Irish would murder them all."

Robert nodded as he and Horace had previously had the same thoughts as they searched for the stolen frigate.

"When they found that some of the crew were press-ganged and some were Irish boys keen on going home, they brought in a fishing vessel that took around twenty and sailed for Derry. Two American whaling boats that came into the loch under cover of darkness took fifty or so with them. The Irish rebels have strong links with the Americans. When the men heard the frigate, *Providence*, would sail for Boston, some were interested and joined the crew. After the attack, the republicans locked up fifteen to twenty of those who would not work with them on a deserted old farm north of Gearach. I assume they are still there."

"What of the rest of the crew?"

"The Irish told them that if they laid low for two weeks, they would release them. The week before the mission, they transferred groups to Port Askaig. I am not sure how they did it, but they are all now in Scotland."

"Would you show us where this deserted farm is, where the crew members are locked up?"

"No, Laddie! Why do you think I am wearing this balaclava? If anyone sees my face, I am a dead man. But I will draw you a map."

Robert was surprised at the amount of information this man was divulging. Was it the truth, or was it fiction? The map and the farm would confirm the fact.

"Mr Fenton. Some ink and paper, please?"

Soon Callum was drawing a crude map of the farm's location. He passed it across, and Robert examined it.

Robert quickly decided it was sufficient and asked, "Do you know the names of the whaling ships?"

"The 'Mary Chowan' and 'Tarquin Explorer' out of New Bedford."

"Why did the Irish execute all the officers except the captain?"

"When the Irish took *Providence*, the officers mounted the resistance. The crew were half-hearted and quickly surrendered. Most of the officers died in the battle. One of the Irish leaders later murdered the remaining officers. I have met this executioner, and he is a cold-blooded murderer. It is not a war for him. He enjoys killing!"

"So, where does your information come from, Mr Smith."

"Oh, here and there!"

"So, do you have any more information for us?"

"There is a lot more, Captain South, but first, we must strike a bargain."

"No bargains, Captain South!" A booming voice came from behind Robert. Major Coombes, in bare feet, wearing only his trousers and leather braces, joined the conversation.

Callum looked up at the large man now confronting him and asked, "And who might you be, Sir?"

Horace ignored the man and pulled Robert away from the conversation. Out of earshot, he quietly said, "I do not like this fellow, Robert. How do we know he is telling us the truth?"

"We might never know that! But he has a real Scottish accent and has shared some interesting information. We must visit the farm he has described on this map first thing in the morning! I suggest we play him for everything we can. He has been working for the Irish but has had a change of heart. Probably because of the humiliating defeat they have suffered. He wants some insurance."

Horace thumbed his chin and took another look at the man. As Major Coombes considered Smith, Swanton appeared with a coat and placed it around Horace's shoulders.

Horace turned and frowned at Robert, saying, "We will test this gentleman's story!"

Approaching Callum, Major Coombes quietly said, "For passage with us, Mr Smith, you must choose your side. If we visit this farm tomorrow and find nothing, it will be the gallows for you. So, tell me, who was the Irish leader here and where he came from?"

"I have already chosen my side, Sir. By being on this British deck, I have put my life in danger. I will tell you the details you require and more if you guarantee the safe passage of myself and my partner. But I prefer speaking with Captain South as I know his name."

"Well, you are talking now with Major Coombes, and if you tell us the truth, you will have safe passage. If not, then there is no agreement. I take it your partner is a female?"

"That is correct."

Callum looked at both Major Coombes and Captain South. Robert looked away. Clearly, the Major was in command, and Callum must make a final decision on who he could trust. He took a deep breath and answered.

"Major Coombes, the Irish leader, was a fellow called Aiden who comes from Cobh. I never heard his last name. He is about five foot ten inches, has a thick build, brown hair, and green eyes. He has a bad temper, and he executed your remaining officers himself.

All the Irish rebels were from Cobh and have returned there now. But there are others still on the island who I have not met. That is how they work – they are a secret society. They use Islay as a safe route into Glasgow. I can assure you they are watching.

You will understand now why I need your protection."

"Assuming you have told us the truth, I will provide you and your girl with safe passage. Be alongside late Saturday night in your boat, and we will give you accommodation. If you have been lying, we will find you before then. So, is there anything else, Mr Smith?"

"No. I will be off then, lad. See you Saturday night."

Callum turned and slowly climbed over the ship rail. He then descended into his boat. As he rowed away into the darkness, Robert observed, "Well, if he is telling the truth, then we now know what happened."

"Robert, I doubt his story, but we will test it tomorrow. I will take a large detachment with me in case it is a trap. He said the Irish are still here. So, where are they? Perhaps at Gearach! Double the guard tonight and keep it doubled until we leave on Sunday. While I am on this wild goose chase in the morning, you should start loading the barques. The sooner we are on our way home, the better."

Safe House, Port Charlotte, Isle of Islay ...
"Ruthy, wake up! I have some good news."

Ruth Walsh turned over and opened her eyes. The night at the pub with Lieutenant Sam Peters had been long and exhausting, and she was ready for a long sleep.

Callum checked that Ruth was fully awake before he began, "How did things go at the pub?"

"Got the information Dan wanted. I have hidden it away for you."

"Good, now listen. Do you remember how we talked about insurance, given the failure of the Irish here? Well, I have secured us a safe passage out of here."

Ruth sat up and smiled, "What do you mean, Callum? I thought we were going on the ferry from Port Asking and then into Glasgow."

"Ruth, the Irish have lost this battle. The British will soon round them up, and you know what will happen then. We must disappear. We can find a place in England, settle, and have a family."

"You think the battle is lost, Callum?"

"I am sure of it."

"How do you know that!"

"Ruth, I have met with the navy captain, Captain Robert South and the Army Commander, Major Coombes. They will give us protection for information. We will disappear from the brothers and be free."

"I hope you held back on the information just in case they do not keep their word?"

"I told them very little! But they still agreed. They must be desperate."

"Well, you have set us free then. When do we leave?"

"Saturday night late."

"Darling, come here. We have both had a hard night, but you have scored the most."

Callum pulled off his clothes and climbed in beside her. She pulled up her nightdress and let him pull her close.

"I love you so much, Ruthy! We will start a family and make a new life."

Ruth whispered, "Yes, Callum. A new life!"

She pulled him closer and opened her legs as he kissed her breasts and mounted her.

Callum never saw Ruth pull the knife, thrust it up through his throat into his brain, and then twist it as the instructor had taught her. His eyes opened in horror, and then they dulled as he died on top of her, the blood rolling down her face.

She grunted as she pushed him onto the floor, "You, damn traitor! Good riddance!"

Ruth washed, changed her dress, and packed as fast as she could. Time was now her enemy. She ran out the back door and hitched up the horse. She would make the early morning Glasgow ferry from Port Ellen if she started now. Ruth whipped the horse into a canter, the cart flying away towards the other side of Islay. She must warn Michael and the other brothers that trouble was coming. She did not look back.

The Grand Hotel, Kingston, Jamaica ...

Lady Clarissa Wendarm climbed into the carriage, seated herself and then looked down upon Fiona Green, who stood beside the open door.

"Now, Fiona, will you not embark with me? My business here is complete, and the estates are sold. I will be in London within two months, and we could celebrate the sales together. I will be so lonely on the trip home without you!"

"Someone must remain with Sir Hugh. He has no support here, and I may be of assistance in case of his death. He looks even worse today. I think Doctor Cowper's advice is, unfortunately, correct."

"Fiona, you are not a nurse. You are making a mistake! The man will be dead within a few days. Doctor Cowper will employ a nurse for his care. Come with me and depart this horrible place. There is still a day before the ship leaves. Plenty of time for packing and boarding the ship."

"No, Clarissa, my mind is made up. I will probably be on next month's ship, so I shall soon follow. Join me for a few days in Bedfordshire once I return. Have a nice time today."

Fiona closed the door and watched as the carriage moved away. As it sped up and headed towards the cricket club, Clarissa frowned and wondered why Fiona would waste her time on Sir Hugh. From Doctor Cowper's advice, Clarissa was under no doubt that Sir Hugh's health would fail in the next day or two and that Fiona would be left with the mess of his affairs. After all, he had an attorney who would clear up all those issues. The trouble with her friend was that she was too kind-hearted for her own good.

As the carriage stopped at the club, Mr Polkinghorne awaited her.

"I say, Lady Clarissa, I hear your friend Sir Hugh is unwell. I hope it is nothing serious?"

"Unfortunately, Stephen, poor Hugh may not last more than a day or two. The disease is fatal. Fiona, who was far closer than I with Sir Hugh, will remain in Kingston, oversee the arrangements, and attend the funeral. She will travel on the ship next month. I am afraid it was the climate – it was too much for him. Some fever, I understand."

"His family will be most upset on hearing the news."

"Yes, unfortunately, that job is mine. It will be a sorrowful occasion. However, I must do my duty."

Stephen Polkinghorne could see the distress on Clarissa's face and hugged her, "Oh, you poor thing! Perhaps you would care for some dinner with me tonight. We should toast this unfortunate fellow. It is the least we can do."

"Thank you, Stephen. You are so thoughtful and kind!"

"Now, come in quickly. We will have time for a quick lunch and drink before the players walk on for the second innings. Perfect day for it."

The Funeral of Mrs Eleanora Turner ...

The Reverend Andrew Taggart watched the Turner family quietly walk down the centre aisle towards the coffin. The Turner's home staff also joined them.

Madeline held Marcia's hand, with William following them. The church was packed, and the seven-year-old boy felt the eyes of the congregation watching him as they found their seating. For William being in church was an uncomfortable time as it meant sitting still and not talking. He often wondered why he was there as he had never heard God speak in here. William wondered if anyone else heard God speak. He must say something as they all enjoyed their time in church. But William thought God must be a dull person if he lived in a building such as this. It was cold, dark and had many things called crypts for famous dead people. The only living thing inside the church was the candles.

He sat at the end of the second row, near his mother's coffin. He wondered what it would be like lying in a coffin. It must be very cramped in there. How would his mother breathe? Marcia sat forward with her hands on the next pew, watching her father. William lent behind her and asked Ethel, "How would Mother breathe in that coffin?"

Ethel leant over and whispered, "She has passed away, William. You do not breathe once you are with Jesus." Unfortunately, William lifted his leg as he listened, accidentally knocking Marcia off the seat. She fell and then burst out crying in a loud voice.

Immediately Jonathan Turner looked behind him and found William looking down at Marcia, who stood up with a slight amount of blood on her lip where it had hit the tiled floor. Anne wiped Marcia's lip with a handkerchief, but it did not console the small five-year-old girl. Anne lifted her over the back of the pew and placed the child on her lap. Marcia, with her arms around Anne's neck, continued whimpering quietly.

With his rage growing, Jonathan asked, "Ethel, would you take him out into the vestibule, please? Make it quick before he causes any more trouble."

Ethel glared at Jonathan, clearly protesting, 'It is his mother's funeral, Mr Turner. Please, do not treat your son in this way!'

Jonathan ignored the look and insisted as he continued calming a crying Marcia.

A grim Ethel stood and escorted William out. William was glad of the direction as he became restless as the Reverend Andrew kept speaking and speaking. Ethel was embarrassed as she walked with William under everyone's eye in the church. She was aware of the comments passing between husbands and wives as they passed each pew.

Ethel and William found a seat in the vestibule where they could see straight up the centre aisle.

"Father always blames me for everything!"

Ethel, beside William, was glad they were now out of earshot and could talk privately.

"Your Father is stressed today, William. He is most upset about losing his wife. It would be best if you took care and did not annoy him."

"It does not matter what I do; he always punishes me. One day I will punish him."

"What do you mean, William?"

William looked up at Ethel thoughtfully. It took him nearly a minute before he answered.

"Anne told me I must not tell anyone outside our family about it. But you are family now, Ethel."

Ethel Nibley was both pleased by his answer and curious. She was about to speak when William continued, "Last year, I could not sleep and went downstairs peeking into mother's room. I was frightened as I saw father beating mother with his hand. He heard the door creak and saw me. I ran and hid in my bed upstairs. In the morning, after he had left for the bakery, I heard mother moaning, and there was lots of blood, and Anne sent for the doctor."

"He beat your mother?"

"Yes, I think he had done it before, as Anne told me. Ever since he saw me peeking in, he has hated me. He strapped my legs once so hard I could not stand up until Doctor Neville carried me into the kitchen and bathed my legs with salty water. I was so afraid."

"I am sure you were."

They sat in silence as the service continued.

"Ethel, why is Thomas standing up there, talking? It is usually Reverend Taggart talking."

"He is giving the eulogy, William. He tells everyone about your mother's life and how your family loved her."

"I know what a eulogy is. Father made a eulogy once for Doctor Stephens, who died. That day I was kept at home with Simeon. He had a broken arm. I did not mind as we were playing checkers."

"Shush, little man! We must not disturb the service."

Ethel sat there, wondering about what William had said. She knew Jonathan Turner disliked William in particular, but given what William had just told her, it took on a new perspective. Ethel had not been aware that Jonathan had beaten his wife. As far as she knew, he was a devoted husband and loved his wife dearly. She must treat this knowledge carefully. When the time was right, she would verify it with Mrs Jennings.

Ethel felt a tugging on her arm.

William whispered, "Can we play pirates at the river this afternoon?"

Ethel smiled, "Perhaps, but probably just a few of us, not everyone."

"Will you come, Ethel? I like you! I like talking with you."

Ethel smiled back at William. Then she looked up. The congregation were on their knees, praying. Sitting at the end of the pew beside his wife's coffin, Jonathan Turner turned and looked directly at William. There was no love in the look. It was cold and hinted at a slight hatred. Then he glanced up at Ethel, and the expression changed to a smile of thanks.

Ethel shivered. The look he gave William was frightening and from a man who wielded much power in this community. There were issues here that might be best left unsaid. It was clear that William would need protection. Protection from his father!

Ethel put her arm around William and pulled him close, "Yes, we will visit the river this afternoon. Perhaps, Simeon, Clemmie and Maddie might also come."

PART 2

"The sun peers through the clouds,
Our hearts are lifted, and warmth is all
around!"

February 1827, Isle of Wight

Chapter 9

Shanklin, Isle of Wight, off Portsmouth, England …

Anne and Robert wandered hand in hand down the hill from the small beach cottage they rented in Shanklin on the Isle of Wight. The February day was freezing, but the sun was out, and the ocean's vast glistening blue waters stretched away in front of them into a misty horizon.

"You were fortunate spending all your boyhood vacations out here, Robert!"

'It seemed normal at the time, but now I appreciate it even more! It is a beautiful place."

As they reached the steps down onto the beach, Anne let go of Robert's hand and ran off, kicking away her shoes and dipping her feet in the icy water. It was cool and refreshing, and she waded in further, wetting the brim of her dress as she enjoyed the sensation.

"I could stay here forever!" In her nineteen years of life, this was Anne's first experience of the seaside.

Turning, she saw Robert on the beach, removing his shoes and stockings. She giggled as he wrestled with them. Soon he was beside her.

Anne spoke her thoughts, "I wish we could be together here forever!"

"We could, as my family own a small residence just along at Luccombe Bay, but I decided on neutral territory for the first two weeks of our married life. No family, no servants, just us! Except for Molly Carter, of course! I felt we should employ a cook for the honeymoon, and she lives elsewhere, so why not?"

Anne gazed up into Robert's smiling brown eyes. "Would we have time this morning for a visit? This small mansion where you spent your boyhood holidays sounds interesting."

"Certainly! After lunch, I will arrange a carriage, but it will only be the verandahs as it is locked in the winter. I think you will enjoy seeing its position. Even better, we could stay there when I return from the Mediterranean! Father sends a team of servants down in early spring for yearly maintenance and cleaning. We shall plan a vacation there with both our families?"

"That would be wonderful. My brothers and sisters have never seen the sea. The time here has been a dream, Darling!" She moved closer, kissing him gently on the lips.

Anne imagined, "When we have children, do you think they will have brown eyes like you?"

"Perhaps. With your blue eyes and my brown, they may have green or grey eyes!"

Anne stood back from Robert with a mischievous grin on her face. Then suddenly, taking Robert by surprise, she lunged forward and pushed him into the shallow water.

Not expecting this, Robert fell heavily backwards, and the freezing water drenched him. He screamed, "Oh, that is cold!"

Jumping up quickly, he started smiling, "I think it is time, Lady Anne South, for your first swimming lesson!"

"No! No, Robert – it is winter and too cold!"

With that, he sprang upon her amazingly quickly, and despite Anne's effort at escape, he caught her, swinging Anne up into his arms. As she screamed, squirming and kicking madly, he carried her further into the deeper water.

"Don't you dare, Robert!" she screamed with joy.

"You do not want the boys ahead of you in their swimming lessons, do you? Now, remember, Anne, pinch your nose and hold your breath!" With that, he dropped her screaming into the water.

Anne went totally under and surfaced like a drowned rat. She gasped as the waist-deep water was like ice. Despite the wet clothes clinging against her body and struggling with her footing, Robert could see the determined expression on her face. He backed towards the shore, laughing as Anne chased him onto the beach.

Other holidaymakers joined them at the water's edge as the sun gradually rose in the sky, slightly warming the day. A breeze from the sea chilled them through their wet clothes, and Anne called a truce, pointing towards their seaside cottage.

It was a week since the wedding in Guildford, and Robert was enjoying being a married man. As an aristocrat on the family estate near Petersfield, he had little companionship in his childhood except for his brother, sister, and a few family acquaintances. When he met Anne by chance, his world changed.

He would always be thankful for Anne's younger brother, William Turner, whose influence on events last year had forever changed his life. Since joining the navy, he, of necessity, had mixed with all classes of society but found the middle class a refreshing change from the tightly guarded relationships of the upper class. He was still proud of his position in life but clearly understood that the world was changing, and with the advent of steam power, a revolution was occurring. The changes in industry would issue in a new era of entrepreneurs who would become the wealthy of the nation.

As they walked hand in hand back up the hill, they were not short of conversation, and Robert loved talking freely with his vivacious wife.

"Anne, I wonder if farming estates like my father's at Fintelton will survive in the coming decades. What is your opinion?"

"Where did that come from, Robert? We are on our honeymoon! Surely you should be thinking about how beautiful your bedraggled wife is or what we can do during our last week?"

"Well, I am thinking about other things as well."

Anne knew Robert was most concerned about the financial affairs of his father's estate. He was a dedicated son and still felt his duty keenly despite not being the heir. She smiled, thinking about what a good man he was.

"I think given the right management, they will survive! Improved productivity from new technology and science will assist. As my father is experimenting with steam in his new flour mill, your father must invest in new machinery. But Robert, right now, I need some warm, dry clothes and a wonderful breakfast overlooking the ocean."

"What do you think of the ocean, Anne?"

"I love its vastness and the different blue colours that mix and match as the passing sun shines at different angles. It is beautiful. But it also scares me as I know you will soon be sailing out of sight, and I will be alone."

She hugged him hard as she trembled with the thought.

"I am sorry I cannot take you to the Mediterranean, but the Admiral would not hear of it for some reason. Perhaps next time! I hope Neville has arranged that house for us. We will only have a few days setting up before I must be off."

"Then we will make the most of it, my Darling!"

"I wonder if Molly has cooked more of that crispy bacon this morning! The ocean air has made me hungry."

"Me too. Come on! Let's find out."

They hurried up the stairs and onto the front porch of the cottage. Robert stopped and looked at Anne with the sea behind her.

"I will remember you right here, right now. It will be what I think of each day as we are apart."

"Oh, Robert, do not go. Leave the navy and stay with me forever?"

"You know I can't, Anne. But we are together now and let us make as many memories as we can, so we keep close while I am away."

He wiped away the tears from her eyes and gently pushed her cheeks into a happy face. She burst out with the most beautiful smile, half laughing, half crying as they held each other close.

"Sir Robert, Sir Robert, there is an urgent letter here for you. Lady Anne, come in and change before you catch a cold. Let me help you with those wet things. There is a lovely breakfast ready, Sir Robert."

Anne kissed Robert and took Molly's hands, "Thank you, Molly. You have taken such good care of us!"

The little lady blushed and squeezed Anne's hand before following her into the bedroom.

Robert inspected the envelope with interest. "Ah, a letter from the Admiral!"

Opening the letter, Robert found a short note advising that the Admiral required him back earlier than expected. There was an immediate change in plans which directly affected HMS *Shadow*. The Admiral requested his presence next Tuesday morning.

"New orders! Now, where are they sending me?"

The Bassington Household, Guildford, Surrey …

Bethany came into the breakfast room yawning and hugged Neville. He kissed Bethany and then concentrated on finishing his bowl of hot porridge before leaving for the surgery.

"Oh, I slept so well, Neville. I am so glad you purchased this house for us. I feel like it is our home now."

"I wish it could be larger; however, that will come in time."

Bethany smiled, "I am so happy, Neville. The house we have is perfect."

Neville looked around and called the housekeeper, "I say, Mrs Goodhew! Mrs Bassington is down for breakfast."

Ivy Goodhew poked her head around the corner, "Very well, Doctor. It will be ready soon."

"Thank you, Ivy."

"Darling Bethany, you know I would spend every minute of my life with you, but I must visit London the week after next. I am meeting with several hospital surgeons who allocate the treatment of trauma accidents. They have heard of my naval experience and are seeking a meeting. It is an opportunity to gain clients in London. Will you join me at my parents' home as they are keen that we both visit? From there, we can easily attend the memorial for Mrs Steele on the Friday."

"I understand, Neville, and I will miss you too. How the time has flown; it seems no time since our October wedding! But I promised Anne I would be here when she returned. She will struggle with Robert being away so soon after their marriage. So, I must remain here. Perhaps we might come up together and meet you at the memorial service. This may help Anne cope with Robert's departing for the Mediterranean."

"That is a fine idea. We can all share a coach back after the service. I hope Robert and Anne are happy with how we set out their furniture at 'Porting'. But now, I must be off. Many appointments are waiting for me at the surgery today!"

Bethany waved him goodbye as he strode off with his medical bag towards the town centre. She was thankful for her husband and their sweet and simple life. It was time for breakfast and checking on her father and his household.

As Bethany was eating her egg, she felt a strange, unpleasant sickness in her stomach that kept increasing. Then she rushed from the room. Ivy Goodhew was surprised as Bethany ran past into the mudroom and vomited in a large wash basin.

Ivy helped her young mistress and made sympathetic comments.

Soon Bethany felt somewhat better and stood up, "My goodness, Ivy. I am sure it was not breakfast. Perhaps I am sick!"

Ivy Goodhew smiled knowingly, "Perhaps not, Mrs Bassington. Right time of the morning! I think I know what it is!"

The Turner Household, Guildford ...

Jonathan Turner sat at the dining table with Thomas and Marion as Mrs Jennings and Aggie served morning tea.

Marion admiring the setting, commented, "Thank you, Mrs Jennings and Aggie. It looks scrumptious!"

Jonathan, keen on continuing the conversation, nodded in agreement, "Yes, it does! That will be all now, Mrs Jennings and Aggie. Thank you."

Once the staff were out of earshot, Jonathan asked, "So, it sounds like the time you spent in Scotland with James McPherson turned rather ugly?"

"No, Father, we had a splendid time with James, but when Mr & Mrs McPherson arrived, James quietly suggested we dine out the first night, allowing him some time with his parents. Hamish and Marjorie were somewhat shocked by his news. They had not met Isla before, and James was unsure they would understand their relationship. He was correct on that issue!"

"Was the girl the cause of the problems?"

"Yes and No. It appears both James and Isla are content with not marrying. The issues of religion are too great for them, so they decided to ignore our society's traditional expectations. Given his position in the company, I fear he has displayed a lack of judgement. James's determined stand took Mr McPherson by surprise. I understand Mr McPherson tried to avoid any argument as best he could. He must love his son dearly, given how much he suffered in maintaining the relationship. I think James and Isla are pushing too hard."

"Thomas, do you understand why James is so determined?"

"Well, how long have you got, Father? It is quite complex. We left the day after, rushing back for Mrs Steele's funeral and then here for Mother's. Much organisation was required in Woolwich as Mr Steele's household was in a mess!"

Marion smiled, "Thomas is kind, Mr Turner, about our household in Woolwich. The house looked like a battlefield, and I think my father had words again with the boys. It is all sorted now. I hope we see some of them visiting down here soon."

Thomas continued, "I only spoke with him at times, but in James' position as General Manager of a brewery, his attitude could destroy the trust relationship with their customers. The population is mostly Presbyterian, and relations with the Church of Scotland and the Catholics are strained."

Jonathan smiled but seemed far away, "Marion, I am glad all the difficulties are solved. Now you and Thomas, please join us for dinner as I must hear about your honeymoon. Especially Paris, unfortunately, I never took Mrs Turner there …!"

Jonathan sat uncomfortably in his chair in a slight daze. It was obvious he was thinking of his wife and now needed space.

Marion heard the baby crying and excused herself. She was keen on seeing the little one fed as she had high hopes of having a baby soon. Not that she had told Thomas this yet.

Once she was gone, Thomas looked at his father and said, "Father, I know that you still grieve for mother. Please be assured that Marion and I are here for you. You are not alone, Father."

Jonathan looked up and smiled, "Thank you, Son. I will recover in time. Be patient with me for a few months, please. Thomas, I will not attend Jennifer Steele's memorial service next week. I fear I may break down on such an occasion. Please make my apologies and tell Alexander that it is too soon for me. Too soon."

Shanklin, Isle of Wight …

The weather had closed in during the late afternoon, and a slight rain fell. Robert sat beside the fire gazing out the window across the calm sea. The coach ride around Luccombe Bay was enjoyable, and further inland, the mansion provided a total surprise for Anne. The house was immense, with large expansive verandahs and ocean views. Anne wondered about the cost of maintaining such a property. She began understanding why the estate must make money as the overheads of a holiday mansion and a city house would increase the already spiralling Fintelton estate expenses.

As Anne joined Robert with a cup of coffee, she was fascinated by the view of the sea, "Look, Robert, the colour of the sea was blue, but now it is grey. It is vast, cold and frightening!"

"Sorry, Anne. I was not watching. Yes, it does that as the clouds come over!"

"Robert, you were miles away. What is bothering you?"

"I was thinking about my last voyage. I am still unsure how the Irish discovered our precise route details. How did they know where we would be and with enough time to marshall such a force? Sorry, Anne. Would you like some red or white wine?"

"No, thank you. I have coffee here. You are off in your navy world again! But what do you mean by 'how did they know'? I thought a crew member gave them the information?"

"Well, both Foster and Hughes had orders setting out precise routes and staging points. In both cases, the Irish were waiting for them. There was no way the crew could have known their orders in advance and passed the information off the ship. Along the way, there were no ports of call, so no opportunity there. Somehow, the republicans knew in advance of their precise movements.

In my case, they had men on the ship and tried entering my cabin. I had always thought they were after my orders. Looking back at it, given Lieutenant Small was an Irish republican, perhaps they were not after my orders at all but planned on killing me that night and taking control of the ship. Also, how did they know in advance that Portsmouth was our destination? The attack on the return journey may have been a planned second attempt after the first action failed."

Anne was worried about what Robert disclosed but also considered the facts, ordering them logically in her mind. If it were a business problem, how would she address it? Perhaps she could help.

"So, you are confused because there are similarities?"

"Yes. I can't get past how the Republicans knew our routes for each mission in advance."

"Let me assist but forgive me if this is simplistic."

"Anne, sometimes the most complex problems are solved by a simple conclusion that we have all disregarded."

Anne sat back, looking away from the sea, and faced her husband, "The first step is clearly understanding the problem. In this case, the problem is how the Irish knew your orders. This is the common thread."

"Yes."

"It seems that there are only two possibilities. The first is that on each occasion, a crew member alerted the republicans."

"I agree, but there was no opportunity. I spoke with Foster and questioned him about that; he was adamant there was no chance. In the report made by Hughes, there were similar statements."

"Robert, let us say that Foster and Hughes kept their orders secure. We also know yours were secure. So, we can assume no persons had access before the ship's departure."

"Yes, Anne, I know that. What is the other possibility?"

"Well, it is simple, Robert. Someone ashore who had access spilled the beans!"

Robert looked hard at Anne. He had assumed that the Fleet Commander's offices were secure. Yet, he had no proof confirming this.

"You mean someone in the Navy ashore leaked this information?"

"Yes. Some person in the Fleet Commander's offices. After all, Lieutenant Small was an Irish sympathiser!"

Robert stood and again gazed at the horizon, now masked in clouds and fog. Was this possible? Surely the Republicans had not infiltrated Fleet Headquarters. But what other explanation was there?

"Anne, I think you have raised an alternative I have discarded from the start. I have always believed the internal workings of the navy are secure. Perhaps that is a naïve assumption. Now I must revise my thinking on this. But if this is true, where do I start?"

"Robert! Given what has transpired, it may be preferable not to trust anyone until you are sure of their honesty. I may not be much help as I know little about the navy. Usually, over time, anyone who is dishonest will make a mistake. Something will show up. Until then, you must take care. I will let you consider that, as the navy is not my department. But your father's estate now is, and I will need your assistance on Monday before we leave Portsmouth."

Robert was still thinking about the Fleet Commander's Office. He was still not convinced.

"Robert! I will need your help on Monday, please!"

"Certainly, Anne. What is it you have in mind?"

Anne explained the conversation with the Lions Bank Manager before their wedding. The situation was delicate as the evidence pointed towards Sir Hugh's involvement with the Estate's shortage of funds. Having been married only two weeks, she would not blame Robert's brother at this stage. It would be better if Robert came to that conclusion himself.

"Robert, I suspect that Mrs Constance is somehow involved. Mr Meyhew gave me, in confidence, the details of her referees. I must visit each of them on Monday morning, and I would like you with me for support. There may be a connection as Mrs Constance was at the bank when the money disappeared. If that is the case, we must find out what her involvement was."

"So, once you have this further information from the bank and the information from the referees of Mrs Constance, we may find where the missing money has gone."

"Possibly, but I may need to make more enquiries. I am now sure that it is not the tenant farmers. Their accounts are fully paid up except for the two Mr Stem is currently managing."

"Anne, the Admiral has requested my presence on Tuesday morning, so it may be best if we take some accommodation in Portsmouth. Unfortunately, I will not be able to accompany you to Fintelton. I am sorry, but I must leave the setting up of our house for you. Anyway, let us see what the Admiral requires on Tuesday. I will send a rider with a message if the change is significant."

The River Wey, Guildford …

Simeon and William walked along the riverbank towards their favourite spot for sailing the *Ellena*. Taking them by surprise, two boys were already present with another sailboat. William recognised one of the boys as Archie, who had joined them several times before.

Simeon called out, "Archie! Archie! We are here!"

Archie Watson stood up and welcomed them, "Hi, Simeon and William. Meet my friend Levi Spencer. He attends the Free School with me."

The boys nodded at each other but were more interested in the sailing boat that Levi held.

William said, "Hey, that's the boat we saved up for before Christmas. How did you get it?"

Levi said, "It was a Christmas present."

"It is a beauty. We asked the shopkeeper if there was another, but he told us not until next year. So, Doctor Sopwith helped us build a boat. The '*Ellena*.'"

William held up their little sailing boat with much pride. The boys spent some minutes admiring each other's boats, questions flying between them.

"Levi, show us how your boat sails!"

The boys watched as Levi carefully launched his sailing boat, pointing it parallel to the riverbank. The model sailed along beautifully, and soon the boys organised races with much cheering at each finish.

A sudden gust of wind blew Levi's boat towards the centre of the river. Levi waded into the deeper water but soon found himself floundering as the current pulled him out.

"I can't swim!"

The boys watched with open mouths as Levi disappeared beneath the surface. William wasted no time and dived into the water and pulled him up.

Grabbing William, Levi shouted again, "I can't swim!"

"I can! Hold on, and we will drift into the bank."

Levi was a bit taller than William and was panicking. He hugged William tight, pulling him down, and suddenly they both submerged. Simeon gathered a branch and ran along the bank beside them. When William's head came up, he called, "Here, Will. Grab this!"

The branch was long enough and gave William some stability as he pulled up Levi, who was coughing up swallowed water. Simeon and Archie helped them onto the bank, and the two boys stood there shivering from the cold water.

Levi was still coughing as Archie asked, "You swim well, Will? Who taught you?"

"Doctor Sopwith and Dr Bassington!"

Simeon added, "We learnt in the Mens Club's pool. The water is heated, and it is fun. William is a better swimmer than me. But we both can swim well now, and we will improve in July when we holiday on the Isle of Wight."

Archie explained, "Wow, I wish I could swim. My father never taught me that."

Levi piped up, half coughing and spluttering, "Me too!"

Simeon said, "Let's recover your boat from under that weeping willow, and then we can ask Doctor Sopwith about lessons. If we use this branch, we might reach your boat. No more swimming in the river, hey!"

They all agreed and set off on their mission.

The Guildford Medical Practice …

Doctor Neville Bassington, knowing David Sopwith was currently free, poked his head around the door.

"David, before you see your next patient, I should remind you of my being away the week beginning Monday twenty-sixth of February. I will be addressing a group of doctors in London and visiting some hospitals that week."

David smiled, "Yes, I had that in my diary. You will be back the following Monday, given my wedding is coming up?"

"Yes, you can depend on that."

"That should be fine, Neville. I will need you available in Petersfield on Thursday afternoon for the rehearsal and then Friday evening. You will be the best man if Robert does not turn up!"

"I have not forgotten, and I will be there."

"Fine then. I hope it all goes well."

"Thanks, David."

After Neville had left, David sat back and considered the coming weeks. He was somewhat worried as he knew that operating the practice with one doctor was becoming difficult. From his experience of Guildford, he knew that a sudden rush would usually follow when appointment numbers were low. He would need some help while Neville was away.

"Doctor Sopwith, four young boys are begging if you would see them." Jenny Swift, the practice nurse and receptionist, smiled, waiting for his response.

"Four boys! Who are they?"

"Two of them are the Turner boys. I'm not sure who the others are."

David checked his appointments and found he had ten spare minutes, "Bring them in, please, Jenny."

The nurse was back in a few minutes with the boys. William and Levi had towels wrapped around them.

"Good afternoon, Simeon and William. Who are your friends?"

Simeon took a big breath and said, "Doctor Sopwith, please meet Archie Watson and Levi Spencer. We were down at the river sailing boats, and Levi fell in. William dived in and pulled him up, and I held out a branch, and we got him ashore."

"Good morning, Archie and Levi. I was wondering why you and William had towels around you. Are you all right, boys?"

"Yes, Doctor, but a bit cold." Levi was shaking slightly.

"Levi, sit down beside the fire and warm yourself up. You sit beside Levi, William! It is dangerous sailing boats in the river if you cannot swim. Perhaps you should find another spot?"

Seeing his opportunity, William said, "Doctor Sopwith, would you include Archie and Levi in our swimming lessons? Neither of them can swim, and they need lessons."

David Sopwith sat back in his chair, surveying the eager young faces. He did not have time for this, especially with Neville away in London next week and his wedding coming up. But Levi had already fallen into the river, and the boys understood the danger. They were being responsible with their request.

"Let me see!" David opened his diary and turned over several pages. He found the date he was looking for, "Our next lesson is on Monday at five pm. Ah, sorry! Now I remember another appointment that clashes with that. If we make it the Tuesday, that should be fine. There is, however, an issue. I cannot look after all four of you at once, so I will need your fathers present for the lesson and their prior approval. They must see me before next Tuesday, please. How does that sound?"

The boys all nodded in agreement, and David could see the excitement on their faces.

"Good. Your fathers must give permission and understand what we are doing. Please make sure they visit me. Understood?"

They all agreed.

"Good! Now I must go as I have a patient coming soon. Levi and William ask the nurse for another towel each and go home quickly and get on some dry, warm clothes."

"Yes, Doctor Sopwith."

The boys excitedly thanked the doctor and then quietly left his office. David was impressed by their good manners.

The Grand Hotel, Kingston, Jamaica …

Nurse Jackson gave an early morning knock on Fiona Green's hotel door, "Mrs Green, Doctor Cowper has nearly finished Sir Hugh's examination. He wondered if he might consult with you?" Fiona rushed down the hall in her dressing gown before the doctor left. Doctor Cowper carried a grave face as he explained, "Mrs Green, I am amazed Sir Hugh has lasted this long. His condition is considerably worse. I must advise you that the crisis is coming quickly, and I fear the disease will claim him today. If I do not receive a message from you, I will not return until late this afternoon. The nurse on the next shift will return within the hour."

"Thank you, Doctor. I am sure that Sir Hugh could not have better care anywhere else. I am most grateful."

The Doctor gave a slight smile as he left while Nurse Jackson remained stationed near Sir Hugh's bed, ensuring that a young boy, cord in hand, kept a fan waving from the ceiling.

After breakfast, Fiona Green met with Lady Clarissa Wendarm, who was checking out of the hotel. Fiona and Clarissa had booked return tickets, but Fiona cancelled at the last minute.

"Fiona! Are you sure you will not change your mind and come home with me? There is still plenty of time. If you packed quickly, you could make the port in time."

"No, Clarissa! As I said last night, someone must remain with Sir Hugh as he has no family here. The Doctor expects he will not last the day, and I must stay with him until the end. I will probably catch the ship next month."

Clarissa sighed and started waving her fan quickly, "Fiona, you are under no obligation. I think you are making a mistake, but of course, you always did have a good heart. Send me a note when you have returned."

As they walked down the front steps, Fiona said, "When I return, please visit me at Bedfordshire, and you might stay a few days. Here is a letter for Sir Hugh's parents advising them of the situation. Would you mail it as soon as you reach England? They must be made aware of Sir Hugh's condition."

"Certainly, Fiona!"

A tall, handsome man suddenly appeared from the waiting carriage. Stephen Polkinghorne greeted Fiona.

"Good morning, Fiona. It is a beautiful day for travel. I hope you are well?"

"Yes, thank you, Stephen. I must advise that it may be a sad day."

"Ah! I understand you are concerned for Sir Hugh?"

"Yes, the end is very near."

"Fiona, might I say I am impressed that you are remaining by his side. Given the circumstances, I think you are very gallant."

Lady Clarissa was becoming impatient and scolded her travelling companion, "Well, Stephen, we must be on our way. We share the carriage, Fiona, as Stephen is travelling on the same ship today. What a pleasant coincidence! Well, I shall see you in London."

With that, Stephen Polkinghorne doffed his hat and boarded the carriage as Clarissa tapped the roof. Fiona watched as the coach moved off and descended the hill, turning the corner towards the port. She sighed, feeling the heat increase from the hot sun.

Nurse Jackson tapped her on the shoulder, "Mrs Green, please come quickly. It appears the crisis has come."

"Oh, No!"

Fiona followed Nurse Jackson up the stairs and found another nurse wiping Sir Hugh's face with a cold washer. He thrashed and groaned in his sleep, calling out, "Kathy, Kathy! You must not. Never again, please!"

Fiona sat silently as Sir Hugh fought against the fever that racked his body. He occasionally ranted in his delirium and called out for this girl, "Kathy, Kathy!"

Nurse Jackson sat beside Fiona and quietly asked, "Do you know who this 'Kathy' girl is?"

"No, I am afraid not. I only met Sir Hugh on the way from England, and his main companion was Lady Clarissa. I know little of his history except for this Kingston trip and some details of his plantations. Oh, and of course, dinner with the Governor."

"I see."

Sir Hugh suddenly sat up straight on the bed and shouted, "The Countess, The Countess!"

Nurse Jackson and Fiona took one of his shoulders each and lay him back down. They wiped his brow and face, and Hugh fell into a deep sleep.

Guildford, Surrey, England ...

Doctor Bryan Watson sat at the dinner table, saying, Grace. Being an active Presbyterian, he enjoyed saying a long Grace, but Archie despised them. When Archie was hungry, he often wondered where his father found all the inclusions in the long prayer of thanks before the meal. Once finished and dinner began, Archie raised the issue of swimming lessons with his father.

"Father, I think it is essential that I have some swimming lessons. Levi could have drowned today except with the help of Simeon and William. What if it had been me?"

"It would not have been you, Archie, as you are smarter and would not fall in the river."

Bryan was tired and worried. They had been in Guildford for nearly four weeks with little work or prospects, and their financial reserves were running low. The shortage of money would soon force their relocation. Plenty of jobs were available in the London hospitals, but living in the city again was not attractive.

"Bryan, I think Doctor Sopwith's request is generous. I am sure he is busy, and his offer to sacrifice his time is well-intentioned. Also, it would be good if you met another Doctor in the community rather than at work."

"I'm not so sure, Jessica. I had no response from Dr Sopwith or Dr Bassington about my employment enquiry. I feel they are a bit self-important and rude, so I cannot but think poorly of them. Surely, a simple reply stating they had no staff vacancies at present was not too much to ask?"

"Bryan, are you sure they received your letter?"

"No, but I am certain they would have."

"Well, go and meet this Doctor Sopwith and discuss the swimming lessons. While you are there, ask about your letter."

Archie held his breath as his father sat back and reconsidered if he would swallow his pride.

After two minutes of silence, he said, "Cannot hurt, can it? I will meet with Doctor Sopwith and discuss the swimming lessons. Archie, we can discuss the outcome tomorrow night at dinner. Now no more about this tonight, please."

Archie smiled at his mother and then heartily attacked his dinner. Jessica Watson was pleased that her husband would swallow his pride.

In the morning, Bryan decided he would see Doctor Sopwith before calling at Woodbridge Hill. He was unsure if Doctor Chenning would provide him with any work today, but it was worth the trip as he required employment.

On entering the surgery, he was impressed with the decor and the friendly receptionist.

"I wonder if I might quickly see Doctor Sopwith, please."

"I am sorry he is not taking appointments as he visits his country patients this morning. Might I give you an appointment for tomorrow?"

"Forgive me, please! I should have explained. I am Doctor Bryan Watson. It is a private matter about swimming lessons for my son Archie. The Doctor asked if I would call."

Jenny Swift looked up in recognition, "Certainly, let me see if I can catch him."

The nurse quickly walked down the hallway, entering the second doorway. On returning, she smiled, "Follow me, please."

Doctor Sopwith stood and shook Bryan Watson's hand.

"Please have a seat, Doctor Watson. I have been expecting you for some time. You enquired in early December about employment, and I replied but have heard nothing since. I am glad you came in. How are you enjoying Guildford?"

Bryan Watson was surprised by the welcome and enjoyed the talk with Doctor Sopwith, which lasted for about fifteen minutes.

"The reason for our move requires explanation. I would appreciate your keeping this confidential, but Port Charlotte was taken over by Irish nationalists early last November. They captured an English frigate and hid the ship in the bay there. The English came and retook the frigate but not after a bloody battle. Following this, the Irish held my son hostage, threatening his life if I did not tend to their injured. Of course, our profession aims to preserve life, so I would have helped anyway. However, before they left Port Charlotte, they made death threats if I ever mentioned any names.

The threat encouraged our relocation and our disappearance from Scotland. I had memories of Guildford as a boy and thought I would return here and seek work. I considered it far enough away from the Irish."

"I understand how terrifying that would have been, and I will keep it confidential. So, do you have work?"

"Only when Doctor Chenning has too many patients, which is not often. I am thankful for the work, but it is not the type of opportunity I am looking for."

"I see. Well, my partner, Doctor Bassington, will be away the week after next in London. Then, I will be away on my honeymoon for six weeks. I am worried about one Doctor handling the workload over the next two months, so I am looking for assistance. Would you come next Monday, meet Doctor Bassington, my partner, and do a week's trial with me? After that, we can talk about the future. You could advise Doctor Chenning you will be unavailable next week but back on call after that. No point in cutting the ties before we decide."

"I would much appreciate the opportunity, Doctor Sopwith. I am off there in case they have any appointments for me today. I will advise Doctor Chenning and present here on Monday morning."

"And the help with the swimming lessons? There will be no charge, but I need the assistance of yourself and Mr Spencer if possible."

"Yes, I will be there."

"I usually have Doctor Bassington with me, but I understand he is unavailable that day. He is a fine swimmer and a good instructor. My methods are more practical. Do you swim, yourself?"

"A little! It has been some time, but I remember the basics. I swam in the river near the University of Glasgow[15], but it was as cold as ice. Certainly, the temperature of the water encouraged fast swimming."

"The water at the Men's Club is heated, so that will not be a problem. If Archie does not have swimming trunks, then a pair of old shorts and a towel will be fine. We start at five pm. No patients will be booked here after four-thirty so we can get away."

"That is a good plan."

"Are you heading for Doctor Chenning's surgery at Woodbridge Hill? My first patient is near Worplesdon. Might I offer you a ride in my carriage?"

"Thank you, Doctor, that would be most kind of you."

David Sopwith was a good judge of character and liked Bryan Watson. The problem he foresaw would be convincing Neville. Perhaps a financial incentive might help.

McPherson Residence, Greenwich ...

The Butler, Jenkins, made the introduction, "Mr McPherson, Mrs Stubbington."

"Janet, good morning. Your discussions with the directors must have been prompt. I will welcome your advice."

"Good day, Hamish. How was the Fintelton wedding?"

"It was a marvellous affair and so many guests. Marjorie was so pleased with the contacts she made. She is running a charity now for the countess. Lady Jane requires a quieter life due to the Earl's health and will seldom visit London in the future. So, Marjorie readily agreed with the plea for help."

Janet Stubbington smiled but was not one for straying and said, "Hamish, it would be best if you visited Guildford soon. Jonathan Turner and his son Thomas need your counsel."

"That will not be necessary as Jonathan and his son will attend the London memorial service for Jennifer Steele. I will talk with them then."

"Hamish, I think you will find Jonathan has declined the invitation. I would advise you to depart on Saturday and meet with him Monday. Your business partner mourns his wife and requires someone with the strength who can snap him out of it. See if you can help him, please!"

Hamish McPherson agreed and wondered what Janet would say next.

"You will recall our conversation last week. At length, I have discussed your son James's marital status and nonconformist lifestyle with my directors. They agree that he cannot continue in Glasgow. We suggest expanding your brewing operations with James as the General Manager for Ireland. This business expansion will give the Grey Line a legitimate reason for regular voyages in and out of Cobh. Purchase a warehouse and a few pubs and see

---

[15] University of Glasgow was established in 1451. See 'www.gla.ac.uk'

what develops. While you construct your brewery in Guildford, we suggest Thomas Turner resides in Glasgow as the new interim manager. He should work under the supervision of Lachlan. It will be some excellent mentoring for him. Also, he can visit Guildford regularly and review the brewery's construction."

Hamish had partially hoped for what Janet suggested. This path would avoid challenging James over his radical views on marriage and continue their good relationship. His wife, Marjorie, would also be pleased with this outcome. Mrs Stubbington's suggestion that Thomas Turner's move north was one he had not predicted, but he liked the idea.

"I think your suggestions have merit, Janet. I will act on them! Please assure me you will not involve James in any political skullduggery?"

"I cannot do any such thing, Hamish. As I said at our last meeting, James is his own man and will decide where he stands. It would be advisable if you are not heavily involved in the Irish move, please."

Hamish could see they had something in mind for James. He would not argue the point now, but he must find a way of warning his son.

"Also, Hamish, while you are in Guildford, please chat with young Anne Turner, now Lady Anne South. If I am correct, Jonathan's recovery will be drawn out. Lady Anne is an impressive operator, but she will need a mentor. She is young and lacks experience. The bakery business must continue growing. While Jonathan regains his countenance, Lady Anne will lead that organisation. You and I know just how hard that will be for a woman. With your business knowledge, I am sure you can assist her with mentoring on this.

Lady South has a friend who is vitally interested in fashion. Perhaps the time is right for an expansion of Hursts into London. We will ensure she gains the right clientele. With the countess and your wife as contacts, the business will flourish.

I will leave this in your hands, Hamish. Now I must be off. Much on the Agenda for today. Thank you for your time."

The Turner Household, Guildford ...

Ethel waited until the children were in bed and peace had descended on the household. Since Mrs Turner's death and Anne's marriage, Ethel's duties had increased significantly. She spent much time with the children reassuring them of their security. Jonathan Turner had become a recluse, locking himself away in his study most nights. It was time for a discussion with Mr Turner about her future duties.

She went to the study and knocked.

Jonathan Turner opened the door, a handkerchief dabbing his eyes, "Ah, Ethel. How may I be of assistance?"

"Please forgive me for disturbing you, Mr Turner, but we should talk as there are issues you must address. I understand your great loss and that overcoming the grief is difficult, but I must clarify my duties with you while I remain in your service."

"Why, Ethel, we could not survive without you! At present, you are holding this family together. I struggle with the loss of Eleanora and worry that if I have too much contact with the children, I will make things worse."

Ethel remembered the difficult years after the loss of her husband. She realised Jonathan's grief would not be short-lived, but the children needed their father now.

"Mr Turner, as you know, I lost my husband some years ago, and I, too, went through a grieving process. My situation left me in dire circumstances, which increased my feeling of loss. Being with my daughter somewhat lessened the effect as we both encouraged each other. I think by locking yourself away, your anguish may increase. At present, your daughters are struggling with the loss of their mother. They need a hug from their father often during these times. More contact with your children will also help you."

"I had forgotten your situation, Ethel. I am ashamed of my selfishness. Thank you for reminding me of my role. Let me summon some strength overnight; tomorrow, I will be with them more. Our family has benefited greatly from the comfort you provide. I have not those skills, Ethel."

"Thank you, Mr Turner, for the compliment. You will recall that my position is Mrs Turner's lady's maid with various other household duties. Please excuse me for asking this. As Mrs Turner is no longer with us, I need clarification of what services you require, and if so, in what capacity."

"I am sorry, Ethel. I have been concentrating on myself and have disregarded the family. What do you suggest?"

Ethel took a step backwards as she considered an answer that would not stir anger in this man. She was becoming aware of his rage problem, which confounded his grief. But she needed communication on what his expectations were regarding the household.

"Mr Turner, I am unsure what the future will be, but at present, your children need an ordered household where they can find stability and love. Firstly, your ongoing contact with the children is crucial, particularly for the struggling girls. The boys are adjusting, but I am unsure what lies under the surface. They come to me for reassurance, aware that you are indisposed. However, there is only so much I can give them, Mr Turner. I am no substitute for their father or mother. Sir, you must come out of your study and be with them more. You are the one who provides their security, comfort, and leadership. They hunger for meaningful communication with you.

For the household, I would like your permission for my position to become the Housekeeper. Someone must control the staff. Mrs Jennings is an excellent cook; however, she does not have the skills required by a housekeeper. Please forgive me for asking this; it is not a quest for power. Your household is large, with six children still at home, one being a baby who requires a Nanny and a wet nurse. The house needs maintenance, cleaning, and supplies. The staff require direction. Also, there is much daily attention and care needed for the children. Mrs Turner managed all this even in her sickness. I know you do not have the time for these duties. But someone must take on the role and quickly.

Both Thomas and Bethany have responsibilities in their households, and Anne is newly married and setting up her home. With Jeremy being a baby, there may be another fifteen years of care required for your children, so stability and care now are essential.

Please, might we try these new arrangements for the next month? This way, I can arrange the household and bring some order and regularity back for us all?"

"Ethel, I am so glad you have suggested these measures, and I agree with them entirely. I will speak with Mrs Jennings in the morning, so there is no confusion in her mind. The last thing we need is Mrs Jennings becoming upset by a reorganisation she is unaware of in advance. I will let you counsel the other staff members, including hiring a Nanny.

You are now the Housekeeper, and tomorrow at dinner, you must join us. I know this is a bit radical, but I believe it essential considering your close relationship with the children. I will announce the new arrangements during dinner and allow the children time for questions. As Clementine and Rosalind are such good friends, I hope we see your daughter more often here. I will have a word with Anne on her return, and she will double your remuneration as of tomorrow. Now, if you would excuse me, other matters require my attention."

"Of course, Mr Turner."

Jonathan Turner gently closed the door, and Ethel stood there with her mouth open. Mr Turner had been very generous and understood that her duties must change. He required no trial period and agreed with all her requests. She was somewhat confused as Jonathan Turner was frugal with his money. Ethel smiled as she now saw a kinder side of this complex man that had not been apparent before. There was a challenge here in returning the house to order. Firstly, she would arrange dinner for tomorrow night with everyone present.

Anne and Robert entered The Rows United Bank branch in Portsmouth and asked if they might see Mr Francis Hadley, the Manager. The receptionist requested on behalf of Mr Hadley the nature of their inquiry. Robert advised that he was the son of the Earl of Fintelton, and it was confidential.

An elderly gentleman soon greeted them and led them into an interview room down the hallway. Mr Hadley carried a grim expression and seemed somewhat disturbed by their arrival at the bank.

"Good morning, Sir Robert and Lady South. May I congratulate you on your recent marriage? There has been good coverage of the wedding in the society columns here. Your families must be pleased."

"Thank you, Mr Hadley, for seeing us without any notice. We took the opportunity today as we return from our honeymoon and pass through Portsmouth."

"I have been expecting Lady South as Mr Meyhew, a good friend, alerted me that you may call and instructed me on what you would be requesting."

Anne was not expecting this as she and Mr Meyhew had agreed the issues would be confidential.

Mr Hadley continued, "Mr Meyhew explained the confidential nature of your inquiries and the interest the Lions Bank of Guildford has in resolving these issues. He asked for our co-operation in this matter. Might I say that without his notification, a meeting such as this would have been impossible? You may also be assured of our confidentiality!"

Anne spoke up, "Thank you, Mr Hadley. That is most reassuring as it is also a difficult matter for the Estate and the South family, and we hope it has some simple explanation. However, we are early in our enquiries, and your information will be most helpful."

Mr Hadley sat there with a look on his face showing he was somewhat uncomfortable; however, he understood he must assist in these matters for the bank's good.

"I understand you are interested in speaking with Mrs Constance's referees from our bank."

"That is correct."

"I have reviewed the matters with the staff involved, saving us time and ensuring your inquiry is confidential. Mr Stillsen, our Head Teller, and Mr Hankerton, the Supervisor in the Ledger Department, have been most helpful and confirmed their comments at that time. Also, I have been the manager here for the last thirty years, and I recall Mrs Constance well. She was a handsome lady, and her husband, an Army sergeant in India, fell in battle many years ago. She needed more income as the army pension was meagre; we showed some sympathy and employed her. The remuneration from the bank and her Army pension allowed her to support her son.

Our decision was beneficial for both the bank and Mrs Constance. She possessed strong writing and mathematics skills; her first position was as an assistant Ledger Clerk. We employed her for ten years, and she was promoted through the ledger department and then onto teller work. We were most impressed by her, and she was well-liked by our customers. We were sorry when she left for Petersfield."

Robert was interested, "It appears that Mrs Constance was the ideal employee, Mr Hadley?"

"Yes, we were most impressed with her work. She was very dedicated and punctual. I was surprised that she never married again as she was an attractive young lady, and I would have thought her quite eligible. Perhaps it was her son. He sometimes proved a handful, but what boy isn't these days!"

Anne was satisfied but asked, "Mr Hadley, are you aware of her current address? We might contact her in the future."

"Certainly, I understand some of the staff remain in contact. I believe Mrs Constance works for another bank in London and lives in Wimbledon. I do not have the address with me, but I shall forward it care of Fintelton Estate."

"If you would please mark the letter 'Private & Confidential', that would assist! Thank you, Mr Hadley, this has been most helpful."

Robert required one more piece of information, "Mr Hadley, would you be aware if Mrs Constance ever had any contact with my brother, Sir Hugh South?"

"Not that I am aware of Sir Robert. Sir Hugh rarely visited the bank here, and I am unsure if he was ever in contact with Mrs Constance."

"But Sir Hugh did attend the bank here on occasions?"

"Yes, it would have been some ten to fifteen years ago and on several occasions. The Estate took out a loan to purchase a property in London and fully repaid it over five years. Sir Hugh occasionally visited for repayments or checking on the balance."

Robert was unaware of any property owned by the family in London except 'Harting'. He could not recall the Earl or Sir Hugh discussing the property; however, he had been away in the navy so long there would be many Estate details unknown to him.

"Mr Hadley, would you have the details of that property, please?"

"Certainly, Sir Robert. I will include it in the letter."

"Thank you, Sir. You have been most helpful."

"It is a pleasure, Sir Robert. I hope you find the resolution you desire. Good day."

Mr Hadley was keen on ending the conversation and stood, showing them the way out.

Outside, Anne was confused and said, "The bank references for Mrs Constance are sound, but it still does not explain why Hugh gave her such an outstanding character reference."

"Also, why did they take out a loan for an unknown property? I must ask father about that, but I will run out of time. If Hugh returns soon, we must ask him."

"Well, Robert. One more visit, and then you may take me out for lunch. Now, onto the church at Portsmouth, and hopefully, the Reverend Ison will be available."

Safe House, Dublin, Ireland ...
Aiden Reid and Dan O'Leary sat with Braydon Kelly and Iain Murphy in a safe house some ten miles from Dublin along a country road.

"When did you set this house up, Braydon? I have never visited here before."

"Recently, Dan! We must move regularly; otherwise, the watchmen[16] see a pattern and then raid the place. We know we are safe here as it is a long way from the road and a quiet area. As far as we know, the watchmen have never been here."

"Good. Aiden and I were feeling a bit nervous, walking up a country road alone at night. If anyone had passed us, we would have stood out as strangers."

"You were safe, Dan! No one comes up that road at night. It leads nowhere—a dead end. There is a back door out onto a trail avoiding the road for about a mile. A good escape route, if needed."

"What have you got for us, Braydon?" Aiden was still feeling nervous about this location in the country. He preferred the city, where they were inconspicuous.

"I visited our friends in Scotland, and it took them some time to gather the information. Sorry for the delay. It appears that around ten men are working for the brothers in Glasgow. Only three of these are involved in recruitment. The man who spied the strangers that night is a docker on a friendly wharf and is not involved."

"Yes, we remember."

"It appears the three who were recruiting were all working in pubs those nights in the docks area. Their names are Iain Hughes, Robert Murray, and Ian Doyle. We thought we would leave the interviews for Aiden. They all reported contacts on those nights, some successful and some not. So, it is a similar story for all of them."

Aiden sat up straight as his interest increased, "So it could have been any

---

[16] In 1827 the traditional establishment for a constabulary was a part time paid Parish Constable supported by casual watchmen who would be paid for their services by the local council.

of them?"

Braydon always felt uncomfortable in Aiden's presence as he knew Aiden was a cold-blooded killer and was kept on a short lease by the Committee in Cobh. Before the meeting, he and Iain had agreed that Aiden must brief the Glasgow committee before acting. They were not keen on an arbitrary execution if there was no clear evidence that the brother had knowingly broken the pledge.

"It may be one of them or perhaps not any of them. Sit down with these men and find out what transpired that night. Aiden, before taking any action, you must discuss the information with the Glasgow Committee."

In a deep, quiet voice, Iain Murphy calmly said, "Aiden, we know you are grieving for your brother, Sean. If you prove that one of these men was responsible for leaking the information, the Committee will authorise the action. But we do not want an unexpected execution that may jeopardise the members in Glasgow. If it is needed, then it will be done carefully. If you disregard this warning, then it might be you who goes for a walk next. Do you understand?"

Aiden focused on Iain with a steely, lifeless stare, "I understand. But where do we find these men?"

Braydon handed over a sheet of paper. After reading the details, Aiden folded the paper and placed it in his pocket.

"We have a method of moving people into Scotland undetected. Go with Braydon tonight, and he will show you the meeting point. The boat will leave tomorrow morning. When you reach Glasgow, find the Dublin Tavern at the docks, and ask for Molly Maguire. She will take care of you. Good luck."

Braydon stood, indicating that it was time. They both left by the back entrance. Iain Murphy looked at Dan and thought carefully about what he would say next.

"Dan, you know, Aiden better than I. To me, he looked like a man possessed. He grieves for his brother and cannot let it go. I am worried that his character has changed."

"I don't see much of him except at meetings. Michael would be a better judge, but I agree that he has been moody of late."

"I agree, lad! Michael and Aiden are close. Would you give Michael this message, please?"

"What is it, Iain?"

"Michael must keep a close watch on him. Aiden might use the brothers for his purposes. I have seen it before. Tell Michael that if he cannot control Aiden, he must take him for a walk. It will be Michael's job – make that clear! We cannot have a brother who jeopardises the complete network for their revenge."

Dan sat there without saying a word. Iain had not convinced him that Aiden Read was out of control. These directions confused him, as Aiden was a loyal brother who carried out orders without question. He risked his life often for the brothers, including at Islay. Why would Iain require him executed?

"Now, Dan, they need about an hour's start before we leave. Would you care for a drink, my boy?"

Chapter 10

Cobh, Ireland ...

The day was miserable, with thick dark clouds overhead driven by a freezing north-westerly wind racing across the sky. The small packet ship[17] docked in the busy harbour late in the afternoon after arriving overnight from Bristol. Ruth Walsh had secured a corner bunk in the large cabin keeping her distance from the other stowage passengers. It was an uncomfortable crossing, and she welcomed being on dry land again.

Ruth struggled with a worn old cloth case bursting full of clothes and held her grey-coloured woollen coat tight, protecting her from the cold. Looking up, she realised it would rain soon. Reaching Auntie Madge's house before the downpour was doubtful unless she could find help with her case. The docks were busy with at least seven or eight packets and luggers either disembarking or loading. People were everywhere, and as she exited through the dock gate, she thankfully heard the familiar voice of Daniel Magee over her shoulder.

"Well, Ruthy Walsh. How would you be then, girl?"

Ruth turned and saw the friendly smiling face of Daniel looking down at her from a covered store verandah beside the road.

"Come here, Dan, and make yourself useful!"

Dan hopped down and walked over, kissing her on the cheek. Smiling, she pressed on him the heavy bag letting him feel the weight, "Seems like you got a lot of clothes here, Ruth?"

"T'is what cases are for, Daniel!" Ruth was keen on leaving the crowd behind. She tidied her lovely reddish hair and walked off towards the path that led up the hill.

"Slow down, Ruth. This case is heavy!"

"You need more exercise, Dan. I can carry it! Wait at the Walsh home,

---

[17] Packet ship – In sea transport, a packet service is a regular, scheduled service, carrying freight and passengers. The ships used for this service are called packet ships or packet boats. The seamen are called packetmen, and the business is called packet trade. Wikipedia .

please, as I have some business in town. It will not take me long. If my case is delivered safely, I will give you a kiss later."

Daniel Magee was not that popular with the girls, and the promise of a kiss was more than enough persuasion. He smiled and waved, but Ruth had already turned and sped off on her mission. As she crossed the park, she stopped in the middle pretending her bootlaces needed tightening. Carefully Ruth looked around, checking if there was anyone following her. She then walked back the way she had come, north beside the docks, until she found the road leading up a slight incline ending at Hannigan's pub.

Finding the rear staff entrance unlocked, she sought out Lester Sloan, the Staff Manager.

"Mr Sloan, would you have a minute, please?"

'Why, Ruth! Not seen you for some time. After a job then, lass?"

"Yes, Mr Sloan and a kiss!"

Lester bent down and gave her a peck on the cheek. Ruth whispered, "Dan O'Leary, soon as you can find him!"

She kissed him back, "I have been up country, but back now. It would be good if my old job were still there, please?"

"Leave it with me, Ruth, for a day or two. But before you go, let me check the rosters."

Mr Sloan walked across the kitchen, checked the roster on the wall, turned and shouted, "Come back and see me tonight at seven. Jamie O'Callaghan is sick, and I need a replacement. I will see you then. Do you need a livery, girl?"

"Yes, Mr Sloan. That would be helpful."

Ruth smiled and headed off home as the rain started sprinkling down. She found Daniel sitting outside the front door, smiling.

'Well, thank you, Daniel. That was kind of you carrying my case. Let me check inside."

Ruth produced a key and unlocked the front door. She stuck her head inside and called, "Auntie Madge!"

There was no reply.

"Now, Daniel, you are a lucky boy! Auntie must be still at work. Come in out of the rain, and I will give you a kiss and maybe a bit more!"

Daniel was not slow when offered a gift and quickly carried Ruth's bag through the open entrance. From the half-open front door, Ruth scanned the street for anything out of place, satisfying herself no one was watching. Closing the door, she took Daniel's hand and led him down the hallway.

The Turner House, Guildford ...
Mrs Ethel Nibley and Mrs Jennings were nearing the end of a hard day's work, ensuring everything was ready for the family dinner. Rather than feeding the

younger children in the kitchen, Ethel brought forward dinner time so all could attend in the dining room at six-thirty. Bethany and Neville were also coming, but they did not expect Anne until Tuesday evening so she would miss this occasion.

"I'm glad Mr Turner has made these decisions, Ethel, as it has been far more difficult since Mrs Turner's sad passing. I still grieve for her and have appreciated your support in the last few weeks. It must have been terrible those many years ago when your husband died, and you coped alone with a child."

"Thank you, Mrs Jennings. It was particularly hard, but with my situation here, life has improved considerably. I was worried today that you would be upset when you heard I would become the housekeeper."

"No, no, Ethel! I am relieved. I am not sure if I am coping either. The decision is grand as the house needs far more organisation, especially with the new baby."

"I think if we do not provide more help for Nanny Smithers soon, she too will be overcome. The baby needs care all day and night, poor little thing."

Bethany entered the kitchen, "How are the preparations going, Mrs Jennings? May I assist with anything?"

"That is kind of you, Bethany. Oh, sorry, I should say Mrs Bassington!"

"No, Mrs Jennings, we have been family since I can remember. I insist you always call me Bethany."

"Well, dear, you could stir that soup every so often. That would help."

Ethel asked, "Is Doctor Bassington with you?"

"Yes. Neville is in the study with father. He is still most upset and finds it hard facing the world. Neville will encourage him."

"His encouragement will be welcome! Mr Turner struggles greatly with his grief."

Ethel noticed the time, "Now, it is six twenty, so I will gather all the children, Nany and Jeremy, and seat them at the table. I will be quick. Perhaps, Bethany, would you assist Mrs Jennings with bread on the side plates? Once that is done, we should tell your father and Doctor Bassington that dinner is ready, please."

Ethel left the kitchen in search of the children.

"Mrs Jennings, I think Ethel is a bit stressed tonight. Do you know why? Is it anything I have done?"

"No, Beth. It is an important dinner tonight, and a pity Thomas and young Mrs Turner are not attending."

"Why is it so important, Mrs Jennings?"

"I must hold my tongue! Sorry, Bethany. You will hear all within a few minutes at dinner."

"Oh!"

Grand Hotel, Kingston, Jamaica …

Fiona Green watched over Sir Hugh as he slept peacefully. It was two days since the crisis when they had all expected the end. But Sir Hugh survived. Fiona had finished her morning tea in the lounge downstairs and returned, allowing the nurse a break for half an hour.

"Good morning, Mrs Green. How is the patient today?"

"Morning, Doctor Cowper. He sleeps peacefully but has not woken yet."

"Mrs Green, this has been a fascinating case. Sir Hugh must have a strong constitution to survive that crisis. I admit I was amazed. But this is the nature of the disease. It is not predictable at all."

"Yes, it was also drawn out in my late husband's case, but he died during the first crisis. I think he gave up hope. Do you think hope makes a difference?"

"I am sure it does!"

Sir Hugh stirred and said, "What does?"

Doctor Cowper approached him with a smile, "Sir Hugh, I am Doctor Cowper, and this is Mrs Green, who you know. She has been looking after you for the last three weeks. I am glad you can talk with us again. You appear far better today."

Hugh looked around and registered that Fiona Green was sitting by his bed. He was surprised that a doctor was present.

"Three weeks?"

"Yes, you only avoided death by a whisker! Your recovery will take some time. The fever was severe, and we struggled to keep up your liquids. You must keep drinking and slowly take small portions of food as your body recovers. Fortunately, you are alive, Sir."

Hugh blinked, drank some water and said, "Thank you, Doctor. Lifting the arm for the drink has exhausted me. I must…." With that, he fell asleep.

"Mrs Green, as I explained, Sir Hugh will need a good two-month recovery time before he travels. Given his resilience, he may recover sooner, but I doubt it. He will require care for most of this time. I will make the nurses available. There is still the chance of another crisis, but hopefully not. Someone must accompany him on the return voyage, as it will be challenging. In the meantime, I will call on him weekly. Please call me if his condition deteriorates."

Turner Household, Guildford …

Jonathan Turner sat at the head of the dining table with the children down either side. Sitting at the other end, Bethany and Neville noticed an empty chair beside them.

"Before we start dinner tonight, I must ask for your attention. Mrs Nibley has agreed to join us tonight because what I say concerns her and all the family members. Clemmie, would you find Ethel, please!"

Bethany allowed Marcia some bread as they waited on Ethel. Quietly nudging Neville, Bethany asked, "What is this all about?"

"Your father will make an announcement. Be patient!"

Once Ethel took her place, Jonathan continued.

"Thank you for joining us, Ethel. Now I wanted everyone here, so I could explain the future staff structure we are putting in place. With the unfortunate death of your mother, we are in a difficult position. Bethany now has her own home with Neville, and Anne will return Monday next and live at 'Porting' with Robert. While Bethany and Anne are still close, they will have their own homes to manage. So, we must change the roles of the staff for the foreseeable future.

We will all benefit from these changes. Stability and care are what we will need in the coming months. I, too, am grieving, and I have found the loss of your mother distressing. Neville has been most helpful, and I feel I will overcome some of the depression that has come upon me since your mother's departure. But this will take time!"

Marcia, carefully listening, blurted out, "Do you mean Mama's death, Dada?"

"Yes, Marcia, that is correct." Jonathan smiled at the little one, calming her.

"From today onwards, Mrs Ethel Nibley has been appointed housekeeper and will take a far more active role in our family affairs. I cannot look after you all alone, and I need Mrs Nibley's assistance."

Marcia shouted again, "What is a housekeeper, Dada?"

Jonathan explained, "Someone who looks after the staff and all our arrangements daily."

"Like Mama did, Dada?"

"That's right, Marcia."

The children sat there, wondering what this all meant. Neville stood and showed his appreciation for Ethel by clapping and saying, "Marvellous!" Bethany joined him, and then the children followed. Ethel blushed and thanked them all.

"I have asked Ethel if she would join us at dinner each night, particularly if I am away on business. Our being together will ensure consistent communication among the family members. I am sure you will all give Mrs Nibley your full support, and our family will quickly return to a normal routine. Now let me say, Grace."

After Grace, Neville leaned over and quietly said, "Well done, Ethel. It will be a big challenge, but I am sure you are most capable of handling it. Beth and I will give you as much help as we can."

"Thank you, Doctor Bassington. I miss Mrs Turner as well and would prefer she was still with us. Sadly, we must make these arrangements, and I will do my best!"

The dinner went well, and there were various discussions about improving the household routine. Simeon and William were worried they would have more chores, but Jonathan reassured them that Doctor Bassington had convinced him to appoint a man for house maintenance. One of his jobs would be the firewood."

The boys sat back, feeling more relaxed, until Jonathan smiled, "Of course, this will allow you both more time on your schoolwork!"

While Simeon was content with that comment, William was a bit perplexed. He had hoped for more free time outside, mainly once spring arrived.

Later in the evening, Clemmie talked with Beth before the married couple left for home.

"Beth, do you think father is thinking of marrying again? Will he marry Ethel?"

"No, Clemmie. Of course not. Father misses mother dreadfully. He is a bit lost at present. What he has announced tonight is wise. The family needs stability, and it will help each of you. We all love Ethel as she is kind and trustworthy. I think she will do a grand job."

"But do you think father will marry her?"

Bethany stood and thought about what Clemmie said. She was sure her father had not even considered the prospect of remarrying, and marriage required agreement from both persons. From Clementine's question, it was clear that Clemmie was alarmed. It would be best if she comforted her at present.

"No, I am sure that will not happen. What he wants is stability and comfort for you, little sister."

As Neville and Bethany walked home that night, Bethany asked, "Neville, it is strange that Ethel joined us for dinner tonight. I wonder if your father has in mind marrying again?"

'No, not at all. From my discussions with your father, I am sure he struggles with understanding himself. The prospect of marrying again is not on his mind at all."

Guildford Medical Practice ...
As Neville arrived on Tuesday morning, David quickly jumped up from his office and joined him.

"Morning, Neville. I would have informed you about my decision last Friday, but you were out yesterday with country patients.

You will be away next week and the week after will be my wedding. I will be on my honeymoon for six weeks following the wedding, so we need a replacement Doctor. I talked with Doctor Watson on Friday; he has a pleasant personality and sound experience. I think he is suitable for our practice."

"David, we can't afford it yet! I understand you are worried about being overrun with patients, but we must also keep the costs down."

"Yes, Neville and I appreciate you are worried about costs, but I have decided to pay for this myself. You will bear none of the cost. I know the practice cannot afford it, so I will personally finance this initiative. If you step back and think about the benefits, you will understand. Anyway, I asked him for a trial starting yesterday. It will benefit me as I will not be worried about being run off my feet."

Neville stood back and saw the concern on David's face, "This is kind of you, David! There is no need, but what can I say – if you feel it is for the best, your offer is accepted! However, I am uncomfortable as it will benefit me more than you."

"No, it will benefit both of us. Anyway, Neville, I am not short of money. So, let us say it is an investment in the general health of Guildford. It will also ensure I have a worry-free honeymoon!"

"Then it is a good investment, indeed! Meeting Doctor Watson will be a pleasure."

The Men's Club, Guildford …
Before five in the afternoon, fathers and sons arrived at the Club, waiting for Doctor Sopwith and Doctor Watson.

Jonathan was encouraged to find Terry there, "Why Terry, you will also be an instructor. I hope you can swim as I am a beginner. Good afternoon, Levi, and who is your friend?"

"This is Archie Watson, Mr Turner; he is Doctor Watson's son. Doctor Sopwith and Doctor Watson are coming together. I think Doctor Bassington is also coming."

"Ah! Well, Good afternoon, Archie. Are you learning as well?"

"Yes, Mr Turner. Simeon and William saved me from drowning last week at the river. So, we all agreed we should have swimming lessons."

"I see….!"

As the doctors arrived, David introduced everyone and quickly gave a rundown of the lessons before entering the Club.

The swimming went well, with the boys learning a lot by watching Jonathan Turner making his first few strokes in front of them. David Sopwith was impressed that Jonathan made the effort to attend, which might divert his thoughts away from his grief. Bryan Watson proved helpful as he was an accomplished swimmer and added some coaching expertise. Bryan taught

Archie and Levi breathing techniques so they were not afraid of sinking below the surface. By the lesson's end, the boys enjoyed blowing bubbles and floating on their backs.

Neville noted how Jonathan Turner was more relaxed in the warm water and enjoyed the men's conversation as they learned together. Terry and Jonathan laughed as they spluttered in the water with some encouragement from Bryan Watson. The Scottish doctor fitted in well and did not force himself into the conversations, only occasionally commenting. Neville reconsidered. He may have been wrong about the new recruit.

Hannigan's Pub, Cobh …

Dan O'Leary climbed the stairs at the back of the pub around nine in the evening and made the standard knock. The door opened quickly, and his sister, Ruby, pulled him inside.

'You are late, Dan! I have been waiting for half an hour."

"I am just back from Dublin, Ruby, and catching up. A few other things are happening tonight as well. I am here now! Call Ruth up, please."

Ruby was not pleased with her brother but said no more. She disappeared down the stairs finding Ruth working in the bar. Dan made his way into the dark meeting room, lit a candle, and made himself comfortable on a chair. He thought Ruth was still in Port Charlotte as the committee had not recalled her. There must be trouble if she was back in Cobh.

Ruth Walsh rushed into the room, "Dan, thank you for coming."

"Ruth, I am glad you are safely home, but why are you here?"

"There was a dangerous problem, and I fled Port Charlotte quickly!"

"But what about Callum? Where is he?"

Ruth looked away from Dan in fear. Suddenly she was trembling and overcome with tears as she cried out, "He is dead, Dan. I killed him as he was turning against us. There was no other choice!"

Dan O'Leary stood there with his mouth open for a few seconds and then closed it as he took in this news. He stood up and put his hands on her trembling shoulders as she continued crying.

"Sit here, girl. Now tell me all about it."

Gathering another chair, he sat beside her, passing across a small hand towel from the wall table.

"The English came back and searched the town for any republicans. They also found the grave. They were still there asking questions when I left."

"But why would you kill Callum?"

"Callum mistook our relationship for love. I tried several times explaining that it was our job and that he should not read too much into it. But Callum was convinced that I loved him. He traded information with the captain of the British frigate for our safe passage out of Port Charlotte. When Callum returned late at night and told me we were leaving the next day for England, I became angry as I worked hard that night, getting information from a British Officer. I was disgusted when I heard from Callum that he was negotiating with the British. I know I acted hastily, but I thought there was no other option."

"So, we do not have the information the committee requested?"

"No, not at all. I gathered all that." Ruth pulled out an envelope from under her apron and passed it across. "I am not sure how much information Callum gave the English. But we must scatter as they will come here soon for sure."

"That is if they find Callum. Where did you bury him?"

Ruth fearfully looked at Dan and said, "I did not bury him! I left him in the bed where I killed him."

"So, he is still in the safe house."

"Yes."

"Well, that could become a problem, but not for now. Ruth, you should have let him fall asleep and left quietly."

"I could not, as he was a light sleeper, and perhaps he would have killed me if I had not agreed with his plan."

"I doubt that! Callum was a brave man but not a killer. How did you disappear?"

"Once I was out of bed, I found his blood all over me and my nightdress. I stripped, washed, and changed into a clean dress. Then I rugged up, packed what I could, took the cart and set off for Port Ellen. I arrived in time for the Glasgow ferry. Then I worked my way back here through Bristol."

"Where did you leave the horse and cart?"

"At Fleming's Stable. I told them I would return in a month or two. I paid five pounds for stabling and exercise. The cart is there as well."

Dan sat there, thinking about what she had told him. The locals would soon discover their dead Scottish brother, so their safe route through Port Charlotte was compromised. He must quickly advise the brothers in Dublin before that path was used again. Then he realised that Aiden Reid was either there or now nearing Port Charlotte. If the locals had found Callum's body, Aiden might be in danger.

"Ruth, best if you worked tonight, but keep out of sight as much as you can. If you want a rest, go inland and join Michael on the farm. All the brothers around Cork have been stood down for two months or more. If Callum told them about the men from Cobh, we are in for a hard time. You decide if you continue working here or leave for the farm. You have earned a rest, and I am sure you will be welcome at home."

Ruth frowned but then asked, "Dan! Will the brothers' committee believe me?"

Dan O'Leary held up the envelope Ruth had given him, "This should help!"

"Thank you, Dan."

"A pleasure, Ruth! Now, you go first."

When Dan came down, he beckoned Ruby and led her outside.

"I will be gone for a day or two. Keep an eye on Ruth if you can. She needs some support."

"Why?"

"She can tell you when she is ready. You will understand then. I am off tonight and will be back Friday."

"Where are you going, Dan?"

"Dublin."

Turner Business Offices, Guildford …

Clementine Turner knocked and entered her father's office, "Father, Mr McPherson has arrived."

"Mr McPherson!"

"Yes, he asked if he could meet with you."

"This is a pleasant surprise!" Jonathan Turner, who had been watching the river flow past, quickly placed a few papers on his desk as if he had been working.

"Show him in Clemmie."

"Father, you should not call me Clemmie here at the office. It is Clementine!"

"I am sorry, Clementine! I was not thinking."

She disappeared out the door, and soon Hamish sat across the desk and sipped a scotch.

"Hamish, I did not expect you here today. When did you arrive in Guildford?"

"Last night, but I decided to visit your office this morning."

"It would not have been a disturbance, and I would have enjoyed your company at dinner last night."

"Thank you, Jonathan, but preferably we should speak alone. How are you coping without Eleanora?"

"Not well. Not well at all. I find I can think of nothing else. I have not thought about the business since Eleanora died. I find I cannot concentrate anymore. Neville tells me it is a normal reaction, and I will recover in time, but he thinks it is more severe in me than he has encountered before."

"I was worried for you, Jonathan. We have much business together, and I am concerned about your recovery. There are some changes in my business that we must discuss. Best if we quietly discussed it together before the changes become more widely known. I also have an offer for you."

Jonathan was jolted out of his depression and wondered what the changes and offers were that Hamish would reveal.

"I am not sure if Thomas has advised you of the difficulties in Glasgow I am encountering with my son, James?"

"He has mentioned James. I understand there are different opinions, but that was all he told me."

"Let me explain, and I will keep it brief. James's unwise relationship with a young Irish lady has created a situation in Glasgow. I will solve this by Lachlan taking control of the breweries in Glasgow and James becoming our General Manager in Ireland.

As the brewery's construction here in Guildford will take at least a year, we will appoint Thomas as an assistant manager with Lachlan, and he will manage the brewery James is leaving. He and Marion will take up residence for a year or so. Lachlan will suitably mentor him. As we are business partners Jonathan, I was keen on briefing you before giving Thomas the excellent news."

"But what of his involvement in the Guildford Brewery?"

"He will regularly visit and check the building plans and progress. I think this will be a better way of developing his brewing knowledge. Lachlan has vast experience and works well as a mentor."

Jonathan sat back in his chair and took a sip of whisky. He wondered what his son's reaction would be. Glasgow was a long way from Guildford. Thank goodness Eleanora had passed away - she would have missed him terribly.

Hamish interrupted his thoughts, "Marion will love it. They will have James's house in Glasgow, which is centrally located. She will enjoy the social set, and Thomas will learn much from Lachlan. The move will be good for him, Jonathan. I will leave London with Marjorie after the charity ball on the third of March. We will sail for Glasgow, where I will implement these new arrangements. I also have an offer for you, Jonathan. When Marion and Thomas come two weeks later in March, I think you should join them. Once you are in Glasgow, we shall explore the country together. It will refresh your mind. Think of it as a friendly time of therapy."

Jonathan was surprised by the generosity of Hamish's offer. Since the funeral, he felt the need for some time off but was unsure what to do. He was finding the grief was draining his energy levels, and he had lost focus.

"Jonathan, Anne will manage! She is the Managing Director now and has a good team under her. Let her prove herself. I think you will be surprised. Lachlan will have no difficulties holding the fort while I am away. He will enjoy it."

Leaning across the desk, Jonathan filled Hamish's glass with whisky and poured his own.

"The offer is generous, Hamish. I have pleasure in accepting. Presently I am a lost soul, and the break will do me good. I will look forward to arriving in Glasgow."

Their glasses clinked together as they toasted their forthcoming trip.

Portsmouth, England ...

As the sun slowly rose over the horizon and lit their room, Anne watched Robert peacefully asleep beside her. She knew she would not see him again for some time, depending on the new orders he would receive this morning. But he was here now, and they were married. Her life had changed forever, and she would make the best of their time this morning before the coach pulled out for Petersfield and then Fintelton.

She pulled herself up on her elbows and kissed his cheek.

"I love you, Robert South!"

Robert opened his eyes and stretched, "I am glad of that, Lady Anne South; otherwise, I would be in big trouble."

A broad smile appeared on his face that lit the day up for Anne, and she moved close beside him.

Robert suggested, "How about I take you out for breakfast, my Darling? I must show you off again."

Anne raised herself onto her knees and hit him with her pillow, "No! I will show you off, but you can pay the bill!"

Robert laughed and pulled her close as the sun drenched the bed warmly and enticed a long embrace.

At breakfast, Robert asked, "Anne, are you prepared for your return? I know the loss of your mother was hard, and being alone in Guildford will be difficult. I wish I could make it easier for you."

"Mother and I had many conversations in the weeks before she died. We knew it would happen soon, so I had already said my goodbyes. I cried many a night for the weeks before. I think God prepared me for it."

"So, you will cope?"

"I am not sure, but I will try. Certainly, the new house and the business will keep me busy. But the separation from you will be the greatest challenge, Darling. I think I will spend much time with Beth."

"As soon as I know my orders, I will send a message. Even if the Admiralty delays the mission, there are pressing issues on *Shadow* that must be solved. It may be some days before I join you in Guildford. Let us hope it is a substantial delay so we can spend time together in our new home."

"I will wait for your message. Do not forget you are David's best man on the tenth of March. He will need your support, so no gales in the Channel, please."

"I will not forget."

Anne waved from the coach's window as it moved away down the street and around the corner, and Robert disappeared out of sight. She sat back and then thought about Fintelton and what kind of reception she should expect there. It would be a new beginning with the Earl and Countess as their daughter-in-law.

The Admiral's Flagship, Portsmouth Harbour ...
Robert pulled himself up the first-rate's side with Commodore Jacobs and Captain Graham welcoming him on the quarter-deck.

"Good morning, Captain South. Welcome aboard! I will let Commodore Jacobs escort you. The Admiral is waiting."

"Thank you, Captain. I am sure you are glad the refit is complete!"

"Not quite. We have not had the ship at sea yet. There are still many adjustments that the Sailing Master must make. Perhaps later this week, we will have the chance."

Robert smiled and followed the Commodore.

"Commodore, I understand there has been a change in orders."

"Yes, the Admiral will explain. It will be straightforward!"

Robert followed as Jacobs led him into the great cabin in the stern of the flagship.

"Captain South, welcome aboard!" The Admiral gave his usual warm welcome and offered Robert a chair. Jacobs joined them.

"Admiral Sutherland, it is a pleasure finding you back on board your flagship, Sir."

"You are right, Captain. I am far happier here. Give me the sea any day! How was your honeymoon, Sir? Lady Sutherland will require a full report from me when I see her tonight."

"We spent an undisturbed week on the Isle of Wight, Sir. You will have been familiar with the weather, and of course, the Isle is beautiful at any time. We are fully rested and ready for the year ahead."

"Good, good! Sorry about pulling you away early from the honeymoon, but there are new orders, and you may get more than an extra week once you are in Woolwich. I would issue a dinner invitation, but time has overtaken us. Now we must quickly discuss your orders, as I am sure pressing matters will await you on *Shadow*."

"That is kind, Sir. But Lady South left for Fintelton this morning and then travels onto Guildford tomorrow. And you are correct, Admiral! I have the officers working the men hard on *Shadow*, and much training is still required."

"Ah! Robert, this marriage will be interesting, with your wife active in commercial activities. It will be a challenge. But from my knowledge of her,

I think she will make a success of it. Commodore Jacobs, the orders, please."

Commodore Jacobs passed the orders across. Robert accepted the envelope and noticed his name printed across the top.

"These are your orders, Captain. There has been a change, and you will not join us in the Mediterranean until July. The Admiralty has another urgent task for you, which requires your special skills. Admiral Crouch will brief you in London next week."

Admiral Sutherland checked the time and then continued.

"A high-ranking government mission has been appointed and will depart from Woolwich on the seventeenth of March. The mission aims to improve conditions for Irish tenant farmers. Various members of parliament from both houses will constitute the mission committee, so they will require protection. I understand that Lord Dawlting will lead the mission and has requested that you attend to him as the naval commander. You will assist with security and join many of the community inspections in Ireland."

Robert was both surprised and confused by the decision.

"Admiral, I am disappointed I will not be with you in the Mediterranean. I feel my duty lies there."

"Your duty, young man, is where the Admiralty directs you! We will hopefully see you in the Med in July at the latest. This new mission will only last a few months, giving you time with your new wife before sailing. Now you will board *Shadow* and finish victualing. I want you away quickly, Robert. Best provide yourself with plenty of time for navigating up the Thames.

There will be a dinner at Admiral Crouch's residence on Friday, the second of March. The following night a ball will celebrate the mission, where you and your wife will accompany the First Sea Lord and his wife. The tickets are in with your orders. I understand that you are the best man at a wedding on the tenth of March, so I was fortunate to persuade the Admiral that there should be a slight delay in the departure date from Woolwich.

The Admiralty have agreed that Lord Heffron's barque[18], the *Chalk*, will carry most of the official party. Another barque, the *Eventide*, will bring the remainder of the party. *Shadow*, supported by *Restless*, will provide support and security. Colonel Scott, the Admiralty Chief of Security, will travel with a small contingent on *Chalk* but liaise with you. Major Coombes will join you again in Woolwich with a squad of marines. He will travel with you on *Shadow* but be under Colonel Scott's command while ashore. As Captain of *Shadow*, you will take responsibility for the security at sea and in the ports of call.

Lieutenant Ham on *Restless* will support you, given the difficulties we have

---

[18] A barque, barc, or bark is a type of sailing vessel with three or more masts having the fore- and mainmasts rigged square and only the mizzen (the aftmost mast) rigged fore and aft. Wikipedia.

experienced lately in the Irish Sea. Ham will join your small flotilla with extra marines on board, boosting the numbers of Major Coombes's contingent. While we do not expect any difficulties, it is better if you are prepared for action.

It appears this will be another feather in your cap, Robert. A special request for you from Lord Dawlting will not go unnoticed. Also, the experience of being a flotilla commander will be a new challenge. I am sure Major Coombes will enjoy being at sea again." The Admiral had a chuckle about this.

"Everything is in the orders, Captain. I suggest you join your ship and prepare for the voyage. It would be best to arrive in Woolwich by Thursday night, allowing time for the functions on Friday and Saturday. Sail as soon as you are ready once you have taken stock aboard.

I shall request your presence on the flagship when you arrive in the Eastern Mediterranean."

"Thank you, Admiral. I will read the orders with interest and might your voyage across the Med[19] be safe and successful."

Robert took his leave and followed Commodore Jacobs onto the quarterdeck. Jacobs stopped him before he tackled the ladder down the side.

"Captain South. You will recall our previous meeting and viewing the various mission orders. I took the liberty of reviewing them as well. This time I was more thorough. I must apologise, as I found some similarities that I think are worth discussing. If I can find a time, might we discuss it before you sail? I shall send you a note advising of the day."

"I would welcome the opportunity, Commodore. Let us say eight tomorrow morning."

"Excellent. I will have the mission orders ready to review them together."

They shook hands, and Robert quickly descended into his cutter, which cast off and headed for *Shadow*.

Fintelton Manor, East of Petersfield ...
Anne enjoyed the view of the Manor as the coach approached, and this time saw it in a different light. This large Estate house was the home of her husband's parents. She was now part of the family by marriage and wondered if her relationship with the Earl and Countess would change.

As the carriage approached the Manor, Anne noticed that the butler had assembled the staff at the front entrance. Anne wondered what the occasion was. The carriage slowed over the last fifty yards and pulled up in front of what Anne thought must be the entire staff standing in neat rows.

After the carriage stopped, a footman helped her down near the Earl, the Countess, and Lady Emma. The Earl took a step forward and took Anne's

---

[19] Med. Sailors often refer to the Mediterranean as the 'Med'.

hand, "Welcome, Lady Anne, Robert sent a rider, and we have been expecting you. My, you are beautiful today! We are all eager to hear how you and Robert spent the honeymoon."

"Your Lordship, this welcome is far too grand for me. I am overwhelmed!"

The countess came forward and gave Anne a hug and a kiss, "Anne, you do not know how much I have been waiting for this moment. Welcome back, and you must treat the Estate now as your home."

Lady Emma also rushed forward and hugged and kissed Anne.

They embraced, and Anne blurted out, "Emma, the wedding is less than three weeks away – we will be talking all night about the preparations!"

"First, I must hear about the honeymoon, but after the welcome." Then Emma stood back with a smile on her face.

The Earl then explained, "Before we go in, Pike will introduce each staff member. It is a tradition I started when I brought the countess home as my wife some thirty years ago. A pity Robert is not here, but we must soldier on."

Thomas Pike stepped forward, "Lady South, congratulations on your marriage, and if you would join me, I will make the introductions."

Surprising Pike, Anne smiled and shook his hand. Emma walked beside Anne and quietly said, "A smile and saying good afternoon will do!"

Pike, slightly disturbed by Lady Emma's comments, took a deep breath and then made the first introduction, "Lady Anne South, may I introduce our housekeeper, Mrs Cora Walsh."

"Good afternoon, Mrs Walsh; thank you for coming out and meeting me."

Mrs Walsh gave a slight curtsy, "Welcome, Lady South. It is a pleasure."

"Do I detect an Irish accent, Mrs Walsh?"

"Yes, Ma'am. It was a long time ago. I hope you do not mind?"

"It sounds lovely. I love the Irish accent. Thank you, Mrs Walsh."

A pleasant smile came over Pike's face as he moved along for the subsequent introductions.

Emma was surprised as Anne conversed politely with each household staff member. Once Pike finished the introductions, the Earl escorted Anne into the warmth.

"Now tell me, Anne, Robert advises that his orders have changed. Are you aware of the details?"

"Not as yet, your Lordship, but he promised that a rider would bring a message this afternoon."

"Good, good. Now I must meet with the Estate Manager and discuss the rose garden. I will leave you with the Countess and Lady Emma."

"Thank you for the lovely welcome, your Lordship."

"It was a pleasure, my dear. It is not every day that you welcome a daughter-in-law into the family. Now I must be off with Mr Stem."

As Anne reunited with Lady Jane and Lady Emma, they talked about the honeymoon and the various places on the Isle of Wight were mentioned. Around five in the afternoon, a rider delivered a message for Lady Anne South.

The butler appeared, "Lady South, a letter for you."

"Thank you, Pike."

Anne took the letter from the butler and waited until he had left the room.

"It is the message from Robert." They were all eager for Robert's news.

"He is not sailing for the Mediterranean yet but has a new mission in Ireland. They sail early next week for Woolwich, and Robert and I must attend a dinner on Friday, the Second of March and then a ball the following night. These appointments are well-timed as they coincide with Marion's mother's memorial service."

Lady Jane was pleasantly surprised, "I am sure the ball you mention will be the Irish Benefit Ball. Marjorie McPherson sent an invitation for the Earl and I, but we have not responded yet. Emma, you must have David attend as well. We shall make up a party."

Emma was immediately excited, "I shall write today, and Anne may deliver it tomorrow."

"Anne, I am unsure if you know Marjorie McPherson's involvement in the Irish Benefit Charity."

"No, Lady Jane, I am not!" Anne listened with interest.

"When you last left Harting at St James's Square, you will recall I asked your advice on how I should manage the friendship with Marjorie. She visited Harting for afternoon tea that day."

Anne recalled the meeting, "Of course, you asked me for a strategy, and we agreed on one."

"Yes. Your strategy was that Marjorie replace me on one of my charity committees. My Dear, your suggestion has worked well, and Marjorie is now firmly embedded on the Irish Benefit-Charity Committee and is much involved with the ball's organisation. I believe she, her husband and one of their sons will attend."

"I am sure the son will be James. He often visits Greenwich."

Lady Jane looked somewhat concerned. Emma asked, "What is the matter, Mother?"

"I was considering your father's health before I accepted or declined Marjorie's invitation. Now that I know you and Anne will attend, it is more enticing. However, the wedding is so close, and the distance may challenge your father's health, Emma. It may be too strenuous for him."

"I am sure, Mother, if you took the trip one stage at a time, he would cope. A stop in Guildford, then Epsom, and onto London. Plan for three stages."

"Yes, yes, Emma. But I also must consider your wedding! If we set off on Sunday morning and did the three stages again. I am sure the Earl will cope with that, and David will be there in case his health comes into question."

Anne added, "Robert will be there as well. In the note, he says the Admiral approved him being absent from his ship for some days so that he may return with us."

"Then it is settled we shall all travel together and arrive at Harting on Thursday night, allowing you girls time for the memorial service on Friday. We shall have a lovely time and leave for home on Sunday."

Emma smiled, "I am sure David will demand to be back seeing patients that week before the wedding. Now Anne, let me tell you all the wedding details and when the rehearsal is! After dinner, I have a special surprise – the wedding dress! It arrived from Mrs Smith at Hursts on Monday. While you were away, Victoria Sopwith and Mother helped me with the fittings. I must give you a viewing after dinner."

Anne was amazed that Lady Jane had decided on a wedding dress from Hursts. Having the countess as a client was a significant step forward in the clientele of the Guildford establishment. "Why wait – let us go up now? There is enough time before dinner." The countess, Emma and Anne rushed off upstairs, calling their maids as they went and giggling in excitement as they talked.

In the morning, Anne rose early and quickly dressed as she had requested a meeting with Mr Malcolm Stem, the Estate Manager, before breakfast. She would meet with him alone and not worry Lady Jane or Emma with Mrs Constance's details. She required more information before deciding if the lady was involved.

The Estate Manager found Anne in the Library as arranged. "Good morning, Lady South. May I offer my congratulations on your recent marriage? I wish you and Sir Robert much happiness in the years ahead."

"Thank you, Mr Stem, you may. I am sorry our meetings are always at such an early hour. My stay at Fintelton is short as I leave for Guildford today. So, I apologise for the early hour and the short notice."

Mr Stem smiled, "I assumed it would concern the Estate finances."

"Yes, I continue my inquiries. You will recall our previous meeting."

"Yes, Lady South."

"Mr Stem, some other information has emerged which may be helpful. It may be a coincidence, or it may have meaning. I am not sure at this stage. If you would keep it confidential, please, as it involves a lady, and I would not want anything hurtful said if the information is purely coincidental."

"I understand, my Lady. I agree with your sentiments."

Stem, as usual, was displaying a helpful and understanding manner.

"Mr Stem, might you recall if Sir Hugh had any relationship in the past with a Mrs Constance at the Lions Bank in Petersfield?"

The Estate Manager scratched his head, thinking back through the years, "I recall Mrs Constance as we met regularly at the Petersfield bank. As I previously shared with you, I assembled the banking and visited the branch as required. Sir Hugh did not accompany me. I would always see Mrs Constance and found her most helpful and efficient. As far as I know, Sir Hugh may have visited the bank occasionally but not often. He may have met her then. He never confided in me that he knew Mrs Constance."

"Mr Stem, if we go back further, do you recall if Sir Hugh ever did any banking in Portsmouth before 1821?"

"He visited Portsmouth regularly in the decade before 1821. I am sure of that as I accompanied him on several occasions. He did visit a bank there, but I cannot recall its name. But when I accompanied him, it was more estate business than banking. Does that assist?"

"Would the bank's name have been 'The Rows United Bank'?"

"Yes, that is it. I remember it on the High Street near the Garrison Church end."

"Yes, that is the one. Mr Stem, were you aware why Sir Hugh was visiting the bank?"

"On one occasion, he did mention something about a property. However, it was a bit of a grumble, and I was unclear about what he said."

"There is nothing else you can tell me about Mrs Constance?"

"No, my Lady. As far as I know, Sir Hugh did not have a relationship with Mrs Constance. However, he did find plenty of company in Portsmouth. It was not hard finding that kind of company there."

"Might I ask if Mrs Constance was a handsome lady, Mr Stem?"

"Very handsome indeed, Milady. There was always a queue at her teller station."

Anne was concentrating hard on what Malcolm Stem had told her as Pike entered the room.

"Lady South! Breakfast is served. Will Mr Stem be joining you?"

The Estate Manager stood and replied, "Thank you, Mr Pike. But no, I have already had breakfast and must be on my way. Milady, please let me know if you require any further information."

"Thank you, Mr Stem. I am most appreciative of your help."

With that, Stem nodded and made his way out. Pike remained and gave a slight cough.

"Yes, Pike!"

The butler spoke carefully and with great respect, "Lady South, please forgive me if I intruded too far, but it may be more appropriate to have someone with you rather than meeting alone with gentlemen early in the morning. I understand you are making inquiries and that your meeting was quite innocent, but sometimes people draw the wrong conclusion. I remained outside the door, ensuring your protection. Any details I heard will remain confidential. I hope you will excuse me?"

Anne understood the gentle lesson Pike provided and was thankful for his concern.

"You are correct, Pike, and I had not considered that issue at all. My apologies, and thank you for your concern. I trust you will keep my conversation with Mr Stem confidential."

"Certainly, Milady. Now there is a delightful breakfast awaiting you. I am sure Lady Jane and Lady Emma will join you presently."

Turner Household, Guildford ...

The children sat at the breakfast table in the kitchen, discussing what they would do for the day. Reverend Taggart would be at a meeting with the bishop and had cancelled school until the afternoon.

William spoke first, "Ethel, where is Anne's new house?"

Ethel thought for a moment and then answered, "I think it is up behind where your sister, Bethany, lives. I have the address in my room. Why do you ask?"

"Might you take us over there this morning so we can see it?"

"William, there is so much happening here today. Perhaps we could go on Saturday or Sunday?" Ethel was still working out the best routine for everyone and could not afford the time.

Clementine suggested, "I can take a few hours off work, Ethel. I will take them over if that is all right?"

Ethel was not convinced, "Anne will not arrive until this afternoon. She sent a message yesterday. There will be no one there."

"That is fine! We will walk around the garden and peep in the windows. We will not take long as I should be at work by ten if possible."

The children, including Marcia, cheered Clementine's suggestion.

"Well, children. If Clementine goes with you and you all stay together, please make sure you are back by ten in the morning."

Madeline said, "I wish Anne would be there as I miss her so much!"

Ethel understood that of all the sisters, Madeline confided the most in Anne. She was a gentle child and often depended on Anne's guidance with decisions. On the other hand, Clementine was fiercely independent, usually made the wrong decision, and never wanted any helpful advice. Working at the bakery had helped Clemmie as she slowly understood that most things were connected, and bad choices had consequences.

At that moment, Jonathan Turner entered the breakfast room and cuddled Marcia.

"Dada, Dada! We are going for a walk and visiting Anne's house this morning!"

Jonathan said, "Well, you will all be thirsty when you arrive. Madeline, knock at the back door, and Mrs Kirby will give the children a drink of water each. Mind the back fence, as it requires some repair."

Ethel explained, "Oh! I forgot about Mrs Kirby. I thought there would be no one there. Sorry, Mr Turner, I should explain! Clementine will be walking with them. I will remain here as they return by ten in the morning."

"I see. Now, Clementine, you are expected at work by eight-thirty, so how will you fit this in?"

"Father, I will spend the time wisely with my brothers and sisters and finish my work in the afternoon."

Jonathan could see the eager expressions on all the children's faces and was mindful of Ethel's advice that they needed more time together. He was angry that Clementine thought she could wander into work whenever she desired. But this was not the time for a debate. The outing should be positive for all of them.

"I shall join you as well. We will all meet at Anne's house."

Clementine lifted her eyes as she regarded herself capable of leading this expedition. The last thing she wanted was for her father to attend.

"That is not necessary, Father. I will take good care of them."

"Yes, Clemmie, but I would enjoy visiting 'Porting' and spending more time with my children. I will visit the office first and advise Audrey you will be late. Then I will collect some buns and ask Sophia for some croissants. We will have morning tea there."

Ethel smiled, and the children all cheered. Despite not wanting her father along, Clementine could not argue with a splendid morning tea, so the expedition set off.

After a reasonable walk past Guildford Castle and the Bassington's house, they turned right and followed a road that ended at a front gate. On one of the gate posts, there was a nameplate with the word 'Porting'. Opening the gate, Clementine said, "It has a beautiful yard, but what a strange name for a house. Plenty of room for children's games. Let us go around the back and call on Mrs Kirby."

The two boys ran off, with Simeon chasing William around the trees and Marcia following behind, waving her toy bear, 'Buster'. Madeline walked beside Clementine as they gazed up at the two-storied house.

"Big, isn't it?" Madeline was amazed that Anne would have such a large house.

"Well, she married into the nobility. Appearances are important! Ours is a similar-sized house but appears smaller as 'Porting' stands alone. Our house on High Street has houses on either side."

Madeline thoughtfully said, "I wonder if she will be lonely when Robert is away?"

"I think so. I am sure Anne will come home often. I hope she does, as it will keep Ethel under control."

As they rounded the corner at the back of the house, a welcoming voice rang out, "Well, who have we here? I think it is Mrs South's brothers and sisters. And little Marcia as well and Buster. How is the little one?"

Marcia flew into Mrs Kirby's arms and excitedly told how well-behaved Buster had been on the walk. Clementine and Madeline each hugged Mrs Kirby and said Mr Turner would join them for morning tea.

"I am glad you are all here. You can help me make some cakes as Mrs South will arrive this afternoon and I need a good afternoon tea ready for her. I am sure she will dash off somewhere for work, but perhaps she will have time for a cup of tea and a cake!"

As Mrs Kirby talked with the girls, William found a hole in the back fence and was straight through. Simeon followed. They stood on the other side and looked across a sizeable woodland with no houses in sight.

"I was not aware there was so much woodland up here. It is almost a forest!"

William walked forward with exploring in mind, "Do you think someone owns it, or is it the King's?"

"Not sure – come on, we should go back!"

"Sim, why not walk over as far as that first bunch of pine trees? We might see a house from there."

Simeon was reluctant but followed William. Of course, once William reached the pine trees, he immediately progressed onto the next clump of trees, but there was still no sign of any house. Gazing down the slope, William could see what he thought might be a track or a driveway.

"Come on, Sim; there is a path down there."

Simeon was carefully keeping watch on their bearings in case there was a need for a hasty retreat. Glancing to the right, William could not believe his eyes. He spied a toy fort about ten feet high with a moat, drawbridge, ramparts and flagpole one hundred yards away.

"Hey, Sim, look at that! It is a pirate fort. Come on."

The boys, entranced by what they saw, forgot they were on someone else's property and rushed eagerly towards the most magnificent fort they had ever seen. They were inside the fort, exploring the rooms and ramparts in less than thirty seconds.

William was already defending the fort from invading pirates when Simeon noticed a house in the distance.

"Hey, Will! There is a house down there. They probably own this land. We should run for Anne's house before they see us."

William stopped and gazed down in the direction Simeon now faced. William saw a two-storied large mansion with a flat green lawn five hundred yards down the hill. On the lawn, a solitary figure in a white dress was chasing her dog.

As soon as William saw the little girl in the white dress, he thought of Olivia, a young chimney sweep who died in an accident at their house. At the time, William was attracted to the little chimney sweep despite her being dirty and smelly. She was so gentle and unprotected that he felt a sense of duty towards her. The last he saw of her was Doctor Stephens wrapping her body in some white linen Anne had brought from the house.

The dog stopped and looked towards the fort and started growling and barking.

"Will, we must go quickly. Come on!" Simeon was away. He did not fancy being chased and eaten by some large dog.

As Simeon strode off, William turned and looked again. The little girl in the long white dress stood gazing at him on the fort battlement. She had long brown hair flowing down her sides to below her waist. The dog was running towards the fort, but she called it back. Then she smiled at William.

William stood up straight from his crouching position and smiled at her. She waved, and he waved back. Then she went inside, followed by the dog.

"It must be Olivia. She is back!'

Simeon's hand grabbed William's shoulder, "Run, Will! While we have the chance. Come on."

William took one last look and sprinted after Simeon, who was now well ahead.

Chapter 11

L ate in the afternoon, a carriage pulled up outside the residence of Doctor Neville and Mrs Bethany Bassington. A chilly westerly wind drove low dark clouds quickly across the sky with the threat of imminent rain. The footman assisted Lady Anne South as she left the carriage.

"Thank you, James. We must reach 'Porting' before the rain. I will only be here a few minutes, and then we are on our way."

"Yes, Milady!"

Anne rushed up the front steps onto the verandah and knocked quickly on the door. As she waited, she enjoyed the splendid view out across Guilford. She breathed in, relishing the country aromas; she was home again but without her husband.

On Tuesday, Anne had been teary for much of the trip from Portsmouth. By her arrival at Fintelton, she had gathered her spirits, but the previous night missing Robert had nearly brought her to tears at dinner. Talking late into the night with Emma was a good tonic and cheered her immensely. But now, she was in Guildford without Robert, feeling as if nothing had transpired over the last two weeks. Anne was determined she would steel herself and be strong.

Mrs Goodhew answered the door, "Lady South, welcome back! Mrs Bassington has been expecting you. Come in, please."

"Thank you, Ivy. I still struggle with my new surname, but it will become normal in a few months. Now how is Bethany?"

Ivy Goodhew appreciated Anne's friendly approach but understood that could only happen privately: "She is well, but I will let her tell you the news!" Anne could see the look of excitement on Ivy's face.

Bethany rushed into the drawing room and hugged Anne, "You look so well, little sister. I am so glad you are back. Neville is on a late call and is not home yet. Now, I have planned on you joining us for dinner! Is that correct?"

"Yes. I must go and warn Mrs Kirby and arrange accommodation for the coachmen. The Earl insisted I take a coach with me for the next few months.

If this continues, Robert must plan a renovation for the old stable at the back of the house. Mrs Kirby will find the groom and footmen some accommodation at Porting in the servant quarters. There is plenty of room."

"Your business role at the bakery will require daily commuting. A stable may not be such a bad idea. The business offices are quite a distance from here, especially if it is raining or dark!"

"Yes, I suppose so. Life was so relaxed before I was married, but now my diary has become complicated. I had no idea what was confronting me. But Mrs Goodhew tells me there is some good news?"

Bethany looked innocent momentarily but then burst out with a guilty laugh, "Neville and I were keeping it a secret for another four weeks, but I will tell you if you promise....!"

Anne could see that her sister was radiant and so excited, "Beth, you are not?"

"Yes. Isn't it wonderful?"

"I am so glad for you, Beth! When is the baby due?"

"August."

"Wonderful, Beth, Congratulations! Is Neville happy?"

"Over the moon!" Beth was almost crying with joy.

Anne hugged her hard but asked, "I thought you planned on waiting for a while?"

"So did I!"

They both burst out laughing.

"Oh, Beth, this is so wonderful. I will not tell a soul, but it will be hard. When should I return for dinner as I must brief Mrs Kirby on my movements for the next week? She will be glad of the peace when we leave for London next Wednesday. I will tell you all about the honeymoon over dinner."

"Be back at seven, and Neville may have returned home by then."

"I will be here at seven on the dot."

Anne kissed her sister goodbye and rushed off to the waiting coach. She felt far more composed, having talked with Beth, and heard the good news.

"Now off to 'Porting'! Please, James!"

"Yes, Milady!"

The Rectory, Guildford ...

A frowning Reverend Andrew Taggart arrived at the front door of the rectory. He quietly sat on the porch bench, placing his hat beside him, considering the implications of the meeting with the bishop. The clouds were gathering, and it would soon rain. As the temperature dropped, he hugged his coat tight and took some comfort in this afternoon solitude, where he could gather his thoughts.

Andrew knew he was overcommitted and needed help with the church school. On several occasions, the bishop had declined his request for an assistant curate, but today, with no counter arguments, he had strangely agreed. Andrew was pleasantly surprised and most thankful despite not having any say in the appointee's selection. He was worried other reasons might have swayed the bishop's decision.

The school, housed in the church building, was experiencing increasing enrolments, and soon a separate school building away from the church must be considered. Discussions with the bishop concentrated on the need for a curate to manage the school, allowing him more time to focus on pastoral care.

Andrew sighed. God was good and had answered his request; however, he wondered if the new curate would cope with the job. He must keep an open mind and be thankful that he finally had some help.

Taking his hat in hand and standing, the reverend entered the rectory.

"Andrew, you are home. I was not expecting you until after dinner."

"The bishop had a dinner engagement and dispatched me home, Laura! No matter, I prefer your company. The meeting went well, and an assistant curate will commence in two weeks. He will be taking over running the school."

"Wonderful, Andrew! That will be a great help."

Laura Taggart noticed the dull expression on Andrew's face. "What is worrying you, Andrew?"

"I had no say in the selection, and we must accept this curate sight unseen. I shall make enquiries, so I know something of this gentleman's background."

"Perhaps, Andrew, you should trust the bishop and accept this assistance with an open mind. I am sure the bishop has made a good choice."

Andrew, in other circumstances, would probably agree with this suggestion from his wife. However, he was suspicious of this appointment and wished he could ignore his doubts. He must reconsider his feelings tonight and spend some time in prayer. It would be unforgivable if he doubted a fellow priest. Indeed, the recommendation from the bishop should be enough.

"So, Andrew, what is the name of this new minister joining our team here?"

"The Reverend Philip Hotspur. He will be coming from London in a few weeks."

The Bassington Residence, Guildford …

That evening Anne was most thankful for Beth and Neville's company. The dinner distracted her from thinking of Robert and gave her time to settle her thoughts. At nineteen years of age, she was still young and became agitated without her husband. Now the influence of her big sister and Neville was reassuring.

"We visited their mansion on the island. It was huge and would easily accommodate several families. I had no idea they had so much property."

Neville recalled the property, "Yes, once, I think when the fleet was in during July, Robert invited me down there for a week. It was an impressive house with many servants. I think they transfer the staff from 'Harting' down there for the summer. I hope you have many happy holidays there, Anne."

"I hope so too, Neville, and you and Beth must join us there."

As Ivy Goodhew cleared the dinner plates, Neville said, "Thank you, Mrs Goodhew. That was a delicious dinner."

Anne also thanked the cook, "Yes, thank you, Ivy. It was magnificent."

The little lady curtseyed and left the room with a pleasant smile.

"Now, Anne! I served in the navy for over thirteen years and appreciate how hard it is for married officers to part from their wives. It was a sacrifice I could not make, so I left the navy when I met Bethany. I assure you Robert is thinking of you tonight and yearning for you at 'Harting'. I understand he will join us in London on Friday next week. Well, that is better than waiting six months for him. Perhaps after Ireland, he will have more time off."

Neville smiled as he thought his words would considerably cheer up Anne. Unfortunately, they had the reverse effect.

Anne smiled and rubbed her nose, struggling to keep the tears at bay. She became emotional and could hardly find any breath, "I will count each day till then."

Bethany took Anne's hand and said, "The time will pass quickly. You will be busy, and the time will fly past."

"I know, and I am trying. But it is so hard, and I want Robert here!" Anne started sobbing and then burst into uncontrollable tears. Bethany took her in her arms and comforted her.

"There, there, little one. Robert is probably finding it hard, as well. We are here with you, and you may call whenever you wish."

Anne hugged Bethany hard, letting all her sorrow out on her sister's shoulder. Neville was amazed by this display of grief, and Bethany indicated that he should withdraw. Bethany sat there for several minutes, caressing her little sister as she slowly controlled her feelings.

"That is better. There is nothing better than a cry. I find it helps!"

"Sorry, Beth. With our mother dying and Robert away, it all came together, and I could not control my feelings. I am usually made of better stuff than that." Anne wiped her nose with a handkerchief as she leaned back on her chair.

"Everyone in times of need feels better after a good cry."

Anne smiled thankfully and said, "Even better if you have your big sister's shoulder available."

"Careful or big sister might be the next one crying!" They both giggled.

"How about you stay here tonight? We can talk all night if you wish."

"Thank you, Beth, but I must go home. I will be away early in the morning as much requires review at the office. A business needs constant attention."

"Do not push yourself too hard, Anne!"

"I will rest better tomorrow night, knowing the work is in hand. Three weeks is the most I have ever been away, and I worry about what awaits me."

"Surely the staff have it in hand?"

"Probably the routine work, but I wonder if father has made any strange decisions while I was away. He has not recovered from mother's death, and I must discuss that with him tomorrow. I think I will be in for a long talk."

"I am not sure he will ever get over mother's death. But he will adapt – he can still grieve and cope with life. I understand he has made plans with Hamish McPherson. The trip will help his recovery."

"That is good news, indeed."

Bethany gave Anne an update on all that had happened while she was on her honeymoon.

"Beth, do you know who owns the land behind 'Porting'?"

"I am sorry, but no."

"It is funny, but this afternoon before dark, I was in the kitchen and looked out towards the back fence. A young girl, probably eight or nine years old or perhaps older, was standing there with her dog. She had long dark hair reaching her waist and a lovely white dress. Her grooming was immaculate, and she smiled at me when she saw me looking at her through the kitchen window. I smiled back, but when I went outside, she was gone.

The dog was still there and friendly. It was the same breed as Nosey and behaved similarly, putting its head between my knees for a pat. The collar was engraved with the name 'Ralph'. I peered through the fence, but I could see no one around. Then I heard a whistle from somewhere on the property, and the dog raced into the forest."

"Strange! You would have expected she would introduce herself."

"She had a beautiful smile. It reminded me of someone, but I can't think who."

"Well, Anne. I am sure you will meet her soon."

Neville came back in. Anne rushed over and hugged him, "Thank you for your concern, Neville. I will get through this. Tonight, has been wonderful. I hope I can return the favour soon."

"Anne, I know I am always giving advice, but please trust me. Next Friday week at Harting will be wonderful for you and Robert. Until then, we are here if you need us. You are stronger than any of us, Anne South. You will manage this."

Neville hugged Anne, and with that, they walked her outside, and helped her into the coach.

At 'Porting', Anne once again found the dog sitting there. He licked her hands, gave a little wail, and shook like Nosey. Anne patted him and said, "What are you doing here, Ralph?"

The dog gave another little wail and then rushed off into the dark. Anne could hear someone whistling.

Glasgow, Scotland …

Aiden Reid pulled his coat tight around him as he walked down the busy Glasgow Street. People were everywhere, and he enjoyed being inconspicuous in the crowd as he followed his directions by memory. He veered left into a small road and carefully looked for the sign he was told would be halfway along the road on a two-story building.

Strolling quietly, he missed the sign at first, given the number of advertising boards for taverns, barbers, tobacconists, fishmongers, and other shops. Then he saw it. The sign read, 'Glasson's Boarding House'; the building was neat and in good repair. Entering, he found the reception area small but well-lit, and a smiling young lady greeted him.

"May I help you, Sir?"

"Yes, please. I am seeking Mr Angus Smith. We are repairing his yacht down in the harbour, and there are a couple of issues that I must clarify with him."

"Certainly, Mr….?"

"Reid."

"Mr Reid, please take a seat, and I will be back directly."

The receptionist smiled and exited through a door and down a hallway. Soon she returned and gave Aiden a piece of paper with an address.

"Thank you, Miss."

The receptionist did not reply but smiled, walked across and opened the front door for Aiden. Taking the cue, he was off and searching for this new address.

'Porting', Guildford …

Norma Kirby knocked on the door gently and entered the master bedroom with a tray of hot tea and buttered rolls.

"Mrs South, it is five o'clock, and I have your tray here as you asked."

Anne was fast asleep and did not stir.

Mrs Kirby put the tray on a side table, made up the fire, and lit a few candles. Completing this, she saw that Anne was still asleep, so she gently nudged her mistress's hand.

Anne sat up in shock and then saw the friendly face of Norma Kirby looking down at her, "It is just past five, Lady South. There are some rolls and a cup of tea here for you. What time would you like breakfast, Milady?"

Anne yawned, "Oh, Mrs Kirby. Sorry, I was fast asleep. Thank you for waking me. Breakfast at six, and please have the coachmen ready by seven. I must be at the offices early today. Is that rain I hear?"

"Yes! It is pouring down outside. Hopefully, it will stop later."

Mrs Kirby needed a word with her mistress. Seeing that Mrs South was still waking up, she decided it could wait until after breakfast. This young lady needed more time in bed to gather her thoughts.

Anne sat back after Norma left and enjoyed the tea and rolls. A heavy rain squall knocked on the windowpane as she gazed at the crackling fire and felt some relief from her sleep. Last night Anne had tossed and turned without Robert by her side, but some sleep must have come as she felt refreshed and ready for the day at work. Before leaving for the bakery offices, she must ensure Mrs Kirby knew all her appointments for the coming week.

As Anne sat there, she looked at the room's décor and decided it was a bit dated. The house needed some redecoration. Victoria Sopwith was the perfect person to help her. She had an eye for fashion, and Anne was sure she would also be good at home decorating. While thinking about Victoria, Anne suddenly realised she would need dresses for the coming London trip. Hopping out of bed, she opened her wardrobe. It was empty. Her clothes were still at home. What would she wear at the memorial service? Anne's mind kicked into action, and the plan for her day developed.

After discussing the following week's activities with Mrs Kirby at breakfast, Anne sent a message advising the butler at 'Harting' she would arrive on Thursday afternoon and remain till Sunday. She was unsure of Robert's movements but advised that Sir Robert would join her at the latest on Friday. Anne also arranged an afternoon tea invitation for Victoria Sopwith at the office. Anne wondered how she would cope with all these engagements and her work during the day.

"Lady South! Might I have a word?"

Mrs Kirby had also considered Anne's busy schedule and how tired she had looked last night when she arrived home.

"Yes, Mrs Kirby. Please excuse me for eating while you talk, but time is in short supply this morning."

"Milady, I have never been employed by a Lady who worked before. I thought about our discussion last night about all the appointments you will have this week and your London trip next week. It seems you have not planned for any relaxation time."

"I'm not sure I need relaxation time, Mrs Kirby, or I will start lamenting Sir Robert not being here with me."

"Milady, I would not pry, but with your workload, somehow, we must provide you with more help. You need a lady's maid! I am afraid I do not have the time or the skills for that, and my duties as a cook are full-time. It would help if you had a skilled maid. It will save a lot of time. I apologise for putting this so bluntly, Milady, but everyone needs rest, and you are not allowing yourself that."

"Thank you, Mrs Kirby. I understand your goodwill in these comments and appreciate them. I will give them some consideration today. Now, that was a delicious breakfast, but I must run."

"Milady, you have not had the second course yet!"

"Sorry, Mrs Kirby, there is no time left. While I am upstairs, would you ensure the carriage is ready?"

"Yes, Milady."

Glasgow, Scotland …

"Why have you been wasting my time with these different addresses?"

Angus Faulkner regarded Aiden Reid and could see the intensity in this man. The committee from Dublin had warned him about Reid, and he now saw why.

"We were expecting you, Aiden. We had you followed from Glasson's Boarding House, ensuring no one was trailing you. Much is at stake here, and we cannot be too careful. The British have watchmen everywhere; our complete network will be discovered if we make one mistake. You are not in Ireland now. Only a portion of the population supports us here."

Aiden Reid regarded Angus with a look of contempt on his face but said nothing.

"Fergus will take you out back and show you where you can bed down. Stow your things and be ready by seven o'clock. He will introduce the recruiters and assist with questions where he can. Remember, Aiden, no action here unless the committee approves it first. I will meet with you again around midday tomorrow and hear how you went."

Angus Faulkner put on his coat and cap and left through the front door of the café, disappearing down the road.

Fergus Taylor said nothing but walked off, leading the way. Aiden was disgruntled with this almost hostile reception in Glasgow but held his tongue and followed. At the shop's rear was a stairway down into a basement. Several bunks lined the walls, and a large table stood beside a wood heater in the centre of the room.

After indicating which bunk Aiden should use, Fergus said, "I will be back at seven. Be ready, then. Grab a meal from upstairs before the café closes at five. Stay here till tonight. If there is an emergency, the back door is right there."

Fergus pointed at the corner of the room. "There is a wee ally outside. Get out quickly and head for the docks. Find the offices of the Grey Shipping Line and walk up the alley beside the building. At the far end, go down the stairway and wait in the shadows below. Someone will be there during the night. But only use this place in a dire emergency. Got it?"

Aiden nodded.

"See you here at seven."

Fergus moved off and climbed the stairs, Aiden hearing his footsteps above as he walked towards the front of the café.

Turner Business Offices, Guildford …

Anne was in her office, checking her mail, when her father arrived around eight in the morning. She looked up as Jonathan entered her office.

"Anne, you are back early. Why did you not come home for dinner last night?"

"Unfortunately, Robert was called back a week early by the Admiral. However, they have granted him extra time for David and Emma's wedding and a couple of extra days in Guildford before his ship departs from Woolwich. I had arranged a dinner with Beth and Neville in advance. Perhaps tonight, Father?"

"Yes, come tonight, please. How was your honeymoon?"

Anne smiled, "Everyone asks me that at the moment." They spent several minutes catching up on the family news.

"Your Uncle Richard and Aunt Sarah leave for South Africa on Wednesday next week. Clementine and I will say farewell to them at Southampton. Katherine will return here and join Clementine in her bedroom."

"It is funny that I have been away only a week and a half, and now my room is Clementine's!"

"Anne, you are now married and have your own house. All the family still loves you, but time moves on for all of us. I hope Clemmie and Katherine will re-establish the good relationship they enjoyed at Huntley. If not, I may need help from you and Beth settling any differences."

"Father, I think Ethel will come in handy there. Let her work with the two of them if there is a difference of opinion. Ethel is very balanced and patient."

"She is, indeed! I rely more and more on her every day. It makes me realise how much I miss your mother."

"I miss her too, Father. In time we will both cope better. We must have plenty of time together as a family for now."

"Oh, I should tell you, Anne! Hamish McPherson has invited me on an adventure he proposes in the Scottish Highlands. Their company is reorganising, and I understand he will announce the details when he visits Glasgow. Hamish asked that I join him in Glasgow, from where we will set off. I agreed and thanked him for the invitation. I need the break as I find it hard to concentrate on the business now."

"How long will you be gone for, Father?"

"I am not sure. Hamish will advise me of the dates soon, and then we can plan for my absence. Have you run through the figures yet?"

"Yes, at a cursory glance, the cash flow seems far better than I expected. The navy biscuit contract payment was helpful, and that ten thousand pounds you banked made a great difference. What was that for, Father?"

"Ah, yes, I remember that. It might be better if we discuss that one at home tonight. It is time I explained that fully. As you will be managing while I am away, you must be aware of a certain agreement."

"Is the agreement here? I could read it now, saving time tonight!"

"No, it is in my study. Better if we go through it there together. Tonight, after dinner!"

With that, Jonathan withdrew, ensuring the conversation was finished. Anne was intrigued but realised she must wait. She scribbled a note advising Mrs Kirby she would not be home for dinner and found the receptionist downstairs, "Daisy! Would you have that delivered, please?"

The office was a scene of activity, with clerks rapidly counting yesterday's takings and readying the money for banking. Audrey was talking with Clementine at her desk.

"Morning, Audrey! Morning, Clementine!"

Audrey broke out in a lovely smile, "Miss Anne. Welcome back. Oh! I must apologise. I should call you Lady South. I am sorry."

"No matter! In the office, please call me Anne. But when there are non-staff present, probably Lady South. I am finding it hard as well. It is confusing changing your name. Now, Clementine! How are you settling in?"

"Welcome back, Anne! Why did you not come home last night and see us?"

"I was tired, and Beth had already arranged tea for me. Don't worry; I will be home for dinner tonight."

"Good, now William and Simeon are here. I knew you were with Father, so I held them back in the waiting area. They asked if they could see you before school starts. Should I send them upstairs?"

"No, I will collect them. Thank you, Clementine."

Anne joined the boys in the reception area. William raced over and hugged Anne, and Simeon was not far behind.

"Anne, you are home! We have missed you so much."

"And I have missed you as well. Now, why are you here?"

Simeon seemed quite excited, "Anne, we visited 'Porting' yesterday with father and found a forest behind your back fence. We explored some of it and found a pirate fort, the best we had ever seen. May we come home with you today and play in the fort again?"

Then William added, "Yes, Anne, it was the best. You must see it."

Anne considered the request and remembered the strange girl she had seen in the twilight yesterday. They should gain permission before invading the property again, but she was unaware of who the owner was.

"Perhaps not this afternoon, boys, as we should first seek permission. Do you know who owns that property?"

"No, but we could see a house in the distance from the fort. Someone must be living there as we saw a girl playing on the lawn. She waved."

"She looked much like Olivia, but she was older. Perhaps she is a relative."

Anne took pity on her young brother's enthusiasm, but also, she was interested in knowing who owned the property and who the young girl was.

"I shall make enquiries today, and we will discuss it tonight at dinner. Now it is time for school. The Reverend Taggart will be wondering where you are."

As Anne sat at her desk, she noticed a letter from Hamish McPherson in her mail. Opening the letter, she read:

McPherson Brewing Company
Woolwich, England

Lady Anne South
Managing Director
Turner Milling and Baking
Guildford

Dear Anne

Just a quick note saying how much Marjorie and I enjoyed your wedding in early February, and we look forward to renewing our acquaintance with you and Robert in the future.

If possible, might I reserve a time with you mid-afternoon at 'Harting' after Jennifer Steele's memorial service? As you will be aware, your father and I are planning a trip, and I hope it will assist in his recovery from the loss of your mother. As you will be running the business in Guildford without your father present, I thought it might be helpful to discuss how our companies might assist each other at this time.

Please reserve from three in the afternoon until four if you would be so kind. I am sure we will have a lively conversation. Please advise me if Friday, the second of March, is not suitable, and I will suggest another time.

Yours respectfully
Hamish McPherson

Anne noted the appointment in her diary and sent a note accepting the invitation.

Portsmouth, Admiral Sutherland's Flagship ...

"Captain South, welcome. Admiral Sutherland enjoys being back at sea; however, I must admit the larger office ashore was a luxury I preferred!"

"You should have remained a Captain, Commodore."

"Precisely, South, something you should also keep in mind before they promote you again. Now, I have the reports here."

Jacobs closed the door and lowered his voice slightly, "I went through the three different reports and realised the impossibility of the rebels knowing the voyage routes before embarkation. In your case, it was less likely as your destination was the navy dockyards at Woolwich. It may have been an intelligent guess, but I doubt it. It appears we must think outside the box here. If the crew were not responsible, then who was?"

"Precisely, my thoughts, Sir."

"Well, Captain South! Did your thoughts take you any further?"

"I have considered this for some time, Commodore. There are various possibilities, but I have not taken it further."

Commodore Jacobs sat back in his chair and considered South. Jacobs could clearly see the captain was now suspicious of those ashore and unsure who he could trust. South suspected that someone within the navy ranks ashore must have gained access if it was not the crew. So, either someone within the Admiral's staff or someone above who had privileged access. This proximity complicated their relationship as South was unsure if he could trust the Commodore.

"I understand your reluctance, South. However, for all our sakes, this mystery should be solved quickly. Once I was convinced that there must be someone outside of the ship's crew leaking this information, I checked every member of my staff. I went back through each man's history and family background. I came up with nothing. I am not saying that my checks were perfect, but it seems unlikely that one of my staff was the culprit. Now that leaves only one alternative."

'Surely not, Commodore. There could be many alternatives."

"Yes, that is true, but the probability of it being someone distant is remote. It is more likely that the deception comes from above!"

Robert was still unsure he could trust the Commodore and held back from sharing his opinion.

"South, I understand you are treading very carefully here as you are unsure who you should trust. Particularly as your life may depend on this, I can say that I suspect that the culprit who gave away the route information was either the Admiral or someone above the Admiral. I, for one, have complete trust in Sutherland, so I would say that it came from a higher source."

Robert felt he must give some comment, "That is reasonable."

"Then, Captain South, it appears I may not be of any further assistance. The fleet embarks for the Mediterranean soon, and you will be in Ireland."

"What would you suggest, Commodore?"

"I am sure I need not speak on this any further as I would assume you understand my precise meaning. All I can say, Captain, is, be careful and trust no one. We both agree that there is a connection between the Irish rebels and someone well-placed in England who has either access or influence with the Admiralty. It may be that someone is manipulating the Irish for some other purpose. Given your success in combatting their previous attempts, it may be that you are now a target."

The Commodore said nothing for a few seconds, allowing South time to consider his comments. Then he continued.

"I will say no more on the matter. I wish you success on your Irish mission and hope you join us soon in the Med. Take care, Captain South."

"A moment, please, Commodore."

"Yes, South."

Robert asked, "Sir, might I ask if Lord Dawlting was involved in planning the Irish missions?"

The Commodore looked away, considering if he should reveal this information. Turning back, he said, "I believe he has had some involvement. I understand you are having dinner with the First Lord on the second of March. Making the most of that opportunity with the Admiral may be prudent. He may shed some light on the situation." Jacobs raised his eyebrows and smiled.

"Thank you, Commodore."

With that, Robert saluted, left the commodore's office, walked across the quarter-deck, and found his cutter below. Captain South, taking his seat, watched with interest as the crew hauled up the sail and got her underway towards *Shadow*. As the cutter raced back, Robert carefully considered Jacobs suggestions. If the Commodore were the leak, he would make sure his staff were clear of any suspicion. But could he trust what Jacobs told him? At this stage, Jacobs was still under suspicion. However, what he said about the information coming from above was also sensible. Robert did not suspect Admiral Sutherland for one moment. He had known Sir Tristan for too long and respected his integrity. Those above the Admiral were far from clear in Robert's mind. Could this be some powerplay from above, and he was a pawn in their game?

Turner Household, Guildford ...

At ten o'clock, Anne took a break for morning tea. Leaving the office, she briefed Daisy about visiting the Turner house and walked towards the High Street. On arriving, she knocked on the front door, but there was no answer. Anne tested the door and found it unlocked. Venturing inside, she heard staff talking in the kitchen.

"Mrs Jennings and Aggie, we must discuss the dinner menu for the next two weeks. What have you planned? Mr Turner will be away from Monday but will return with Clementine and Miss Katherine on Thursday. We will need clean sheets on the beds." Ethel held a large piece of paper on which she had drafted a timetable for the coming weeks.

Mrs Jennings was puzzling over the timetable as Anne peaked her head around the door, "Sounds impressive, Ethel. I wonder if Mrs Kirby does that."

Ethel turned in surprise, "Miss Anne, welcome back. You are looking very well, indeed."

"Thank you, Ethel. I am well. Did father tell you I would be at dinner tonight?"

Realising that Anne, now a married woman, should be addressed with her new title, Ethel replied, "My apologies, I should have said Lady South. Unfortunately, he has not, but we expected you might, so we are prepared."

"Good. I must apologise for barging in, but I need clothes. Are my dresses in my room?"

"No, I moved them into the guest room for when you returned. I am afraid Clementine is putting her stamp on your room. But you will easily find them in the cupboard upstairs."

Mrs Jennings and Aggie hugged Anne and asked about the honeymoon. They talked with great excitement for a few minutes before Anne refocused the conversation, "Now I am short of time at present, so we can all talk again tonight. I must check my dresses and then return. Ethel, would you have a minute as I need a favour?"

"Certainly, Lady South."

Ethel followed Anne into the drawing room, where they could speak alone.

"Mrs Kirby is already complaining that she cannot cope with my busy schedule. I understand she was employed as a cook, which is fine, but I need extra help surviving this married life. My parents employed you through an agency, Ethel! I need a Lady's Maid. Would you please assist me, as I do not have the time for this?"

"Yes, certainly. I have all the agency details and will contact them today."

"Thank you, Ethel. You are a darling. We can talk more tonight at dinner. Now I must check the dresses and then visit Hursts. You can see why I need a Lady's maid!"

With that, Anne was off upstairs and soon sorting through her clothes.

Ethel found Mrs Jennings and Aggie pouring over the new timetable in the kitchen.

High Street, Guildford …

Simeon and William rushed home from school and soon caught up with the girls walking ahead. Madeline was deep in conversation with Dawn Luckett and Sophie Watson, "Ruby must be sick if she stayed away from school. We will introduce you once she is back. How did you enjoy your first day, Sophie?"

"I liked it. The Reverend Taggart is kind, and I love Mrs Taggart. She is so sweet."

Simeon and William ran past the girls, racing for home.

Madeline dodged the boys, nearly being pushed over, "Hey! Watch out, you boys! What is the rush for?"

Simeon ran behind William, turned, gave Madeline a wink and a smile and mouthed, 'Sorry!' He chased William along the High Street, barely maintaining a grip on his bag.

The girls, who had stepped aside, watched them run away. Madeline was suspicious, "They normally do not rush home for their chores. They are planning something. We should go and find out."

William reached home first and raced through the front door, down the hall and onto the back verandah. By the time Simeon arrived, William had the axe ready and a piece of wood on the chopping block.

Simeon called, "Let me chop the wood, as I am faster. Will, keep bringing out the blocks to me. We can stack it later." William darted off with Nosey following, tail madly wagging and searching for a pat.

Simeon took the first swing and perfectly hit his target, chopping the woodblock into four or five fragments, ready for the fires. As he lifted another piece onto the chopping block, the girls strolled out onto the back verandah and watched. Simeon did not look up, concentrating on his next axe swing. Within ten minutes, the pile of wood splinters reached a respectable size, and William decided he should stack some in the woodshed.

Soon the girls lost interest and withdrew into the kitchen, where Aggie put out afternoon tea. Ethel asked how Sophie's first day at the church school went.

"I think I will enjoy the school, Mrs Nibley. Mrs Taggart is arranging some reading for me that I have never heard of before. I think I will be learning far more here than if I had stayed in Scotland."

"Sophie, my understanding was that you came from Glasgow. Is that correct?"

"Not exactly. For the last five years, we have lived at Killarow, on the Isle of Islay. It is very remote, and my father was the doctor for the Isle. The school was small, with only eleven students and often no teacher. So, some of the mothers stood in and did their best. My mother gave me additional schooling at home."

"I have never heard of the Isle of Islay, Sophie. It must be remote."

Madeline was also interested, "We have an atlas in the drawing room. Come on! We can look it up!"

Dawn and Madeline rushed off for the atlas, while Sophie said, "Thank you, Mrs Jennings, for the lovely warm quiches. They were delicious."

"Thank you, Sophie. That is nice of you." Ethel and Mrs Jennings were impressed with Sophie's kind comments and good manners.

Simeon stopped chopping and inspected William's pile in the woodshed.

"That is enough, Will. Father will be satisfied. We can now gather some afternoon tea and be off."

The boys darted into the kitchen and explained that they would chop wood for Anne at 'Porting'. Ethel considered their request as they quickly munched on the crisp, tasty quiches.

"Does Mrs South know you are chopping wood there?"

"No, it is a surprise for Anne, but Mrs Kirby knows. They do not have a man yet for that work. We will take Nosey with us. He needs a walk."

Ethel felt the explanation was reasonable, but she still had doubts, "Do not stay there too long. Lady South has a lot happening, and she will be tired when she comes home. Make sure you stay together and are back before six o'clock."

Simeon and William each slid a quiche into their pockets and rushed out the back leading Nosey off towards 'Porting'. Ethel watched as they hurried away.

"They seem in a great hurry, Ethel!"

"Yes, Mrs Jennings, they do. I will leave you and Aggie with the dinner preparations and take a walk. Perhaps I will visit 'Porting' myself. I have a feeling these young fellows will get into trouble."

Mrs Jennings nodded in agreement, "My thoughts exactly!"

Turner Business Offices, Guildford ...
"Victoria, thank you for coming. Would you take some tea or coffee?"

"A cup of tea, please."

Audrey knocked on the door and entered, "Excuse me, Lady South and Miss Sopwith. Here is the information you requested on your neighbour." Audrey passed across a sheet of paper and quietly backed out of the office.

"Thank you, Audrey."

As the door closed, Victoria said, "The name, Lady South, sounds lovely! How are you coping with the change?"

"At present, with great difficulty. But I will adapt in time. It felt rather funny the first time someone greeted me in that way. Please excuse my pride here; I was proud of becoming Robert's wife and accepted the name with honour. It is the start of a new life for me."

Victoria smiled and said, "I understand it is a strong tradition that a woman must take on her husband's name in marriage. I am not sure I could give up my name. With the loss of my father, mother, and brother, I feel a kind of duty to remain a Sopwith."

"If you find the right man, you might change your mind!"

"Do you think so? It would mean giving up my inheritance, and I would feel insecure being dependent on a man. I am not sure I could love anyone that much."

"Victoria, soon we should talk at length about that. I agree you should not give up your inheritance. The lawyers can arrange that. Before you marry and find a man you love and respect, you should explain that the inheritance will remain your property. That will certainly flush him out if he is a gold digger."

"Oh!"

"Now, I must ask you for some help. I have been looking at 'Porting's décor, which is very dated. All the rooms require redecorating. I wondered if you would assist me and allow me to benefit from your advice."

"Yes, please, Anne. What a treat. We will have some fun doing that!"

"Thank you, Victoria. I have some colour skills but am far more comfortable with someone advising me. Mother and Beth have always been good at that. But circumstances have changed, so I am excited that we can do it together."

"I am glad you are back, Anne. I missed our conversations while you were away."

'Me too!" Anne picked up her cup of tea and took a sip.

'Porting', Guildford, ...

William led Simeon and Nosey through the fence and towards the first clump of trees.

"All clear, no sign of Pirates." William was looking for the fort. On the other hand, Simeon was looking for the property's owners.

"No sign of that dog, which is good." Simeon gave Nosey a pat making sure the dog did not bark.

"Sim, which way is the fort?"

"Over that way." Simeon pointed at a clump of trees around a hundred yards on their right.

Quietly the boys darted across and soon spied the fort fifty yards ahead. They rushed over and ran through the entrance. Taking a breath in the fort's safety, they stopped and looked around.

A voice came from behind them, "I thought you would be back. Is school out?"

Turning, they looked straight at the young girl they had seen the previous day. She stood in the same white dress, holding a leash latched onto Ralph. The dog stood motionless, with its tail straight up in the air. Being a relatively friendly dog, Nosey ran over and started smelling Ralph.

The girl said, "OK!" Ralph immediately relaxed and started smelling Nosey.

William asked, "Who are you?"

The girl replied, "More importantly, why are you on my father's land?"

"The fort! We have never seen such a good fort before. We like playing pirates."

"What are your names?"

"I am William Turner, and this is my brother, Simeon. We live on High Street but are visiting our sister Lady South, who lives at 'Porting'. Do you mind if we play in the fort?"

"No, not at all. But my father might become angry."

"Who is your father?"

"Mr Benjamin Petherton. He is an important businessman in London. We live in Guildford as my father says it is safe here, and the air is cleaner."

"He is right. I visited London twice last year, and the air smelt of smoke and bad stuff. I would not live there either." William noticed that the girl was slightly taller than either himself or Simeon. She had very fair skin and magnificent long dark brown hair. "What is your name?"

"Clare."

"Do you often play at the fort, Clare?"

"Not that often now. Before my brother Mark died, we would play here every day. But now I do not come here much at all. My father has the gardener keep the fort clean and ready for use. Father comes up here sometimes, sitting alone and remembers Mark. I think he is still sad about him dying."

"How did your brother die, Clare?" Simeon was interested in her story.

"He fell from a horse in the paddock on the other side of the house. Father says the fall broke his neck, and he died instantly. It was a sad time, and I still miss him. When I saw you yesterday, I thought you were Mark coming back."

"Really! That would be hard if he is dead!"

"Yes. I realised later it was not Mark, as the flag was not up. Mark always put up the flag when he was in the fort. That way, father knew where he was."

The children looked up at the Union Jack flying from the flagpole.

William was surprised by Clare's comment. "I thought you were a girl called Olivia; I saw her die in one of our chimneys. She suffocated because she swallowed too much soot!"

"Was she a chimney sweep?"

"Yes. Olivia's parents were poor and sold her to the Master Chimney Sweep. He treated them terribly. She was filthy and smelly when I first met her, but I felt sorry for her."

Clare noticed William became downcast as he spoke about Olivia. Simeon said, "William liked Olivia, and he took some time getting over it."

"I did not!"

Clare changed the subject, "From whom did you acquire your dog? He is the same breed as Ralph."

"Nosey was a present from a friend of the family, Mr McPherson from Greenwich. Burglars killed our first dog, 'Snups', one night. Mr McPherson is a kind man, and he got us another dog. We called him 'Nosey'."

Clare smiled, "How old is Nosey?"

"I think he is nearly one. When did we get him, Sim?"

"I think six months would be closer."

Clare patted Nosey, "I thought he was more of a puppy than Ralph." Clare's dog looked up at the mention of his name.

"It is time you were home, Miss Clare!" A tall lady with spectacles appeared in the doorway of the fort. William and Simeon looked up with some surprise.

Clare said, "This is Mrs Preston. She is my Governess. Mrs Preston, this is William and Simeon."

"What is your surname, boys?"

"Turner."

"No relation of the bakery man, Turner?"

"Yes, he is our father."

"Do you boys know this is private land? If you play here, you will need a formal introduction and permission from Mr Petherton. Please, do not come back here without that. Now, where did you come from."

"We came through the back fence of our sister's home, Lady South of 'Porting'."

"Are yes, I know of 'Porting'."

"Well, you tell your sister what you have been doing and that Mrs Preston will be seeing her. So, make sure you tell her. Now boys, off you go home."

Mrs Preston lowered the flag and placed it in a box beneath the walkway. Clare appeared upset that Mrs Preston would be so forthright with her new friends. She urgently said, "Simeon, have you a sister around my age?"

"How old are you, Clare?"

As Mrs Preston led Clare away, the girl called, "Eleven."

"Yes! Madeline is eleven."

Clare shouted, "Tell your sister mentioning Madeline will help! Bring her when you next come."

Mrs Preston, holding Clare's hand tightly, led her off towards the house. Clare looked behind and, with her free hand, waved. Then she whistled Ralph, who stopped smelling nosey and immediately sprang after her.

Ethel and Mrs Kirby stood looking at the vegetable patch as the boys climbed through the back fence. Ethel said, "Did you find what you were looking for, boys?"

Simeon and William stood there with their mouths open, looking guilty.

Dock's Area, Glasgow ...

Fergus Taylor led Aiden Reid into the last pub for the night. They sat at a table at the rear of the bar area, waiting for Ian Doyle to arrive. It was clear that the previous two recruiters had not contacted anyone suspicious.

As Fergus' drink arrived, he said, "Are you sure you will not have a drink, Aiden?"

"Positive. I must keep my head clear for the interview, but you go ahead."

Fergus had now deduced that Aiden had little small talk. An attribute probably ideal for a brother's member, but it made developing a relationship rather difficult. Fergus could not understand this man. As Aiden questioned Iain Hughes and Robert Murray, the questions came across like orders, and he expected quick answers. Perhaps this was what was required when you were in a leadership position.

As the night went on, the smoke in the pub created a mist that gave each table a certain amount of privacy. Approaching eleven more men entered the bar, and the noise levels continued increasing. But there was still no sign of Ian Doyle. Fergus was becoming uncomfortable as Aiden was not drinking, not talking, and becoming impatient. Thankfully, at that moment, Ian Doyle strode into the bar and stood at the counter waiting for his usual.

"That's him!" Fergus nodded in Ian's direction. Aiden placed a hand on Fergus's arm and said, "Wait a bit and see what he does". This confused Fergus even more as he thought Aiden wanted answers straight away.

Ian Doyle took his drink and joined a group of men who looked like sailors. As he sat at their table, the conversation went through introductions and quickly became more jovial. Ian had already finished his first drink when one of the sailors fetched another. That drink also disappeared quickly.

"Likes his drink, does he?"

"Aye, he drinks scotch but only Isle of Islay scotch. He said he discovered it some months ago. Won't touch anything else."

Aiden looked hard at Fergus as he considered that comment. Then he sat back in his chair and continued watching the small man for another ten minutes. During that time, Ian Doyle put down another three scotches.

Leaning forward onto the table with his hands held together, Aiden quietly said, "Fergus, I think this will be our man. You order at the bar and bring back some scotch malted at Islay and three glasses. When you bring him over, you say nothing and sit there and listen. When we finish, follow me out of here and stick with me. You understand."

Fergus nodded in agreement.

"Go get the scotch, Fergie!" Aiden gave him a wink as he stood.

When Fergus returned, Aiden poured three glasses of whisky. "Go get him!"

Aiden leaned back, thinking about how he would handle this. Slowly a small smile came across his face.

In a few minutes, Fergus and Ian returned. Taking their seats, Fergus leaned over and introduced Ian quietly, "Aiden, this is Ian Doyle. He does a lot of good recruiting for us here in the docks."

Aiden and Ian shook hands, "Ian, good meeting you, lad. Thanks for all these fellows you send through and the ones we send over here that you care for."

"A pleasure, Aiden."

"Ian, I have been briefing the committee here on what happened with our last mission. You may not have heard, but that does not matter, as it was a huge success. Fellows like you who supply us with fine recruits make all the difference. We thank you for that. How about we toast that."

Ian Doyle, hearing the praise, relaxed and took his glass willingly. He guzzled the drink down in one go. Smiling, he said, "We do the best we can. How about another?" He whispered, "To a free Ireland!"

"Aye!" Aiden filled Ian's glass again, and he and Fergie joined him in the toast.

Fergus Taylor was amazed at the complete change in Aiden Reid's personality. He was charming, friendly, and good company. Aiden smiled as he talked and had Ian Doyle in the palm of his hand. Fergus realised then that Aiden was a dangerous man.

"Ian, I gave the committee here all the information they requested, but one thing came up. They asked me if I knew two Irish sailors searching for a working passage home last Christmas. They described them as a medium-height man of normal build and a tall, muscular man who did not say much. They are skilled sailors who know their ropes soundly. The committee wants them for a job they have in mind. I have not met them and cannot provide any information, but I have been asking around while here. I, too, would welcome a meeting with them. Their skills would help us greatly."

Ian Doyle scratched his head and sat back, "Aiden, let me think. Do you know if they are still here?" Ian tapped his finger on the empty glass as he thought.

Fergus filled the glass.

Keeping the conversation flowing, Aiden added, "Well, Ian, they could be back in Ireland by now. So, I will ask around at home once I get back. It is of no consequence if you are unaware of them. As I meet our recruiters, I ask them, as the committee is sure these men came through Glasgow. I will help the committee if I can."

Ian skolled his glass, licked his lips and tapped the glass with his finger.

Fergus was impressed with how Aiden controlled Ian's thinking, with the lad now thinking he was doing Aiden a favour.

As Aiden filled Ian's glass, he said, "My Ian, you like this scotch, man!"

"Aye, it is Isle of Islay scotch. I never drank it before last October when I visited the island delivering some recruits. Best whisky I have ever tasted. Do you like it?"

Aiden confided in a low voice, "Yes, I like it, but I am a bit of a slow drinker. I have my health problems, you know. Weak bladder!"

"Fair enough." Ian Doyle was now thoroughly convinced of Aiden's sincerity.

He gazed around the room and lowered his head, "I think I met these men you describe. I am not sure where they are now, but I can tell you what I know. Make sure you mention my name when you talk with the committee, please. A little bit of praise always helps."

Aiden and Fergus leaned forward with interest, "Definitely, Ian."

"The big man did not say much at all. They were both drunk and crying, sad about getting home for Christmas. It was long since they had seen Ireland, hard-pressed into the navy as sailors back in eighteen-ten. After the war, they were paid off and signed on an Indiaman, the 'Duchess', out of Bristol. Come mid-year, they worked on the farms and saved for a passage home."

"Where was home?"

"Gweedore. Michael O'Flaherty's father owns the pub there. Mick Ryan was tagging along with Michael. Said he had no family."

"So, were they interested in working for us."

"Yes, we talked about a passage home and a ship that would soon depart."

"Ian, what do you mean a ship that would soon depart?"

"As I said earlier, I visited Islay in October, and there was a ship there that the brothers were working on for a mission. They were searching for more crew members who had sailing skills."

"But you did not tell them where it was? Did you?"

"Oh, no! I am a bit cagier than that. At first, I was not sure of them; you never are with recruits. After a few rounds of drinks and getting under their guard, I was sure they were good Irish boys. They were interested in a passage on an Irish-bound packet, and we talked and drank for most of the night. They were good company."

"Ian, who bought all the drinks?"

"They did! They spent a bit of money that night. I told them I would only drink Islay scotch. Just like this one tonight. Ha, ha!"

"So, what happened the next night?"

"Well, they never came back. I expect it was the fight we had in the bar. Some Scottish lads came in looking for a fight. I led the charge from the Irish side. The two disappeared out a side alley, and I never saw them again."

"Thank you, Ian. I will let the committee here know, and I will also use these details in Ireland. I hope we can contact them as they have skills we can use."

Ian Doyle sat back and skolled another glass of scotch. He seemed pleased with the information he had provided. Fergus also sipped at his drink, relaxing and thinking Reid was satisfied. Aiden excused himself and visited the toilet at the back of the bar. On his return, he suggested, "Ian, the night is young, and I have finished for tonight. How about you show us a few of the dock bars where you find these recruits? We could all use some more scotch. The drinks are on us."

Ian Doyle was all for this suggestion and led the way out of the bar and towards the docks. Aiden and Fergus followed, checking exactly where they were.

"It is a bit dark down this street on the left." Ian strode out as if he had not had any drink at all. Aiden caught up with him and walked beside him. As they passed a dark side road that ended at a pier, Aiden called out in alarm and pointed, "Hey, what is that!"

Ian looked in the direction that Aiden was pointing as a pistol's heavy barrel cracked the top of his skull. He fell instantly, hitting the ground hard. Aiden quickly crouched down, facing Fergus with his finger across his lips, signalling silence. They carried Ian Doyle along the dark road and placed him in the shadows on the pier.

After standing there for five minutes, they agreed they were alone. There was no movement on the dock, and the tide was high.

"Help me lift him onto the pier's edge in the shadows over there."

Fergus followed Aiden's orders, scared of disagreeing with this man. They laid Ian down at the edge of the dock, where they could easily roll him into the water. Aiden pulled out his pistol again and covered the gun with a thick woollen cloth. Fergus watched in horror as Aiden put the weapon against the side of Ian's head and fired.

The pistol shot was deadly, but surprisingly the woollen cloth muffled most of the noise. Reid pushed the body into the water, followed by the pistol and cloth.

Quietly moving Fergus back into the shadows, Aiden said, "Time we split up, Fergus. Tell the committee I will not be back. I have no time for their endless meetings. The story of the two men was crap. Any intelligent officer could have made that up, and by chance, I know that the pub owner at Gweedore is Sean O'Flanagan, a strong supporter of the brothers. He has been there for twenty-five years. A decent recruiter should have either checked this out or picked it up. Ian Doyle told them more than he should have. You heard him talk about how he only drinks Islay whisky. Islay was the critical bit of information they were after!

Ian Doyle was responsible for the death of thirty-seven good Irish boys and several gravely injured others.

You can have fun telling the committee. Also, let them know their safe house in Islay is compromised. I found Ferguson dead on his bed. It looks like his girl companion knifed him. There was blood all over the nightdress she left. I cleaned the place up and buried him. The British will never find the grave.

The committee should send someone quickly and secure the site. Tell them it will be a waste of time looking for me. I will surface again in Cobh when I am ready."

Chapter 12

Turner Business Offices, Guildford …

By mid-afternoon on Friday, Anne had reviewed the Turner Bakery accounts and was satisfied that everything was in order. However, one trend worried her, the increase in revenue they had experienced in the previous year had eased. Sales were now flat, and without an increase, they may not meet their bank commitment of refreshing their reserves.

As she considered the problem, there was a knock on her office door.

"Lady South, I wonder if I might speak with you?"

"Certainly, Jeb. What may I assist you with?"

Jeb Hiscock, the bakery manager, and a good friend of Anne nervously moved forward and placed an open letter on her desk.

"The Magistrate's Court has requested me as a witness at the London trial of the arsonists. It states that the trial will start on Wednesday, the twenty-eighth of March and may take three days. The Court has also called our Mill Manager, Terry Spencer and the Parish Constable, Michael Rawlins."

Anne read the letter, "The Court will require you for three days and the travelling time as well. You must not worry, Jeb! It will be an open and shut case. But, if you tell the truth, which I am sure you will, justice will be served."

"Lady South, the furthest I have ever travelled from Guildford is Batton Place, where my parents live. I walk there every night. Some nights I stay with the Stern family, which saves me the walk home. London is a long way from Guildford, Ma'am."

Anne realised the challenge Jeb was facing in his mind. After all, it was only last year that she visited London for the first time. For Jeb, this would be the longest trip of his life. Moreover, the Bakery had a responsibility towards him as an employee.

"Jeb, I have spoken with my father about the trial. We agreed that I would attend and support you, Terry, and Constable Rawlins and find accommodation for you and the others. If necessary, I can meet with you each day at the Court. You will not be alone, as Mr Blake Wood, our attorney from Guildford, will be with you daily. Mrs Smith from Hurst's will fit you and Terry for gentlemen's outfits for the trial."

"Thank you, Lady South. I appreciate that greatly."

"While you are here, Jeb, I need your opinion on the sales trend. I have been reviewing the figures and noticed that sales are not increasing. Have you noticed this?"

"Yes, Miss. I mean, Lady South!" Jeb stopped talking for a moment as he thought about the question.

"Last year, Thomas and Mr Turner spent much time visiting the landholders and convincing them there was better value in purchasing our products. Since Mrs Turner's death and Thomas leaving on his honeymoon, no one is visiting the landholders. There were many new people in Guildford last year, which is not happening this year. It is winter at present, so it may be that we will see greater crowds and sales as spring returns. Have you checked the sales for last winter?"

Anne was interested in what Jeb said, "That is a good point, Jeb. I will do that, and I agree with your comment about contact with customers. There has been a lot of change, and we have not kept our focus on the customers. Thank you for your insight."

"A pleasure, Lady South. Now I must be on my way. It will be dark by the time I reach home."

Jeb excused himself, and Anne packed up as she was due at the Turner household, where she would visit Ethel and check the progress of the new Lady's maid. But, before she left, Audrey Stern came into Anne's office with some papers and a message recently delivered. The writer had neatly wrapped it with a wax seal initialled, 'CC'.

As Anne opened the message, she wondered what 'CC' meant.

Mr Benjamin Petherton
Cloverdale Chase
Guildford, Surrey

Lady Anne South
'Porting'
Guildford, Surrey

C/- Turner Bakeries
Guildford

Dear Lady South,
I understand that you and your husband, Captain Sir Robert South,

have taken possession of the property 'Porting' which adjoins my property. Please accept my congratulations on your recent marriage and a welcome from your neighbour. I hope that in the future we shall enjoy good neighbourly relations.

A matter has arisen which I am sure we can resolve. I understand that your young brothers, William and Simeon, have been entering my property from 'Porting' and playing on the toy fort I constructed for my son Mark. Unfortunately, my son died in a tragic horse-riding accident two years ago, and the fort holds dear memories for me. I have restricted the fort's use for my daughter Clare under supervision as I sometimes visit there and spend time remembering my son.

Clare has requested that I grant your younger brothers and sister permission to play with her at the fort. Clare is eleven years of age and understands that Simeon and William have a sister of a similar age. My daughter is home-schooled and has a governess. I prefer keeping my dealings in the community private. However, I will allow your brothers and their sister, Madeline, access on the following conditions.

Firstly, I would ask that you join us for morning tea at eleven on Saturday morning for formal introductions. This meeting would meet my requirements for an acceptable introduction.

Secondly, I shall ask that any times for play are booked in advance, ensuring my daughter is accompanied by either her Governess, Mrs Irene Preston or my Head Gardener, Mr Samuel Grey.

These arrangements will ensure the propriety of any meetings and satisfy my requirements.

Please send a note of acceptance soon so my staff can make the catering arrangements. I look forward to meeting you and your siblings for morning tea.

Your Neighbour
Mr Benjamin Petherton.

Anne considered the note and thought Mr Petherton's request seemed reasonable, and it appeared he was keen on satisfying his daughter's request while ensuring her protection at a young age. She smiled, knowing this news would solve the issue of the boys' request. However, Madeline may require some convincing.

Knocking on her father's office door, she entered, "Father, I have a letter here from a Mr Benjamin Petherton. It concerns Simeon and William."

Jonathan looked up with interest. Anne briefly explained the situation, including the boys' incursions onto Mr Petherton's land. Anne could see her father becoming agitated.

"Father, please keep calm. They were doing what boys do, being adventurous. It is good for them, especially Simeon. The boys did not harm anything, and Mr Petherton seemed friendly and encouraging. Do you know him?"

"Yes, I have come across him often at the Guild meetings. He has a large wine and spirits business in London but lives in Guildford, keeping a low profile."

"Why would he keep a low profile?"

"He is a Catholic. It has not been easy for him over the years, and he takes care that his competitors have no opportunity of defaming him. A wise decision, as his life in Guildford is spared the scrutiny of city life. I find him a pleasant gentleman and have enjoyed working with him on several Guild projects."

"Then you approve my accepting his invitation for morning tea on Saturday. I wanted your agreement before I raised it with Madeline, as I intend to take the children with me in my carriage."

Jonathan sat there looking out the window, considering the proposed outing. William always found a way of embarrassing him on such visits, and he would prefer to avoid further issues.

"I feel no good will come of it! Please oversee William; I would not wish my relationship with Benjamin Petherton destroyed. Will they all fit in your carriage?"

"Yes, and we shall be a merry party."

"Then I leave it in your capable hands, Anne. Please advise Ethel. She confided in me the other night that she had been watching the boys when they visit you at 'Porting'."

Anne smiled and withdrew from her father's office. Anne was unaware that her father and Ethel knew about the boy's exploits at 'Porting'. Ethel's interest in the boys was pleasing, and she decided to speak with Mrs Kirby, ensuring she received reports on these events.

Guildford Medical Practice ...

Neville Bassington and David Sopwith talked over a cup of tea.

"What are your thoughts on Bryan Watson's performance this week, Neville?"

"He is a far better Doctor than I at first imagined. He is also good with patients – he develops trust quickly. Certainly, he is dedicated and works long hours. I am happy with him."

"Good. Emma has requested that I join her in London for the Charity Ball. It seems that Lady Jane is organising a table for all of us. I would not be surprised if you find an invitation when you return home tonight. So, I will be leaving earlier than planned."

"I had no idea that this was coming up! Lady Jane is unaware of the disruption she causes with her requests. No matter! So, Bryan will be left alone running the practice while we are both away." Neville became quiet as he considered the risks. "When will you be leaving?"

"Probably the Thursday morning and return by Monday evening."

"So, it will be for five days. Bryan will cope, David!"

"Good. I agree with your assessment. If client numbers increase, he would be a good prospect for a full-time position."

Neville grinned but did not elaborate and said, "Let us see how he copes by himself."

Turner Household, Guildford …

As Anne arrived, Mrs Jennings was setting out the afternoon tea for the children. She could hear Aggie calling Simeon and William from the wood chopping and Clementine's voice loudly advising where everyone should sit. Anne thought, 'Some things never change.'

As Anne entered the kitchen, she noticed Sophie Watson sitting beside Madeline.

"Hello, Sophie! It is lovely seeing you here."

"Thank you, Lady South. Madeline and I have some painting materials on the back verandah. We are working on a project about rivers!"

Madeline added, "At school, we have been learning about the rivers of England, and we thought if we copied the globe, we could create a map. Of course, the River Wey would be the centre of the map."

"How exciting. Do you have some painting paper?"

"Yes, Mrs Watson purchased some from Stanton's General store."

An excited Sophie said, "May we show you the paper, Lady South?"

"Yes, I would like that! But first, I must ask something."

The children were quietly crunching biscuits as Anne pulled out the letter.

"I received a letter from Mr Benjamin Petherton today who has invited Simeon, William and Madeline to morning tea at Cloverdale Chase tomorrow at eleven."

Madeline called out, "Why me? I don't know him, and I will be painting with Sophie tomorrow morning."

Anne somewhat expected this reaction from Madeline and asked Sophie, "Would you join us for morning tea at Cloverdale Chase, Sophie? I am sure Mr Petherton would welcome you, and we will all travel together in my carriage."

"I would like that very much, Lady South."

Madeline looked at Sophie with her mouth open but then turned and questioned Anne, "But ....!"

"Let me explain, Madeline. Mr Petherton has a daughter named Clare, about your age. She needs some new friends. Simeon and William met her at the fort at Cloverdale Chase. Her father requests an official introduction before the boys and you girls are invited there again. So, we will do it tomorrow at morning tea."

"That is a fine idea, children. You will not feel like you are sneaking in from 'Porting." Ethel directed her comments at Simeon and William.

Madeline looking disappointed, gave a sulky pout. Sophie said, "It will be lovely, Madeline. We can paint tomorrow afternoon. I am sure my mother would allow that."

Madeline was worried and not keen on joining the party, "I don't know if I will even like this, Clare!"

Anne then said, "Sophie and Madeline! Following afternoon tea, you may show me your painting paper, and then I will take you both in my carriage. We shall visit Sophie's home and ask permission if she may visit the Pethertons with us. I will bring you back here, Madeline, after that."

"May I come too, Anne? I have not had a ride in your carriage yet!"

"Certainly, Clementine. You shall sit beside me."

The girls then started chattering excitedly about the coming carriage ride. Ethel noticed Anne's persuasive approach and assisted by saying, "Well, girls. As you will be young ladies riding in a carriage, I think you will each need a hat. So, Clementine and Madeline, you run upstairs and gather your hats. Sophie, I think I have just the hat for you in my room. You come with me, and we will try it on."

Anne sat down and sipped her tea, knowing that stage one of this expedition was complete. William knowingly grinned at her raising his eyebrows, thinking, 'That was clever, Anne!'

Grand Hotel, Kingston, Jamaica ...

"Milady, Milady! There is an urgent message here for you. It is from the Governor, Milady."

"Thank you, Sandy. What time is it, please?"

"Six o'clock, Milady. The sun will be up in twenty minutes. There is tea and toast for you on the side table. I think you will rise early today when you read that message."

"Sandy, have you been reading my messages?"

"Yes, Milady. The message was open! I do not know how it happened. But it is most important, and I must take the best care of you, Milady. You are so good and take care of Sir Hugh, and you deserve good care too."

"Sandy, you are so naughty! But you take good care of me, for which I am most thankful."

"Now, you have your cup of tea, and I will tell Sir Hugh that you will see him at seven. I will make sure he is awake by then. Breakfast will be ready downstairs at eight o'clock. Would you like some help with your hair?"

"Yes, I would! If you would be back in half an hour, please. Thank you, Sandy."

The maid quickly exited and left Fiona Green enjoying a cup of tea in bed as the sun rose. Smiling, she opened the message noticing the seal was already broken. There were no secrets in Kingston. When she read the letter, her eyes opened wide.

The Office of the Governor of Jamaica
The Right Hon. Sir William Wade, Bt.

Mrs Fiona Green
Grand Hotel
Kingston

Mrs Green
I write on behalf of the Governor of Jamaica and advise that Sir William Wade was most distressed on first hearing of Sir Hugh South's infirmity. Doctor Cowper informed the Governor of Sir Hugh's recovery and reported that you, Mrs Green, have been a tower of strength for Sir Hugh during this time. The Governor would like to thank you personally for your selfless service to Sir Hugh.

The official party should arrive at the Grand Hotel by eleven and call upon you and Sir Hugh. I have arranged that morning tea be served on the verandah outside Sir Hugh's room. This way, the Governor will have a private discussion with Sir Hugh and then meet with you on the verandah.

My apologies for the short notice, but the opportunity has arisen in the Governor's diary. We shall have the pleasure of meeting at eleven in the morning.

Yours in the King's Service
Major Walter Ponsonby
Aide-de-Camp

Fiona took a deep breath, a bite of her toast and a sip of tea. Leaning back on the pillows, she thought about the day ahead. There would be no difficulty entertaining a Baronet as Fiona was the daughter of an Earl and understood the etiquette. However, she worried about Sir Hugh as he had not ventured out of bed and slipped back into sleep quickly after a short conversation. His recovery was taking longer than expected.

The hot Caribbean sun was slightly below the horizon and lit up the cloud base with pink and crimson shades across the sky as she watched. It was a magnificent display of nature, and she thanked her Lord for witnessing such a spectacle. Then the sun rose over the horizon, illuminating her bedroom, and the blinding glare forced her eyes shut. Fiona hopped out of bed, put on her light dressing gown, walked along the verandah, and knocked on the door of Sir Hugh's room. There she found nurse Jackson giving Sir Hugh a body wash.

Calling from the outside corner of the doors, she said, "Would you cover him up with a sheet for a moment, please, Cynthia?"

Hugh called out, "Ah, Fiona, I hear the Governor visits this morning. I am hopeful he will have some advice for me on my plantations. Once I have that, I can decide what business decisions I should make. Will you join me for breakfast this morning?"

"No, thank you, Sir Hugh. I will wait until you gain enough walking strength. The staff will have my breakfast ready downstairs, and then there will be preparations."

"What preparations are needed?"

"I must check my wardrobe and prepare myself. Also, the verandah will need suitable furniture and dressings. We do not want the Governor sitting in the sun. Now I will leave you with Nurse Jackson, and make sure you exercise before your morning nap, Sir Hugh."

With that, Fiona smiled and quickly walked down the verandah, entered her room, and started sorting her clothes.

"Your friend, Mrs Green, is a fine woman, Sir Hugh. You are fortunate you found her."

Sir Hugh yawned and said, "Strangely, Nurse Jackson, I share your admiration for her. Ow! Hey, watch where you place that soap, Nurse!"

Cynthia Jackson giggled as she continued washing the helpless man at her mercy.

The Barque 'Manson', Atlantic Ocean, Nearing Ireland …
Mr Stephen Polkinghorne walked beside Lady Clarissa Wendarm as they paced out around the quarter deck, heading towards the stern. It was perfect weather as the ship held a long tack heading directly towards Ireland's southern tip.

"The captain advised me at breakfast that we should see Ireland within a few hours."

"I was not aware that we were so close, Stephen."

"Oh, yes! This 'Manson' is quite a fast barque and usually completes the trip back in four weeks. The winds are with us in this direction. I assume you ported at New York on your way over. Why most companies take that route, I am not sure. It usually means at least an eight-week trip. The direct route is far faster."

"I see. When will we reach Southampton?"

"I expect we will be in Cobh overnight and reach Southampton within two days. Of course, that depends on this good weather holding."

Clarissa became thoughtful. She enjoyed Stephen's company and had lost concentration on her strategy prepared for the Earl and Countess of Fintelton. Her story was believable, but her credibility would rise substantially with Stephen's assistance. She must play Stephen carefully, ensuring he was not scared off.

She stopped and faced him. He was surprised at the change in expression. Instead of being pleasantly relaxed, Clarissa appeared determined, which he associated with a business discussion.

She carefully said, "I must explain some details before we dock in Ireland. I have become very fond of you, Stephen, and I would be most disturbed if you thought badly of me."

Clarissa's companion was a businessman through and through. He had amassed plantations in the West Indies and tobacco farms in Virginia through hard work and starting with nothing. His products were transported across the Atlantic and sold from warehouses across England. Stephen's focus had been on the success of his business, but this attractive woman was now making him think twice about his marital status.

"I, too, find myself most comfortable in your company, Clarissa, and there is something I must ask you....!"

Clarissa gently put her hand over his mouth, "Hear me out first, Darling, before you say any more. I must tell you all, and I think you will understand."

Stephen was somewhat confused but remained silent.

"I am worried about commencing a relationship so soon after Sir Hugh's death!"

"But surely, Sir Hugh was only an acquaintance?"

She placed her hands on his shoulders and gently said, "Please, Darling. Let me explain this. My first husband, Sir David, died in a drowning accident on the Thames. I loved him dearly, and David's death left me distraught for a long time. Finally, I recovered enough strength and embarked on an inspection tour of my Jamaican plantations. During the voyage, Fiona Green introduced her acquaintance, Sir Hugh, and through many card games, we became good friends. Fiona's relationship with Sir Hugh was purely platonic, and by accident, Sir Hugh turned his attention towards me. During the stay at Kingston, we fell madly in love and secretly married."

Clarissa stopped, appearing overcome by emotion and gave a quiet sob. The display deeply moved Stephen, and he offered her a handkerchief. Drying her eyes and taking a deep breath, she continued, "Once again, my husband died!

This time Hugh, as you know, became desperately ill and insisted that I abandon our marriage as he felt I had suffered enough. He knew he was dying and insisted I leave. I completed my business there but pleaded with him that I should remain until the end. However, he would have none of it and pushed me away, insisting my memories should see him as a fit and healthy man. He was very gallant, and it took all my courage to remain calm the day I departed Kingston. But now he is dead and buried, and I must start again. So, you will understand why I must ask for more time. I am a free woman, but I feel a duty towards his family. I must visit his mother first and break the terrible news."

As she said these last few words, Clarissa commenced sobbing. Stephen took her in his arms and comforted her.

"Dear Clarissa, I had no idea. You should have told me sooner. I would have made suitable arrangements, and we might have stayed in Kingston. You poor thing. You must suffer terribly?"

"Thank you, Stephen, for your understanding. You are such a wonderful man."

Stephen found himself helpless and kissed her for some time, assuring her of his love until she recovered.

"You shall have all the time you require, my Dear. You must visit Sir Hugh's mother. She will be shattered at the loss of her son but glad that she has his wife by her side. It will give some relief in the grieving."

"Thank you, Stephen. I could not have wished for more. But there is one more issue!"

Stephen wondered what else there could be, "Tell me, Dearest?"

"I bear Sir Hugh's child! So, it is most important that I meet with the Earl and Countess of Fintelton."

Cloverdale Chase, Guildford, England …
The carriage slowly drove along the tree-lined entrance road, revealing a well-situated large house with an aspect facing the north. The children had not realised they were visiting such a magnificent property. As they neared the house, Simeon and Madeline counted at least fifteen gardeners tending various areas.

"Mr Petherton must be rich, Anne?"

"I am not sure, Madeline. Perhaps the property is rented! Still, we must not enquire about that as it would be rude. Let us enjoy his kind hospitality."

Anne imagined what the children would say if they saw 'Fintelton'. She must brief them beforehand if a visit eventuated – which it surely would. This expedition taught her quite a lot about people's impressions and opinions. As the coach neared the house entrance, a footman descended the steps and stood ready for their arrival.

"The girls giggled as the footman assisted them from the carriage. Then, William and Simeon bounded out, followed by Anne. Fortunately, the weather had cleared, and they gazed at the beautiful property before entering.

As the butler announced them, Mr Benjamin Petherton and his daughter Clare stood ready in the drawing room.

"Lady South, may I introduce myself? I am Benjamin Petherton, and this is my daughter, Clare."

Anne gave a slight curtsey as she took Mr Petherton's hand, "Delighted, Mr Petherton and good morning, Clare. You are a pretty young girl." Anne gave a little compliment that she thought might assist.

Clare smiled as her father said, "Thank you for accepting our invitation. I was not sure if I had approached this situation the correct way. However, I was keen that we start well as neighbours."

"I should thank you for your hospitality, Mr Petherton, as I feel that my young brothers have imposed on you unfairly, and I extend my apologies. I have only recently returned from my honeymoon, and with business commitments and setting up a new home, my care for the visiting children was somewhat lacking. Again, I apologise for this."

"Now, now, Lady South. I understand that William and Simeon only did what all boys would do. I had a son myself. Mark would have done the same, and there is no harm in their antics."

He asked the children, "Now, I am Mr Petherton, and I assume you are William, and you are Simeon?" He shook the hands of both boys. They politely said, "Good morning, Mr Petherton." Clare smiled as she saw their good manners.

"And you must be Madeline, young lady?" He approached Sophie and extended his hand.

"I am sorry, Sir, as I am Sophie Watson, one of Madeline's friends."

'Well, welcome, Sophie Watson." Mr Petherton gently shook her hand. He then found Madeline beside a display case.

"Welcome, Miss Madeline. My daughter Clare was most excited that you would come. Let me introduce you and Sophie."

Clare came forward with a lovely smile and grasped Madeline's hands with hers, "Madeline and Sophie, I am so glad you came. I have been waiting eagerly for your arrival. But, Father, before we have morning tea, may I please show my friends around the grounds quickly?"

"Yes, Clare, but only five minutes, please."

"Thank you, Father."

Clare took Madeline and Sophie's hands and led them out a double door onto the patio. The girls talked excitedly about the beautifully manicured gardens that surrounded the house. William was still standing there admiring the vast collection of empty bottles that lined the room's walls.

"They are many of the wines and spirits I import from all over the world, William. The bottles are a good reminder of the wine and spirits merchants I deal with – it helps my memory. When we have time, I will show you some of the important ones."

"Thank you, Sir."

Anne quickly said, "Now, run along with the others, please, William." He walked briskly out of the room, following the children.

"Lady South, I am impressed with the children's manners. They are well educated, indeed!"

"My mother took great care in ensuring they understood our society's expectations; however, they also have their moments, especially when they become excited."

Benjamin Petherton nodded, "Sir Robert is not with you. I take it he has sailed for the Mediterranean?"

"No, Sir. There was a change in orders, and he will now escort a government fact-finding mission. I understand they will visit Ireland. We will meet in London next Thursday."

"Please give him my regards, and I hope to meet him soon."

"I will do that, Sir."

"Have a seat, Lady South. I must explain my motives here. At first, I was most disturbed hearing that your brothers were venturing onto my property and playing at my son's fort. Thankfully, I took my time considering my response.

Since his sad passing, I have treated the fort as my son's memorial. It is a place that holds dear memories for me. Clare also misses him, but she has coped better with the situation than I did. Her mother, Miriam, died in childbirth eleven years ago, so she never knew her mother.

I know your father, Jonathan. He is a fine man and has, on several occasions, assisted me in my business dealings. However, I am sure he has advised you that I keep a low social profile for specific reasons. So, I have probably become overprotective of Clare."

"She seems a fine young girl, Mr Petherton. I would say you have been a caring father for her."

"Probably taking too much care but thank you for the kind comment."

Benjamin Petherton stood up and started walking around the room, "Lady South, do you mind if I stand? I find I think better if I am on my feet."

"Not at all, Mr Petherton."

"William and Simeon's exploration of my land has been strangely beneficial. On reflection, I have realised I have been living in the shadow of grief, and I must break free from it. This has affected Clare as she has been locked up here for far too long, and I think I should slowly introduce her into society. What I am saying is that I feel I have been over-protective."

"That is quite understandable, Mr Petherton."

"As for the children playing on the fort, I am afraid my first thoughts were misguided. Clare expressed her feelings by saying she wished I knew them better and was this the proper way of dealing with neighbours? After that, I spent considerable time reviewing my motives.

I was protecting her by hiding my daughter away from the world. Of course, this is not fair to Clare, as she needs society so she might flourish.

I am saying, Lady South, that I welcome your brothers and their friends coming onto the property and playing at the fort, and Clare might join them on occasions. I was delighted that Madeline and Sophie came today as Clare has no female friends besides her governess."

"That is sad, Mr Petherton."

"Yes, please come and view them from the doors here."

Anne stood up and joined Mr Petherton at the drawing room's open doors onto the patio. The girls were merrily talking, laughing, and enjoying each other's company. Simeon and William carefully watched the goldfish in a large pond adjoining the patio.

"That is the type of friendship I cannot provide for Clare."

Anne nodded and thought deeply about this well-mannered but quiet man who cared deeply for his daughter. She felt that despite his great wealth, he must be very lonely.

"Mr Petherton, I would have no difficulty in fostering the friendship. I am sure my father would also endorse this. But we must let the children decide for themselves. There are no guarantees in the friendships of children. I think that is one of the reasons schools are such a benefit. The children seek out and find their friends. Have you considered a school for Clare?"

Benjamin Petherton stood there silently, enjoying the sight of his happy daughter with her new friends. He felt he had made the right decision by inviting young Lady South and the children. Now, he was surprised again at what she had suggested, something he had fought against for many years. It would be a great challenge to release his daughter into the care of a school for several hours a day. He was not sure if he could cope with the risks involved.

After standing there silently beside Anne for a few minutes, he quietly said, "I understand the argument you are advancing, Lady South. It may take me some time before I can answer that question. But it is a helpful suggestion. Thank you."

After the children had taken morning tea, Mr Petherton proposed an expedition to inspect the fort. The children cheered and were quickly ready, with Clare leading the way. Anne and Mr Petherton followed at a more sedate pace.

"You mentioned that your wife died in childbirth, Mr Petherton! How long were you married before she died?"

"Some six years. We married in eighteen hundred and ten. Those were the happiest years of my life."

Anne said, "My father lost his wife some two months ago. He grieves greatly for her."

"Yes. I sent Jonathan a condolence letter. When the time is right, I will meet with him and share my experiences. It may help, and it may not. We all grieve in different ways. Immersing myself in my business took much of the pain away. However, I should not indulge you in these morbid thoughts as you still revel in being a newly married woman."

"Thank you, but by marrying a navy man, there is also joy and pain. I long for Thursday when Robert will join me at 'Harting', St James's Square. We will spend some time here at 'Porting'. He will have nearly a week before his ship departs from Woolwich. They sail for Ireland on the seventeenth."

"Then, while he is here, please walk over one day at morning tea and introduce me. I will be at home next week."

"That is a kind offer, Mr Petherton. I am sure he would welcome your company."

"Lady South! I suggest the children plan for a Saturday morning if they intend a long visit. That way, they may join Clare for morning tea at the house. However, I am relaxed if they visit you and spend some time at the fort on any day of the week. There is one condition – they must raise the flag if they are playing there. That way, the gardener who watches the grounds will know who is there."

"That is most kind of you, Mr Petherton. I will ensure the children are made aware of your condition."

Anne smiled as she looked around the beautiful gardens. The sunshine warmed her, and she felt as if she could throw away her wrap, run with the children, and play. But as a married woman on an important social occasion, Anne refrained from embarrassing Mr Petherton. The meeting had been far different from what she expected, and she was glad her new neighbour was so open in his conversation.

"Mr Petherton, please do not answer this question if you so choose, but since the death of your wife, have you ever consulted a woman about Clare's education?"

"No. I have few female contacts, and I would assume the governess would always have some bias, so I avoided that. Why do you ask?"

"I am no expert Mr Petherton, but I think women have a far higher opinion of schooling than men. It is probable that men only think of the more robust attributes of education, whereas women understand the importance of social contact with other children in their community. I cannot help thinking that your wife might have adopted a different approach for Clare's education."

Benjamin Petherton stopped walking and stood there thinking about her comment.

"Lady South, you are the first woman since my wife died who has discussed the merits of my approach to Clare's education. I have always feared handing my daughter into the control of educators. Perhaps I have been overprotective, but I am proud of my daughter's present confidence and demeanour. I appreciate your gentle suggestion about social contact. It is radical, and I must admit I have never considered it. As Clare talks with Madeline and Sophie, the enjoyment I see will certainly make me carefully consider your comment. Thank you, Lady South. Your visit today has been beneficial in many ways."

Hannigan's Pub, Cobh, Ireland …
Ruby O'Leary was leaving work late and saw Ruth Walsh walking ahead.
"May I walk with you, Ruth? Better not being alone on the streets late at night."

Ruth smiled and took her hand, "I could do with the company."

They walked silently down the cold dark street with the occasional working gas lantern illuminating the ageing side-by-side cottages that probably held families of eight or more now fast asleep.

"Cobh is a bit depressing at this time of night. Was it the same in Islay?"

"It was colder, but the place has a unique charm about it. At first, I thought it was so remote that I would never see anyone. But there is a strong community around all the distilleries there. I have never seen so much scotch whisky in my life." She gave a little laugh. "I worked a few hours a day in a distillery and some nights at the pub. It gave me a chance to make friends in the community."

"If it were that cold, I probably would have stayed in bed too long. I do not rise early in winter!"

"It was warm in bed once you were rugged up, especially when you had Callum beside ……!" Ruth stopped talking and remained silent. Ruby could see she was shaking.

Putting her arm around her, Ruby asked, "Ruth, are you cold?"

"Thank you, Ruby, but you know what the matter is."

"Dan told me a little but not the whole story. Was it bad?"

Ruth took out an old, crinkled hanky and blew her nose. They walked on in silence for another ten paces as Ruth took a deep breath and breathed easier.

"I thought I loved Callum, but I was not sure. I had never before felt that way for someone. We even made plans for marriage, children, and a farm somewhere. I think I did love him, but now it is all gone."

"Men can let you down so easily! It happens so often. Someone else will come along, Ruthy."

"No, you don't understand!" Ruth held Ruby's hand tight, stopped walking, turned, and faced her. Ruby was astonished at the strength in her grip. Then Ruth shouted in her face, "No, Ruby! You do not understand! No one does. I killed the man I loved, and now I am nothing. There is no future; there is no hope. I have lost him, and it is all my stupid fault."

Ruby O'Leary stood there in disbelief. She was not aware that Ruth had killed Callum, "But Ruth. Surely not. He was your partner. A Brother!"

Ruth held her face in her hands and cried. Then, she turned away from Ruby and walked away. As Ruby followed, she turned and yelled, "Go away, Ruby! I know you mean well, but I must be alone now. I need my family at Garranes. I don't know if I will be back, but please leave me alone now."

With that, Ruth ran off, wiping the tears from her face.

HMS Shadow, Portsmouth, England ...

At the head of the table in the great cabin of HMS *Shadow* sat her commander, Captain Sir Robert South. The ship's officers had joined their captain while the midshipmen took the watch.

"Mr Fenton. Is *Shadow* ready for sea?"

"Captain, the sooner we are underway, the happier the crew will be. The preparations are complete."

"Good. Gentlemen, this mission will take us first into the Channel, where we will continue our training and canon practice, then onto Woolwich, docking for several days and complete some minor repairs. We depart on the seventeenth for Ireland. We will escort the civilian barques *Chalk* and *Eventide* during the mission. *Restless* will make up the fourth ship in our flotilla. This voyage will be an excellent opportunity for testing *Shadows'* battle readiness. Most of the crew are new, and I am sure we are all keen on seeing what she can do."

There were several comments of agreement from his officers.

"Mr Miles, have the Yeoman signal *Restless* that we sail in half an hour. Raise the Blue Peter[20], please."

---

[20] The Flag named the Blue Peter is a blue flag with a white square. The flag signalled that the ship was ready to get under way or its departure was imminent.

"Aye, Captain." Miles stood and rushed out of the cabin.

'Well, Gentlemen, the Channel awaits us. Mr Fenton! You may prepare the ship. I will join you on the poop at three o'clock. Thank you, Gentlemen."

The officers stood and quickly moved out, keen on mustering their men.

"Swanton, my telescope, please."

The captain's servant quickly opened the captain's sea chest and checked for the prized possession. Then, removing it from a velvet cover, he brought it over.

"These are better quarters than on *Restless* or *Providence*, Sir. The servant's quarters here make my old cabin on *Restless* look tiny."

"*Shadow* is slightly larger than *Providence*, and I am told she is faster. We shall see if we can manage this crew well and tune her sails. I am glad you are satisfied, Michael. What is your assessment of the crew so far?"

"The Officers are all inexperienced, and the crew has many Irish lads. I would not be surprised if some abandoned ship once we dock in Ireland. Most of them are supporting families, so they should be safe. I have not heard anything suspicious yet."

"Good, keep an eye on them, Swanton. The Admiral specifically told me that we should trust no one. Not much of a confidence booster before embarking on a mission, was it! I hope our time at sea is calmer this time."

"Leave it with me, Sir. We can trust Midshipman Collins and our Sailing Master, Mr Trotters. Glad you brought them with us, Sir. Trotters is capable and reliable."

Captain South was distracted by a thought, "By the way, Swanton, how are you at riding a horse?"

"As I was in the infantry, Sir, we mostly marched. But I have had experience with horses, and I have the skills."

"Good, as you will be riding with me when we do these inspections that the mission requires. You will be watching my back, Swanton."

"Don't you trust the Marines, Sir?"

"You are the Marines, Mr Swanton!"

"Beg your pardon, Captain, but I thought Major Coombes was joining us with some marines."

"Yes, he will be with us but is joining the ship at Woolwich. We will be in port for over a week there. Firstly, this mission has some official functions, and then I am ducking off with my wife for a few days in Guildford. During my absence, please further acquaint yourself with the crew. We set sail on the seventeenth."

"Aye, Sir." Swanton passed across the captain's telescope.

"Well, Swanton, hearing your assessment of the crew so far, it sounds like I have some work ahead of me getting this lot trained. Time we were at sea!"

Robert donned his hat and left the great cabin for the poop deck.

Swanton was unsure, but he had a feeling that wherever Captain South was, that was where the action would be. Time would tell. With the officers upstairs managing *Shadow*'s departure and the dinner preparations already complete, he had time for an hour of scrimshawing.

On the poop, Robert watched Lieutenant Fenton and the other officers bring the ship to life. Steward Fenton was five years older than Robert and had the experience this ship needed. Captain South was fortunate in snaring him from another frigate undergoing a refit and was confident Fenton would sort out the crew. He ran *Shadow* competently on their Islay voyage with no mistakes, and the captain had high hopes that Fenton would be as competent as Lieutenant Ham had been on *Restless*.

Fenton was unaware of how hard his captain would push the crew in the next few days. Robert must discover how his men would react under pressure and cope when tired. He also wanted them so busy there was no time for any mischief that might emerge. During the next two nights, there would be little sleep for them. They could rest in Woolwich. What he did now might be crucial for all their lives in the days ahead.

"Mr Fenton, please take her slowly through the Admiral's fleet at Spithead. Use the jib, topsails, and spanker until clear of the Blue. We will salute the Admiral's flag as we pass by. Please have the officer's form upon the poop. Once past the Admiral, I want every sail up. Let us see what this little ship can do, shall we?"

The Capstan party were singing as they hauled up the anchor. It was a bit too relaxed for Robert, but he refrained from any comment. He would brief Fenton in private.

Midshipman Collins rushed over, addressing the First Officer, "Harbour Master's Flag is up, Mr Fenton."

'Thank you, Mr Collins. Mr Trotters, please raise the jib and spanker. Then let go of the topsails."

Robert felt the anchor let go, and the capstan party started working harder, bringing the anchor up quickly.

"Mr Miles, please find out what is happening with that fore staysail and ensure Kennedy has the anchor secured properly. Quickly man!" At Fenton's command, the second lieutenant rushed onto the quarter deck and sprinted away.

"Mr Trotters, where are those sails?"

Trotters was madly yelling orders above through his megaphone. The foretopsail suddenly let go, and immediately *Shadow* started making way. Robert knew this was a good sign as she was off quickly under one sail only. Then the main topsail let go and set beautifully. Robert thought, 'A bit late but filling nicely'. *Shadow* accelerated, and the sailors became more animated as they enjoyed her making way. Robert noticed that the jib and the spanker remained furled, and Trotters was now yelling himself hoarse, finding out why they were not up. Slowly the spanker was raised and took its shape. Yet, there was still no jib! Fenton approached the Master and asked, "Mr Trotters, please go forward and sort out whatever is going on up there." Trotters was off quickly.

Fenton came across and saluted the captain, "My apologies Sir. I am sure Trotters will solve the situation."

"Thank you, Mr Fenton."

As 'HMS *Shadow*' quietly proceeded down the harbour towards Portsmouth Point, Midshipman Collins approached Lieutenant Fenton, "Sir! A cutter is rapidly approaching us with an Army officer waving."

Fenton quickly turned and looked from the stern at the cutter under full sail, rapidly gaining on them. He could hear the man yelling, "Slow down, you Navy buggers!"

Captain South came across and said, "Major Coombes. I expected him in Woolwich!"

Fenton nodded. Robert smiled and said, "Let us see if the Army can catch us!"

For the first time Robert could recall, Fenton gave a broad smile, understanding this might be a bit of friendly rivalry. The Lieutenant said, "We shall welcome Major Coombes aboard, Sir. If he catches up?"

Meanwhile, Trotters ordered winching a man out along the bowsprit to untangle the fore staysail, which remained furled. There was much shouting and pointing as various sailors shouted instructions, and the seaman, straining his muscles, pulled the ropes free. Then, with a cheer, the staysail suddenly appeared and gave a slight increase in the ship's way.

At precisely that moment, Horace Coombes was jumping across from his cutter beside *Shadow*'s Jacobs ladder. He lunged out and grabbed the ladder rope but fell hard against the hull with half his body immersed. Holding on hard, Horace pulled himself up the side of the ship, appearing with a great smile. He then arranged with one of the hands for the transfer of his sea locker.

Major Coombes then walked along the quarter deck, climbed the ladder onto the poop, stood at attention and saluted.

"Captain South, Major Coombes reporting for duty, Sir."

Robert returned the salute and replied, "Welcome, Major. I did not expect you until Woolwich. As you are now onboard ...." Captain South took a breath before continuing and noted the Major's wet uniform, "You may join us in saluting the Admiral's Flagship, and then please see my servant below about your accommodation."

"It would be a pleasure, Sir."

"If you would join me, Major!"

With a grin, Fenton lined the officers up, ready for the salute.

As they passed the Admiral's flagship, Robert could make out the Admiral standing with his Officers on the flagship's poop.

"Have the ensign raised, Mr Fenton and three cheers for the Admiral!"

A lone sailor, standing near the local Tavern at Portsmouth Point with a copy of the London Gazette, watched the frigate and schooner proceed through the fleet anchored in Spithead. Drifting on the breeze, he heard the faint cheers of *Shadow*'s officers and crew, "Hurrah, Hurrah, Hurrah!"

Noting the time, he walked off up the road towards the business district.

Chapter 13

Country Catholic Church, Garranes, Ireland …

The sound of singing drifted out of the little country church's front door as the congregation finished the first hymn. The Walsh family had set off from their farm near Garranes, enjoying the warm sunny day. The weather was mild, and Michael's two young brothers enjoyed the walk, excitedly asking him about Cobh. It was a special day as Ruth was home after being away for nearly eight months. The girls were chatting happily with Ruth about the rugged beauty of Islay as the church came into view.

Continuing with the Mass, the priest announced the second hymn. Beside Michael sat his sister, Ruth, who had not sung the first hymn. Her thoughts were far away in Islay, where the look of horror on Callum's face kept reappearing in her memory. The brothers' committee had sent her six months in advance as part of the team that would hide the British frigate at Port Charlotte. She worked with two other women who infiltrated the community and provided feedback on who could be trusted and who should be locked away.

The brothers housed her at the Safe House with Callum Ferguson, who moved men safely through Ireland's network into Scotland. As soon as Ruth met Callum, she found herself interested in him. Tall and thin, with a lovely personality, Callum was fun and different from the men she had known in Ireland. He was optimistic and always talked about the farm he would own one day.

Soon she felt a kind of love growing between them, and she moved from the spare room into his bed for love and warmth in the bitter Islay climate. Did she love him? She was not sure. She, too, wanted a future, and the idea of a farm was something they romantically shared. But he was now dead. She had killed him!

Pushed over the edge by her Irish loyalty, she acted hastily without considering the implications. The man she might have spent the rest of her life with was dead, and she felt as if she had committed a sin that God could never forgive. The tears rolled down her cheeks – she could not put aside what she had done.

Her older brother noticed her tears and held her close with his arm around her shoulders. Michael commanded the brothers' section in Cobh, a healthy group of men of all ages, closely knit and of one mind about Irish freedom. Cobh and the surrounding country produced no shortage of volunteers. Even men from Cork joined them, preferring the strong bonds that existed down in the port area.

The failure of the mission in Islay had hit the community hard. Thirty-seven men were dead, and many were wounded and would need continuing care. Michael had spent much time comforting the parents, wives, and children of those deceased and injured. He felt the pain intensely, which made him more determined for their cause of releasing Ireland from the English landowners' shackles.

Mrs Maeve Malone, sitting beside Ruth, pulled out a handkerchief, moved closer, dabbed the tears, and quietly comforted her. There were no secrets in this community – the Irish people stood together. It was the only way they could survive under the English persecution.

As the congregation stood for the following hymn, a man slipped into the seat beside Michael Walsh at the pew's end. Michael moved aside, allowing the newcomer some space, raised his eyes and found himself focusing on the smiling face of Dan O'Leary.

Dan said nothing but slipped Michael a note from under his open hymn book. Taking the message, Michael quickly pressed it into his coat pocket. They continued singing as the congregation found its voice with an uplifting tune. Michael smiled at Mrs Malone as she kept her arm around a silent and tearful Ruth. Looking around for Dan, he found the seat was now vacant, and the open hymn book rested on the pew.

The singing always seemed stronger after communion. Michael took heart from the family and friends around him here in church. Resting his eyes on the crucifix above the altar, he prayed for freedom and that his Lord and Saviour might deliver them from this bondage under the English. Michael Walsh knew what would be in Dan's message and decided against reading it now. He was sick of the pain and misery from this war and would rather throw the note away. But Michael knew he must read it, and it would contain orders.

Grand Hotel, Kingston, Jamaica …
At around eleven, Fiona Green entered Sir Hugh's room and checked on the patient. The nurse was downstairs disposing of the laundry and would

not return until after lunch. Hugh was sitting up in bed gazing out the open French doors onto the verandah, taking in the view of the bay. The day was clear, with a refreshing soft breeze and a temperature lower than the average oven-like heat.

"How is the patient today?"

Sir Hugh turned and smiled, recognising Fiona.

"Improving every day, thank you! How was church, Fiona?"

"Fascinating! They certainly have enthusiasm in their singing and prayer here. It is different from home in Bedfordshire. The English ladies would be shocked if they found themselves in such a joyous congregation. I enjoy the fellowship with the women here very much. It makes me think that the less material wealth people have, the more they enjoy life. Certainly, the friends I am making here will be life-long. I will have far more correspondence once I return to England."

"I agree. Material wealth can lead one astray. I had always believed that wealth was my right rather than a privilege. I have learnt a great deal from this illness." Hugh paused and then asked, "Do you miss England?"

"Occasionally. But how is your health, Sir Hugh?"

"Fiona, we have known each other for two months or more. I think it is time you called me Hugh. After all, we are not in court!"

Fiona thought about that and smiled, "As long as you are not including any romantic notions, Hugh!"

"I am indeed not. Why, it is if you are like my sister, Emma. Only she and you could take care of me so well."

"I will take that as a compliment. But I do need an answer about your health. It is important as we cannot remain in Kingston forever."

"Yes, I understand what you are saying. I am most thankful that you remained with me, Fiona. I will never forget that. As for my health, I feel my energy returning! A walk in the park would be nice today. A pity there is no park! But there is a dirt road we could struggle along."

Fiona decided to test him because Hugh's desire may be more optimistic than his current physical ability.

"In that case, give me a demonstration. Can you stand by yourself?"

Hugh was always one for a challenge. Pulling the sheet off, he carefully swung his legs over the side of the bed.

"Excuse my pyjamas!"

He gritted his teeth and pulled himself up on his feet. As soon as he reached full height, he started wabbling and fell backwards onto the bed. Fiona rushed across, ensuring he did not roll onto the floor.

Looking down at the pained face and closed eyes, she said, "Good try, Hugh. You are most brave. I think you are making progress. A week ago, you could not move your legs at all. Standing up today was quite an achievement."

Hugh, smelling her perfume and his eyes opening, finding Fiona's smiling face close, said with a cheeky smile, "Then, I think I deserve a reward. Perhaps a soft kiss?"

"You are impossible, Hugh. Remember, I said no romantic notions."

"Of course, of course."

She moved away from the bed and sat down.

"Cover yourself up, please. I have some documents from the Governor. He left them with me after his visit. As you feel so much better, perhaps it is time for some reading. It appears your agents here have not been entirely truthful."

She passed the documents across.

Arranging against his pillows, Hugh sat up, took the papers, and commenced reading.

"I will leave them with you, Hugh. I must change my clothes and freshen up. As the temperature rises, the staff will move you onto the verandah, where we will have lunch together. You can advise me then on what you wish done with the Governor's discoveries. I will be back in an hour and a half. Also, I think I know of some special equipment that may assist your walking. I saw one in a home where my Aunty resided. I shall have one acquired and delivered."

"There is no need, Fiona. I will be up and about soon."

"Hugh, if you fall and break your leg, it will delay our departure another two months. This equipment will provide support and using it on the verandah daily will speed up your recovery. Forgive me for saying this, but it would be best to regain strength in your skinny legs before we embark. Trust me! The apparatus will work."

"As you say, Fiona! But now I must read these papers before lunch."

Fiona realised that Hugh was a shadow of the man she had met on the *Frogmore* several months earlier. He had lost much weight during his sickness. She left him reading his papers and hurried off downstairs, where she would arrange a healthy lunch on the verandah. He must put on some weight before considering the arduous trip across the Atlantic.

Turner Residence, Guildford ...

Anne joined her family for Sunday lunch at the Turner residence, assisting Ethel in bringing some normality back into the household. It pleased Anne that she found Rosalind, Ethel's daughter, sitting beside Clemmie at the table. Mr Turner had invited her for Sunday lunch as Ethel had missed seeing her last Sunday. Anne agreed with Ethel's wishes that her father would spend more time with the children.

"Father, now that lunch is complete, I suggest we recommence our family riverside visits. We should also invite Bethany, Neville, Thomas, and Marion this afternoon. It will be our last chance before you leave for Southampton."

William and Simeon were most excited about the chance of a pirate game at their favourite spot. Marcia was already crying out pirate commands, and the girls were smiling about how Marcia mixed up her words. Jonathan sat there in a world of his own.

From the other end of the table, Ethel said, "Mr Turner, what do you think of Anne's suggestion? It is the first clear day we have had in some time. We may see some sunshine at last."

Stirring from his thoughts, Jonathan said, "What was the suggestion, Ethel?"

Anne repeated her request, "A visit beside the river and some afternoon tea!"

"Oh, I see. Yes, that would be good for the children. Shall we venture down there? Let us say at three."

"Yes, Father. Madeline, you may accompany me in the carriage as we tell Beth and Thomas about the picnic. Go up and quickly change and meet me at the front door. Clemmie and Rosalind, would you help the children into old clothes, please? Ethel, I will return here around two forty-five, and we can load some food and drink into the carriage. Father, you could join Ethel and me if you wish."

"No, Anne! Thank you for the offer, but I will walk with the children. I need the exercise, and William and Simeon have asked for some time with me. It is about this fort at Cloverdale Chase!"

Fintelton Manor, Outside Petersfield, Sussex …

Lady Fintelton discussed the packing for their London trip with her maid, "Margaret, no need for the heavy chest this time as this will be a short visit."

Lady Emma appeared at the bedroom door, "Mother, Mr Stem is asking if he might have a word. He also requested my presence. He is downstairs in the drawing room."

"Certainly, Emma. I shall come now before the afternoon becomes too busy. Margaret, I will be right back. Perhaps you would check with Pike about the coach's departure time on Tuesday."

They proceeded downstairs and met Mr Stem in the drawing room.

"Thank you for seeing me, Lady Fintelton. I understand the Earl is asleep, so I did not disturb him. Also, I felt you might best handle this matter."

Mr Stem looked around and noticed several servants present, "Might we discuss this in a private place, my Lady?"

Lady Jane, who now understood that the matter might be confidential, obliged and said, "Please, follow me."

She led them through the lounge area and into her private writing room. She closed the door and asked, "Now, Mr Stem, how may I be of assistance."

"Lady Fintelton! On Sir Robert's recommendation, Lady Emma and Lady Anne asked me about the missing funds from the estate accounts. Knowing that you were both aware of these matters, I was keen to inform you of the current position. There are urgent reasons for this which I shall explain."

Lady Jane quickly responded, "Thank you, Mr Stem, for your consideration."

The Estate Manager nodded and continued, "On Friday, I made out the bank draft requests for the staff wage payments. I had assumed sufficient funds would be available in the bank for the drafts. The bank informed me late on Saturday that there were insufficient funds. As we must pay the staff wages by Wednesday next, I thought we should act quickly.

I would have asked the Earl; however, I thought it might be prudent if you, your Ladyship, and Lady Emma were made aware of the situation. I have the forms here requiring a signature authorizing a transfer of five hundred pounds from the reserve account. The Earl usually transfers around that amount every second month."

Lady Jane and Lady Emma considered the documents.

Lady Emma spoke first, "Mr Stem, I am assuming you are telling us that the Estate's working account is empty."

"Not empty, Milady! But there are only a few pounds available in that account. The reserve account is where the Earl maintains the estate's remaining funds. I understand the balance is a few thousand pounds."

Lady Jane had been quietly considering the forms in the background, "So, Mr Stem. We have a few thousand pounds in the reserve account. How many thousand pounds is a few?"

"Three, Milady."

"And what is the cost of funding the estate each year?"

"Eight thousand pounds, Milady. Also, there is the expense of 'Harting' in London and the Isle of Wight residence."

Lady Jane and Lady Emma looked at each other in horror.

Mr Stem added, "My Ladies, there is income due in the future. Income from the winter crops is due in April, and the summer crop in October. Also, I understand there should be regular payments from the estates in Scotland, Ireland and the Indies. Then there will be the tenant farmer payments in May and October."

Lady Emma quickly asked, "Mr Stem, might I ask that you provide me with an estimate of these payments by tomorrow morning, please? I will take them with me as the countess must speak with the bank manager in Guildford as we break our trip there. We shall have the Earl sign the documents tonight, and

I will leave that for you tomorrow morning. I trust the sum of five hundred pounds will be sufficient?"

"More than sufficient, Milady. Thank you for seeing me."

Mr Stem slowly backed away and left the room.

After Emma was sure Stem was out of hearing distance, she said, "Mother, I have been remiss. I should have taken the warning Robert gave more seriously. Thank goodness we will be in Guildford tomorrow. We can meet Anne there and discuss our options. In the interim, Father must sign these documents tonight. Have you read them?"

"No, you do it, please, Dear. I suddenly have a severe headache. Please ask Pike to send Margaret upstairs with some tea. I think your father, taking a nap, is more sensible than us. Perhaps a short sleep before dinner may help me."

Lady Jane slowly left the writing study. Emma sat down and placed the documents on the desk. She put her head in her hands and shed a tear, 'Oh Anne, I need your advice. I am not sure what we should do!'

The Banks of the River Wey, Guildford, England ...

As the coach slowly drove down the High Street towards the river, Ethel said, "Thank you, Lady South, for suggesting the river visit. It is what the children need, and time for Mr Turner with them. Why we may even see Mr Turner smile this afternoon."

"I had the same thoughts, Ethel. Thank you for the wonderful job you are doing at home. I am not sure you receive the appreciation you deserve, but rest assured, I am impressed with what you are achieving there."

"You are too kind, Milady. I am only doing my job."

"Well, that is being done very well. Please, Ethel, when we are alone, call me Anne. We are friends, Ethel, and it shall never be different. Now tell me about progress with the new maid."

Stunned about the level of familiarity Anne allowed, Ethel was uplifted by this gesture of friendship.

"Well, Anne!" They both laughed., "The Agency can send someone next Wednesday for an interview."

"That is fine, except I will be travelling that day. Would you interview her, please, with Mrs Kirby? I had no idea how complex life would become after marriage, and I require a maid quickly. There is never enough time for every-thing. I am exhausted!"

"You are handling it all well, Anne. We are excited about what you are achieving. But, yes, I will do the interview, and I am sure you will have a maid by the time you return from London."

"Thank you, Ethel."

The coach stopped beside the riverbank, where the children were playing. The footman, James, opened the coach door and helped the ladies down. They decided on a sunny spot and carried the afternoon tea over.

Neville Bassington and David Sopwith were brandishing arms with the children defending their imaginary pirate ship on a mound of dirt beside the river. Marcia was screaming with delight and holding Neville's left leg for protection. There was much giggling and shouting as the game went on.

Beth, Marion, and Thomas were sitting on a rug watching the antics, and Anne placed another blanket beside them and asked Ethel if she would join her. Standing at the river's edge, Jonathan Turner came up the bank and sat opposite Anne and Ethel.

Jonathan commented, "Rosalind is enjoying the skirmish on the bank, Ethel. She seems proficient with a sword."

Ethel smiled, "She probably inherited that from her father. I can assure you it was not from me."

Marion inquired, "Ethel, was your husband in the army?"

"Yes, he served in the Peninsula war with Wellesley[21] and then was stationed at Sandhurst[22], where he trained new officers." Ethel watched the children wielding their swords. "I am not sure, but I believe he was involved in fencing. So, he may have made a good pirate." Marion and Ethel laughed.

"That must have been an exciting life for you. Did you visit Portugal?"

"No, I met Andrew when he was home on leave, and we married before he left for Portugal. He insisted that the Peninsula was no place for a woman and that he would return soon, which he did. We were apart for two years before he took up his position at Sandhurst. Rosalind came along some ten months after he returned. Absence makes the heart grow fonder!" She laughed with the others while Jonathan turned away, thinking about Eleanor.

Ethel, noticing the dull look on Jonathan's face, said, "My apologies Mr Turner. I am sorry if my comment brought back sad memories for you."

"No, no, Ethel. It is I who should apologise. I am not one for good humour at present. The talk of your recovery from the loss of your husband comforts me that I will recover in time."

"It has taken a long time Mr Turner. But it does happen eventually."

Beth announced, "Time for the Turner family riverside feast. Anne, you may hand out the biscuits, and I will take care of the drinks. Ethel, you may enjoy the scenery as you packed all the refreshments. You enjoy some time with Rosalind."

---

[21] Arthur Wellesley, 1st Duke of Wellington, rose to prominence as a general during the Peninsular campaign (1807 – 1814) of the Napoleonic Wars.

[22] The Royal Military Academy Sandhurst, commonly known simply as Sandhurst, is one of several military academies of the United Kingdom and is the British Army's initial officer training centre.

Marion laughed and said, "You are not leaving me out, Beth. I will hand out the buttered rolls. I might have one myself, as they look delicious."

Jonathan Turner and Thomas needed some quiet space and decided to walk along the riverbank, where they discussed his appointment as brewery manager in Scotland. They both enjoyed watching the swans and ducks paddling majestically along the river.

Turner Household, Guildford, Surrey ...

On Monday morning, Jonathan and Clementine left for Southampton to farewell Jonathan's brother and sister-in-law, who were embarking for South Africa. Richard and Sarah had agreed that Katherine would remain with the Turners during their stay in Africa, which may be too dangerous for a young girl. Still unsure if this was a wise decision but duty-bound by his agreement with his brother, Jonathan had planned the trip carefully. Katherine would be comforted by Clementine, and the two girls would reside in the same room at Guildford. Clementine was unsure how effective she would be, but she reassured her father she would do her best.

As the coach pulled out, Clementine waved excitedly, this trip being a significant event for her. She had never seen the sea, and being alone with her father, she expected to be somewhat spoilt. On the other hand, Jonathon would enjoy Clementine's company and relish the reading time he might fit in during the trip.

"She is excited, Ethel!"

"Yes, Mrs Jennings. It will be a lovely trip for her. I am not sure Mr Turner understands how talkative she has become. Clemmie can be over-enthusiastic at times."

Mrs Jennings laughed, "She prepared a list of talking points for her father. Poor Mr Turner will be exhausted by tonight." They both smiled.

"While she is away, Mrs Jennings, we can give the room a good clean out and spruce it up before they return with Katherine. If you can spare Ivy and Jess for a few hours this morning, we will make a start?"

"Yes. There is no one here for lunch today. But I will need the maids by four for the dinner preparations."

They watched as the coach disappeared down the High Street.

"Another young lady will be living here, Mrs Jennings. The dynamics will change again."

"Let us hope she has a gentle nature!"

They both laughed as the children slowly walked inside, wishing they were going as well instead of attending school.

In the coach, Clementine sat up as they entered the countryside, "How long will the trip take, Father?"

"We will not push the horses too hard, Clementine. Winchester is far enough for today. We will reach our destination in daylight. Did you bring a fine reading book with you?"

"No, Father! You know that I become travel sick if I read in a coach. It would be best if you talked with me for the whole journey. I have prepared a list of topics we may discuss. We shall have a merry time discussing the world's problems." Clementine passed across the list.

Jonathan took a quick look and then said, "Oh!"

"We should start with the Russian Tsar and whether he will invade the Ottoman empire."

"I was not aware you were interested in politics and world affairs, Clemmie."

"I wasn't until I started reading the newspapers you receive at work. 'The Times'[23] is particularly interesting. We learnt a little about world affairs at Reverend Taggart's school, but I was more interested in talking with the girls then. Now I read the newspapers and find them fascinating. Perhaps one day Father, I might become a journalist like Megan Bassington. Perhaps I might join her in New York. I could stay with her and learn journalism?"

"I thought you enjoyed your job at the bakery?"

"It is a bit dull! All those figures every day. Only a special person like Anne enjoys that! She revels in the figures as the world goes by. I am sure she is brilliant and quick with the figures, but the work is the same each day, and I complete my work on time. I think being a journalist would be far more interesting and exciting."

"But why America, Clemmie? What is wrong with London?"

"A woman would never get a job as a journalist in England. In America, it is a new world. Women can have careers. The articles Megan Bassington has published here on women in America are fascinating. Mr Bassington receives articles from Megan regularly. Some are published, and some are not. However, she has far more success reporting on the English Aristocracy in New York. The American newspapers publish everything she writes as the people there are mad about the English upper class."

"Is that right!"

"I am fourteen this year, Father! How old must I be before I could visit America?"

"I am not sure, Clemmie – probably at least twenty-one. You may be married by then and settled with children."

"Never, Father. I am not like the other girls in the office. All they do is talk about the boys. You know that Jeb brought a flower in for Audrey last week, and they talked for quite some time. He stays overnight at the Sterns'

---

[23] The Times was founded on 1 January 1785 as 'The Daily Universal Register'. After 940 editions the publisher changed the paper's name on 1 January 1788 to 'The Times'. Wikipedia.

house some nights rather than walking home. I would not be surprised if they marry later in the year. She seems sweet on him."

"Really!"

"Yes, and Sophia is keen on Aaron. They chat sometimes, but I am not sure if Aaron is that keen on her. We will see when the church fair comes along this year. It is always interesting seeing who the couples are."

Jonathan Turner was surprised at the education he was receiving from Clementine. Unaware of his staff members' private lives, he felt awkward and would prefer not to know these details.

"So, we should commence at number one on your list. The Russian Tsar! What do you know about his intentions?"

"Well, Father, the previous Tsar, Alexander, as you know, died in 1825, and his brother Tsar Nicholas took over. This new Tsar is far more warlike and plans on expanding his empire by invading the Ottoman-held parts of Greece. The Greeks have been fighting for independence for the last ten years. It was their land before the Ottomans came along. Our government is reluctant to help the Greeks. Why would they not support the Greeks, Father?"

Jonathan was familiar with recent world affairs, so he ventured a guess, "Probably the Prime Minister, Jenkinson, does not want a war!"

Their conversation continued for nearly an hour, with Clementine moving slowly down her list of topics. Jonathan was desperate for a break.

"Now, Clemmie. I need some quiet time to think about what I must do in Southampton while we are there. Perhaps a break from our talk and quiet reflection time might be in order."

"Father, I thought you would need a break, so I brought my timepiece." She pulled out a small fob watch so he could see it. "You may have a fifteen-minute break, and then we should start again. There are still many points left." Clementine grinned at her father, feeling quite satisfied with their progress on her list.

Jonathan reluctantly said, "That is very generous of you, Clemmie!"

The Church Rectory, Guildford …

The Reverend Andrew Taggart sat at his study desk rereading the letter he had received from the Reverend Charles Upton, from Woking, regarding his confidential enquiry about the Reverend Philip Hotspur. The Uptons would join them for lunch today, breaking their trip here at Guildford. Their journey involved visiting a desperately sick relative in Farnham, who was a dear friend and would soon depart this world. Andrew had offered them accommodation, but they declined, explaining the urgency of their trip.

Before speaking with his wife, Andrew pulled out another letter from Archdeacon Rufus Handle at Greenwich. He had met the Archdeacon at the

Turner-Steele wedding last November and formed a friendship. The letter read:

Archdeacon Rufus Handle
Rectory
Greenwich

Dear Andrew
I write a short note congratulating you on your optimistic message about the new staff member. The Reverend Philip Hotspur comes from a notable London family of booksellers. I understand the family inheritance rests entirely with the older brother, Kevin Hotspur. It appears that Philip is estranged from his father for some mysterious reason and will not receive any inheritance. A pity as Philip is a likeable young man who will make a fine Rector given a sound mentor such as yourself. He will find more interest in our profession as he refines his churchmanship.

Philip was betrothed to Miss Mary Rochedale. She is the daughter of a wealthy merchant, Mr Miles Rochedale, who attends Deptford parish. The couple sometimes visited for morning tea, and she is a delightful young lady. Mary has an endowment of twenty thousand pounds which will pass with her at marriage.

Two months ago, a problem with the relationship developed, and her parents removed Mary. She now travels with her mother to Italy. I believe the parents informed Philip that the engagement had ended. I know little more than this.

Concerning ministry, Philip will require some sermon-making tuition before you let him loose in the pulpit. I am sure with your mentoring, he will gain concentration skills and improve dramatically.

If you pass through Greenwich, please stay with us at the Rectory. Felicity and I have a warm affection for you and your dear wife, Laura.

Yours in His Name
Rufus Handle

Andrew Taggart recognised that Rufus had spelled out carefully that there was a problem with this young clergyman. Rufus wrote the letter masterfully, so if it fell into the wrong hands, there was no room for misinterpretation. He would keep Rufus's thoughts private, but today he must test these comments against Charles Upton's views. The Uptons had previously served in a London parish and had made Philip Hotspur's acquaintance.

Lions Bank of Guildford …

Anne rushed along Quarry Street and turned into the High Street towards the Lions Bank. Already expecting a fully booked day of appointments, she received a note from the bank manager requesting an urgent meeting before lunch. Anne had rebooked some of her late-morning appointments and was approaching the bank. At least it was not raining, making the dash a bit more comfortable, but she was due straight after lunch at Hursts, where Lady Emma and another bridesmaid, Miss Lily Richards, would be waiting. She prayed for no further adjustments, completing the fitting process. Anne also hoped the two dresses ordered for her London visit would be ready.

Anne now understood the difficulties of a woman remaining well-groomed for different occasions and maintaining a career. The employment of a lady's maid was essential so she could be free from organising her wardrobe. This time-saving would be most beneficial, particularly for her stress levels.

"Anne, you are in a rush! May I be of assistance?"

Jolted out of her thoughts, she found Victoria Sopwith and her maid standing before her.

"Hello, Victoria. Hello Judith."

Victoria Sopwith's maid replied, "Good day, Lady South."

"Thank you, Victoria, but I have an unexpected appointment at the bank. It could not have come at a worse time, but I must attend."

"Are you coming for the dress fitting at Hursts after lunch?"

"Yes, depending on how long this bank meeting goes, I will be there."

"Oh, you poor thing! Come and join Lady Emma, Lady Lily, and me for lunch. I have a table booked for one o'clock at the Fox and Hound. It is twelve now, so I am sure your appointment will last no longer than an hour. That means we will have an hour for lunch before the fitting. Hursts is close by, so it will be convenient. May I place your order and have it ready?"

"Oh, Judith, your mistress is so sweet!" Judith smiled in agreement.

"Thank you, Victoria. Please, some assorted sandwiches and a cup of tea would be delightful. I will need a rest, as today has been hectic. I must go. See you at one!"

They waved as Anne rushed off for the bank. Anne slowed before the entrance, sorted herself and then entered.

"Lady South, I am sorry, but Mr Meyhew is running five minutes late."

Anne raised her eyebrows, breathed in relief, and replied, "Thank you."

"Please have a seat."

Ten minutes later, Mr Meyhew opened his office door and politely beckoned to Anne.

"My apologies for the delay, but I was verifying some of the figures with

Mr Appleby, our High Street Branch Manager. Lady South, may I introduce Mr Appleby."

Anne shook hands with the banker and then took a seat.

"Mr Meyhew, I must be away by one o'clock as it is a hectic day."

"We will be no longer than half an hour, Lady South. Might I offer you a glass of water as you appear flushed?"

"That would be extremely kind, Sir. I have run all the way here as I was late."

Mr Meyhew opened his office door and said, "Miss Morton, a jug of water, please and three glasses, thank you."

Soon Anne sipped some cool, clear water as Mr Meyhew began, "You will recall our last meeting, Lady South. You requested a listing of all the transfers between the Estate bank accounts, of which there are three, and Sir Hugh's Accounts. Mr Appleby, please!"

"Thank you, Mr Meyhew. Lady South, we have examined each of the three Estate bank accounts and tracked all the transfers for the last three years. We found a pattern that might be consistent with your enquiry about the missing money. The money is not missing but was transferred into one of Sir Hugh's accounts. Two accounts are involved, and I numbered them one and two.

When I detected the pattern, Mr Meyhew agreed we should compile a list of all the transfers. You will find every transaction dating from eighteen hundred and twelve – some fifteen years ago in this document."

Mr Appleby passed the paper across.

"The bank transferred three thousand pounds per year from the estate's working account for five years into the number one account. The years involved were 1812 to 1816. In addition, the bank has transferred three hundred and six pounds per month from the Estate working account to the number two account for the last fifteen years. The years involved were 1812 to 1826. The total transfers amount to some seventy thousand and eighty pounds.

I have not included the 1827 year, but I have noted that the same pattern continues for the number two account for this year. We expect the subsequent transfer to occur this Wednesday when Mr Stem arrives with the banking instructions in Petersfield."

Anne was initially shocked but excited by the amount of missing money the bank investigation had revealed. She asked several questions, which Mr Appleby carefully explained.

Mr Meyhew, confident that Mr Appleby had fully explained the figures, said, "Thank you, Mr Appleby. That will be all."

The High Street Branch Manager nodded and quietly left.

Anne said, "My goodness. It has all gone into his account. Interestingly, no one from the Estate had noticed until last year when Sir Hugh forgot the wages and paid them late. Mr Meyhew, we must stop these transfers at once!"

Mr Meyhew sitting back in his chair with his hands clasped across his waistcoat, said, "Lady South, it may be prudent waiting until all the facts are known before any conclusions are made. At least we know that the bank has not lost the money. Persons with the proper authority have made the transfers. The question now is, what has become of the money?"

"Surely it is either in Sir Hugh's account or it is spent."

"But on what? And how do we find that out? I think the contents of this letter from Mr Hadley at Rows United Bank, Portsmouth, will assist."

He passed Anne the envelope.

"I am not sure you will gain any further information from Mr Hadley unless Sir Hugh authorises the release. Gaining his authority may be problematic, given he is in the West Indies. You will need authorisation for the bank draft changes to stop the transfers. The Earl or Lady Fintelton will have authority for this."

"How do I gain more information on the property? What would you suggest?"

"Find someone who might give you the transaction date for the original purchase of the property and the price paid. Perhaps start with the Earl's solicitors. You will have explained the fifteen thousand pounds if the purchase price matches the total transfers in the number one account. I cannot assist you with the remaining amount at this stage."

Before leaving, Anne opened the envelope from Mr Hadley and read the contents.

"The address of the property purchased is in Wimbledon, and the address for Mrs Constance is in Wimbledon too!"

"It may be a coincidence, or it may be significant! Lady South, I know you are energetic in your inquiries and will probably visit these addresses. I would strongly suggest that if you intend further research, you do so in the company of someone who can protect you. I may be overreacting, but there is a lot of money at stake here, and if someone is desperate, there is no guessing what may result. Take care, Lady South. Make sure you fully discuss this with Sir Robert before proceeding."

Anne put the letter back into the envelope, "Thank you, Mr Meyhew, I will take your advice gladly. I think reinforcements are required."

As Anne left, she glanced at the clock. It was one o'clock. She turned in the direction of the Fox and Hound and dashed off. Spying Victoria as she entered, she rushed across and sat in the empty chair.

"Sorry, I am late, Victoria! There is so much happening at work today!

Emma, you have arrived. Wonderful! Did Mrs Kirby show you your room?"

"Yes, Anne, I left my luggage there. May I introduce Lady Lily Johnstone from Hampshire?"

"It is a pleasure, Lady Lily." Anne, with a warm smile, nodded across the table.

From an ancient and respected family, Lily would not normally associate with commoners. She bore a condescending expression and took her time in responding.

Lily finally said, "Lady South! Good afternoon. So, you work, do you, Lady Anne?"

Grand Hotel, Kingston, Jamaica ...

Nurse Jackson placed the wooden gadget beside Sir Hugh's bed as Fiona Green explained the contraption. The unit consisted of two tea chests joined together, one with the bottom taken out and securely strengthened with a wooden frame on either side, giving it rigidity. A folded blanket draped over the rough edges along the top, protected against any injury.

Sir Hugh looked at the contraption with some doubt, "Where did you get this thing from, Fiona? It looks like a small coffin standing on its end."

"I remembered my Aunty had some trouble standing after an injury. It took her a long time to regain her strength and balance. The first hurdle was gaining strength in her legs and then having her stand for a few minutes at a time."

"So, will it give me some support when I stand up?"

"Yes, Hugh. Your body has lost the strength to stand. So, we start slowly and build your strength again. It will adjust with practice. There is no use in you remaining in bed – we need you on your feet and rebuilding your leg muscles. I know it looks crude, but it worked for my Aunty."

"Where did you get it from?"

"I had a carpenter make it up for me. He made some innovations, making it slightly stronger and higher."

Hugh shook the box-like gadget and found it stable, solid and light.

"Well, there is no time like the present. Up you get, Sir Hugh."

Hugh gritted his teeth and pulled himself onto the contraption as his legs shook, "I am feeling giddy, Fiona. My head is spinning."

Fiona and nurse Jackson helped him back down onto his bed.

"Well done, Sir Hugh. You were on your feet. Perhaps for only ten seconds, but you were up there." The nurse was very enthusiastic about the equipment. "That is great progress. I must show Doctor Cowper this contraption. It is so simple but helps."

"Don't show him yet. I want a few more attempts before we start boasting."

Hugh pulled himself up again and stood there for twenty seconds. "We will walk down that road before you know it, Fiona!" He slumped and shook, and they gently assisted him onto the bed.

Fiona smiled as she said, "Perhaps, that is enough for today."

Sir Hugh was asleep, exhausted from the effort. Fiona whispered, "I will return later and check on him, nurse. We will talk about tomorrow then."

With a look of appreciation, Nurse Jackson said, "He is most fortunate to have a friend such as you, Mrs Green."

"No, no! I saw what my husband went through. The worst is still coming. We are on that ship for England if we can get him mobile. At least he may have time with his family before things develop further."

"I still think he is very fortunate, Ma'am."

Fiona smiled as she walked away. She knew that Clarissa would have delivered the first letter by now, and the Earl and Lady Fintelton would be desperate for more news. Fiona decided to write again today. This letter would have far more positive news for Sir Hugh's mother.

The Bridesmaid's Dress Fittings, Hursts, Guildford ...

There was time for discussion while Mrs Smith and her helpers sewed the adjustments required from the initial fittings for the bridesmaid's dresses. Anne took the two dresses she had ordered for London from their boxes, and while they waited, she tried on the black mourning dress.

The dress for Mrs Jennifer Steele's memorial service looked stunning once adorned by Anne. She asked Victoria for assistance with her corset, "I wonder why we put ourselves through this agony just for fashion. It must not be too tight. If I cannot breathe, that would defeat the purpose."

Victoria laughed, saying, "One day, fashion will rid us of these corsets. What a day that will be!"

Anne pulled on the dress over her head and corset, and Victoria helped her straighten it out. Emma and Lilly could not resist and came over and felt the material. Emma said, "A black muslin, it feels nice. The waist is lower than your previous dresses, Anne?"

Mrs Smith answered, "The fashion is changing, Lady Emma. The waists are going down."

The skirt was wide at the bottom, only showing the points of her shoes, and the narrow waist was emphasised using a day sash. Anne chose a wide-brimmed bonnet with black flowers. The dress was simple but effective, and Emma and Victoria were impressed.

Emma asked, "Mrs Smith, would you have another like this one I may try? Anne's dress makes the one I packed rather dull."

"Certainly, Lady Emma, follow me into the measuring room here, and I will measure you up. We can have the first fitting if you come tomorrow at eleven. It will be finished before you leave for London. If you need a bonnet, Mrs Marsh will assist you with that in the millinery section at the front of the shop."

"Thank you, Mrs Smith."

Anne was in her ball gown when Fiona Smith completed measuring Emma. The other girls admired an excited Anne gazing into the mirror. She spun around, letting the silk fly out in a circle brushing against Victoria's and Emma's legs.

"Oh, I love the pink silk, Anne, and the sheer full-length sleeves. Do you think it needs some shoulder pads, or are you comfortable as it is?"

"No, Emma, I love it as it is. Anyway, I have no more time for any changes. The dress will do for the ball; if it does not measure up, I will hide behind you."

Victoria smiled, "There will be no need for that, Anne. It is a beautiful dress, and you will shine in it. I wish I could be a fly on the wall."

Understanding Victoria's disappointment that she would not be with them in London, Anne said, "We must have a ball here in Guildford soon. Once we are through this busy period, we will discuss how to arrange one."

"That would be nice but don't feel sorry for me as I have told William, Simeon, Madeline and Sophie that I will be their chaperone at morning tea on Saturday at Cloverdale Chase."

"Excellent, so we will not feel guilty about leaving you in Guildford."

Lily, who had watched with interest as Anne tried on the ball gown, said, "I had no idea that gowns such as these were made outside London. Mother and I usually visit London for dress fittings. That ball gown is a quality garment. Mrs Smith, do you have any other ball gowns as I may purchase one while I am here in Guildford?"

Mrs Smith said with a smile, "Certainly, Lady Lily."

Later at Porting and after dinner, Mrs Kirby announced that Doctor Sopwith had arrived.

"Please show him in, Mrs Kirby."

Emma was excited that David had come as she had not seen him since the previous Sunday. As he entered, she threw herself into his arms. David gave her a soft kiss and then looked up.

"My apologies, Lady South, I do not normally make an entrance like this."

"Apology accepted, Doctor Sopwith. You make me quite jealous as Robert is not here."

"David and Anne, you are very formal tonight?"

"We are putting on our good English manners for you, Vicky!" David smiled and then kissed Emma again.

Anne, with sparkling eyes, said, "Come, Victoria, we shall have a game of cards before bed and leave these two alone. Doctor Sopwith, I must request that you leave at a respectable time."

"Only if I may take Emma with me!"

Anne and Victoria laughed as they moved into the drawing room.

The Walsh Farm, Garranes, Ireland ...

Michael Walsh looked across at Ruth, who lay asleep in bed beside her two younger sisters. They were warm all together and peaceful. Ruth had not been herself all day, and Michael was glad she was finally sleeping peacefully.

He had avoided opening the message from Dan, but he could not put it off any longer. Would this be the end for Aiden Reid? He found a small piece of paper inside the envelope with a short note in Dan's handwriting. He held it near the candle and read:

> *Michael*
> *Tell Ruth! There is a job for her as soon as she feels ready. Hopefully, she can come to visit Hannigans by Wednesday morning.*
>
> *Aiden Reid disobeyed orders and disappeared. When he shows up, the committee wants him in Dublin. They have a job for him. I am sure they think you know where he is.*
>
> *The committee wants you in Dublin as soon as you can. I will see you there.*
>
> *Dan*
>
> *PS Burn this letter!*

Michael sat there wondering what kind of a job they would have for Aiden Reid after he had disobeyed orders. It must have been important as Dan was also attending, and his letter sounded urgent. Something big must be happening, and they needed him as an organiser.

Michael smiled. Aiden Reid had got away with murder again. How long would this last?

Hopping out of bed, he went across and lightly dropped the message into the fireplace. Michael watched as the message burned and turned black within the warm orange flames. Satisfied, he hopped back into bed, snuggling up beside his two brothers, who were fast asleep.

'Best, get a good night's sleep. Tomorrow would be busy.' He prayed, 'Please, Lord of Hosts, protect my family. Forgive us for our sins. Please provide us with some food tomorrow and protect us from danger this night and tomorrow. Mother Mary, pray for our safety tonight. Amen."

With that, Michael blew out the candle.

In the morning, the first thing he heard was several horses cantering towards the small cottage.

"Walsh! Come out here! Walsh!"

Michael's father opened the door and went out.

"Seamus, I have a letter here from Lord Kellwick. The Lord also sent down some potatoes for your family!"

The land agent dropped the letter and the potatoes at Seamus Walsh's feet.

"Thank you, Mr Higgins. We appreciate the potatoes."

"You probably will not like the letter."

With that, the land agent galloped off on his next call.

Seamus bent down and picked up the letter and the potatoes. He opened the letter and asked Michael if he would read it. Michael quickly read the letter and said, "He has raised the rent from six to seven shillings a week, commencing on the first of April." Michael screwed the letter up and threw it in the mud.

Seamus spat on the ground and watched the land agents galloping off.

"That does it. We must emigrate! Kellwick has no sense. Perhaps the ribbon men[24] will teach him a lesson after we are gone."

Michael patted his father on the back, "At least he gave us some potatoes!"

They stood together in silence as they watched the land agents dismounting at the next tenant farmer's cottage.

Seamus turned and asked Michael, "We will starve if we stay here, Michael. You find out from the brothers. Ask them how we arrange emigration. If we stay here, Kellwick will steal every cent we own. You and Ruth can join us when you can. I think we will try for Boston. We have family there. Make sure you are careful here until you come. Take care of Ruth. Her mind is not good at present."

"Right, Da! We will be with you before you know it."

Turner Coach Approaching Southampton …

As the steeples of Southampton came into sight from the carriage, Jonathon took a deep breath of relief. They had breakfasted early and left before eight. The roads were good, and little traffic at the turnpikes, making their progress fast. After their stop at Eastleigh for morning tea, Jonathan distracted Clementine by asking for a list of topics for discussion with Katherine on the

---

[24] Ribbon men: The Ribbon Society was principally an agrarian society, whose members consisted of rural Irish Catholics. The society was formed in response to the miserable conditions in which most tenant farmers and rural workers lived in the early nineteenth century in Ireland. Its objective was to prevent landlords from changing or evicting their tenants.

return journey. Fortunately, Clemmie decided she could write a list without becoming travel sick.

"Clemmie, when we reach this next rise, you should see the sea. If you turn and watch ahead, you will see it." The horses struggled to climb a short steep hill and then sped up again as the coach reached the summit.

"It looks like a bay, Father. I thought it would be larger than that?"

"It is! Southampton is at the top of a long bay called Southampton Water. It extends until reaching the Solent, the channel between the mainland and the Isle of Wight. You see that island far down there."

"On the horizon? Is that the island?"

"Yes, that is it. Now beyond that is the English Channel."

"Reverend Taggart taught us about that at school. The English Channel enters the Celtic Sea, named after the people who settled in Ireland. They came from Europe. Ireland is an island, Father, settled by different people, not the English. Why is it not a different country, Father? If I were Prime Minister ..."

Jonathan interrupted Clementine on her tangent, "Yes, yes, Clemmie, if you turn right at the bottom of England, that will take you out into the Atlantic Ocean. The second-largest sea in the world. What is the largest ocean in the world? You would have learnt this at school."

Clementine thought for a moment. Then she smiled, "The Great Southern Ocean."

Jonathan was confused, "I am sorry, as I thought it was the Pacific Ocean. The one that Cook explored. But you may be right. We must check up on that. Anyway, you will soon see Katherine, Uncle Richard and Auntie Sarah."

Clementine gazed at her father with a pained expression, "I think this will be a sad time for Katherine. I know I would be heartbroken if I were leaving home and possibly never returning. How will I help her, Father?"

Jonathan sat back in his seat and thought about Clementine's comment. His daughter was giving him an insight into how William might feel if Jonathan sent him away. He put it out of his mind.

"Be her friend and talk about all the wonderful fun you and she will have together. Tell her it will be a bit like boarding school but far better. Her mother will be returning in two years and staying with us. She will be reunited then."

Clementine nodded and looked out the window again, searching for the Southampton Water.

HMS Shadow, English Channel ...

Robert sat with Horace Coombes in the great cabin, each sipping a hot cup of coffee. Michael Swanton came across and placed a plate of Turner's Biscuits on the table before Horace.

Horace smiled and quickly took one. "Thank you, Swanton. Best biscuits this side of India. I hope the navy lodges a permanent order for the biscuits, Robert. I would like them in the army rations kit."

"If I had my way, it would be done!"

"Damn shame about the Admiral cutting your time short on the honeymoon."

"Yes and no, Horace. I will have a week off while we are in port at Woolwich, giving me some time with Anne, and I will see my Guildford residence for the first time. I bought it unseen, given the lack of time before the wedding. Anne inspected the place and advised me it was suitable. You must come and stay once we both find some free time ashore."

"It won't be next week, Robert, as I will be working with Colonel Scott on the security arrangements for this trip. I understand there are four ports where we stop. Cobh, Dublin, Belfast, and Derry. Security will be a nightmare. We may need more soldiers from the local barracks, as I doubt we have enough for every possibility. Did you know that the Earl of Dawlting intends to make various country visits while we are in each port?"

"That is probably normal, Horace. He intends an in-depth study gathering as much information as he can. The government's aim is improving the tenant farmer's lot in life."

"You don't believe that do you, Robert? These politicians are only interested in building their nests. It is more like they are finding a means of impoverishing these poor Irish beggars further. If they improved their lifestyles, it would only assist their struggle for independence. I cannot see that happening."

Robert had understood the mission's aim at face value and was honoured by his appointment by the government. He also felt some sympathy for the Irish people. "That is a bit cynical, Horace!"

"Think about it, Robert. How many of these politicians have estates in Ireland? They call them absentee landlords and have land agents acting for them. Why do they have estates here? To earn income! I would not be so bold and say they oppress the people working their estates, but I am sure they are not acting in the tenant's interests.

Have you seen your father's tenants' conditions at Fintelton?"

"No."

"Well, you should. The Irish living conditions are far worse. You should be more critical in your thinking about this. The romantic idea of improving the peasants' welfare is generous, but it may not be the actual outcome of this mission."

"Your views on this are interesting, Horace. I admit that my life in the navy has distanced me from the realities of the agrarian workforce. I need more information on this before I can form an opinion. Perhaps this mission will be an eye-opener for me."

"Good, your attitude is well-directed. We shall continue our discussions on these matters as we see the evidence. In the meantime, I suggest you keep your thoughts private. The politicians may become somewhat agitated if you become too accommodating, especially for the Irish."

"Good point, Horace. I did not tell you about my conversation with Captain Foster of *Providence*."

"Poor fellow! How is he recovering?"

"Slowly. I visited Foster at the naval hospital in Gosport. He was somewhat melancholy but glad of the company. I wanted the specific details of his mission when the Irish republicans boarded and took his ship. I have been continually thinking about how they knew in advance the precise movements of his initial voyage."

"I, too, wondered how they knew he was heading straight for Donegal." Horace was interested.

"The fact that they were expecting him was clear in that they had a chain across the channel. They also had six cutters full of men hidden beside the shore. For that level of preparation, they must have known in advance."

"So, what was his opinion?"

"He was sure the orders were secure, and no crew member had access. These facts made me think I should compare Foster's orders with Captain Hughes, who was also attacked. I visited the Admiral's office in Portsmouth, asked for both missions' orders, and carefully reviewed them."

"I'm surprised they released them."

"Commodore Jacobs was reluctant but agreed that a review might help. I found an interesting similarity in each of the orders. The captains' orders specifically stated they must sail directly to their first staging point with no stops. Mine was different as the Irish attacked us on the way back from Portsmouth. But you will recall that Swanton detected someone attempting a break-in of my cabin on the first night of the trip. So, my experience was the same as the others. The crew made a failed attempt, but it was during the first direct leg of the trip."

"So, if the crew were unaware of the route, how did the information get out?"

"That is precisely what I have been asking myself. I discussed it with Anne during our honeymoon as it was worrying me. She suggested that if a crew member did not leak the information, then there was only one other place it could have come from."

"Surely not! The Admiral is a truly loyal subject. There is no question of that."

"I agree. But when the Admiral originally gave me command of *Restless*, he dismissed the Commodore from our discussions and gave me additional orders. He commented that these orders came from a higher source than him."

Major Coombes sat back and finished his coffee. Taking another biscuit, "I don't like what you are thinking, Robert. If you are correct, we are all in danger."

"Perhaps I am paranoid, but I cannot find any other explanation for who leaked the information."

Horace slowly said, "There is also another indicator that we may be in trouble. The Admiral changed your orders from sailing with the fleet at the last minute. Also, the fact that I received new orders and was assigned here is suspicious. It may be a coincidence, and it may not."

"The Admiral told me that the Earl of Dawlting requested us personally. Our experience with the Irish and success on the last mission influenced his decision. I think he expects trouble."

They both sat there for a moment, thinking in silence.

Major Coombes greatly liked Turner biscuits and took another as he sipped his coffee.

Robert sat back and enjoyed the movement of *Shadow* through the waves. He relished the calming motion of a ship. "Seems like the crew are settling for the night, Horace!"

"They need a rest. You worked them hard today."

"That was necessary! I am not happy at all with their current performance. They are slow and not precise in their actions. In a battle situation, we would struggle. That is not how you gain the advantage at sea. I must have them dramatically improve before we venture back into the Irish sea."

"You suspect whoever leaked that information for the previous missions will try the same tricks again?"

"The thought has crossed my mind, Horace. Think about it. Whoever it is, remains well hidden from scrutiny. You and I are the ones who undid their plan for *Providence*. I would suspect that these traitors do not hold us in high esteem. We may even be targets now. I would not put it past these republicans."

Horace scratched his head and crunched another biscuit, "Surely not. We uncovered their plot and stopped them in their tracks."

"Perhaps, Horace, but hear me out. For some reason, the traitors need a major incident for publicity. We think they desire it so the republicans gain support at home in Ireland. A display of how independence is inevitable for Ireland. But what if someone higher is manipulating this for other purposes? Who knows what? The Irish may be pawns in a far greater plot that we may discover unintentionally. So, they will kill two birds with one stone. If you understand my meaning?"

"They get rid of us and carry out their plot. But what is the plot?"

"That is the question, and I am afraid we must find the answer!"

Swanton came in and asked if they required any further coffee.

"Swanton!"

"Yes, Captain."

Robert hesitated and looked at Horace for a few seconds.

"Call the Master at Arms, please and quickly. We need some backup. I can't have you staying awake all night again."

"Do you expect trouble, Sir?"

"Not sure, but I am keen on waking fresh in the morning …… refreshed!"

"Aye, Sir." Swanton quickly left the captain's cabin and disappeared on his mission.

"Now, Horace, the crew have had an hour off since we last drilled. It is now ten-thirty. They are well-fed and probably settling in their hammocks, expecting some rest. Time for the next exercise. Will you join me on deck as we put them through their paces?"

"It would be a pleasure, Captain."

There was a knock on the door.

"Enter!"

The Master at Arms, Mr Fulcher, said, "You requested my presence, Captain."

"Thank you, Mr Fulcher. Unlock the armoury, please, and issue the marines with their arms. Have two marines stand guard outside my cabin door now on shifts for the rest of this voyage. Liaise with Swanton on the security arrangements, please. On your way Mr Fulcher."

"Aye, Sir."

"Swanton, keep this cabin door locked at all times during the night, please. Major Coombes is the only officer with authorised access besides myself and Lieutenant Fenton."

"Aye, Sir."

"When I go on deck, Mr Swanton, I will order battle stations. Keep a good eye on our quarters here. If there is any funny business, take care of it and let me know. I will require breakfast at five in the morning. The crew will be at battle stations again at five-thirty.

Will you join me, Major Coombes?"

Robert was out the door and heading for the poop deck.

As Major Coombes put on his coat, he looked at Swanton and raised his eyebrows.

Swanton quietly said, "Here we go again, Sir."

Chapter 14

'Porting', Guildford, England ...

Lady Emma South slowly pushed the door of Anne's bedroom open and crept in, standing beside the large double bed. It was five in the morning, and Anne was fast asleep.

Emma gently nudged Anne's shoulder and whispered in her ear, "Anne! Anne, wake up. We must talk!"

Anne opened her eyes with a start, "Who is It?"

"It is Emma. I must talk with you."

Anne relaxed, sat up and checked her clock in the dim light, "Emma, what are you doing here at this time of the morning? It is only five o'clock!" Then Anne heard Emma's quiet sobbing.

"Emma, come into my bed and cover yourself. You must be freezing." Anne hopped up and lit a candle. The fire was almost out, and she quickly made it up.

"That will keep the fire going until Mrs Kirby comes." Anne could now see a distraught Emma sitting in her bed.

"Pull the covers over you, Emma, and we will warm each other until the fire heats the room. Mrs Kirby is an early riser, so I will ring the bell and stretch the friendship. Some tea and toast will keep us going until breakfast."

"Thank you, Anne."

Anne left the bed and pulled on her dressing gown, "I should go down and explain why we need the tea so early. Otherwise, Mrs Kirby will become curious. She means well but often gives too much advice. I will be quick." With that, Anne was out the door and away down the stairwell.

Emma pulled the sheet and blankets over her and watched the crackling fire as it warmed the room. Anne was soon back.

"Now, tell me what is bothering you, Emma?"

"I could not say anything last night as David and Victoria were here. Mr Stem, the Estate Manager, requested a Sunday meeting with mother and me.

He advised that only three thousand pounds remained in the Estate's Reserve account and only two or three pounds in the Working Account. The staff wages were due, and he needed five hundred pounds transferred into the Working Account. My mother arranged the transfer, and my father signed it.

When we asked Mr Stem about the costs of running the estate, I realised from his answer that I could no longer ignore this problem. Anne, I am afraid that the estate is now unfinancial. Father is old and no longer capable, Hugh is away in the Indies doing who knows what, and the situation genuinely stressed mother on Sunday night. She retired with a headache."

Emma wiped her eyes and then blew her nose.

"Emma, I was not aware that the finances were so low. Did you obtain the bank balances I asked for?"

"No! I am sorry. I forgot."

"No matter! We shall ask the Guildford bank manager for them this morning. I have authority from your mother."

"But Anne. Mr Stem would not be wrong. What can we do?"

"Calm down, Emma. I have slowly been assembling the information I need. Soon we will understand how we can keep the estate running."

"I am not sure that is possible. I am marrying David in a week and a half, and he thinks he is marrying a well-off daughter of an Earl. If I ask him for money before we marry, he will think the worst of me."

"Emma, that will not happen! You know the trust money that will soon be available once you are married."

"Yes, but I will be away on my honeymoon for six weeks and will not have access. By the time I return, the Estate will run out of money. Unless we have a plan, my mother will be beside herself."

"Emma, we will not let that happen. There are plenty of options. We will find the right one!"

"You sound so sure, Anne. I have no experience in these things, and it frightens me."

"Emma, you must be positive about the future. You are marrying a wonderful man who would never allow you or your family to be hurt. The future is bright for you, and your wedding will be wonderful. We will have a wonderful time over the next week, and then you will be off touring the continent and Ireland. There will be plenty of money."

Emma calmed down slightly and smiled at Anne.

"That is better, Emma! When you smile, you light up the world."

"With a friend like you, Anne. It gives me confidence. But what can I tell David?"

"I thought you had already told him everything. If not, Emma, it is time you did. David is no fool. He has probably already realised there are financial problems. You must trust him and share your life with him openly. He will be your most trusted partner in life."

Mrs Kirby knocked on the door and entered with two cups of tea and some buttered rolls.

Emma jumped out of bed and assisted her with the tray, "Thank you, Mrs Kirby. That is so nice. I had a bad dream and needed company until I calmed down."

"Ah, pre-marriage nerves, Lady Emma. A nice cup of tea will settle your nerves." Mrs Kirby smiled and quickly left.

They both took a sip of their teas, and Anne had a bite of her roll, "Um, that is better!"

"I thought about telling him everything, but I decided against it. I was afraid I would lose him. He has told me of his fortune and has done so openly. Now, I feel guilty that I have not been so open. I must marry David, Anne. I love him so much."

"And he loves you too, Emma. You must trust him!"

"I will. Mother and father arrive here today, so I asked Mr Stem if he would provide my mother with a listing of the estate's annual expenses and the cash income he expects. Mother will bring it with her. We must see the bank manager and ensure enough money is accessible until I return. I will then deposit my trust money into the Working Account, so the bank does not take action against the Estate."

"I am sure Mr Meyhew will see you and your mother, Emma."

"Anne, you must come as well. The team must present a united front. I need this done before David and I leave on the honeymoon; otherwise, I will be worried, and David will think I am not enjoying myself."

"I shall, but first, we must discuss it tonight with your mother. Then, if necessary, we shall all visit Mr Meyhew and set things straight. He has been my father's bank manager for as long as I can remember. He will assist us."

Emma smiled and took another sip of tea.

"Emma, there is another issue that worries me. I have great fears about Saturday night. The ball will be my first venture into society with Robert, and you saw how Lily treated me yesterday at the Fox and Hound. I am afraid the city ladies will tear me apart!"

"I will be with you, Anne. Lily will be there for your support as well. I have already had words with Lily. She will help protect you from the carnivores at the ball. They can be most cutting, but remember, it is the game they always play. They must be superior, or they have failed. After all, they are only ac-quaintances, and you may never see them again."

"I admit I am dreading the ball. It is not my world; I have no aspirations for their society. Lily considers herself superior but cannot add up two plus two. How would she survive if her father withdrew her money?"

"Does it matter, Anne? I know your first ball is a frightening prospect, but if you enjoy yourself and remain with those you know, there is nothing they can do."

"I think there is a lot they can do, and it will take all my strength to remain polite in such an environment."

Southampton, Hampshire, England …
Jonathan Turner woke and found the light slowly brightening his room. The suite they booked was still, and there was no noise from Clementine or Katherine, who slept in the adjoining bedroom. Richard and Sarah had decided that the girls should bond by staying together before their departure. The friendship should help Katherine once the parents had sailed and during the return journey with Jonathan and Clementine.

The day would be busy as Richard and his wife had arranged the loading of their luggage in advance. They had planned on being with Katherine for the remainder of the day before they embarked early the following morning. Jonathan and Clementine would join them at the ship, with the girls re-establishing their friendship. The process had worked well, and the girls had talked late into the night.

Keen for some breakfast before they visited the docks, Jonathan leapt out of bed and poured water into his washbasin. Then, after having a quick body wash, he was soon putting on his clothes.

The girls were still fast asleep when he entered their room.

"Clementine and Katherine! It is time you were stirring and readying yourselves for breakfast. We have a busy day ahead of us."

Jonathan found himself met with cries of woe and discontent. Showing no mercy, he walked across and pulled aside the curtain, letting in the bright sunshine, and ending the girl's peaceful sleep.

"I will be in the breakfast room, girls, and I will expect you down in fifteen minutes, please." Smiling, he exited the room and rubbed his hands in expectation as he set off for his favourite meal.

Reverend Taggart's Rectory, Guildford, Surrey …
The ladies had adjourned into the garden, and the Reverend Charles Upton and the Reverend Andrew Taggart freely talked about their church business.

"Sorry for the delay, Andrew, but one of my parishioners fell critically sick on the day we were leaving last week, and I decided I must call on him. I had decided to defer our departure by the time we finished the visit. Then I heard the sick relative I was visiting in Crawley had died. So, we cancelled the trip for a week. Now we are attending his funeral."

"A shame, Charles, but I understand how busy a clergyman's life is."

"No matter, these things happen in life. So, I welcome the fellowship we share with you and Laura today."

"You are most welcome. It has been a long time since we met in person, Charles. We must make the most of our time together. Now, there is a subject we might discuss while we have some privacy."

"Ah yes, I received your letter and decided not to write but that a private conversation may be sufficient. Andrew, I understand you ask for some information on Philip Hotspur."

"Yes! I have been requesting the addition of a curate here for several years. The bishop has always indicated a lack of funds and felt no need. Strangely, on my last request, there was no discussion but a quick agreement with my proposal for an assistant curate. I learned that Philip Hotspur would be joining us here at Guildford soon. I was not involved in the selection process."

"I see!"

"I have made a few other enquiries, and one response was carefully written but intimated that there might be a problem with this young chap."

"What sort of problem, Andrew?"

"Well, I am not sure yet. The response implied Philip lacked experience and did not concentrate on his profession. Also, it revealed that, for some reason, his fiancé broke off their engagement. There was also a reference that his future bride would have brought a substantial financial benefit into the union."

"I have heard the same."

Charles Upton lifted his cup of tea and drank. He smiled as he placed the cup on the saucer.

"I think whoever your source was, and I would never ask who it was, is quite accurate in his or her description."

Andrew sat upright, staring at Charles, "You mean this young man has all these problems?"

"I am sure he does not consider them problems but lost opportunities. Perhaps his calling is not so much a vocation but the benefits of his position."

Andrew thought hard about the comment. He stood, walked across, and glanced outside into the garden where his wife and Mrs Upton talked as they enjoyed the roses. Turning back towards Charles, he said, "I understand what you are saying. Is there any other advice I should hear?"

"In strict confidence, yes, there is!"

Walking back across, Andrew sat again and sipped his tea.

"Oh, blast this tea. Here, Charles, we shall have a glass of sherry. I am afraid I will need it."

"Thank you, Andrew. A little fortification would assist."

They both took a half-full glass of sherry and emptied them quickly.

"Andrew, are you aware that Philip is the bishop's nephew?"

"No, the Bishop had not disclosed that."

"Then it is good that you know, but perhaps it may be prudent if you did not mention it."

Andrew nodded in agreement. He then filled both glasses with sherry.

"What will Hotspur be doing in your parish?"

"I asked for someone who could take care of the school."

Charles Upton sat back and drank half the glass of sherry. Licking his lips, he said, "Philip Hotspur may not be the best person for the school.

Children require constant supervision. Philip cannot concentrate on issues in which he has no interest. I have heard rumours that he aims to find a wealthy young lady, marry her, and then retire from the ministry. He has no interest in a spiritual vocation."

Andrew Taggart was now particularly concerned. He needed a curate who would eventually manage the running of the school. The bishop was fully aware of this. However, he was now receiving advice from Charles that the man was not suited for this type of role.

The Reverend Taggart opened his mouth, but Charles Upton cut him off, "It is best, Andrew, if I say no more. You and I have been friends for over twenty years, and I value your confidence. But, for your career, I beg that you tread very carefully here. The man may not be a dedicated minister, but he has connections. Employ him in a position where he cannot do any damage. If he is working with children, he will also need supervision. If his role involves contact with the parish's eligible young ladies, keep a close eye on him. Philip's approaches will have only one aim: purely financial. We both know this is not a good basis for establishing a marriage relationship. I can say no more than this. Now I must collect my good wife, and I am afraid we must be on our way. I aim to arrive at Crawley before sunset."

"Thank you for your advice, Charles. It is most appreciated."

"Thank you for your hospitality and the sherry, Andrew. A good drop if I do say so myself."

Charles Upton shook Andrew's hand, and they walked out into the garden and joined the ladies.

The Walsh Farm, Garranes, Ireland ...

Ruth sat on a tree stump, quietly talking with Orla, one of her younger sisters, as the setting sun gave a little warmth through their tightly wrapped coats.

"America will be wonderful. The sun always shines, and there is work for everyone. People have bread on the table instead of potatoes. I heard that girls attend school till year eight, and you can study history and maybe attend a university. I read it in the paper we found left in a garbage can in Garranes, Ruth. I kept it as it was the first newspaper I have ever seen."

"Is that what you want, Orla? Travel across the sea and live in a new country."

"Why not, Ruthy? You worked in Islay. I support my father's decision. We are starving here, and if there is another bad winter, perhaps poor Tara will not survive. She gets no good food, only potatoes. Sometimes in the mornings, I think she is dead, but then her eyes open, and I breathe a sigh of relief. There is an opportunity for all of us in America. There is no future here. The landowner treats us as if we were his slaves."

"One day, Orla, Ireland will be free!"

"Not in my lifetime, Ruthy."

"Farmers will own their land. The land the English took from us. Is that not worth fighting for?"

"Not if we can live somewhere else and have a good life. We do not have a life here at all. The ways of the landholders will never change. We are their slaves, and they enjoy our misery. In America, we can be free. Freedom Ruth – don't you understand what that means? We can earn money, send it home, and support those struggling here. I could get an education and become a teacher or an office worker. I would leave with father tomorrow if he can find a way."

Ruth looked away and considered what her sister was saying. She understood bitterly what the word freedom meant. She craved it in another way. But if everyone left for America, would Ireland ever be free? Then she thought of Callum. Ruth realised that her actions were too hasty and had taken his life in the heat of the moment. She had not been honest with him and sacrificed the man she loved for Ireland. Callum and all those Irish boys were now dead. Now, her family was leaving, and soon she would be alone. She could never leave her homeland and waste the sacrifices that she had made. The tears started falling down her cheeks.

Orla stood and moved closer, sat beside Ruth, and hugged her.

"You loved him, didn't you?"

"I think I did. I am not sure. Callum was so much fun; he dreamed of owning a farm and marrying me. But I took his life. The look in his eye as he lay on top of me. He was saying, 'Why Ruth? Why?' I will never be free of it. Can I ever be forgiven?"

"Father O'Doherty says there is no sin our Lord cannot forgive."

"Does he just!"

"Ruth, if you ever free yourself from this war, join me in America, and we shall travel, learn, and do things you have never imagined here."

"Little sister, you are so sweet. I would love it. But at present, I am a lost soul. I can never be free until God forgives me. I don't know how that will ever happen." Ruth broke down and started shaking as the tears flowed down her cheeks.

Flann Walsh, Ruth's mother, came out and hugged them both. Flann whispered, "Give it time, Darling! You will find peace again."

Michael Walsh took his knapsack and opened the front door. When he saw the three women in the pasture hugging each other, he knew Ruth needed more time. She may never recover from her ordeal.

Seamus walking up from the pasture, slapped his son on the back, "You are off then, Michael?"

"Should be dark by the time I reach Garranes. If the chance comes, I will hitch into Lissarda and catch a coach. By travelling at night, it will be easy to avoid the watchmen."

"Good. Now send me a note on what help the brothers will give towards our emigration. I must have the family out of here before summer."

"I will, Father. Ruth is not ready yet. She may never be ready. You take her with you. She needs a new start."

"Don't we all, boy?" Seamus gripped his son close and hugged him hard.

"Bye, Da!"

"Take care, Michael."

Michael Walsh turned and walked off down the road with his bag over his shoulder. He was not sure if he would ever see them again. A small tear dropped down from his left eye. "Blast it!" he said as he pulled out his hand-kerchief, wiped his eye and blew his nose.

The Fort, 'Cloverdale Chase', Guildford, Surrey …

Madeline, Sophie, Simeon, and William galloped down the slope through the clumps of trees and headed straight for the fort. Excitement was all over their faces as they tumbled through the gate and climbed the rampart.

"Raise the flag so Clare knows we are here," Madeline cried. William quickly opened the flag box, took it out, attached and raised the flag so it filled in the light breeze.

"Pirates attacking from the north! Stand ready!"

The children grabbed their sticks representing spears and lined the fort's walls.

Simeon yelled, "Ready!"

Everyone raised their stick or branch, waiting for the command.

"They are in range. Fire!"

The children thrust their sticks and branches into the air, followed by whatever ammunition they had collected on the hillside. Screams of delight were heard as the melee unfolded.

"They are breaching the gate!" William cried, "We must repel them!"

The small party rushed down the steps and formed a defensive line at the gate, encountering the imaginary enemy. Without thinking, William grabbed a large stick and started spinning, hitting Madeline in the cheek.

"Ow!" Madeline felt her cheek and found blood on her fingers. "Oh, no!" she screamed.

The battle stopped as everyone looked at Madeline, whose fingers pressed on the bleeding scratch.

Sophie asked, "Do you boys have a handkerchief?"

They both answered, "No". Simeon looked down towards the house and saw Clare and Mr Petherton walking up the hill.

Simeon called, "Come on, Madeline, Mr Petherton will have a handkerchief."

Soon they found themselves sitting on the patio at Clare's residence, each having a cold drink of water and the maid helping Madeline with her cut cheek.

"William, you struck Madeline with a nasty blow. Please be more careful in future!"

"I am sorry, Mr Petherton. It was an accident. We were in the middle of repelling the pirates from the fort's gate."

"I'm sure you were, but remember, a gallant soldier always keeps the presence of mind during a battle. That way, you can always outsmart the enemy. By blindly spinning, you make yourself an easy target. I hope you will learn from this accident."

"I shall, Mr Petherton."

"I'll bet," Madeline said with a scowl.

Clare spoke up, "It is good that William has said he will try, Madeline. I am sure he will be careful in the future."

Madeline gave a polite smile.

William asked, "Mr Petherton, while we are here, would you show us some of your bottle collection."

"Certainly, William. It is time you head home, but another five minutes will not matter. Come with me!"

'Porting', Guildford, Surrey ...

Lord and Lady Fintelton arrived at around four-thirty, approached the entrance, and rang the doorbell. There was a noise of running feet inside, and the front door flew open. Emma and Anne rushed out with screams of delight like children as they hugged and kissed the Earl and Countess.

"Why this reminds me of when the children were young, Jane. What a pleasant welcome. Thank you, Emma and Anne."

Lady Jane wiped a tear from her eye and gathered her thoughts after such a show of affection.

"Now, Anne. Let me see this property that Robert has acquired for you. It looks quite interesting but a bit small."

Anne smiled, "I'm not sure Robert has even seen it yet, Lady Jane. But it will suit us very well."

"Well, show me around, young Anne. I am eager for a tour."

Mrs Kirby came around from the back, waited until the guests were shown in, and then approached the footmen and advised the arrangements. Soon the second coach arrived with the Earl and Countess's staff and some more luggage.

Anne glanced over her shoulder through an upstairs window and noticed the two coaches outside and the luggage and staff. She thought, 'I think Robert must renovate the stables.'

The Grand Hotel, Kingston, Jamaica ...

Sir Hugh stood holding his balance contraption and took one step away. He stood there without assistance for twenty seconds and then moved back, grasping the support apparatus.

"What do you think of that, Fiona!?"

Fiona Green and Nurse Jackson clapped and cheered.

"That was wonderful, Hugh. You are gaining your strength faster than Doctor Cowper thought you would. If you can take five steps unassisted by the end of the week, I shall book us onto the ship that leaves in early May. Now we must talk about your plantations."

They assisted Sir Hugh into a chair on the verandah. He sat there smiling, most content with his progress.

"Fiona, I have an idea. The standing frame has been a great success, as I can now remain upright and move my legs for several minutes. But the gadget does not move. I have an idea. Here at the hotel, we have this long verandah!"

Pointing at the verandah rail, Hugh explained, "But the rail is too low for my purposes. Why not install a temporary higher rail making it safe and allowing me support along the verandah? I can feel my strength returning, and I will surely walk freely within a week. The cost of the installation will not be significant. What do you think?"

Fiona was most encouraged, "Hugh, that is a grand idea. I will discuss it with the hotel manager and then employ the same carpenter who created your frame. If you walk again soon, we will journey down the road together in the fresh air. Now that will be a welcome experience for you."

"You are right. I was wondering if I would ever see home again. Yet strangely, I have a steadily growing attraction for England. When I left, I was a lost soul. Let us say I had a reality check. I was unsure where I was heading."

"That sounds most strange, Hugh. I have always considered you a confident, outgoing man, safeguarding your father's estate, and checking on your investments regularly."

Hugh laughed, "That is very flattering, Fiona. If only it were true. I am no better than your run-of-the-mill thief keen on using whatever he can of his father's money."

"I do not believe that Hugh. You have good manners, and you care for people."

Hugh was amazed, "You see that in me, Fiona! I must tell you about myself and clear the air. I am not what you think. My attempts at redeeming myself have failed!"

Hugh spent the next half hour relating his personal story. They sat together on the verandah, sipping lemonade and ordering more when needed. At times Hugh would stand up and use his contraption while continuing the story. At times, they would laugh with Fiona identifying parts of Hugh's story with her own life.

"When Doctor Sopwith told me I had the pox, and there was no cure, I initially did not believe him. But then I had an episode, far milder than the one I have recovered from here. I suddenly realised my life might end soon, making me think about what I had achieved. When I made those awful remarks at my friend's stag party in a drunken stupor, I finally realised that I had reached rock bottom."

"What did you do, Hugh?"

"I sat in Reverend Taggart's church all night, and he found me in the morning. I was a mess and quite dishevelled. I am sure he would have been most displeased as he was preparing for a service. But do you know what he did?"

"Tell me."

"He sat there silently and waited as I explained. It was one of the most meaningful conversations of my life. No, it was the most meaningful."

Fiona noticed for the first time since she had met Hugh that he was becoming emotional.

"After much discussion, he asked me a question that he said I must answer." Hugh shuddered slightly and gritted his teeth as he struggled with his emotions. He wiped away a couple of tears.

Fiona gave Hugh some time as he calmed himself and gently asked, "What was the question, Hugh?"

"He asked me if I liked myself."

Hugh could not speak any further for a few minutes and looked away in embarrassment as he wiped away the tears. Fiona realised that this had been a life-changing moment for Hugh.

Hugh continued in a shaky voice, "After several minutes of avoiding his question, I realised it was a question of such importance that I must answer. I knew then what I had been thinking for a long time. I hated myself! I had lost all sense of what my purpose in life was. It was – how can I say it – a moment I shall never forget."

"What did he say when you answered his question?"

"He said that I had made the first step in redeeming my life and that my honest answer had taken great courage."

Hugh once again stopped talking and took a sip of lemonade. He gazed out across the bay, noticing a ship entering the harbour.

"It sounds like Reverend Andrew Taggart is a remarkable man. I hope he had his sermon prepared beforehand."

Hugh laughed and wiped his nose, "I do too. I left him no preparation time at all. He is one of the most remarkable men I have ever met. You know he never judged me once. Reverend Taggart sat there, put aside my shortcomings and befriended me. The whole experience so moved me."

"So, what has been the outcome, Hugh?"

"The outcome was that despite my best efforts, I failed. I tried but always fell back into the comfort of my failing ways. So, in the end, I decided that I would visit the Indies and probably die here rather than have my family deal with the trail of destruction I have left behind me."

"Oh, dear! Hugh, you must not think that. Your family love you."

"I know! I was running away from the mess I had made of my life. I thought it might help. But it did not. I found myself in more trouble."

"What kind of trouble, Hugh?"

"Well, I was enchanted by Lady Clarissa as soon as I was on the ship. I should have known better, but I fell again. That reminds me, why does she not visit me? I thought she had genuine feelings for me."

Fiona groaned, "Oh, Hugh. You and every other man on earth! She is a great actor and has little sense. I tried warning you, but there was only so much I could say. I am afraid she left for London with another man in tow. She is probably in London now."

"Oh!"

"After we have returned, I would enjoy making the acquaintance of this Reverend Andrew Taggart."

"So, you shall, Fiona. When we return, I insist that you stay at Fintelton with me, and then we shall visit Guildford and see him at church. Of course, I assume you do not have someone waiting for you. My apologies if I have spoken too freely."

"You have not, and I will be pleased to meet your family, Hugh. But you must ensure that they understand that we are not in a relationship but are good friends. I will also ensure you receive the care you need on your return journey."

"Of course, Fiona. You have my word on that. Now we should discuss the plantations. It appears the Governor's men have uncovered some difficulties?"

The Docks, Southampton, England ...

Jonathan Turner moved uneasily around the packet's deck that would be the start of his brother and sister-in-law's adventure. Seeing the vast deck area under the four square-rigged masts, he was amazed at the ship's size. The accommodation was well-planned and comfortable, and the passenger bar served delicious meals.

After exploring every corner of the public areas, Katherine, followed by Clementine, entered the cabin. They found Katherine's parents and her uncle in deep discussion.

Clementine, totally enthralled by the romantic nature of travel, was openly saying, "Uncle Richard, I wish I were going with you. May I visit you in South Africa once you are settled? I would love a sea voyage on a ship such as this."

Richard lifted his eyebrows and glanced at Jonathan, "I am not sure it is the place for a young girl, Clementine."

Immediately picking up on Richard's cue, Jonathan sought out Clementine and took her aside.

"Clemmie, that sort of talk will not assist Katherine. Remember, she is losing her parents for the next five years. The last thing we want is for her begging her father that she should accompany them."

"Sorry, Father. I had not thought of that."

"Well, please be a bit more circumspect."

"I will, Father."

"Now, let us visit the passenger bar with Uncle Richard, Auntie Sarah and Katherine and have afternoon tea. Soon after that, we must say our final farewells."

The Barque 'Manson', Docking at Southampton Harbour, England ...

The Manson slowly moved up the harbour and approached the docks. Onboard the packet *Cape Cradwell*, Clementine spied the large sailing ship approaching the docks and urgently requested, "Father, look at that large ship going past. It must be docking. Might Katherine and I go on deck and watch, please? It is so exciting."

"Yes! But finish your orange juice first. That cost me a pretty penny."

"I have finished mine, Uncle Jonathan. Thank you, it was delicious and most refreshing."

Jonathan was pleased with Katherine's refined comment.

Clementine upended her glass and swallowed the contents in one go. Jonathan watched in horror, noting her bad manners. The girls then excused themselves, Clemmie giving a large burp as they rushed off.

"They are excited, Jonathan. They are young; this is the first time Clemmie has seen a port."

"Yes, but I pray it leads her nowhere else."

Sarah smiled and then became more serious. She waited until Richard stopped speaking and then addressed Jonathan.

"This may be our last chance, Jonathan, before we leave. The ship will sail on the high tide at four am tomorrow morning. I must say something, please, if you will allow me?"

"Certainly, Sarah, we are family!"

"Jonathan, it has been nearly two months since Eleanora died. I know it has been a difficult time for you, and in many ways, I am glad that Katherine is remaining here as the chaos Clemmie and Kathy create in your household will take your mind away from the grief."

Richard and Jonathan smiled at the suggestion.

"Jonathan, you are still young and have many years ahead of you…."

"Sarah, no …."

"No, Jonathan, I must say this. You are still young enough and should marry again. It may not be what you wish but remember the children and a baby at home who require care. Eleanora would want you remarried. She would not want her children left without a mother. I know it is painful, and I know you miss Eleanora deeply. But soon, you must move on. I am afraid the past is gone. There is no harm in having happy memories about the past, but your children will live in the future. They need the care of a mother. You should carefully consider this, Jonathan. Please tell me that you will?"

Sarah's address had moved him. Given the protective role he played for Clementine and Katherine today, he had forgotten his grief for Eleanora. He felt ashamed, yet the suggestion sounded familiar. He must face the facts soon and drag himself from his melancholy.

"Sarah…" Jonathan struggled with his words, ensuring he was polite. "I understand what you are saying and will consider your suggestion. I am most flattered that you are so kind in your thoughts towards me. I will write and tell you the direction I have taken. But I need more time. Please, you must understand. I am making progress, but I need more time."

As the *Manson* moved into position near the dock, crew members threw many lines ashore where waiting workers hauled the almost stationary ship against the pier.

Lady Clarissa Wendarm stood beside the rail, wondering where Stephen Polkinghorne could be. They had agreed to watch the docking process together. What was keeping him? She must check his cabin as he may still be packing. The thought of dinner at the up-market hotel they had booked and spending the next few nights there with Stephen was uppermost on her mind.

Clarissa moved towards the internal stairs, attracting several gentlemen's attention, who raised their hats as she smiled and strutted along the corridor. Finding Stephen's room, she knocked gently and opened the door. Clarissa was surprised when she found the cabin empty. All the clothes were gone from the cupboard, and a letter was left on the bed. She noticed her name above the address, being her cabin number. He must have left it for the porter. She broke the seal, opened the note, and eagerly read:

My Dear Clarissa

I have enjoyed the voyage and the time we spent together in Jamaica and onboard. I have found your company charming.

You were open and honest with me during the voyage and revealed your troubles with your first husband, Peter, and your second, Sir Hugh. I thank you for this. When you told me of your blessing of carrying Sir Hugh's child, I thought deeply about our future together.

On reflection, I thought it best that you join Sir Hugh's family, and they have the joy of welcoming his son or daughter. As the child will be the estate's legitimate heir, it will be essential that they reside either on or near the estate. So, I am sure it is best if we suspend our relationship for the present time.

I appreciate your honesty. I leave this letter with a heavy heart, but I feel it is for the best. I will contact you in a year, and we might discuss the future then.

Love Stephen

Clarissa was fuming, "You Cad! I will fix you."

She rushed out of the cabin and onto the deck. Soon standing beside the rail, she saw the crew moving the gangplank into place. The first passenger disembarking was a tall, quickly walking man carrying a briefcase and coat. It was Stephen!

As he rushed along the pier towards the Departures Hall, Clarissa unleashed an almighty scream, "Stephen, you Cad!"

He stopped in his tracks and looked up at the fuming face of Clarissa, who looked as if she could tear him apart.

He politely raised his hat and looked away, escaping into the crowd with a smile of relief.

After Dinner at 'Porting', Guildford …

Lady Jane was impressed with the house. She sat in the lounge room before the fire and sipped some sherry. The Earl was making himself comfortable before attacking his glass of scotch, and Lady Emma was tinkering with the piano.

The Earl said, "Anne, that was a marvellous dinner. I am now most relaxed, and a little music will suit me fine."

Anne, not keen on demonstrating her lack of skill, said, "Then Emma should play first as she knows the music you will enjoy."

"Anne, I have not heard you play yet, so you start, and Emma may follow. Given all the other pursuits you achieve with excellence, I do not expect a great piano rendition. But a little music would be most welcome."

"I will try, Lord Fintelton, but please forgive me for my mistakes."

As Anne arranged herself, the footman lit more candles and stoked the fire.

Lord Fintelton commented, "Jane, this is a lovely room for a young married couple. It is cosy and warm. It reminds me of when we were first married and our time away on the continent. Venice, I think. Do you remember the canals and the view from the hotel? I can see it as plain as day. What a wonderful time that was."

"Well, David, I think Anne has rightly pointed out that the wallpaper is dated, and there is a need for redecorating and new furniture. But it has the potential for being pretty indeed."

The Earl was already far away, drifting down a canal in Venice, watching the gondolas pass. Lord Fintelton was content, and given his hearing, it would not have mattered what tune Anne played. The music was in the background as he relaxed, enjoying his scotch and the warm fire.

Anne chose a simple but elegant piece and commenced playing. As the tune unfolded, the Earl's eyes drooped, and he soon put his empty glass down, rested his head against the wingback of the chair, and nodded off, enjoying the comfort of rest.

The countess said, "We need a few grandchildren here to keep him awake!"

Lady Emma chuckled, "Well, hopefully, he will see some soon. He has taken the first day well, Mother. I think our plan is working."

"I am confident that he shall arrive at 'Harting' rested and well, Emma. Anne, having a family stop at 'Porting' is now a great asset. Perhaps soon, Emma, you will have a similar house, giving us more reason for Guildford visits. I think your father is quite enjoying having daughters in Guildford."

"Once there are grandchildren, Lady Jane, we will often visit Fintelton. I understand that travel for you and his Lordship will become far more difficult as you age. I would not want you missing out on the joy of your grandchildren."

"You are so sweet, Anne. Perhaps, two or three would be sufficient!"

They all laughed as the Earl grunted and shifted his head.

In a softer voice, Lady Jane said, "Now, Anne and Emma, here are the figures from Mr Stem."

She passed the envelope across, and Anne opened the letter and quickly read it.

As Anne read, Lady Jane said, "We must overcome this financial crisis, girls! We cannot rely on the men, so we are the team who must ensure Fintelton's survival."

Emma was impressed with her mother's comments, "Mother, you sound far more positive and confident tonight."

"I am Emma. Have a look at the figures Stem has provided."

Anne passed the letter across.

"It appears the income from the winter harvest will almost cover the estate's working expenses for the next three months. The problem is keeping the cash flow reserves large enough, so the bankers do not panic. A happy banker is full of confidence."

Lady Jane agreed and asked, "What do you suggest, Anne."

"We do not have any idea about the plantations in the Indies and must wait for Hugh's return for that information. The estates in Scotland and Ireland are also unknowns. Emma, David has estates in Ireland. He would understand the finances of an estate, and I am sure they are well-managed. We must ask him for advice."

"Anne, you know I do not wish him involved. Not before the wedding."

"It is time he was made aware of the situation, Emma. He may not be pleased if he finds he could have been helpful."

"Anne is right, Emma. David is a wise man and will cope with any situation. You underestimate the wonderful man you are marrying. We should include him in our team. The more minds working together, the stronger we become."

Emma sat there, toying with the idea. She was not yet convinced but warmed towards the concept.

"I would be happier if we had agreed upon a plan. That way, David would have greater respect for what we are doing. I would rather that he was not involved financially."

Anne smiled and said, "I have a plan for us. I am certain it will be sufficient until you return from your honeymoon and probably longer."

Emma and Lady Jane looked up, "Tell us, Anne!"

"Firstly, Emma, tell me you will include David in our team."

Emma sighed, "Are you both happy that he joins our secret counsel of war?"

Anne quickly replied, 'Yes, of course! He will soon be your husband, Emma, and I greatly respect him."

"I too, Emma. David will be thankful that you trusted him." Lady Jane felt the time was right for David's inclusion.

"Then, I shall discuss it with him at 'Harting', but I am terrified that he might misunderstand me."

"And I am terrified, Emma, of the ball society we shall meet in London. We shall support each other as we move forward."

Emma smiled and came over and hugged Anne. "Sister, I will be beside you every inch of the way. We are strong together."

"That is the spirit, girls. Now, Anne, what is the plan."

"Well, the current problem is a cash shortage. The bankers will become worried if the reserves further decrease. With the men all away, we need a short-term solution. I have two promissory notes that provide short-term loans of two years or less, depending on the needs. One is an advance of three thousand pounds from my money, and the other is four thousand pounds from the Turner Bakery money. These drafts will put seven thousand pounds into the Estate working account, and with the three thousand pounds already there, it will cover one year's working expenses. But we must sort out this financial situation by eighteen twenty-eight, at the latest. At that time, the estate may repay the notes. There will be no interest charged."

"Anne, are you sure about lending three thousand pounds of your own money? That is very generous of you."

"I am now the Managing Director of my father's company, and he pays me a salary far exceeding my needs. I can spare the money easily, Emma."

"Anne, you have been very generous here, and I thank you for saving us in our time of need. I think you can be sure that Emma and I are determined that this financial situation will be solved. Now, how do we put your plan in place."

"You both should carefully read the promissory note wording and then sign them with a witness. The witness will verify your signatures. I will have Mrs Kirby come in once you are ready. She can read and write and is well educated."

Emma said, "Give us ten minutes, please."

"Of course, and tomorrow morning I will deposit the monies into your working account before I leave for London. When we meet at Epsom, I will confirm it is all in place."

Dublin Safe House, Ireland …
Michael Walsh arrived earlier in the day and sat looking out over the pastures as he waited for the arrival of the others. The brothers had found a secluded house not that far from Dublin. The tenant farmers in the area would keep their secret, and the land agents would not be game, knowing if they revealed

the house's position, they would suffer at the hands of the Ribbon-men.

Michael thought, 'Why would any landholder want an estate in Ireland? They would be up against so much opposition and not know who they could trust. Perhaps that was why there were so many absentee landholders. Then again, it must be profitable as they would not relinquish their estates without a fight.'

There was a tap on Michael Walsh's right shoulder, and he spun around in surprise, finding a pistol pointed at his face. Ian Murphy smiled and lowered the gun, "Did no one tell you? You should wait inside out of sight – it is broad daylight, man, and the owner is only here at night."

"Sorry, Ian, I forgot."

"If the watchmen find you here, you will never forget it while you live. They will tear you apart. Finding a brother's coordinator would be ripe picking for them. Use your sense, man. Now inside out of this cold."

As they entered the house, Michael commented, "Ian, I was wondering why the English desire landholdings in Ireland. The only reason could be it is highly profitable?"

"You are right. In our world, anyone who owns large landholdings is a member of the Ascendancy[25]. They can use the land for their purposes and cheat the tenant farmers out of everything they have. We will change that system one day when we win back the country!"

Michael nodded in agreement, "One day soon, I hope?"

"Now, Michael, do not get your hopes up. The republic is a long way off. I have been working full-time on this for thirty years, and there is still no clear way ahead of us. I will not see it in my lifetime, but you may."

"I hope so. I received your message and came straight away. Ruth is still in a bad way, so I left her on the farm. My father has decided to emigrate. We have relatives in Boston. Ruth and I will stay, but the rest of the family will go. Would the brothers help him with the process?"

"Yes, lad. The brothers will kick in some money for the fares. I will have Dan O'Leary set it up and speak with your father. We have plenty of contacts in Boston. Now I am concerned for Ruth. She is an excellent operative, and we need her in Dublin. Poor thing! It was her first killing, but it becomes easier after that."

"I am not so sure. I think a role out of the action may be better for Ruth."

Ian Murphy was surprised by that comment, "Why do you say that Michael?"

---

[25] The Ascendancy was the political, economic, and social domination of Ireland between the 17th century and the early 20th century by a minority of landowners, Protestant Clergy, and members of the professions, all members of the Established Church (Church of Ireland or Church of England). Wikipedia.

"She is a girl, Ian. Only nineteen, and her whole life is ahead of her. But at present, she is a lost soul. She is full of remorse. That boy she lived with meant more than she realised. Now she wonders if she can ever be forgiven."

"She will recover. They all do. Now, Dan and Braydon are bringing some dinner. They should be here soon after dark. So, it gives us some time to plan the mission. The British have a committee of inquiry that will visit Ireland. They plan on improving the situation of Irish tenant farmers like your Da! Would you believe that?"

"Sounds unlikely!"

"That's right. The British will probably use anything they discover against us rather than help. Our contact advises they will visit Cork, Dublin, Belfast, and Derry and stay with landowners on their estates. They plan on visiting and talking with tenant farmers. There will also be functions like dinners where various landowners, high-ranking officials and some tenants will be invited along."

"They will invite the tenants. Which of their rags will they put on for the dinners?"

"The landowners will assist with some new clothes. I wonder if the clothes will be a gift, or they must pay for them?"

"At least they will look the part. The modern Irish tenant!"

"But listen, Michael! The British warship's Captain and the Marines' Major, who took our frigate, will be attending. The committee requires them assassinated at one of the functions, creating publicity that will strengthen our support in Ireland. That's why we are searching for Aiden Reid. The committee considers him a lost hope and will sacrifice him on this mission. It kills two birds with one stone. He has the pleasure of killing this Captain and Major, and Aiden is captured by the British, and they will hang him. Very neat!"

"Where will they carry this out?"

"We decide on that at the meeting tonight. Probably Cork, as Aiden lives in that area. But he has vanished."

"No, it must not be in Cork! The last thing we want is the British tearing our homes apart, searching for conspirators. We have many men recovering from their injuries from the battle at Islay. They must not connect our area with that battle."

"Good point! The Red Coats would have no pity and execute the men."

"Aiden Reid does not like the country. He prefers working in the cities. It will give him confidence if he feels he can fade into the crowd. He is a master at that, and as we can't find him, the British will never find him."

"That is not what the committee wants, Michael. They want him found. The British will try him with much publicity, and it will be something that the London public enjoys. Aiden will become a hero in Ireland and no longer be a problem for us."

"Then, we must carry it out in Dublin. That is our largest city, and Aiden will feel comfortable there. He will carry out the job. He wants revenge against that English Captain."

"There is only one problem, Michael! Where is Aiden Reid?"

"How long have we got?"

"Three weeks."

'I will find him for you."

Turner Household, Guilford, Surrey ...

Having made good time from Winchester, the coach arrived at around five-thirty in the afternoon while it was still light. The girls' conversation had been lively during the journey, and Jonathan found them in good spirits as they pulled up in front of the house.

Aggie, sweeping the entrance, noticed the coach approaching and called inside for the children. A welcoming party soon assembled and greeted their cousin, Katherine, as she joined the family for the next five years.

Before the coach stopped, the two girls were out and running into Madeline and Marcia's arms. Both William and Simeon received gentle hugs followed by polite conversations with Mrs Nibley, Mrs Jennings and Aggie. It was a warm welcome, and Ethel was surprised that Katherine was so content and happy.

Following the excitement of dinner and the tales of their adventure at Southampton, the girls headed for their room upstairs, unpacking and finding their bedclothes before it became too late. Clementine was one step behind Katherine every inch of the way and pointed out precisely what cupboard space was hers.

Ethel took the opportunity and talked with Jonathan.

"Katherine seems calm and in such a good mood, Mr Turner. I was worried that she might be missing her parents."

"I am glad you mentioned this, Ethel. I, too, had the same worry. Yet, strangely, there has been no sign of loss at all. Even when we departed the ship, she bid her parents farewell as if it was a matter of course. Strange indeed! I cannot fathom it. Perhaps it will come tomorrow. We must be ready when the time comes."

"I will be ready."

"Thank you, Ethel. I will leave it with you. Let me know if you require assistance."

Upstairs, Clementine, Katherine, Madeline, and Marcia, jumping from bed to bed, were having a merry time.

"Where do you sleep, Madeline?" Katherine was interested as she recalled Anne had her own bedroom, and Madeline and Clemmie shared.

"Father cleared the old storeroom upstairs beside Simeon and William's room. The room was cleaned up and redecorated. It is now my and Marcia's bedroom."

Marcia added, "And Buster's!"

In a motherly tone, Katherine asked, "Well, little one, it is past your bedtime. Shall we go up with you and help you to bed."

"Madeline puts me to bed now. I miss Muma, but Madeline is nice. I think Buster loves Madeline as well. But you can help if you wish."

They all walked up the stairs towards Madeline and Marcia's bedroom. As they passed the boys' room, Simeon came out and asked, "Katherine, now you are staying with us. Will you be doing some sewing again?"

"I hope so. Perhaps we can have Rosalind visit?"

"Oh! I should tell you. She is here quite often now."

"Is that right?"

"Yes, I will tell you about it later."

Once the girls had Marcia settled down in bed, she soon fell asleep hugging Buster. Clemmie rushed off with something in mind. As Katherine stood up, she felt something roll under her feet and fell back on Madeline's bed.

"Oops!"

Katherine knelt and felt the cloth her foot had disturbed. A small bottle was lying under the fabric.

"I am sorry, Madeline. I have stood on a bottle of yours. My apologies."

"That is fine, Katherine. It is just a bottle I found that I like. I will put it away."

Katherine smiled and quietly left in search of Clemmie.

An innocent smile fell from Madeline's face, and she quickly retrieved the bottle and placed it in a small box at the rear of her wardrobe's top shelf. She sighed in relief and then changed for bed.

Lions Bank of Guildford, Surrey …

"Thank you for seeing me, Mr Meyhew, at such an early hour!"

Anne had knocked at the door of the bank at nine o'clock. Lady Jane, the Earl, Lady Emma, and David Sopwith had left half an hour ago. Rushing down High Street, Anne held the documentation, hoping Mr Meyhew would see her first.

"It is a pleasure, Lady South. Now, how may I be of help?"

"Mr Meyhew, I am leaving Guildford today for London. I have business there and will remain until Sunday before commencing the return journey. I need some urgent banking completed before I leave."

"Certainly, Lady South."

"I have two promissory notes signed and witnessed last night. I will leave these with you for the Turner Bakery's strongbox, please. The first agreement is a withdrawal of three thousand pounds from my account and deposited into the Fintelton Estate's working account. The second deposit is a withdrawal from the Turner Bakery's account and deposited into the Fintelton Estate's working account."

Mr Meyhew took the documents and quickly read each of them. He sighed and said, "Lady South, I understand that you are now a member of the family, and you are keen that the Fintelton Estate prospers. However, I would advise against these transfers."

"Why is that Mr Meyhew?"

"Lady South, given our previous discussions regarding the loss of monies from the Estate and our working together on this problem, I will speak with you confidentially. Please, it must go no further."

"Thank you, Mr Meyhew."

"The bank has been carefully monitoring the decline of the Fintelton Estate's finances over the past ten years. Unfortunately, the Earl and his heir, Sir Hugh, are not good businessmen. Despite repeated warnings, neither gentleman has changed their ways, and the Estate still uses the outdated practices they were using fifteen years ago. The Earl lives in a dream thinking the productivity he harnessed twenty years ago is sufficient for the present.

There is no monitoring of expenditure, and their lifestyle is extravagant. Why does the family have a full-time butler in London and at Fintelton? One must wonder what the London butler does most of the year while the family is in the country. Surely a housekeeper would be sufficient in London. The Earl ignores the financial accounts, and the son, Sir Hugh, has other expensive passions. There has been no accountability for many years, and the money is almost all gone.

The bank will soon send a letter advising the Earl that no credit will be available until they present us with a viable recovery plan. Several other great Estates have fallen into debt, and the bank now does not extend credit where we see the same pattern. However, these loans will only forestall this happening. Lady South, you will lose your money. I would strongly advise against this investment."

Anne was taken aback by Mr Meyhew's stern warning. She could see the truth in what he was saying, but now was not the time to discuss this at length.

"Thank you for your advice, Mr Meyhew. I assure you that the Fintelton Estate will return a healthy financial result in the years ahead! Sir Robert will be addressing the productivity issues. You have my word on this."

"Lady South, given the Turner Bakery's financial position, I would have thought you had enough on your agenda. I will assist you where I can, but my financiers in London may have a different opinion."

"Thank you, Mr Meyhew. I will visit you once I return from London, and we might discuss this further. I insist that you make the transfers today, and now I must rush for my coach. Good day."

Chapter 15

HMS *Shadow* arrived at Woolwich by midday, closely followed by HMS *Restless*. Once docked, Lieutenant Ham waited until *Restless* was secured and then walked along the pier and boarded *Shadow*, joining the officers at Captain South's request.

The First Lieutenant assembled a piping party for Ham as he came on board, and the officers exchanged salutes. "Welcome, Lieutenant Ham. A splendid trip along the coast, Sir. I hope all the training was not a problem for you."

"Not at all, Lieutenant Fenton. I also took the opportunity to exercise my crew but kept the powder dry. Once we are at sea again, we should compete for the fastest broadside. I think we can achieve our stations within two minutes now."

"I cannot match that good time, Sir. Give me another month, and we may become competitive. We will be doing some exercises in port while the captain is away. Perhaps you would join me and give me some pointers."

"Certainly, Mr Fenton. It would be my pleasure."

Fenton smiled and felt some advice from a mentor like Ham would be helpful. Ham was ten years his elder and had many years of battle experience behind him. Being proud of his achievements, Fenton was not so arrogant that he would miss out on the advice of a well-proven mentor.

"Thank you, Lieutenant Ham. Now, if you would follow me, the captain expects you."

Ham obediently followed as Fenton led him towards *Shadow*'s great cabin at the stern. The Captain of *Restless* was impressed with the activity he saw as they walked along the quarter deck. A washing party was scrubbing the decks, and some sail mending at the rear of the poop deck had commenced. Below he could hear the midshipmen preparing an inspection party to examine the ship's hull. The captain kept this crew busy and gave them no opportunity for mischief.

Captain South stood as Lieutenant Ham entered the great cabin, "Welcome, Ham. A good trip from Portsmouth?"

"Yes, thank you, Sir. *Restless* behaved herself."

"Good, now let me introduce Colonel Scott, Chief of Security for the Admiralty. Colonel Scott will manage the security operation ashore in Ireland."

Colonel Scott stood and shook hands with Lieutenant Ham.

"You know Major Coombes, who will lead the Marine detachment. Lieutenant Stanley White will assist Major Coombes with the Marines. I would ask that you accommodate Lieutenant White on *Restless* with twenty marines. That should be a challenge for the cook. Ha, Ha!"

"Yes, Sir. I will order in some more provisions."

"This is Captain Russell Hastings, who will be assisting Colonel Scott on board Lord Heffron's packet, *Chalk*."

Ham saluted and then took his seat.

Now satisfied that everyone knew each other, Robert introduced the colonel and then found himself a chair.

The colonel stood and, with a smile, said, "Gentlemen! Thank you, Captain South, for the introductions and for hosting this meeting on *Shadow*. As you know, I will be leading the security operation ashore. I hope this will be a reasonably quiet mission, but I could be wrong, given the problems the Irish have recently been causing us. Lord Dawlting insisted we have significant security on this trip, fearing the Irish may try for a publicity stunt. Possible issues could be as simple as a pie in the face or an assassination. So, we must be on our guard.

We have a long week ahead of us working on the security plan, Gentlemen, while Captain South finishes his honeymoon!"

The gentlemen joined in respectful laughter and light comments as Robert cheerfully responded, "I will be with you in spirit, gentlemen. I shall rejoin you on Friday the fourteenth of March."

"Bring some of those famous Turner biscuits with you, Robert!" Horace said, with a grin on his face, and threw a biscuit at Robert. "We will be doing all the work while you are at play."

"Not quite, Horace. I am expecting you all at the ball on Saturday night. Lord Dawlting has requested the pleasure of our company."

Colonel Scott, laughing, brought the meeting back on track, "Well, Gentlemen! I expect Lord Heffron's ship here tomorrow, and *Eventide* will follow. Places are reserved along the pier, up from *Shadow*. I will take my lodgings here with Major Coombes tonight, and we will work on into the night. Perhaps a few scotches as well. Also, Captain South, I would appreciate it if I could impose on you for a bunk for Captain Hastings tonight."

"I will have Lieutenant Fenton organise this for you, Sir."

"Gentlemen, a lot of work is required before the marines arrive on Saturday. I will have a complete outline of the proposed security plan by tomorrow morning. Please be here by eight o'clock sharp, and we will commence discussions over breakfast."

Robert stood, "Gentlemen, lunch will be served here in ten minutes, and this will give us an opportunity for fellowship before we break for the afternoon."

With that, the meeting was over. After lunch, Robert found Horace pacing the poop deck.

"The Colonel seems relaxed, Robert. Perhaps he is not expecting trouble. The only problem is the hair on the back of my neck is already standing up. When that happens, I know something is brewing."

Looking forward along the deck, Robert watched the crew busily working, "I agree, Horace. The fact that Lord Dawlting asked specifically for us has raised suspicion in my mind. But we are here and will make the best of it. I will ensure Lieutenant Fenton keeps guards on the officer's doors while I am away. Also, make sure Swanton watches your back. As Commodore Jacobs said, "Trust no one!"

"I do not like it when you get paranoid, Robert. The problem is that you are usually right! So, if we see some action, I brought the crossbows."

"Good man! I will be back late next week."

Hammersmith, London ...

After Lady Clarissa Wendarm's carriage arrived at Hammersmith, she carefully supervised as the porters unloaded her luggage and delivered it to her apartment. Sitting at her late husband's desk, she pensively gazed out the window at a partial view of the Thames.

Clarissa was still lamenting Stephen's escape. She should have kept her dealings with Sir Hugh secret, especially her carrying the son of the Earl's heir. Stephen seemed so loving and compliant, yet he must have been wary and frightened off by her revelations. The disappointment of missing out on a few nights of being waited on hand and foot in an upmarket London hotel made her miserable. Now, the evening meal was fish and chips in the dingy flat that Peter had acquired with the little money left after paying off his gambling debts.

Lady Wendarm's modest circumstances encouraged her to act quickly. Clarissa must write today and inform the countess of her plight. She must be installed at Fintelton as soon as possible. Sir Hugh's death was convenient, but it was a pity he was gone. His lovemaking was superb, not that she would ever tell him that. It was best if these men were kept guessing. A satisfied man would wander.

She pondered what approach would stir kindness in the countess's heart. The letter must be convincing and most sorrowful. Perhaps a plea for fellowship in her time of grief. Lady Clarissa pulled out paper, ink, and quill and began composing. She would triumph over the Souths first, then contact Stephen and again offer the companionship she knew he craved. He would not escape this time.

Now, where was the Fintelton Estate – Clarissa had the address somewhere. Pulling the borrowed letters from her unpacked suitcase lying on the bed, she checked the countess's address on the note. Checking if it had a wax seal which it did not, Clarissa carefully opened the envelope and took the letter out. She sat back and read it. The news in this letter would not do as it had nothing about Hugh's death but only that he was ill, and they hoped he would recover soon. Clarissa folded the letter and placed it in her travelling case. She picked up the envelope and copied the address onto the start of her letter.

Ah! There is a townhouse in St James's Square. That did sound fascinating. The estate must be significant, indeed, and the Earl wealthy. Clarissa smiled as she penned the first few words.

Box 55671
Piccadilly Post Office
London

The Right Honourable
Countess of Fintelton
'Harting'
St James's Square
London

Dear Lady Fintelton
Sadly, I must advise you of the untimely death of your son, Sir Hugh South, in Kingston, Jamaica.

Since embarking from Southampton, I have been your son's closest companion and nursed him through the last stages of his illness. Sir Hugh contracted a disease called 'malaria', more commonly known as swamp fever. He was actively visiting plantations and reviewing their progress during his visit. Unfortunately, the doctors believe that this is where he would have contracted the disease.

Hugh and I became close on the voyage and married in Kingston. As he deteriorated, he begged that I leave Jamaica and make a home with you in London. I refused and nursed him until the end. When he finally died, I cried and cried for nearly a week. My grief was inconsolable, but after burying Sir Hugh, I finally embarked for England and decided I should make your acquaintance.

There is one consolation in that I carry Sir Hugh's child and your grandchild. I was unaware of this until after his death and will keep this confidential until we meet. I felt you would be so glad that Hugh has left you a grandchild who will carry on the family line.

I will visit you at St James's Square or Fintelton so we might become acquainted. Perhaps you would send me an invitation and a coach, as I am in a delicate condition and will require assistance.

I eagerly await your response.

Yours faithfully, your daughter-in-law,
Lady Clarissa South

Clarissa read the letter several times, making a few adjustments and then said. "Perfect!"

'Harting', St James's Square, London ...

"Welcome, Sir Robert. You are earlier than I expected."

"Thank you, Staines. I planned on arriving before my wife. Tomorrow afternoon will be a special occasion when we are together again. I will be preparing a few things before she arrives."

"Ah! I see, Sir. Come in, please and let me carry your bag."

"Now, Staines, which room will you place us in?"

"In the blue room, Sir! It has a private bathroom and a larger bedroom area. The view is exceptional from the second floor out over the square."

"That sounds fine, Staines. Now, I will visit the room and decide what flower arrangements are required for tomorrow, and if you would please bring up some candles, I will try them in different places tonight. Tomorrow will be the start of the second week of our honeymoon, so I must make it as romantic as possible for her."

"I understand, Sir. Please let me know if we can assist in any way."

"Thank you, Staines."

Later in the evening, after dinner, Staines came into the drawing room and asked, "Is everything satisfactory, Sir Robert?"

"Yes, Staines, I think I have everything prepared. Perhaps a bottle of champagne on ice would be nice for the afternoon, depending on when they arrive."

"I shall have it prepared. Is there any news of Sir Hugh?"

"Not that I am aware of Staines. I assume you have still not met with him. He will certainly visit London on his return."

"The thought did cross my mind, Sir! Given that there has been no news, and her Ladyship has only received one letter since he left, perhaps Sir Hugh may have encountered difficulties?"

"I am not sure what you mean, Staines?"

"Jamaica is not known for its comforts, Sir. It is a hot and sweaty place. It may be that Sir Hugh has contracted a disease."

"Ah! I see."

Staines loitered in the room, attracting Robert's attention.

"Is there anything else, Staines?"

"Sir Robert, once again, I must ask if I may speak openly with you as a matter has arisen that requires either the Earl's attention or someone with control of the estate."

"Please ask, Staines. I assure you of my confidentiality."

"Sir Robert, the staff are usually paid monthly on the first of the month. The draft for the pay did not arrive at the start of February. So, we have not paid the staff for January yet. The draft usually arrives on the Wednesday before the first of the month. I checked today, but the draft has still not arrived. Might I enquire if the estate is in financial difficulties, Sir?"

Robert was shocked by this news. He had been remiss in not checking the financial situation before leaving for Woolwich. He believed sufficient money was available for the staff pay, but perhaps he should have checked. Surely, Stem would have advised him if this was not the case.

"Staines, I am as surprised as you about this situation. I shall send a rider tonight for the draft. If he rides all night, he should reach Fintelton by midday Thursday. We should see a response by Saturday morning. I will address the staff in the morning and explain the situation. Although I, too, am unsure why this has happened. My sincere apologies, Staines. If you call for a rider, I will write a letter requesting Mr Stem at Fintelton dispatch a draft immediately. Tell me, Staines, what is the cost of wages for a month?"

"Thank you, Sir. Around fifty-seven pounds! It varies depending on what staffing levels are needed. I keep the staff bill as low as possible. Might I ask for a sovereign for the rider, Sir? I am afraid the London working account is empty!"

Robert quickly found a sovereign in his pocket and placed it in Staines's hand. It appeared that this financial shortage was far worse than he thought.

"Staines, if there is no money in the working account, how are you keeping this townhouse operating?"

"There are some suppliers who are allowing us credit, Sir. The bank will not provide us with further credit unless the Earl provides an authority to transfer monies from another account. However, I have my ways of finding goods that will keep us going while the Earl and Countess are here."

"My goodness! I am so sorry this has happened, Staines. I will soon be away for a few months, so I would ask that you notify my wife immediately if there are any financial problems. She has sound business knowledge and will solve any problems that come up. If I am not away, please call me directly. A situation such as this must not happen again. My apologies, as this is embarrassing for us all."

"Thank you, Sir Robert. I shall find a rider. If you would complete your letter, Sir."

Robert spun around and found a writing desk. He pulled out a quill, ink and paper and jotted an explicit message requesting the draft urgently. He also decided to deposit fifty-seven pounds of his money and ensure Staines immediately paid the staff. Robert, once again, bristled with anger that Hugh had let the estate fall into such a position. Where was Hugh? Why was he not back here looking after things?

Dublin, Ireland …

Michael Walsh sat in a Dublin city pub across the road from the River Liffey. He sipped a hot coffee and crunched a pasty while he watched the traffic crossing the bridge from the northern bank of the river. After a hike from the safe house starting before light, Michael recalled Aiden's comment about how you stand out on the country roads. Aiden may have been a killer, but he gave some excellent advice.

Michael remembered that Aiden had an aunt and uncle in Dublin up at Portobello past the cathedral. He and Sean had visited there twice some years ago. The relative's house seemed like a logical place where his search should start. It was now nearly nine in the morning, so he should be there by nine-thirty if he left soon. The house was not far away, but he would carefully steer clear of the castle and the cathedral where people congregated. It would be safer if he stayed out of sight.

On finding the street, he walked along until he reached number eleven. Tapping on the door, he stepped back and gazed about, checking if anyone was watching. He saw several curtains drop back into place in houses nearby. As this was a solid catholic neighbourhood, Michael was not that worried. But then, at the end of the street, two men came around the corner, both wearing reasonably new coats.

Michael was sure they must be watchmen, and he backed himself up against the door staying out of sight. As the door opened from inside, he fell into the hallway. Looking up from the floor, he said, "Quick, Mrs Reid! Close the door."

Mrs Máire Reid gazed down in surprise and then, realising the situation, closed the door gently.

"Michael Walsh, I haven't seen you for a few years, love. What brings you here?"

"I am looking for Aiden, Mrs Reid."

Before he could say anything else, there was a knock on the door. Máire saw the worried look on Michael's face and whispered, "Out the back. Quick!"

Michael quietly rushed down the hallway and disappeared into the kitchen. Once Mrs Reid was sure he was out of sight, she answered the door.

There was a tall older man and a shorter younger man. The older man stood back and let the younger man talk.

"Mrs Reid, I am Peter Smith, and this is Fred Herston. The local Constable has asked us if we would make some enquiries. There has been some trouble down in Cork and some mention of Sean Reid. We know he is your nephew and wonder if he has visited lately."

"Why no. I have not seen Sean for nearly two years now. I hope he is not in any trouble?"

"Thank you, Mrs Reid. Please, contact the local Constable if he should visit. We think he has information about some disturbances in Cork."

"If I see him, I will let you know."

They nodded and left, walking away quickly in the direction they had come. Máire Reid closed the door securely and walked back down the hallway into the kitchen.

"Would you like a cup of tea then, Michael? Those watchmen don't even know Sean has passed away. You must have done a good job on that!"

Michael Walsh crawling out from behind a drying rack with various towels and other clothes hanging from it, said, "Well, we said he was in England working. A cup of tea would be nice, Mrs Reid. It would indeed!"

After a lengthy talk with Aiden's aunt, Michael found a spare bed in one of the bedrooms and took a nap. He knew the night ahead would be long and tiring, and returning to the street now was useless as the Watchmen would still be in the area. Mrs Reid indicated she could reach Aiden safely. After lunch, a friend would call, and they would go shopping together. As Aiden was not far away, she would deliver the message this afternoon.

Máire asked, "What is the message?"

Michael replied slowly, "The White Pony Bar near the Carlisle Bridge, late!"

The McPherson Household, Greenwich …

The children were out of the coach, rushing towards their grandparents, hugging and yelling greetings. Lachlan McPherson helped his wife, Taye, from the coach, and they walked across, enjoying the excitement.

"Welcome, Lachlan. The children are so excited. It is wonderful that you and Taye are here now."

Hamish McPherson hugged his son, and as soon as Taye had finished with Marjorie, he gave her a welcome kiss.

"It was a long trip for the children, Father, and they are so glad we have arrived. I am sure we must remain a few weeks before venturing back. We shall give mother plenty of time with them. Taye planned it well with a stop for a couple of days in Manchester with some friends. The business issues will hold until we return, giving us time to plan strategy."

Marjorie and Taye were already climbing the steps with the children streaming past them into the house. As Hamish and Lachlan followed, Hamish said, "We were leaving for Glasgow next week, but I will defer for a week or two. There is no rush."

"Father, I brought a case of Islay scotch whisky with me and another scotch that a new distillery makes on the mainland. It is an interesting drink without the bitter taste of peat. I think you will like it."

"Sounds interesting, Lachlan. We shall have some later. Now, I must brief you on our dinner guest tonight. Mrs Janet Stubbington has been a business associate of mine for many years. It is time you met her."

"Is she part of the brewing industry, Father?"

"More into security and information!"

Lachlan turned with a puzzled look, "You amaze me, Father. Security and information, she sounds like a spy!"

They both laughed and went in.

The White Pony Bar, Dublin ...

The band was packing up, and the bar staff were stacking the seats from outside. The few patrons left inside were making signs of moving on, and Michael Walsh wondered if he had wasted his time tonight. Perhaps the message did not get through. He would check with Mrs Reid again tomorrow. Now he must find accommodation for the night. The safe house was too far, and the Reids would have already retired. A boarding house would do back down towards the docks.

He waved as he passed the barman.

"She might turn up tomorrow night, Mate!"

Michael laughed as he exited the bar saying, "I should have known better!"

He headed down D'Olier Street and would pass the University as he headed for the docks. As he neared the College building, a familiar voice came over his shoulder, "What is a Cobh boy doing in Dublin?"

Turning, he found Aiden Reid following him, dressed in a long black coat.

"I was not coming into that bar, Michael? It might have been a trap."

"Well, it might have been, but it wasn't!"

Aiden walked closer and held out his hand. Michael clasped it and shook it hard.

"You are a hard man to find, Aiden Reid!"

"There is a good reason for that, and it all revolves around trust."

Michael did not answer but shrugged and asked, "Where can we talk?"

"We talk as we walk along. If I do not like what you say, I will be gone, and you can forget me."

"Aiden, the Brother's Committee in Dublin have a job for you. A British Government Delegation will soon visit Ireland, and included in the party are your friends, the Commander of *Restless*, and his Army Captain. The committee wants them assassinated during one of the dinners planned for the tour. It will be a great victory for Ireland and show the British that we will never give up on our quest for freedom."

"How is little Ruth after her troubles in Islay?"

"What do you mean?"

"When I got there, and with no warning from your committee, I found Callum dead in his bed. It appeared that Ruth knifed him in the throat, and blood was everywhere. She must have been terrified and fled. I cleaned up the mess and buried the young man. His grave is over the hill by about a hundred yards. If you are searching, you will know where to look. The Scottish will never find it; they are not that smart. Anyway, what will the Committee do with Ruthy?"

"Why do you ask?"

Aiden Read stopped walking, put a hand on Michael Walsh's shoulder and pulled him around so they were closely facing each other.

"I am asking if they will execute Ruth or not. Do you understand? I assume they will take me for a walk once I surface?"

"I think the Scottish Committee would like that done. They seemed somewhat agitated about losing one of their good men."

"Good man! He signed the death warrant for thirty-seven of our men and my brother, Sean. Ian Doyle was an amateur and had a loose mouth. He was a danger that needed silencing quickly. But what about Callum? He was trading information with the captain of *Shadow* in return for protection. The brothers trusted him while he was deserting them for the British. Ruth did what was needed. But it appeared she panicked after the event. If Callum had boarded that warship, he probably would have told them about the complete network in Ireland."

It was clear that Aiden Reid knew far more about what had happened than what he had been briefed on, "How did you find this all out?"

"I have my contacts!"

"Will you meet the Committee and be briefed on this job?"

"Michael, do you think I am stupid? South and Coombes are intelligent officers and will have deduced they may be targets. Is it surprising they are on this delegation? They will have in-depth security. Whoever tries will die needlessly. The brothers' committee needs change. Iain Murphy is yesterday's man and does not think strategically. He should stand down."

"Just asking, Aiden!"

"You know, and I know the committee has signed my execution warrant. The brothers' plan is flawed, Michael. They have no chance of assassinating South and Coombes, and the brothers who try will be caught by the British and executed. The outcomes are obvious."

"That is about it!"

"But think, Michael. Why would they execute loyal brothers' members like Ruth and me? Who is driving this?"

"What do you mean, Aiden?"

Aiden took a few steps away and then turned and considered Michael.

"Of all the brothers, Michael, you are the only one I trust. They probably know that, and that is why they sent you."

Michael would have spoken, but Aiden raised his hand and indicated several young men were approaching. He moved quickly into the shadows down an alleyway, and Michael followed.

Michael whispered, "How did you know the names of South and Coombes?"

"Ruth must have spent some time writing it out as there were several half-finished copies. She screwed up the paper on the first few attempts and threw the copies in a bin. I would say that Ruth was tired and hopped into bed without burning them. When Callum arrived home, their cosy relationship must have ended. As I cleaned the place up, I found the papers."

"Then surely this is a great opportunity. I am sure there must be a way of escaping!"

"No, Michael. Good try! I will choose my own time if I decide to take revenge. Perhaps one day, I might find trust in the brothers again, but they are heading in the wrong direction for my liking. They think I am a bloodthirsty killer. I can only assume they are afraid of me."

"I think you are right."

They stood there in silence, waiting for the pedestrians walking past.

"Michael, you and I go back a long way. I have been watching your back since you were a kid. I must disappear for a while, and you will be on your own."

"I can take care of myself, Aiden."

"Can you? Have you considered all these failed missions over the last few years? So many of our brothers are dead. And now they are mounting a suicide mission at some castle dinner. There is a pattern here, Michael, and you should take notice."

"What do you mean, Aiden?"

"Someone is manipulating the brothers for their purposes. I have never trusted Iain Murphy, but I have no evidence except our continual failures. This latest plan will fail again and result in much pain and misery for our people. Also, he wants members like Ruth and me executed. These ideas do not come from Iain. Someone is giving him instructions which he willingly obeys. The question is, why?"

Michael Walsh had not considered this before but agreed as he recalled many failed missions in the past few years. Aiden had raised an issue that he had missed.

"You think Murphy is manipulating us?"

"No. Iain is not that smart. Someone is using him and manipulating us. I am not sure how it works, but I would not be surprised if he were on the take."

Aiden fell silent as Michael took all this in.

"Michael, watch your back, friend! I do not trust Murphy. He is efficient at getting our brothers killed but not good at planning missions. He is a dangerous man with the power of the committee behind him. We cannot continue as we have operated over the last few years – no one will be left. Get Ruthy out of Ireland quickly. They will execute her for sure. She knows too much. If they execute her, you will be next."

Michael looked at Aiden in disbelief, "Are you sure, Aiden?"

"I am positive!"

"I will pass the message on to the Committee."

"Better than that, tell them you could not find me. I will be gone for a long time, Michael. When you hear Murphy is dead, you will know I am on my way."

"You will kill Murphy?"

"In time, when I have the proof."

"Where will you go when you disappear?"

"I will let you know. Now head out and check if the end of the alley is clear."

Michael walked carefully out of the shadows and looked each way up and down the street. He turned and signalled Aiden the all-clear but found the alley behind him was empty.

Michael Walsh smiled. He knew the brothers would never catch Aiden Reed, as he was invisible!

'Harting', St James's Square, London …
The coaches pulled up around four in the afternoon outside Lord Fintelton's townhouse, and Robert eagerly came out and greeted them. Anne's coach was the last, and Robert ran, opened the door, and hugged her as she descended.

"Anne, we are together again!"

"Robert, I have missed you so much."

The others soon surrounded them and shared greetings as they moved inside.

Not being allowed a drink all day, the Earl eagerly asked the butler, "Staines! Is my glass of scotch ready?"

"Yes, Lord Fintelton. Ready and waiting in the study."

"Good man!" The Earl rushed inside.

Lady Jane was annoyed, "Staines! I am sure you mean well, but you should not humour him."

Staines smiled, "Welcome, My Lady. I understand your comment and plead forgiveness as I must obey my Master. Welcome back, Lady Fintelton! I hope you had a pleasant journey."

Lady Jane understood the difficult position she had put Staines in but did not smile, "Yes, we took three days, a precaution ensuring the distance did not overcome the Earl. It may have worked too well!" The countess noted how spritely the Earl became when mentioning a glass of scotch.

"We shall both watch his input of scotch, please! Have you given Sir Robert and Lady South a private room?"

"Yes, My Lady. They have the Blue Room on the second floor."

"Excellent, Staines. Please have the footmen assist Miss Lane with my luggage."

Later in the evening, after the Earl and Countess had retired, the four young people sat in front of the fire catching up on old times. Robert decided this was a good opportunity to discuss the estate's financial situation.

"David, I hope you don't mind, but I have a burning question for Anne and Emma, and I think you should be involved in this as well. In less than two weeks, you will be part of this family, so I would like you as a member of our team."

David Sopwith sat up and enquired, "What team is this, Robert?"

Emma took hold of David's hands and almost cried out, "Oh, David. I should have discussed this with you long ago. You recall at Fintelton when I unfairly dismissed you. I am ashamed when I recall it."

"Not at all, Emma. You were most disturbed by some serious family problems. Anyone would have reacted in the same way. I was the one in the wrong by insisting on my way."

"Darling, you are always too kind. I am sorry, Robert, but I must brief David first, or he will think badly of me!"

Robert sat back and waved his upturned hands, indicating that Emma should continue.

"David! Pike, the Fintelton butler, approached Robert some time ago and revealed a money shortage at the estate. The Estate Manager had insufficient money for the staff wages. At first, we thought it was Sir Hugh's mismanagement of the estate, but it became more serious after further inquiries. We agreed that Anne should review the books and found some seventy thousand pounds were missing from the estate's revenue over fifteen years."

David repeated with astonishment, "Seventy thousand pounds! That is a small fortune."

"Yes, and we have been slowly investigating it ever since. We have a plan for recovering the money."

David was most interested and said, "Well, if I can be of any help, count me in."

Emma was greatly relieved.

Robert then offered some new information, "David, Staines advised me yesterday that he has not paid the staff for January or February. It appears the Harting account is empty."

David was now particularly concerned and sat up.

Robert continued, "I had wrongly assumed that my father would have arranged for sufficient money in the bank. I put two hundred pounds into the household account here this morning so Staines could pay for the wages and incidentals. We must keep the household running until we sort out this problem."

Emma then told Robert about the promissory notes she and her mother had signed bolstering the Petersfield bank accounts.

David said, "Surely, we must check who has authority for expenditure and ensure there is careful cross-checking of expenditure from here on."

Anne said, "It is not easy as the Earl has ultimate authority. Even Lady Jane must have the Earl sign for expenditure."

David rubbing his chin, said, "I see! That must change, given his poor health and state of mind."

Robert was keen on hearing the results of Anne's investigation, "Anne, would you brief us all on the results of your enquiries through the bank, please."

Anne breathed deeply before saying, "This will take a little time, so everyone, please grab a drink."

As Anne slowly explained the outcome of her investigation, the other three became more and more interested. The focus was turning towards the ex-bank teller at the Lions Bank branch in Petersfield.

David asked, "So this Mrs Constance now lives in London? But no facts are implicating her. She must be a smooth operator?"

"That is correct, yet I suspect there is a direct link. I am proposing, Robert, that we spend an extra day in London and visit the addresses provided by the bank for the properties concerned."

David added, "That is a good idea. Unfortunately, Emma and I may not join you as I promised Lady Jane, we would be close by as the Lord travels. She is most concerned about his health with the wedding coming up."

"That is fine, David. We can probably do it on the way on Sunday morning and then catch up with you at Epsom. Anne, I am sure it will only take an extra hour as Wimbledon is on the way, and we must spend some time together at 'Porting'. What do you say?"

"I think Sunday morning we should stop in Wimbledon. However, I am worried about what we may discover."

"With the present financial situation, Anne, I am not worried at all. We must clear these matters up quickly and re-establish the estate on a firm footing." Robert chuckled and said, "David and Emma, if you would excuse us, Anne and I have some honeymooning we must catch up on."

Emma and Anne giggled, and David Sopwith smiled and raised his eyebrows, "I have only eight days before I am in the same position. I am envious of you, Robert!"

Emma slapped David on the shoulder and hugged and kissed him, "You will last until then, my love."

Robert helped Anne up and said, "We shall join you at breakfast. I think the memorial service commences at eleven in the morning."

As they entered the blue room, Anne's eyes opened wide in surprise at the twenty candles lit and placed in strategic points and the magnificent bundles of red roses, one lying on the centre of the bed, others on the side tables. The room shone with the theme of love, and on a small coffee table sat a bottle of champagne on ice and two flutes.

Robert quietly closed the door behind them. With a naughty grin, Anne turned and said, "This will be an exciting night, Darling!"

The Grand Hotel, Kingston, Jamaica ...
Hugh stood beside the raised verandah rail. He held his breath as he turned, freed his hands, and managed five steps before grabbing the rail again. He was happy with the slow but consistent progress he was making. The strength in his legs was returning. However, he was unsure if he would be ready by the first of May. Gaining enough strength before the voyage home weighed heavily on his mind.

At his present recovery rate, it was more likely the first of June would be the date. Dr Cowper came onto the verandah from Hugh's room, saying, "How are you today, Sir Hugh?"

"Much improved, Doctor. As a result of your excellent treatment, I am growing stronger daily. But not as fast as I had hoped. This pox has been devastating. I never understood it would be so bad. Some days I feel like an old man."

"Your progress has been faster than I expected. Make sure you do not push it too hard, or you may suffer a relapse. It is time for your weekly examination. Let me help you into the bedroom."

Hugh consented, put his arm across Doctor Cowper's shoulder, and slowly walked towards the bed. The examination took around ten minutes, and then Hugh was helped back into a chair on the verandah.

Doctor Cowper leaned against the verandah rail and took a minute, enjoying the magnificent view of the bay. He turned and watched as one of the hotel staff served the morning tea. Moving back, he sat beside Sir Hugh, taking a cup of tea and sipping it until the waiter left.

"Sir Hugh, it is time we spoke. You are now well enough and will understand what I must explain. I would encourage you to book your return trip home on the ship leaving on the first of May."

"I was considering the same issue this morning, Doctor. However, at the rate of progress I am making, I might not be ready by then."

"You will be ready enough! I am pleased by your progress, and there are eight weeks before the ship leaves. That gives you plenty of time. I predict you will be walking steadily by then."

"You are confident I will be steady enough for a ship journey?"

"Probably as well as you will ever be! Sir Hugh, the likely course of your condition is not that hopeful. From experience, I can assure you the disease will not let you go. It already has a significant hold on your body, and if a relapse occurs, it is ninety per cent likely that will end in death. Your condition's good news is that you have no deformities yet, despite the advanced stage of the disease. Your condition might change anytime, and if deformities occur, you will probably decide to withdraw from the world."

"So, there is no hope, Doctor?"

Doctor Cowper shook his head, "Not much!"

"What if I have a relapse on the ship?"

"I suggested that date because I will finish my term here and return home on that same ship. I would be available during the trip and assist with your care, at no cost, of course, and perhaps play a few hands of cards."

Hugh laughed, "That is a kind offer. I will have Fiona arrange the tickets. Tell me, Doctor. Why do you leave Kingston? It appears there is much work here for you."

"I originally signed a contract for three years and have stayed five. The opportunity here has provided experience with tropical diseases, but my interest is holistic health. So, I have applied and successfully gained a position at Sydney Cove. I have a great interest in the study of convict diseases. The contract will commence in January 1828, so I would like some time at home with my parents before I venture around the world again."

"I see. Your decision is very timely for me, Doctor."

As Hugh spoke, Fiona Green arrived on the verandah.

"Good morning, Ronald. I see I am in time for some tea."

Doctor Cowper had the greatest respect for Fiona, given her many months of selfless care for her friend, Sir Hugh.

"Here, Fiona, let me pour some tea for you."

"Thank you."

"I have just convinced Sir Hugh that it is time to book his ticket home. I will be travelling on the ship on the first of May, and he has agreed we will sail together. I hope you will join us as well?"

Fiona raised her eyes from her cup, "Nothing would give me greater pleasure, Doctor Cowper and Sir Hugh. I long for the green hills of Bedfordshire again."

Hugh was interested, "Pray, Doctor Cowper. Where is your home in England?"

"Truro, in Cornwall."

"Well, I hope you might both stay a few days with me at Fintelton in Sussex before you head home. It is the least I can do given the kindness you have shown me here."

The Doctor and Mrs Green welcomed the invitation and hatched a plan for activities around the Fintelton Estate.

Hugh felt stronger given the expectation of returning home and the excellent company he would have, "It appears I have a deadline. By the first of May, I shall be walking freely." He stood, walked the four steps freely across the verandah, and grabbed the rail. He turned around and raised his hands in the air with happiness. Doctor Cowper and Fiona Green clapped politely before assisting him back into his chair.

Turner Household, Guildford, Surrey ...

Victoria Sopwith walked up the stairs and knocked on the front door. She waited for a minute before the door opened.

"Morning, Mrs Jennings, I am here for the interview for Lady South's lady's maid. That is, I will assist Mrs Nibley."

"Yes, Miss Sopwith. Please come in. Let me show you the way."

Victoria followed Mrs Jennings along the hall and into the parlour, where Ethel and Mrs Kirby discussed the resume for the applicant they would interview today.

"Miss Sopwith, welcome!" Ethel stood and took Victoria's hand. "Thank you so much for assisting us with this."

"It is a pleasure, Ethel. Good day, Mrs Kirby. I am sure we will enjoy navigating through the process together."

Mrs Kirby smiled but said nothing. She gave a slight curtsy and then resumed reading the resume.

Ethel broke the embarrassing silence, "I thought Mrs Kirby would be most useful as she and Lady South have discussed the requirements. Have you read the resume, as we still have ten minutes? I will call for some tea."

"Thank you, Ethel! Some tea would be welcome. I am sorry, Mrs Kirby, but is there a problem?"

"Please excuse me, Ma'am, if I sound rude, but I do not understand why there are three of us here?"

"I see, Mrs Kirby!"

Victoria could see that Anne's housekeeper resented her presence and decided to clear the air, "I have had a personal lady's maid since I was thirteen. I have changed maids several times and been involved with all the interviews. I hope I bring some good experience with me."

"My apologies Ma'am. I was not aware."

Victoria picked up the resume and began reading it. Ethel smiled at Mrs Kirby and then poured the tea.

Once the applicant arrived, the interview proceeded well, and Ethel was glad she had invited Victoria. Miss Sopwith focused her questions on the support the maid would provide for her mistress. At the end of the interview, they all agreed that Miss Mary Hedge would be competent in the position.

Harting, St James's Square, London …

After a long memorial service for Jennifer Steele, the party arrived back at Harting around two o'clock. The church at Greenwich was packed, and Archdeacon Rufus Handle had managed the service well. His final sermon was inspiring, and many attendees shed tears as the procession left the church.

Despite the nibblies offered after the service, Emma was desperate for food, "Staines, I hope you saved some lunch for us?"

"I was not sure if lunch was required, my Lady, but I arranged a light lunch for everyone in the breakfast room. The Earl and Countess have already eaten and have retired for an afternoon rest. You will find the food all set out on the table."

"Thank you, Staines."

Emma and David went through, followed by Anne and Robert.

"Well, you girls matched well in your dresses. Who copied who?"

"I copied Anne. Mrs Smith at Hursts produced this simple but beautiful black dress for Anne, and when I saw it, I loved it."

"I thought you both dressed perfectly for the occasion." Robert poured himself a cup of coffee. "Would anyone else like one?"

Anne and Emma nodded. David Sopwith seemed preoccupied as he ate a sandwich.

Anne asked him, "What are you thinking about, David?"

"I was reflecting on how we have all lost loved ones over the years, and more will follow as life goes on. It is strange how people can be there one day and then gone the next. I thought Archdeacon Handle described it well when he said we should cherish each other's company each day. None of us knows how long we have on this earth."

Anne replied, "Yes, I agree, but there is also hope through our faith that we will all be reunited in heaven again. We are created in the image of God, so I assume we will recognise each other in the next life!"

"That is reassuring, Anne, but I am not sure if your theology is correct. I struggle with the question of the physical resurrection quite often."

Robert was interested and opened his mouth, but Anne spoke first, "Why do you struggle with it, David? The gospels mention how many witnesses saw our Lord physically rise into heaven."

Emma coughed as she swallowed something backwards, "Excuse me!"

David had a curious look on his face, "I will need further discussion with Andrew Taggart. He is a knowledgeable man, that one."

Anne checked the time on the sideboard clock, "Robert, I must be quick as Hamish McPherson is calling this afternoon at three. He brings his son, Lachlan, and wishes for a conversation about our business with him."

"Should I attend?"

"Best if I see Mr McPherson and Lachlan by myself this time. I am sure they will say hello before they go."

"Yes, then we visit Mayfair tonight and dine with Admiral Crouch and his wife."

Emma excitedly chirped, "Well, David has booked a table at the Bath Hotel for tonight. Mother and Father will come with us."

Anne gushed, "Oh, Emma. You will have a wonderful time."

The Grand Hotel, Kingston, Jamaica …
Fiona and Hugh sat at a table on the verandah, pouring through the documents the Governor's men had supplied.

"It appears, Hugh, that either your friends at Stephenson's Attorneys have been inept in managing your affairs over here or are involved in fraud. This schedule indicates the managers have understated production by sixty per cent.

They have done it cleverly by reducing the production figures by around ten per cent each year over a long period.

This document estimates the underpayment for sugar to be around ten thousand pounds per year for ten years. Surely someone was monitoring the records when they reached Fintelton?"

"I am afraid not, Fiona! My father is elderly and lost some of his faculties several years ago. I should have realised he may have lost his way. He often asked me if I would take more interest in the overseas plantations and perhaps visit them. If I had been less interested in women and wine and taken on more responsibility, I might have alerted myself about his failings."

"You were more interested in women! Was there ever a woman you cared for except your mother and sister?"

Hugh looked up from the document he was reading with a thoughtful expression.

"There was a young lady many years ago. She was slightly older than me but beautiful, intelligent and refined. I was madly in love with her and asked if she would marry me, but she declined. I was young and became quite downcast, and I think she took pity on me and gently explained why it would be impossible. She was a commoner and had no desire to enter the upper class. I came across her again during a business meeting, but I kept the meeting circumspect despite still having feelings for her. I thought I was wiser then, but perhaps not, and that was about it. A pity in many ways. Perhaps if her answer had been different, my life might have changed for the better."

"What was her name?"

"Kathy!"

"Katherine is a lovely name, but your story is sad!"

"Yes, but we do have some joy on the horizon. The Governor's men have appointed a new manager for my plantations and found me some reliable Agents. It appears that income from the plantations should increase substantially from now on. They have also recovered some of the lost funds."

"How much more will you receive?"

"Well, if the estimates are correct, they will recover some twenty thousand pounds, and future revenues will be between forty and fifty thousand pounds a year."

Fiona sat up in surprise, "That is a lot of money, Hugh!"

"Imagine what we have lost over the last ten years. I should have listened to my father."

"So, you have achieved your purposes here, Hugh. Now, you must become stronger so we can return home. Up you get and do some walking. From now on, we shall have at least five or six walking sessions daily."

"But Fiona, Doctor Cowper said slow, steady, and not too hard!"

"Piffle, Hugh! Twelve sessions a day is hard. You can easily manage five or six sessions a day."

"Wonderful!" Hugh groaned.

Hamish and Lachlan McPherson entered the Earl's study and commented on the morning's memorial service.

"It was a fitting service, Anne, and I assure you that Marion is relieved it is over. She was in a state this morning. She and her mother were always close, and it will take many years before she adjusts. I am thankful for Thomas. He has shown great care since her mother passed away. He has taken Marion walking this afternoon, a diversion helping her cope with the loss."

"My brother has a gentle streak in him and will keep Marion close while she suffers. He will respect Marion's close affection for her family. This affection is not a bad quality in a woman, Mr McPherson."

"Well said, Anne. Now we have limited time so we must discuss business. I wanted Lachlan here with us so you could meet him today, and I could explain the transition happening in our company. It will affect both our businesses. Given the more significant role you will play in the future, I am also offering you, our assistance.

Firstly, Anne! Thomas will reside in Glasgow soon and manage one of our breweries there. My son James, the previous brewery manager, moves with his lady partner and becomes our managing director in Ireland. They will rent in Cobh for the first year but settle in Dublin, where they will start setting up pubs. He will be responsible for our expansion in Ireland."

"I was unaware that James was in a relationship."

"Yes, the young lady's name is ....!"

Lachlan quickly said, "Isla, Father."

"Yes, Isla. They are expecting their first child."

Anne realised Hamish had not forgotten the name but struggled to say it.

"That is a surprise, Mr McPherson. Please pass on our congratulations when you see them."

"Yes, it is a surprise. Thank you, Anne. Now, Lachlan will replace me as Managing Director of the company, as I will step back but continue as Chairman of the Board. Lachlan will remain in Glasgow this year and probably move his family down here in March next year. Douglas will take over managing both breweries in Edinburgh. Lachlan will spend time mentoring Thomas during the next six months. So, a major structural change will occur over the next two years. I understand your company will have similar growing pains with the new bakeries in London and Reading."

Anne smiled, "We are far smaller than your company, Mr McPherson. I know of the new bakery in London but not the one in Reading. My father has not mentioned this!"

"He soon will, Anne. Over the next five years, we will need far more of your products between here and Bristol. The challenge for both our companies is growth. A business must grow, or we stagnate. There is no in-between! If we lose focus, we become a soft target for our competitors."

Lachlan spoke and explained their plan further, "Anne, at present, you are a small organisation, but that has many strategic advantages. We can help you grow your business profitably in ways that will also assist our business. Our company is established in London with around ten pubs and another ten sites purchased ready for pub builds over the next five years. We are also expanding across the southern counties and will commence our first pub in Bristol next year. This expansion will involve another ten new pubs. Once that is complete, we will move into the midlands. Liverpool, Manchester and Birmingham.

Your products complement ours. No other baking company in England will have the reach our network will provide for your company. With a well-managed expansion, Turner Bakeries could become the largest baking company in Britain within ten years."

"These are grand plans, Lachlan, but how would we finance such a development?"

Hamish quickly said, "You are attending the Irish Benefit Ball tomorrow night?"

"That is correct."

"There will be a guest at our table, Mrs Janet Stubbington. I will introduce you. She is a business associate of your father and has been helpful in the development of our company. Janet manages an investment fund that provides the finance at very reasonable terms. Your father and I have already had preliminary discussions on this. Tomorrow night, when the opportunity arises, I will bring her across and make the introduction. If you would spend ten minutes with her, I think you will be impressed with her proposals."

"Certainly. I would be pleased in making Mrs Stubbington's acquaintance, but we should conduct proper business conversations in private, as we are doing here."

"I agree but consider this a first meeting and gather some preliminary information. Your father and I had dinner in Reading last year, and I introduced Janet then."

"I have never heard my father mention her."

"Talk with him once you return home. He will explain the business relationship. But tomorrow night will be informal and a pleasant opportunity for discussion."

"I will try my best, Mr McPherson."

"Thank you, Anne. We could ask for no more."

They continued their conversation for some time, Anne enjoying the discussion on strategy. She found Lachlan pleasant, and he was genuine in his helpful suggestions. Finally, after an hour, the conversation came to an end.

"I will think about your proposed strategy, Mr McPherson, but I must talk with my father first. I am sure he will be genuinely interested."

"We would ask for no less, Anne. Thank you for your time this afternoon. Marjorie is excited about meeting you tomorrow night at the ball."

Admiral Crouch's Residence, Mayfair, London …

The evening proceeded well, and again, Anne stunned the Admiral and his wife with her beauty, complemented by her dazzling dress and jewels. She had used the best in her wardrobe, mindful of presenting well in front of her husband's superiors.

Lady Katherine Crouch had been particularly friendly towards Anne and advised her on what was expected of a navy wife when dealing with the higher echelons.

"My dear, it was horrible for me at first. The Admiral was a lieutenant, and the captains required us at dinners where I had no idea what to say. I had not even been on a navy ship and was confused by their navy terminology. I had nightmares."

"I have similar feelings, Lady Katherine. I have nightmares about being among the aristocracy. I am terrified about tomorrow night."

"Do not worry, Anne. We will arrive together as a fleet and keep you safe in the middle. I will tell you what the standard procedure is. You see, it is like this….!"

While the ladies talked in the drawing room, Robert and Admiral Crouch were still at the dinner table drinking port.

"I am glad you are here tonight, Robert. This dinner may be my last one for some time. There is major trouble brewing in the eastern Mediterranean. Best you are out of it. You have had enough difficult postings in the last year."

"Are you concerned about the Russians, Admiral?"

"Yes, this new Tsar is becoming difficult. He is far more warlike than the previous Tsar. The government is also forced into a corner about the next First Lord of the Admiralty appointment. They are unsure about the proposed appointee and will keep me on as an admiral, providing some support. It is a bother as I yearn to retire on my estate in Hampshire.

By the way, how is your father? I have a few weeks off in May, and I thought Katherine and I would pay them a call."

"He is improving considerably, Admiral. He will walk Emma down the aisle next Saturday. If you are coming in May, remember that they usually travel to the Isle of Wight in late May. Perhaps you could join them at the seaside?"

"Of course, of course! I forgot about the wedding. Kate organises my social events now, and I follow instructions. I will see you there and keep in mind the Isle of Wight. Now about this future mission. These outings where we support the politicians can become strenuous exercises, particularly when dealing with the House of Lords. There are vested interests, and it may appear that the politicians are taking advantage of their positions. Which quite often they are.

Let me explain the specific responsibilities you have during the mission. Colonel Scott will handle the most taxing problems. He is a good man and understands these men of power. Become close to Colonel Scott and learn from him; you will probably be doing more of this type of work in the future. The request from Lord Dawlting that you join this mission was not by chance. He sees great diplomatic skills in you, Robert.

Ensure you keep well in the background and do not enter any politics. Our role is to uphold the government and the rule of law. As military men, we must serve our government as commanded. It is non-negotiable. In Ireland, you will see a situation that is entirely out of control. The people live in miserable conditions and are oppressed by our peerage, who have vast landholdings. Your father has an estate there, so see what occurs under his stewardship.

We have intelligence that the Irish are planning on disrupting the mission. Some of our informers have heard faint rumours that planning is underway and various assets are being gathered. Now at this stage, we have no more information than this. You will be visiting estates with the committee and speaking with the tenants. Use this time well and confer with Colonel Scott on any information you gather. Scott will have large security assets under his control. We have information that the Irish may attempt an assassination. The target will probably be one of the Lords. Let us hope not but be prepared in advance.

As I expect trouble, you will need all your skills during the next two months. With the Colonel and Major Coombes, you have a good team. Work together and cover every angle and keep the mission safe. The aim is helping the Irish people and not letting anyone undo our purpose."

Robert listened carefully, and as the Admiral went on, he realised the gravity of his situation. This mission was far more dangerous than he had first thought.

"Admiral, might I ask why Major Coombes and I were selected for this mission?"

"Lord Dawlting wanted officers familiar with the Irish situation who understood the dangers. It was no use sending some pompous ass along who would ignore the people and put on a show. The mission could easily become dangerous, and we wanted our best. He conferred with me and several others, and we decided that you and Coombes, who had recent experience with our friends in Ireland, were the best people for the mission."

"Admiral, I have thought long and hard about the previous mission and discussed it at length with Captain Foster and Commodore Jacobs. There are similarities between the missions, which, in my opinion, explain some of the outcomes. Would you have time for a discussion of my conclusions?"

"Certainly, Robert. Go ahead!"

Over the next ten minutes, Robert explained the similarities between each mission's orders and the events. He explained how each ship's crew would find it impossible to transfer the information ashore. Then he raised his suspicions of the bigger picture with an influence manipulating the Irish nationalists for some other purpose.

Admiral Crouch said, "So you think there is someone or perhaps several people with vested interests who are playing the Irish nationalists for fools and using these uprisings for their agenda."

"Sir, you will recall how adamant the politicians are that Ireland will never gain independence. Our system's ascendancy is responsible for the Irish tenant farmers' poor conditions. But the reason is purely for the gain of the landholders. Those who hold the land would maintain their possession even if it meant fighting for it."

"I see where you are coming from, Robert and it is well thought out. Our decision to appoint you is showing merit already. Discuss these details with Colonel Scott. He is trustworthy and will appreciate your insight. I am disturbed by what you are saying as you imply that someone inside the government manipulated the Admiralty's orders. Of course, we have all assumed this is impossible, but you have raised valid concerns. I will think about your suggestion and how I might test it. If you are correct, we are dealing with some clever operatives protected by their positions."

"It is only a theory at this stage, Admiral. But this mission may provide the opportunity to test our suspicions."

"Your suspicions, Robert! At this stage, I have doubts despite your argument having merit. Let me think about this. I will have more intelligence available by the wedding in Petersfield. We shall spend some time together there, and I will update you. Now, I think that is enough for your briefing tonight. It is time we joined the ladies and enjoyed their company."

"Thank you, Admiral, for hearing me out tonight. I appreciate your trust in me."

"A pleasure Captain South. We have great confidence in what you will achieve in Ireland."

As they walked together from the dining room, the Admiral advised, "Now, we shall pick you up at seven o'clock tomorrow night. The ball commences at seven-thirty, and it is a short ride into London from St James's Square.

Colonel Scott and his wife will meet us there. Admiral Bird and his wife, Patricia, are also joining us. You will recall her from a previous dinner."

"Yes, Sir."

"By the way. Katherine will stay close to Anne tomorrow night and keep her safe. These balls are fun, but society can be challenging. I understand this will be Anne's first venture into these circles, so we shall keep her well-protected. Mind you, I expect from my previous meetings with her; she will outshine us all. Ha, Ha!"

"Thank you, Sir. I appreciate your concern for Anne."

"Robert, we in the navy must always support each other. It is our strength."

Chapter 16

Cloverdale Chase, Guildford, Surrey …

"Good morning, Mr Petherton. I am Miss Victoria Sopwith, and I believe Lady South advised you that I would be bringing the children this morning. She is in London until Tuesday next!"

"Miss Sopwith, you are most welcome. Yes, I received the note from Lady South and was disappointed that she was unavailable. But I am pleased the children are here with you. I was not aware that Guildford has so many handsome young ladies."

"Thank you, Mr Petherton!" Victoria blushed as she heard the compliment.

"Do I detect an Irish accent?"

"You do. I only moved to Guildford a few weeks before last Christmas, and I live with my brother, Doctor David Sopwith. I will settle here and acquire a residence in due course."

"My apologies, Miss Sopwith, as I should have recognised the name. Doctor Sopwith is my physician, a fine man, indeed. Please come in! I see Clare has already taken the children through. She delights in their visits."

Victoria followed Mr Petherton through the spacious vestibule, along the hall and into the drawing room with large glass windowed doors overlooking a patio and a manicured garden.

"My, you and your wife have a grand vista here. It is a beautiful house."

"Thank you, Miss Sopwith. My wife chose a large house with grounds as she had in mind a large family. Unfortunately, she died in childbirth when Clare was born. Now, I have some coffee here that is somewhat unique. It is part of my business, and I import it from the mountains of Columbia."

"I am sorry about the loss of your wife. I was unaware."

"It was eleven years ago now, but it seems like yesterday. But thank you for your kind wishes. Now, would you enjoy a coffee with me?"

"Yes, the Columbia coffee sounds interesting. I would enjoy trying it, please, Mr Petherton."

The children circled the pond beside the patio and were amazed at the size of some of the goldfish. Clare and Madeline watched from further along the pool.

"Clare, what do they eat? There are so many of them you would think they would run out of food."

"They have some special food that Father gives them, but they also eat some of the plants in the pool. Some of the larger goldfish are older than me, nearly fifteen years old."

"When do you feed them?"

"Father does it each evening when he is here. Come inside, and we will find the food and feed them. They become far more active when there is food on offer."

Madeline followed Clare inside. Simeon was gazing into the water as William peered into the distance. He saw a slight movement and screwed his eyes up, identifying the shape. Then, suddenly, a large deer with antlers came into view, followed by several does.

"Look, Sim, over there!"

As the buck moved towards the house, both the boys backed up. Simeon, particularly remembering last year's incident where a deer broke his arm, edged towards the patio doors.

As Clare and Marion came out, Clare asked, "What is the matter, Simeon?"

"Some deer are coming!"

"They will not come close. It is the short grass that the deer seek. They love it! They never come near the house."

The boys sat down on a couple of chairs near the drawing-room windows. Clare stood beside the pond and sprinkled the fish food over the water. Instantly there was a commotion on the surface with goldfish thrashing the water, fighting for food.

As the butler organised the staff serving morning tea, Mr Petherton and Victoria joined the children.

"Are you boys tired today? I notice you are sitting down."

"No, Mr Petherton! We are watching the deer. Last year we had a bad experience with them, and Simeon's arm was broken."

"The deer never come much closer than where they are now. They come out most days from the King's Forest and feed on the short grass. Now, come across and take a drink and some food. You might as well eat while you are watching the animals."

Simeon and William happily accepted and selected some biscuits while maintaining a watch on the deer. Clare and Madeline went inside again, returning the fish food.

"So, Victoria, how do you like Guildford?"

"Very much, Mr Petherton. I particularly enjoy walking along the riverbank. It is most refreshing when the sun comes out."

"Well, it is now the third day of Spring, so you should soon see far more of the sun. You will enjoy the English summer; it is a wonderful time of year."

Clare came across from the table and whispered in her father's ear. Mr Petherton regarded his daughter and smiled.

"Miss Sopwith, my daughter, has requested if Madeline might remain for luncheon. They have a plan to sew together this afternoon. I would ensure her safety and bring her home by coach by four o'clock."

"I am sure Mr Turner would find that acceptable. Madeline, please be on your best behaviour. Now, Mr Petherton, since we have finished morning tea, would you show me the famous fort the boys have told us about?"

"It would be a pleasure, Miss Sopwith!"

"Perhaps, a short visit, as we must not take up too much of your time."

Mr Petherton smiled, looked up, checked the weather, and asked the butler for some umbrellas.

"It is a fair walk, so we should take some protection in case of rain. Shall we?"

Mr Petherton led the way and welcomed the deer disappearing into the forest as the party walked up the slope towards the fort.

William asked, "Mr Petherton, after the fort, might you show us more of the bottle collection? As we came in, I noticed the biggest bottle I have ever seen."

"Yes, William. I know the one you mean. I like that one as well."

Dublin Safe House, Ireland …

It was nearly ten o'clock that evening before the last committee member arrived. Iain Murphy stood outside the closed front door, waiting as his eyes were accustomed to the dark. He saw the tall frame of the man rushing up the path towards the cottage. Slightly moving back into the shadows, he drew his knife and kept it out of sight.

Braydon Kelly stopped four yards short of the house, seeing the shadow of a man beside the door.

"It is Braydon!"

"Why are you so late, lad? We expected you an hour ago."

Braydon breathed a sigh of relief and moved forward towards Iain. He stopped as Murphy pulled out the knife from behind his back.

"Sorry, Braydon! I was not sure who it was in the darkness. Glad you said your name."

Looking at the knife, Braydon said, "So am I!"

Putting away his knife, Iain chuckled and said, "Come out of the cold."

Braydon Kelly followed the brothers' leader inside. As the door closed, one man took a candle and moved towards the fireplace.

Braydon quickly said, "Hold on, man!" He went around all the windows checking they were completely covered. Once satisfied, he said, "I don't want any light getting out tonight. You may light your candle now as the windows are covered."

Iain Murphy was confused about Braydon's caution. They were well hidden here in the country, surrounded by farms supporting the brothers.

As Braydon sat beside Michael Walsh, he cleared his throat, drank some water, and said, "I am not sure when the rest of you set off, but the streets are full of watchmen and soldiers. With this British mission coming, they are stepping up their security activities. We will probably see more red coats on the streets soon and some pitch capping. Everyone must be away by midnight and take alternative routes home. Michael and Dan, you should come with me and stay at my house tonight."

The information was welcome as Iain and the others had set off earlier by various routes and had not noticed the increased police presence.

"Thank you, Braydon. That is useful information. So, men, we have less than two hours. Firstly, Michael Walsh, I understand you found Aiden Reid."

"Yes, Iain. I tracked him down through relatives in Dublin. He is not interested in the job. He thinks it is a setup and said he would appear in good time."

Anger appeared on Iain's face, "Damn him! He is a brother's member. What is wrong with him?"

"He is not stupid, Iain! He knew the committee would react the wrong way. He told me he was disappearing and would surface in a few years. We were standing in an alleyway in Dublin, keeping out of sight of passers-by. I checked if the alleyway entrance was clear, and when I turned around, he was gone. Disappeared!"

The group sat silently for a few minutes as Murphy considered Michael Walsh's response, "You are sure he was gone, or are you protecting him?"

Michael was offended by the question, and he replied through gritted teeth, "I would not be here unless I were sure!"

Iain paused and said, "Thank you for your efforts, Michael. Now we need a replacement for Reid. I need someone good at killing for this job. Possibly two men, so we make sure at least one of them hits the target."

The conversation continued for another hour and a half before Iain

Murphy called a halt. Then one by one, the members left, disappearing into the darkness.

By midnight there were only four of them left in the cottage. Dan O'Leary and Braydon Kelly were outside, accustoming their eyes in the darkness, and Michael and Iain were sitting at a table drinking scotch.

Iain Murphy said, "Michael, thank you for your work with Aiden. But it seems he is afraid if he will not talk with us face to face and has broken his pledge. We cannot risk him taking another side. You understand what I am saying?"

"No! Hold on while I put out some candles so my eyes will adjust better." Michael blew out three or four candles.

"Michael, we are fighting a war. Brother's members must obey orders. Aiden Reid has chosen a path away from us. He has broken his pledge. If we let him do this and word gets out, it will affect other brother members when the pressure mounts. He is a deserter."

"He took care of that lazy recruiter in Glasgow who was responsible for the death of thirty-seven of our men and many injured in Islay. Is that so wrong, Iain?"

Braydon O'Leary stuck his head halfway through the door, saying, "My eyes are right. We will take the front way - it seems clear. Come on, Michael."

"Just a moment, Braydon!" Iain hopped up, quickly checked outside the door, and closed it. He sat down again and faced Michael.

"Take Aiden for a walk and execute him, Michael. That is an order. Someone will deliver you a pistol soon. Keep it somewhere safe and be ready when he shows his face again. From now on, tell him nothing about our business."

Michael Walsh nodded.

"I need more than a nod, Michael. Will you do this?"

"Yes, Iain. But I am not sure when or where he will surface."

"His mother is in Cobh. He will surface there someday, and you will be ready for him. Good lad! Also, I have the information for your dad. The money for the fares is in the envelope. There are also brother contacts in Boston who will help them set up a house. I am sad they are going, but it is better than starving."

"Thank you, Iain. This will allow them a new start in Boston. I am most thankful."

"Now you and Ruth are staying, aren't you?"

"Yes."

"Good! We have a job for Ruth and you in Dublin when the mission comes. Bring Ruth with you next week. Braydon will find a safe place where you can stay."

Michael felt uneasy but concealed his feelings as he thought of Aiden's warning about Ruth.

Iain stood and patted Michael on the shoulder, then shook his hand. "Now, off with you before those watchmen find us. New meeting place next time in Dublin central. We will see you both then."

Michael shook Iain's hand and hugged him before disappearing out the door into the darkness. As he carefully followed Braydon and Dan along the road, he thought about Aiden and the execution order from Iain.

As Michael grew up in Cobh, Aiden and Sean always looked after the younger lads. Many a night, Aiden had saved Michael from a belting at the hands of various watchmen and ruffians. Most of the Cobh lads thought of him as a big brother figure. It was true that Aiden had changed in the last two years, but they all had, including Iain.

The fight for freedom took a more serious turn, with the landowners raising rent and requiring increased production from the farms. Last year, the potato crop had nearly failed, and the tenant farmers had little money for their dues. Many would have left their tenancies if it had not been for the Ribbon Men. But it was a hard decision to leave your tenancy and move your family somewhere else. It seemed that revolution was the only way forward.

They lost the battle against the British in Islay. So many of their local lads had been killed or gravely wounded. Aiden had watched his wounded brother slowly die. Who would not be affected? The brothers should be more mindful of the effect killing has on a soul. It was tearing Ruth apart as she grappled with what she had done. He was sure it was the same for Aiden.

If this was what the future held here, then perhaps America was a better option. He had the emigration information for their family. Best if he set off now and discussed it with his father. America might be a better option for Aiden, as there was no way Michael would execute his friend.

Turner Household, Guildford, Surrey …
Mr Petherton walked up the front stairs with Madeline and Clare and knocked on the door.

"There is no need, Mr Petherton. My Father will not be expecting you."

"Your father will appreciate my calling in, Madeline. I always insist on being notified when my daughter is delivered home. It is our society's expectation when dealing with young ladies your age."

Aggie opened the front door and smiled, "Miss Madeline, you are home!"

Mr Petherton stood back, allowed Madeline past, and asked, "Would Mr Turner be home? I am Mr Benjamin Petherton from Cloverdale Chase. I might take the opportunity of greeting Mr Turner as we are here."

"Certainly, Mr Petherton, please come in."

Aggie led Mr Petherton and Clare into the drawing room, where a warm fire was burning. "Please have a seat while I advise Mr Turner that you have arrived."

Mr Petherton sat and carefully inspected the room, smiling in approval. It was a fair-sized room with beautiful wallpaper and was well-furnished. The room was meticulously clean, and the seats were comfortable. Benjamin Petherton was impressed.

As he relaxed, Clare's voice softly interrupted his thoughts, "Father, may I go upstairs, please, as Madeline wishes to show me her room."

"Yes, Clare, but not for long, as this is a short visit."

The girls scampered off! Madeline was carrying her bag, and Clare took in everything as they enjoyed each other's company.

Jonathan Turner hurried into the room, followed by Ethel.

"Benjamin, this is a surprise. Welcome, Sir."

"Thank you, Jonathan, and who might this handsome lady be?"

"Of course! May I introduce my housekeeper, Mrs Ethel Nibley? Mrs Nibley and I were discussing the arrangements for my forthcoming trip. I will visit Scotland with Hamish McPherson."

"It is a pleasure, Mrs Nibley."

"Thank you, Sir. Would you care for some tea?"

"That would be excellent. But Clare and I will only stay a short time, so please, if it is a bother, don't worry."

"It is no trouble at all, Sir." Ethel turned and walked off down the hallway.

"Jonathan, I have not had the opportunity to express my sympathy over your good wife's loss. I sent a card, but a card is no substitute for the personal encouragement of a friend."

"Thank you, Benjamin. It is a difficult time, and my family has been most supportive. Eleanora had been ill for over two years. The disease finally took her, but I hoped she would last another year. Nothing can prepare you for this."

"I felt the same when my dear Miriam died after childbirth. It is eleven years now, and I still yearn for her soft voice and fragrance. I find it harder to recall her now, but the memory remains. I wonder if one ever recovers!"

Ethel returned with the tea and set it on a small table near the gentlemen. She poured two cups and left them with the milk and sugar.

"Thank you, Ethel."

Benjamin Petherton nodded his thank you as Ethel left. "She seems a very competent housekeeper, Jonathan?"

"Yes, in the last few months, Ethel has been more a mother than a house-keeper. She was Eleanora's lady's maid, and after my wife's death, we all agreed that Ethel should become the housekeeper. She has been marvellous with the children. I am not sure what I would have done without her."

"You are fortunate, indeed, then, Jonathan. It is hard finding a woman of such fine character."

"Why do you say that Benjamin?"

"Since I lost my wife, putting my house in order has taken many years. I am now employing the third governess for Clare, and I am still not satisfied with the lady's performance. Perhaps my expectations are too great as I expect the governess maintains a close relationship with my daughter. Far more than a teacher-student relationship at school."

"I see. Is Clare your only child?"

"Now, she is! My son, Mark, died of a tragic riding accident two years ago."

"I am sorry, Benjamin."

Mr Petherton smiled, and momentarily, Jonathan saw he was far away.

"When you return from your trip, Jonathan, would you join me for dinner? We can talk more then. At present, I must take Clare home. If one of the staff could fetch her, that would be kind."

"Yes. I would enjoy that."

Jonathan asked Aggie if she would advise Clare that Mr Petherton was leaving.

"Clare finds Madeline delightful company. Thank you for allowing the friendship."

"I think you should thank Madeline. I give her free reign in choosing her friends."

Later after the Pethertons had left and Madeline was alone in her room, she quickly reached into her bag, pulled out another small bottle, and placed it in the back of her wardrobe with the others.

Harting, St James's Square, London …

The butler dashed into the drawing room and advised Sir Robert that Admiral Crouch's carriage was rounding the square and would soon be outside. Lady Emma's maid slipped a light coat over Anne's ball dress as Anne and Robert left the house.

"Here, Ma'am, you will need this tonight as it is chilly with that breeze."

"Thank you, Jane. That is very thoughtful."

Anne walked towards the front coach but soon found her path blocked by an Army Captain. The officer politely asked if they would follow him. Admiral Crouch appeared through the open door and welcomed them, "The front coach is carrying the security detail. A precaution, of course, but best we have them with us."

A footman assisted Anne up into the coach, and she sat opposite Lady Katherine Crouch. As the carriage pulled away from 'Harting', they recommenced their conversation from the previous night.

"Well, Anne. Ready for the big occasion. I am sure you will enjoy yourself."

"I am sure I will too. Will many people be attending?"

Admiral Crouch happily answered, "It seems the committee has done a good job raising support, as there will be quite a crowd tonight."

The trip was short, and Admiral Crouch quickly briefed his guests as they approached the Strand.

"Now we have a navy table, and Admiral Bird and his wife, Patricia, will be joining us, as well as Lord Dawlting and his wife, Hannah. I understand our table is beside the official table, and the prince will be attending."

"The prince!"

"Yes, he assists many charities and is interested in the plight of the Irish."

Robert added, "I am glad the charity is holding this ball. Hopefully, there will be enough money raised so that we may leave a legacy from our mission."

"A gallant thought, Robert." Admiral Crouch was looking ahead. "Anne, you will now see the advantages of rank!"

As the coach approached the entrance, Anne quickly asked, "Lady Katherine, how do I address him if we speak with the prince?"

"You give a small curtsey, and then if he offers his hand, you respond with 'Your Royal Highness'. Take my lead and follow what I do – it will be very relaxed tonight."

"Thank you." People were everywhere, with many standing in a long queue along the street.

"Admiral, should we not stop and join the queue?"

"Anne, you are a special person tonight. We represent the Royal Navy, and our hosts expect us at the head of the queue."

The carriage crossed into an entry courtyard and stopped, where footmen opened the doors and assisted the ladies out. The queue of guests extended right across the square and through another entrance backing onto the Strand. Anne placed her hand around Robert's arm for strength as she marvelled at the many lanterns lighting the courtyard walls, which shone like a fairy wonderland.

Admiral Crouch and Lady Katherine led the way, and Anne reflected on her current position. They entered the ball as official guests and sat at the front of the room. Anne feared this would make her more of a target for the carnivores waiting for her inside. Edging closer, she said, "Stay with me, Robert. I am terrified but also excited!"

Admiral Crouch's party was issued past the queue, straight through the entrance, and followed a circular stairway to the ballroom. Anne's eyes opened wide as she saw the height of the ceiling, some thirty feet above. At their end of the room, ten tables surrounded the official party's table, with footmen standing along a roped-off barrier between this area and the crowd in the great room. A large, raised platform positioned at the head of the room supported the orchestra, who were already playing a lovely waltz as guests arrived.

Anne heard the rhythm of the music and started smiling as she glanced at Robert and he at her. Passing across the dance floor towards their table, Robert took Anne in his arms, whirling her around him in a waltz[26]. "Just a quick practice, Anne. They are allowing the Viennese Waltz tonight. The prince loves it."

"You may practice as much as you like." She smiled into his eyes, and he breathed in her sweet scent and felt the softness of her dress.

"I will take particular notice when you reveal your new dress."

Anne smiling, raised her eyebrows and replied, "Well, you will soon see."

Admiral Crouch looking over his shoulder, saw Robert twirling Anne around as they followed. With a smile on his face, he took Katherine's hand. She said, "Young love, Franklin. It is wonderful."

As they arrived at their table, they found the other guests seated. The gentlemen immediately stood up, and Admiral Crouch made the introductions.

"Now, Sir Robert and Lady South, you are good friends with Lord and Lady Dawlting."

Lord Dawlting came straight around the table and gave Robert a warm handshake.

"I will rest well on this mission, knowing you are with me, Robert. I am sure it will be a worthwhile exercise."

"I will do my best for you, Lord Dawlting."

"And that is all I ask. Ah, Anne. You are looking most beautiful, indeed." Then with a smile, he kissed Anne on the cheek and escorted her around the table, where Lady Dawlting greeted her.

"Anne, we enjoyed the wedding so much. I am so pleased you are here with us tonight. I have often wondered how we might assist the Irish poor."

"Yes, Lady Dawlting. It will be a wonderful occasion. Admiral Crouch honours us with his kind invitation."

Hannah Fowey was a beautiful, sophisticated lady and most affectionate of Anne, as was her husband, Lord Dawlting. She kissed Anne on the cheek and hugged her, releasing Anne so the Admiral could introduce the other guests.

---

[26] The waltz became fashionable in Vienna around the 1780's, spreading to many other countries in the following years. It reached England in 1791. During the Napoleonic Wars, infantry soldiers of the King's German Legion introduced the dance to the people of Bexhill, Sussex from 1804. It became fashionable in Britain during the Regency period, having been made respectable by the endorsement of Dorothea Lieven, wife of the Russian Ambassador. Diarist Thomas Raikes later recounted that "No event ever produced so great a sensation in English society as the introduction of the waltz in 1813." Wikipedia.

"Sir Robert and Lady South, may I introduce Admiral Bird and his beautiful wife, Lady Patricia."

Lady Patricia protested, "Admiral, you are too kind."

Robert and Anne quickly greeted the Admiral and his wife, Lady Patricia, who shared some comments with Anne. Admiral Crouch stood ready and introduced the next guests.

"Our special guests tonight are the Marquess and Marchioness of Questlow. Sir Robert and Lady South, may I present Lord and Lady Questlow."

Once again, Robert and Anne moved around the table and greeted the Marquess and Marchioness. Anne was not sure of the etiquette for a marchioness, so she took a guess, "It is a great honour meeting you, Lady Questlow." Anne curtseyed and rose with a beautiful smile on her face.

Lady Questlow, a lady of the same age as Anne's mother-in-law, was most taken with her and took her hand and laughed, "You are most welcome, my dear. Now tell me all about yourself as we have not met before. I know Lady Jane but was unaware that Robert was married. How wonderful. Now, do you enjoy art?"

The conversation continued as Robert stood beside Anne and enjoyed watching his wife's wonderful gift of intelligent speech enthralling this lady, a great supporter of the Arts.

"My dear, we must talk more, but I think the prince is entering, so we must finish now. We will talk later."

Anne and Robert quickly approached the table and stood beside Admiral Crouch. Anne, glancing behind her, saw Lady Jane and the Earl at the next table, with Bethany and Emma smiling at her. She turned, gave a little wave, and told Robert they were at the table beside them. As the official procession entered with the prince and his lady following the master of ceremonies, Anne felt her confidence growing.

Being the first occasion, she had ever been present with royalty, Anne stood quite still, watching the other guests and would follow their lead once the orchestra finished playing the national anthem. At the end of the anthem, the table guests took their seats while the several hundred guests on the other side of the footmen remained standing.

"Robert, where will the other guests find a seat and have dinner?"

"There is not enough room in the exhibition hall, so tables have been set up in the rooms on either side. They are large rooms and can easily accommodate everyone you see here. There must be a huge staff downstairs preparing the food for this lot."

The master of ceremonies stood, introducing the prince and his lady. There were cheers and a rousing round of applause, the crowd genuinely showing appreciation for him attending the ball. The prince responded with a smile and a wave and stood at the podium as the guests fell silent.

The prince first acknowledged the official party, including the First Lord of the Admiralty, and warmly welcomed all those attending. He then made some brief comments about the challenges facing Irish tenant farmers and how the monies raised by this charity would significantly impact their lives. He encouraged everyone attending tonight to dig deep and contribute generously, as this was a worthy charity. A hearty round of applause once again followed his comments.

The ball began with a lovely waltz, and Robert and Anne relished the opportunity to fly around the dance floor together, bumping into an awkward Neville and Bethany. Neville shouted, "They never trained us for this in the Navy."

"You are doing very well, Neville. Mind you don't tread on Beth's toes." Beth agreed as they drifted apart. Next, they met Emma and David, with David whirling Emma around the floor as if he were a professional dancer. Robert smiled, and Anne raised her voice, "David is a fine dancer, Emma!"

"Pity I am not." They whisked away across the floor.

After several dances, Robert led Anne out onto the terrace that looked across the Thames, and as drinks were offered, they both took a glass of champagne.

"Robert, what a grand view. The Thames must be cleaner tonight as it does not smell."

"Perhaps the tide is in –the water is quite high tonight. It may smell a bit as the tide runs out."

As they admired the view, Hamish McPherson appeared with an unknown lady.

"Anne and Robert! Marjorie was so glad that you could attend. I think Marjorie is meeting the Marquess and his wife at present. Please, may I introduce Mrs Janet Stubbington? Janet is a friend of your father, Anne, and a business associate of mine.'

"Good evening, Mrs Stubbington. What business are you in?"

"My husband was in butchery until he died a few years ago. Now I am into investments."

Hamish added, "Janet has investments in several of my pubs and is making a fine return."

"Hamish, perhaps you would talk with Sir Robert while Lady Anne and I stroll along the terrace."

"Certainly, Robert might tell me about the coming Irish visit."

Janet Stubbington walked away along the terrace and indicated that Anne should join her. Anne found she had no choice.

"That is a pretty dress you are wearing, Lady Anne. Did it come from Hursts?"

"Yes, it did. But how did you know of Hursts?"

"I met your father at church one Sunday before your mother died, and she informed me of the establishment. I was most impressed and purchased some dresses there. You should open a shop in London. With your connections, it would do well."

"Mrs Stubbington, it appears you know my parents well, but I have not heard of you before. So, you will understand why I am somewhat timid."

"Call me Janet, Lady South. If I may, I will call you Anne."

"Certainly, Janet."

"My investment company has a contract with your father, which I am sure he has not discussed with you. However, you will recall the ten thousand pounds that appeared before Christmas in your bank account and the confirmation of the navy biscuit contract."

Anne was stunned that Janet would be so familiar with their business. She nodded in agreement.

"Your father has changed his position in your company, and now you are the Managing Director. It is time you were made aware of our contract with your father. Do not be alarmed; we are friends, and our interests are mutual. Hamish agreed to introduce us tonight, so you know who I am. Please discuss our meeting with your father; he will confirm our agreement. Soon after he leaves with Hamish McPherson for Scotland, I will visit you, and we might talk business. Hamish McPherson is also a client of ours. He will verify our organisation's beneficial interest in his company."

"Janet, this is all so sudden. I am not sure what I should say."

"You need not say anything. We shall talk soon in Guildford. Please do not worry, Anne, as we will become close friends over time. We should rejoin Robert and Hamish as I understand the waiters will soon serve dinner."

Anne welcomed the suggestion, "I agree, Janet."

"Have you enjoyed dancing? The orchestra is wonderful tonight."

"Oh, yes. I felt like I was flying above the floor. The waltz is romantic."

Robert picked up on the last remark and added, "She is a nightingale, Mrs Stubbington."

"She can sing then as well?"

"Yes, she sings well but is a wonderful dancer."

Anne took Robert's hand and led him off, wishing Hamish and Janet well.

"What was all that about, Anne?"

"I will tell you later. First, let us have some dinner. I am starving."

The dinner was five courses and started with a delicate pumpkin soup, precisely what Anne needed with the cold from the terrace now seeping into her. She concentrated on her soup and finished before the others. Anne was in a world of her own. Who was this woman that claimed she had an agreement with her father? How did Janet know about the ten thousand pounds her father had still not explained or the navy order? Anne took a deep breath as she finished her soup.

Admiral Crouch, sitting beside Anne, gently said, "The cool air on the terrace gave you an appetite, Anne. It is the same at sea. We keep our sailors well-fed to bolster their strength against the cold weather in the oceans."

"I did feel a cold chill out there, Admiral. I am still feeling a little cold."

The Admiral quickly beckoned a footman who fetched Anne's coat and politely helped her put it on.

"Thank you. That feels much warmer. I am sure I will be warm enough soon."

As waiters removed the soup bowls, Robert watched as the next course was brought out from the kitchen entrance. He was impressed with the fine serving of dishes and the waiter's skill as they deftly held between four and six plates each while navigating the tables. Then Robert noticed one waiter serving at the table straight in front of the head table. There was something different about the man as he seemed taller, and his vest was fuller than the others. The waiter carried four servings and placed them down with care. As he leaned down, placing the last plate, Robert saw his vest slightly open, and the butt of a pistol appeared.

For a moment, the world stood still as the adrenaline kicked into his body, and his muscles tensed for action. Robert's complete attention was now focused on the waiter as he propelled himself out of his seat and at the man. After placing the last serving on the table, he pulled a pistol out from his vest. He saw Robert closing from the corner of his eye as he drew the second pistol and pointed them towards the prince. Robert was ten feet from the man when the first pistol fired, missing the target but hitting the wife of the Master of Ceremonies, with whom the prince was actively engaged in conversation.

The lady was shot in the shoulder, the impact forcing her backwards, knocking her chair over, and falling heavily on the floor. The prince, watching her in shock, turned and faced a waiter now raising another pistol. A shocked silence fell over the room. By this time, Robert was at full sprint, closing fast on the gunman cocking his pistol. Robert leapt forward with his left hand outstretched and coming upwards, knocking the gun towards the ceiling.

It was as if the world was in slow motion as Robert leapt through the air, crashing into the man as the pistol went off virtually in his face. Then a silence followed as the gunman's shot flew above the prince's head. Robert and the gunman collided with an unfortunate gentleman sitting at the adjoining table, crashing onto the floor. Screaming broke out as the gunman, still holding a pistol in his free hand, bashed the butt down on Robert's head, knocking him out cold and blood gushing from his forehead. That was the last Robert remembered for a few minutes.

As soon as the first shot was heard, security guards and marines came from all directions converging on the floor's wrestling men. The gunman was quickly overpowered and arrested. Anne screamed as she saw her husband lying limply on the floor with blood rushing down his face. Admiral Crouch held her back, keeping her where it was safe.

David Sopwith and Neville Bassington offered their services as doctors and soon attended to Robert's injured skull. He was still unconscious, and David was concerned about a concussion. Neville called for a hospital medical cart so they could move him. Security soon had a stretcher organised and covered Robert with blankets. Neville was also concerned about Mrs Fortescue, who was shot in the shoulder. He left David with Robert and attended to her. David also quickly checked the gentleman with whom the gunman had collided. The poor chap had two broken ribs, which would be very painful. So, they ordered another medical cart.

David signalled through the crowd of marines and security staff that Anne should come over. She ran across and hugged her husband, who lay limply on the floor. As they lifted Robert onto the stretcher, his eyes flickered and opened, seeing Anne's beautiful but teary face.

He said, "Have they served the second course yet? I am hungry!"

Anne hugged him tight as Robert gazed blankly into the face of the prince standing high above him and Anne, "Thank you, young man. That was well done!"

Cloverdale Chase, Guildford, Surrey ...

As Benjamin Petherton sat quietly in an easy chair in his study after dinner, he thought about his young daughter's future. She was eleven, and he would soon turn fifty. Benjamin had known for some time of his heart condition and was aware that many men died at his age. While doctor Sopwith had controlled his condition with various potions, he still worried about the consequences of his early death.

If he passed away, it would leave Clare on her own. He had no extended family or suitable relations who he trusted. If he had remarried, this might have solved the problem. With a large inheritance, Clare would be financially secure, but she would still be at the mercy of her Trustees. He must find someone who had Clare's best interest in mind. She was his only child, and he would do anything for her happiness.

She now had some good friends with the Turner children. Perhaps Anne South's suggestion about the school had merit. At least this would provide some continuity for her in the next few years. Enrolling Clare at a Church of England school would be a major step as he was a Catholic and had never thought about changing religion. He saw no need. His penance was regular, and he attended mass every week. Surely there was no need for change. But Clare's friends were Church of England. He saw little difference between the two denominations. They were both Christian and with Catholic emancipation coming, Clare could quickly revert in later life if that were her wish.

He would visit Reverend Taggart tomorrow and discuss enrolling Clare. She would still have her governess but also schooling during the day.

Benjamin stood and walked upstairs. He quietly opened Clare's bedroom door and sat beside his sleeping daughter. She was beautiful as she lay there fast asleep. The joy of youth flowed from her like a halo, and she reminded him so much of Miriam. How he missed his darling wife! They had been so happy, and then she was gone. It was a tragedy, and then Mark died.

Clare was all he had left. Closing his eyes, he thanked his Lord for all His blessings and prayed for both health and Clare's happiness.

Then he felt Clare's soft touch on his hand and opened his eyes. She was awake and watching him.

"Father, what is the matter?"

"I was lonely, Clare, so I thought I would sit with you for a moment or two. There is nothing wrong. Go back to sleep."

Clare yawned and smiled, "Just like when I was young, you sat with me, so I was not afraid."

"Yes, Darling."

Clare turned over, and soon she was asleep again. Benjamin sat there for nearly half an hour and then returned downstairs. As he walked through the drawing room where part of his bottle collection was on display, he noticed three small bottles in the lower left-hand corner of a display case were missing.

He quickly searched the room, thinking a maid may have moved them. But there was still no sign of them. 'That was strange,' he thought. Tomorrow morning, he must ask the butler if he knew where they were.

'Harting', St James's Square, London …

The four coaches and carriages entered St James's Square in a row, the first pulling up outside 'Harting' quickly. The security detail of marines was out promptly as they took up stations around the entrance. Admiral Crouch's carriage stopped next, with the Admiral hopping down quickly and watching as two marines assisted Robert into the house. David Sopwith, who accompanied Robert with Anne, was concerned that his friend was still a bit giddy, and rushed inside the townhouse alerting Staines.

The next carriage carried the Earl and Countess and Lady Crouch. The fourth carriage brought Emma and Beth but without Neville, who remained with Mrs Dorothy Fortescue at the hospital.

Once Admiral Crouch was satisfied, Robert was inside; he went outside and assisted the Earl and Lady Jane. Katherine Crouch entered with Emma and Bethany, who were avidly discussing the events of the evening. They found Robert protesting as David rechecked him for any signs of a head injury that so often occurred after a severe knock.

"Follow my finger, please, as I move it. Do not move your head."

Robert focused on the finger but lost sight as it moved away. David tried him again. The same thing happened. Robert then sat back and closed his eyes, "I am a bit tired, David."

"Relax for a while and drink water, please. No alcohol. Staines a jug of water and a glass! Robert, you need to remain awake for at least three hours for observation. I will be with you, and we shall play cards. You must not sleep yet."

"Why not? I am sleepy and would like a rest."

"I must be sure that your brain or blood vessels have no internal injuries. If there are, they will appear in the next three hours. After that, the probability lessens very significantly."

"It is quarter past eleven now, so we are playing cards till two fifteen!"

"Looks like it, old fellow!"

Lady Jane chastened Robert, "Do as the Doctor asks Robert! David knows what he is doing. Be sensible and agree, please."

"Yes, Mother. Someone find the cards!"

Admiral Crouch said, "Robert, I think Lady Jane has a sensible suggestion there. But I must say that Lord Dawlting is sure he recruited the right man for this future mission. But perhaps, for Anne's sake, you might use more delegation in the future."

Anne hugged Admiral Crouch, "Oh, yes, Robert. Please obey the Admiral, please."

Robert stood and turned around, "I am sorry, Admiral, I forgot you were here. I shall follow your instructions, Sir, and of course, my wife's." The wide, friendly smile that Robert usually wore returned, and a sense of relief came across the whole party.

"Now shuffle those cards, Robert. I suggest everyone has a sleep-in tomorrow, and I will check on your condition tomorrow afternoon. I shall take Lady Katherine home now, and we wish you all a very peaceful night."

Several conversations started as Lady Jane and the Earl accompanied Admiral Crouch and Lady Katherine outside.

As the Admiral followed his wife out, he swung around and said, "Lady Jane! You know that your son saved the prince's life tonight. It will not finish here. There will be consequences. Good ones!" He smiled, waved and boarded the carriage.

The Earl said as they came inside, "Staines, I think I will have a scotch."

"Oh, no, you won't, David! You are retiring like the rest of us. Come, dear. We need some sleep before reorganising our plans tomorrow. With Robert's condition, we must delay our departure."

Lady Jane led a muttering Earl away and up the stairs.

Bethany briefed Staines that Neville would appear sometime in the next two hours from the hospital and apologised that someone must remain up and let him in.

Staines replied, "That is my duty, my Lady. It will be a pleasure, and I will also assist Doctor Sopwith."

"Thank you, Staines."

Around three in the morning, a knock came on the front door. Assuming it would be Doctor Bassington, Staines opened the door, finding a messenger outside. The man passed across the letter and explained it was a special delivery. Staines took the envelope and closed the door.

He read the front of the envelope and saw it bore the address of the countess. He then checked the back and read it was from Lady Clarissa South. He raised his eyebrows, wondering who Lady South was. Staines, carrying the letter into the servant's hall, placed the letter in Lady Jane's pigeonhole. He thought, 'We have had enough excitement for one night. It can wait until the morning.'

Staines returned and sat in the foyer, waiting for Doctor Bassington.

Braydon Kelly's House, Dublin, Ireland ...

"Dan! Dan, are you awake?"

"No!"

"Dan, there is something I must ask you?"

It was three in the morning. The walk back into Dublin had been slow as the watchmen were still on the streets detaining anyone who looked suspicious. Keeping well in the shadows, the three brothers had taken an extra hour before reaching their destination.

"What is it, Michael?"

Michael Walsh rolled off his bunk and knelt beside the next bunk where Dan O'Leary slept.

In a low voice, he said, "Iain Murphy gave me an order. He wants Aiden Reid taken for a walk!"

Dan stirred, saying, "What!"

He pushed himself up on his elbow and could faintly see Michael's face in the darkness.

"Why would he want Aiden dead?"

"He says he is out of control, Dan, and we must get rid of him before he causes trouble."

"I know he is grieving Sean, but he is not out of control. The man is a magician. He can disappear into thin air!"

"I know it happened last week here in Dublin when I saw him. I am more worried about Iain."

"What do you mean?"

"Better if we talk somewhere else back in Cobh. I was not sure how you would react. I can see your thoughts are the same as mine. Keep it confidential, Dan. Time for sleep."

With that, they both lay back down on their bunks. Michael Walsh was still confused. He was not sure now who he should believe. The sooner his family was out of this mess, the better.

Grand Hotel, Kingston, Jamacia ...

Sir Hugh South sat in bed and watched as a dim dawn light grew on the eastern horizon. Hugh was restless and yearned for an early morning ride in the crisp air of the pastures at home. He found he was sleeping too late each day and slipping behind in his quest to restore his fitness. It was less than two months before the ship departed, and Hugh had his affairs in order. If he could only increase his stamina enough and properly walk again, he would recover far quicker.

He swung his legs out over the side of the bed and sat up straight. The next hurdle was standing upright without his contraption. Closing his eyes and gathering all the strength he could muster, he thrust himself upwards. Opening his eyes, he found himself standing but leaning slightly forward. He wavered around a bit, finding his balance.

Now upright, he slowly moved his left leg forward and walked across the verandah, grasping his exercise rail. Halfway there, he felt giddy but fortunately regained his balance. Holding onto the raised rail, he breathed deeply, feeling his lungs fill with fresh air. It felt good. Hugh was pleased with his achievement as he stood there, knowing he had mastered it himself.

He enjoyed standing, taking in the faint light as it increased slowly. He considered that the sun must have risen a million times over this horizon since the earth began. How many people had watched the sunrise since creation, and most were now dead? Generation after generation kept passing away. There was no escaping the inevitable. He shivered as he knew he should be dead. Why had he survived?

His mind wandered, retrieving scant details of his discussions with the Reverend Andrew Taggart. The man was so gentle but full of wisdom. What was it that he had said? "The battle is won! All you need is faith." What was the battle – what was he talking about? Then Hugh remembered Andrew Taggart had given him some notes. Where had he put them? Hugh decided to find those notes today and read them. But first, he must conquer the return walk. Refusing the thought of crawling back, Hugh decided to beat this and walk back!

Perhaps he could find some help. 'Please, God, if you exist, help me walk again and show me your way!"

Hugh took a step and shuddered. Then some more faltering steps, and as he felt giddy, some hands held him up, guided him across the floor and gently lowered him into the bed.

"Fiona, I would not have disturbed you, but I had no idea I was making such a racket. Sorry!"

Hugh moved his legs onto the bed and lay back on the pillow, smiling. He looked up for Fiona, but there was no one there. That was strange. She must have quickly left the room.

He lay there exhausted, drifting back into sleep and found himself laughing and running with Robert through Fintelton's golden pastures towards the threshing room as the bright rays of the summer sun warmed their chests.

'Harting', St James's Square, London ...

Robert was the first at breakfast with his head bandaged, ready for a hearty meal after missing out on dinner last night.

Staines enquired, "How is the head feeling this morning, Sir Robert?"

"Fine, Staines. Thank you."

"Very good, Sir! You will find the various dishes in the serving trays. Would you like tea or coffee, Sir?"

"Tea, thanks, Staines."

Except for Neville, the rest of the family and guests emerged fairly soon. Beth explained that Mrs Fortescue had lost a lot of blood, and fortunately, she survived the night. Neville did not arrive home till six am and was now fast asleep. He would rise at twelve and then revisit the patient in the hospital.

Lady Jane was impressed, "The doctors work long hours for our good. I am very thankful for Neville and David. The Earl and I have put off our departure until tomorrow. We shall still have enough time for the final wedding arrangements. Now, Beth, I understand you and Neville will arrive on Friday. We have a room for you at Fintelton."

Beth nodded, confirming the date.

Emma said, "Mother would you mind if David and I, Robert and Anne, went off for a carriage ride this morning? David will observe how the fresh air and a ride will affect Robert's head."

David looked up in surprise, and Emma quickly continued, "Now, Beth, you said you would visit your parents-in-law. Perhaps we could drop you off along the way."

"Thank you, Emma, but I will wait for Neville. He only plans a short visit with Mrs Fortescue, and I will accompany him. We will go on from there and have dinner with the Bassingtons and return later tonight if that is suitable, Lady Jane."

"That would be excellent, Beth, as it would be a great relief if the doctors were with us in case of any medical emergency with the Earl."

Lord Fintelton sat up from his bacon and eggs and muttered, "Piffle, Jane. I am as fit as a fiddle today."

Later in the carriage, Emma explained, "David, remember the bank teller in Petersfield? Somehow, she and the Wimbledon house are connected. We must inspect the property, as it might provide the necessary information."

"Ah, sorry, I forgot. I assumed Anne and Robert were doing that."

Anne answered, "We were, but now we all stay an extra day. It would be safer with four than two."

David Sopwith was somewhat concerned, "You understand that Wimbledon is quite a distance. There will be less traffic as it is Sunday, but this trip will take us the rest of the day."

Emma explained, "David, we must do this. Consider it as a necessary examination of a patient. We shall stop and have lunch with my Auntie and Uncle and then search out the addresses. Wimbledon is a nice country area. It is green and spacious with large blocks of land for sale, and Uncle John has built a delightful home there."

Robert agreed, "It is almost a castle. I think he went a little overboard."

David smiled, "Then we shall have fun doing the research!"

Emma was relieved and snuggled up beside David and kissed him. David said, "More, please!"

After visiting the relatives for an early lunch, the carriage finally reached the first address. It was a large two-storied house on land with a pleasant aspect. A small artificial lake and some wooded areas at the back gave it a country charm. A sign on the front fence indicated rooms or suites for rent, and the rental charges were displayed.

Anne tapped the roof and stopped the carriage.

"The sign says apply within. David, would you accompany me, please, as I shall inspect the property? Robert, with your injury, it may be best if you remain in the carriage."

"But I have recovered!"

"Please, Robert, remain here with Emma. I have a good reason for this request."

David grinned as he exited the carriage and said, "If we are not back in twenty minutes, call the police, please. Why am I doing this?" David obediently followed an energised Anne, who opened the entry gate, walked confidently down the path, and knocked on the front door.

A young lady quickly answered the knock, "Yes?"

"Good afternoon. I read the sign on the front fence and decided to call. Might we inspect the rooms advertised? I am Mrs Boswell, and this is my husband, Doctor Boswell. He is thinking of commencing practice in Wimbledon."

"Oh, of course. You will need some temporary accommodation. My name is Fanny. I am one of the maids who keep the place clean and running. We have two families here at present and four single women. There is one suite left. It is upstairs, and I am afraid it is the most expensive. However, please come in, and I will show you through."

"Thank you, Fanny. If you would lead the way."

David said nothing but followed Fanny and Anne as they quickly climbed the internal stairway. On the way up, David noticed the large drawing room adjoining a reading room with a small library on the ground floor. But there were no people in the house as far as he could see.

David asked, "Where are all your tenants, Fanny?"

"It is Sunday, Doctor Boswell! When our guests find the chance, they enjoy the sunshine. I expect some back around four when we serve afternoon tea. You are most welcome for a cup of tea if you intend to reside with us. I can assure you we carefully select tenants. We very rarely accept single men. Mrs Constance is very particular."

Fanny showed David into the suite and opened the blinds. The owner had beautifully decorated the living area, and Anne liked the wallpaper.

"Where did you find that wallpaper, Fanny? It is beautiful."

Fanny smiled and replied, "Mrs Constance picked the wallpaper and would know. She does all the decorating. Her son David does the work around the house for her. He is indentured to a builder and is doing very well."

Anne and David then looked through the other rooms, including a large bedroom with a four-poster bed. Anne murmured, "Very comfortable indeed. Fanny, do you have the application form?"

"No, sorry, Mrs Bolster. You must see Mrs Constance for that. She is out this afternoon. I understand she is in London. But her son David should be there."

"It is Mrs Boswell, Fanny. Where would we find Mrs Constance's son?" Anne was sure Fanny was far more intelligent than she let on, and the name slip was intentional, testing whether the applicants were genuine.

"Sorry, Mrs Boswell. It is close. They live directly behind this guest house. The house fronts onto the next street, and the number is twenty-one. If your carriage proceeds around the block, you will enter the street behind this one and easily find it. Also, for your information, we have a stable and groomsmen who will care for your carriage and horses."

"Why, that was the next question I was considering. Thank you, Fanny. We will drive around and ask for the application form. Hopefully, we will return soon."

"That is a pleasure, Doctor and Mrs Boswell. "

With that, Fanny showed Anne and David out the front door. David was impressed with Anne's subterfuge and said, "You are cool under pressure, Anne. That was well done. I am glad Emma is marrying me. I could not handle you!"

Anne laughed as they climbed into the carriage. She briefed Robert and Emma on what they had found as their carriage circled the block. Since Mrs Constance was out, Anne was keen on meeting the son.

"Why must you meet with the son, Anne?" Robert was unsettled and felt that remaining here any longer was unnecessary.

"I have a suspicion, Robert. I must satisfy myself, or I will not sleep tonight."

As they approached the house directly behind the guest house, Anne was impressed again at the neat little cottage with a well-kept garden and plenty of space for future development if required. David noticed Fanny leaving the back of the house and walking towards the guest house.

"I think the young man will be there. I can see Fanny walking back." David Sopwith pointed her out.

Anne replied, "She wasted no time."

The carriage stopped, and Anne and David hopped down again and walked up the front path. Anne quietly said, "Let me do the talking, please."

She knocked on the door, which quickly opened. A tall young man around eighteen years old appeared. He was well-dressed and had a beautiful smile.

Anne stood there, dumbfounded.

In a refined voice, he asked, "May I be of assistance? I understand you are Doctor and Mrs Boswell. Fanny told me of your enquiry. I have the application form here. After receiving the application, we usually require two weeks to check references; however, we might make that shorter in your case. We require a bond of four weeks' rent, which must be paid in advance."

Anne stood there silently, mouth open until she felt her throat drying, and then slowly closed the mouth. The young man held out the application form and looked at Anne and David in turn. David noticing Anne's predicament, said, "Thank you, Mr ...?"

"Constance. I am afraid my mother is in London at present. Otherwise, she would greet you."

The young man hesitated, wondering why Anne looked at him strangely, "Dr Boswell, is Mrs Boswell unwell? She seems somewhat surprised."

"No, no. She was not expecting such a handsome young man. We must be on our way now."

Anne quietly said, "Good day, Mr Constance."

David Constance looked hard at the Doctor's wife and wondered what the matter was. Taking a final glance, he slowly closed the door.

As David and Anne reboarded the coach, Emma and Robert eagerly awaited the details.

Anne sat there in stunned silence, thinking deeply. David gave her time to digest what she had seen. Anne looked at David, knowing he could not have missed what she had recognised. Anne remained silent.

Robert said, "Please, one of you, tell me what happened?"

David quietly said, "If I am not mistaken, Robert, and I am sure Anne will support me on this observation. Robert and Emma, it appears you might have an unrecognised nephew!"

Robert sat back, and Emma said, "What, you must be mistaken?"

Anne gathered her strength and said, "He was almost Hugh's twin. I think we now know the connection. Hugh has a son, of whom your parents were unaware. There can be no other explanation!"

'Harting', St James's Square, London …

Staines was passing the servant's hall when he spied the unopened envelope in Lady Jane's pigeonhole. He had forgotten the letter this morning and suddenly remembered it had come in the early morning hours as he waited for Doctor Bassington. Quickly picking up the letter, he sought out the countess, knowing she was probably writing while the Earl had his after-lunch nap.

Staines reread the back of the letter and wondered who Lady Clarissa South was.

He walked through the drawing room, down a small passage, and into Lady Jane's writing room. Finding his mistress at her desk, he said, "Your Ladyship, I must apologise. This letter was dropped off by courier early this morning, to be exact, at three in the morning. I put it aside as I understood everyone needed their sleep."

"Thank you, Staines. I agree with your decision; everyone needed their sleep. I am still somewhat tired myself."

"Thank you, My Lady." With that, the butler withdrew.

Lady Jane picked up the letter and read the details of the sender. Lady Clarissa South! Who was that?

She opened the letter and read it. Slowly she sat up straight, saying, "No, it cannot be. No!"

As Lady Jane read, she was horrified. She considered waking the Earl but understood he needed his rest. A tear slowly ran down her cheek, dripping onto the blotting paper. She sat there for several minutes thinking about her dear son, Hugh. She loved him so much despite his failures in life. He was her son, and she felt in her bones that he was alive and well. She, of all people, would know if he was dead.

"Staines!" There was no answer.

She pulled the cord for the servant's hall. Soon Staines was with her.

"Staines, some tea, please. No, I think it should be coffee. Quickly please!"

She took the letter again and reread it. These claims must be fraudulent! A fraud of an unmeasurably despicable degree. Who was this, Clarissa South? Then she remembered her son's letter informing her of Lady Clarissa Wendarm. Her sister-in-law, Lady Angela Philps, had warned her of this lady, and Lady Jane had written to Hugh, hoping she was in time, but there had been no reply. It was March, and she had expected him home from Jamaica by now. The facts in the letter were from an unknown woman claiming the honour of being Sir Hugh's wife and that her son was now dead. It could only be a fraud!

At first, she felt a pang of sorrow for her son, but she realised this news could not be accurate. Hugh would never let this happen. From deep inside, she felt revulsion towards this lady's playing with the truth. With gritted teeth, Lady Fintelton said aloud, "This woman shall never enter my house!"

PART 3

"It was if something had exploded inside
him,
A joy so unexplained that wonderfully
filled his heart!"

1827, Guildford, Surrey, England.

Chapter 17

'Harting', St James's Square, London ...

The Earl gently placed the letter back in front of Lady Jane and then, with a slight amount of anger in his voice, complained, "This is preposterous, my Dear! Hugh would never marry someone without letting us know first. There is no word about any sickness; the governor would have written directly if Hugh had died. It is a fraud, and we must avoid this woman at all costs."

Lady Jane took heart from hearing that her husband was of a similar view, "Thank you, David. Before leaving, I must ask our solicitors for advice on this lady's claim. I shall write this morning. They will be aware of the legal issue and will advise us. Unfortunately, Hugh's absence complicates the situation, but I am sure we will hear from him soon."

Anne looked up and said, "Lady Jane! Robert and I would be only too happy dropping off the letter on our way. We will probably catch up with our party by lunch or in Epson tonight."

Robert opened his mouth, but Anne continued, "My father asked if I would discuss some company issues with the solicitors." Anne rested her hand on Robert's arm and made a pleading glance at him.

Robert taking the hint, added, "It would be no bother at all, Mother."

"Certainly, Anne. That would be most helpful."

Anne gathered some writing paper, ink and quill and jotted out a quick note. She advised Mr Finchley at Manifold & Stout Attorneys they would call and asked if he would report on an urgent matter.

"Staines!"

"Yes, Milady."

"Would you have a rider deliver this as soon as possible?"

"Yes, Lady South. I will have it dispatched at once." As the butler turned, he looked hard at Sir Robert and gave a slight cough before leaving the room. Robert excused himself and followed Staines into the hallway.

"I am sorry, Sir Robert, but the cash box is empty as over Saturday and

Sunday, the bank is closed and does not reopen until after ten this morning. Might I ask for a half-crown for the rider, Sir?"

In a calm voice, Robert quickly said, "I understand, Staines. This cash shortage is the family's fault. Here take this change and put it in the box." Robert cleared his pocket of several crowns, half-crowns, and other coins, placing them in Staines's hands.

"Thank you, Sir!"

As Robert returned to the breakfast room, he noticed Anne standing in the doorway watching.

"They have no money, Anne, until after the bank opens this morning!"

"Robert, we must solve this financial crisis quickly. I suggested visiting the attorneys to discover more about Mrs Constance's property. Please, do not mention it at breakfast, as your mother has enough on her mind."

"I thought that might have been your reason. We should finish breakfast and pack. Then we will set off and visit Manifold and Stout."

As they took their places at the breakfast table, David Sopwith said, "It appears the weather has cleared, so we should have a good run today. I understand, Anne, that your cousin is the manager of the Epsom pub we are staying at?"

"Yes, Oliver is most experienced in the business now, and my father is half-owner of the pub. Robert has not seen 'Porting' yet, so if the weather holds, it will be a picture."

Robert broke out in his magnificent smile and laughed, "I will carry you over the threshold, Anne. I missed that opportunity when you first arrived alone, but we shall do it together this time."

Lady Jane was excited, "We shall enjoy watching, Robert and Anne. Perhaps a little champagne as well. Now, your Lordship, it is time we finished the packing."

The Earl was ready, wiping his hands on the serviette and leading Lady Jane upstairs. Anne, waiting until she was sure they were out of earshot, quietly said, "At the attorneys, we will check on the Constance property. I am sure they will have some information."

David apologised, "I am sorry that we cannot be of more help. We will be out of contact on the honeymoon for the next six weeks. Perhaps Lady Jane's suggestion of not corresponding with this woman may be prudent. After all, there is no proof yet. We need evidence. The first step is finding out from the governor in Kingston about Sir Hugh's state of health."

Robert, without hesitation, said, "No need for an apology, you two. We understand completely. The problems will be sorted out before your return. But, David, you make a good point about delaying any meeting. Anne must work closely with Lady Jane on delaying this, Lady Clarissa."

Standing on the far side of the room, Staines gave a slight cough, "Sir Robert, might I have a word?"

David and Robert looked up from their conversation, "Yes, Staines! What is it?"

"Sir, Might I ask who Lady Clarissa South is?"

Robert replied, "The Lady claims a family membership as Sir Hugh's wife. We have no evidence of this or any communication from Sir Hugh. She also claims that Sir Hugh died in Jamaica and that she carries his child."

Staines stood there taking it all in and swayed backward and forward as he thought.

"Sir Robert, the Lady would not be the first to make this type of accusation. However, there are ways and means of dealing with it. Certainly, Sir, I have seen how other families deal with these situations, and there is no need for haste. Sometimes it may take several years, given death is involved, before the family gives any recognition."

David put down his coffee and sat back in his chair, "Robert, I think Staines' comment has merit. He will be helpful in these circumstances. Let me draft a reply letter that Lady Jane may sign. The coaches will not leave before morning tea, and we might still reach Epsom in plenty of time."

Staines replied, "Thank you, Doctor Sopwith. I would assume that if the lady desires lodging with the family, she will likely arrive here and ask for assistance. In this case, it would be best if the family resided at Fintelton. I will ensure she does not gain entry here."

Robert nearly choked on some toast remembering an incident when he first met Staines. He gave a slight cough and smiled, saying, "Excuse me! I am sure, Staines, you will do an excellent job on that!"

Offices of Manifold & Stout, Attorneys ...
"Thank you for seeing us at short notice, Mr Finchley."

"It is a pleasure, Sir Robert. Fortunately, I have a light workload today. I say the papers are full of your gallant exploits on Saturday night at the charity ball. I am glad you are uninjured."

"Well, I hope that type of event does not occur again. But thank you for your comments."

"Certainly, Sir. Now, how may I be of assistance."

Robert said, "Lady South will explain."

Mr Finchley focused on Anne, "Lady South, I must congratulate you on your change in status. You were engaged and visited with Lady Emma the last time we met."

"You were most generous in allowing my participation in that meeting, Mr Finchley, and I must thank you. I believe my father and mother became clients of yours."

"Yes, they did. Please accept my condolences on your mother's passing. Unfortunately, I understand that it was expected?"

"Yes, but not quite so soon. Now let me explain our enquiry."

Anne took Mr Finchley through the complete story of the staff not being paid, arousing Sir Robert's concern, and then discovering the missing money. Mr Finchley's facial expression became grave as the story continued.

"We visited Mrs Constance's house in Wimbledon and found that her residence was directly behind the property that is in question. The bank has assured us that the estate paid for the property; however, we are unsure who owns the property. Would you be aware of who the owner is?"

Mr Finchley took some time before he made his reply.

"Sir Robert and Lady South, I assume you are talking of the property in Wimbledon acquired by the Earl some fifteen years ago?"

"That is correct, Mr Finchley. However, we thought Sir Hugh acquired it."

"Sorry, I assumed it would have been Sir David who acquired the property as Sir Hugh at that time would not have had the authority. However, the specific purchaser is not the issue. Yes, we do hold the title of that property here with the other estate titles."

"Then it is an estate property?" Robert was fascinated that there was an additional property he was unaware of.

"Yes, that is correct. It was an excellent investment as property values in Wimbledon are rising quickly."

Anne, relieved they had solved a missing part of the puzzle, sighed, "Well, we have found where fifteen thousand pounds of the missing money has gone."

Robert was confused, "Mr Finchley, why is this Mrs Constance living there if it is an estate property?"

"These provisions are usually contained in a codicil in the will. I must be careful here as I may not reveal the details of Sir David's will without authorisation. I can discuss the estate, and in this case, we hold an agreement that stipulates that Mrs Constance may reside during her lifetime at the property and that all income from the Wimbledon property remains the property of Mrs Constance during her lifetime tenancy. As the Earl is alive, any codicil will have no effect, and the agreement takes precedence. On Mrs Constance's death, the estate regains the management of the property."

Robert and Anne sat there in silence, digesting this new information. Robert finally said, "Might we see the title, Mr Finchley?"

"Certainly. I will have one of the clerks bring it in." He quickly called his secretary, asking for the title.

Anne said, "Robert, this opens up more possibilities!"

"We shall discuss them in the carriage, Anne."

A clerk arrived with the title. Mr Finchley passed it across. The survey showed the land extending between the two streets they had visited the previous day. The Fintelton Estate was noted as the owner.

"Mr Finchley! Are you aware if one or two buildings were on the property when purchased?"

"As far as I am aware, there was only one building."

Robert looked at Anne and raised his eyebrows, "It appears there are two buildings now and stables!"

"Sir Robert and Lady South, I should not say any more than I have disclosed this morning. I understand your concern; however, I suggest you discuss the issues with the Earl. He and possibly Sir Hugh will have the full details."

Anne quickly said, "Thank you, Mr Finchley, you have been most helpful. Here is a letter from Lady Fintelton requesting your services on another matter." Anne passed across the envelope.

Mr Finchley opened the envelope and read the letter.

"Oh, dear! I am indeed sorry about the news of Sir Hugh. I shall have letters of inquiry written today and sent off. However, dealing with Kingston may mean we do not have any confirmation for two months or more. I shall explain this in the correspondence with the countess and advise her of the timing."

"Thank you, Mr Finchley."

Anne noticed her husband's worried face in the carriage: "Robert, this may mean that young Mr Constance may either be your nephew or your half-brother."

"That did cross my mind, Anne. But surely not a half-brother! I would say that Hugh has got this lady into trouble, and Father has helped Hugh out of a most difficult situation."

"Robert, that is one of two possibilities. We are discussing an affair that may have occurred some twenty years ago. If your father was involved, I think it may be prudent to refrain from discussing this with your mother until we are sure."

Robert sat there with a glum look, "It may be better if we never say anything at all."

The Local Church School, Guildford ...

"Boys and girls! May I introduce the Reverent Philip Hotspur? You will call him Mr Hotspur."

The children said, "Good morning Mr Hotspur; May God bless you!"

Philip Hotspur was quite taken with the lovely welcome from the children.

"Mr Hotspur will assist me with the school here and teach many of your classes from today. He is well educated, coming from Oxford, and this allows an expansion of our curriculum, including introducing the Latin language and some higher mathematics."

The children ceased smiling at the thought of more work, except for two boys halfway down the row of desks, who remained smiling.

"I am glad, children, that Mr Hotspur brings this knowledge with him as he will greatly help in the future. As I have a pressing appointment, I will leave Mr Hotspur with you, and please behave."

As Reverend Taggart left, he asked his wife, Laura, "Keep an eye on him, Laura. I must know if anything difficult happens."

Laura Taggart nodded in agreement and placed herself where she could see the class.

"Good morning, children! I always enjoy meeting young people. Over the coming week, I will talk with each of you and assess your skills. But first, as we must become acquainted, I thought we might discuss where you tell me about yourself and Guildford. I am sure there are many things here you are proud of, and we can have some fun learning about them."

Dawn Luckett was the first with her hand up, and the Reverend pointed her out and asked, "And what is your name?"

"Dawn Luckett, Mr Hatspur."

"It is Hotspur! Perhaps I should write it up on the blackboard. Where is the chalk? Here it is."

The Reverend quickly wrote his name in large letters on the blackboard.

"Now, Dawn, what will you tell us about Guildford."

Dawn standing straight, excitedly said, "My father has a farm outside town up over the hill, and he milks the cows!"

"Wonderful, Dawn. We know where our milk comes from now. Thank you."

Philip Hotspur noticed two boys still smiling in the middle row, "Boys, what are your names? Stand up and tell me, please?"

The boys stood up and said in turn, "William Turner, Sir." And "Edward Wood, Sir."

"You boys seem entertained by something. What was it?"

William said, "We thought your name was funny, Sir!"

All the boys and girls laughed and waited for Mr Hotspur's reaction. Simeon put his head in his hands, knowing that this would not go well for William.

"Well, William Turner and Edward Wood! My name is an old English name that goes back centuries. I am proud of my surname, as I am sure you are proud of yours. We should all refrain from making fun of anybody's name, please."

With that, the discussion continued.

Turner Business Offices, Guildford …

Mid-morning, a rider jumped down from his horse and quickly entered the building, delivering Mr Jonathan Turner a message. The receptionist promptly took it upstairs, knocked on Mr Turner's door, and entered.

"A special delivery Mr Turner. The rider is here now and waiting for a response."

Jonathan raised his eyes, and said, "Give it here, Daisy. It must be urgent!"

He took the message and noticed it was from Hamish McPherson.

"Ask the rider to wait, Daisy. I will write a reply. He will have it in a few minutes."

Jonathan commenced reading.

McPherson Breweries
Greenwich, England.

Dear Jonathan

I hope this letter finds you well. I am afraid my circumstances have changed, as my son Lachlan and his family have arrived here, and I have delayed my departure for two weeks. This way, Marjorie may enjoy the grandchildren, and Lachlan and I will discuss business at length.

I have rearranged my travel arrangements and thought you might be interested. I propose leaving Greenwich on the seventeenth of March on one of my ships, and I am sending this invitation that you might join me on the voyage. Marjorie will travel with Lachlan and his family on their return journey by coach. We will meet them in Glasgow.

I can assure you that the trip will be most informative. We will visit two ports on the way. Firstly, Bristol, where I have decided on some sites for pubs. You would enjoy seeing them, and we should survey some sites for your first bakery there if you are inclined. Then into Liverpool and a marvellous view of the Mersey River. From there, our next destination will be Glasgow.

I hope you will join me, Jonathan, as you will enjoy the voyage. Please advise me of your decision, and I will arrange your passage on our ship.

Your friend
Hamish

Jonathan was excited. The invitation was generous indeed! This was an opportunity he would not miss. Quickly writing a reply, he called the receptionist.

"Here is a half-crown for the rider, Daisy. Ask that it is delivered directly."

'Porting', Guildford, Surrey ...

Robert lifted Anne into his arms and carried her across the threshold at Porting. As he slowly let her down, they kissed, hugging each other closely.

"Do you think this will be where our first child will be born?" Robert beamed with anticipation.

"I hope so, darling. But you must have the stables repaired and expanded, as your mother and father will visit on that occasion."

"Show me through the house first, and then we shall inspect the stables on our walk before dinner. My parents should be arriving soon, so it may be best if I meet Mrs Kirby first."

Anne smiled and said with a laugh, "Follow me, Sir Robert!"

As they entered the kitchen, Anne noticed a young maid with Mrs Kirby.

"Welcome back, Lady South."

"Thank you, Mrs Kirby. May I introduce my husband, Sir Robert South?"

Mrs Kirby and the maid gave curtsies. Anne noticed that the maid was thin and young with a smart black dress and brown hair curled neatly in a bun. She was around twenty and quite handsome.

"Please, Mrs Kirby, who is this young lady?"

"This, Milady, is your new lady's maid, Miss Mary Hedge."

"Welcome, Mary. I am so glad you are here! I certainly need your assistance."

"It is a pleasure, Lady South!"

"Do I detect a slight Irish accent?"

"Yes, Milady! My parents left Ireland in eighteen fifteen and settled here when I was ten. I have never completely lost the accent from my speech. I am sorry if it worries you."

"Not at all, Mary. Your accent is soft and sweet on the ear. I will talk with you later, but we must welcome the Earl and Countess. I hear their carriage arriving."

Later in the afternoon, Robert and Anne walked around the garden, with Anne particularly interested in showing Robert the dilapidated stables.

As they approached, Robert said, "I say, they are a bit run down and small. Is there any accommodation attached?"

"I believe so as James the footman resides there. He is good with the carriage, but I decided on hiring two footmen for tonight's dinner while your mother and father are here."

"Good. I will have Mr Stem come up from Fintelton, and he will advise me on what repairs are needed. Once we have his advice, we will employ either a local builder or bring a team from Fintelton."

As Robert looked away from the barn, he felt a dog nudging his right leg.

Anne called out, "Hello, Ralph. How did you know we would be coming?"

With his tail wagging madly, Ralph left Robert and commenced licking Anne's hands.

"I am sorry, Lady South! I should have had him on a leash. He is over-friendly. My apologies."

"Mr Petherton and Clare! What a lovely surprise. Please meet my husband, Sir Robert South."

"Sir Robert, it is an honour. We were walking the dog on our property, and I heard you might be returning this afternoon, so I took the chance, and here you are. I am your neighbour, and this is my daughter, Clare."

Robert offered his hand and said, "I am honoured to make your acquaintance Mr Petherton and you too, Clare."

Clare gave Robert a slight bow, rushed over, and hugged Anne, "I have missed you, Lady South. When might you come and have morning tea with us again?"

"That is kind of you, Clare. We will return late Sunday evening. Sir Robert will be here until Wednesday morning when he leaves for Woolwich. You were fortunate catching us here, Mr Petherton, as we are home overnight, and then tomorrow morning, we rush away to Fintelton estate near Petersfield. Sir Robert's sister will be married on Saturday, and Robert is the best man, and I am the maid of honour."

"Then this is a happy coincidence! Might I offer a lunch invitation for next Tuesday? I understand it may be the only opportunity for some time."

"You are correct, Sir. I sail on the seventeenth and will not return for some two months. We would be honoured to attend for luncheon."

The Rectory, Guildford, Surrey ...
The Reverend Andrew Taggart sat in his office facing Mr Benjamin Petherton. Andrew Taggart was surprised as he knew Benjamin was a regular Catholic worshipper and wondered why he had come in.

"Benjamin, it is an honour having you visit this morning. How may I assist?"

Benjamin Petherton had met Andrew Taggart many times during his residency in Guildford and held a high opinion of the man. He always found him trustworthy and, despite his different denomination, felt he could confidently talk with him.

"Andrew, you understand that I am a Catholic and being here is quite a step for me. We have met on many social occasions, and I value your friendship. What I will say might be seen as a betrayal by my fellow believers, so we must keep it between you and me."

"I understand."

"Since my son, Mark, died, I have focused on keeping my daughter, Clare, safe. I have kept her out of public view and what you might consider almost a prisoner on our estate. She does not think of it that way as she knows nothing different. Despite many requests from our priest, I have kept her away from the Catholic school. In some ways, I regret this now."

"Why would that be, Benjamin?"

"She has had little company with other children in her first eleven years. I have now allowed a developing friendship between the Turner children, Sophie Watson and Clare. They often visit my home and play with her. I see now that she has benefited greatly from this fellowship. Friends of her age are what she craves, yet I have resisted it."

Andrew Taggart could see the struggle Benjamin Petherton was facing. If Benjamin kept Clare away from other children, how would she face the world when she was an adult?

Andrew suggested, "I know these children, Benjamin. They come from good homes with parents of similar beliefs as you. Certainly, they come from a different denomination, but their intentions are for the best."

"I agree! That is why I am here, Andrew. I wish those relationships might continue, so I am proposing the enrolment of Clare in your church school."

Andrew was staggered. He sat back and looked Benjamin in the eye, "This would be a difficult move for you and perhaps for Clare as you have raised her in the Catholic tradition. Are you sure about this path, Benjamin?"

"My responsibility as Clare's father requires me to educate her in fear of our Lord and ensure her safety. I have taught Christian ethics as best as possible without damaging my relationship with her. The denomination she chooses in later life will be her decision. My aim is that she has friends around her that share our beliefs and enjoy education."

"Benjamin! I would happily enrol her, but I must point out a few issues. Despite taking every precaution, I cannot guarantee a child's safety in the schoolyard. Children have immature intentions, and we must help them mature. She will have differences of opinion with other children, but she has good friends, which is a fine start."

"I understand that, Andrew. I know perfection is not possible. After all, we both agree that is why our Lord died for us on the cross."

"Yes, that is true. It may also be prudent to brief Clare well on any possible issue resulting from the children finding out she is from a Catholic background. I will observe and do my best to protect her against unfair criticism."

"That is all I ask, Andrew. Her friends will also look out for her."

"When would you propose that she start here?"

"Andrew, I was thinking of next Monday if that is possible. That would be the twelfth of March."

Later in the morning, Miss Daisy Eltham knocked on Jonathan Turner's office door and entered.

"Mr Turner, Mr Benjamin Petherton, is in the reception. He asks if he might have a word."

"Certainly, Daisy! Please show him in. Also, would you arrange some morning tea and coffee, please? Bring it up as soon as you can."

Benjamin Petherton sat in Jonathan Turner's office a few minutes later, enjoying coffee.

"Jonathan, I understand you will attend the Fintelton wedding this Saturday?"

"Yes, Anne is the maid of honour, and Robert is the best man."

"These biscuits, Jonathan, they are fine biscuits. Are they a product of yours?"

"Yes, they are produced across the road in the bakery."

"They are tasty! Might I purchase a supply before I leave?"

"Certainly, Benjamin. I will arrange that for you, and there will be no charge."

Benjamin quickly replied, "We can arrange that later, Jonathan. There is a more important matter!"

Jonathan sat again and let Benjamin continue.

"As you will be away on Saturday, I thought I should ask you this question early in the week. I am keen that the friendship between your children, Madeline, Simeon and William, continues with Clare. I propose they stay the night at Cloverdale Chase on Saturday. That way, they could stay for dinner and play games with Clare on Saturday evening. I would have them at church on Sunday morning and return them home. It would be best if one of your staff attended in case of any sickness or incidents where a familiar face might help."

"Benjamin, by church, do you mean the Catholic church?"

"No, Jonathan, it would be at your church in the High Street. I have enrolled Clare in the church school run by the Reverend Andrew Taggart. It would further help her friendships and give her some worldly exposure."

Jonathan realised what a great sacrifice this man was making for his daughter's welfare. An appearance at the Turner's church would cause criticism from his home church.

"Benjamin, are you sure you have thought through the implications of what you are doing? Some of your congregation may not approve."

"I have Jonathan, and I have my reasons! I am intent on Clare having friendships with children from like-minded families."

"Then it shall be, Benjamin. I will have it arranged, and Mrs Nibley will accompany them."

"And I shall provide you, Jonathan, with some of my Columbia coffee. You may find the taste smoother than the blend you are using."

They both laughed. Jonathan's admiration for Benjamin Petherton was growing indeed.

The Barque 'Mistral', Entering Bristol Harbour …

Aiden Reid, wearing a long black coat, leaned on the barque's gunwale, watching as the ship was slowly towed into the docks in the middle of Bristol. He was amazed at the activity and the hundreds of people working and visiting the harbour docks. There would be no shortage of crowds in Bristol where he could disappear.

Grabbing his bag, he followed the other stowage passengers off the ship, along the quay and onto the street. He first needed an Irish pub where he could ask for directions. As he exited the dock, he carefully threaded through the crowd of people, carts and trolleys and crossed the street. It was far busier than Dublin, and not knowing exactly where he was heading, he followed the traffic.

"Hey, mate! You look a bit lost. Where are you heading?"

Aiden turned, finding a tall man in shaggy overalls with an Irish cap looking down at him. The man seemed genuine in his assistance.

"Looking for the nearest pub, man!"

"Two blocks down, mate, in the other direction and around the corner on your right. But if you are from Ireland, then you should follow me."

Aiden was not expecting these instructions and wondered who this stranger was.

"I will try the pub two blocks down."

As he moved off, another man appeared and grabbed his left arm. The first man firmly gripped his right arm and pushed him towards an alley. Aiden suddenly realised they were mugging him, but their firm grips held despite his resistance. Another man appeared and punched him hard in the stomach as they entered the alley, winding him.

Now lying on the ground, Aiden protected himself with his arms as the men kicked him hard from three directions. As he heard a police whistle and other footsteps approaching, a hard blow on his head was the last thing he remembered.

Opening his eyes sometime later, Aiden found himself on a bed with someone dabbing his forehead. He sat up in a start, pulling his fists up in defence.

The young woman beside him edged slightly away and said, "You are safe now. The police brought you here for safety. You can relax while I clean your forehead. That is a nasty cut you have there."

Aiden focused on the girl and found her smiling face comforted him, "Where am I?"

"Saint Peter's Hall near the docks. We run a mission for those needing help. Now let me bathe that cut. You will need a bandage."

Looking around, he saw several other men resting in the large room with windows looking out onto a small landing below street level. The sun was partly shining in and was warming the room.

"The local thugs mugged you. Luckily the police were nearby and scared them away before you were seriously hurt. You are not the only one! The gang has been hard at it today, and the police have brought in three others."

Aiden saw a man on the next bed, bandaged and fast asleep. He looked in a bad way.

The girl reached out with a clean wet cloth and dabbed his cut. Aiden pulled his head back, unsure of what she was doing.

"I will not hurt you. It would be best if we cleaned this up, or it may become infected. Sit still, please!"

As he focused, he noticed that she wore a nun's habit.

"You are a nun!"

"That's right. I am in training. So, sit still and let me clean this up."

Aiden relaxed, and the nun completed her work.

As the novice finished, she said, "Lunch will be in an hour. There will be some hot soup."

"Lunch! What time is it?"

"It is eleven-thirty in the morning. You were asleep for nearly three hours."

Aiden lay back down, shutting his eyes. The day was half gone – he must change his plans.

"Here is your money. The muggers missed it. You were lucky. They did not find it in the bottom of your boots."

"Thanks! Thanks for all you have done. Do you know where I can catch a Portsmouth coach?"

"Yes, but most of them leave in the morning. There is only one late at night. So, please stay here till morning, and we can direct you tomorrow. Father O'Reilly will come and see you in a minute."

"I need directions to find the coach terminal, …. please!"

The nun frowned and said, "When you go out, turn left and walk for three blocks. Turn right and go six blocks, and you will see the coach terminal. If you need accommodation overnight, there are several boarding houses nearby. But they are not safe. You would be better off staying here."

The bandaging finished, the novice collected her materials and moved off towards the back of the room. She found Father O'Reilly and talked with him, pointing towards Aiden's bunk. When she looked again, her mouth opened. The bunk was empty.

Polkinghorne Imports Building, Isle of Dogs, London …
Stephen Polkinghorne sat at his desk watching the traffic on the Thames. His attachment for Lady Clarissa steadily grew, and he could not put her out of his thoughts. Indeed, the prospect of marriage had entered his mind. He was now regretting how they had parted at the docks.

He took fright from the details she had confidentially explained about her relationship with Sir Hugh. Stephen was a little ashamed of his behaviour on the ship's arrival at Southampton, given he had continued his relationship with her until then. But perhaps he had acted in haste.

He said aloud, "Damn the woman!" He knew she had entered his heart, and he yearned for her company.

The senior clerk knocked, and half opened the door, "Mr Thurgood has arrived for his appointment, Sir. Might I bring him in?"

"A moment, please, as I must write a note. I will give you a call in a few minutes. Jephson, have a cup of coffee made for Mr Thurgood, please."

"Yes, Sir."

Stephen pulled out his ink, paper, and quill and quickly scribbled a note, folded it, and sealed it in an envelope. He then wrote the name Lady Clarissa Wendarm clearly on the front.

Rising from his desk, he opened the door and beckoned his clerk, "Jephson, have your investigator fellow find this lady. I believe she lives in Hammersmith. Then have this note delivered."

"Certainly, sir."

"Now show in, Mr Thurgood, please."

Cloverdale Chase, Guildford, Surrey …
On Wednesday afternoon Benjamin Petherton noticed the flag at the fort flying well in the breeze.

He asked, "Mrs Preston, who is at the fort?"

"Clare and the Turner children are playing together. Clare asked my permission, and I consented."

As it was near afternoon teatime, Benjamin decided on some exercise and set off for the fort.

As he approached, he heard the melee inside as the children ran around the ramparts fighting invading marauders. Wondering where they found the energy for their continually exciting games, he alerted them of his presence, ensuring he was not the recipient of one of William's accidents.

"Ahoy, castle. May a lowly citizen enter, please?"

There was a sudden silence inside the fort, and the gate opened. The children ran out and greeted him.

"Mr Petherton, we beat the invading Vikings and drove them into the North Sea."

"Well, William. You must be tired, hungry and thirsty after that. Come and have some afternoon tea."

The children cheered, and an active conversation continued until they reached the patio, where bread rolls and water were ready.

Madeline put down her bag, took a glass, and gulped down the water. The other children were just as thirsty and chose the water first. As the maid served the buttered rolls, the focus switched, and they enjoyed the aroma of the hot bread.

Simeon licked his lips as he held a roll close to his nose, "These rolls smell beautiful, Mr Petherton."

"They should, Simeon! They are fresh from the Turner bakery today."

Clare asked Madeline, "Might we tour the bakery one day? I have always wondered how they make the bread."

"I will ask my father. I think he will be pleased to arrange a tour. I like the pastries section the best. The pastry cook, Sophia, is a special lady. She always gives us a pastry."

"I like the pastries too!" shouted William with a mouth full of a buttered roll.

"Slow down, William, or you will choke!" Mr Petherton enjoyed William's enthusiasm. It reminded him of his son, Mark.

"Children! Mr Turner has accepted my invitation that you will spend Saturday night here with Clare. Please bring your favourite game, and we will have a games night after dinner."

The children cheered and started discussing which games they would bring.

"I have also invited Sophie Watson. She is a good friend of Clare and Madeline's."

Madeline picked up her bag and asked if she might use the bathroom. Mrs Preston showed her the way.

Simeon excitedly said, "That will be fun! My father and others will be away at Emma and Doctor Sopwith's wedding. So now we can have fun on Saturday night. Thank you, Mr Petherton."

"What is your favourite game, William?"

"I like checkers, but only two can play. For everybody, my favourite would be Blind Man's Bluff. I like pinning the tail on the donkey."

Benjamin Petherton was surprised at how a seven-year-old would consider what would benefit the whole group of children, "Well thought out, William. I think we will have a lot of fun. Now perhaps another half hour in the fort, and then it will be time for home."

The children were off in an instant, running up the hill.

Mr Petherton noticed that Madeline had left her bag behind. He picked it up and heard a clink as it knocked on the seat. Looking inside, he found one of his small bottles from the collection beneath a cardigan.

Mrs Preston noticed him holding the bag and said, "She is not a convincing thief, is she? I was watching Madeline inside without her knowledge. She picked up one of the bottles and hid it in her bag. I would have advised you later."

A frown came over Benjamin Petherton's face. "She is a child, Mrs Preston. Sometimes children do strange things. There must be a reason for it."

Mr Petherton had not expected such behaviour. The children's conduct had been perfect, but this act by Madeline was most concerning. Now fifty years old, Benjamin knew from experience that quickly drawing conclusions was dangerous. There may be many reasons for this behaviour, and Madeline may offer a reasonable explanation.

He returned the bottle to Madeline's bag and asked Mrs Preston if she would deliver it.

"Tell them it is time they were home, please!"

Mrs Preston looked at Mr Petherton in surprise, "Will you not reprimand her?"

"No. I will let this continue, Mrs Preston. There may be a valid reason, and we might find Madeline needs assistance. It may be simple childish jealousy driving her actions. Who knows? And Mrs Preston, please see that Clare comes directly home."

Hammersmith, London …

Lady Clarissa Wendarm was still fuming about the letter from the Earl of Fintelton's Attorneys. The Earl and Countess had refused her claim and would not entertain any visit from her. They advised that any documentary evidence she held should be made available for testing by their attorneys. They also stipulated that she must address all future correspondence to their attorney, Mr Evan Finchley of Manifold and Stout.

'We will see about that!'

Clarissa jumped up from her small breakfast table, cleared the dishes into a washbasin and ran into her bedroom. Despite feeling somewhat tired this morning, she prepared her best clothes before dressing. Lady Wendarm smiled as she considered the visit, she would pay at St James's Square.

As she was about to dress, a knock came at the door. Clarissa was not expecting anyone but decided the caller may be of importance. Putting down her makeup, she covered herself with a dressing gown and answered the door. The doorman of the unit block stood there with an envelope in his hand.

As the doorman passed her the small envelope, he said, "A message delivered for you, Lady Wendarm!" She checked the sender's address on the back of the letter, which read, Polkinghorne Imports PLC, West India Docks, Isle of Dogs. Clarissa immediately knew the message must be from Stephen. She smiled and commenced reading, turning and closing the door on the doorman's outstretched hand, ready for a tip.

Polkinghorne Imports Plc
West India Docks
Isle of Dogs, London, UK

Dear Clarissa

I apologise for not writing sooner and must explain why I departed the ship in such a hurry. Since then, my business commitments have been demanding, and it is only now that I can address this matter with the attention it deserves.

I am dining today at the Bath Hotel on Piccadilly at one in the afternoon. I understand this is short notice; however, I would enjoy your company. There is no need for a reply as I will still be dining even if you cannot attend.

I would welcome your company and hope I might explain my situation as we enjoy lunch together.

Yours sincerely
Stephen Polkinghorne

Clarissa smiled, 'Caught and bowled! – Well done, Clarissa!'

The Grand Hotel, Kingston, Jamaica …

Fiona Green sat at her desk with a quill pen, carefully considering the best information she could provide Sir Hugh's mother. She had no intention of alarming the countess by setting out the details of the near-fatal illness but decided to send encouraging comments advising of Sir Hugh's recovery.

She recalled what she had written in her last letter sent with Lady Wendarm and would update all the information for the countess. Fiona felt sure that Clarissa would have delivered the first letter by now. The countess must be greatly concerned, and who would blame her? A mother was always deeply concerned for her children. She slowly laboured on with the letter searching for encouraging words for his mother.

The Grand Hotel
Kingston, Jamaica

The Right Honourable, The Countess of Fintelton
'Harting'
St James's Square
London

7 March 1827

Dear Lady Fintelton,

Please find an update on my previous letter sent via Lady Clarissa Wendarm in early February. I am pleased that I may report Sir Hugh has survived the crisis in the disease that struck him down and is making a slow but steady recovery.

Sir Hugh spent over a month bedridden from the latest attack of his disease and lost much weight and strength in his muscles. His physician, Doctor Ronald Cowper, has provided excellent care for your son and calls regularly.

Our priority is now the strengthening of Sir Hugh's body. We replicated a machine one of my aunts used that appears as two tea chests joined together. The gadget is positioned in an upright manner and provides support for Sir Hugh while standing. It has worked well, and I report that Sir Hugh is now standing for considerable periods and has commenced taking one or two steps at a time.

Given his continuing improvement, I have booked passage with him on a packet sailing from Kingston, departing here on the first of May. I understand the standard voyage time is four weeks, so we should arrive in Southampton near Tuesday, the twenty-ninth of May.

By coincidence, Doctor Cowper has finished his contract here in Kingston and will return with us on the same voyage. He has volunteered his continued care of Sir Hugh while we all travel home. By the time we reach England's shores, I hope your son will have made a recovery allowing his full mobility.

Sir Hugh has asked if Doctor Cowper and I might visit you on our return. We propose spending two days with you, allowing Dr Cowper enough time to hand over your son's care. He assumes you have a local doctor and asks that he may be present for a briefing.

Kingston, Jamaica is far distant, and I understand a reply in time before we depart Kingston will not be possible. If Doctor Cowper and my attendances at Fintelton are inconvenient, we will easily find accommodation nearby in Petersfield. After visiting you, I will depart Fintelton and head for my estate in Bedfordshire. Dr Cowper intends to stay with his family in Cornwall before leaving for a contract at Sydney Cove.

Please keep us in your prayers during the Atlantic voyage as we return your son. I wish you the best and hope we make your acquaintance towards the end of May this year.

With kindest regards
Lady Fiona Green

Fiona took the letter and placed it in an envelope. She dressed and left for the post office, ensuring she mailed it today.

The Bath Hotel [27], Piccadilly, London …

Clarissa mentioned her name at the restaurant entry and asked for Mr Stephen Polkinghorne. The waiter immediately led her away through the tables. As they approached, Stephen caught a glimpse of her and stood giving a wave.

"Lady Clarissa, please have a seat!" Stephen kissed Clarissa on the cheek and remained standing as the waiter assisted her with the chair.

"I am glad you came. You look so beautiful. Being back in London must agree with you?"

Clarissa was in no mood for the delay and focused directly on the point. She said in a low but firm tone, "Stephen, I was most embarrassed by how you deserted me at the docks. During the voyage, I expected from your intentions that we would have come ashore together and continued our relationship. What must I think, Stephen? What must I think?"

Stephen swallowed backwards and realised this conversation would not be easy. Yet, he desired peace with Clarissa and wanted her back in his life.

"I must apologise for my actions, Clarissa. Your revelations were somewhat overwhelming as we approached England, and I needed time to understand them. At first, I must admit that I could not assist you with the issues. Yet, I now understand that I was wrong. Nevertheless, my intentions have not changed, and if you accept a humble dinner with me, I will explain as best as I may."

"I will accept dinner, but I might not accept your apology until I am convinced of your goodwill."

Clarissa could see from his comments that he was desperate for her love. She decided that a show of hurt and anger would achieve her aims with him. Holding out and letting the man squirm before she capitulated would be best. But Stephen was wary, realising that Clarissa was manipulating him. Lady Wendarm had underestimated Stephen Polkinghorne, a man with a good heart and a significant amount of wisdom.

"Clarissa, you may be assured of my goodwill. That is why I am here today. Now shall we order, and then we can talk."

Clarissa relaxed slightly and focused on the menu as the waiter explained the different choices.

During the meal, Stephen said, "Now tell me, Clarissa, the details you advised me about on the ship. Was that all that you intended to tell me?"

---

[27] The Ritz, London, was built on the site which had been first the Old White Horse Cellar, also known as Hatchetts' White Horse Cellar. Hatchetts moved across the road facilitating the building of the Bath Hotel on that site. This in turn was sold to the financial backers of the Ritz in 1902. The financial backers of the Ritz felt that they had secured one of the prime sites in London for their project. Wikipedia.

"What do you mean, Stephen."

"If we both seek a future together, I must know what transpired between you and Sir Hugh and why a devoted wife would leave him a day before he died."

"I have already told you. There is no more. I have said it all."

"Then I shall take that at face value and not ask again. However, I think it will be an uphill battle convincing the Earl of Fintelton that you are now one of his family."

"It will be no problem as I have a certificate of marriage. So that will carry the day, and my baby, if it is a son, will be the next Earl."

"How far are you advanced in the pregnancy, Clarissa?"

"Three months. It is now showing."

"You hide it well. I was impressed with your figure as you entered."

"Thank you. I will take that as a compliment, as I have always found you genuine. Now, as we have re-established our relationship, there is something that you might assist me with."

"What would that be, Clarissa?"

"After lunch, we might travel in your carriage and visit the Earl's close-by residence in St James's Square, where I will call upon them."

Stephen Polkinghorne was highly sceptical that Clarissa's marriage certificate was genuine but refrained from inflaming the conversation. The thought entered his mind that she might be delusional.

"Of course. Consider it done."

"Thank you, Stephen. That is most considerate of you."

Around three-thirty, the carriage arrived in front of 'Harting', and Clarissa and Stephen, standing at the front entrance, knocked.

There was a slight delay, and then a butler opened the door, stood blocking the entrance, and asked, "May I be of assistance?" Matthew Staines was not tall, but he stood five feet eleven inches in height and was reasonably muscular. He appeared as a brick wall in front of Clarissa.

"I am Lady Clarissa South, widow of the late Sir Hugh South, and this is my friend, Mr Stephen Polkinghorne of Mayfair. Please let us enter as I must talk with the Countess of Fintelton."

Staines looked down at Clarissa with a sneer and politely said, "I am afraid, Madam, that I am not aware of the recent passing of Sir Hugh. The countess informed me that Lady Clarissa Wendarm might call. I presume you are Lady Wendarm?"

"Yes, that was my name before my marriage."

"The countess instructed me that this story of your being the wife of Sir Hugh is a fraud and that she sent you a letter instructing that all further communication between you and the family must be via the Earl's attorneys,

Manifold and Stout. You will find their offices at Cursitor Street off Chancery Lane. I apologise that I may not allow you entry, and you will understand that I must obey my employer's instructions."

Enraged by this comment from a man of lower station, Clarissa retorted, "Now, hear this, my good man! I have every right of entry into this …"

Stephen, seeing the situation becoming embarrassing, intervened, "Lady Clarissa! I think it may be advisable if we depart."

Clarissa stood there with her mouth open and now fuming.

Stephen, avoiding any further embarrassment, said, "Thank you, my good man. Sorry, we bothered your afternoon. We will depart now."

Matthew Staines gave Mr Polkinghorne a smile of thanks and slowly closed the door when Clarissa broke free of Stephen's restraint and pushed the door open, rushing Staines and attacking him. The butler, stepping backwards in complete surprise, used all his strength, pushing Lady Clarissa back out of the doorway. Before he could manage it, she bit him on the arm and flew at him, clawing his face with both hands. Overcome by the unexpected naked aggression, Staines retreated as the Lady entered the mansion.

"Now, Mr Butler, where is the countess? I must see her!"

"Madam, I must ask that you leave at once, or I will have no alternative but to call on the police."

Lady Clarissa started laughing and commenced a search of the ground floor rooms.

"Please, Lady Clarissa, the family is not here. They are at Fintelton Estate in Sussex."

Stephen knocked and entered, "Butler, what pray is your name?"

"Matthew Staines, Sir!"

"Staines, my apologies for Lady Clarissa's behaviour. Let me take care of this. I will remove her now!"

"Thank you, Mr Polkinghorne."

Stephen saw Clarissa returning after barging into every room on the ground floor. Polkinghorne quickly moved across the stairway and grabbed her around the waist as she eyed the stairway. In a surprise move, he carried the struggling and kicking woman through the front door and placed her into the carriage. Clarissa was yelling at him, "What are you doing, Stephen? What are you doing?"

"I am saving what small amount of reputation you have left, my dear!"

With that, he tapped the roof, and the carriage was quickly underway.

Staines stood at the front door with a resentful expression. He was sure the lady was mad and that she would now attempt to interrupt the wedding at Petersfield. He must warn the family before Lady Clarissa caused any more damage.

"You had no right touching me, Stephen. How dare you! Did you see the wealth these people enjoy? It was a magnificent house, and that was just their townhouse. They owe me, Stephen! They owe me a living as their daughter-in-law."

Stephen was amazed at what was coming out of Clarissa's mouth. Rather than argue, he would let her settle down and call for a doctor. A tranquilliser and some sleep would do her the world of good. But, if her claims were valid, there was a process that she must follow, which would take some time. It appeared that Clarissa had no adviser or family except Fiona Green, who she had left in Kingston.

"Clarissa, do you have family in London?"

"I see! You will now get rid of me again?"

"No, not at all, but I thought since you returned, you might have sought some advice from your family."

"Fiona Green is the only family member who speaks with me now. As you know, she is in Kingston."

"If that is the case, you must calm down, and we will discuss your situation tonight. You are not approaching these people in a way that will be successful. So, I will take you home, and you may pack and then visit my house at Mayfair for dinner. We will then talk about how we should manage this process. If your health is sufficient tomorrow, we must write and apologise to the family. When the Earl hears of your behaviour, he will have the police involved. Where do you live?"

"Hammersmith!"

Stephen tapped the roof of the carriage. The driver quickly turned and waited for instructions.

"Hammersmith, please. I will provide more instruction once we are near."

Clarissa felt the rage leaving her body. She would enjoy a stay at Stephen's home. Her anger had somewhat dissipated, and a smile came across her face.

"Thank you, Stephen. That shall be quite pleasant."

Stephen nodded and thought about how he would convince Clarissa of the need for a medical examination. Given her delicate condition, she would not refuse some care to assist her baby. The doctor could provide some potions that would make her sleep tonight. As they travelled, Stephen thought, 'Tomorrow will be an interesting day!'

Chapter 18

The Polkinghorne Residence, Mayfair, London ...
Stephen Polkinghorne entered his drawing room and found the waiting doctor sipping tea. Putting his cup down, he stood as Stephen approached.

"Well, Doctor Arrowsmith, what did you find?"

"You were correct, Sir. The lady is suffering from hypertension. I gave her some strong potions to make her sleep well into tomorrow. She will not rise until the afternoon."

"Was an examination carried out?"

"Yes! I asked if I might assist with her health and make an examination. She agreed and advised me that she felt tight in the chest and had some congestion. She also complained of extreme tiredness. However, I found another issue of concern. Might we both sit, Sir, as we discuss this?"

Stephen nodded, and they sat at a coffee table near the fireplace. The butler entered and asked if Mr Polkinghorne would like some tea, "Yes, thanks, Nottle."

"Sir, I am not sure what your relationship is with this lady, but I assume you support her?"

"That is correct, Doctor." Stephen felt he should explain the nature of their relationship. "Her family is all gone, and the only close relative is presently in Kingston, Jamaica and will not return for at least a month or two. I met her in Jamaica, where we formed a friendship. We travelled back on the same ship. So, I have taken on that responsibility."

The Doctor took a deep breath and continued, "Mr Polkinghorne, I did not proceed far when it became clear that the lady has the advanced stages of the French pox.[28] I will explain this carefully."

Stephen sat back with a look of horror on his face. The doctor understood he would need a full explanation of this tragic diagnosis.

---

[28] Syphilis.

"Are you sure, Doctor?"

"Yes, one hundred per cent sure. The Lady covers up her rash very well with her powders, and the wig hides the hair loss that has started. But, as I said before, she is at an advanced stage, which means she has been infected for many years."

The Doctor paused as if thinking profoundly but said, "Mr Polkinghorne, pardon me for asking this, but if by chance you have had sexual relations with this woman, then I would recommend an urgent medical examination."

"Thankfully, there is no need for that, Doctor. I have been very prudent in that area."

"That is a relief. I would say that the stress of the disease has caused some of the delusional activities that have taken place. Also, she may not know she has contracted the disease, although I highly doubt it. If she continues without medical help, death will follow within a month."

"The disease is that advanced?"

"Yes! There is a mercury ointment that will assist, but I recommend employing a nurse for its application. A patient without a carer usually does not use it. The ointment may help, but there is no cure. She will soon die. I am sorry, but you must be made aware of the danger."

"This has come as a great shock, Doctor. What should I expect in the weeks ahead?"

"I would suggest that Lady Wendarm will lapse now into fever and extreme tiredness for some time. There will be a crisis; if she survives, she may live on for many months before another crisis hits. However, I doubt that she would survive another crisis in her frail state."

"And the baby?"

"There is no baby, Sir! That also must be a delusion she has convinced herself of."

"Or concocted for a reason!" Stephen was becoming more disappointed in Clarissa.

The doctor stood, pulled out a jar of ointment labelled mercury, and passed it over.

"I will call again in the morning. Might I arrange a nurse for Lady Clarissa?"

"Yes, that would be appreciated, Doctor. Thank you for your service and advice. It is most appreciated despite the diagnosis. Oh, doctor! Is travel out of the question?"

"Yes, she must rest. If Lady Wendarm makes a recovery, it may be possible!"

With that, Stephen walked with the doctor and wished him a good night at the front door.

As he returned and sat in the drawing room, he considered what he should do now. He had no information about her relatives or when Fiona Green was returning. He was now heavily involved with a woman who had trespassed into an Earl's property and insulted Lord Fintelton most irresponsibly. At least the police would not know where she was. But they would! The butler, Staines, had his name. So, the police will probably arrive tomorrow.

Stephen sighed. He was ready for dinner and a quiet night. He wondered what would have happened if he had not lunched with Clarissa. She probably would have died alone at her Hammersmith flat. There was now no alternative, and she desperately needed help. He would keep her comfortable until the end.

Sitting alone eating his dinner, he weighed up the best ways of diffusing this situation. An apology letter must explain the situation and suggest a meeting with the Earl and Countess. Perhaps, he should first seek an appointment with their attorneys. What was the name the butler had mentioned? 'Manifold and Stout'- that was it!

'Harting' St James's Square, London …

In the early hours of Saturday morning, Matthew Staines put on his coat and opened the front door.

"Mrs Falconer, no visitors should gain entry in the next week, and you may bring in any supplies through the back lane. Please keep the front door locked. I should be back from Fintelton by next Tuesday. Make sure all the staff understand that no one may answer or open the front door until I return."

"Yes, Sir. I will ensure it is kept shut."

"No! Locked Mrs Falconer."

"Yes, Mr Staines."

Matthew Staines rushed down the front steps and into a waiting carriage, whisking him away towards Fintelton Estate.

The 'Red Dear' Hotel, Petersfield …

Anne rolled over and noticed Robert was fast asleep. She would allow him another hour as he needed sleep after David's bucks party. Quietly hopping up, Anne put on her dressing gown and entered the hallway. On reaching Emma's room, she knocked. The hotel's top floor was reserved for the family, and there was no movement in the corridor.

Soon after the gentle knock, Emma, fully awake and in a dressing gown, opened the door.

"I thought you might be awake."

"I did not sleep well, Anne, with all these issues happening and my going away for six weeks. I must tell my mother about the financial state of the estate. She must know."

"Yes, Emma, but leave that with me. Today is your day, and you may forget about all that until you return. I will spend some time with your parents while you, David and Robert are away and keep an eye on them. So, they will be safe."

"Anne, you are so thoughtful. You are the sister I always wanted, and God has blessed our family with you."

Anne smiled, "You might also give Robert a bit of credit!"

"Yes, of course." They both giggled.

"Now, Lady Emma, are you ready for your name change today?"

"I have never been more ready."

"Good, as we must start the preparations. I take it you have ordered a room service breakfast for us."

"I forgot!"

Anne smiled, understanding Emma had many things on her mind today.

"There is plenty of time. I will go downstairs and arrange it. You wash and slip into a comfortable dress. Meredith and Lily will arrive at eight, so we can easily be ready by then. I will be back in five minutes." Anne opened the door, rushed back along the hall, and wore a respectable dress before going downstairs and ordering breakfast.

Later as the girls ate together, someone knocked at the door. Emma jumped up and answered.

A young lady staff member in a pristine uniform said, "Lady Emma, a message for you."

"Thank you."

Emma took the message and closed the door. Intently reading, she looked up at Anne with a smile, "It is from David. It is for both you and me. Here, you have a look." She passed the message across.

Dear Emma

I know it is bad luck on the day of the wedding to see the bride before the service, so I thought I should write a quick note. Please, share this with Anne as well.

By the time you receive this letter, I know you will be busily preparing for the wedding. So, I will be quick.

Yesterday I deposited ten thousand pounds into the Fintelton Estates bank account. My reason for doing so is I am sure we will not solve this situation until after Sir Hugh returns. That said, I did not want you, or Anne worried about the estate finances while we were away. With the existing balance and this extra deposit, the bank will not question the stability of the estate.

It will also provide Staines or Pike with petty cash if they must send an urgent message. Ha, Ha! Not likely while we are in Europe and Ireland.

So let us enjoy the day. I love you dearly and will wait for you at the end of the aisle!

All my love.
David

Anne took a deep breath.

"You are marrying the right man, Emma! Imagine him doing that and telling you on your wedding day, setting your mind at rest. I think he deserves an extra kiss tonight."

"I know, and he will receive it!"

Cloverdale Chase, Guildford, Surrey ...

William laughed as the other children turned him around and around. Even with a blindfold, he found he was steady as he reached out like a blind man feeling for the paper sheet with the donkey's outline. The girls stood aside as William carefully felt out in front of him. Simeon could see that he was now wildly off track and nudged him in the right direction.

"Thanks!"

He moved forwards and finally touched the sheet of paper showing the donkey. Stepping closer, he felt the paper's edges and deduced where the tail should go. Then, with force, he pushed the pin through the paper and into the cushion behind.

Everyone clapped, including Mrs Preston, impressed with how William found the correct position.

"Well done, William!"

Mr Petherton removed the blindfold, and William saw he had pinned the tail halfway down the donkey's back. "You were closer than the girls and nearly hit the right spot." William, pleased with his performance, wondered how Simeon would go.

His older brother was now being spun and looked slightly giddy as he tried standing still. At first, he put his hands out as far as they could reach and felt around him. Then, Simeon's hand touched something soft that went, 'Ow!'.

"That is Clare?"

"No, it is not!" Sophie giggled.

Simeon stood there for a second and then said, "Sophie?"

"Yes."

He thought about where Sophie stood and walked around her towards the doorway. There was much laughter until Mr Petherton brought him back in front of the Donkey.

Simeon reached out and felt the paper, "Ah, here it is."

Slowly he put his hand up and pinned the tail on the donkey's belly.

"Well done, Simeon! Nearly as close as William."

After finishing the game, Mr Petherton gathered the children around him and addressed the issue of the mislaid bottles.

"Children, I have discovered that some of my bottles are missing, and I can't find them?"

William asked, "Which ones are they, Mr Petherton? We could mount a search."

"There is no need for a search, William. I have already had that done. Perhaps one of you might have seen them somewhere and could help me?"

There was no response from the children.

"Well, thank you, children. Now, I think Mrs Preston has another game for you. It involves making up funny words. Off you go."

Mr Petherton ensured that Madeline knew he was aware the bottles were gone. Perhaps they would mysteriously reappear, but he knew this would take time. Nevertheless, he was hopeful of resolving the situation without needing confrontation.

The 'Red Dear' Hotel, Petersfield …

The Countess and the Earl could not have wished for a better wedding for their daughter. The church had been full of friends and relatives, the weather fine, and the bridal party was glamorous. The reception had gone well with superb food and much happy banter as the Earl, the groom, and selected guests gave traditional speeches.

Towards the end of the reception, Robert sat with Admiral Crouch at the far end of the room.

"We should talk now, Robert, as with the situation in the eastern Med hotting up and you off on your mission next Saturday, we may not have another opportunity. I have some more intelligence concerning your Irish visit. Unfortunately, the news is not good!

We are now sure of an assassination attempt either in Dublin or Belfast. It seems the nationalists are keen on setting an example of what they can achieve. We are unaware of who the target is, but the game is on. Colonel Scott will be planning for heavy security at each banquet location. The Irish will count on gaining the maximum publicity from disrupting a public event.

These dinners will become complex functions, so Scott will need as much assistance as you and Coombes can provide. Be careful, Robert, and ensure you and the major protect yourselves!"

"We will handle it, Sir. We have beaten them before, and we shall do it again."

"Good! I was never happy with this Irish mission. The politicians think they can help a people who hate us. As I said some time ago, this Republican movement will not stop until the country has independence. The problem is the ascendancy, which creates the turmoil that we see. What about you, Robert? Your father has an estate in Ireland. How do you feel about the plight of the Irish?"

"My father has never explained the details of the estates we own. So, as my elder brother, Sir Hugh, will become the next Earl, I have never considered it. This mission and my previous one has interested me in the Irish. From my Christian beliefs, I understand our Lord would expect that we care for the poor. If the Irish are unfairly treated, then we must remedy that. However, I am unaware of the facts and will take an interest in the mission's aims and findings."

"Robert, I think you will make a good contribution but take care. The politicians want the glory. If you make suggestions, it must be carefully done so they consider it their idea. They will not appreciate anyone else taking credit for the mission outcomes."

"I understand this, Sir. I think I can manage it."

Robert felt he could trust the Admiral and asked, "Admiral Crouch, have you considered what we discussed previously at dinner about Foster and Hughes's orders?"

Admiral Crouch looked at Robert strangely, and then some recognition came across his face. He checked the room, ensuring no one was within hearing distance.

"I think your suggestions were well thought out, Robert and have merit. However, even I understand where this takes us may be forbidden territory. It may be best if we say little of it at present. The Irish situation continues to unsettle the ascendancy, who reject the proposition of an independent Ireland. They fear losing their landholdings. Your father may agree. So, the government must deal with various stakeholders on this matter. Take my advice and tread carefully and learn from what you see. If there is an internal problem, we shall solve it in time."

"Thank you for the advice, Admiral. In the event of personal conversations, have you any advice on who may be trusted?"

Admiral Crouch took a deep breath and looked around again.

"A difficult question, Robert. All I can say is that from my experience, trust no one, especially politicians and their advisors. If you put yourself out on a limb, they will think nothing of cutting the branch off!"

"Thank you, Sir. I see that this will be a challenging mission."

"Robert, now you will understand why I was content with your appointment. Bring them all back in one piece, please."

They both smiled and shook hands.

"Take care, Robert! There are some murky waters ahead!"

Joining the conversation, Lady Katherine Crouch advised, "Excuse me, Sir Robert, and your Lordship. It is time you both ended this private discussion as His Lordship and you, must be ready for the farewell festivities."

Admiral Crouch welcomed his wife's interruption, "You are correct, my dear. We have finished! Robert, off you go and look after Lady Anne. She is a picture tonight. I am sure she will welcome your attention."

"Oh, yes, Robert. She was beautiful in the bridal procession. I am so glad that you found her."

"Thank you, Lady Katherine. I shall willingly take your advice."

Fintelton Estate, Sussex …

As the light faded late Saturday afternoon, an unexpected coach arrived with a single passenger. He opened the coach door without waiting for a footman and carried his bag up the steps.

Matthew Staines knocked on one of the solid wood front doors. The Fintelton butler, Thomas Pike, soon answered and asked, "May I be of assistance, Sir."

"Yes! I am Mr Matthew Staines, the Earl's butler from 'Harting' at St James's Square. My apologies for coming unannounced, and I understand we have never met before, but I presume you are Mr Thomas Pike, the butler here?"

"That I am, Mr Staines. How can I be of assistance?"

"I have some urgent information regarding Sir Hugh that I must discuss with the Earl, Countess, and Sir Robert. The information will probably also affect you, Mr Pike. I understand that His Lordship and the Countess are attending Lady Emma's wedding reception but will return tomorrow. So, I must meet them in the morning and promptly return to London with their instructions. I will need a room in the servant's quarters tonight, please."

"Mr Staines, you are welcome. Come this way, and we shall arrange a room for you. You are in time for the staff dinner!"

Local Church, Guildford …

The service of Holy Communion had reached the time for the sermon, but today Andrew Taggart had another priority for the congregation. He and Laura had rushed away from the wedding reception at Petersfield soon after the speeches finished. The Rector had decided it was essential he should return home for the Sunday morning service. So, they had travelled at night, arriving in Guildford in the early morning hours.

"Good morning, everyone. We have a special occasion this morning as I have the pleasure of introducing our new Curate. The Reverend Philip

Hotspur has joined our team as Assistant Curate and will be heavily involved in the church school and many other ministries. Mr Hotspur joins us from London, and this is his first appointment outside the city.

Would you please welcome the Reverend Philip Hotspur?"

The congregation was surprised, but there was a gentle round of applause for the new staff member.

Following the service, the mayor's wife, Mrs Marjorie Smith, invited several folks, including Mr Hotspur, for lunch. The Assistant Curate was more than willing and readily accepted the invitation as he was sure Mrs Smith might assist him with his inquiries.

"I hope you are enjoying our little country town, Mr Hotspur?"

"It is far from little, Mrs Smith. The town is growing, and business is brisk. I am enjoying the warm fellowship of the congregation as it is far more friendly than London."

"Wonderful, Mr Hotspur. Please, let me introduce some of the guests."

The Reverend Philip Hotspur carefully sought out the ladies of note in the congregation as he understood their influence and the generosity of their future patronage. He was not disappointed as the ladies attending were all wives of notable men in the town. His prime objective was eliciting future invitations where he could assess eligible young women as future spouse material. His previous betrothal now ended, leaving him in new territory seeking a favourable match for himself.

"Mrs Smith, if I may be so bold, I would ask you about some of the younger women in our congregation. I am keen on making their acquaintance as well. I did notice several young ladies this morning but missed the opportunity of an introduction."

"I understand! You are of eligible age, Mr Hotspur, and you need a fine wife. I am sure many young ladies here would be most interested in an introduction. Let me arrange a morning tea and invite some. Would that be appropriate?"

"You are most kind, Mrs Smith. That is an excellent offer, and I would certainly attend. Now, if you would excuse me, I must discuss some issues of importance with your fine husband, the mayor."

Philip Hotspur gave a slight bow and drifted away towards a group of men surrounding the mayor.

Marjorie Smith was delighted that this young man, a newcomer in their town, would empower her to organise a morning tea for the young women in Guildford. Charmed and honoured, she excitedly gathered some friends and began planning.

Seeing a lapse in the men's conversation, the Reverend Hotspur took his opportunity, "Mr Mayor, your grace, I wonder if you would do me the honour of providing some advice?"

"Certainly, Mr Hotspur. How may I assist?"

"As you know, Sir. I will be most involved with the church school here. The problem facing us is the rising number of students and the current space available for them at the school. The church needs funds to purchase land and construct a purpose-built school. Surely, we must leave no stone unturned to provide our students with excellent accommodation?"

"Of course, of course! I agree wholeheartedly, Sir. We must form a committee!"

"That is correct, Sir, and I shall put forward the proposal at the next Parish council meeting. I am sure, Sir, that our Rector will suggest you as the committee chair."

Rupert Smith was already puffing up his chest, seeing the political benefits of being on such a committee. The smile on his face broadened as Philip suggested that Rupert should be the Chairman.

"Please advise me, Mr Chairman!" They both chuckled at the suggestion. "Are there any great families in our parish? Let me be more specific, families with the financial resources who would make significant contributions towards the land and building."

"Certainly, Sir. We have many business families in our town who would willingly help. Let me consider this, and I will give you a list. See me at my office on Wednesday, and I will have it ready for you. Of course, please keep the list confidential!"

"Of course, Sir. I appreciate your support of such a worthy project."

As the new assistant curate walked home after lunch, he was satisfied with his morning's work. Next, the mayor's wife would gather the eligible young women for his inspection, and the mayor would provide a list of the town's wealthy families. He would then narrow his focus onto the young ladies with a large dowry and the prospect of a reasonably sized inheritance. He smiled as he lifted his hat, acknowledging a family he had met earlier at the morning service. Perhaps it was now time for some relaxation before attending Evensong tonight.

Fintelton Manor, Outside Petersfield …

The family had attended church in Petersfield and farewelled David and Emma on their honeymoon before returning to Fintelton for lunch. The Earl was tired when they reached the estate and was keen on an early lunch before the prospect of a quiet afternoon nap in his bedroom.

On arriving, Lord and Lady Fintelton were somewhat surprised by the sudden appearance of their butler from 'Harting' in London.

"Staines, this is a pleasant surprise, but what brings you here?"

"Your Lordship and Lady Fintelton, I bring urgent news on Lady Clarissa Wendarm, who suggests she is now one of the family. It might be best to discuss this with Sir Robert and Lady South, who are arriving. It would also be preferable if Mr Pike joined us."

"Certainly, Staines. Pike, please have Sir Robert and Lady South attend."

Within a few minutes, all were present, and Staines began.

"I am afraid that Lady Clarissa arrived at 'Harting' on Friday afternoon and forcibly staked her claim. A gentleman by the name of Mr Stephen Polkinghorne accompanied her. Unfortunately, the lady somewhat lacks in manners."

Lord Fintelton said, "Oh dear!"

"The Lady introduced herself as Lady Clarissa South and demanded entry. I explained that there would be no entry and she must send all correspondence via your attorneys. She did not accept this and became very loud and brash with her protests.

I noticed Mr Polkinghorne was shocked by her behaviour and stood well back.

As I was closing the door, she attacked me. You will notice the scratch marks on my face. She forced her way through and began searching the rooms on the ground floor."

Lady Fintelton was appalled, "My goodness! Lord Fintelton, this is trespass and assault. We must call in the police!"

The Earl nodded in agreement but was in no rush and asked, "My dear, let us hear out Staines, as he has come a long way, and I feel he has more information for us."

"Thank you, my Lord. There is an interesting outcome. This gentleman who accompanied her is of sound mind and good manners, and he entered and apologised for her behaviour and then forcibly removed her from the premises. She screamed at him, 'What are you doing, Stephen?' I heard him reply, 'Preserving what remains of your respectability, Lady Clarissa.' I think it may be worthwhile initiating discussions with this gentleman. He is on a first-name basis with Lady Wendarm. It might be that he was in Jamaica and has information we are unaware of about Sir Hugh. He appeared as Lady Wendarm 's protector and was in disbelief at the rude behaviour."

On Staines completing his report of events, there was silence among the group.

Robert broke the silence, "I think you have acted most appropriately, Staines and thank you for travelling down and for your advice. The account given is most helpful. Let us as a family discuss these developments, and I will give you directions later in the afternoon. I take it you have quarters here?"

"Yes, Mr Pike has been most helpful, Sir."

"Thank you, Pike. If you would excuse us, please."

"I shall wait downstairs in the servant quarters, Sir Robert. I have instructed the maid at 'Harting' that the front door remain locked while I am away. I considered calling the police but thought it more appropriate to consult your Lordship and Lady Fintelton first. Thank you, Sir."

With that, Staines and Pike both left the room, Pike leading the way.

Robert smiled and said, "My goodness, it must have been an event. The poor chap was quite rattled by it and the scratches on his face. My admiration for Staines has grown as he has stood up for the family well."

Anne asked, "Robert, I was interested in what Staines said about the gentleman, Mr Stephen …"

"Polkinghorne!"

"Yes, Staines may be making a strategic point here. If this gentleman is the protector of Lady Clarissa, he may tell us far more than we know now. He may have news if he also returned with her from Jamaica. It is worth a try."

Lord and Lady Fintelton listened with interest, and then Lady Fintelton said, "This woman has broken into my home, insulted our family and assaulted our butler. If she is of the upper class, she has been most remiss and appears desperate. Her behaviour indicates a sickness of the mind. Perhaps this Mr Polkinghorne is far more than a minder. I agree with Staines that some discussion should take place but in a safe environment and with the prior knowledge of our attorneys."

The Earl muttered, "Throw her to the dogs, I say. The damn cheek of the woman. Breaking into our house and assaulting our butler. Damn cheek!"

Anne sat there thinking, and Robert could see a comment coming.

"Your Lordship and Lady Fintelton, might I make a suggestion?"

The Earl looked at his daughter-in-law and smiled, "Of course, my Dear."

"I understand the hurt you must be feeling from what Staines has told us. Also, Lady Wendarm's breaking the news of the possible passing of your son in a most disturbing and uncaring manner. I, myself, do not believe there is any truth in the tale and will wait for the advice from the Governor."

She took a long breath.

"I will visit London soon for the trial of the arsonists captured at my father's mill. Perhaps while I am there, I could discuss this with Mr Stephen Polkinghorne. It is two and a half weeks until that date, so we might contact the attorneys in advance. It would also be advisable if someone accompanied me, ensuring respectability."

Lady Jane volunteered immediately, "That is a fine suggestion Anne, and I will most certainly join you."

Robert, looking concerned, questioned, "But Mother, if you are there, we defeat the purpose of keeping our distance from this woman."

"Oh, fiddle-faddle, Robert! I must support Anne."

The Earl could see the error in Lady Jane's suggestion, "My dear Jane. I think Robert has a point. There is no rush, and this meeting will be less confrontational if you are not there. Now, Anne, did you have someone in mind?"

"Yes, my Lord. I might ask Victoria Sopwith if this meets your approval?"

River Wey, Guildford, Surrey ...

The children were immersed in the pirate fight as Ethel and Mr Petherton watched with interest. Despite being early spring, it was still a cool day, and Benjamin Petherton thanked Ethel for the cup of hot soup she offered him.

"You are most capable, Mrs Nibley, providing hot soup on a day like this."

"Thank you, Mr Petherton. My husband was in the army, and we often went camping. He taught me, with minimum equipment, how hot soup was possible at a picnic. There is a rug here if you care for a seat while you enjoy the soup."

"Mrs Nibley, you think of everything. It will be a pleasure sitting with you. I hear William often becomes overexcited in pirate games, and accidents occur."

"Yes, he is a free spirit and loses concentration at times. I was told that once, he was running directly at the Countess of Fintelton with a stick twirling. Lady Fintelton has a strong voice indeed and stopped him in his tracks. A strong rebuff will have the desired effect if he advances with signs of danger."

Benjamin Petherton laughed at the thought, "You have a sound understanding of Mr Turner's children. What about your child and your husband? They must miss you, as you are in service."

"My husband is dead, Sir. He died of the consumption. Rosalind visits often and lives with my mother on Southampton Road, slightly out of town. Mr and Mrs Turner were most kind and welcomed Rosalind."

"My apologies, Mrs Nibley. I was unaware of your situation."

"There is no need, Mr Petherton. You were not to know. It is many years since Andrew died, and I have accepted it."

Benjamin nodded as he recalled his grief at the passing of his wife. He quickly realised that this woman had gone into service after losing her husband and was now her family's primary breadwinner.

"Mrs Nibley, while the children are playing, I must say ... It pleases me seeing Clare enjoying herself so energetically. Please understand that I would not be opposed if Clare and Rosalind strike up a friendship."

"Thank you, Mr Petherton."

"Now, as I was saying, there is a subject we must discuss."

Ethel wondered what Mr Petherton would say.

"Mrs Nibley, as you know, the Turner children and Sophie Watson often visit my house for entertainment. The friendship with Clare has been highly desirable, and I believe she has grown in maturity. There is one difficulty. That being, some of my bottle collection has disappeared."

"Oh!"

"The bottles are insignificant, and I am not upset at the disappearance. However, it would be best if we solved the problem. I think it might be one of the children, and there may be a reason for it happening. Clare's governess, Mrs Preston, has identified Madeline as the culprit."

"Did she catch Madeline in the process?"

"She was watching unnoticed and witnessed Madeline picking up a bottle, wrapping it with a cloth and depositing it in her bag."

"Oh! I must apologise, Mr Petherton. This behaviour is not what we expect of her. She is usually gentle and most helpful around the house."

"I agree, Mrs Nibley. I have found her the same, and I struggle to understand why she would do this or what may influence her. There will be a valid reason, and if we can discover that, we might assist her in changing the course of action she follows."

"Mr Petherton, you are most generous in your outlook. If we could work together, we may identify the cause."

"My thoughts exactly, Mrs Nibley. I must discuss it with Mr Turner, but I understand he is away at a wedding."

"Yes, we expect him home tonight. But Mr Petherton, might I ask that Mr Turner might not hear of this yet, please?"

Benjamin Petherton found this comment surprising and looked at Ethel, waiting for an explanation.

"It is that Mr Turner has struggled with a rage problem and has only now found a way of controlling it. A suggestion that one of his children is stealing might set off another bout, and the child in question may suffer greatly. It would be best if you allowed me time, and I will search for the bottles and talk quietly with Madeline."

"Would not Mr Turner feel that I was going behind his back?"

"Not if he was not aware!"

"He is the children's father, and we should not hide Madeline's behaviour from him."

"I agree, but he soon embarks on travel with his friend for four weeks. Mr McPherson takes him on his ship, and they visit Scotland. It would be disappointing if he set off with this in his mind. He has suffered greatly from losing his wife and needs recovery time. I feel the trip will be of great benefit to him."

Mr Petherton sat there silently for some time, watching the children play. He considered carefully what Mrs Nibley said. There was wisdom in her suggestion, and he respected that.

"Mrs Nibley, you have a far better understanding of the Turner family than I do. I trust your judgement on this matter, but in time Mr Turner must be made aware of this."

"Mr Petherton, you have my word on that."

"I am away in London tomorrow and will not return until the Saturday next. I shall call next week, and we may discuss Madeline further."

The Turner Household, Guildford …

William took an entire mouthful of water and spat it out, then went hard with his toothbrush[29] cleaning his teeth. His mother had always reminded him about brushing his teeth before bed. The process had become a good habit, and Doctor Sopwith had told him that he would have better teeth in later life if he continued the practice. He liked Doctor Sopwith as much as Doctor Bassington, and they both cleaned their teeth. If doctors did, then he should.

He remembered leaving his jacket downstairs as he finished and would need it first thing in the morning. It was already chilly, so he raced from his washbasin into the hallway and downstairs. William found his jacket beside Madeline's bag and, knowing she was in bed, decided to take it upstairs for her.

As he rushed up the stairs, he heard a clinking noise as it brushed against his legs. Stopping on the first landing, he looked inside the bag. There he found two bottles individually wrapped and placed beneath the other contents. He looked at one of the bottles and immediately realised they were from Mr Petherton's collection.

William placed the wrapped bottle into the bag and raced upstairs.

"Sim, I know where Mr Petherton's bottles are! Look here!"

Reading by candlelight, Simeon looked up from his book, "You should not be looking in Madeline's bag. She will be angry."

"But look here!" William took out a bottle and removed it from its wrapping. Simeon also recognised the bottle as soon as he saw it.

"Will put it back in Madeline's room, or we will all be in trouble. If Father finds out, he will flog us. Perhaps she found them somewhere and was returning them. Who knows? Put the bag in her room quickly."

Simeon was all too aware of how violent his father's temper could be. Over the past months, with treatment from Doctor Bassington, his father had re-strained himself well. Simeon was keen that this continued. He knew that if one of the Turner children were the culprit, the shame inflicted on the family might precipitate his father's temper returning. Who knew how his father might react?

William bundled the bottle into the handkerchief and carefully placed it

---

[29] In the UK, William Addis is believed to have produced the first mass-produced toothbrush in 1780. Pig bristles were used for cheaper toothbrushes and badger hair for more expensive ones. Wikipedia.

in the bag. He then carried it on tiptoe down the hall and quietly opened Madeline's bedroom door enough so he could slip the bag in and gently place it on the floor. He then retreated quickly.

"Say your prayers, Will."

"But it is cold! I will say them in bed."

"You know the rules. If I must do it, you do as well."

William grunted, hopped out of bed, knelt and said the Lord's prayer. He then scampered back under his blanket.

"I bet God is somewhere warm. I bet he says his prayers in bed."

Simeon closed his book and blew out the candle.

"Think of it this way, Will. Mother would be pleased that you said your prayers."

William lay there thinking about his mother. He remembered her soft touch and the warmth of her embrace. He had tried talking with her after she died, but there was no answer. She was gone, and Anne was gone. They had left him at the mercy of his father. He shuddered, and a small tear ran down his cheek.

'Mother, if you can hear me, I miss you so much. Please come back and hold me tight. Please talk with me like Reverend Taggart said you would.' As he kept his eyes tightly shut, he remembered the warmth of her arms around him and her soft, goodnight kiss. He remembered the beautiful scent she wore and her reassuring smile as her long hair brushed across his face. He heard her saying, "God protect you here tonight, my little one!" Slowly his breathing became deeper as he drifted off into sleep, his blanket tightly wound around him.

Turner Household, the following afternoon …

William stacked the wood quickly in the woodshed as Simeon steadily continued chopping.

"Do you think Ethel will let us visit, Anne?"

"Not sure, Will."

"I thought Father was hiring a man to chop wood?"

"Well, he has not yet. Perhaps he will when he returns from his trip."

"Sim, while Father is away, is there a need for so much firewood?"

Simeon stopped and looked at William. He scratched his head, thinking about William's question. With a loud voice, Mrs Jennings, standing on the back verandah, said, "Yes, boys, you do! So, we can boil water and cook your food!"

The boys put their heads down and continued their chores.

Ethel slowly walked along the hallway, carrying some ironed clothes, and hoping Madeline would be talkative. She opened the bedroom door and found Madeline on her bed reading.

With a smile, Ethel said, "Madeline, everyone else is downstairs, so how about we chat?"

Madeline appeared disinterested and asked, "Why do you always want a chat, Ethel?"

"Mr Petherton and I had a conversation on Sunday afternoon. He advised me that he discussed the disappearance of some small bottles from his collection with you and the other children on Saturday night. Could you tell me about his collection and if you know where the bottles have gone?"

Madeline looked at Ethel with innocent eyes and said, "I'm not sure where the bottles went. How does he know they were stolen? It could be that the maids put them somewhere by accident."

"He nor I suggested they were stolen! Mr Petherton only mentioned that they were missing. Is his bottle collection extensive?"

"Oh, yes. Mr Petherton has bottles from England, Scotland, and Ireland, many from Europe. There are some beautiful bottles. I imagine he is quite upset that some are missing."

Ethel was amazed at how composed Madeline was, given the implications involved.

"Madeline, I took the liberty of searching all the children's rooms today. Before I continue, are you sure you have nothing to say?"

Madeline suddenly became angry, "Ethel, you have no right searching our rooms? You are the housekeeper, not our mother. Our rooms are private, and you should leave things alone. I shall tell Father about this."

"Well, we must clean your room, Madeline. A search is not much different. Now tell me, is there anything else you want to say?"

Madeline sat there with her arms crossed, biting her bottom lip. Ethel could tell she was much put out but would not admit anything.

"Madeline. If we can help Mr Petherton find his bottles, it will be a great help. He is not angry that they are missing. He is more concerned about helping whoever misplaced them. I, too, would like to help. There will be no punishment."

Madeline sat there with a stubborn look and spat out, "I have no idea where the bottles are, and I do not care who did it. That is all I know, and I would thank you if you left now!"

Mrs Nibley was disappointed with Madeline and was now certain that Mr Petherton was correct. Madeline was the culprit. Ethel had searched all the children's rooms today with the help of Marcia. Of course, the little one thought they were cleaning. When Ethel found the bottles neatly wrapped and deposited on the highest shelf at the back of Madeline's closet, she realised who the culprit was. But why would gentle little Madeline do such a thing?

What would Madeline do now that Ethel had discovered she was the culprit? The obvious thing would be she would hide the bottles somewhere else. However, Mrs Nibley, understanding young girls' behaviour, decided that the stolen bottles would be safer somewhere Madeline would not find them. This way, she could not move them into another bedroom and blame one of her brothers or sisters.

The mystery still was why Madeline would do such a thing.

'Porting', Guildford, Surrey, …

Victoria Sopwith sat with Anne South as they enjoyed a lovely afternoon tea provided by Mrs Kirby.

"Thank you for inviting me, Anne. Since leaving Fintelton on Monday morning, I have felt a little lonely. David's house seems quiet now that he has left on his honeymoon with Emma. My maid, Judith, always cares for me, but it can never be like a sister. Molly Lane is a good companion, but she has her duties, and I feel embarrassed spending too much time with her. So, it is pleasant sitting here with you again."

"You are always welcome here, Victoria. Let us make the most of our time together. There is a pressing matter we must discuss. Perhaps David did not share this news with you, but Lady Clarissa Wendarm has returned from Jamaica and claims she is Sir Hugh South's wife. She also claims that he died in Kingston, and she has returned bearing his child and desires recognition."

Victoria was alarmed, "Now I realise why there were so many side conversations on Sunday night. I thought there might be a problem but was afraid of asking. I can imagine the distress of the Earl and Countess. I am so sorry for them. But at least they might have an heir."

Anne talked at length and related the complete story.

"I have requested that someone attend with me when I talk with this Mr Stephen Polkinghorne. I suggested that you accompany me without your permission, and the Earl and Countess approved my request. Would you feel comfortable coming with me, Victoria?"

"It would be a pleasure, Anne. I am honoured that the Earl and Countess would entrust me with knowledge of their private matters. It is kind that you suggested me, but I am unsure what I may add."

"The fact that you are with me will be a great encouragement, and it would not be proper if I saw the gentleman alone. I will feel far more comfortable if you are with me."

"I shall do my best."

"We leave for London on Monday, the twenty-sixth of March. I thought it might also be an opportune time to explore the city. We might as well have fun there, so I suggest some serious shopping."

Victoria was of a similar mind, "This trip is sounding more attractive all the time."

"But before we go, we must start redecorating 'Porting'. Perhaps we could walk around the grounds now. I am afraid this will take much of your time this week."

"Anne, as I said earlier, I am glad of your company!"

As they walked around the grounds, Victoria commented, "It is a beautiful position, Anne, and the views are splendid across the forest. Do you envisage the furnishings reflecting this natural beauty, or should the colour scheme be a more traditional theme?"

"I am not sure, Victoria, so we must consider both."

Walking together, they encountered William and Simeon running up the driveway. William ran straight for Anne and hugged her tight. "Anne, Anne! I am so glad you are back. Will you be at dinner tonight?"

"I must dine with Robert here, William, but I will come another night. Perhaps Victoria will come as well."

"Yes, please come, Victoria, and we can play blind man's bluff. Can we play on the fort, please? But first, do you need any wood chopped? Mrs Jennings will be cross if we do not chop some wood. Hello, Miss Sopwith."

"Go around and find Robert in the stables, boys. Robert is with Mr Stem discussing plans for the renovation. He will tell you if there is any wood needed. Then off and play."

The boys rushed away, and Anne said, "Perhaps you will not be as lonely as you thought this week, Victoria."

Mayfair, London ...
Stephen Polkinghorne stood outside Lady Clarissa's room and knocked on the door. The nurse, Miss Eliza Best, answered.

"Nurse Best, I enquire about our patient's condition today."

On Thursday night, Lady Clarissa had fallen into a deep sleep that continued off and on for four days. Her condition deteriorated daily, and a worried Stephen Polkinghorne called the doctor twice. Unfortunately, the opportunity for a discussion since the invasion of the Earl's home in St James's Square had not eventuated, and Stephen was keen for the earliest chance.

"Lady Clarissa is asleep, Mr Polkinghorne. Shall I call you when she wakes?"

"Yes, thank you. There are pressing matters I must discuss with her."

The nurse nodded and then closed the door.

Carefully considering the situation, Stephen decided that even if Lady Clarissa woke, it was unlikely that she would be capable of logical reasoning, given her state of health. He decided to write, asking the Earl if he could repair the damage.

Polkinghorne Imports Plc
West India Docks
Isle of Dogs, London, UK

The Right Honourable, The Earl of Fintelton
'Harting'
St James's Square
St James, England.

Dear Lord Fintelton
I sincerely apologise for the uncivil behaviour of my friend, Lady Clarissa
Wendarm, recently at your London Townhouse in St James's Square.
Since this embarrassing event, I have learnt that Lady Clarissa suffers
greatly from an advanced state of infirmity, and it would be remiss of me
if I did not write and explain the situation.

I first met Lady Clarissa at the Grand Hotel in Kingston, Jamaica. I
understand your son Sir Hugh South was also a guest there. Unfortu-
nately, I did not have the pleasure of meeting your son, who suffered from
a severe illness and remained isolated.

Lady Clarissa and her travelling companion Lady Fiona Green
became friends of mine during my stay there. We dined several times, and
I was impressed by her fine manners and refined speech. Lady Wendarm
and I departed Jamaica on the same ship arriving at Portsmouth in early
March.

During the voyage, Lady Wendarm advised me that she and Sir Hugh
had secretly married before she left for England. I understand that Sir
Hugh did not accompany her due to his illness. Strangely Lady Fiona
Green remained in Kingston caring for Sir Hugh while Lady Wendarm
returned home.

Since landing in England, Lady Wendarm and I were not in contact
until we lunched together the previous Thursday. Lady Wendarm advised
me that she was expected at your address and asked if I would accompany
her. The request seemed reasonable, and I agreed.

Her behaviour at your premises was inexcusable, and I apologise
profusely for the intrusion. I removed Lady Wendarm as soon as possible
and found that she suffers from a disease that may cause delusion.

If it is your desire, I will make myself freely available and explain the
details of the situation to your representative. I apologise again for Lady
Wendarm's out-of-character behaviour.

Kindest Regards
Stephen Polkinghorne

Jonathan Turner was in a festive mood, given his daughter, Anne, and her new husband were attending dinner. In addition, Bethany and Neville had also joined the group, and Neville told the story of the swimming lesson he had supervised on behalf of David Sopwith.

"Anne, your father is making good progress. We are proud of him."

Jonathan laughed and said, "Neville, if you call swimming along the bottom of the pool good, then we must celebrate."

Bethany quickly replied, "You have made the effort, Father, and that is the point. Many other fathers would not have. I am proud of you."

"Then, Bethany, you have made it worthwhile for me. Thank you."

Simeon excitedly said, "Levi and Archie are also making good progress. They can take several strokes along the surface. One day we should start a swimming club."

Clementine complained, "Only if it is a male and female swimming club!"

"Perhaps the Mayor may be interested in this." Jonathan could see that swimming was a skill all children should learn. "But on another subject, I will be on a trip with Mr McPherson in Scotland next month. The ship leaves this Saturday, and I will depart Guilford on Thursday morning and join Mr McPherson at his company's Woolwich wharf. I hope, children, you will behave for Mrs Nibley while I am away."

Madeline, looking at Clementine, frowned and lifted her eyebrows. Clementine slightly nodded back but kept a sweet expression on her face. Bethany could not help but notice the girl's unsaid protest about Ethel and wondered what was driving this. As far as she knew, the children were thankful for Ethel's care.

William was fascinated at the thought of a voyage, "Father, you are going by ship. How big is the ship?"

"I am not sure, William, but I will tell you when I return. I am glad you are back, Anne, as the company will need hands-on management next month."

Robert added, "Mr Turner! My mission leaves on Saturday for Ireland. We are docked at the navy wharves at Woolwich and will embark around lunchtime with the high tide. There are four ships, and you should easily see us."

"I will keep a watch, Robert. If I see you, I shall wave."

Later that evening at 'Porting', Robert mentioned, "Anne, before we left Fintelton, I agreed with Stem that the banking for Mrs Constance would not continue. As there is no indication of the timing of Hugh's return, we should try flushing her out. It will not take long before she realises the money has not arrived."

"Is that wise, Robert? If we do that, she will suspect someone knows what is happening and take action."

"Yes, but what will that action be?"

"It could become violent! I do not wish that to happen when I am alone here."

"Well, I thought about that as well. David and Emma are away, and I leave tomorrow. Why not ask Victoria Sopwith if she would come and stay with you until I return? She would enjoy the company, and so would you. If anything occurs, you will have Mrs Kirby, the other staff, and Victoria with you."

"That is a wonderful idea. I agree, and I will ask Victoria tomorrow."

Robert smiled, "Perhaps you might help her find a property. David and Emma will want their privacy when they return."

"So will we!" Anne was already thinking about Robert's return.

"Now, the payments go out on the first of the month, so it will not be until around the first week in April that Mrs Constance realises something is wrong. The week after that is when she will act. I suggest you and Victoria spend that week at Fintelton. It will be near Easter, and my mother and father will enjoy your company. They will be pining for your arrival."

Anne thought about her appointments coming up next month and relaxed. There were very few, and she was unsure of the exact dates without her diary. However, she could see the logic in Robert's thoughts.

"That should work. If there are any appointments, I will change them, and my father should be returning the week after. You think the repercussions will happen at Fintelton?"

Robert fingered his chin as he thought, "I would say so, as there is no history of her being in London when these events occurred. I know she lives there now, but that may be because there is more demand for accommodation. I would not be sure she even knows about 'Harting'."

"Robert, I am still uneasy about this as you will be away."

"I thought you would, so I have briefed Stem, Staines and Pike in advance. They will keep it confidential. You will be safe during your time at Fintelton. They are also watching for any mail that may come demanding payment."

"Robert, you have been thinking about this for some time. Why did you not tell me?"

"We have all been so busy with Emma's wedding that there has not been time. But now it is time we solve this puzzle once and for all."

Chapter 19

HMS Shadow, Woolwich Navy Dockyards …

The Captain of HMS *Shadow* stood silently on the poop deck as the crew waited for departure orders. Robert was amazed at how quickly the week had passed since Emma and David's wedding.

"Mr Fenton, the wind is gusting from the northwest, and we have an incoming tide nearing high water. What sails do you suggest?"

"Captain, it will be tricky this afternoon until we near the estuary, so I suggest we use the fore staysails, the spanker and the fore topsail."

"Good. I suggest you keep a sail crew on the main topsail if we need some additional way at short notice. I have sailed this river a few times, and it is tricky. Ham is already making good time in *Restless* – he will be almost out of sight once he rounds the bend at Thamesmead. *Chalk* and *Eventide* are edging out, so we may proceed. Before we embark, call the Master, please."

Fenton spied Trotters on the quarter deck and shouted, "Mr Trotters! Report to the Captain, please."

With a smile, Robert said, "Mr Trotters, I trust we will have no problems with the staysails today?"

"Checked and double-checked, Captain."

"Good, thank you, Master."

As Trotters walked away, he crossed his fingers. Robert soon noticed a midshipman racing along the quarter-deck towards the bow.

The captain took a final look at the two packet ships, which were already unfurling their sails. He was satisfied his small fleet was safely underway.

"Take her out, Mr Fenton, and keep it clean."

"Aye, Sir."

Fenton started screaming orders, and the ship instantly changed from an inanimate object into a vessel teaming with life. Officers were calling everywhere, sailors running, sails unfurling, and the land party singing as they pushed the frigate away from the dock. As soon as the jibs and spanker caught the north-westerly gusts, *Shadow* responded and made way, moving quickly from the wharf.

Standing at the leeward rail on the quarter deck, Major Coombes turned, climbed the stairs, and joined an extremely alert captain on the poop.

"Exciting this leaving port. Pity there is no one waving us goodbye."

"Enjoy it here, Horace! I doubt there will be any folks waving in Cobh. If you would excuse me until we reach Gravesend, we will encounter some nasty bends ahead, which are tricky. River sailing is always dangerous."

"Certainly, Captain. I shall watch with interest."

Robert stood with Fenton as *Shadow* moved out into the middle of the river, where the wind gusts seemed stronger. Within five minutes, the wind dropped significantly, leaving the sailing master guessing the direction of the next blow of wind. Trotters hoisted himself up a few yards on the port rigging, keenly watching the rippling water approaching from behind. From his higher position, the Master could discern a large gust approaching from two hundred yards behind them. Trotters yelled, "Captain, large gust coming from Greenwich." Captain South alerted his first lieutenant, "Fenton, unfurl the main topsail. We must make the most of this next gust."

Fenton screamed the order, and as the sailing team grappled with the unfurling sail, the wind snapped it open with a large crack! The main topsail set quickly in the breeze, and with the other sails full, *Shadow* leapt forward as if she was a horse under the whip. The crew were relieved by the increasing way, which allowed steerage in these tricky conditions.

After several hair-raising episodes of losing wind and almost making no way, *Shadow* reached Gravesend, where the Thames significantly widened. The north-easterly became more constant, giving them far more ability to control their course.

As *Shadow* ploughed on towards the estuary, Robert watched for the two packet ships following around the last river bend. *Chalk* was in plain view making good sail, but there was no sign of *Eventide*.

"Damn!" Robert had been dreading a mishap along the river. "Mr Fenton, have Lieutenant Peters launch the whaler and sail back past Gravesend. I fear *Eventide* may be in trouble. That last bend is particularly dangerous; even the best sailors have difficulties there. His message for the captain of *Eventide* is that we will wait off Margate until he confirms their situation. Lieutenant Peters should also check with the captain of *Chalk* before he returns."

"Aye, Captain."

Robert saw Horace watching the sailors wrestling and hoisting the whaler into the water.

Horace commented, "I see what you mean about the sharp bends. It was a bit tricky back there!"

Robert was relieved they had reached Gravesend without mishap, "Why did they not depart from Portsmouth or Southampton? Woolwich is always a difficult port. The trees and hills beside the river make the wind variable, and the currents and eddies change at every bend. As ships become larger, a journey starting from Woolwich is not for the faint-hearted."

"Robert, you are dealing with politicians. They like their comfort. Ha, Ha! It is convenient. They let the navy solve any navigation problems as you have done. Where did you learn your skills at river sailing?"

"Foster taught me. He was an exceptionally skilled sailor. Let us hope *Eventide* is not aground. Otherwise, it may be late tonight before we leave Margate."

Horace and Robert watched as the whaler sailed upriver, searching for *Eventide*.

"Well, it is time for a coffee and some Turner biscuits. Will you join me, Captain?"

"Not yet, Horace. Give me a half hour, please? I must see us past Westcliff before I come down. With this breeze, we will make good time. I may not be that long."

Horace approached the quarter deck and turned, saying, 'I will warn Swanton!"

Robert was already discussing the course with Fenton, "Signal both *Restless* and *Chalk* we will wait off Margate. Hopefully, Peters will sort this delay out. Now, make way for Westcliff, Mr Fenton. You may put up as much sail as you see fit."

"Aye, Captain."

Robert watched proceedings closely as *Shadow* carefully edged along the river. The tide was now high, and it was the best time for exiting the Thames. *Eventide* must have gone aground. That would be a bad start for the mission, and sailors were superstitious about the journey's beginning. A ship running aground in the river would breed all kinds of rumours forewarning of danger. As they passed Westcliff, he moved from the rail and spoke with Mr Fenton.

"I will be in my cabin, Mr Fenton. Let me know as soon as Lieutenant Peters returns."

"Aye, Captain."

Robert joined Horace in the captain's cabin, where coffee and biscuits awaited him.

"Still no sign of *Eventide*. I would say she lost the wind and went aground."

"From what I saw, Robert. It might easily happen."

"When I was aboard *Eventide*, I met with the captain and his officers. They seemed a well-experienced crew. But, still, stranger things happen."

As Swanton came in with more coffee, Robert asked, "While I was away,

Swanton, what did you find out about the crew?"

"Major Coombes will agree that they all seem loyal and well-behaved. I have not seen anything suspicious but will keep my eyes open, Sir."

"Good, it is usually at sea when they start their mischief. Once we are around Land's End, I will arrange some target practice. Horace, your Marines may have the first turn. Swanton, this mission requires us ashore and over-nighting in various estates. You will ride with us and keep an eye on our backs."

Robert checked that the cabin door was firmly closed. He then sat at the table and quietly said, "We have information that an assassination attempt is in play and that the Major and I might be the targets. When staying ashore overnight, Swanton, you will be keeping us safe. I want every possible vantage point an assassin might use covered by our security."

Horace stopped crunching a biscuit and protested, "I thought that was Colonel Scott's role?"

"It is, but I would like a little assurance for myself and you, my friend. I am determined that we shall return home after this mission."

A knock came on the cabin door, and the First Lieutenant entered, "*Eventide* insight, Sir. She is making good way. The whaler is still beside *Chalk*. I would assume Peters will soon join us again."

"Thank you, Mr Fenton. I will join you on the poop in ten minutes."

"Aye, Sir."

Fenton left the cabin, and Robert turned and focused on his servant, "Swanton, ensure a guard is on my cabin door during each watch. Also, I always want lanterns alight in the corridor outside. There must be no chance of anyone gaining entry. While we are ashore at each port, this cabin must be kept secure. The Master at Arms will take responsibility; Fulcher will under-stand. Swanton, you may organise the security with him."

Horace was confused, "Robert, Swanton has already advised you he thinks the crew is safe. Why the need for this extra security?"

"I am taking no chances, Horace. I have no time on this mission to fight any Irish nationalists on board. Your marines may take care of them this time. We need a backup as they will be with us ashore. Fulcher is trusted and performed well on Restless. I brought him onto this crew for that precise reason."

"So, you are expecting trouble onboard?"

"Not sure, Horace, but this ship has a larger crew. There is more chance, but we will see. Making it as hard as we can for them will not hurt. Now, gentlemen, the first dinner will be held at Lord Kellwick's estate outside Cork. Scott has provided the details of the Manor house. Horace, what are the plans for security?"

Portsmouth, Hampshire, England …

Aiden Reid stretched after he climbed down from the back of the coach. The driver threw down his bag. Aiden caught it and then tipped his cap.

"Which way are the docks?"

The driver looked down from the other bags on the coach and said, "Follow this road until you meet the High Street. Follow it down as far as Lombard Street, and then right. The docks will be in sight."

"Thanks."

The clouds were darkening as they rolled in from the west, shutting out the sun. Lamplighters were on the streets, busy at their work. Aiden knew if he did not hurry, the clouds would open, and the storm would drench him before reaching his destination. The Irishman was well-rested after spending nearly three days on coaches from Bristol. Now he had arrived, he would search for his contact and find the information he needed.

Swinging his duffle bag over his shoulder and pulling his cap down, he ventured towards the docks. It was far warmer here than in Cobh, and he felt a light humidity. A storm was quickly building, so he quickened his pace along the High Street. Keeping his distance from other pedestrians rushing away from the storm, he watched for anything that appeared even remotely suspicious as he searched for the pub sign, he knew.

After a twenty-minute walk, he saw the Black Whale Pub sign. Taking off his cap, he went in and approached the bar. The ceilings were low, and the pipe smoke was thick as the late afternoon crowd sought shelter from the rain. Finally, catching the barman's attention, he asked, "Would Michael McGinty be in, please?"

"Would you like a drink while I find out, Mister?"

"Thanks, a glass of water if that's not too much trouble."

"And who be asking for McGinty, then?"

"Aiden Reid!"

The barman looked hard at Aiden and then passed him across the water.

"Take a seat down the back there and wait."

Aiden nodded, took the water, and slowly edged between patrons towards the back of the bar. He welcomed the seat as the day had been long, and he could hear the storm approaching as the light rain started and rattled against the windows. It was now dark outside, and the approaching lightning lit the sky occasionally.

After half an hour, Aiden finished sipping his water and became self-conscious. He was the only man at his table, and some other sailors occasionally glanced at him. Then a thick-set man wearing a long coat tapped him on the shoulder, beckoning him. He exited through a door past the kitchen and out the back of the pub. Here a tiny sheltering roof protected him from the rain pouring down.

As Aiden came through the rear door, two men grabbed him and pushed him hard against the pub's wall.

"Who be looking for McGinty then, Mr Stranger?"

"Aiden Reid from Cobh."

"What do you want?"

"Tell, Michael! It is about importing pigs!"

The man asking the questions sneered at Aiden and then turned and went. The other pushed him into a chair nearby and stood watching him.

"Aiden Reid! It has been nearly four years since I have seen you. What brings you here, lad?"

Appearing from nowhere, a small attractive woman about forty years of age and dressed as a kitchen hand stood beside him.

"Biddie Quinn! I am glad you are still here, girl."

"Not many call me a girl anymore, Aiden. Thanks for the compliment. Now, what do you want?"

"Is there somewhere private where we can talk?"

"Follow me." She led him across the small laneway into a stable, then up some stairs into a room hidden from below. Closing the door, she lit a candle and raised her eyes with a frown.

"You are taking a risk coming here, Aiden. Did you know they are looking for you? A message has come through requesting a report if you show up."

"I know, but they will never find me. Give it some time, Biddie, before you tell them."

Biddie Quinn looked up into his face with a smile and said, "They will come for you, Aiden."

"I know. But I will not be here, will I? Nor will you. It is nearly time for America."

Aiden gently pulled her close and lightly kissed her on the lips. At first, she did not respond. Biddie had last seen Aiden when he passed through Portsmouth on a brothers' mission four years ago.

"You think we can continue as if you had never been away?"

"I did my duty, and now it is time for us."

She kissed him back hard, raising her arms around his neck.

Biddie's voice trembled, "I was not sure you would ever return."

"I was not sure either, but the brothers are planning something that will be their end. For some time, I have thought that Ian Murphy in Dublin has not been thinking right. He makes great statements about what we will achieve and then orders missions that always fail."

"What kind of missions?"

"After several failed attempts, we took an English frigate hostage and prepared it as a fire ship. The objective was Portsmouth Harbour, where it would burn the fleet. But the English found us before we could set off. Thirty-seven brothers died. More men have died of their injuries since. Now he is planning an assassination against an English mission in Ireland. He claims it will make a point about the brothers' power and bring in more members."

"Wouldn't he be right, Aiden? Any victory would bring fame and more members."

"Possibly! But what do you think the British will do if we assassinate one of their politicians? First, they will tear the island apart, searching for the Republican boys. Then, the English might execute hundreds of innocent Irish men because of Murphy's orders."

"You are right! Heaven helps them if they assassinate someone. It may start a war."

"I think there is more than that, Biddie. Murphy is dumb but not that dumb that he knows a challenger, so I have led him on a merry chase. He sent Michael Walsh after me offering me the assassination mission. It would have been my death sentence. I refused and told Michael I would surface in a few years. But Michael thinks I am after revenge which I don't mind him thinking!"

"Well, why are you here if you want revenge."

"They think I am after the Navy Commander of the British frigate who killed all our men in Port Charlotte. I do not mind if they think that. So, I will leave a trail for them, which will be a dead-end. But before they find that dead-end, I will be back in Ireland and pay a visit. Ian Murphy will not be expecting me!"

"I don't want that dead-end being here, Aiden!"

"It will not, Biddie. Once you get the information I need, I will lead them on a merry chase."

"But why kill Murphy?" Biddie could not understand the argument.

"I don't trust Murphy. I have been thinking about this for a long time. We have lost every mission over the last few years, and many good young men have died. Why? What has been the plan? It seems there is a plan afoot that will cement the British in Ireland rather than force them out. I think Murphy is working with the British and sending our men on missions they cannot win. Why would he want me killed when I took care of a useless recruiter who gave away our position at Port Charlotte and resulted in so many brothers dead? It does not make sense."

Biddie considered what Aiden was saying. She was now becoming greatly concerned.

"We must warn them! If it is a trap, we must warn them."

"No, Biddie. It is already in action. What they have planned will come about. But the brothers and our people will pay dearly for it. If we want a free Ireland, then the traitors must die. Murphy will be the first."

"You are saying there are more?"

"Yes, Biddie! The path I have been following leads right here."

"If that happens, Aiden, they will also come here."

"Yes, and that is part of their plan. The Brothers will not spare you, Biddie. You know too much. So, for us, it is nearly time for America. Do not worry; the British will not find this place for a few months yet. By the time they come, we will be on our way. But first, there is some business I must finish. I need some information, Biddie, and you will know where I can find it."

High Street, Guilford, Surrey ...

Ethel Nibley walked past the marketplace and down towards a small coffee house near the riverbank. She was nervous as she rarely left the Turner house before Mrs Turner died. She should venture out more often as the house-keeper, but Ethel still felt vulnerable on the streets.

Since the loss of her husband some eleven years ago, it was a constant struggle fending off poverty. For the first six years, she worked with her mother in the seamstress business but found the returns were not enough for the life she wanted. Her husband had left little savings, and these were soon gone. Rosalind was two when Andrew Nibley died, and Ethel was thankful that the child remained with her mother once she entered service.

Her first job with the Jessops near Camberley proved challenging because one of the family's sons was over-friendly, and she and many of the female staff relied on the butler and housekeeper for protection. After five years of service there, she left, thankfully, without an incident. The job at the Turners had been like a dream come true, with good pay, reasonably regular duties, and safe accommodation near her mother's house. Yet, since losing Andrew, she had lost much of her confidence and continually wondered what life would bring upon her.

Now she was solving the problems of another man's children. Mr Turner seemed incapable of understanding his children unless they were working in a business with him. She sighed. Making decisions for the children was not her role, but with Jonathan Turner distracted by his grief, no one else took on their interest.

As she entered the coffee house, she immediately saw Mr Benjamin Petherton sitting at a table near the front window. He stood and waved, and Ethel smiled, acknowledging the wave. She navigated between tables and breathed a sigh of relief as she sat across from Mr Petherton.

"Thank you, Mrs Nibley, for meeting with me today. I was keen on an update on your progress with Madeline. May I order you a tea or coffee?"

"Yes, please, a black coffee would be nice."

Benjamin drew the attention of a waiter and ordered the coffee.

"I am afraid I'm making little progress with Madeline. I sat with her the other night and asked if she could tell me anything about the missing bottles. Instead, she became most defensive and would not say much at all. I think there is a problem, and it may be her mother's death."

"I see." Benjamin Petherton sat there with a sombre expression. "I am not an expert on children as I struggle enough with Clare. Might it be that she is seeking attention?"

"Quite possibly. Madeline and Anne are close, but with Anne now married, Madeline is left with only Clementine and Marcia at home. Clementine is extremely independent, often in a world of her own or fighting for some cause and has little time for deep friendships. Marcia is too young and requires much attention. Perhaps Madeline feels left out. I am not sure."

"You know the children well. I am impressed."

"You must remember, Mr Petherton, I work there from dawn till dusk. I am not a family member. I am a servant. So, I probably know them too well for my good."

Nodding in agreement, Benjamin Petherton asked, "And the bottles, did you find them?"

"Yes! They were on the top shelf at the back of Madeline's cupboard. I removed them, and they are now carefully hidden. If she repositioned them, I felt she might blame one of the boys rather than own up. Is this one of them?"

Ethel pulled one of the bottles from her bag.

"Yes, that is one of them. A wise move, shifting the bottles. But Madeline will now know that you have discovered them."

"Yes, and she seems not to care."

"I think you are correct, Mrs Nibley. She is looking for attention. Perhaps her mother's death has affected her more than the other children. It may also be that she resents Simeon and William being friends with Clare. Young girls get some silly notions in their heads at times. She may feel shut out by her brothers. Let me think about it for a week or two."

"Mr Petherton, I thought you were away this week in London?"

"Yes, I was due there on Monday but put back my appointment until Thursday. I leave tomorrow and return the week after next. The children may play at the fort. The gardeners are alerted, and they will watch out for them."

"That is most kind of you, Sir."

"Not as kind as you, sparing this time assisting me with my enquiries. Now Mrs Ethel Nibley, might I tempt you with a slice of tea cake?"

The Local Church, Guildford …

Anne sat with Victoria Sopwith in the Turner's pew on Sunday morning. Reverend Taggart gave a splendid sermon on prayer and its benefit, while the Reverend Hotspur sat quietly out of sight but with enough access to survey who was in the congregation. He gained interest when he noticed Anne and Victoria in the pew five rows from the front.

He was impressed with their beauty and dress. They were quite an improvement on the introductions he had received the previous Sunday. After the service, the mayor's wife monopolised his time with arrangements for the coming dinner.

Marjorie Smith asked, "Mr Hotspur, are you free on Saturday the twenty-fourth of March? It appears that most of the young ladies are free next Saturday."

"That would be eminently suitable, Mrs Mayor. Should I arrive by six?"

"Yes, that is a very respectable time, and I will expect you then."

"Thank you, Mrs Smith. Forgive me for asking, but the two young women talking with your husband. Who might they be?"

"The fair-haired Lady is Lady Anne South. Sir Robert is a Captain in the navy and is presently away. Anne married him some months ago and resides here in Guildford. The lady with the dark hair is Miss Victoria Sopwith. She is the sister of one of our local doctors and stays here with her brother, Doctor David Sopwith. David is recently married and on his honeymoon."

"I see. Excuse me, Mrs Smith, I recall something I must discuss urgently with the mayor." Philip Hotspur left Marjorie with the women surrounding her and ventured across, hovering beside Mayor Rupert Smith.

"Four weeks! I am sure you will be glad when they return, Victoria. Ah, but here is our new young Reverend. Mr Hotspur, please join our conversation."

"Thank you, Mr Mayor. I hope I am not interrupting, but I must discuss an important point with you, Sir."

Anne and Victoria looked up at Mr Hotspur, who appeared most excited and ended their conversation.

Anne ventured, "We will leave you with the good Reverend, Mr Smith. Thank you for your advice."

Philip Hotspur quickly replied before the ladies could depart. "Please, ladies, forgive my interruption. Mr Smith, perhaps you might introduce me."

"Certainly, Reverend Hotspur. May I present Lady Anne South and Miss Victoria Sopwith?"

"Delighted, ladies. I must have missed you last Sunday."

Anne was not impressed by the young man but politely replied, "We attended Victoria's brother and my sister-in-law's wedding last Saturday at Petersfield. We were absent from Guildford on Sunday."

"Then the church missed the company of two most handsome ladies. It is a pleasure meeting you here today."

Anne smiled and replied, "I am glad we have improved your day Mr Hotspur, but you must excuse us now as we have a pressing engagement. Good morning."

Anne took Victoria's hand and led her towards the Turner's house.

Philip Hotspur gave a polite bow and smiled as they walked away. Then turning, he enquired of the mayor, "They are most handsome ladies, Mr Smith. Please tell me some of their backgrounds?"

Rupert Smith was not the brightest among men, but he did realise the value of having the clergy onside. He was slightly suspicious of the clergyman's enquiry but decided there was more value in providing the information than withholding.

"Lady South is the daughter of Mr Jonathan Turner, a local businessman with substantial business assets. Anne married Sir Robert South, second son of the Earl of Fintelton, some six weeks ago. Victoria is the sister of Doctor David Sopwith. David is a respected local Doctor."

"Do you feel that either of their families might provide a school building fund donation if asked?"

"Mr Turner, or should I say Lady Anne's father, would have that capacity. I am not sure about Doctor Sopwith. He set up practice here some two years ago, coming from London. I understand the practice is growing, but they still struggle financially."

"I see."

Standing nearer the church's door, the Reverend Andrew Taggart carefully watched his curate's sudden interruption of the conversation between the Mayor, Lady South and Miss Sopwith. Knowing of Philip Hotspur's previous broken engagement, Reverend Taggart was concerned that his curate might have decided on a new target.

The Turner Household, Guildford, Surrey …

Anne and Victoria talked as they crossed the road and walked towards the Turner house.

Victoria said, "I am sure he meant no harm, Anne. He was simply meeting more members of the congregation. After all, you are from a prominent family in town, and your father is the chair of the Parish Council."

Anne stood on the bottom front step of the Turner's house, "I think he was a bit too eager to interrupt. The man intended to force an introduction, and it was clear we were the focus of his attention, not the mayor. A clergyman should have more manners."

"Perhaps!"

They ventured inside and sped into the kitchen, where they found a large bowl full of eggs and another wooden box with eggs covered by straw on the kitchen table.

Ethel and Mrs Jennings looked up as the two women entered.

"Lady South and Miss Victoria, welcome! We have been expecting you. The children are upstairs changing and will be down presently."

"Ethel, why are all these eggs here?"

"With Easter coming, I thought I would teach the children the egg dance. It is some fun for after Easter Sunday lunch. The children will enjoy blowing the contents out of an egg, drying the shell, and colouring them. It is four weeks till Easter Sunday, so we have enough time to prepare plenty of eggs."

Anne was inspired, "What a wonderful idea, Ethel! They will love this."

"Please excuse their old clothes, as I thought we could start blowing the eggs before lunch."

Victoria was fascinated, "I have never seen eggs blown or heard of the egg dance!"

Anne had some recollection of the dance, "I only remember my mother doing it once when I was young. I think you stick a pin in the egg. Is that right, Ethel?"

"Well, if you put on aprons, so your good clothes are not spoiled, I will show you."

Mrs Jennings passed the ladies an apron each and then organised the children as they arrived. William rushed and hugged Anne tightly. Anne noticed Madeline looking displeased as William continued hugging her.

"May I stand between you and Victoria, Anne?"

"Certainly, William."

Victoria tapped William on the head and said, "What about me?"

William smiled and hugged Victoria, but not as tight as Anne's hug.

"Now, everyone, I will show you how the contents are blown out of an eggshell."

Clementine and Madeline, who had previously seemed uninterested, suddenly focused on Ethel holding an egg.

"First, you put a small square of cloth over one end of the egg and very carefully insert a needle through the cloth into the egg, making a small hole. The cloth prevents the egg from cracking, but not always, so you must do it carefully. Now, wiggle the needle around like this, making the hole slightly larger and helping break up the yolk inside the egg."

As Ethel carried out the process, the children were fascinated.

"Now repeat the process of making a hole at the other end of the egg." Ethel dug the needle through another cloth at the other end of the egg. After removing the needle, she said, "Keep a finger on each hole, shake the egg, and turn the yolk into liquid." She gently shook the egg and then pretended to drop it on William.

"Ah!" he cried, and everyone laughed.

"Now, I will blow the contents out of the egg." Ethel positioned the egg over a bowl, put her lips on the cloth covering the upper hole in the egg, and blew. The contents ran out of the lower hole and into the bowl.

"Wow!" The children were amazed and keen on their turn.

A group of children's heads almost obscured Ethel's view as they inspected the contents of the bowl. Quickly the egg became empty, and the children were amazed at how easy it appeared.

"Now, it is your turn." Ethel began giving out the eggs and small cut pieces of cloth.

Soon eggs were being pricked and blown out all over the kitchen. There were many jovial comments and laughter as each succeeded or failed and tried again. A small mound of empty eggshells appeared.

"Now, we must let all these eggshells dry before colouring them for the dance."

Madeline was fascinated by the process and, forgetting her hostility for Ethel, asked, "How long, Ethel, does it take before they are dry?"

"Usually about a week. Then next Sunday afternoon, we can decorate them."

"Oh, Victoria and I will be in London. That is not fair." Anne was disappointed.

Ethel quietly said, "I am sure we can save a couple for you. Lady Anne."

William called out, "I only smashed two of my four eggs. May I have another go, Ethel?"

"Yes, William. Here, please have another." She carefully placed an egg in William's eager hands.

Madeline quickly said, "May I have another go as well, Ethel?"

"Certainly, Madeline." Ethel smiled as she placed the egg in an excited Madeline's hands, realising there was an opportunity to break down some of the barriers with this young girl.

Polkinghorne Residence, Mayfair, London ...
The nurse entered Mr Polkinghorne's study.

"Sir, Lady Wendarm is awake and requests your company."

"Thank you, Nurse ...."

Stephen cleared his papers, put them away and climbed the stairs. He had been dreading this moment as he knew it was time to ask Clarissa about the veracity of her claims. The fact that she contracted a fatal disease made it more critical as this Lady needed time to prepare her affairs before departing.

The doctor treating Clarissa had delivered a chilling verdict when he advised that Lady Wendarm was not carrying a child. Stephen was disturbed about her sharing this untruth. Was it because she was desperate for security or genuinely delusional? He was unsure.

She pulled herself up in bed as he entered the room and smiled.

"Stephen, thank you for your care. I was unaware of how sick I was. I hope I shall soon be better and no longer impose on your hospitality."

"I was concerned for you, Clarissa. The doctor has advised me of your condition. I am afraid you must rest for some time. The disease you suffer from is serious, and you will need support. It would be best if you remained here until ……. Well, let us say until there is an outcome."

"Nonsense, Stephen. I will be well in a few days. Now you must dispense with the nurse as I do not need the ointment she applies. I will care for myself and solve this situation with the Souths as soon as further documentation of Sir Hugh's death arrives."

Stephen was now unsure if Clarissa was aware of how sick she was. However, she appeared intent on continuing her campaign.

"Clarissa, the doctor warned me that your condition could prove fatal very soon. I think you are underestimating the seriousness of your condition."

"There is no need for concern, Stephen. I have had these rashes before, and they clear up quickly."

"The doctor advised me that there is no child! I was confused by this, Clarissa. Are you sure you are bearing a child?"

Lady Wendarm turned her head and looked out the window. The smile disappeared, and she quietly said, "Then the doctor must be mistaken, Stephen. I bear Sir Hugh's child, and he is my husband. It is scandalous that Lord and Lady Fintelton do not receive their daughter-in-law. It is a sad way of starting a relationship."

"I agree, but your behaviour at St James's Square may not encourage any relationship. I find it hard to understand why you would leave your husband in Kingston on his deathbed and return home without informing the Earl and Countess. Surely a joint return or letters from Sir Hugh might have cleared the way."

"There was no time, Stephen. Hugh pleaded with me that I return and join the family. I have the marriage certificate, which I will present in due time. Notification of Hugh's death will come soon from the Governor. My child will follow his father and be the next Earl of Fintelton. You will see. But now, I must admit I am exhausted from this conversation. Perhaps you would leave me now as I am tired."

"Certainly, Clarissa. Please ask the nurse if there is anything you require."

As Stephen Polkinghorne walked down the stairs, he nodded his head.

The lady maintained her unlikely story and seemed hell-bent on joining the Earl's family. She was either correct in her claims or delusional. Stephen was convinced it was the latter.

Turner Business Office, Guildford, Surrey ...
Anne sat gazing out the office window at the brown water of the River Wey passing the Turner wharf. She smiled and said, "Victoria, I have a question for you. Robert suggested this, and I agree with him. Would you consider joining me at 'Porting' while Emma and David are away? It would be lovely for me and keep me company. If I dwell on Robert being away, I become most depressed. I miss him dreadfully, and your company would be so refreshing."

Victoria, surprised by the suggestion, "I would indeed, Anne. That is most generous of you. I am lonely in the house without David and have considered moving out. Emma and David will want their privacy when they return."

"I am glad you agreed so readily. We shall have a lovely time together. We might even commence a search for some premises for you."

"I was thinking the same thing. When would you suggest I move in?"

"This afternoon would be good as I have another suggestion you might consider over the next few days."

"That is generous, but I will need a little more time. Say Wednesday late morning. I am curious about your other suggestion."

"Let me explain. My mother left me with a controlling interest in Hursts. I have restructured it as a company and am the major shareholder. The other shareholders are my brothers and sisters. My father has no ownership at all. So, I have some plans for developing the business, and I will start with developing fashion skills. Would you consider working with me in design and fashion?"

"Anne, I know nothing about business."

"Yes, but you know so much about fashion and design. You will teach me far more than Mrs Smith could ever achieve."

"That is flattery indeed. So, this would mean that I would work during the day."

"Yes, you would have an office beside mine in the Turner Bakeries building. I understand we both desire time off for our family life. Our positions would be structured, allowing us this freedom. I can guarantee you will never be bored or lonely again."

"You need not worry about marriage as no one is in sight yet. Would I be reporting to you, Anne?"

"Yes, at the start, but that may change. Hursts is a chain of three shops my mother's parents set up. They recruited Mr Lionel Wall, a tailor responsible for the chain. In addition, he manages the Woking store and resides above that shop.

I have plans for a store in London, but I am afraid Mr Wall is not keen on my ideas for growth, so there is a problem ahead. But with you and Mrs Smith, we could meet the challenge and create something new that would interest many women in London. So, we would start off working together on new designs."

"This sounds most exciting. But will the new store only cater for women?"

"No, we shall maintain a focus on both men and women. I am sure Mr Wall will supply everything we need for the men." Anne smiled, and Victoria giggled.

"Mr Wall must be very traditional?"

"Yes, he will not change, but that may be advantageous. Men's fashions are traditional. It is in women's clothing where we can make a difference."

"I will join your venture, Anne. I have been looking for a role that would keep me busy. The thought of endless morning teas, lunches and dinners is somewhat tiresome. My interest is in fashion, so this will be all-consuming. Thank you for this opportunity. Now, I must be off, as I need a few things from Hursts. Tell me, does Mrs Smith know yet?"

"No, I have not advised her. I will do so in the coming days, but I thought I must advise Mr Wall first. I would not want him taking fright and thinking his position is at risk. So, please say nothing for a week or so."

"I shall, Anne. I will wait until you give the all-clear."

Anne noticed Daisy waiting as Victoria Sopwith left, "What is it, Daisy?"

"Lady South, a rider left this envelope for you. I believe it is an urgent message from the Countess of Fintelton."

"Thank you."

Opening the envelope, she found two pages enclosed. One was a message from Lady Jane, and the other was a letter from Mr Stephen Polkinghorne for the Earl and Countess. Anne read Lady Jane's message first.

The Countess of Fintelton
Fintelton Manor
East Harting
Sussex

My Dearest Anne,
I hope this letter finds you well and you are not missing Robert. Please remember you are very welcome at any time here at Fintelton.

Attached you will find a letter from Mr Stephen Polkinghorne explaining the unexpected intrusion by Lady Wendarm into our home in St James's Square. It appears Mr Polkinghorne is a reasonably-minded gentleman who may have more knowledge of Sir Hugh's and Lady

Wendarm's situations than detailed in his letter.

As you arrange a meeting with this gentleman, I will visit 'Porting' and stay overnight. There are some questions I wish answered, and Mr Polkinghorne might enlighten me on these issues.

I shall arrive on Thursday afternoon with my lady's maid. The Earl will remain at Fintelton, so I shall have dinner with you and perhaps hear some news of Robert. Also, I may visit Hursts on Friday morning before returning home. It would be most reassuring if you would accompany me and point out any new fashions Mrs Smith has discovered.

I am excited about my Guildford trip and spending time with you.

With much love
Jane Fintelton

Anne smiled as it appeared Lady Jane was keen on advising her before the meeting with Mr Polkinghorne. She then recalled that Victoria would move in on Wednesday morning. Anne wondered if the presence of Victoria would be uncomfortable for the countess. Surely not, as she was an in-law now.

Quickly scribbling a note advising Mrs Kirby of the pending visit, she walked downstairs and asked Daisy, "Please have this delivered!"

"Yes, Milady."

"Daisy, would you also advise Jeb and Terry that I am ready for their requested meeting."

Anne returned upstairs and took out the bakery and mill figures. Thankfully, the financial situation had improved in the last few weeks. But she was worried about the business while Jeb and Terry were in London. The court case and Anne's other commitments would keep them away for a week, and while Anne was confident in Peter Hammer and Aaron Hall looking after the bakery, she was unsure who would manage the mill in Terry's absence.

As the gentlemen arrived, Anne could see Jeb wore a huge smile.

"Come in, Jeb and Terry. Thank you for coming so quickly. Have you been fully fitted out for our London trip yet? Also, Terry! During your absence, who will manage the mill? With Mr Turner away, we may be short on people."

Terry could not hold his tongue and quickly said, "Lady South, before we proceed any further, there is some good news that Jeb should tell you before he bursts."

Anne sat up straight with an inquisitive expression, "Well, Jeb?"

"Lady South, Miss Audrey Stern and I have announced our engagement today."

"Jeb! Jeb, that is wonderful!" Anne stood and rushed around her desk and hugged Jeb hard.

"When will you marry and where?"

"We thought in late May, Lady South, as Sir Robert may return by then. We were keen that you both attend the wedding. We shall wed in Reverend Taggart's church as Audrey has attended there all her life. Her parents were keen on that church as well."

"Jeb, this is wonderful. I will go downstairs and congratulate Audrey as soon as we finish our meeting. Now, I have a list of issues we must discuss. Firstly, have you both been fitted with appropriate gentlemen's clothing for the trial?"

Later, after the meeting and congratulating Audrey Stern, Anne visited her parents' home and lunched with Ethel Nibley. She was concerned about Madeline and what Ethel told her about the missing bottles.

Turner Household, Guildford, Surrey ...

"Anne, I shall set another place, and we can share some of the quiches Mrs Jennings has made this morning. It may be best if we lunch in the dining room, and Marcia might stay with Mrs Jennings and Ivy."

"That would probably be better, as we should keep our discussion about Madeline private."

"Certainly. If you would wait in the dining room, I will have Aggie set the table."

"Let me help, please. I am not above all that, Ethel. It is good being home."

Anne took the cutlery, wandered into the dining room, and set the table. Ivy came in with a jug of water and two glasses.

"How have you settled in, Ivy?"

"I love working here, Lady South. Mrs Nibley and the other staff have been kind, and the family is well-mannered. I am so glad Mrs Nibley offered me the job."

"That is wonderful, Ivy. Have you studied any courses at the Institute yet?"

"What do you mean, Ma'am?"

"The Institute has courses for all types of jobs. I am sure they would have one on service staff. It would help if you were doing a course each year, so you improve your qualifications. Mr Sharples will be of great assistance. We have employed many young people from Guildford who have bettered themselves at the Institute."

"Thank you, Ma'am. But my reading is not that good. I would struggle."

"They have courses for improving reading, Ivy. Do not underestimate yourself. I think you would do well."

Ethel entered with two plates of warm miniature quiches and salad, "Please do not train her too quickly, Lady South. We do not want her escaping now she is employed here." They all laughed, and Ivy gave a slight curtsey and rushed back into the kitchen.

"I feel she has great talent, Ethel."

"Yes, she does, but she lacks confidence. I am not sure she is treated that well at home."

"I see. Perhaps we can discuss that another time. Now, about Madeline. How is she coping with her situation?"

"She is still claiming innocence despite my having found the bottles and hidden them away."

"It may be prudent if you returned the bottles and explained the situation. This would ease Mr Petherton's mind, but it will not excuse Madeline's behaviour."

"Strangely, he is more concerned for Madeline than for his bottles. He is a kind soul and wishes Madeline to learn and grow from this situation. I have been impressed with his understanding of young people."

"I, too, am impressed with the man. He certainly thinks through everything he does very carefully. Perhaps that is why he has made a fortune. Still, I think you should return the bottles. That way, Mr Petherton or his staff will notice any further disappearance of bottles immediately. Our next task is to discover why Madeline did this. I assume none of the other children know?"

"That is correct, although I suspect the boys may be aware of something. They were not involved in the stealing, but they seemed knowledgeable about the situation. Perhaps one discovered a bottle in Madeline's bag at some stage."

"Well, good on them for not saying anything. Please take the family coach tomorrow and return the bottles. I would be uncomfortable if they were still here when my father returned. He would react the worst way, and there could be some punishment. Fortunately, he seems more balanced with the girls than the boys."

Ethel looked hard at Anne and wondered if she should ask.

"Anne, I have heard about Mr Turner's rage several times but never seen any instances since I arrived. However, I have noticed that he certainly favours the girls. I know it is a delicate subject, but it would assist me if you provided some background on it."

"Ethel, where do I start?"

"Perhaps at the beginning!"

Anne was only too pleased explaining her father's history and how the family had finally confronted his rage problem. She clarified that her father was reformed, but Anne clearly said there is no guarantee it may not reoccur. He had admitted his past failings and suffered greatly from his wife's death. Anne was encouraged by Hamish McPherson's kind offer of the Scottish trip and hoped her father might return further reformed and free of his grief.

Local Church School, Guildford, Surrey …

Mr Hotspur sat at his desk near the front of the room. His head was down as he peered at the detailed instructions the Reverend Taggart had left him. After a late night, Philip Hotspur felt somewhat flat and was keen on the school day ending. The children had returned from lunch and the curate had them quietly reading.

Philip found the responsibility of caring for the children exhausting, and with his lethargy from a late night, he struggled to decipher the instructions. "Six-year-olds reading blue books; Seven-year-olds practising spelling; Eight-year-olds basic grammar from brown books; Follow the notes; Reading and Grammar." 'What notes?' he thought. 'I am sick of this teaching school. I did not join the clergy for this rot!'

Edward Wood raised his hand and asked, "Sir, May I be excused, please?"

The Reverend Hotspur was not in the mood for answering stupid questions. He continued looking at the desk, head cradled in his hands, and ignored the child's plea.

Edward looked at William and whispered, "I forgot at lunch, and I have to go!"

"Walk out quietly! He has a headache or something. He will not notice. If he asks where you are, I will tell him."

Edward could wait no longer, so he hopped up and walked quickly towards the toilet. The Curate saw him walking past and grabbed him by the arm, "Where do you think you are going?"

"The toilet, Sir. I must go!"

"You little brat! You do not move from your desk without my permission."

Reverend Hotspur then raised his hand and belted the boy across the face with such force that Edward fell onto the front desk, knocking his head and falling unconscious on the floor. The child, in shock, urinated on the floor and lay there motionless. William, at his desk, was stunned that a minister would hit a child. It brought back all the memories of his father beating him.

"Get up, you brat! You are messing up the floor. Get up."

Dawn Luckett and Ruby Bowers stood, came around their desks and knelt beside the boy.

"Edward, are you alright?" Dawn turned him slightly over and saw his eyes were closed and blood running from a deep cut above his eyebrow.

"Sir, he is bleeding! I think he is badly hurt."

"Oh, rubbish! He is just playacting. You girls, pull him over beside the wall. Simeon Turner!"

"Yes, Sir."

"Go fetch a bucket, mop and water, and you can clean this mess up. Now you girls, start reading again at your desk."

Reverend Hotspur then looked down at the table and put his head on one of his hands as he continued the quest of unravelling his instructions.

Ruby Bowers whispered, "Dawn, was he breathing?"

"Yes, but just. We need Mrs Taggart."

Ruby raised her hand and said, "Sir, may we call Mrs Taggart?"

In a rage, Philip Hotspur spat back at the children, "We do not need Mrs Taggart. He is playacting. Get up, Edward, and you can clean up that blood trail you are leaving." The Teacher then looked down at the notes on his desk again.

As Simeon fetched the mop, he entered the other class area and whispered in Mrs Taggart's ear, "Edward Wood is lying on the floor and bleeding!" Simeon then rushed off with the mop.

Laura Taggart stood up with a confused look and peered around the corner into the other classroom. She saw a prostrate Edward unconscious on the ground and bleeding from the forehead and Philip Hotspur ignoring the boy and reading his notes. Mrs Taggart rushed across and rolled Edward over. She quickly pulled out a handkerchief and pressed it onto the wound.

"Samuel Birch, run and get Doctor Bassington. Quickly!"

The Curate looked up from his desk and saw Mrs Taggart tending the child. He stood up and went over, rubbing his eyes as he asked, "There is no need Mrs Taggart. Edward tripped and hit his head at the front desk. He is just playacting. He is not hurt."

"The child is unconscious, Mr Hotspur. Did you check him?"

"Two of the girls checked him. He was alright."

"Well, he is not now. Please bring a blanket and a pillow. Quickly!"

Philip Hotspur had said enough. He made his way from the classroom, wondering where to find a blanket and a pillow. Missing the sick room, Philip wandered into the church, looking around. As he was halfway along the central church aisle, Reverend Taggart came in the other direction.

"Ah, Philip! I will assist you with the school before the day's end. Everything going well?"

"Yes, Reverend Taggart. A little hiccup – Edward Blake tripped and hit his head on the front desk. Your good wife is taking care of him. I am looking for a pillow and a blanket."

Reverend Taggart wondered why Philip was in the church, "Did you try the sick room?"

"The sick room! Where is that?"

"Near the classrooms, Philip. I have shown you before."

"Oh!"

Cobh, Ireland, …

Major Coombes enjoyed the feeling of being back in the saddle. He was an army man through and through and was not keen on transport by sea. If Horace could avoid navy ships, he would. He disliked accommodation that was crowded, noisy and never stopped moving beneath his feet. However, he had no complaint about sharing the captain's cabin with his friend Sir Robert South.

"Captain, I welcome some time on horseback. Too much of this sea life cannot be good for you. You will be sore tonight, my friend."

"I'm not sure about that, Major Coombes. We often ride at the estate. But I must admit most of my travels of late have been by coach."

"Ha, ha! Just as I said, Robert, you are getting soft. Let us see how you are tonight when we reach Lord Kellwick's estate."

Robert, Horace, and Swanton watched as the main party of politicians and their wives, followed by the staff and baggage carts, proceeded from the pier and out of the port. Many an Irishman and woman stared in amazement as they saw the fine procession of coaches, horsemen and carts full of marines proceeding from Cobh through the city of Cork and into the country towards Lord Kellwick's estate.

Robert pulled his coat around him tight as the wind rose in strength and a slight rain started falling. It was ten-thirty in the morning, and it felt like the temperature had dropped ten degrees.

"Horace, the temperature is falling. It looks like heavy rain in the distance."

"Probably! The weather here is fickle in March. You need good shelter at night. It has not made up its mind if it is still winter or coming into spring. But it is bracing, Robert. Good for you!"

"Give me the sea any day, Horace, some coffee and Turner's biscuits."

"Well, Robert, I cannot help you there except I have some of the biscuits Lady Anne sent. Swanton pull a few from your saddlebag. Captain South is looking decidedly hungry. We must ensure he does not fade away on us."

Swanton laughed and passed across a few Turner's biscuits.

Robert crunched away, saying, "That helps! Thank you, Swanton."

"I would hate marching through the wilds of Scotland with you, Robert. You may not like what they feed you there. Ha, ha!" Horace was enjoying the banter.

After three-quarters of an hour, the road curved around a bend, and a sizeable fertile valley extended before them. Colonel Scott came riding back and saluted.

"Major Coombes, that is Lord Kellwick's estate in the distance. You can see the Manor house."

They all looked ahead and enjoyed the fair prospect of the pleasantly situated three-story mansion beside a river that expanded like a lake. Green creeping vines adorned many parts of the building, and large patios extended from several ground-floor rooms.

"I think we shall be comfortable there, Colonel!" Horace imagined a few good nights' sleep on a stationary bed.

"Do not think about your comfort yet, Major. Please move ahead quickly and check the security before we arrive. You should find two squads of marines there commanded by Lieutenant Hinton. Please ensure the butler has the house staff assembled out front for the arrival. On your way, Major."

"Yes, sir!"

Horace saluted, and Robert and Swanton followed as they galloped off ahead of the line of coaches. After they passed the leading coach containing Lord Dawlting, Lord Kellwick and their wives, Lord Kellwick asked, "Who are those officers, Dawlting?"

"Major Coombes and Captain South. South was the captain who recovered HMS *Providence* from the Irish nationalists. I asked for them particularly. South knows the Irish situation well and will ensure we are protected."

Lady Kellwick added, "Lord Dawlting, I understand Captain South saved the life of the Prince at the Charity Ball last Saturday. Is it the same man?"

"Yes, Lady Kellwick. We are in good hands with Sir Robert in our security detail. You shall meet the officers at dinner tonight."

Lady Kellwick smiled and continued talking with Lady Dawlting.

As Horace and Robert galloped down the road towards the Manor house, Robert glancing at the fields, noticed the tenant farmers at work wearing brightly coloured tunics. The low stone walls and green hedges were a picture with some gorse bushes already coming into yellow flowers. He was surprised by the countryside's neatness, pleasantly groomed cottages in the distance, and thin plumes of smoke rising from chimneys. It seemed an ideal place where a tenant farmer could develop a good living.

At the Manor, they slowed their horses, trotting closer and noticed the small guard of marines assembled, ready for the official party. A sole lieutenant came forward accompanied by his sergeant.

Horace shouted as he dismounted his horse, "Lieutenant Hinton!"

Hinton stood at attention and saluted, "Yes, Major."

"Lieutenant, I am Major Coombes, and this is Sir Robert South, captain of HMS *Shadow*."

"Welcome, Major and Captain."

"Thank you, Hinton. Now I take it that you have the security in place for Lord Kellwick's arrival?"

"Yes, Sir. The squad here is guarding the front area of the house, and the other squad is in the rear. I am satisfied we have it covered, Sir."

"What about the inside, Hinton."

"Excuse me, Sir! What do you mean?"

"Have you checked each member of staff? Do you know the number of staff and their recruitment dates? Have there been any changes in staff within the last few weeks?"

Lieutenant Hinton stood there without an answer.

Horace quickly gazed at the staff. He thought, 'There must be twenty-five to thirty staff standing in that line.'

"Hinton, have your Sergeant check with the butler so we can check the security of this welcoming committee. What is the name of the butler?"

"O'Neill, Sir."

Realising they were running out of time, Major Coombes approached the butler and quickly asked, "O'Neill, I am Major Coombes and looking after security here for the British government. Tell me quickly if this assembly of staff welcoming the Lord is necessary and if you have employed any new staff in the last month."

O'Neill looked at the giant man before him and decided it was best to accept his claim on trust and comply, "Major Coombes, the assembly is a tradition and one the Lord and his guests will expect. In terms of staff changes, there are three. Two stable hands and one maid."

"Are any of them present here?"

"Yes, Sir. All are present."

Horace urgently asked, "Please, ask them that they attend the foyer immediately, where Sergeant Swanton will check them. Have your housekeeper attend the sergeant; she may check the maid."

O'Neill thought this was taking the situation too far and bit his lip as he considered whether he should object.

Horace noticing his hesitation, said, "Mr O'Neill, we only have minutes before your Lord arrives. We must carry out this search for his safety."

O'Neill agreed and called out the staff, who quickly followed Swanton. Horace looked around and noticed Robert holding the reins of the horses.

"O'Neill, when your stable hands come back, one of them may take our three horses. Sergeant Swanton will accompany him and check the stables. Lieutenant Hinton, please send a marine with Sergeant Swanton."

Horace could see that the coaches were now only five hundred yards away. Swanton returned and gave the all-clear as the staff retook their places in the welcoming committee. The stable hand took the horses' reins, leading them off. Swanton and the marine followed.

"O'Neill, we will stand at the corner of the house and observe. You may manage the welcome. If anything unusual happens, yell for us loud as hell!"

"What do you mean unusual, Sir?"

"A possible attack on any member of our party."

O'Neill raised his eyebrows with an amused look. "I can assure you, Major Coombes, you are safe here. We are particular in whom we employ on the estate, and our tenants are happy and thriving."

"Thank you, Mr O'Neill. That is most assuring."

"Lieutenant Hinton! Please stand at the other end of the Manor and watch from there as the guests arrive." Horace walked off, not waiting for an answer from Hinton and indicated that Robert should follow.

"I don't like this, Robert. We know nothing of the people here or who we can believe. That Lieutenant is green behind the ears, and I must sort him out on security. Not his fault, as I felt Scott would have sent advance instructions. The first thing Hinton should have done was check the staff. At the next Manor, we must be there a day earlier. I will speak with Scott about it."

As the coaches pulled up, Robert noticed no smile or a pleasant face among the assembled staff flanking the front door. The one exception was the butler, who grinned as he welcomed each coach as it pulled up.

As the guests stepped onto the driveway of Kellwick Manor, Horace murmured, "Ha! I have never heard of tenant farmers in Ireland being happy and thriving!"

Chapter 20

Lord Kellwick's Estate, outside Cork, Ireland …

Robert was ready early and decided on a quick drink downstairs before the official party gathered for dinner. He was keen on learning as much as he could about this estate and making it the benchmark for comparisons against other estates. There was also some self-interest involved as he intended to visit his father's estate in County Down while the mission was in Belfast. Some education about the running of an estate would be helpful.

As he reached the bottom step, the butler, Mr William O'Neill, greeted him.

"Sir Robert, you are slightly early. Might I suggest some time in the drawing room, and I will provide you with some refreshments?" O'Neill pointed out the way.

"Thank you, O'Neill. Have you recovered from our first encounter yet?"

"Major Coombes was very direct, Sir! I understand he was acting in the Lord's and his guests' best interest, but some warning on his security requirements may have assisted."

"I understand, O'Neill. I hope our security requirements did not cause you any embarrassment?"

"Thank you, Sir. We now have the situation under control."

"It must be expensive managing an estate like this. I only ask as my father has an estate in County Down, and I intend a visit while we are in Belfast."

"I see! We minimise the expenses by only keeping a small staff of twenty-five here, managed by a housekeeper. Mrs Maeve Carroll manages the household in our absence."

"You are not normally here then?"

"No, Sir Robert. I travel with Lord Kellwick. Usually, I arrive a week in advance, depending on which estate we visit. Lord Kellwick employs a housekeeper at each estate and prefers the continuity of the one butler as he visits. In this way, he receives the same level of service he expects at home."

"And where is home, Mr O'Neill?"

"My Lord's home estate is Kellwick Manor in Essex, Sir Robert. He spends most of his time there or in London."

"May I ask how long he spends in his other estates each year?"

"Lord Kellwick would spend two days twice a year in each estate. He feels the estate manager and the land agents manage well enough. Mind you, this is generous compared to other absentee landlords. I hear that some have never visited during their lifetime, leaving the land agents in charge."

"Thank you, O'Neill. That information will be most helpful when I visit County Down in a few weeks."

"A pleasure, Sir Robert. Now, do you have a preference for drinks?"

Later at dinner, Robert sat between Lady Dawlting and Lady Kellwick, which seemed an honour beyond his position.

Lady Kellwick, enjoying the dinner immensely, commented, "Sir Robert, this is my first visit here. I have never visited Ireland before. Lord Kellwick usually travels alone when visiting his estates and leaves me in Essex. I am finding your company refreshing, Sir Robert. I must say, I was impressed with your quick actions when you saved the prince's life at the Irish Charity Ball."

"Thank you, Lady Kellwick, for your kind words. I am sorry the proceedings were spoiled."

"Not at all, Sir Robert. England has another hero!"

"It was a duty rather than heroism. We train all the time for that sort of thing."

"But how did you know he was an assassin? The first thing we saw was you flying through the air at him and then the terrible scuffle on the floor."

"He failed in his disguise. I was enjoying the quality of the wait staff when his slightly different movements drew my attention. When a pistol under his tunic became visible, I was sure he would soon act."

"We are most grateful that you attended, Sir Robert. Certainly, we feel more relaxed on this trip given the tight security we have."

"Lady Kellwick, I thought you would have felt safe being on one of your husband's estates?"

In a softer voice, Lady Kellwick said confidently, "Far from it, Sir Robert. I am well familiar with the history of this island. The people resent the British despite what we have done for them. Since we arrived in Cobh yesterday, there have been far more angry faces than friendly ones. My husband is relaxed, but I am worried if I will ever see England again."

"I can assure you that Colonel Scott, Major Coombes and I will take every precaution for your safety. Also, I think you may misjudge the Irish people. Those I have met have been most hospitable and friendly."

Lady Dawlting, who had been listening, added, "I agree with Sir Robert,

Susan. I find the Irish people most accommodating, and I love the accent. I am sure you will be safe during our trip. Now, Sir Robert, you must tell me about your honeymoon, and how is Anne?"

Robert moved his chair back so both ladies could be involved in the conversation, "She is well, Lady Dawlting. I assume she is working hard now and probably redecorating our new house in Guildford."

"Sir Robert, Earl Dawlting and I loved the wedding, and Anne was so beautiful. We were very thankful for the invitation. Your father was looking so well and pleased with the proceedings."

"Yes, that was the plan, Milady. As you know, my father has suffered from bad health, and we were keen that before anything else resulted, he would have the joy of attending our wedding. Please, Lady Dawlting and Lady Kellwick, call me Robert. We are among friends and will spend much time together on this mission. I am quite comfortable with my Christian name only."

Lady Kellwick did not hesitate in accepting Robert's offer, "That is kind of you, Robert. Now you indicated that your wife would be working hard. Do I correctly understand that she has a profession?"

"She now manages her father's business interests. Anne is the Managing Director of Turner Bakeries and Milling. She also is the major shareholder in a chain of Tailors and Seamstresses called Hursts. This uniform I am wearing came from Hurts."

"That is most unusual that your Lady works! It is quite novel. She must enjoy this work?"

"She is addicted, Lady Kellwick. However, I do not mind as it is comforting knowing she is busy while I am away."

"Susan, she is a darling and extremely intelligent and beautiful. I will be entertaining at Dawlting Estate soon. I will include the Earl and Countess of Fintelton, Sir Robert and Lady Anne on the guest list. Would you and Lord Kellwick attend as well?"

"Hannah, we would be delighted. I am sure Lord Kellwick would enjoy the shooting. Robert, I must meet this Anne of yours. She sounds most interesting."

"I share your opinion, my Lady. That is why I married her." The three of them burst into laughter, with all the other guests turning around, wondering at their delight.

When the gentlemen had finished their after-dinner port and re-joined the ladies, Lord Dawlting took Robert aside, "Thank you, South, for looking after the ladies at dinner tonight. I think you have some admirers in those two. Now, how are you enjoying Ireland?"

"It is far more friendly than my last visit, Sir!"

Lord Dawlting smiled, "Kellwick runs a good estate and looks after the tenants far better than on other estates. Not as well as our English tenants, but better than most Irish tenants. Learn as much as you can while here, as we will use Lord Kellwick's tenants as the base standard for our evaluations. I am keen that these poor Irish receive some assistance as many have suffered greatly."

"What remedies do you intend to propose, my Lord?"

"Well, once we have made our inspections, the committee will meet and make proposals. I am unsure yet, but I will be making suggestions. I think the concept of 'tenant right', as they use in Ulster, may be of assistance."

"I shall assure you I will be energetic in my quest for Irish knowledge. My father has an estate in County Down, and I know nothing about who or how it runs."

"Then this mission will be of much assistance. Sleep well tonight, as tomorrow will be our first banquet, and I hope the security will be tight. I will join you at breakfast."

"Yes, Sir. Goodnight, Lord Dawlting."

The Wood Household, Guilford, Surrey ...

The Reverend Andrew Taggart stood beside a desperately worried Mr Blake Wood and his wife as Doctor Bryan Watson examined Edward. It was now several hours after the incident, and the boy remained unconscious.

Doctor Watson turned and spoke softly, "I am afraid all we can do is wait. Nothing indicates an injury except the laceration on his forehead. I expect that came from knocking his head on the desk. Sometimes the body maintains a state of unconsciousness until it can recover. I am unsure, but I hope this is the case. He may recover at any time, but it also might be several days before he regains consciousness."

"Doctor, what if he does not recover?"

"Mr Wood, I think he will. He is a strong, healthy lad; from what you have told me, he has a good mind. I think his body is protecting him from some pain presently. I will stay with him for the next few hours and monitor his movements."

Bryan Watson knew the lad had made no movements, which was not a good sign. The child was seriously hurt but resting comfortably. There was nothing else he could do. Doctor Watson hoped his diagnosis was correct, but there would be no harm in gaining a second opinion. Doctor Bassington was available and had far more experience in accidents involving trauma.

"Mr Wood, I would like a second opinion. Would you have someone call at our medical rooms and ask that Doctor Bassington attend, please? Mrs Wood might remain with me as we watch over Edward."

"I shall fetch him myself, Doctor."

Ethel said grace, and then everyone commenced their dinner.

Marcia asked, "When will Papa be home, Ethel?"

"In about three weeks, Marcia?"

"How many sleeps is that?"

Clementine said, "About twenty-one. I am sure Father will bring you a gift when he returns. Might be a kilt!"

Marcia was confused, "What is a kilt?"

"The men in Scotland wear short dresses. It is the tradition up there."

Madeline giggled, "I wonder if Father will come home in a kilt."

"I doubt it!" Simeon was unconvinced, "He would be embarrassed being seen in public with a kilt on."

Ethel thought about that and added, "The trip may have helped him with his grief. If he is feeling more relaxed, he might do it. But I agree, Simeon, it would be a bit out of character. William, how is Edward Blake?"

"He was still unconscious when I left their home at five-thirty. Reverend Taggart was there, and both Doctor Watson and Doctor Bassington. No one was smiling."

"Tell me, what happened at school?" Ethel was interested in how the child was so seriously injured.

Madeline cut off William and said, "Edward tripped and hit his head on the front desk."

Sitting with his mouth open, William seemed annoyed. Madeline gave him a stern gaze, and William shut his mouth. Ethel could see that the children were not telling the complete story for some reason.

"Was that all?"

Madeline nodded, and the others said nothing.

"Well, in that case, I think we should all say a prayer for Edward. Simeon, would you say the prayer, please?"

Simeon agreed and prayed, "Dear Lord Jesus, please help Edward recover and not let his family cry. Amen."

"Thank you, Simeon. Now, children, it is time for…."

Mrs Jennings came in, followed by Doctor Bassington.

"I was on my way home, but I thought you would all be anxious about Edward."

"Oh no! He hasn't….?" Ethel was thinking the worst.

"No, Ethel, he has woken up and seems fine except for a bit of a headache. Doctor Watson is still there and will monitor him for several hours yet. Edward should make a full recovery. I was sure the children would be pleased."

"Thank you, Doctor Bassington! We are all relieved. Praise God that Edward has recovered. I felt so sad for Mr and Mrs Wood, but now I can rejoice. Now children, off you go and get ready for bed. It has been a big day."

Neville watched as the children went off. Marcia wanted a hug and a kiss, so he kissed her, and then Madeline led her off. Marcia turned and said, "Papa is coming home in a kilt!"

Neville smiled as Madeline led Marcia up the stairs. The doctor was curious and asked, "Ethel, have the children said anything about Edward's injury at school today?"

"Just that he tripped and hit his head on the front desk."

Thinking aloud, Neville said, "That is what Reverend Taggart said, but the depth of the laceration on his forehead makes me question what is being said. I am concerned that the children may be covering up what happened for some reason."

Portsmouth Docks Area, England …

The lamplight shone down, giving the laneway entrance a misty look. Well concealed in the shadow of a doorway across the road, Aiden Reid had been watching for two and a half hours. The rain had stopped, and the temperature dropped as the early morning hours passed.

The message had come by post. The Black Whale pub had been established for many years and was owned by a man known as Michael McGinty, a landlord in absentia. McGinty died in action during the battle of Vinegar Hill in seventeen ninety-eight, but his death was not reported. Rumour had it that he set up the pub and installed a manager, and since then, no one had ever seen McGinty again.

Biddie Quinn took over the pub's management eight years ago from another brother who was required back in Dublin. She had no idea who owned the establishment and worked hard to keep a low community profile while building up the business. Michael McGinty was the code word used by brothers' members if they needed shelter in Portsmouth.

Aiden Reid had met Biddie fifteen years ago, and they had fallen desperately in love. Marriage had become a forgotten subject as the years passed, with Biddie stationed in Portsmouth and he in Cobh. She had given up hope of a relationship, only seeing Aiden fleetingly during the last eight years. After kissing him, she found her love was still as strong as when she was twenty-five. But was he the same man, and could she trust him?

Biddie had briefed Aiden on the drop-off system used at a pre-determined spot. He should follow the pick-up courier, whoever he may be, and find the following link in the delivery process. The Irishman was intent on tracing the source and who was at the top end of the message chain.

Aiden was tired. Some hot coffee would give him more energy and delay the stiffness in his body from the cold. However, he dared not move as this would give away his position. As he concealed a yawn, he saw a movement out of the corner of his eye. A gentleman in a top hat was stationed further down the road, partly concealed, and surveying the street. The man was stationary like Aiden and carefully positioned, watching for anyone else present.

Ensuring his body remained still, Aiden slowly moved his head, left a fraction of an inch, gaining a better view. The man wore a top hat, coat, and tailored suit. Strange dress for this time of the morning. He continued in his position for another fifteen minutes, ensuring the street was empty.

Reid was sure this was the courier, and the man would soon come along the street, enter the alleyway, and pick up the message. To Aiden's surprise, the gentleman disappeared after another five minutes, and a lone sailor quickly walked up the street and entered the alley. He reappeared within a minute and exited the way he had come.

'Clever, they think they have every angle covered'. Aiden opened the door behind him and darted through the unoccupied house and into the back alley. Sprinting along the back alley, he peered around the corner and saw the men. The sailor was now exchanging packages with the gentlemen who had surveyed the street. They separated, and the gentleman, who Aiden was now sure was the courier, walked away towards the Portsmouth business area, and Aiden carefully followed.

After fifteen minutes, the courier entered a two-level terrace house west of the town centre. Now accustomed to the man's profile, Aiden felt he would know him even if he changed his clothes. Quickly checking his timepiece, he noted it was four in the morning, and Aiden felt a growing need for sustenance. However, he must continue his observation and found a small garden further up the street where he could conceal himself.

Around nine in the morning, the man remerged from the townhouse, dressed in the same clothes and walked off towards the town centre. As the courier reached the High Street, he entered a coffee house and ordered breakfast. Now extremely hungry and desperate for a coffee, Aiden entered the establishment and noted the man's physical details as he passed. He chose a table at the rear of the coffee house from where he could see the courier.

Aiden ordered a large breakfast and picked up a broadsheet, holding it high while he checked the back entrance. As he enjoyed his hot meal, Aiden noticed several navy officers entering and leaving the café. It seemed a popular spot for navy staff living in the area; however, there was no contact with the gentleman he had followed. Then from the rear of the building, a navy officer appeared and passed by Aiden. With perfect timing, the courier placed the envelope at the aisle side of his table, and without stopping, the navy officer swooped it up and concealed it in his jacket.

Reid's suspicion was correct. There was a direct link with the British

Navy. He finished his breakfast and left the café, walking along the street and finding a spot to observe from near the corner. Aiden saw the courier emerge and continue down the road in the opposite direction for around fifty yards before entering an office building. He waited a reasonable time before casually walking past the building, noting the single-tenant directory sign – 'Carricks' Attorneys'.

Local Church, High Street, Guildford ...
At eleven on Thursday morning, The Reverend Andrew Taggart welcomed attorney Blake Woods into his study, receiving a message from him early in the morning that he required a meeting.

"Blake, I am always happy to welcome one of my parish councillors. How may I be of help?"

"I am surprised you ask that question, given Edward's injury yesterday."

"My apologies, Blake. It was thoughtless of me. How is your son?"

"Not well. Edward has bouts of dizziness and remains nauseous. He will not be leaving the house today. Doctor Watson has requested that he rests at home for the next week. I have talked at length with both doctors, and they believe that the laceration he received could have only happened if someone struck the child."

"I see."

"Reverend Taggart, it is important that you investigate this incident and discover the cause. I fear that your new man, the Reverend Hotspur, hit or attacked our child. However, I have no evidence as the school children in his class are reluctant when questioned. Could it be that Mr Hotspur has threatened them?"

"That I am not sure of, Blake. But I will find out. I will be investigating the incident this morning, and I will keep you fully informed. My wife has taken on that class for the time being, and Mrs Glossip, who has taught here before, has replaced Laura. Give me a few days, Blake. The children will open up. They always do."

"Reverend Taggart, I have great faith in you, and I thank you for your investigation; however, I must advise that my son will not return as long as Mr Hotspur is in any way associated with the school."

The Black Whale Pub, Portsmouth ...
"Biddie, have you ever heard of Carrick's Attorneys? They have an office on the High Street."

"Yes, some office clerks come here for a drink regularly. Sometimes I overhear them speaking about business."

"But no connection with the brothers?"

"Not that I know off."

Biddie's answer was unconvincing, and Aiden suspected she was not telling him the complete story. He knew he must trace the navy man's whereabouts so he could confirm his suspicions. But it may be best if Biddie thought he was leaving. It would not be long before the brothers were hunting him here.

"I will be away for a few days, Biddie. Would you stow some of my gear for me? I will collect it before we leave."

"But you said we were leaving for America?"

"We are, girl! But first, I must leave a trail with no end. That will be our protection."

"Aiden, I am nervous about staying here for too long. The brothers will come for you. I must not be here when that happens."

"They don't know I am here yet, so we are safe. I will be back in good time."

Polkinghorne Residence, Mayfair, London, …

"I am surprised at her recovery Mr Polkinghorne, but I mentioned that it was a strange disease. She is still weak from the fever, and now that it has broken, I suggest she will be mobile again within a few weeks. However, Lady Wendarm will require significant care as she regains her strength. I advise you to maintain the nurse for at least the next few weeks."

Stephen Polkinghorne took a sip of coffee as he sat across the table from the doctor. He, too, was surprised by the speed of Lady Wendarm's recovery and was quietly pleased that he would soon have her companionship again.

"I take it that now she is recovering, there is the possibility of several years of life?"

The Doctor frowned and leaned back in his chair.

"It is possible, but the disease is advanced. I think the delusional episodes indicate that there could be a sudden decline at any time. If Lady Wendarm is fortunate, perhaps two years at the most." Doctor Arrowsmith paused and thought, "It may be a mercy if she quickly went as if she lingers on, then the disease will cause her great distress."

"I shall ensure that she has the best of care."

Doctor Arrowsmith enjoyed the intense aroma of the coffee as he tasted it again.

"May I take a liberty, Stephen?"

"Certainly, Doctor! You have been the family doctor for many years, and I count you as a friend. Please ask what you wish."

"Stephen, you provide this lady with great compassion. I am sure your parents would be astonished if they were alive. She is obviously of ill repute, yet you provide her with protection in your home. Why do you show this interest?"

Stephen Polkinghorne sat up straight and looked the doctor in the eye, "That is a good question, Doctor. As you know, I have given up everything in life while building up my business. My parents' initial help with some small financing made me exceedingly successful. That success has come at a cost. I am a lonely man without a wife or offspring. It is only now that I have realised the implications of this situation.

I met Lady Wendarm by chance in Kingston. The attraction was mutual, and we enjoyed some jolly good times together. I immensely enjoyed her company on the voyage home but let me be clear our relationship was platonic and without blemish. We were never physically intimate. I felt for the first time in my life that I was in love. I would have revealed this the day before we entered port, but she spoke first and told me of her husband in Kingston, who had recently died and that she carried his child.

As I considered the implications and her claims on the South family, I took fright and deserted her at the docks. On reflection, I was ashamed of my behaviour as I still had intimate feelings for her. So, knowing she had no other family, I decided to rekindle the relationship. You know the rest of the story."

Doctor Arrowsmith nodded in understanding, "The ladies have a great effect on us, do they not? I am surprised you protect her, but I will not condemn you for your charity. I hope there may be a chance for some fellowship with her in the months ahead. I am afraid her life span may be short indeed. Be prepared for the worst, Stephen. In this way, you will protect yourself, minimising your disappointment."

"I shall, Doctor. Thank you for your kind words."

Porting, Guildford, Surrey ...
The countess kissed Anne and then Victoria as she entered the house and looked around with a pleased look.

"I think I am growing fond of this house, Anne. I see you are already making changes."

"Victoria and I are working on redecorating. She has some good ideas I would never have thought of."

"Then Victoria, you shall help me with Fintelton. It needs some refreshing. But first, I must rest before dinner. The coach trip was long and tiring. I am not that young anymore, and I find travel tiring. Margaret will assist me in changing into something more comfortable, so I might rest before dressing for dinner. I am sure we will catch up over a fine meal tonight."

With that, Lady Jane was off upstairs, followed by her maid.

Anne whispered, "Victoria, if you would excuse me, I must talk with Mrs Kirby about tonight's dinner and tomorrow morning. I must keep my mother-in-law happy."

"I understand, Anne. I heard the children play at the fort, so I shall visit them."

"Thank you, Victoria. That would be a load off my mind. It would be best if they returned home early this afternoon."

"I will see what I can do."

Victoria walked through the well-kept gardens, down the gentle incline toward the fort. She could hear the children talking with raised voices as she came closer. Not seen yet, she listened as they discussed the Reverend Hotspur.

"We can't tell, or Mr Hotspur will take it out on us. He has a violent temper, and I do not want him hitting me."

"But Madeline, unless we tell, he might hit all of us. I think he is a horrible man."

"Madeline, Clare is right!" William was overly anxious. "If we do nothing, he may hit Edward again, and this time he might not wake up."

"I am not sure, Will. He is stronger than he looks. It may be safer if we say nothing, at least for now."

Victoria quietly walked through the fort entrance. She noticed that as soon as she entered, the children stopped talking. There was no customary joyous welcome but only forlorn faces.

"Hello, children. I thought I heard you talking and came in. This is a lovely fort! When I was growing up in Ireland, I had a walk-in doll house with dolls everywhere. It was my magical place. I was fortunate as the servants cleaned it up after I had been there."

Madeline asked, "Did you have friends that played with you?"

"Very seldom. When visitors came with children, it was exciting. Most of the time, it was only my brothers who were not keen on dolls." Victoria grinned but noticed the children kept solemn faces. She sat on a box near Clare and could see they were not their usual relaxed selves. It was apparent that the incident at school was on their minds.

Victoria carefully said, "My parents spent a lot of money on my dolls, but I would have preferred friends. One day I became so lonely that I became angry and smashed all the dolls into pieces. When my parents saw the mess, I lied, saying the servants did it and should be punished. I was nine or ten and was avoiding the shame of what I did. My parents, of course, were aware I was the one who smashed the dolls. A few days later, my father sat beside me and explained that telling the truth was the best course. He said there would be no punishment, but it was better for me if I told the truth so I would not worry about telling a lie."

Madeline quietly asked, "What did you do?"

"I confessed. After that, I felt a lot better as I hated lying and could not stand the guilt."

Victoria sat there and let the children think about the lesson she was telling them. Then she said, "I also realised I did not want the servants punished for what I had done."

Clare said, "I thought your parents were dead, Miss Victoria?"

"They are. But this was a long time before that."

The children were quiet, but William said, "Mr Hotspur struck Edward so hard that he fell on the desk and hit his head."

Simeon followed, saying, "He asked if he could be excused, but Mr Hotspur ignored him. Edward was desperate and walked out, but Mr Hotspur hit him, knocked him down, and left him on the floor."

Victoria was shocked that Philip Hotspur could demonstrate this behaviour in front of children, "He did not help the boy? He just left him on the floor bleeding?"

Clare said, "I was so afraid I could not move, but Dawn and Ruby stood up and checked him, and he was unconscious. Mr Hotspur said he was play-acting and shouted at him, 'Get Up!' But he just lay there. I thought he was dead." She began sobbing, and Victoria put her arm around her.

"Children, why did you not say this before? No one would have blamed you for telling the truth."

Madeline said, "Mr Hotspur is a nasty man. He is not like Reverend Taggart at all. If we do anything wrong, he punishes us. We were afraid he would hit us as well."

"I see. But this is serious, especially for Edward. It would be best if you told the truth, children. I will ensure you are protected. Let me talk with Reverend Taggart. He will understand and solve this problem. Please, you must tell your parents about this tonight."

Clare said, "I cannot tell my father as he will take me out of school, and I will lose all my friends."

"No, Clare. I am sure he will not. It is more important that you tell him exactly what happened. This way, Mr Hotspur may be set straight about his behaviour. Your parents will be far more understanding if you tell the truth. Now, come with me. We shall walk Clare down the hill and find Mrs Preston, and then I shall take you three back home in my carriage. As Mr Turner is away, I think it may be best if you all speak with Mrs Nibley about this. She is very understanding and will help you."

They all stood and walked off towards the house. Later as they climbed into the carriage at 'Porting', the children were noticeably quiet. Madeline sat beside Victoria and the boys across from them.

Madeline started sobbing as the coach moved off down the hill and then cried bitterly. William and Simeon were surprised, and Victoria put her arm around Madeline and comforted her.

"You do not understand, Victoria. There is more, and I will be in so much trouble."

"What trouble would you be in for telling the truth, Madeline."

"It is because I have not told the truth. I have been stealing Mr Petherton's bottles." Madeline hugged Victoria hard and wailed, crying her eyes out. The truth was all coming out, and the child could not bear her guilt.

Victoria asked, "What bottles are these?"

She sobbed, "From Mr Petherton's bottle collection."

Simeon passed Madeline a handkerchief and explained, "She has been taking a bottle from his collection, one at a time. We found one in her bag some weeks ago but said nothing. I am not sure why she did it."

As they arrived at the Turner house, Madeline was still crying and in the arms of Victoria.

"You boys go inside, and I will bring Madeline in soon."

Simeon and William jumped out and ran up the front stairs and through the entrance leaving Victoria with Madeline.

"Now tell me, Madeline, why did you take the bottles?"

Madeline sobbed and then said, "No one loves me anymore. My mother is dead, and my father is gone away. No one cares about me, and I can talk with no one. They make me look after Marcia, and no one puts me to bed or kisses me good night. I am so alone!"

She started crying uncontrollably again, and Victoria knew the sorrow of losing her mother was too much. The eleven-year-old girl desperately needed affection.

"There, there, little one. I think your family love you very much, but they are all struggling with the loss of your mother. It is not an easy time for you or them. I remember when I lost my mother, father and brother. I was devastated for some time and would never let my brother, David, out of my sight. He was all I had left. I cried for months wanting my mother back, but after a time, I realised she was not coming back. It was a hard time, but it passed. You will come through this, Madeline."

"But no one loves me, and I cannot talk with anyone."

"You can talk with me whenever you wish. And I know that Mrs Nibley cares for you very much and would help if you let her into your life. She will protect you and help you through this."

"No, she won't. She bosses me around and thinks she is in control."

"I think she must do this, Madeline. Someone must hold the family together at present. You are not the only one missing your mother. Ethel misses her as well."

Madeline sat up and looked Victoria in the face, "How could she miss my mother? She is a servant!"

"I understand they were good friends. Your mother did not distinguish between people by class. She accepted them as they were. She was a wonderful mother and kept your family together. She would be so happy if she knew you were supporting Ethel. And from what I have seen of Ethel, she is also very loving. She has protected you so much during this crisis in your life. She is your best friend now, Madeline. Do not push her away from you. She needs you as much as you need her."

Ethel came down the steps as they talked and quietly waited beside the coach. Victoria could see her there but let Madeline regain her countenance before she opened the carriage door again. Madeline looked up and wiped her red face.

"Thank you, Victoria. I am sorry for crying so much."

Madeline hopped down from the coach, ran past Ethel without a word, and entered the house.

Dinner at 'Porting', Guildford ...

Lady Jane, who had greatly missed her daughter's company since the wedding, welcomed the occasion with Anne and Victoria for dinner.

"It has been hard for me at Fintelton without Emma's companionship. I now know how much I relied on her. Being here is refreshing, girls, as you cheer me up exceedingly. Now Anne, please tell me about this redecorating."

As the dinner courses came and went, the conversation was non-stop with suggestions for colours, wallpaper, changes in furniture and possible stable renovations. As they had coffee Lady Jane addressed the subject of Lady Wendarm.

"Victoria, I understand you will attend to Anne while she speaks with Mr Polkinghorne about Lady Wendarm. This Lady claims she married my son before he allegedly died in Kingston, Jamaica. Now you must support Anne, so she is strong with this man and delays any action on the subject until we hear from Hugh. I do not believe a word Lady Wendarm says, and, in my heart, I know Sir Hugh is alive."

"I will support Anne as best I can, Lady Fintelton."

"Good. Victoria, please call me Lady Jane! After all, you are one of the family members now, and I am comfortable with that form of address."

"Yes, Lady Jane."

The countess nodded in appreciation, "Anne, how will you start the conversation?"

Anne sat up straight and said, "I will commence by explaining that the news was unexpected and delivered in a most uncaring manner. The family's attorneys must assess Lady Wendarm's claims before any conversation occurs. The enquiries may take some time before the attorneys establish the veracity of the claims. I am sure they will not argue with that."

"I would be far happier if you first saw our Attorney, Mr Finchley. He will give you good advice on the best approach. If Hugh is dead, I will delay this lady as long as I can before she receives any recognition."

"Lady Jane, I will see the attorneys in London. Please be patient, as Mr Finchley has written and asked for confirmation from the governor in Jamaica—the time delays for gaining this information work in our favour. Lady Wendarm can do nothing until her claims are verified. I shall visit for Easter, and we can discuss it further then. Perhaps I might bring Victoria if it is not too much trouble."

"Victoria, you are most welcome, and Anne, bring some of your brothers and sisters. It is so quiet at the manor; some young people will be good for the Earl. It has been so quiet since Hugh and Emma left."

A tear ran down Lady Jane's cheek, "I feel within myself that Hugh is not dead, and we will solve this situation in time. If only he had found someone like you, Anne, or Victoria long ago, he would have solved all these problems for the family. There is nothing worse than a nobleman who does not marry. It allows the circulation of all kinds of false stories. The gossip chain in our society is far worse than the local church gossip. If you would excuse us for a little while, Victoria, I must talk with Anne privately."

"Certainly, Lady Jane. I have a book I am reading, and I will find a snug chair in the study."

Victoria excused herself, walking off in search of her book.

"Victoria is such a pretty young thing. She will make a wonderful catch for some young man one day. Is there anyone on the horizon, Anne?"

"Not that I am aware of, but I am sure that will change as she becomes better known in society."

"I am sure you are correct." Lady Jane looked at the fireplace and thought for a moment.

"Anne, before Emma left on her honeymoon, she gave me a quick update on the estate's finances and your enquiries. Who is this, Mrs Constance?"

Anne felt it was only fair to explain where the enquiries had led them. The countess listened with interest and said, "Anne, you have done a fine job. This lady appears to be involved, but I would prefer we proceed no further! I am worried about the Earl's health. He has been beside himself since he heard of Lady Wendarm, and I would be most reluctant to inform him of this, Mrs Constance. Who knows where it may lead? Best if we let the past rest. Surely, we should accept that the money is gone and find a way of continuing with the estate through income from its resources?"

Anne was now confused. Why this sudden change of heart from the countess?

"Lady Jane, until we find out Sir Hugh's situation, solve the financial issues with the estates in Scotland, Ireland and Jamaica and finalise a budget for Fintelton's produce, we are unaware of how much money is available. Mr Stem assures us that there will be more income from the winter crops, but I am unsure the money will last further than mid-summer."

"Precisely, Anne! Hugh will have returned by then, and we will understand the financial position of the farms in Jamaica. I am sure they will be healthy. Why sugar is very sort after here in England."

Anne was confused as this change in mind by the countess without Robert or Emma's knowledge would put her in a difficult position. It may also jeopardise the estate if the reserves decreased further and the bank became sceptical of the estate's future.

"Lady Jane, I am having difficulty understanding what you suggest. Are you saying we should not further investigate the estate's finances?"

"Yes, we know there are problems, but we cannot find any further information until Hugh comes home. I am sure he will return soon, and I am worried about the Earl. This incident with Lady Wendarm affected him terribly. He sits in the rose garden and mutters about her constantly."

"Come, Lady Jane. Let us sit together by the fireplace in the drawing room." Anne led the countess out and found some comfortable seating where they could talk.

With a calm voice, Anne asked her mother-in-law, "Now tell me, Lady Jane, why do you wish the enquiries into the disappearance of the money stopped? Are you worried that we might uncover something detrimental affecting the family in the past?"

"No, No, I do not know what you mean! I worry about the Earl and his health and Robert in Ireland. Who knows what trouble he will meet on that estate in County Down?"

"I am sure he will be safe. He will have Horace Coombes with him and a detachment of marines. That should deter anyone with any nasty thoughts. Now you should enjoy a little sherry and relax by the fireplace. We have made substantial progress on the enquiries, and as you say, Hugh and Robert will soon be home. We will finish the enquiries then."

Anne decided it would be best if she humoured her mother-in-law and did not reveal that Robert had already put moves in place that may elicit a response from Mrs Constance. He would insist that the action be continued, and she remained confused by Lady Jane's comments. Anne suspected the countess was withholding something she already knew about the missing money. Lady Jane's hesitancy made Anne even more curious about what had occurred many years ago.

Victoria joined them and said, "My, that sherry looks good. May I join you?"

Lady Jane's persona changed utterly, and she cheerfully said, "Oh yes, dear. Come and tell me more about the suggestions for redecorating this room."

Victoria had a cheeky grin, "First Lady Jane, I must tell you about the Easter eggs we made with Mrs Nibley. We blew out their insides without damaging the shell and are painting them this weekend, preparing for Easter and the egg dance!"

"Well, I never! I have not seen the Easter egg dance in many years. I am envious."

Turner Household, Guildford …

As the children readied themselves for bed, Madeline entered the boy's bedroom and sat on Simeon's bed.

"I was unaware you found one of the bottles in my bag. How did you find it?"

William looked up and said, "I left my jacket downstairs and fetched it. I noticed the bottle in your bag as I climbed the stairs. It scraped my leg! When I saw it was one of Mr Petherton's bottles, I showed Simeon. We said nothing, as we did not want you getting into trouble. You know what father is like."

"Thank you for not telling on me."

Both boys gave a smile. Then Madeline asked, "Did either of you tell Ethel?"

They both said, "No."

Madeline sat there and rubbed her red eyes. Simeon could see that something was bothering her.

"Have you been crying, Madeline?"

"What is it to you?"

"Sorry, I was feeling sorry for you."

"Oh!"

Madeline sat there thinking and asked Simeon, "Do you trust Ethel?"

"Yes. Why would I not trust her?"

"I don't know!"

William said, "She always looks after us and protects us from Father when he becomes angry. I trust her more than Father!"

Madeline shrugged and sat there for a while, looking around the room.

"Why do you always read, Simeon? Don't you get bored with books?"

"Never, they are so interesting. This one is about a man stranded on a desert island and how he survives. It gets scary as well."

Madeline sorted through a few more of Simeon's books, seeing if anything was interesting when Ethel quietly entered the room. She said, "I was checking on Marcia. She is sound asleep. Thank you, Madeline, for putting her to bed. It is nearly bedtime for you three. Make sure you snuff out your candles before you retire, please. Goodnight."

William called out, "Goodnight, Ethel. Thank you for looking after us."

Ethel smiled and closed the door.

Madeline quickly stood and followed Ethel out. As she entered the hallway, she called, "Mrs Nibley, I am sorry about today!"

Ethel stopped and turned, "Madeline, you know you can call me Ethel, so this sounds serious. What is the matter?"

Madeline walked along the hallway and placed her hands on the rail near where Ethel stood.

"I took the bottles from Mr Petherton's collection. I was scared that I would be in trouble if I admitted it. Also, I failed Edward Blake and his family by not speaking out against Mr Hotspur. I am ashamed of myself and did not confess when you asked."

"Madeline, I have been concerned for you and wondered why you would do this. I was sure the other day that you were aware that I knew the truth. Confessing that you have done wrong takes a lot of courage, and I am very proud of you. Now, we can help you set this right. But tell me, do you know why you took the bottles?"

Madeline knew she was losing control of her emotions and whimpered, "I felt alone and wanted my mother back!" The tears started rolling down Madeline's cheeks as she sank back into thoughts of her mother. She cried out, "Mother is not here anymore, and I miss her so much!"

"You are not alone, Madeline. You have a very loving family, and I also have great affection for you."

Madeline rubbed her nose and said, "Do you really?"

"Yes, Madeline, you are very dear to me."

"Might I hug you, Ethel?"

"I would love that very much, little one."

Ethel Nibley went down on one knee and cradled the crying girl in her arms. Madeline hugged Ethel with all her might and cried her eyes out on Ethel's shoulder.

"Let it all out, little one. Let it all out. You are loved so much by all of us."

Lord Kellwick's Estate, outside Cork, Ireland ...

Robert, Horace, and Swanton entered the stables before dawn and assisted the stable hands in saddling the horses. It was still freezing for early spring, and as they spoke, the steam shot out from their mouths.

"You are sure about this early morning ride, Robert? It is freezing out there, and some of those puddles are frozen. It will probably rain!"

"I thought you army men were not affected by the cold." Robert grinned, "Anyway, Horace, you have a fine coat to keep you warm. Swanton, is he this worried about the weather when out on manoeuvres?"

"No, Sir. When there is a battle coming, he is focused!"

Robert walked nearer Swanton's horse and asked quietly, "You have the muskets and pistols?"

Swanton checked that no stable hands were near before answering, "Yes, Sir. One musket and a rifle musket that I thought we might try out. Also, three pistols in the saddlebag."

Robert nodded and then shouted at a mumbling Horace, "Think of it as a fact-finding patrol. You will forget about the cold that way."

Pulling on his gloves, Robert mounted his horse and led the Major and Swanton out of the stable yard and up a hill trail behind the manor house leading towards Garranes.

William O'Neill appeared and asked the stable manager, "Where are they going?"

"Not sure, Mr O'Neill. But they did mention fact-finding."

O'Neill shook his head and returned the way he had come.

Over the low hill behind the manor, the country opened into a sloping plain that levelled out beside a faraway river.

Robert raised his hand and halted his horse.

"Gentlemen, Lord Kellwick encouraged me to learn from our visit here, so we are doing that. We have an opportunity to hear uncensored accounts from the tenants nearby. So hopefully, we can find someone who will talk with us."

Horace steadied his horse and said, "Those tenants we saw in the bright tunics yesterday. They were a set-up. I have never seen tenant farmers so well dressed in England. Lead on, Robert!"

They cantered their horses across the plain towards the first tenant's house in view. The house was small, with only two rooms and a damaged thatched roof. No smoke was coming from the chimney, and the cottage looked deserted. Robert dismounted and knocked on the door. No answer came, and the scene was silent except for the wind rustling through the loose thatch.

He pushed the unlocked door open. Peering inside, he could see the cottage was deserted.

"No one living here!"

In the meantime, Horace had been scanning the adjoining fields and noticed a larger cottage some thousand yards further down the hill.

"There is smoke coming from that cottage over there. There will be tenants in that one."

Robert mounted again, and they rode on.

As they neared the cottage, a man in his fifties opened the front door and came out, peering across at the approaching riders.

"This looks more hopeful, Horace. We have a welcoming party."

As they neared the cottage, two children came out and peered at them from behind the farmer's legs.

"Good morning, Sir. We have come from the manor house. May we speak with you?"

"Well, Sir. It will depend on what questions you ask."

Robert could see the distrust on the man's face.

"We are part of the mission from London examining the situation of Irish tenant farmers. We desire true accounts of the challenges faced by the tenants. From our enquiries, we hope our recommendations can improve the conditions of farmers such as yourselves."

Robert dismounted and walked towards the tenant farmer with his hand held out.

The farmer took his hand and shook it. Swanton breathed a sigh of relief as this was at least a show of friendship.

"I thought the Lord would ask these questions tonight at the dinner?"

Robert smiled, "Ah, Lord Kellwick invited you?"

"I was, Sir. But I handed in my notice as I decided to emigrate to America. The Lord has withdrawn my invitation."

"Then you, Sir, are precisely the person we need. Would you tell us about the challenges of being a tenant farmer here? We would be most obliged. I am Sir Robert South, Captain of HMS *Shadow*. May I also introduce my colleague Major Horace Coombes and my servant, Sergeant Swanton? Whom would I be addressing, sir?"

"Walsh. Seamus Walsh."

"Mr Walsh, might you spare us five minutes and tell us your story?"

"Well, it cannot hurt now as we are leaving for America." Seamus looked at the men and was confident they meant no harm. He found he liked this Sir Robert, who seemed somewhat more friendly than any other Englishman he had met.

"You better come in and share a tea around our kitchen table. I cannot offer you more as we have little food enough for the children."

"A tea would be most generous, Mr Walsh, thank you. Swanton, please keep an eye on the horses."

Robert and Horace followed Seamus Walsh into his house. As Horace entered the doorway, he knocked his head hard on the lintel and bent low in pain.

"Are you missed your footing, Major Coombes? That lintel is rather low. My apologies. Ruth, bring some water and a rag, please."

Horace limped into the cottage's main room, which seemed a combined entry, kitchen, and drawing room all in one. In the end wall, a fireplace held a cooking pot hung above a crackling fire that warmed the room.

Seamus Walsh offered them each a chair around the family's dining table.

Taking a seat, Seamus said, "May I introduce my wife Frann, daughter Ruth and my eldest son Michael? The other children are still in bed. You are early visitors, Sir Robert."

Michael Walsh joined his father at the table with the two visitors. Ruth left the wet cloth with Horace and moved away, placing the bowl on a window bench. She remained there looking out the window.

"My apologies for our early visit, Mr Walsh, but we felt it was the only way of gaining an independent view of the conditions for Irish tenant farmers."

"Well, you can see the size and condition of the house, Sir. It does shelter us, but as it belongs to the estate, we do not improve it as we have no tenant rights.

The farm is twenty acres with five dairy cows, which I must milk soon. The land is barely enough to support the cows, other cereal crops and vegetables we plant. We bring in some thirty pounds a year from the sale of milk and vegetables to cover the rent of six shillings a week, Lord Kellwick demands. So, we have around four pounds a year that we live on, plus anything we can gain extra from the farm."

"My goodness, how do you survive?"

"We cannot anymore. That is why we are emigrating."

Robert and Horace were both fascinated as the conversation continued and asked several clarification questions.

"Do you receive any recompense for tenant rights when you leave?"

Seamus laughed and said, "I wish."

Swanton opened the doorway, "Major, riders approaching."

Horace removed the wet cloth from his forehead and moved outside.

Swanton returned and passed Robert a wrapped package. "Just in case, Sir."

Seamus stood and said, "Excuse me, Sir Robert. I will deal with these men."

Robert had noticed that Michael Walsh was in his late twenties and appeared like a farmer. He wondered if he would take over the farm and stay.

"Will you be going with your father, Michael?"

"We all will, Sir. We have relatives in Boston and will make a new start there."

"I see! We visited the cottage further over and found it empty. Where are the tenants."

"Lord Kellwick threw them out for non-payment of their rent. The farm was only five acres, and they could not survive. They are in Cork seeking work."

"So, what happens with that tenancy now?"

"Nothing. I would expect you have heard of the Ribbonmen[30]?"

---

[30] The Ribbon Society was principally an agrarian secret society, whose members consisted of rural Irish Catholics. The society was formed in response to the miserable conditions in which most Irish tenant farmers and rural workers lived in the early 19th century. Its objective was to prevent landlords from changing or evicting their tenants. Members were called Ribbonmen. Wikipedia.

Robert and Michael heard shouting outside and a thud as if someone had been hit.

"What is going on?" Robert quickly looked out the window and saw Seamus Walsh lying unconscious on the ground. The men on horseback were pointing their guns towards Horace and Swanton. Before Robert could move, a man kicked the door of the cottage open and rushed through, grabbing Ruth at the bench and pushing her, belly first, against it.

"I have been waiting for you, Ruth. And now, it is my turn. I will give you a going-away present, darling!" He held a pistol in his hand and looked around the room. In his rush, he could not see Robert behind the opened door.

Pointing his pistol at Michael, he yelled, "You! Do not move, or I will blow your head off, you Irish bastard."

With that, he pulled the girl's skirt up and pulled down her underclothes. Ruth screamed as she was shoved into position, the man laughing as he dropped his pants.

Suddenly the man felt the barrel of a pistol press hard against the side of his head, and a hand gripped his hair tightly.

"You make one more move, and I will blow your brains out. You here, me, fellow!"

The man froze with his blinking eyes glancing sideways.

"Michael, come and take your sister into the other room."

Michael Walsh instantly came across, took the man's pistol from his hand, and put it on the table. Robert pulled the man back from Ruth and slammed him hard against the wall head-first, breaking the skin and bloodying the wall.

"Now, my poor fellow, we are going outside, and you are first. Forget your pants, and I will keep hold of your collar and remember my pistol is in the back of your head. Try anything at all, and you are dead!"

"Who are you?"

"Sir Robert South, a guest of Lord Kellwick."

Kingston, Jamacia …

Holding the verandah railing firmly, Sir Hugh South took a deep breath. He slowly let go of the rail and walked the distance of the verandah. At the far end, he stopped and turned without grasping the railing. He then walked back until reaching his room and firmly grabbed the rail. An excited nurse, Jackson and Fiona Green applauded his achievement.

"I never really appreciated the importance of walking. It is like being given one's freedom from jail. A new beginning."

"Hugh, the next challenge will be tackling the stairs. I am sure you will be ready for that soon."

"Fiona, I think I need some consolidation before the stairs. I will walk on the verandah this week and gain more strength. Perhaps by next Saturday."

Hugh carefully walked over and sat beside Fiona. She could see he was still weak, and the walking today had taken a lot out of him, yet his leg muscles showed definite signs of improvement.

"You did well here today, Hugh. You will get there and probably sooner than you think."

"Thank you, Fiona. You are always optimistic and have a smile on your face. Why is that?"

"I have every reason for being happy, Hugh. Soon I will be home in England, and it will be spring! A wonderful time in our country. I will see all my friends again. I am sure you will have so many people waiting for you. Returning home is a blessing we might both enjoy."

Hugh sat there with an uncomfortable look and did not smile.

"What is wrong, Hugh? You do not seem happy at the prospect of returning."

"I …." He could not speak for a moment or two. "I return home for my death, Fiona. For the first time in my life, I am afraid. I sound weak and cowardly, but I have suffered so much in the last few months, and my life is turning around. I would like a few more years if it were only possible."

"And so, you shall, Hugh. You have made wonderful progress in the last few months. I think there are still a few more adventures for you in life. You must come and stay with me in Bedfordshire and see where I live."

"I shall do that, Fiona." Hugh looked across the verandah and out into the bay and breathed in the fresh Jamaican air. "I shall do that."

"Hugh, there are only five weeks until we depart Kingston. It is time you wrote a letter home and explained your last three months' lack of correspondence. There is a ship leaving next Saturday for England. If you post it tomorrow, it will be delivered home in four or five weeks. Your mother will receive my letter within a week or two, but she must crave a message from you."

Fiona turned her head away from the view and glanced at Hugh. He was asleep in the chair beside her. She sighed, "Sleep now, my dear. Regather your strength, for we will be away and home soon."

Chapter 21

Lord Kellwick's Estate, outside Cork, Ireland ...

Colonel Scott, Robert, and Horace sat across the table from Lord Kellwick and Lord Dawlting, discussing the morning's incident.

"You are charging Hartwig with assault and attempted rape, Sir Robert! Are you saying that the victim of this attempted rape was Seamus Walsh's daughter?"

"Yes, my Lord. Joseph Hartwig would have raped Ruth Walsh in front of her mother and their children if we had not stopped him. The man was like an animal."

"But surely, he was playing a practical joke, Captain South. The man is my chief land agent."

"I would not call knocking her father unconscious, breaking into their house, and holding her family at gunpoint friendly behaviour, my Lord. He grabbed the girl and ripped off her dress, forcing her against a bench. He had dropped his pants and was forcing himself on her when I intervened. It was not a pleasant meeting."

Lord Kellwick frowned and then said, "I see."

"My Lords, if it was your daughter, would you hesitate for one moment about charging the fellow?"

Lord Kellwick was not amused and argued with a severe face, "But we are talking about a jolly Irish peasant girl. Her parents are troublemakers, and they are giving up their tenancy and leaving for America. For years, I have employed Joseph Hartwig as my chief land agent and can vouch for his good character. Perhaps, Sir Robert, he was provoked as this report of his behaviour is most out of character? I say let the matter lie. I will issue him with a warning and guarantee the safety of the Walsh family until they leave for America. I can assure you this will not happen again. Now let that be an end to it, and we shall go and enjoy the dinner tonight."

Horace Coombes asked, "Lord Kellwick, you say they are troublemakers. What trouble have they caused?"

Lord Kellwick was insulted that a mere army major would dare question his integrity. He spat out, "Well, they are always behind in their rent."

"That does sound strange, given they have told us they have always paid their rent on time. Now, how many years have they been tenants of yours?"

"Seamus' father was here many years ago when I inherited the title. I would say around thirty-five years."

Horace smiled, "Thank you, Lord Kellwick. It appears they have been good tenants for this estate for more than a lifetime of service. As I am sure you know, we look after our tenant farmers in England if they face difficulties. Given their poor circumstances, I think it would be fitting if you gave them some recognition for their service. Let us say ten pounds for every year of service. I am sure that would settle matters."

"That is out of the question, Major. Completely out of the question."

Horace stood and responded with a firm but quiet voice, "Lord Kellwick, I am a Major in the King's Army. I witnessed everything Captain South has reported here. These men made an armed attack on military men, held us at gunpoint, knocked an innocent man unconscious and then illegally entered the Walsh residence and attempted to rape Mr Walsh's daughter. These charges are serious and will carry a heavy penalty.

This meeting is adequate as a military court conducted under the control of Colonel Scott. I, for one, agree with all the evidence provided by Captain South."

Lord Kellwick retorted, "Rubbish, you were outside. How could you see what went on inside?"

"Your man Hartwick nearly kicked the door off its hinges in his enthusiasm for the girl. The door was wide open, and I had a clear view. Colonel, would you agree that we have jurisdiction here?"

"Yes, Major. The parliamentary mission acts under the control of the British government while in situ. The local community are under the protection of the military. As such, we have jurisdiction."

"Then Colonel, I will agree with my fellow officer and find Hartwig guilty of grievous crimes against British citizens. The penalty is death by hanging. I suggest we get this out of the way before the banquet. Do you agree, Colonel Scott?"

Colonel Scott swallowed backwards and said, "I concur with your findings, Major, and agree with the sentence."

Lord Kellwick looked hard at Lord Dawlting and gasped, "Are they correct here at law, Lord Dawlting?"

"I am afraid so, Lord Kellwick. They have jurisdiction."

Lord Kellwick was turning a shade of light red as his anger grew.

Horace continued, "Now, Lord Dawlting, we will see your estate manager and find some rope. But of course, and correct me if I am wrong, Colonel Scott, the army has some discretion in this matter. The military court may pass the prisoner and the matter to the civilian authorities for prosecution. But given Lord Kellwick's reluctance to accept the evidence, we must continue the military proceedings."

Colonel Scott smiled and said, "I agree with you entirely, Major Coombes."

Lord Kellwick stood there fuming, knowing he was soundly beaten. He turned and looked out the window onto an expansive view of his magnificent estate.

Lord Dawlting strolled across and quietly advised Lord Kellwick, "Mason, they are offering you an alternative. You might save Hartwig's life. I would take it if I were you. There is no time left!"

Lord Kellwick listened and considered what his close friend, Cecil Fowey, had said. He turned and faced them, "Colonel Scott, I would ask that the military hand this man into my care for civil prosecution. I will ensure the safety of the Walsh family until they leave for America and will compensate them ten pounds a year for each year worked on this estate. There you have it, gentlemen. Are we agreed?"

Colonel Scott and Horace both looked at Captain South. Given the situation, Robert knew it was not what he wanted, but it was the best solution available, and it would be wise not to ask for more.

With some resignation in his voice, he said, "We have an agreement, gentlemen."

Robert and Lord Kellwick shook hands.

Lord Kellwick said, "No hard feelings, South?"

Robert answered, "Sir, I can assure you I will always do my duty. I will protect you and your Lady with my life during this mission. My feelings are not my duty, Sir! I will always serve my King with honour."

"Thank you, Robert. I admire your commitment and that of your colleagues here. Let us all enjoy tonight's banquet in harmony."

Lord Dawlting smiled and said, "Here, here!"

Portsmouth, Hampshire, England ...

Aiden Reid spent the previous two days watching the coffee shop from a spare room in a boarding house further down the street. As the window in the front room gave a clear view of the establishment, he was confident of recognising the man if he appeared. Aiden arrived before dawn each day, watching until eight o'clock when he would venture across the road and eat breakfast. After finishing, he would again take up his position across the street. There had been no sign of the navy officer. The gentleman from Carrick's attorneys had breakfasted there on the second morning, but there was no pickup, and Aiden was sure it was a casual visit.

He recognised the navy officer the following day as he entered the coffee house at eight in the morning. Aiden needed a closer view of the man's face for more detail and decided to risk breakfast at the coffee house. Rather than entering from the front, he walked down an alley and found the café's back door. He noticed the weather was clearing, and it was slightly warmer today. As he entered, a kitchen staff member met him in the hallway.

"Sorry mate, I lost my way! Should have come in through the front door."

"Cheers, mate. Pop through, and we will take your order in a minute."

Aiden waved his thanks and walked through. From the back of the establishment, he could see the man sitting three tables along and facing the front of the shop. He was taller than he recalled, or it might be because he was sitting up straight. Aiden slid into a booth directly behind him, ensuring he could hear any conversation.

The café was quiet, but then several navy men entered, and three of them squeezed into the man's booth. One said, "Move over, Russell!" Aiden was not sure if it was a surname or a Christian name. He concentrated on his breakfast, coffee and newssheet while carefully listening. Then he heard the Christian name Martin used. He was unsure whether it was the navy man's name or one of his friends.

At nine o'clock, the four officers left and walked towards the navy district. Aiden paid his bill and walked away from the café casually in the other direction. Once they were around the far corner, he sprinted around the block and watched from a distance as the men continued walking, joking, and gesticulating about some subject they enjoyed.

As they entered the Portsmouth Navy gates, they waved and split up. Aiden watched as the man continued with a friend deeper into the base until they turned a corner and disappeared. He noticed a guard at the gate watching him, so he faded into the crowd walking towards the business area.

In the afternoon, the Irishman returned, searching for a vantage point to mount a watch. Down the street, he found a building with stairs up the side, partially hidden from the guards at the main gate. Soon after five, many officers walked through the gate, moving off in all directions. As the light faded, Aiden strained his eyes, checking each officer. Fortunately, the man soon appeared and walked quickly towards the High Street. Rushing down the stairs and onto the footpath, the Irishman kept in contact as the man strode on, crossing a park and entering a small general store.

The navy man soon reappeared and walked off towards the residential district carrying a bag of groceries. Aiden deduced from this that he probably lived alone. As the man reached his front gate, he stopped and surveyed up and down the street as if he were checking for someone following him. The Irishman was glad of the poor light and carefully kept out of sight as the officer disappeared into his house. Next, he took note of landmarks that would identify the position of the residence later. After checking for a back lane, he waited an hour before casually walking along the street and pinpointing the house. He was sure it was number twenty-seven.

Content with his work, Aiden Reid disappeared into the growing darkness, keen for a hot meal and a good sleep at his boarding house. He would return in the early morning and wait until the officer had left for work. That would be the opportunity to enter the house and discover his identity.

Turner Household, Guildford …
"Children, while you are having breakfast, I must tell you that Miss Victoria Sopwith and Lady Anne are coming in their carriages, and we are all going for morning tea at Cloverdale Chase. Mr Petherton and Clare are expecting us at nine-thirty."

The boys cheered as the fort's novelty had not diminished, and they enjoyed their friendship with Clare. Marcia rushed up and asked, "Me too, Ethel?"

"Yes, you too, Marcia. Now go upstairs with Clementine, and she will wash and dress you. You can wear your prettiest dress and take Buster with you."

Marcia rushed across and grabbed Clementine's hand, and her big sister gave her a hug. Clemmie smiled at Ethel and asked, "Am I included as well? You said children, and I am no longer a child, so I wondered if the invitation included me."

"Yes, of course, Clemmie. I am sure Mr Petherton would want you there. It is morning tea for all of us."

Clemmie smiled again and led Marcia off upstairs.

Madeline asked Ethel, "I am afraid Mr Petherton will be angry with me."

"No, no, Madeline. He is very understanding and will help you. All you must do is apologise for taking the bottles. They are all returned, and he is most satisfied with the outcome. He is very generous and loves children, so I would treat him as a friend."

Madeline seemed satisfied with this and rushed off.

Mrs Jennings came and stood beside Ethel and whispered in her ear, "One solved and another starts. Girls are definitely more trouble than boys!"

Ethel understood Mrs Jennings's meaning but put it aside as it was a fine day, and the prospect of a lovely morning tea was most attractive. Hopefully, Clemmie would not cause any trouble.

Boarding House, Portsmouth ...

The navy officer left for work, and Aiden Reid carefully approached the back door from the rear alley and slipped the lock. His movements inside were careful and deliberate, keeping out of sight in case any neighbours were home. Before commencing his search, the Irishman watched for curtain movements in the neighbouring houses, but there were none.

He searched the man's house until locating the wrapping of the latest delivered message, which he recalled inspecting at the Black Whale pub with Biddie. The wrapping was all there, but the message was gone. Checking through the navy man's papers, he confirmed his name was Martin Russell, and he was a Lieutenant in the Royal Navy.

The house search was long and painful as Martin Russell seemed a stickler for tidiness. Aiden replaced everything precisely as he found it, ensuring Lieutenant Russell did not suspect a break-in. Carefully surveying the neighbouring houses, he quickly exited and disappeared down the alley.

The events of the last few days had confirmed his suspicions. Someone in the brothers was communicating directly with the British. This revelation changed everything. If it were Iain Murphy, then he would need proof. He must carefully plan how he would acquire this. Perhaps he could use the British and trick Murphy with a false message.

It was time he planted his final trail to lead the brothers nowhere. A coach was leaving Portsmouth after lunch destined for London, and he would be on it. He would break his journey at Petersfield and see what information he could find on South.

As he approached the High Street, thoughts of Biddie came across his mind. He was unsure where her loyalties lay. It had been four years since he last saw her, and it was more likely that she was harbouring thoughts of mistrust against him. It might be best if he gave her some thinking time. Aiden quickly wrote Biddie a note, tucking it in his pocket. He would send a boy with it before he boarded the coach. The question now was how he should use this new information. He would consider this on the coach. There would be plenty of time for thinking as it would be three hours before they reached Petersfield.

Cloverdale Chase, Guildford, Surrey ...

Madeline and Mr Benjamin Petherton could easily hear the excited voices through the open study door as the guests talked and enjoyed a fine spread of morning tea and cakes. Their discussion had lasted for several minutes, and the young girl found herself comfortable in Mr Petherton's presence. She could not help comparing him with her father. If her father had sat opposite her, she knew his reaction would have been far different.

"Thank you, Madeline, for telling me why you took and returned the bottles. I am glad you feel better about your situation, and remember that if you ever need a confidant, the door is always open here. Now I think it is time you joined the others."

"Thank you, Mr Petherton, you have been very generous and kind. I will always remember this."

With that, Madeline hopped up, walked back into the dining room, and placed some cake on her plate.

Ethel came across and said, "How did it go, Madeline?"

"You were right, Mrs Nibley. I feel far better now I have told the truth." Madeline hugged her and then was off talking with Clare and Victoria.

"Mrs Nibley, I believe you handled that situation very well."

"She had us all worried for a while, Mr Petherton, but I believe this will be a new start for Madeline and me. I feel there is a deep friendship developing."

Benjamin Petherton nodded in agreement, "I see a change in the girl already. She is more confident."

They watched as the girls laughed, and Victoria shared some of her stories of Ireland.

"Mrs Nibley, I wonder if you would take lunch with me on Wednesday next week. I understand you have many household duties; however, you might delegate for an hour or two. I must thank you for the service you have provided my family with and the restoration of the bottles."

"That is kind, Mr Petherton, but there is no need. Your friendship is quite sufficient."

"I insist, Mrs Nibley. There are some other private issues I must discuss with you."

"Oh, I see! Well, in that case, I would be honoured."

'Harting' St James's Square, London …
The butler gave the footmen some quick instructions about the luggage and then escorted the ladies inside.

"Thank you, Staines! Now, which rooms are we in?"

"Lady South, you will be in the same room you shared with your husband previously, and Miss Sopwith, your room is beside Lady South's room. I shall guide you there now. I hope your trip was pleasant?"

"It was indeed, and this is Miss Sopwith's first London trip since she was a child, so besides late afternoons when our attorney will update me on the court case, we will be busy for the whole week fitting in sightseeing and shopping. I fear I have little experience finding my way around London, but I know Piccadilly."

"Lady South, if you are visiting diverse venues, I think it might be advisable if I send a footman with you who is knowledgeable of London's landmarks. This city appears safe but can be deceiving, and Sir Robert would be upset if anything untoward happened."

"I accept your offer as we will probably need a navigator and protector as you have suggested. Now, Staines. A special request. Might we have dinner at seven o'clock rather than eight? We country people eat far earlier than the society here."

"Certainly, Lady South, I will arrange it, and also, there is an urgent message for you from a Mrs Stubbington." Staines passed over the letter.

"I understand she will call at six o'clock today."

"Today!"

"Yes! It appears the matter is urgent, Lady South. Should I set another place for dinner?"

"No, that will not be necessary." Anne thought for a moment, then walked towards the stairs.

"Staines, please have my luggage brought up quickly and ask the house-keeper for Mary Hedge, my maid. I am sorry, Victoria, as I must leave you and prepare for this appointment. I was not expecting her until Tuesday or Wednesday." Anne rushed off as it was now five in the afternoon, and she knew how punctual Janet Stubbington was.

As the clock struck six, Mrs Stubbington arrived, and Staines showed her in. Anne had requested the use of Lady Jane's writing room, which provided the privacy she required.

"Lady South, thank you for seeing me at short notice. I apologise, as events take me away from London early tomorrow morning, so I needed to move our meeting time forward."

"Welcome, Janet. Please call me Anne as we agreed at the dinner."

"Certainly, Anne."

"Now, how may I be of assistance?"

"Anne, I am sure you recall our conversation at the Charity Ball. Have you discussed and read the agreement your father signed with our organisation?"

"I have not discussed it with him; however, I located the agreement amongst his files and read the document. I must admit I was somewhat confused by it?"

"Let me explain. My organisation acts on behalf of the government, and our task is gathering and interpreting sensitive information. We are not spying, but we are an intelligence organisation. Hamish McPherson has held an agreement with us for many years, and we have invested a considerable sum of money in assisting with building his company. We signed an agreement with your father as insurance and to protect our investment. Your father was uniquely positioned and would provide information about Hamish McPher-sons' business activities."

"Yes, they are now close friends."

"The problem now is! Pardon me if I put this bluntly. Your father suffers greatly from the loss of your mother and has lost his focus on business activities. I am sure he will regain this focus, but it may be some time before he recovers. He has provided little information despite our investment. We believe that you will fill in the gaps for us."

"Thank you, but I can assure you that my relationship with Mr McPherson is nowhere near that of my fathers."

"That is true, but your father and brother work closely with Hamish!"

Anne was unsure where this was leading, "How then does this affect me, Janet."

Janet Stubbington was impressed at how calm Anne was. She was now positive that Anne would fit the role they had planned for her.

"Anne, you are uniquely positioned in society and understand the effects industrial change is having. Correct me if I am wrong, but you attend London while the court hears the arsonist's case. You know firsthand our countrymen's differing views on industrial change."

"Yes, they continue and affect us all."

"That is correct, Anne. The government does not wish for the same fate as occurred in France. We wish for a more ordered future for Britain where all our people will benefit. The government employs our organisation to collect information to assist in managing situations."

"I understand this, but why do you wish me involved?"

"Firstly, we ask that you and your father continue providing information on the McPhersons. Hamish McPherson is aging, and within the next few years he will step down, and Lachlan will take over the firm's leadership. You will be working closely with Lachlan. He will be a great mentor for you.

Secondly, your profile will significantly increase through your social and business connections. Our organisation will ensure that happens; however, let me say that I am sure you will achieve this without our help.

Thirdly, your husband is destined for greatness; from that position, you will be given privileged access to society. You and Sir Robert will mix in an ever-expanding circle. The contacts you make contain many people in whom we have an interest. I am sure you will support your husband, government, and King in this way?"

"I will, but what do you expect of me?"

"Provide us with information! The same as your father is doing. As your stature in society grows, we will ask for information from other areas. However, at present, our focus is on the McPhersons."

"Who are these senior partners?"

"All I can say is they represent the government at the highest levels."

"How do I know I can trust you, Janet?"

"Anne, your father asked me the same question. The question is a fair one."

"I am always cautious about who I work with."

"That is wise. I understand that you are making enquiries about a certain Mrs Constance?"

Janet's question stunned Anne, "How did you know about that?"

"Anne, our business is intelligence. Now, we might assist you with that. Is there any specific information you require?"

Anne thought about this and then asked, "I need her date of birth, date of marriage, date and circumstances of her husband's death, and the date of birth of her son, David."

Janet confidently said, "I shall have the information delivered before you leave here for Guildford. Please keep all we have discussed confidential. I will leave you with this agreement. I would ask that you read it carefully and then sign it. When do you return home?"

"We leave on Saturday."

"I will have one of our staff here on Friday evening. He will pick up the agreement and provide the required information."

"Janet, I am unsure if I should be happy or terrified about what you requested tonight."

"Anne, please do not worry. There is no need. After all, there is nothing more secure than a government job! Now, if you would excuse me."

"Thank you for coming, Janet."

"Oh, one last thing, please. If you hear anything at all about the Irish situation, please let me have the information immediately. Here is my card with my contact details. The card is for your use only."

"You know of the changes happening with the McPherson Breweries management structure?"

"Yes, we have discussed them with Hamish."

Anne nodded and then said with a tremble, "Is Robert in any danger?"

Janet smiled, "Anne, you know your husband! He is always in the thick of it."

Janet departed, leaving Anne with a package on the desk. Anne decided she would open it tomorrow.

Staines knocked on the open door, "Lady South, there is mail for you here."

"Thank you, Staines."

Anne opened the letter and found it was from the defence attorneys acting for the accused, Henry Creek. He was the arsonist's group leader, committed for arson and attempted murder at the Turner mill. She noticed a message written on the top of the letter from Ethel saying, 'Dear Anne, this letter came late on Saturday night for Mr Turner. I sent it immediately on knowing the urgency.' The letter read,

Camston Attorneys
Chancery Lane
London

Mr Jonathan Turner
Turner Bakeries and Mill
Guildford, Surrey.

Dear Mr Turner
Camston Attorneys represent Mr Henry Creek, who the court has accused of the attempted murder of your mill workers and arson of your flour mill. Our client, now having considered his actions, is most remorseful. He and the other accused men never had the intention of causing any loss of life. Mr Henry Creek apologises for his actions against your mill workers, regrets his mistakes, and remains deeply remorseful.

If convicted, the penalty for Mr Creek's action is death by hanging.

Mr Creek will issue a plea for mercy. He has a wife and four children, and in the event of his hanging, his wife and four children would fall into dire poverty.

As Mr Creek's attorneys, we request that you consider making a joint plea of mercy and his sentencing be the lesser penalty of transportation rather than hanging. This sentence makes it possible for Mr Creek's lawful return from transportation in the distant future and reunion with his family.

We feel that the requested action would also benefit the general community, where there is much support for those affected by the industrial change in our country.

Please contact the writer urgently at the address above if you would work with us on this plea. I appreciate your consideration of this request.

Yours faithfully
Douglas Camston
Senior Partner

Anne sat down and shuddered at the thought of a man hanged until he died. She had no desire that any person should be treated in this way. It was a grizzly thought, and the letter was most convincing. Then she realised the writer had addressed this to her father. He was away, and with the time constraints, she must decide.

She drafted a quick note asking Mr Blake Wood, their trial solicitor, if he would meet with her tomorrow and advise her.

With this out of the way, Anne felt she could relax and enjoy dinner. She stood, covered her mouth as she yawned, and entered the dining room, joining Victoria.

"Sorry, Victoria, it took slightly longer than I expected."

"Forgive me, Anne, but Staines advised I should commence without you. Are the meetings finished?"

Anne smiled, "Yes, and the urgent correspondence, as well. I have an appetite, and I shall join you. Staines, I am ready when the cook prepares my meal."

"You shall have it very soon, Lady South."

"Thank you, Staines. Oh, Victoria, I shall sleep well tonight. I am exhausted!"

"Lady South! Would you care for a small glass of wine?"

The Rectory, High Street, Guildford …

There was a gentle knock on the door, and Laura Taggart, the Rector's wife, answered.

"Philip, you are very welcome. Please come in. Andrew! It is Philip Hotspur."

"Ah, Philip, welcome."

"Thank you for inviting me, Reverend Taggart and Mrs Taggart. Your offer is greatly appreciated as I have no wife, and my cook's food becomes somewhat boring after a while."

"Well, we will feed you well tonight, Philip. Bur first come into my study as we have a few issues we should solve before dinner."

Andrew showed Philip the way, and they both sat in comfortable study chairs, Philip with a slight look of concern on his face.

"Philip, I have finished investigating what happened with Edward Wood, and it appears that all the children tell the same story."

"What a relief! So, they confirmed my account?"

"I am afraid not, Philip. It appears they all, including Edward Blake, have confirmed that you struck the boy resulting in the accident he suffered."

Philip heard this statement with shock, given he had warned the children they must not say anything about his involvement or there would be consequences.

"That is most distressing as they must be banding against me. The outcome is most embarrassing!"

"I am afraid it is more than that, Philip. I have discussed Edward's injury with Doctor Bassington and Doctor Watson, and they both believe that someone must have struck the child with considerable force."

"I think they would have difficulty proving such an assertion. It must be that I am a newcomer, and they resent newcomers."

Andrew Taggart was amazed that the young man could be so steadfast in his denial when there was an insurmountable amount of evidence against him. He wondered what influences in his early life might have created such an attitude.

"Philip, given the weight of evidence against you, I find your involvement in the school has become untenable."

Philp Hotspur sat there nonchalantly, thinking he was not that upset if this were the outcome.

"I shall find some other work for you. Perhaps visiting the sick may be preferable. Also, a young clergyman always needs improvement in his sermon-making. So, you shall preach next Sunday for the first time. You will find the bible readings in the lectionary, choose one and preach on it. Would you give me a copy of your sermon, say by Thursday, please, so I may review it with you."

The young priest was somewhat put out by this request and complained, "Reverend Taggart, I must protest. It is far too early in my ministry here for preaching. Why I have not been here for more than a month, and you ask if I will stand before the congregation and preach."

"Surely, Philip, that was your ambition when you took holy orders?"

"Well, yes and no. I see my ministry far more in the pastoral care area. I have no desire to give sermons. It would take all my time just preparing, and I am not sure what quality I would provide with such short notice."

"That is the point, Philip. This opportunity will give you and me an idea of the standard of your sermons. We can work on them together, and by the time you leave this parish, you will be far more proficient in sermon-making."

"I see!"

"Good, now it is time we joined Laura for dinner. Perhaps a drop of sherry before we sit down at the table? What do you say?"

"An embracing thought indeed, Reverend Taggart. Would you, by any chance, have any scotch whisky?"

High Street, Guildford, Surrey ...
Madeline, Simeon, and William visited the Turner Offices, forgetting Anne was in London. The disappointed children began their walk home as a carriage stopped beside them, and a smiling Mr Malcolm Stem recognised them.

Madeline said, "Who is that Simeon?"

Simeon could recall the face, but William said, "Mr Stem, how are you?"

"Well, William. I am well, indeed. This must be Simeon, and I must apologise as I cannot recall your sister's name."

"Madeline!"

"Good day, Madeline. We met the night I assisted your sister Anne to the Fox and Hound for dinner with Lady Jane and Lady Emma."

Madeline suddenly remembered Mr Stem, "I remember you now, Mr Stem; you enjoyed Mrs Jennings' cooking!"

Malcolm Stem slightly blushed as Madeline made him recall sitting with the children and playing checkers while Mrs Jennings kept supplying them with cakes.

"Yes, it was an enjoyable evening. Are you all on your way home?"

"Yes, we forgot Anne was in London, so we are walking home."

"Climb aboard, and I will give you a ride."

The children did not wait for a second invitation and climbed quickly into the carriage, seating themselves like royalty.

Madeline was gaining a liking for carriages since Anne and Victoria had one each, "Thank you, Mr Stem. I enjoy riding in carriages. Do you do this often?"

"Not that often; mostly, I ride a horse. But when I visit the town, I bring the estate's carriage."

Madeline explained, "I see many girls riding horses. Unfortunately, I have never had that opportunity."

William quickly added, "I have not either! If I could ride a horse, I would hunt deer in the forest with Sir Robert! I could be a knight in shining armour."

Simeon said, "William, the armour would be so heavy you would fall off."

As Simeon laughed, William cried out, "I would not! Mr Stem, may I ride up with the driver? There is a better view of the horses up there."

"Certainly, William. But sit still and do not interfere with the driver. George! Pull up for a moment so William may climb up and sit beside you."

"Aye, sir."

With a big smile, William quickly mounted the carriage and dropped onto the bench beside the driver. George said, "Now, Master William, I will explain what I am doing as we go along. First, I will let the brake off and get the horses walking. Come on, Girls! Giddy up!"

The carriage moved off, and William, sitting straight-backed, watched George's every movement. As they slowly climbed the High Street, Mr Stem asked Simeon, "I think the last time I saw you, Simeon, you were recovering from a broken arm. How is it now?"

"Fixed, Sir. It is still not as strong as it was. Doctor Bassington told me it usually takes the bone a year before fully recovering. But I can now do everything I did before I broke it."

"And what will you do when you grow up?"

"I am not sure yet, but I like reading books and sewing."

"Sewing?"

"Yes, I may become a tailor one day. Everyone needs their clothes mended. Father would prefer me in the bakery, but I do not enjoy rising early in the morning. I think a tailor might be better."

Malcolm Stem laughed, "You are right about the working hours. Bakers do get up early in the morning."

Soon they were at the Turner household, and Ethel came out wondering who was arriving in the coach. She rubbed her hands on her apron as she watched the driver carefully helping the children down.

In excitement, William ran up the steps and yelled, "Ethel, I rode in the driver's seat. I can drive a carriage now. Mr Stem rides horses too. He brought us home from the Turner offices."

"What were you three doing there?"

"We were looking for Anne but forgot she was in London. Mr Stem came from the bakery."

Realising he had not met Mrs Nibley, Malcolm Stem said, "My apologies Mrs …?"

"Nibley."

"Mrs Nibley, I met the children and Mrs Jennings one night when Lady South courted Sir Robert last year. I was responsible for escorting her to and from the Fox and Hound. It was a good thing as William had beaten me three times at checkers in the kitchen, and I was keen on leaving before he thrashed me again."

He laughed, and Ethel smiled, "Mr Stem, I am Mrs Nibley, the housekeeper. The Turners employed me after you visited the house. Thank you for bringing the children home. Do you have business in Guildford?"

"Yes, I have been working today with Peter Hammer at the Turner Bakery about the arrangements for the summer crops. I have further business in Guildford tomorrow, selling some of our winter crops. I return south on Wednesday."

William, full of excitement, tugged Ethel's sleeve and asked, "Could Mr Stem join us at dinner and play checkers with us?" The other children all agreed and urged Ethel.

"Well, not tonight, children but perhaps tomorrow night. Mr Stem, if you are free tomorrow night, would you join us for dinner?"

"That would be kind of you, Mrs Nibley. But only on one condition."

"And what might that be, Sir?"

"Only if Mrs Jennings is cooking. I love her cooking."

"Mr Stem, I will arrange that for you. Shall we say six o'clock then?"

"I will be there. Thank you, Mrs Nibley – it is most kind of you."

The Grand Hotel, Kingston, Jamaica …

Sir Hugh South stood at the top of the stairs considering the first landing twelve steps below him. He recalled arriving at the hotel and bounding up the stairs without effort. Now he was terrified of falling if he placed his left foot on the top step and his leg gave way.

Fiona stood three stairs down and encouraged him, "Hugh. Hold the rail tightly with both hands and move down sideways. Do it one step at a time. There is no rush. Take your time."

Hugh gripped the rail and looked down at Fiona, pained, "I can't, Fiona, I can't!"

Fiona Green had seen it before with her aunt. The initial challenge was always the greatest hurdle, and when the patient was afraid, the carer must find an alternative and restore his confidence. She walked up the three stairs and stood beside Hugh. He released the rail and moved slightly backwards.

She encouraged him, taking his hand, "Hugh, you have been practising for days. The strength is in your legs. You can do this. You sit on the landing and put your feet on the first step as a test run. You can reach the first landing one step at a time. Let us see how you are after that."

"I can't. I am afraid of falling." Hugh sat down on the landing, elbows on his knees and placed his head in his hands, weeping. Fiona sat beside him and put her arm around his broad shoulders.

"Hugh, you can do this. You are ready. These steps will be your greatest challenge. I know you can master this, Darling. I will be right beside you. If you can reach that first landing and then return here, I shall give you a kiss. On the cheek, of course!"

Sir Hugh looked up with tears in his eyes and saw her comforting smile, "You do not know how much your care means, Fiona. You are the only person in my life who cares for me."

"I think many people you have mentioned care for you, Hugh. Let us do this for them."

Sir Hugh looked at her and then smiled. He grasped the rail again and pulled himself up. Slowly, Hugh, hanging on with all his might, lifted and then lowered his left foot onto the first step. Once the foot was secure, he followed with the right foot, his arms shaking more from fear than lack of strength.

"Good Hugh, you are on the first step. Now the next one. Remember, if you feel yourself losing your grip, sink onto the step and rest."

"Got it!"

Once again, he slowly raised himself and lowered the left foot onto the next step. Within ten minutes, he was a step above the landing.

As he slowly lowered his left foot onto the landing, Hugh felt a satisfaction he had not known since he was a boy. He screamed joyfully, attracting curious looks from the people passing the bottom of the staircase on the ground floor. Fiona quickly wiped away a tear as she noticed the exhilaration on Hugh's face. It was a defining moment, and he had conquered his fear.

"Now we need you back up there, Hugh!"

"Give me a minute. I must catch my breath." Hugh was standing there with a great smile on his face.

The movement back up the stairs was far more manageable. Hugh was not afraid of falling as he held the rail fast. Once at the top of the stairs, he thought about sitting when Fiona held him up and said, "No, Hugh, afternoon tea will be coming soon. You must reach your room before you rest."

"You are a real taskmaster, Fiona. But I will try."

He surprised himself with the ease of walking on the flat surface, and he quickly entered his room and sat in an easy chair.

"Well done, Hugh." She knelt in front of him and indicated that he should lean forward. Hugh smiled and slowly leaned towards her. She moved even closer, and he could smell the arousing fragrance she was wearing. Fiona placed her hands on his for support, and he felt their softness and the slight dampness from her sweat. As their faces neared each other, she looked deeply into his eyes, and he saw something he had never seen in another woman's eyes. It was a bonding of minds that he had yearned for all his life. Then she leaned closer and gently kissed him on the cheek. It was as if something had exploded inside him, and a joy so unexplained that wonderfully filled his heart.

"You must stay with me always, Fiona. I cannot do this without you."

As she slowly withdrew her face, she smiled and gently said, "I will be with you, Hugh, until the end."

Petersfield, Hampshire, ...

The coach ride allowed Aiden Reid time to consider the implications of his discovery. The brothers were unaware that a traitor was communicating directly with the British navy through McGinty. Someone in Dublin knew about this, probably Iain Murphy. Was Lieutenant Martin Russell a friend of the brothers or a loyal British Navy officer? The question had been going through Aiden's mind since he left Portsmouth.

Slowly taking note of his surroundings, Aiden made sure he dropped his accent as he entered the closest pub he could find. The bar was only a third full, and no doubt, many more would gather here as the afternoon wore on. He confidently approached the counter, dropped his bag onto the floor and rested his eyes on the barman.

"What would you like, Mister?"

Mustering his best Welsh accent, "A half scotch, please."

"Ah, a Welshman. What brings you here, son."

"Work, me man! Looking for work. Do you know of any?"

The barman carefully looked Aiden up and down and said, "Outside work by the look of you! The big estates around here are the best for work. With the cold weather, the spring planting has not started yet. You may be in time if you are quick."

"Where is the biggest estate?"

"Try Fintelton or Plaintbury estates. Try Fintelton first. They have the most fields under cultivation this year. The Estate Manager is a Mr Stem. A nice man, he comes in here some days."

"Who owns Fintelton? Are they good people?"

"Fine people! They have been here for generations. The Earl and Countess of Fintelton are well-liked here in town. Their son is popular here after saving the prince's life. Sir Robert South is his name."

"Does he run the estate?"

"No, he is the second son. Sir Robert lives in Guildford now. He is in the Navy and is away a lot. He decided on Guildford, so his wife could keep her family close."

"A wise choice."

"Aye, lad. Happy wife, happy life! Another scotch?"

"Yes, thanks. Do you have rooms for the night?"

"One shilling, please and includes breakfast. See Margaret at the back, and she will show you up."

Aiden laid down his shilling and drank his scotch, "Thanks, mate."

The barman watched him as he walked towards Margaret, curious about something strange in his accent.

Turner Household, Guildford ...

The dinner was substantial, and Ethel noticed that Mrs Jennings had put extra effort in during the afternoon, ensuring several excellent courses were ready for the meal. All the children were satisfied, and Mr Stem was most thankful. He insisted that Mrs Jennings join them for dessert, which Ethel thought was allowable as Mr Turner was away, and Mrs Jennings had long service with the family.

"Mrs Jennings! The meal was far more than I expected. It was wonderful, and I thank you so much. It was ten times better than I expected at the boarding house."

"Sir! Given the service you have provided Miss Anne, now Lady South, and the children, it is the least I could do. It will also hold you in good stead when you battle the children at checkers in a few minutes. Would you prefer tea or coffee, Mr Stem?"

"Tea, thank you. Mrs Nibley, would playing checkers on the kitchen table be acceptable? That would allow clearing the dinner plates here, and I would feel more comfortable there. Every advantage I might gain would be of help."

"Of course, Mr Stem. You are more than welcome in the kitchen if you desire that."

Mr Stem and the children were already on their way. The move seemed odd, but Ethel complied and said no more, joining them with Marcia in tow.

William set the board up quickly and sat ready for the first game.

Ethel suggested, "William, it may be best if Madeline plays first. Ladies first is the gentlemanly thing."

William hopped out of the way and sat beside Marcia, who was already rubbing her eyes. Madeline had not expected the honour of the first game and was most excited. Clemmie stood beside her, ready with advice. Ethel placed Marcia on her lap and sat at the end of the table. The little five-year-old held her toy bear tightly and snuggled under Ethel's chin.

William informed Mrs Jennings, "Mr Stem has a carriage and rides horses. Archie Watson told me he would be riding a horse soon. I wish I could ride a horse."

Mr Stem made his checker's move and then considered William's comment, "There is a simple solution, Master William. You must convince your sister, Lady South, to visit Fintelton and bring all the children. If you can manage that I will arrange some riding lessons for you. We have some lovely smaller horses that are perfect for children."

"Ethel, may we? I am sure Anne will take us. We must ask her as soon as she returns."

Ethel put her finger across her mouth, "Shush."

She indicated with her eyes at Marcia, and they all noticed the little one was asleep. Ethel whispered, "I will take care of her in the drawing room until you are ready, Madeline, then we will both take her up."

Madeline whispered back with a thank you smile, "Thank you, Ethel."

Ethel noticed the response was genuine, and even Clemmie smiled approvingly.

Ethel carried the child into the drawing room and sat beside the fire with Marcia on her lap. She remembered her daughter, Rosalind, at this age and missing so much of her childhood. What a privilege it was to look after this sweet little one. She could hear the soft breathing as the child was cradled in her arms, resting on her lap. Soon Marcia's grip loosened on 'Buster', the toy bear, and the little hand went limp.

Polkinghorne Residence, Mayfair, London ...
Nurse Best knocked on Stephen Polkinghorne's study door.

"Enter!"

"Mr Polkinghorne, has Lady Wendarm been moved somewhere as she is not in her room?"

Stephen looked up with a confused face wondering why Nurse Best would ask this question.

"No, of course not, she received breakfast in her room, and I was planning on spending morning tea with her in the upstairs drawing room."

"Sir, the room is empty, and some of her clothes are gone."

Stephen stood and rushed out and up the stairs. Walking quickly down the hall, he pushed the half-shut door and entered Clarissa's room. There he found the maid making up the bed.

"Sadie, where is Lady Wendarm?"

"I am not sure, Sir! I thought she might be in the drawing room."

Stephen quickly left the room and sped there. There was no sign of her. He called the maid, "Please search the house and see if you can find her."

Before the maid commenced the search, Nottle, the butler, appeared and advised, "Sadie, please wait."

Stephen would have reprimanded Nottle, but the butler spoke first, "Mr Polkinghorne, Lady Clarissa left about half an hour ago. She advised me that you knew she was taking a walk and she would return in an hour. I took her at her word, Sir. Otherwise, I would have advised you immediately."

Stephen Polkinghorne stood there with his mouth open.

Port of Cobh, Ireland …

The dock was busy, and children ran with excitement amongst the crowd knowing the ship would sail soon. Michael Walsh watched as porters placed his family's luggage on a trolley, ready for loading onboard. Ruth suddenly ran up, pulled her case from the cart, and held it by her side as the porters wheeled the trolley away.

"I am not going yet, Michael. If they have a job for me, I will stay with you. We will do this last mission together."

"Are you sure, Ruth? Mother will need you in Boston; there is nothing for you here now. I think you should go while you have the chance."

"Ireland is here, Michael! That is enough. Now let us get the family onto the ship."

The luggage had gone, and the only remaining step was boarding. At the bottom of the gangway, the crew called out instructions, and the last passengers climbed onto the ship. The family made its way along the dock and stopped at the gangway. Frann hugged her daughter so tight, tears running down her cheeks, until Seamus asked if he could also have a hug.

"Take care of Michael for us, Ruthy. We will wait for you in Boston. You have the details."

Seamus noted the sparkle of youth in his beautiful daughter's eyes before hugging her and praying he would see her again. Then she was free of him and hugging her brothers and sisters. Michael had finished hugging his mother and came and shook his father's hand. Seamus grabbed him and pulled him close.

"Watch your back, Michael. I have a bad feeling about this mission. I have a bad feeling!"

"Leave it with me, Da. Now you take care of the family, and we will both be there in no time."

Michael almost herded them all onto the gangway, and they were up and onto the barque. Within half an hour, the ship was a speck on the ocean as it passed Spike Island and disappeared out of sight.

"Time for a good sleep tonight at Auntie Madge's and then Dublin tomorrow. Are you sure this is what you want, Ruth?"

"No! But I will do my duty. Michael, we are in a war, and I know now that Ireland will not be set free without sacrifice. If God spares me, then I will see them again. If not, I will see them in heaven."

Michael smiled and said, "I had never thought of it that way. Let us see if Auntie Madge is home!"

But Ruth was not listening as she followed. She was miles away thinking, 'I will not leave you again, Callum, my love.'

Lord Kellwick's Estate, outside Cork, Ireland ...

The carriages were loaded, and the passengers were now boarding. Robert stood beside Lord Kellwick's carriage, waiting for the Lady's. He scanned the surroundings looking for anything out of order, but everything seemed in place. Lady Kellwick came out of the front door and walked straight for him. Some distance behind her, Lady Dawlting followed.

Lady Kellwick turned at the last moment and was helped into the carriage by the footman. She then indicated, calling Robert over. He quickly responded and moved beside the coach.

"Thank you, Robert, for watching over us. I am most glad that the first banquet is over. I watched over my shoulder all night, wondering if anything would eventuate. It appears that the security has worked. At least here, we could contain who attended. Having you and the others here for our protection is such a relief."

"It is my pleasure, Lady Kellwick. Now for a quiet return journey and then an enjoyable voyage before Dublin. I am sure you will sleep well tonight."

"I shall indeed. The sea rocks me off very pleasantly."

Robert tipped his hat and moved away as a footman helped Lady Dawlting into the carriage. The two Lords followed. Colonel Scott appeared on his horse and led the line of carriages forward, joining the leading guard party headed by Major Coombes. Robert noticed as they moved off some unhealthy smirks in the staff line. He realised Horace had been correct, demanding a more thorough check of the employees. Still, the visit here was over, and at least this group could no longer harm the party. But he noted the faces in case they inexplicitly appeared again in Dublin.

Lieutenant Hinton was standing near Robert, and the butler William O'Neil was heading his way. Robert turned and smiled at Hinton, "You will join us in Dublin then, Hinton?"

"No, Sir! I will head for Belfast next. Lieutenant Balfour is already in Dublin preparing. I hope for his sake he is checking the staff carefully. I will not make that mistake again in Belfast."

"I think we are all learning as we go along on this mission, Lieutenant."

"Aye, Sir!"

"We shall meet again in Belfast, then Hinton! Perhaps if time permits, we may share a drink."

Lieutenant Hinton seemed pleased by the comment, and he smiled and said, "Definitely, Sir!"

He then turned and led his squad of marines towards the stables. O'Neill was standing close, waiting for a final word.

"Captain, I hope you found the visit enjoyable and informing."

"I did indeed, O'Neill."

"I understand that Lord Kellwick may soon invite you and your good lady into Essex. It appears Lady Kellwick is most anxious this occurs." The butler half-smiled as he said, "Lord Kellwick strangely seems a little half-hearted today! I am sorry that the unfortunate incident occurred during your early morning exploration of the estate. I understand the tenant has left with the required compensation."

"That is most reassuring, O'Neill."

"Sir, might I confide in you quickly before you go?"

"Yes, O'Neill. My lips are sealed." Robert smiled, expecting another discourse about the estates' happy tenants.

O'Neill lowered his voice, "Sir, Lord Kellwick sends me onto Belfast. I will not be in Dublin! This decision is most unusual as I have always been with him since I joined Lord Kellwick's service some twenty-three years ago. This time he has insisted that I am ready for his arrival in Belfast. I am worried for them both, Sir. Please look out for him and his fine wife. She is petrified of this mission and hardly sleeps."

"I will do my best, O'Neill, and thank you for advising me of this information."

O'Neil took a long breath. He took a step away, then turned and said,

"Captain, I am sure you are wondering who you can trust. Lord Kellwick or I bear you no ill will. I have served Lord Kellwick for twenty-three years. He has his faults, as do all men, but I have always found him a fine man. You can trust him, Sir."

With that, O'Neill walked away towards the Manor. Robert called out, "O'Neill."

The butler stopped and turned.

"Thank you!"

Robert watched the genuine expression on O'Neil's face. A guilty man could not make an expression like that. He gathered from the smile that there was more truth in what O'Neill told him than untruth. It was interesting. Robert had found the same wisdom in Pike at Fintelton. O'Neill's comments disturbed Robert as it meant something unusual was happening in Dublin. Perhaps the assassination attempt would be made there.

Swanton came up from behind with the horses. He passed Robert the reins.

"Thank you, Swanton. I have a feeling we will soon be entering the lion's den!"

Chapter 22

'Harting', St James's Square, London ...

Mary Hedge entered the room and opened the curtains letting in the sun through the eastern-facing windows.

"Good morning, Mary! What time is it?"

"Seven-thirty, Ma'am. Miss Victoria has gone down for breakfast. She advised you needed a sleep-in, so I did not wake you. There is a cup of tea and a roll for you here."

"Thank you, Mary. What a glorious day."

"Yes, Ma'am. Not a cloud in the sky and a light wind."

"I shall enjoy it today. We have no appointments until three this afternoon. Please tell Victoria I will be down for breakfast in a few minutes, then come back up, and you can assist me in dressing."

"Yes, Ma'am."

Anne looked at the last letter she had received from Robert. The mission would arrive in Dublin on Friday. She felt cold, as if a northerly wind were blowing on her, and shivered, thinking of her husband far away.

"Please, God, protect him today. Bring Robert home soon so we can be together."

Mary re-entered the room and said, "Miss Victoria sends her greetings and is going for a walk in the square. She will join you for breakfast when you are down."

"Thank you, Mary."

Anne held the letter against her chest and sipped her tea.

Dublin, Ireland ...

As the coach stopped on the outskirts of Dublin, Michael Walsh opened his eyes and noticed the hotel and stables beside them. It was early morning, but the street was not empty. Several soldiers were rushing past the coach, pushing a stumbling man the soldiers had beaten. They hurried away down the footpath goading him as they went.

Michael leaned forward as the driver climbed back into his seat and asked, "What was that all about?"

The driver turned and quietly said, "Seems like there is a bit of a crackdown in Dublin, extending into the suburbs. A government mission is coming, ensuring the population makes no trouble. You best keep a low profile if you value your freedom this morning."

Michael slouched as watchmen brought another man past, this time in chains. As he looked closer, it was clear the man had been pitch-capped and could hardly stand. The authorities were giving the rebels a warning. 'If you protest, we will make your life hell!' The poor fellows arrested were probably innocent, which would have the reverse effect on the people of Dublin.

From the coach's top seat behind the driver, Michael could see the people in the streets were scared. The crackdown was having its desired effect. He considered how best he and Ruth could avoid this heightened security.

There was a safe house on the other side of town, but they should leave the coach earlier and find shelter rather than risk crossing the centre of Dublin by day. Michael felt their chances would be better with Aiden Reid's aunt Máire again. Family networks were essential in Ireland for keeping undercover and out of the soldier's and watchmen's sight. He would rather be on the streets at night, but that was not an option now. The roads would be dangerous if they could not find a hiding place quickly.

Michael leaned forward towards the driver and asked, "Driver, would you let an Irish boy and his lass off early near Portobello, please?"

"God bless Ireland, lad! Make sure you get her out of the coach quickly. Keep your heads down and get out of sight as soon as you can!"

Michael smiled, understanding the driver was a republican as well.

When the coach stopped, Michael jumped and pulled Ruth out of the cabin. The driver threw their bags down, and then the coach was on its way. Having been here recently, Michael quickly surveyed the area and led Ruth toward the Reid house. The number of people out and about was amazing, making fading into the crowd easier.

On finding the correct street, Michael edged his head around the wall of the corner house and saw Mrs Reid standing at her gate, surrounded by several watchmen. The front door was open, and Mrs Reid yelled at a watchman, who stepped back and struck her hard across the face, forcing her down on her knees. As Máire Reid held her face in her hands, the men pushed past and searched the house. Michael realised he had made the wrong decision coming here.

A short, low whistle came from behind them. At the rear of the house, a wiry older man with a fancy cap leaned over the fence and beckoned them towards the back gate. Michael and Ruth quickly approached him.

"Tis the watchmen down there! Quick! If you need shelter go around into the alley and through the back gate. You must get off the street."

Ruth needed no convincing and led the way as the man opened the back door and beckoned them inside.

"Me name is O'Reilly, Patrick O'Reilly, and I was with Emmet back in eighteen-o-three. I thought you might be avoiding the watchmen as they are on the hunt today."

"Thank you! My name is Ruth Walsh, and this is my brother, Michael. We would have visited Mrs Reid down the street, but the watchmen are harassing her."

"Poor woman, they are searching for her nephews. It may be wise if you stay away from her today. They will be watching."

Michael agreed with Mr O'Reilly's suggestion, "Mr O'Reilly, if we could stay until dark, that would be a great favour."

"I will not ask what you are doing as it is best if I don't know. But it should be dark by eight o'clock, so you are welcome. Would you like a cup of tea?"

"Yes, thank you. You say the British are looking for Mrs Reid's nephews. How do you know that?"

"We are old friends, the Reid family and me. We all talk, you know. First, they were looking for Sean. Of late, they are looking for Aiden. They still want them both, but lately, they seem more interested in Aiden. I don't know the full details, but something happened in Scotland. I think the boys were involved."

Michael and Ruth looked at each other. The wiry older man was still quick in his mind and saw the looks of concern.

"You both are involved? Good on you two. I thought you were the way you were peering around that corner. Let me show you something."

He led them into the next room and pointed out a wall cupboard beside a bed. It stood about five feet high with flaking old green paint. Opening the squeaky door, he revealed a couple of old suits and other clothes on hangers. Pushing them aside, he carefully pushed open a concealed door carpentered into the back of the cupboard. It opened into a small room three feet wide and six feet long but extended to the ceiling height. There were two chairs and a box with candles and a tinder box on the middle. Another box piled with blankets sat in the corner.

"Emmet hid here once, and it saved his life. When the watchmen come, duck in here and close these locks from behind, securing the cupboard's back wall. Do not light the candle until you are sure they are gone! They will come and search. They always do as they know I was with Emmet and supported the movement. But they know my age and usually leave quickly. You will be safe. Take your tea in there and rest. I will be out in the garden. If they come, you will hear me shouting at them."

Michael and Ruth ducked into the room, pulled the clothes hangers along the rail, and closed the door. It was pitch dark except for a tiny glimmer of light that came through a crack in the roof. Ruth was shivering, so Michael lit the candle and reached for the blankets. There were three or four blankets on the corner box. He grabbed two blankets and draped them around her.

Ruth looked up, "How did they know about Aiden?"

Michael was asking the same question in his mind, "It was either from the committee in Glasgow or from an informer here in Dublin. The last time I met Aiden, he told me he did not trust Murphy. I think he may be right. This assassination attempt is already doomed. If they are rounding up folks now, imagine what they will do after any assassination. It will be hell in Dublin for a long time. We must stop this, and someone must confront Murphy."

"That may not be a good idea without proof." Ruth was sure confrontation would cause a backlash. "If Murphy is with the British, then he is dangerous. We must find the evidence first and then convince some of the other brothers."

"Easier said than done."

From outside, there was shouting.

"O'Reilly! We will search your house now. You being an old Republican. Are you hiding Aiden Reid?"

"Well, if I were, I wouldn't tell you about it, would I?"

Michael snuffed the candle as he heard them entering the house.

Ruth whispered, "I hope Patrick O'Reilly is who he said he was! Otherwise, these watchmen will torture us."

Michael went, "Shush."

It was a small house with only five rooms, and they could hear the men knocking over the furniture as they searched. Finally, they entered the room where Michael and Ruth were hiding. One of the men opened the cupboard door and pushed the clothes aside. Michael held his breath as they both remained utterly silent.

There was a sound of the man pushing against the back wall of the cupboard, but it held fast. The man closed the cupboard door. "Nothing in here, Tom. Check the shed out the back."

One of the men sounded as if he was leaving, but then the other shouted, "Don't get any ideas of helping republicans, Pat! This is why!" Michael and Ruth heard the watchman severely beating Patrick and someone falling on the floor. They could hear Patrick being kicked repeatedly and the noise of a man groaning. It was all Michael could do to refrain from defending the old man.

"Let that be a lesson, Pat. Do not even think about helping them?"

The door slammed, and the cottage was silent except for an occasional groan. Ruth, alarmed, reached for the cupboard door, but Michael held her back. She glared at him, but he put his finger across his lips and gave her a stern look. After five minutes, she heard someone walking around, and the door closed again.

Michael noticed a slim ray of light coming from the back wall of the cupboard. He leaned over and saw a loose piece of wood covering a peephole. He put his eye to it and saw the two men standing at the back gate and laughing. Then they moved off. He replaced the wood piece and loosened the cupboard door's wooden locks. Once open, they both crawled out.

Patrick O'Neill was lying still on the floor, his face covered in blood. The beating had been ferocious. Ruth quickly grabbed some cloth and a bucket of water and started bathing his face. The little man's eyes remained closed, but Michael noticed his foot shaking slightly.

Ruth gently said, "Patrick, Patrick, can you hear me?"

He groaned, opened one eye and, with a partial smile, said, "Take a lot more than that to keep me down."

"Thank goodness! I thought you might be nearly dead."

"Well, I thought I was in heaven when I saw this beautiful young Irish girl fixing me up, but it will be a while yet."

Ruth smiled at Patrick.

'Harting', St James's Square, London …

"Lady South, there is an attorney here asking for you. A Mr Wood!"

The early arrival of Blake Wood took Anne by surprise. Once again, Anne knew she could not put off this unexpected visitor.

"Staines. Show Mr Wood into the drawing room, please. I take it the fire is lit?"

"Yes, Lady South."

"Tell Mr Wood I will be with him in ten minutes."

Staines nodded and departed. Victoria asked, "Might I keep him company while you freshen up."

"Thank you, Victoria. That would be most helpful. You might ask about Edward's recovery."

Victoria exited, walked along the hallway, and entered the drawing room.

"Mr Wood. Lady South advised me you were here, and I thought I might come and see you before you met with her. How is Edward's recovery progressing? We were all concerned for him."

"Good morning, Miss Victoria. Edward appeared well before I left Guildford. The doctors expect him to recover and commence school again soon."

"Have you withdrawn him from the school at present?"

"Yes, Reverend Taggart advised me of the outcome of his investigation. It appears Mr Hotspur struck my son as he passed by his teacher's table. The force of the blow knocked Edward's head hard against one of the front desks. Then he ignored my son while he lay helpless on the floor."

"That was inexcusable! I understand why you withdrew, Edward."

"It greatly concerns my wife, and I. Edward will return once Reverend Taggart removes Mr Hotspur from the school."

"I see."

Anne entered the room.

"I am sorry for the wait, Mr Wood, but I did not expect you so early."

"Thank you for seeing me, Lady South. Thank you, Miss Victoria, for greeting me."

Knowing Mr Wood had urgent business with Anne, Victoria commented, "I will call on Mrs Wood when I return. I pray Edward's recovery continues well. Please excuse me now."

"Thank you, Miss Victoria. You will be welcome." Blake Wood waited until the door closed, "Lady South, I received your message and came quickly, as there is much work for me with the prosecutor today and tomorrow. I understand your concern for the accused's life, but I would advise that it is preferable if we do not interfere with the judge's deliberations. The defence might also use the plea to our disadvantage – arguing for a reduction in sentences of the other offenders."

"I am not skilled in the law, Mr Wood. But surely, we might make such a plea with the appropriate wording that men of learning might understand that we wish no man hanged."

"Lady South, we all hate capital punishment. I agree that the courts have used it far too liberally, and it is a severe penalty for most petty crimes. But a jointly written plea might divert the judge's attention away from the case and onto the question of capital punishment. It may jeopardise our case if he is an ardent supporter of capital punishment."

"I see."

"My apologies for disagreeing with you, but I hope you will understand my reasoning."

"I do, Mr Wood. But a man's life is at stake here, and we might save him."

The attorney stood there rigidly waiting for the next suggestion from Lady South that he knew would come.

"Mr Wood. What if I met with the judge in private before sentencing?"

"It would be inappropriate, Lady South. The only avenue available is what the defence proposed."

"And you are not keen on that action?"

"That is correct."

"Well, there is no more we can do for this poor fellow."

"Lady South! I understand the attorney's wording in his letter was convincing, but we must keep this situation in context. Mr Hiscock, Mr Spencer, and Constable Rawlins are alive and well due to Mr Henry Creek being overcome and arrested. The accused would have left our people tied up and defenceless to die in the fire. I think it best if the judge, who will consider all the legal arguments, makes the decision. Please, contact me at the court today if you require further advice. Thank you for your time, Lady South."

"Thank you, Mr Wood."

As Mr Wood left, Anne thought, 'May God have mercy on Mr Creek and his fellow arsonists.'

Grey Line Ship 'Matilda' off the Scottish Coast …

The sea was unusually calm as a bright sun rose in the morning sky. Having not sailed before, Jonathan Turner feared being affected by seasickness but had no symptoms. He was pleasantly content as he surveyed the vast ocean around him with a hint of the Scottish hills far in the east.

A megaphone shout came from the poop deck as the sailing master commenced organising another sail far above. Then as the sail unfurled and filled, he felt the breeze stiffening and wondered how the sailing master knew that was coming.

"Jonathan, you certainly have your sea legs now. Up and about early in the morning and taking in the view."

"I am enjoying it, Hamish. Given we are the only passengers on the ship, it is extremely relaxing."

Hamish smiled and stood beside him against the rail. "I agree. It is an amazing feeling on a beautiful day, with the ship moving under your feet. However, it is not always good weather. I have had trips where I remained below until we docked again in port. That can be most sobering."

"I can imagine."

"Now, shall you join me for breakfast? There are developments we must discuss."

They took a final look at the silver sea reflecting the sun into their eyes and then climbed down the ladder into the passenger dining area. A crew member cleaned up after the fatigued night watch officers headed for their bunks.

Jonathan sat facing Hamish at the end of the table. "What were the items, Hamish, we should discuss?"

"What were your thoughts on the site I showed you in Bristol for a bakery?"

"It was a good site and fulfilled all my criteria. It must wait until we are established in London as my cash flows will not currently support it."

"Jonathan, the time is ripe for buying now while the price is low. If you purchase now, the property's value will have doubled by the time you set up your business next year. That gives you options. You either set up your business there or rent it out until you start elsewhere. Bristol is a growing city, and you will not lose your money."

"But Hamish, I do not have the money!"

"Borrow, Jonathan! I can assist you with that, and I will finance the deposit and help you borrow the rest. Janet Stubbington will organise a low-interest loan. She has a facility that you should consider. The property is ideal for serving the pubs I will establish next year."

"I will discuss it with Janet. Anne will scold me when she hears!"

"Good! Once ashore, I will have the attorneys secure the building with the deposit. We shall organise a loan through Janet Stubbington's facility. When Anne sees the figures, I am sure her smile will return." Hamish said this with a wry smile, knowing how risk-averse Anne was.

Jonathan nodded in agreement and asked, "Hamish tell me about Scotland. What is the problem with James?"

"He has made a foolish attachment. The girl is a Catholic and will not marry him, fearing her children becoming Anglican. The problem is they have been living together for over a year, and she is now with child. I will not stand in the way of their devotion to each other, as I have no intention of creating problems and losing the relationship with my son.

The issue for the business is that she would never be acceptable in Scottish society, and our clients will judge him by association. James's primary role in Glasgow has been courting large clients. So, as a manager in Scotland, his career is finished, but she may be an asset in Ireland."

"You will send him there?"

"Yes. I did not intend to establish the business in Ireland, but a good friend suggested it to provide for James and keep our relationship warm. We will both see his reaction when I advise him in Glasgow. It is important that he leaves soon and commences the business there. Otherwise, it will all be happening when the baby arrives."

"I hope it all works for you, Hamish. Your desire to maintain the relationship above all else is correct. I found James excellent company when he visited us last year. He will do well in Ireland."

"And you, Jonathan. Are you recovering from the loss of Eleanora?"

"Slowly. Ethel Nibley, our housekeeper, held the family together while I locked myself away. She lost her husband when her child was young, and lack of finances forced her into service. I should consider myself fortunate as I have a family, property, and income. My problems are self-made, as I cannot forget our life together."

"Why should you forget, Jonathan? You should keep alive your memories of Eleanora and celebrate them. But remember, life goes on. God blessed you with Eleanora as your wife. She was a wonderful woman but would be disappointed if you lamented her and forgot your family and business. Let her be your inspiration and build upon your experience with her."

"I appreciate the sentiment, Hamish. What you suggest is happening slowly. As my housekeeper says, time is a great healer."

While breakfast was served, the two friends continued their conversation.

Cloverdale Chase, Guildford, Sussex ...

Looking across the dining table, Ethel could see the beautifully manicured gardens of the estate in the midday sunshine. There were happy signs of summer coming as the temperatures warmed and fewer clouds adorned the sun-filled skies. Ethel Nibley felt special dining with Benjamin Petherton and wondered what the important issues were he must discuss with her.

"Mrs Nibley, thank you for taking lunch with me today. I had intended we dine at the Fox and Hound; however, I thought it might be more private here for the issues I must explore with you."

"The honour is mine, Mr Petherton. I am most thankful for your invitation."

"Mrs Nibley, I wonder if we might use our Christian names. I feel we have become good friends, and I would always honour you with your correct name in public; however, might the formality be dropped today."

"Certainly, Mr Petherton, if that is your wish. But Sir, please remember I am in service and would not wish you embarrassed by using your Christian name."

"Ethel, I understand you are only in service due to the unfortunate death of your husband and the necessity of making your finances meet your family's needs. You are a gentleman's daughter, and I will treat you as an equal."

"Thank you …… Benjamin!"

They both smiled.

The butler had the footmen bring in the first course. Ethel could not remember when she had experienced so much luxury. It made her feel like the lady she was before her husband died.

"Thank you, Steadman. I will ring when you and the footmen are required again."

"Yes, Sir."

"Ethel, perhaps I might say Grace first?"

Ethel nodded in agreement.

"Thank you, Lord Jesus, for all this beautiful food, the blessings you provide, and your sacrifice for us on the cross. Amen."

'Amen."

"Ethel, I must explain why I asked you here today. Since we first met at the Turner home, I have found you have greater perception and ability than any woman I have ever known. Your compassionate and excellent management of the Turner household brings you great credit. But more than that, I am sure I have found a great friend in you. By relating to me the sad death of your husband, the consequences, and how you handled them has given me the greatest admiration for your wisdom."

Benjamin's generous compliments slightly overwhelmed Ethel, and she feared where this might lead.

"Benjamin, you are far too generous in your kindness. I have my faults the same as any other woman. I can assure you what you have seen of me is probably the good side. Sometimes I am shocked by my thoughts and ashamed of myself. I think you should temper your comments."

"Ethel, I have been amazed at how you handled the problems of young Madeline and the other children. You are so patient and kind. For me, it has been an education. However, there is another reason for my flattery, and I hope you will consider it seriously."

"Benjamin, I would never doubt your sincerity."

"Ethel Nibley, I would ask for your hand in marriage?"

Ethel sat back in surprise as she had not expected this. Why would a man of such stature and wealth find her attractive? She had known him only briefly, and she felt this question was being rushed for some reason.

"Benjamin, you honour me greatly but take me by surprise."

"Ethel, I know there is an age difference, and while I see no difficulties in this, I must be guided by your thoughts. I can assure you that I have thought long and hard before proposing. It is twelve years since my wife died, and I find I am a desperately lonely man. I see in you a fellow traveller, a partner who shares the same ideals and hopes.

But I must be honest with you and disclose that I have serious health problems that may see my demise all too soon."

"Benjamin, I was not aware. You seem so healthy and content."

"It is my heart. Doctor Sopwith closely monitors my condition. The issue with my heart commenced three years ago, and medical treatment has controlled the condition. However, the heart is weak, and the good doctor has warned me that I should be prepared for the worst."

"I am most sorry, Benjamin. I assure you that I will be near and assist you if any distress arises."

"I knew you would, Ethel. That is your character. That is why I have a love for you. We must finish this first course, or the servants will wonder why I have not called."

Ethel looked around and wondered about the great honour this man had offered her. She thought about being the mistress of this estate and his business empire. She felt dizzy with excitement at the prospect.

As they finished, Mr Petherton called for the butler. After the footmen had served the second course and were alone again, Ethel asked Benjamin, "What would become of Clare if I accepted your proposal?"

"I had hoped that if you were my wife, she would be safe with you. However, if you turn me down, Ethel, some trustees will look after her. I have no extended family that she might live with."

"I see."

"Ethel, let me make this quite clear. You are under no obligation here. I understand this proposal is sudden and lacks romance, but I assure you I have a growing love for you and feel you would be a wonderful mother for Clare. I would also welcome Rosalind into the family as a cherished daughter. Whether you become my wife or not, I propose to alter my will giving you custody of Clare after my death. I will also provide ample funds so you might never be in service again from this day forward. I desire restoring you to the status you enjoyed before your husband died and much more. But I ask that you care for Clare as your daughter after I am gone."

It was becoming far clearer for Ethel, and she understood why this proposal had come so suddenly.

"Benjamin, your proposal! Is it driven by your need for a mother for Clare or your love for me?"

"Both, Ethel. I have found in you a woman who I dearly love. I would be content spending the rest of my days with you. However, I also cannot disregard reality and must provide for my daughter. She will inherit the bulk of my fortune. So, Clare will need a guiding hand. With the high regard she holds you in, I am sure she will take notice of your advice."

"Benjamin, this has taken me by surprise. If I accept your proposal, you will change my life, which is somewhat exciting. I would have no difficulty being a stepmother for Clare. She is a beautiful girl, and I am most fond of her. The answer to your proposal will not come today. You will understand that I need to spend far more time with you to know you truly. This will be difficult as I am in service and must serve my employer with loyalty. I cannot disappear from the house without notice. The children require much attention until they accept the loss of their mother.

At present, I feel that I am not familiar enough with you and you with me. We need time together to understand each other. I believe that marriage must be between two people deeply in love. Please give me a week, and I will consider how we can find time for this. At present, Benjamin, I have a warm feeling for you, but that is all. Have I been fair in what I have expressed?"

"That is not only fair, Ethel, but it is generous. A lesser woman would have said yes immediately. You have made the reply I expected. Perhaps we can meet here again for lunch next week. In the meantime, would you mind if I proceeded to make you a trustee for Clare? With my health situation, I must act on decisions once I have made them."

"Have you discussed this with Clare?"

"Yes! She is most excited about the prospect but also understands it is confidential."

"Then I would be honoured if you made me a Trustee for Clare."

"Thank you, Ethel. This is a great relief. Please remember what I mentioned earlier. From today, you will be free to become a lady of means whether you accept my proposal or not. There will be no financial reason why you must continue in service if you wish otherwise."

"Once again, you overwhelm me with your kindness, Benjamin. We might discuss these issues again next Wednesday at lunch. That date would be suitable. As many duties require my attention this afternoon, we must finish lunch within the hour."

"Ah, Ethel. That is what I love about you. You are loyal and hard-working, and you honour your employer completely. It is only right that you are restored to the situation you held before your husband, Andrew, died. I understand that this will be a difficult transition for you, so please send a message if you need reassurance or advice before then."

Brother's Safe House, Dublin ...

Iain Murphy sat at the head of a table with several other brothers working on the plan for the banquet assassination. Braydon Kelly came into the room and handed Iain a message.

Braydon noticed the frown on Iain's face as he looked up.

"It is from McGinty. Aiden Reid is in Portsmouth."

"That was fast. What is Reid doing there?"

"It is obvious! Reid is going after Captain South. He will be waiting a while, given South is arriving in Dublin today. Braydon, are Michael Walsh and Ruth here yet?"

"Yes, they arrived about an hour ago."

"Right! Get Walsh up here quickly, and Ruth supplied with a caterer's uniform. Once she is fitted out, bring her here."

Cloverdale Chase, Guildford, ...

On reaching Fintelton and visiting several other estates, Aiden Reid found no work available but was told Guildford was a prosperous little town with much work available. Knowing Captain South's wife lived there, he decided a visit was in order. He would either work for a blacksmith or find a gardening job at one of the mansions in the town.

At Guildford, he found an alehouse and gained lodgings there. He enquired about work, hearing that a residence over the hill from the castle called Cloverdale Chase was looking for gardeners.

In the morning, he hiked out and found the estate entrance. Spotting a gardener and gaining directions, he continued onto the head gardener's office.

"So, you did some gardening in Ireland then. What kind of work did you do?"

"Mostly weeding, cutting grass, tending roses and flowers. I am good with a reaping hook or a scythe."

"How is your back? Can you work all day?"

"Good, Mr Grey. No issues with all day. But I don't work at night unless it is inside a barn."

"We only work during the day, but we start early."

"Do you have any accommodation?"

"Yes, there are rough quarters down the back here. You are responsible for feeding yourself."

"Sounds good."

"Have you any references?"

"No, I worked on the Kellwick estate in Ireland, but they were not friendly. Never really considered asking for a reference."

"Well, we will give you a trial period of a week, Aiden. When can you start?"

"Tomorrow morning! I will hike back into town today and get my things."

"There is a cart leaving from here in about half an hour. You can catch a lift, Aiden. If you quickly pack your things, you can come back with them and sleep here tonight. Come on. I will show you the way."

The Bath Hotel, Piccadilly, London …
"If you will follow me, ladies."

Anne and Victoria followed the waiter as they entered the first-class lounge area of the hotel. The waiter stopped at a table where a tall, handsome man sat with a broadsheet open. As he saw them approach, he quickly folded the paper and stood.

"Lady South?"

"Yes, Mr Polkinghorne. May I introduce Miss Victoria Sopwith? She is aware of the details of the meeting, so please speak freely."

"Welcome, Miss Sopwith. I am Stephen Polkinghorne. I run an import business based in the Isle of Dogs."

Victoria nodded politely, and Anne commenced, "Let me firstly thank you for your letter, which contained much helpful information. We were most concerned when we heard reports of Lady Wendarm's assault on our butler and her trespass on the property. I am hoping you might shed some light on the situation."

"Certainly, ladies. But first, may I arrange some refreshments? A lemonade or something stiffer?"

Anne and Victoria both agreed and asked for a lemonade each.

Mr Polkinghorne placed the order and continued, "Let me explain my relationship with Lady Wendarm. I first met her at the Grand Hotel in Kingston, Jamaica. Their party were looking for an additional player for cards that night. I never married as I have always been shy of women, and my business has been my life. However, Lady Wendarm took my eye, and we became good friends. Lady South, Clarissa Wendarm did mention your brother-in-law, Sir Hugh, but never in terms of a relationship existing. I have not had the pleasure of meeting him, and it was the day before we arrived in Southampton that she revealed her marriage, and that she carried his child."

"That must have come as a surprise, Mr Polkinghorne?"

"Yes, it did. For a long-term bachelor, I was somewhat overcome with anxiety. I took fright, and we parted at Southampton, and I did not contact her for some time. I felt guilty about how we parted, and we lunched together on the day she misbehaved at your father-in-law's townhouse. The poor butler was surprised, as was I, and it was most difficult to extract her from the situation."

"So, you know of the claims made by Lady Wendarm on our family?"

"Yes! She claims a secret marriage with Sir Hugh and bears his child."

"Mr Polkinghorne, if that were the case, then surely, she would have remained with Sir Hugh till the end. It seems odd that she left Sir Hugh in Kingston and journeyed home without her husband."

"I agree. I found it most strange when Clarissa told me this before we disembarked in Southampton. Are you aware that her travelling companion, Mrs Fiona Green, remained and cared for Sir Hugh? I was greatly impressed by Fiona's compassion for your brother-in-law."

"Might we be clear on that point, please? You say Sir Hugh was still alive when you and Lady Wendarm departed Jamaica?"

"Yes, he was still fighting against some tropical disease. I understood it was most serious, and the doctor expected that he would only live for a few days."

Anne breathed in sharply. This revelation meant that what Lady Wendarm had written was false, but there was some truth in Sir Hugh being gravely ill.

"So, you cannot confirm if Sir Hugh is still alive then?"

"He was alive on the day we left Kingston. But after that, I do not know his fate. If Lady Wendarm was Sir Hugh's wife, she cared little about his situation.

She was more concerned about leaving Jamaica as fast as she could, escaping the place."

"Why was that Mr Polkinghorne?"

"She hated the heat. Also, she had sold her inherited estates and was keen on returning home."

"Mr Polkinghorne, Lady Wendarm advised my mother by letter of Sir Hugh's untimely death and that she had nursed him for the previous three weeks before he passed away. There was another claim that she spent much time settling his affairs after his death."

"No, that is not correct. The man was alive on the day we left. As far as I know, she was never with him. Fiona Green would not leave him and remained in Kingston caring for Sir Hugh. She is an amazing person. Lady Wendarm would have played no part in settling Sir Hugh's affairs. She was more intent on entertaining herself. If Sir Hugh had not survived, Mrs Green would have contacted the Governor about his affairs. The Governor was aware of Sir Hugh being in Kingston. I am quite sure that Lady Wendarm mentioned they, being herself, Sir Hugh and Mrs Green had dined with the Governor."

The situation became clear that Lady Wendarm was possibly using Hugh's unconfirmed demise for her purposes and falsely claiming a relationship with the family.

"Mr Polkinghorne, you have been most helpful, and we are indebted to you for this. I assume that from your openness, you are no longer enamoured of Lady Wendarm."

"Lady South, from my enquiries, I have discovered that Lady Wendarm has no family besides Mrs Green. You have rightly concluded that she did steal my heart in Jamaica, but this came undone with her revelations. Alas, resolving affairs of the heart is difficult, and I feel some responsibility for her. I have been caring for her at my residence in Mayfair. However, a few days ago, she disappeared completely. I have searched for her, but there is no trace."

Anne was suddenly worried, "I hope she does not intend to invade the estate of my parents-in-law near Petersfield?"

"It is possible. Lady Wendarm is delusional and suffers from a difficult disease. I hope she is not dangerous, but your butler may refute this."

"Might I ask, Mr Polkinghorne, what disease she suffers from?"

"In terms of her privacy, I dare not reveal too much. However, I was concerned for her health and had my physician examine the lady. She suffers from a fatal disease, and it is in its late stages. This may account for the delusional outbursts."

"Mr Polkinghorne, does she bear Sir Hugh's child?"

"No, Lady South. There is no child!"

Turner Household, Guildford ...

"Ethel, might we play at the river this afternoon?" William stood there with his sparkling eyes and fidgeted while waiting for the answer.

"The girls must be invited as well?" From the window, Ethel saw that it was a fine afternoon and the riverbank would be enjoyable. "We will stay for an hour, William, but after four-thirty, we must return home. Tell Nanny Smithers we are going; if Jeremy is awake, she should bring him. The fresh air will do him some good."

William rushed off in excitement, knowing everyone would be coming.

"Mrs Jennings, we are playing at the river for an hour. Could we have a basket and some biscuits, please?"

"Watch that, William, Ethel. He can be a devil when he gets too excited."

"I will. But William also needs freedom. I will keep a close watch on him."

The children were immediately into pirate action at the river with sword fights and wrestling for the highest mound of earth, which would be their ship. Their imaginations rapidly replaced reality, and much laughing and screaming developed. Nosey was particularly excited, tail-wagging and jumping up on various children. As he was not often with them, this outing was a rare treat, particularly for the company.

Clementine, finishing off her work, could see the children from the window at the Turner bakery offices. She folded her ledger and told Audrey she would finish for the day. Remembering her childhood fun at the riverbank, Clementine was keen for some excitement after a tedious day of accounting. She rushed off and headed for the assembly on the bank.

Ethel spread a blanket a little back from where the children played and took a deep breath of the fresh air. She placed the basket in the middle of the blanket and sat beside it. As usual, William had a large stick in his hands and was whirling it around his head.

"Put that stick down, William and come here." Ethel was not taking any chances while Mr Turner was away. An accident now might spoil his trip. William stopped running and lowered the stick. He walked across and said, "I was careful, Ethel."

"Give me the stick, and you play without one, please. We do not wish anyone hurt. Off you go."

William turned and sprinted into the pack where his brother, shouting a command, saw him coming and gave him a bump on the shoulder, forcing him backwards away from Simeon's mound of earth. William fell back, not seeing an overly excited Clementine running full pelt for the gathering. Ethel looked up in surprise, seeing Clemmie tripping over William and falling awkwardly on her face.

Once on the ground, Clemmie did not move.

Ethel waited for a few seconds, but there was still no movement. Scrambling onto his feet, William rushed around and tried rolling his sister over.

There was a sudden scream of agony.

Ethel said, "Oh, no!" William knelt beside her and saw the shoulder bone protruding through her dress. He opened his mouth, but before he could speak, Clemmie screamed in pain and fainted.

Ethel ran across, saw the bone sticking out and blood spreading on her dress. She turned and said, "Quick, Simeon and Madeline, go fetch either Doctor Bassington or Doctor Watson."

Madeline grabbed Simeon's hand and ran off. But Simeon held back and shouted, "Look, Ethel!"

He stood there holding a small rock he had picked up from the bank where Clemmie's head hit the ground. Ethel, seeing the rock, turned, and peered at Clementine's forehead and could see the bruise growing.

"Thank you, Simeon. Now, please fetch the doctor."

She took the rock from his hand and watched Simeon and Madeline run towards the Guildford surgery. Within a few minutes, Neville Bassington knelt beside Clementine, checking her condition.

'Harting', St James's Square, London …

"The arcades are wonderful, Anne. There is nothing like it in Ireland that I have seen. I could spend a month here just wandering them. There is so much choice and items from all around the world."

Staines appeared, "Mr Wood, for you, Lady South."

"Show him into the drawing room, Staines. I will join you in a minute."

"Yes, ma'am."

"Tomorrow morning, Victoria, I must attend to our London attorney. After that appointment, we shall have the entire day for wandering the shops. A luxury we do not often find in Guildford. Now I must see Mr Wood."

"While you talk with Mr Wood, I shall start planning for tomorrow."

Anne took a final sip of her tea and left for the drawing room.

"Mr Wood, is the trial complete?"

"Yes, Lady South. It ended well for us but not well for the defence. However, that was expected as it was clear from the start."

"I am sure my father will be most pleased. However, I am not sure it will help the fear of change in the community. Were the sentences as we expected?"

"Yes, the leader of the men, Mr Henry Creek, was found guilty and given the death sentence. The judge found the other four men guilty and received sentences of transportation. So, the trial is complete. I will be leaving for Guildford in the morning."

"I thought the court was sitting for two days?"

"The courts always allow more time than is necessary if the proceedings run longer than expected or other reasons cause a delay. In this case, all ran smoothly, and the accused's attorney struggled with his defence arguments. It was clear cut."

"I see. Mr Wood, I have thought deeply about the death penalty sentence for Mr Creek. I know he is guilty, and the judge gave the correct sentence, but I am mindful of our Lord's command, 'Thou shalt not kill.' So, here is a letter pleading that the judge might reduce the severity of the sentence. Would you be so kind as to deliver this before leaving for Guildford?"

Mr Wood frowned and said, "Lady South, this is a generous attitude, and I can understand your motive. I doubt it will sway the judge. However, I will deliver the letter tonight."

"Thank you, Mr Wood, and I hope we find Edward fully recovered on our return. Do Mr Hiscock, Mr Spencer and Constable Rawlins travel with you?"

"Yes, they will be with me in my coach."

"Please pass on my thanks for their time here."

Brother's Safe House, Dublin …

Michael Walsh sat on the other side of the table from Iain Murphy and Braydon Kelly. Iain had finished briefing the two marksmen to be smuggled into the castle tomorrow night. The next issue he addressed was Aiden Reid.

"Michael, we have word that Aiden Reid has shown up in Portsmouth. We believe he is searching for Commander South and will assassinate him. You advised him of our plans here, so why would he look for South in Portsmouth?"

"Perhaps he has something else in mind. I am not sure."

"You know what the committee wants, Michael. He must not spoil our operations here. Find him and eliminate him. Leave no trace. Braydon will give you the contact details for our people in Portsmouth. Once it is dark, you leave for Cork and then Bristol. Find him as soon as possible and send word when it is finished."

Michael noticed fifteen other brothers listening as this conversation took place. Now was not the time for a confrontation with Murphy. It could wait until he returned.

"I will be ready at nightfall."

"Good man, if you can be on a boat tomorrow morning from Cobh, that will be safer as we expect all hell will erupt here once we succeed at the castle tomorrow night."

Michael stood and reached across the table and shook Iain's hand. He smiled and said, "Good luck tomorrow night and keep your head down until I return."

"Thanks, Michael. Braydon will give you a briefing downstairs."

Michael followed Braydon Kelly down the stairwell and out the back door. Braydon led him away from the house and sat on a knee-high stone fence surrounded by a high trellis giving them complete protection from any enquiring eyes.

"You have a pistol?"

"Aye, back at Hannigan's pub in Cobh. I will pick it up early tomorrow morning."

"A coach leaves at seven from the coach house two blocks from here. Be on it, and you should reach Cork by midday tomorrow."

"I thought Iain was optimistic, thinking I would arrive early in the morning."

"I agree. Here is another pistol. Now come for a walk with me."

Michael took a hard look at Braydon, wondering if he was safe.

"Don't worry, Michael. You have the pistol!"

Braydon Kelly led the way, and they crouched under the hedge and then walked along a path, reaching an outbuilding once again sheltered by bushy trees.

Once Braydon was sure they were well out of earshot, he stopped and whispered, "You, Aiden and I go back a long way, Michael. I have not got much time to explain this to you. There is something wrong here. This mission at Dublin Castle is a suicide mission. It will be Port Charlotte all over again, but this time with many more lives lost. The British will have no mercy. I have warned Murphy of the danger, but he does not listen. What worries me more is he makes decisions without the committee knowing.

Forget about Cork. You will never make it. He was confusing you with his talk about arriving tomorrow morning. Two men will follow you and capture and murder you on the outskirts of town. Murphy has convinced himself there is a plot against him, and you are one of the conspirators with Aiden Reid. You must leave earlier and shake them off. Then find a ship at the Dublin docks and head for Portsmouth.

After tomorrow night, we will all be in hiding, so be on a ship tomorrow or head south and find one in Cobh. Our contact in Portsmouth is the manager of the Black Whale Pub. Her name is Biddie Quinn, but do not mention her name. Ask for Michael McGinty. When they ask what it is about, say, "Importing pigs!" That is the code word. But watch your back, as they are probably working for Murphy.

You will arrive before they hear about the Dublin Castle incident. See if Biddie knows where Aiden is. If you can find Aiden, tell him he was right. I am sure Murphy is working for the British. Aiden and I had a private talk after the Port Charlotte disaster. Murphy's decisions then convinced Aiden that something was wrong. I was sceptical, but now I see he was right. Take him with you when you join your Da in Boston."

"But what about Ruth?"

"You should not have brought her here. She will be at the castle tomorrow night. It will be a death trap but leave it with me. I will be near her and take her with me. I will get her out if I can. Tomorrow night the world will explode here, and I don't intend sitting on the gunpowder."

"Thanks, Braydon. But I must take Ruth with me, now!"

"If you try that, Michael, they will kill you both here. You must escape now! Hopefully, we will all meet up in Boston. Now get going and make out you are heading for Cork. There will be two of them, so you must shake them off your tail. Run fast and lose them!"

Michael stood there looking at Braydon. He was now aware that Aiden was right. The British had infiltrated their movement, and it was a losing battle. They must escape!

Braydon pushed him on the shoulders hard. "Get going before they become suspicious. They will also kill me if they think I am helping you."

"Tell, Ruth. I had no choice."

Turner Household, Guildford …

Neville Bassington carefully watched as Clementine lay in her bed, occasionally twitching. She breathed regularly but had not woken since passing out during the operation. The bruise on her forehead was now evident, and Neville feared something else might be seriously wrong. He looked at the clock and noted it was eight-thirty.

"Thank you, Bryan. Now we must wait and see! Do you think that bump on the head has affected her in any way?"

"It appears to be quite a large bump. Until Clementine is lucid again, we will not know. It certainly did not stop her screaming." There was a confident smile on his face.

"Thanks for the help with that second bone. I could not have handled that without you. Who taught you about supporting bone resets with wire?"

"I taught myself. Out in the country, there is a lot of improvisation. It came in handy on Islay. I used the procedure on some young Scotsmen and several injured Irishmen. It did the trick."

"What about infection?

"Well, that is the only problem. You noticed how I boiled it before the operation. If it becomes infected, then we must remove it and start again. I am confident it was clean, so we wait and see."

Ethel had continually gone through the accident events during the afternoon and into the night. She had never seen such a freak event. The girl had dropped face first, hitting some uneven ground and placing severe pressure on the shoulder. Doctor Watson had assisted Neville with the operation, and Ethel had cried as she heard the screams from the girl and then a deafening silence.

She must recover. It would be a disaster if she died while Mr Turner was away. This family could not handle another death. Ethel was cold as she sat at the top of the stairs. Then she felt Bethany placing a blanket around her.

"There was nothing you could have done, Ethel. It was an accident. They will soon tell us how she is."

Looking sideways, she was amazed at Beth's calm face. Bethany put her arm around Ethel's shoulders and held her close. "You have a great affection for these children, don't you?"

Wiping her nose, Ethel quietly said, "They need someone who loves them."

Bethany nodded in agreement and hugged her harder. She prayed aloud, "Dear Lord, please bring Clemmie through this ordeal and keep her safe. Thank you for Ethel and all the love she gives our family. Through Jesus' precious name, we pray." They both said, "Amen."

Neville emerged from the room, wiping his brow on his apron. There were streaks and blotches of blood on it. He looked tired but still managed a smile.

"Clemmie is resting comfortably. We managed by giving her strong potions before the operation and some more now. She should sleep for a few hours without pain. I fear this will be a long night as she will probably wake early, and there will be much pain."

Bethany felt Ethel shake as Neville mentioned the details. Madeline, Simeon and William scrambled down the stairs in their bedclothes, eager for some news.

Neville continued, "She broke two bones. The collarbone was easy enough to set back in place, but I am worried about the bone attached to the broken clavicle. We set it back into place, but I am unsure if it will heal." He rubbed his eyes.

"In the navy, I saw many breaks of this type. If it takes, the healing will usually require a few months. I have not seen a break like this in a woman before. Fortunately, Bryan had seen a few and was a great help as we reset it. We have put a plaster on her shoulder but will remove it in a week and check for infection. The recovery will be long and difficult, and she will need months of care."

Ethel said, "She will have the best of care."

"Thank you, Ethel. Now I need a bed for a few hours. I think the early morning will be difficult tomorrow. Where can I find a bed?"

Bethany took his hand and led her husband away.

Madeline came across and sat with Ethel. She said, "We will help you, Ethel."

Ethel kissed the top of her head and waved the two boys back upstairs. "Together, we will bring her through this, Maddie." They sat there together, enjoying the warmth of a hug.

HMS 'Shadow' Approaching Dublin Harbour ...

Shadow was two or three miles off the coast at the rear of the small flotilla as they sailed through delightfully calm seas for this area. Robert stood on the poop deck, enjoying the warmth of the early morning sun as it slowly rose above the horizon in the east.

"A beautiful day, Horace. We could not ask for better. I wonder if it is like this at Guildford?"

"You are thinking about that young wife of yours, Robert."

"That I am, and I don't mind saying I miss her terribly. But it will be some weeks before we return, so that is a sailor's life."

Horace smiled and left Robert, as he had worries of his own. While Robert took the liberty of dreaming about home, Horace was more concerned about the security arrangements for tomorrow night's ball at the castle. He was unsatisfied with the precautions taken at Cork and would discuss this in detail with Colonel Scott once they docked. The events in Dublin must have far better security.

Shaking him out of his thoughts, he heard Robert talking with his first lieutenant.

"Mr Fenton, signal *Restless* to enter the port and prepare the moorings. Ham will be waiting for the signal. We will hold out here until late morning and allow the official party time for a relaxed breakfast and some preparations before we enter Dublin harbour."

"Aye, Sir."

Soon the yeoman was hauling up a swathe of flags that appeared like a pretty line of bunting hanging from the foremast. The recognition signal came from Restless, and she came about and glided towards the coast.

"Pretty ship, Robert!"

"She is, Horace. Despite our troubles, I will always have good memories of my first command."

They watched as the sloop made a fine picture under full sail in the morning sun, backed by the green hills of Ireland.

"I can understand why the Irish want their country back. When it is not raining, it is a beautiful place."

With a smile in his voice, Horace replied, "It is indeed. Nearly as nice as Hampshire."

Robert looked at Horace, and they both laughed.

"Get below Major and have Swanton rustle up some breakfast, please. I will be down in a minute for a coffee."

"Aye, Captain."

"Well said, Horace. You sound more like a sailor every day!"

Horace quickly disappeared below deck, shouting for Swanton. Robert thought about what O'Neill had told him. Dublin was more than likely where they would strike trouble. He hoped Colonel Scott's plan for security was adequate. A cold chill ran down his back as he surveyed the country around Dublin. Would he survive this visit? Perhaps Lady Kellwick was not that far wrong with her fear of Ireland. If trouble was coming, he must protect her and the other party members with his life. The event tomorrow night may well be where it happened. It was time he put fear out of his mind and started covering every eventuality that might occur.

"Mr Fenton, I am going below for breakfast. Signal *Chalk* and *Eventide*. We will continue on this course for the next hour. If there is any change in the weather, let me know. You have the ship!"

"Aye, Sir."

Manifold & Stout Attorneys, London ...

"Lady South, given what you have explained about Lady Wendarm, my advice is that her claims are worthless. They have no legal basis. I think the more urgent issue is the welfare of Sir Hugh, who is still missing in action. Once we receive a response from the governor, this should clear the matter up."

"Thank you, Mr Finchley. I must say I am much relieved. However, as I indicated, we are now aware that Lady Wendarm is missing, and she may arrive on the doorstep of Fintelton demanding entry."

"My advice is that entry be refused, and if she declines, then call the local watchmen and have her removed. Sir David still holds a position as a Magistrate, so he can certainly bring swift action against her."

"Given the Earl's declining health, we would prefer avoiding a scene like that," Anne recalled what the countess had asked of her.

"Before you go, Lady South, there is a matter we should discuss. You will recall our discussions from your last visit. I have received this letter from one Mrs K Constance. I thought it would be of interest."

Mr Finchley passed over the letter, and Anne read it, ensuring she understood every word.

Looking up, she asked, "Mr Finchley, how much time do we have?"

"I think we can hold her off for a month. I will write and advise her that I am making enquiries. However, I will require your instructions by this time next month. Am I correct in my understanding that I should not hurry to forward this letter to the Earl?"

Anne read through the letter again and then looked up into his eyes. Mr

Finchley could see that Anne was deep in thought.

"This letter answers some of my questions. I understand you may not discuss the issues with me because of the will. Is there anything you can tell me?"

"Lady South, the best action would be an informal chat with the Earl. It might be best if you did not consult the countess at this time. An even better alternative would be if Sir Robert handled it on his return home."

"Thank you, Mr Finchley. I cannot prevent you from forwarding the letter as I do not hold that authority. However, please hold it as long as possible before forwarding it on. It also would be best if only the countess received the letter. I fear the Earl may suffer an unwelcome decline in his health if he must deal with this matter. May I retain this copy?"

"Yes, I have the original on file. Thank you for coming."

Chapter 23

Dublin Castle, Ireland …

As they poured over the plans of the castle, the faces of the three officers said it all.

Colonel Scott was alarmed at the extent of passageways and entrances. Their security plan would need to be expanded. "The castle is far larger than I expected, and entrances are everywhere. How do we contain this?"

"With soldiers, Colonel Scott." Horace was intent on bringing in more soldiers from the local regiment.

"Yes, but we need some advisers from the castle who will know every nook and cranny. There may even be some secret passageways. Our soldiers will only see what is in front of them. We need more insight and quickly. Lord Dawlting and I will call on the Viceroy's secretary and have someone here this afternoon."

"In the meantime, Sir, Captain South and I will survey the castle."

"Very good, Major. We shall talk at lunch. Please also have a look at the coach house across the gardens." The colonel moved across and grasped the landing rail. He pointed the building out through the window, "You can see it across there."

"Yes, sir."

As they descended the staircase, Horace said, "We need armed men on the balconies at each end of St Patrick's Hall. If I were an assassin, that would be my preferred position. You would have an excellent view from up above the reception. Before we inspect the stables, I suggest we have a good look around the upper courtyard."

They walked through the main entrance and out into the middle of the courtyard. Various squads of infantry were lining up for the ceremonial welcome practice.

Robert turned and asked Swanton, "Sergeant, if you were an assassin, where would you pick as your vantage point?"

Michael Swanton carefully surveyed the Great Courtyard[31] taking a few steps either way before he answered. "The view from both Bermingham Tower and the Record Tower is obstructed by roofing. The preferred spot would be in Bedford Tower. There is almost a complete view of the courtyard from up there."

"My thought exactly! We need a squad of men in Bedford tower and an additional couple of men in the servant's rooms above the entrance from the lower courtyard. One sharpshooter on either side of the roof gable above."

Michael Swanton addressed the Major and Captain saying, 'It will not happen out here, Sir!"

"We must keep all eventualities covered, Swanton."

"I understand, Sir. But it will be dark out here, and a clear shot will be difficult. It will happen in St Patrick's Hall or the anteroom outside the hall. There will be plenty of light in there for a good shot."

Horace could see sense in the suggestion, "I agree, Swanton. I will talk with the Adjutant now and have a list drawn up for the staff attending. The security guards will search each staff member as they arrive tomorrow night." Horace paced off towards the Adjutant's office.

"Swanton! It is time we inspected those stables for any threat. They are probably too distant and will not pose a problem. But we should check them anyway."

"You mean the Coach House, Sir!"

"Yes!" Robert walked towards the stables but stopped and asked, "Swanton, if you were the Republicans and, as you suggest, you wanted a clear shot, how would you set it up?"

"I am not sure how smart they are, Sir, but I would assume they are professional in what they do. I suggest they would use the same process you used at Port Charlotte. They will attack through stealth. The Republicans will know we are checking everything. So, planting a sharpshooter is almost impossible. If I were them, I would insert one or two marksmen during the proceedings while our guard is down."

"How would they do that?"

"I am not sure, Sir, but we must plan for it."

Fintelton Manor, near Harting, Sussex ...
The weather had been unusually fine, and the countess felt the excitement of an early spring strengthening her.

"Good morning, Pike. What a glorious day!"

---

[31] The author acknowledges the kind assistance from the staff of Dublin Castle and refers readers who have not visited this magnificently restored building to the Castle web site at www.dublincastle.ie An understanding of the castle layout will greatly enhance your enjoyment of this chapter.

"Indeed, your Ladyship. Before you commence breakfast, your Ladyship, I must advise you that there was a knock on the front door last night around three in the morning. I found a woman collapsed outside. We have not yet established her identity as she remains unconscious. I placed her in the cottage beside the estate manager's house. Alfred and the young maid, Hope, are attending her."

"It is not Lady Wendarm, is it, Pike?"

"I am not sure, your Ladyship. I was not keen on opening her luggage and searching at that time of the night. Perhaps if she regains consciousness, I will enquire later in the day. Doctor Preston from Petersfield will attend this morning, Ma'am."

Lady Jane forgot the beauty of the spring morning and found herself resentful that this woman would force herself on her family.

"It must be Clarissa Wendarm! Would you please immediately check her luggage for some identification? This scheming woman will ruin our family with her antics. Well, it shall not be so. Once the doctor has examined her, ask that he attend me at the manor. I shall set this straight once and for all."

Turner Household, Guildford …

Ethel stood on the back verandah, taking in the view of the castle ruins. The scene receded into the background as she considered Benjamin Petherton's offer of marriage and the long recovery time that Clementine would need. Perhaps it was not by chance that she was injured. Ethel wondered if God was telling her something.

A slight tugging on her apron attracted her attention, and she found William looking up at her.

"Yes, William."

"Ethel, Simeon says it was my fault that Clemmie broke her shoulder. But I am sure it was an accident. He said I was running at him and protected himself by bumping me away. But he bumped me hard, and I fell over. I did not know Clemmie was coming!"

She looked down into the seven-year-old's earnest young face. It was clear William was frightened of another belting from his father.

"It was an accident, William. It was not your fault. I will explain this when your father returns."

"But he never listens, and he will blame me. He blames me for everything, and the last time he belted me, I nearly lost my legs. He is mad, and he will kill me."

Ethel knelt, and as she held him close, she felt the boy shaking with fear. She was aware of William's brutal punishment over the last few years. It was no wonder the child was becoming paranoid.

"He will not hurt you, William. I will stand between him and you. He will not push me aside. Now, you and Simeon should take Nosey for a walk?"

William seemed content with this answer and the suggestion of a walk. He rushed away, calling for Simeon, who was upstairs reading.

Ethel watched William run off and then shuddered at the thought of leaving him unprotected from his father. She realised how deep the affection for these Turner children had become for her. But what of her future? The offer of marriage from Benjamin Petherton would free her from service. Why would she turn this down? Ethel was unsure how she would resolve this dilemma.

Cloverdale Chase, Guildford ...
The boys and Nosey arrived at 'Porting' and checked in with Mrs Kirby.

"Thank you for telling me you are here, boys. I have some freshly made chocolate cake in the kitchen. Come, and each of you take a piece – it will give you energy for fighting the pirates!"

They thanked Mrs Kirby and went through the back fence and onto Cloverdale Chase. With cake in their bellies, they had more energy, and by the time they reached the fort, the argument about who was responsible for Clementine's accident ignited again.

"William, it was your fault she fell over and broke her shoulder. I would not have bumped you if you had not charged me!"

"But we always bump into each other! Anyway, I never saw her coming."

"You never see anyone coming, but that does not stop you from injuring them."

"That is not fair, and you pushed me."

"Wait till Father hears. You will get a belting for sure."

"Ethel said she would explain."

"You know, Father, when his rage starts. He goes mad and hears nothing. I hope he does not beat you like last time."

William suddenly thought of the severe beating he received last year. He sat beside the inside wall of the fort in the sun, thinking about what Simeon had said.

"William, I am going back to Portland for another slice of Mrs Kirby's cake. Do you want one?"

William did not hear Simeon's question. He was far away, reliving the terror of his father lashing his legs. The searing pain of the lacerations suddenly jarred his mind, and he could not breathe momentarily. Doctor Bassington had saved his legs by holding his father back. His mother had died and left him defenceless. Anne was gone, and Clemmie was now injured. His father would kill him. The tears started, and he wailed in fright. When he looked up, his brother was gone, but Nosey came and lay beside him.

"Good boy, Nosey. You would never beat me, would you?"

Nosey moved closer and licked William's face. The seven-year-old found it hard to hold back any more tears as he imagined what his father would do. The dog turned its head and began softly growling.

"What are you doing in this fort, young man?"

A tall stranger with a rake in his hand stood above William with a stern look.

"Just visiting, Sir!" William held Nosey close.

"Have you permission?"

Aiden Reid noticed William wiping his nose and red eyes, probably from tears.

"Yes, we are friends of Mr Petherton. He lets us play in the fort. I am William Turner, and my sister lives next door at 'Porting'."

"When you say 'we', I don't see anyone else?"

"My brother, Simeon, has gone for more cake from Mrs Kirby at 'Porting'."

"And what is your sister's name?"

"Anne Turner! No, sorry, she married Sir Robert South, and her name now is Lady Anne South."

The Irishman could not believe his luck. He had found the South residence by chance, and it was in easy distance, being next door.

"If you are here, why is the flag not up?"

"I forgot, sir."

Aiden looked around and then put up the flag. He walked back over and sat down beside William.

"Looks like you have been crying, William. Are you in trouble?"

"I think so, Sir. I fell over, and my sister tripped over me and broke some bones in her shoulder. My father will give me a beating when he gets home."

"I doubt that if it was an accident!"

William looked up and wondered who the man was, "You talk funny. Who are you?"

"I am one of the gardeners here. One of my jobs is cleaning up the fort each day. So, I must start sweeping out the leaves very soon."

"Your accent is Irish!" A voice came from the fort entrance. Simeon stood there with some pieces of cake in his hands.

"And who are you?"

"Simeon Turner, William's brother."

"Well, Simeon, you are correct. I am Irish, but I live in England now."

"I like the Irish accent."

William added, "So do I. You sound like Miss Sopwith. She comes from Ireland but lives here now."

"And where does she reside?"

"She lives with my sister, Anne, at Porting while Robert is away. He is a Captain in the Navy and is on a trip somewhere."

"When does he return?"

"Not for some weeks yet."

Simeon clarified, "Three weeks yet. Then Miss Sopwith will move out. Would you like a piece of cake?"

"Thanks!"

Simeon passed Aiden a slice of cake, and William also took one, "Lucky, I brought four pieces. What is your name?"

"Aiden!"

"Is that an Irish name?"

"I guess so. Now, William, you look a bit better now you are eating cake."

William gave a part smile, and Simeon commented, "He is petrified about being beaten by our father."

"It sounds like he has learned from previous experience."

"And what previous experience would that be?" The three looked up in surprise, finding Mrs Preston, Clare, and Ralph standing at the fort entrance. Aiden jumped up and, as he quickly left, said, "Sorry, Ma'am. I was helping the boys."

She glared at him as he patted the dog and walked away.

Clare raced forward and sat beside William, "I saw the flag up and asked if I could come and play. You have red eyes, William. What is the matter?"

The Turner Coach, approaching Guildford …

It was late Saturday afternoon, and Victoria was asleep, her head resting on a pillow against the cabin wall. Anne pulled out of her bag the two letters she must read. The letter from Mrs Stubbington had only arrived in the morning, and Anne had packed them for reading on the trip. The first time she had read the letter from Mr Finchley, it seemed clear cut, but now she realised it was more complicated and would reread it carefully.

Rushing aboard the coach, she had forgotten the letters in her travelling bag. The time had quickly passed during the trip, and she enjoyed discussing their shopping in London with Victoria. They were only an hour and a half from arriving in Guildford, so there was still time for the letters.

She opened the letter from Janet Stubbington and read:

Stubbington Investments
Pall Mall
London

Lady Anne South
'Harting'
St James's Square
St James's, London

Dear Lady South

I am sorry for the delay in supplying the information you requested, as the task proved more difficult than I expected. We only finalised our enquiries last night, and I sent this by special messenger, ensuring it reached you before your departure on Saturday morning.

The information on Mrs Constance is as follows. We searched for Sergeant Constance in the army during the peninsula war and found no such person. But we did find a Private Roger Constance who joined the military in 1792. Tracing his records, we found he was the son of a bank clerk, Mr Clive Constance, and Mrs Amelia Constance of Hammersmith.

Private Constance was born in 1776 and was sixteen when he joined the army. He died in 1808 at the battle of Vimerio in Portugal. Mr & Mrs Constance had another child, Katherine, born in 1786 but never married. The daughter had a son, David, born in 1807. The Anglican church in Portsmouth holds the birth records being Mother, Katherine Constance, Father, unknown.

As far as we can ascertain, Mrs Constance was never married and found work in a bank from an early age. Her father died in 1810, but the mother is still alive.

Let me know if I can be of any further assistance.

Yours faithfully
Janet Stubbington

Anne leaned back against the leather headrest and gazed out the window. David Constance would now be twenty or perhaps nineteen. Mrs Constance would have been twenty or twenty-one when he was born. The right age for childbearing. So, how old would Hugh have been in 1807? He was five years older than his brother, and Robert was born in 1804 and is now twenty-three years old. Hugh must have been born in 1799, so in 1807 he would have been eight or nearly nine.

Hugh could not have been the father, given his age.

The evidence now convinced Anne that David Constance was the illegitimate son of Sir David South, the Earl of Fintelton.

The parts had fallen into place. The Earl had set up a home and an income for the mother so the son could have a proper upbringing. Anne saw this as being consistent, given the caring nature of her father-in-law. Sir David had spent a great deal ensuring the protection of the mother and child, so a deep relationship must have existed.

Anne then thought about Emma. She was three years younger than Robert, so she must have been born in 1807 as well. The Earl was continuing his relationship with Mrs Constance and his wife at the same time. Emma would be distraught if Anne told her this. It may be best explained on Robert's return when the family is together again. Oh! If only Robert was here.

"Anne, you are looking most disturbed. What are you thinking about?"

"Where Robert is. It would be nice if he were beside me soon, but I know that will not happen for some time."

Brother's Safe House, Dublin …

Ten members were around the table discussing the final plans for the assassination attempt. Braydon Kelly sat there quietly, appearing as positive as he could. He was unsure if Iain Murphy suspected him or not.

"The girl will stand beside South at eleven fifteen precisely. You will recognise her as she has a red scarf that tucks under her apron. Anyway, both the marksmen know her from their meeting yesterday."

"How do we recognise Coombes?"

"Once you have shot South, she will stand beside Coombes for protection. The marksmen will shoot him and then run for the tunnel. The British will find the tunnel well after you have escaped."

"Are you sure they don't know about the tunnel, Iain?"

"Positive, it does not appear on any of the plans we have seen. Braydon, Ruth will join you at the bar after we shoot Coombes."

"Why can't we escape through the tunnel as well?"

"There will not be time. As discussed, you and Ruth must run for the Royal Chapel. There is a stairway under the pulpit down into a crypt. An exit at street level leads out onto the lower yard. Head for the university as fast as you can. Once you reach the accommodation buildings, find the designated room in the cloisters. We will have someone there in the morning, so be ready."

Turner Household, High Street, Guildford …

"There were two broken bones which we put back in place. One required some reinforcement with wire. So, we will keep a close eye on that in case of infection. However, I am confident the bones should heal well within three months, and you will be back at work by then."

"Three months!"

"Yes, Clemmie, three months. The break was severe, and the healing process will be slow. The incision should repair itself within eight weeks, given no infection. You are fortunate that it was not far worse."

"It is bad enough for me. I am bored already! So, I am stuck here in bed for three months?"

Doctor Bassington smiled, "No! I expect you up and about in a few days as exercise is important. The pain will subside in a few weeks."

Ethel entered the room with a smile, "Clemmie, you have a visitor."

"Ethel, you should call me Clementine when I am in public."

Smiling at the reprimand, Ethel said, "Doctor Bassington is one of the family, Clementine."

Neville smiled and said, "I will give you some space for your visitor, Cle... Clementine. I will call again tomorrow."

Neville withdrew, and Clementine asked Ethel, "Who is this visitor?"

"It is Reverend Hotspur. He heard of your unfortunate accident and decided to call on you."

Clementine swallowed and sighed, "Oh, alright. Bring him in."

"Before that, let me straighten up the bedclothes. I will remain with you while Mt Hotspur is present."

"There is no need, Ethel. He is a clergyman."

"Oh, I think there is a great need, Clemmie. We must protect your good name."

Ethel finished arranging the bedclothes and went out, returning with the Reverend Philip Hotspur.

"My dear, Miss Clementine, what disaster has occurred that I find you such as this? Here are some flowers. I thought it may improve your day."

Philip passed across the flowers, and Clementine quickly appraised them before placing the arrangement on the bed. Ethel picked them up and transferred them to the dressing table.

"Thank you for coming, Mr Hotspur. I have never received flowers from a man before. That is very considerate of you."

"Well, you are growing older and more beautiful by the day. With my new role, I must ensure good care of the members of our flock. The good Reverend Taggart has realised that my skills lie in pastoral care, not schooling. So, I will spend some time with you and cheer you up. Now tell me about this plaster thing on your shoulder."

Listening from outside the room, Simeon and William came in as he spoke.

Simeon proudly said, "That is a special plaster, Mr Hotspur. The mould restricts the bones in the shoulder from moving out of place while Clemmie is resting."

"Clementine please, Simeon!"

Surprised, Philip said, "Well, I have never seen such a contraption. It must be heavy carrying that around, Miss Clementine. You will be exhausted by the end of the day."

"It is heavy, but not as heavy as it looks. I think I will manage it."

Ethel indicated that the boys should leave. "Time, you boys and Nosey went for a walk. Off you go. You may visit the bakery and ask Jeb Hiscock for some rolls, croissants, and pastries, please. Ask if someone would deliver them. Also, on your way down, please ask Mrs Jennings if she would send some tea and biscuits for Mr Hotspur?"

The boys were off, and Reverend Hotspur seemed uncomfortable as he heard them saying, "Skills in schooling!" and laughing on their way down the stairs.

"Do not be bothered about my brothers, Mr Hotspur. They let silly ideas enter their heads at their age."

With a half smile, Philip nodded in agreement, "Yes, I found that when I was teaching school."

"When they are my sister's age, they will be more sensible. Of course, I am talking of Anne, who married Sir Robert South. At present, the boys are so childish. I find it most distracting sometimes."

Ethel stood by the door, amused by the airs Clemmie put on for this young clergyman.

"And how is your sister, Lady Anne? I missed her in church last Sunday."

"She has been in London with Victoria Sopwith on business for the week. They will return late this afternoon. Victoria resides with Anne, keeping her company while Sir Robert is at sea. They have become good friends."

"I am sure Miss Sopwith would appreciate that greatly, coming from a home of reduced circumstances and living with her brother, the doctor."

Clemmie felt Philip Hotspur must be confused, and before Ethel could warn her, she said, "I must differ on that, Mr Hotspur. Miss Victoria keeps a carriage and rents another for her maid wherever she goes. I believe she came from a well-off family in Ireland."

The Reverend Hotspur was immediately interested, unaware of this information. Ethel could not avoid noticing his heightened interest.

"I thought that Doctor David Sopwith was struggling financially?"

Ethel cut in, "Ah, the tea! Here is Marcia for you, Mr Hotspur."

Marcia burst into the room with her toy bear 'Buster' and hung across Philip Hotspur's legs gazing up into his face, "Buster and I have been helping Mrs Jennings make cakes." Standing, she cheered as Mrs Jennings entered with a tray of tea and biscuits.

Philip said, "Well, this has been a most rewarding visit. Thank you so much, Mrs Jennings."

Ethel edged through the door and called Madeline, "Madeline would you bring the checkers and remain with Clemmie while Reverend Hotspur is here, please? You know why, and I must go downstairs for a few minutes."

Madeline nodded in agreement, "I will fetch them." She ran in search of the game.

"Reverend Hotspur, if you would excuse me, I must return downstairs. Now Marcia, please behave yourself and do not push on Clementine's arm."

With a cheeky smile, Marcia said, "Clemmie will not mind!"

"Clementine, please, Marcia!"

"I will return shortly, Mr Hotspur. Madeline is bringing the checkers and will be here directly. Perhaps a game after your tea?"

"Wonderful, Mrs Nibley. I shall wave in church as I pass the servant's row tomorrow." Ethel was not amused by Clementine's smirk and noted she must speak with Clemmie later.

"Good day, Reverend." Ethel was annoyed by this young man. He displayed the arrogance of the upper class despite his ordinary situation. Perhaps this explained his newfound interest in Miss Victoria Sopwith.

Dublin Castle, Dublin, Ireland …

Ruth Walsh sat gazing out a window at the buildings across the moat. She was amazed at the size of the temporary kitchen room and the number of staff preparing the banquet for tonight. Before arriving, she was briefed on her role and met the sharpshooters again, ensuring they remembered her detail and red scarf.

The Brother's preparations had been meticulous, and their plan was now in action. As they waited for the start of the banquet, Ruth's mind wandered where she found herself strolling across the cold white sand at Port Charlotte's water's edge. Hand in hand with Callum, they had frolicked by the shore, splashing each other, and running along the rocky beach. Sitting on a log, they occasionally kissed, putting on a devoted show for the Port Charlotte community, convincing them of their relationship.

She had enjoyed their time together as he had gently caressed her each night in their warm bed, sheltered from the severe climate outside. But all too soon, she realised that Callum believed their relationship was true love. He was sure she had feelings for him, and over time this attraction had grown, but she was not sure it was love.

On the night he returned with the news they had passage with the British, she realised she could not betray the brothers. Ruth could find no other choice and killed the man she may have loved. She shuddered, remembering the look on his face as the knife slid through his throat and penetrated his brain. She had panicked and dashed away, running for the brothers' protection.

She could hear him calling her repeatedly, "Why Ruth, why!"

The pain was too great for her, and she could not help feeling that on that night, she had given up her place in heaven. She would be eternally condemned, paying for her actions in hell. She had lost her lust for life and would willingly die for Ireland. But then the British officer they all hated so much saved her from being raped. Why would he do that? And Michael was now convinced there was treachery among the brothers. Had she murdered Callum for nothing? She was confused and found the energy seeping out of her. Why not curl up on the floor, close her eyes and hug her knees? Perhaps it might all go away.

"Here, Ruth, have this. It will give you some energy." Braydon Kelly and Ruth had been brought in through the tunnel, avoiding British security. He was now in his caterer's uniform and passed across a hot chocolate.

"The only benefit of working as a caterer is free drinks."

Ruth managed a smile and then took a sip of the chocolate drink. She immediately felt a lift in energy and looked at Braydon's worried face.

In almost a tremble, she whispered, "Are we doing the right thing being here tonight, Braydon? Michael was sure the British were manipulating us. Will we all die?"

Braydon frowned and whispered, "I was unaware he had told you!"

Ruth noticed how Braydon was now fidgeting with his cup and shaking his head slightly as if making some important decision.

"What is it, Braydon?"

"I am not sure, but I think Michael is right. Something is wrong, Ruth! Unfortunately, I think I know the answer, but I must keep it secret. Watch out for yourself tonight! Run for the bar and find me as soon as the shooting ends. There is an escape route ready for us. Under the pulpit in the Royal Chapel, there is a staircase leading down into the crypt. From there, a door opens out onto the lower yard. If I am arrested or fall, make sure you follow the route out and head for the university college. Find the servant's room in the cloisters. Hide there for the night.

Someone from the brothers will come in the morning but expect you in a different room. Keep hidden until they are well gone. Here is the address. Go there. These people are also suspicious of Murphy. They will help you.

But remember, we must escape during the chaos in the banquet hall."

"If you fall, Braydon, I will know the brothers are responsible."

"That is highly likely."

Ruth nodded and then said, "Relax, Braydon. Be your calm self, or they might suspect both of us."

Braydon nodded with a smile, "I have never been so scared before in my life. I am not sure who we can trust."

Battleaxe Landing, Dublin Castle, Ireland …

"Colonel, the security is complete! Please excuse me; I need some time with Lieutenant Peters, Midshipman Collins and Sergeant Swanton. Perhaps, Major Coombes and Lieutenant White, you would also join us."

"Very good, Captain. I must freshen up before I meet with Lord Dawlting. Sir Cecil is arriving with the Viceroy before we let in the guests. He insists that a parliamentary committee member welcomes each guest as they arrive. The Viceroy's staff will identify each guest as they come in before being greeted. They are meeting now, so I must soon join them."

"Very good, Sir."

"We shall meet back here once all the guests have arrived, say eight-thirty?"

"Yes, Sir."

Colonels Scot moved with his support staff along the corridor towards the record tower, where they had been allocated temporary accommodation for the night.

In a low voice, Horace said, "For the first time, Captain, I yearn for *Shadow* and being away from here."

Robert, who had other things on his mind, agreed quickly and commenced their business, "We are still unsure how they will infiltrate. We are running naked, gentlemen. Has anyone a suggestion."

Swanton looking over the floor of the hall below with seating and tables sprinkled around the room, suggested, "Sir, I think we can narrow it down. There are two possibilities." Swanton stood there, fingering his chin, and considering the ceiling.

Robert grew impatient, "Well, Swanton. What are they?"

"Sorry, Captain. Either it will be danger from a guest, or it must come from the ceiling. If a marksman could access inside the ceiling cavity of the hall, they would have an excellent shot, particularly from above the orchestra landing."

Robert was frustrated and said, "But we have looked at that before, and there is no way in for them. We have men on the roof and all around the entrances. There is no other way in except if they tunnelled under the moat and climbed up through the walls."

Horace looked at Robert with a bit of a grin. Swanton raised his eyebrows and said, "It is a castle, Sir!"

Horace added, "I think you may have found the answer, Robert. How do they access the roof for repairs? There must be a massive structure up there holding up the ceiling. We need a plan showing us where the access holes are."

"Who was that historian that we spoke with earlier, Major? He was adamant there were no tunnels or passageways. But what was his political allegiance? Perhaps he is a Republican and not telling us the complete story."

"The plans Samuel! Where are the plans." Horace was keen on rechecking them.

Lieutenant Peters pointed at a different table, which contained construction drawings.

"My understanding is that when they repaired the ceiling last time, they used scaffolding. Here is a diagram of the ceiling structure. Various mighty frames hold the ceiling in place. There is plenty of room for a man but no indication of where he would enter from."

Midshipman William Collins said, "If I were on *Shadow*, I would ask the ship's carpenter! Perhaps the maintenance man would know."

"Brilliant, Collins!" Robert was excited. Why had they not thought of this before? Someone who crawled around the building would know precisely where the entrances were.

"Horace, we need the Adjutant. Where would he be?"

"Probably on his way here in his finest uniform. They are all due by eight-thirty. We can find him as he enters."

Robert knew they could not wait that long. They needed the information now.

"Collins, where would you look if you were looking for the maintenance man?"

"Probably in the stables, Sir. Horses are always breaking things."

Horace was immediately onto it, "Lieutenant White. Take two men and check the coach house for the maintenance man. Quick as you can and bring him back here."

"Yes, Major."

White was running as he responded and disappeared down the stairs with his men.

"Mr Collins, you will remain here and staff the command post. Major Coombes and I must attend the reception. Lieutenant Peters, come with me. Swanton, keep an eye on that ceiling and find the vantage point. As soon as White returns, come and find me. Come, Horace. We must welcome our guests."

"Into the breach, we go!" Horace smiled and took one last look at the ceiling, which was now bothering him.

The Grand Hotel, Kingston, Jamaica ...
Visitors, including locals and people of various nationalities, filled the dining room, creating a rising din of excited conversation and laughter. Sir Hugh South sat nervously at the table flanked on one side by Doctor Ronald Cowper and on the other by Mrs Fiona Green.

"I am still unaware of our guest visitor, Fiona. When will you be advising me? I am becoming nervous."

"You will remain nervous then, Hugh. A little stress will be good for you." She chuckled and glanced at the entrance watching for their surprise visitor.

Doctor Cowper also was curious, "Fiona, he has suffered enough stress in the last few months. We must not test him too much, please."

Fiona giggled, "A few more minutes, Ronald. You will all be pleased."

Hugh took another sip of his water and sat back, enjoying the suspense. It was a long time since he had partaken in a full-service dinner and was keen on making the most of the night. But this was different. For the first time, Hugh was aware of his limits and avoided alcohol.

Fiona waved as a tall man dressed in full ceremonial army uniform appeared at the door. Both Sir Hugh and Doctor Cowper wondered who this fine-looking army man was. Fiona and the gentlemen stood and welcomed their surprise guest.

He took her hand and said, "This is a pleasure, Lady Green. Thank you so much for the invitation. Please, if you would make the introductions."

"Certainly, Major. Sir Hugh South and Doctor Ronald Cowper, please may I introduce Major Walter Ponsonby, the Governor of Jamaica's Aide-de-Camp."

"Sir Hugh, I am glad you are looking so well. The last time I was here, you were a shell of yourself, and now you have put on weight and look most healthy. It must have been all the good work of Lady Fiona and Doctor Cowper."

"Thank you, Major. It is a pleasure meeting you as well. I gather that I must have been sleeping or indisposed at the time. We are honoured that you will join our party tonight."

"Doctor Cowper, we meet again. I have only heard fine reports of your skills, Sir. I understand you are leaving us for Sydney Cove."

"A pleasure Major. Unfortunately, yes. I leave on the first of May." Ronald Cowper raised his eyebrows, "Lady Fiona and Sir Hugh will be my travelling companions."

"I see. Your leaving will be a great loss for Kingston, Sir. But I wish you well in your quest for knowledge."

"Thank you, Major."

"Please let us be on a first-name basis tonight. After all, we celebrate Sir Hugh's recovery, so let us all be close friends."

Hugh strangely enjoyed the Major's conversation and was pleased, "I agree, Walter. Would you please call me Hugh and you too, Ronald? We are all friends a long way from home, and what better fellowship than friends joining together in a dinner."

There was much laughter as they all became familiar, and Fiona enjoyed the privilege of having three refined gentlemen around the table paying her attention. She took a moment to reflect on her friend Clarissa Wendarm who was back in London. 'Poor Clarissa,' she thought, 'She did not understand what she had here in Kingston and ran away again with another gentleman. She will never learn!"

At the end of an enjoyable night, before Major Ponsonby left, he said, "I almost forgot, Hugh. The Governor sends his regards and asks that you, Fiona, and Ronald dine with him before you leave. It would be a lunchtime event avoiding the dangers of returning at night. I will send you an invitation. I hope your fitness program goes well over the next month."

Later as Fiona kept a close watch on Hugh climbing the stairs, he turned at the top and asked, "Fiona, why was Major Ponsonby addressing you as Lady Fiona? I thought you were Clarissa's travelling companion."

"So I was, Hugh. But I thought it better as a travelling companion using the honorific 'Mrs'. It sounded more appropriate."

"You mean you have a title."

"The daughter of an English Earl usually does!"

"Which Earl?"

"The Earl of Calsand."

Hugh stood back and let her pass. This revelation by Fiona took him entirely by surprise.

Fiona continued, "I have a lovely home in Bedfordshire that my brother David has maintained for me. He always felt that Harrold would ruin himself one way or another, and he was right. We quarantined significant funds from Harrold's hands so he could not gamble them away. Harrold lost his estate through gambling, women and alcohol. I remained with him but was not sad when he was gone. My parents arranged the marriage, and there was never any love or children. He was with other women from the start. So now I am free and enjoy life with those I love."

Hugh quietly walked her down the hallway.

At her door, he said, "Then my situation mirrors Harrold's."

"No, Hugh. With you, there are major differences. You are a man who is turning his life around. You are alive, and fate has given you a second chance. Don't waste that, Hugh! You must consider things in a more positive light. Who knows how long you have? But there are far more important issues to consider than this earthly life. The time you spend on this earth is minuscule compared to eternity. You should reconsider the pages Reverend Taggart wrote out for you."

"Perhaps I should. I shall in the morning."

"But do not forget that tomorrow morning, seeing you managed dinner downstairs tonight, we shall commence some short walks outside. It is time you stepped out into the sun, Sir Hugh South!"

"I will join you in my walking clothes tomorrow morning, Lady Fiona. Good night."

'Porting', Guildford, Surrey …
Anne was sleeping deeply when a hand came over her mouth and stopped her from screaming.

A low deep voice whispered, "I will not kill or hurt you, Lady South. But you must remain quiet so that I can explain some complicated issues threatening your husband's life. He is in danger, and you can assist him. But it will only happen if you comply, and then I will disappear, and you will never see me again. Do you understand?"

Anne, terrified, nodded as best she could with the man's hand over her mouth. He slowly released it, and she sat up in her bed. He passed her dressing gown across and sat back in the chair he had placed beside her bed.

Raising herself against her pillows, Anne felt herself shaking. She needed light and reached for a candle.

"I would prefer you did not light that candle Lady South. It would be best if you could not identify me. The glow from the fire is sufficient, and you are in no danger."

Anne was desperately afraid and trembled as she spoke, "How can I help my husband?"

"Lady South, my name is Aiden Reid. I am an Irish nationalist. You will recall the recent battle retaking a British frigate off Port Charlotte in Scotland. Your husband was commanding HMS *Restless*."

"I recall it."

"I fought on the other side."

Anne breathed in quickly in fear. She had heard of the danger that may come from the Irish.

"Do not be alarmed, as I will cause you no harm, but I must ask for your assistance."

"But you are Robert's enemy. Why would I help you?"

"I thought the same thing until recently. Much has transpired since then. Several other members of our movement and I have discovered that the British have infiltrated us. A private source drives espionage and influences your government's decisions. This private group aims to raise English hatred against the Irish people. This way, the ascendancy maintains its hold on their estates. But the facts of the situation are quite different. The Irish are starving and harmless, only wishing for enough land so they can feed their children."

"Why does this affect my husband and me?"

"Mrs South, your husband is in Ireland protecting a British mission investigating how the government might improve the living conditions of Irish families. The leaders of our movement are planning an assassination, and your husband is one of the targets. I know this because I was offered the job. I rejected the offer as I knew it was madness."

"Why would they assassinate my husband?"

"He won a great victory over the Irish in retaking HMS *Providence*. The assassination of a British hero would fuel hatred of the Irish people. It would diminish any government thoughts of land reform in Ireland. The ascendency would maintain their landholdings in Ireland forever, keeping the Irish people in poverty."

"Why should I believe you when you break into my home and threaten me?"

"Your husband is an intelligent man. It was not an easy task discovering where our movement was hiding the British frigate. A daring adventure indeed, and he will probably never tell you the full details. Sir Robert South will survive this assassination attempt. Your husband is a military man, such as me. I am acting on a hunch, and I hope I am correct. I am offering you a way of stopping this espionage! He must receive this letter as soon as possible. It might save many British and Irish lives in the future, including that of Sir Robert South."

"But why would he take notice of your letter?"

"Firstly, he will know you sent it, and secondly, I suspect he is also suspicious of why the military is being used this way. I am sure you have contacts who will assist. Feel free to read the letter, but please have it delivered in haste."

Dublin Castle, Dublin, Ireland …

It was nearing eleven, and the banquet proceeded successfully, with the guests relaxed in each other's company. The catering staff would soon serve the final course, and a bored Lieutenant Samuel Peters stood near a doorway, watching for anything suspicious. Suddenly a young lady carrying a tray of used dishes appeared before him.

"Excuse me, Sir. May I pass, please?"

Samuel backed away, letting her through but then recognised Ruth, the girl he met in Port Charlotte.

"Ruth, it is me, Samuel!"

Ruth stopped, looked at him, smiled, and said, "You must be mistaken, Sir. You must be thinking of someone else. Excuse me, please."

He watched as she walked away towards the kitchen. Peters was sure it was Ruth from Scotland and wondered how she could be here. But why did she not recognise him? Then it struck him. Irish voice. Irish terrorists in Port

Charlotte. The information she coaxed out of him for a drink and a kiss that night. She was one of them, and she was here now.

As he watched her walk into the kitchen, he saw her turn and look directly at him with a frown. She was worried, and Peters was convinced something was wrong. As soon as she entered the kitchen, Peters looked up. Swanton was mouthing at him from the balcony, 'Who was she?'

He nodded and would have dashed upstairs but saw a relaxed Captain South sitting with Lady Kellwick and Lady Dawlting. He was calm and enjoying their company. Major Coombes, drinking a scotch at another table, seemed comfortable as the evening's proceedings were nearly finished. It struck Peters that they were distracted and had lost focus.

The master of ceremonies announced the final course, and the waiters started streaming out of the kitchen, trays in hand with a splendid desert displayed. Peters weaved his way through the approaching wave of trays and ran up the stairs finding Swanton on the balcony. He took a breath.

"There is a girl here among the wait staff who I met in the pub at Port Charlotte."

"Well, that is a nice coincidence, Laddie! Maybe you can see the girl later."

"You do not understand, Swanton. She has an Irish accent and coaxed information out of me later that night."

Swanton looked straight at him and urgently said, "Where is she? Point her out."

Peters desperately scanned the crowd below for her but could not see the girl anywhere. Then he noticed she was at the far end of the room collecting another tray of dirty plates.

"There!" and he pointed at her.

Swanton screwed his eyes, desperately searching the floor for her. Then he sat up straight, "You were right, Peters. That is Ruth Walsh, the girl nearly raped at Kellwick estate."

Peters continued watching her and said to Swanton, "She has changed!"

"What do you mean? Make sense quickly, lad!"

"She has a red scarf around her neck and tucked under her apron. It was not there before! No other waiter or waitress has a red scarf tonight."

"She must be a marker. Get downstairs and quietly warn the Captain and the Major. Do not cause a stir. It is on for sure! Coincidences like this do not happen. Get below and keep a watch on her."

Swanton was up and running for the cupboard where he had deposited the guns. Taking two muskets and a pistol, he raced back, grabbing Midshipman Collins as he went past.

"Take a musket and do as I tell you."

Collins followed and sat beside Swanton at the balcony rail.

"Load your musket."

They both worked quickly, and both guns were ready within a minute.

"Put it beside you. Now you see where the band is playing on the balcony at the other end of the hall. Look above the band at the ceiling. The light is dimmer up there, making it difficult. Your young eyes may see something before me."

"Sergeant, what am I looking for?"

"I expect a hole will appear somewhere high in the ceiling where a man could push a gun through and fire at someone below."

Collins protested, "But we searched up there before! There was no one up there."

"When was that, Mr Collins?"

"About an hour and a half ago."

"Well, I bet there is someone up there now. Keep searching for a hole. I am positive the Republicans are up there."

"I should arrange another search."

"There is no time, Mr Collins. There is no damn time!"

Peters knelt beside Captain South and waited while Lady Kellwick finished her comment.

"This has been a wonderful event, Robert. I feel so safe with you sitting here. Don't you agree, Hannah?"

Lady Hannah Fowey would have responded, but Robert quickly said, "Please excuse me for a moment, ladies."

At the podium in front of all the dinner tables, the Viceroy stood and asked, "Ladies and Gentlemen, if I might have your attention. Quiet, please!"

Peters said in Sir Robert's ear, "Ruth Walsh is here serving as a waitress. She has a red scarf on tucked into her apron."

Robert looked at Peters in alarm and then started searching the room for the girl. There were waiters everywhere filling glasses.

The Governor-General spoke, "Ladies and Gentlemen, it has given me great pleasure hosting this occasion tonight. I am sure the King would not object if we toasted him again. Ladies and Gentlemen, please raise your glasses."

Everyone in the room stood. Peters suddenly saw Ruth approaching their table from the kitchen end of the room. There was no expression on her face, but she carried a shining metal tray ready for collecting glasses.

"Long live King George. The King!"

A loud and robust chorus of voices echoed around the room, "The King!"

The band commenced playing the national anthem, and all joined the chorus.

Ruth stood slightly beside Robert and smiled up into his face. He knew he was the target, and she was the marker. They would be aiming at her and then at him. A marksman's view from the Battleaxe landing would be obscured, so they must be positioned in the ceiling above the band.

"God save our gracious King."

Swanton on the balcony saw the small flap folding open, and the musket barrel poked out. At the same time, another flap folded open on the other side above the band. Swanton pointed it out, and he and Collins picked up their muskets and took aim.

"Long live our noble King."

Robert also saw the holes appear in the ceiling, grabbed the tray from a smiling Ruth beside him, and held the metal tray in front of Lady Kellwick.

The first shot rang out from the Battleaxe Landing, but no bullet hit them. It was followed momentarily by another shot that passed through Robert's hand holding the tray and impacted with such force that it knocked the tray severely into Lady Kellwick's face throwing her backwards and awkwardly falling on the floor. The joyous anthem silenced the noise of the shots. Ruth quickly rushed towards Major Coombes.

"God save the King."

Seeing Lady Kellwick falling, Horace jumped towards Robert as a shot hit him in the shoulder. A fourth shot quickly rang out, following the third. The band stopped playing as the musicians heard musket fire from above their heads.

"Send him .... victorious ..."

Then there was a sudden silence as guests looked around, and screams came from ladies around Horace and Lady Kellwick, who were both lying still on the floor. Guests backed away from the scene and started running for the exits. Peters noticed Ruth was running towards the bar area. He would have followed, but the several people assisting Lady Kellwick and Sir Robert blocked his path. Two more shots came from the Battleaxe landing above, and a man's face appeared in the open flap of the ceiling above the band. A red stain was forming on the ceiling below his face.

"Get after her, Peters!" Robert screamed as he wound several handkerchiefs around his hand. Samuel Peters pushed through the crowd and caught a glimpse of Ruth escaping with a man into the kitchen doors. He ran as best he could through the crowd, who were rushing to the exits. Security staff and guards were running everywhere.

Robert kneeled beside Lady Kellwick, finding her unconscious. Lady Hannah Fowey leaned on him as she knelt and said, "You saved her life, Robert. Now you be off and find those traitors. I will stay with her. Lord Kellwick is finding a doctor."

"Thank you, Ma'am!"

Robert dashed across and found Horace lying on one side with several men assisting him. He smiled at Robert and called, "Get the bastards, Robert. Go, and bag them!"

Dashing in the direction that Peters had followed, he found himself in the kitchen. He glanced behind him and found Swanton following, armed to the teeth.

"Here, Sir. Take a pistol." Robert grasped it with his uninjured right hand.

Stopping a kitchen hand, he yelled, "Did you see a Navy officer run through here."

The man pointed towards the doorway at the end of the kitchen. One of the doors was still swinging. Running through the kitchen, Robert stopped at the doors. He cocked his pistol and carefully opened one of the doors. Swanton rushed through, holding his musket ready.

"All clear."

They moved into a hallway that led into the Chapel Royal. Slowly opening the doors, the vast building opened before them. Robert slowly entered, noticing the chapel seemed empty. A colossal organ stood above the entrance, with balconies along each side of the church. A doorway on the left was probably the organ accessway. He checked and found stairs both up and down. Swanton came up beside him.

South calmly said, "You check the choir stall area. I will follow this staircase down."

Swanton quickly moved along the pews and into one of the choir stalls. At the pulpit, he found a stairway down. The door was open, and Swanton could hear voices below. He stood and beckoned, but the captain was gone.

Quietly descending, he carefully concealed himself as he entered the crypt through an open iron gate. Crouching, Swanton saw the vault contained many thick columns that supported the chapel floor above. Dim light filtered in at the other end, where a doorway must lead out onto the lower courtyard. Slowly as his eyes adapted, he could make out the outline of Ruth Walsh standing and pointing a pistol at someone.

He heard Samuel Peters saying, "Put the pistol down, Ruth. There is no need for more death."

"Your friends will execute me for sure, Samuel. Now, lay down your weapon, or we'll fight it out. Make your decision quickly, as I must get away from here."

Swanton heard Peters placing his weapon on the marble floor, "They will not hang you, Ruth. Probably transportation at the most if you help us."

"Help you!" She lowered her pistol. "Your Ascendancy keeps our people in poverty. You have not seen the children starving as I have. One day Ireland will be free, Sam. Now turn around while I leave."

There was silence, and then Swanton heard Peter's feet move. The sweat was pouring down the back of the sergeant's neck as he realised he had no clear shot. Swanton knew he must jump away from the gate while aiming. Then he saw Ruth's pistol raise from behind a column. He must move now before it was too late.

As Swanton jumped out, his musket hit a column, and he fumbled it. Ruth moved the pistol across, aiming at him. Then there was a shot, and she fell where she stood.

Peters rushed forward and kicked Ruth's pistol away. He kneeled beside her and saw the blood flowing from her mouth. She was whispering, so he leaned down close enough to hear.

Ruth gasped, "I will join Callum now. Long live Ire…" She breathed out for the last time.

Captain South appeared, holding his spent pistol, and asked, "What did she say?"

"Something about joining Callum now."

Swanton appeared and said, "She had a man with her, but I fear he is long gone. If he escaped, there is no way we would find him in the crowd outside." He walked off, intent on checking the lower courtyard door.

Robert noticed a tear in Peters' eye. Samuel carefully placed his arms under Ruth's petite body and lifted her. Her head fell back with her eyes open. Robert gently closed the eyelids.

"Thank you, Sir! She was a warrior on the other side and deserves the same honour as any of our men. There must be respect for the fallen."

"Do you need a hand, Samuel?"

"No, Sir. I will do this myself."

Robert watched Samuel Peters carefully carry Ruth back up the stairs towards the chapel. He realised then there was more between them than he had known.

Chapter 24

Turner Household, High Street, Guildford …

The afternoon tea was ready, and Ethel asked, "Aggie, would you let Nanny Smithers know that Lady South has arrived and if she would bring down Jeremy."

"Thank you, Ethel. I am sure Jeremy has grown since I last saw him."

"He has, and he is learning new tricks all the time. He likes to splash in the bath now, and we all must watch out." She laughed, "He is a cheeky little thing."

Ethel passed Anne a cup of tea and suggested, "Once you are finished seeing Jeremy, you must also visit Clemmie."

"Yes, I will. The shoulder must be improving by now?"

"I think so, but the plaster cast hides everything. Clemmie was up walking yesterday and sitting in the drawing room. But she becomes tired easily and is soon back in bed. I think it may be a long recovery."

"Ethel, you are so good with the children. I am not sure how they would cope without you."

Ethel quietly said, "Anne, I am afraid they must soon!"

"What do you mean, Ethel? Are you not happy here?"

"No, it is not that. Mr Benjamin Petherton has asked for my hand in marriage, and I have accepted."

Anne sat there amazed.

Ethel continued, "You are the first person I have told. We are keeping it confidential until after Easter. That way, I can tell Mr Turner before we announce it."

"Ethel, this is wonderful for you. Congratulations, and I wish you the very best with all my heart. We shall always be best friends, and I understand your decision. How does Rosalind feel about your union?"

"She does not know yet. I will tell her this weekend while you and the children are at Fintelton. I appreciate your understanding. I was not sure how everyone would react. But for Rosalind's sake, I could not refuse."

Anne could see the doubt in Ethel's mind, "Do you love him, Ethel?"

"I am sure I will in time. Let us say that at my age, in my situation in life, and with a mother and daughter who will need care, I cannot ignore the financial advantages he offers. Benjamin Petherton is a gentle person full of wisdom who I imagine will be a fine partner for me."

"I am sure he will. We will be neighbours, Ethel; how exciting."

"Anne, I think I will need your support. It has been a long time since I was not in service. I am not sure the community will accept my new status."

"Ethel, join Victoria and me for morning tea tomorrow, as it will be the last chance before we leave for Fintelton. We will bolster your confidence. I am so glad for you."

"Thank you, Anne. Your friendship means a great deal. I will make sure the children are ready on Saturday morning. When will you return?"

"Probably the Monday after next. Lady Jane asked if we would stay the week, including this Easter Sunday."

"Then I shall pack the Easter eggs for you. Lady Jane will enjoy seeing the children doing the Easter egg dance."

"Thank you, Ethel." Anne understood all the work Ethel had put into preparing the Easter eggs. Now she would miss out on the dance. Despite her engagement, Ethel was still most protective of the children. It was as if she had taken over the role of their mother. However, Ethel did not display the joy of a newly engaged couple, and Anne could not help feeling something was wrong. Perhaps she imagined it. She would reconsider after her return from Fintelton.

'Finteldown', outside Saintfield, Ireland …

The old wooden gate was loosely latched and hung at an angle from the gatepost. Robert steadied his mount and surveyed the surrounding country-side. The rich green pastures looked ideal for farming, and he noticed the seemingly content brown and black cattle quietly chewing the long green grass on fields bound by hedges, some decorated with clumps of yellow flowering gorse.

"Follow me, gentlemen."

Lieutenant Peters and Sergeant Swanton urged their mounts and caught up with the captain's horse cantering off into the property. After five minutes, there was still no sign of a manor house or any buildings, and Robert wondered how large this estate was. As they came over the crest of a hill, they found the manor pleasantly situated, overlooking a small lake with various outbuildings around one hundred yards on their left.

Enjoying the sight, Robert urged his horse into a gallop and pulled it up outside the manor's front entrance. Dismounting, he gazed at the decaying building. It was smaller than Fintelton but still of a respectable size. The façade of the building needed urgent repair, with the stonework badly chipped and crumbling in various places and a well-grown vine covering some of the ground floor windows. As he surveyed the outbuildings, he could see they were in worse repair.

A middle-aged lady wearing a fine coat came out, walked across the portico to the steps, and asked, "Who might you men be then?"

"I am Sir Robert South, and these two men are Lieutenant Peters and Sergeant Swanton. We are part of the government mission exploring how to improve the Irish tenant's situation. I sent a letter last month. Did you receive it?"

"Oh, yes, we received it but threw it away. Your mission does not concern us. We ensure a good situation for our tenants, so please leave at once."

Swanton and Peters were amazed that the lady would speak so bluntly. She was almost hostile and enjoyed the banter.

"I think you must be confused, Madam. Who am I addressing, please?"

"None of your business. You are not welcome, so please leave."

"Madam, we are on government business. I would encourage your cooperation. I will ask once again, who am I addressing?"

One of the entrance doors opened, and three men with muskets came out and stood behind the lady.

She snarled, "I will give you some advice, young man. Ride like hell off this property for your safety. You are trespassing, and my men will deal with you if you do not leave now."

Robert carefully scrutinised the young men who physically looked similar. These men might have been the woman's sons. They stood in a threatening manner with angry faces.

"Certainly, Madam." Sir Robert mounted his horse and said no more. Taking a last look at the men, he saw the eldest one sneering at him with a grin that revealed several lost teeth. There was no point in arguing, given their lives had been threatened. Robert had no interest in continuing the conversation with such an angry woman. Time was on his side.

As they cantered towards the main road, a fully loaded cart entered the estate's front gate. Coaxing his horse into a gallop, Robert approached the cart and stopped. The driver was a lean man with a torn coat and soft cap that he lifted as Robert came beside him.

"Excuse me, fellow! What is the name of the people in the Manor house?"

"Who might you be, Sir?"

"Sir Robert South, member of the British mission working on improving the conditions of Irish tenants in Ireland."

'If I tell you, Sir, they will flog me. Please, Sir. Leave me alone!" The man was shaking with fear and had a pleading, furrowed face. Robert could see that he was far older than he first thought.

"Well, then! Perhaps you can tell me how many tenants are on this estate and how many cattle they each run."

"You can see that by just looking around, so I can tell you that. Fifteen tenants, and they each run around twenty cattle. The plots are each forty acres. The Lord of the manor runs about two hundred and fifty cattle and three hundred sheep."

"And who is the Lord of the Manor?"

"I do not know, Sir. Never seen him."

"Where is the nearest tenant's house?"

Pointing, the man said, "About a mile, that way, but don't go there, Sir. They will see you. There are some much further out. Go at night and be careful. I must go, Sir. If they see me talking with you, they will beat me."

The cart driver flicked the reins and let off the brake handle. The cart slowly moved forwards. The man turned around and shouted back at them, "McKalay!" Robert nodded, and the man whipped the horses into a canter and sped off towards the manor.

"Right, gentlemen. Let us get down onto the road and find a hill. I need a vantage point where I can spot some outlying tenants."

Fintelton Manor, Outside Petersfield, Sussex ...

Lady Jane South stood in the bedroom of the vacant assistant Estate manager's house, peering down at the bed. Lady Clarissa Wendarm lay there lifeless. Her hands were folded across her chest, and the black wig was placed neatly on her head as if she had young hair. One of the staff had placed a flower in Clarissa's hand.

"Your call for assistance was timely, Lady Fintelton. As I had expected, she was not long for this world. It appears the disease overwhelmed her. It is a strange disease in that it comes and goes. Sometimes there is a major crisis, and the body succumbs. I would say the lady was weak from her journey and could not mount the resistance required at this stage of the disease."

Lady Jane stood silently, realising that this woman was likely her son's partner on the Jamaican ship journey. She was attractive and probably well-educated in her manners, given she held a title. What kind of life had she lived that would end this way?

"Doctor Preston, you say that she was well advanced in this disease that took her. Was it contagious?"

"Only if her partner had intercourse with her. Otherwise, there is no danger."

Lady Fintelton was unsure of the extent of the relationship between this lady and her son, Hugh. She was in no doubt of the change in Hugh's attitude, but he was weak and had probably fallen under her spell quickly. The countess knew she must now expect the worst. Sir Hugh may have contracted the disease from this woman, accounting for the stories of him being terminally ill.

"Doctor, I will arrange transport for the body. It will arrive at the undertaker's premises today. I need Lady Wendarm's body dispatched before my visitors arrive on Saturday evening. It is Thursday today, so please ensure the undertaker buries her tomorrow. The burial should be in the Church of England section of the public cemetery. Make sure they do not bury her on church grounds. I insist it is done quickly, please."

"Certainly, your Ladyship. There are no suspicious circumstances, so I will arrange to note the parish records before the body arrives in Petersfield. Usually, the undertakers collect the body, Lady Fintelton. Are you sure you will not wait for them?"

"No! I will have Mr Stem deliver the body as soon as we can. This lady has disturbed our peace for long enough. She must now deal with her maker."

"Thank you, your Ladyship."

The doctor picked up his bag and quickly left.

"Hope, please find a sheet and cover her up completely. I shall now call Mr Stem. When they come for the body, please pack her luggage. Mr Stem will store the luggage until we forward it on." Lady Jane thought about this for a few seconds and then said. "Hope! Before proceeding, please go through Lady Wendarm's bags and search for any letters that involve my son, Sir Hugh. I would not like anything like that falling into the public's hands."

"Yes, my Lady. I shall do that now and bring it across later in the morning."

Lady Jane left, walking out into the sunshine, and quickly made for Mr Stem's estate office.

"Good morning, your Ladyship. How may I be of help?"

'Mr Stem, Lady Clarissa Wendarm passed away last night. I have discussed this with the doctor and agreed that she should be removed from the estate today. We will not wait for the undertakers. Would you please arrange for the removal of the body? Doctor Preston will let the undertakers know you will be arriving this afternoon. We have guests coming on Easter Saturday evening, and we must be clear of this situation by then. Please, if you would talk with the vicar and make all the arrangements. The Estate will pay all the expenses. Please stay in Petersfield and attend the funeral. I am sure you will be the only person there, as we are unaware of any other family. Inform me on your return of the proceedings. I must be satisfied we have finished this incident."

"I shall take care of it, my Lady."

"Mr Stem, have you prepared horses for the children? I am sure they will require lessons in the morning and the afternoon. Do we have enough staff for their training?"

"It is all in place, your Ladyship. We will commence on Monday morning."

"Good. I am hoping the sound of children, here again, will cheer up His Lordship considerably."

The Grand Hotel, Kingston, Jamaica …

In the west, the sun was setting with a cool sea breeze extinguishing the heat from the day. Hundreds of chirping parrots bounced among the trees that dotted the park further down the hillside from the hotel. Many folks were out walking, exercising in the cool late afternoon.

Fiona and Hugh returned from a short walk and asked for drinks on the verandah outside Sir Hugh's room. As they approached the stairs, Hugh said, "Watch this, Fiona!" Hugh, feeling invigorated by the walk, ran up the stairs.

"Rest at the landing, Hugh!"

He ignored her and sped on reaching the top in a few bounds. There he stopped, breathing heavily, but with a broad smile and a laugh, shouted, "I did it. I knew I could. I will be fine for the journey home."

Fiona joined him at the top of the stairs and scolded him, "Doctor Cowper warned you about overexerting yourself. Your body is still recovering from a most serious sickness. You should be more careful."

"Your correct, Fiona. I am feeling a bit strange after that exertion. Come out on the verandah, and we will rest as we watch the sunset."

Sitting back in two easy chairs as the waiter served the drinks, Hugh said, "I enjoy this time of the day when the cool sea breeze drifts in. I think the cooler climate in England will be a bit of a shock."

"You will adapt quickly, Hugh, and we will arrive in spring's last month. It will not be that cold. Did you go through Reverend Taggart's written pages? I am keen to find out what you learned from them."

"I read them several times and was encouraged. I now understand what he was saying. Given our many discussions, Fiona, about the Bible's authenticity, I found comfort in what Taggart was saying. In short, Fiona, I have made my peace with God. I have put my faith in the Lord Jesus for my salvation. Given my life, it was clear that I needed to repent."

"I am glad for you, Hugh. You will sleep well tonight. Now, excuse me for a moment, as I must show you something." She walked away quickly with a smile on her face.

Sitting there sipping a cool drink, he thought back several weeks, remembering the early morning when he first walked across the verandah and grasped the rail. He had faltered on his return, but someone supported him for the last five or six steps. He was still unaware of who had helped him.

He leaned back against a pillow, resting his head. The view of the horizon became a blurred mist.

A man's hand reached out and gently took his. It was warm and friendly and had an unshakeable grip on his. He stood and followed him, almost running into the growing light.

Fiona soon returned and sat down again. She passed him the letter and popped it on his lap.

"It is from your mother, Hugh. They gave it to me as we arrived back this afternoon. I forgot it was in my handbag. I was too busy scolding you for running up the stairs." She took a sip of her drink and looked across at Hugh. He sat there, but she saw no movement.

"Hugh!"

Fiona realised there was something wrong here. She bent over him, grasping his limp hand, and felt it cooling. Hugh was not breathing, and there was no heartbeat. The tears started streaming from her eyes as she knew the man she had grown to love was gone. She stood and gazed down at his face. There was no pain there, and it was as if he was peacefully sleeping.

Fintelton Manor, Outside Petersfield, Sussex …
"Your Ladyship, I found some letters in Lady Wendarm's luggage. I think you should read them!"

Hope Smith passed the three letters across in a bundle with a ribbon tied around them.

"Thank you, Hope. Is the packing all done?"

"Yes, your Ladyship. All packed, and the suitcases are ready outside the cottage. Mr Stem will collect them before departing. I believe they leave within the hour, Ma'am, as Mr Stem wishes to arrive in Petersfield before lunch. Being Good Friday tomorrow, Mr Stem hopes the funeral may be done this afternoon."

"Of course! I forgot Good Friday. Thank you, Hope."

Lady Jane was satisfied that the difficulties with Lady Wendarm were now complete. However, these letters may reveal more information about Hugh's situation. The first letter was her response when Hugh had advised her of a possible attachment and asked for advice. The letter was meant for Hugh's eyes only, and she was disturbed that Clarissa possessed it. The countess sighed in anger as she saw the unopened second letter addressed to Lady Emma. Clarissa had never sent it on once she was in London again. The third letter, also unopened, had the countess's name and address on it. It came from Hugh's hotel in Kingston, the writer being Lady Fiona Green. Once again, Clarissa had not mailed the letter.

Opening the envelope, she noted it was dated January 1827, some two months ago. She read:

The Grand Hotel
Kingston, Jamaica

The Right Honourable
The Countess of Fintelton
'Harting'
St James's Square
St James, London

January 1827

Madam
I inform you of a serious matter and apologise for our lack of introduction. I have taken a courageous step and written as I felt you must yearn for news of your son, Sir Hugh. Please forgive me if I offend you in any way.

My name is Lady Fiona Green, and I am the daughter of the late Earl of Calsand. I met your son, Sir Hugh, aboard the Barque Frogmore out of London and bound for Jamaica. I accompanied Lady Clarissa Wendarm as a travelling companion and stayed at the Grand Hotel in Kingston, where Sir Hugh resided except when he visited his plantations.

Sadly, your son suffers from an incurable disease and has lapsed into unconsciousness for several weeks. He is receiving the best medical attention, and I have employed Doctor Ronald Cowper and various nurses who care for him. When writing this letter, I am afraid he is near death.

I have requested Lady Clarissa Wendarm forward this letter as soon as she reaches London. She departs today on her voyage home. I understand the journey will take around four weeks as it takes a direct course.

I will write again and advise on your son's condition once the crisis ends. We are all praying here for his safe recovery. Unfortunately, Doctor Cowper has asked that we prepare for the worst.

I understand this will be a distressing time for you and your family. Please be assured that I will remain and care for Sir Hugh and hopefully advise you of his recovery soon.

Yours faithfully
Lady Fiona Green

Lady Fiona had written the letter nearly two months ago. Clarissa Wendarm had no intention of sending it on. She had deserted her son and used her knowledge of the family for ulterior motives. Lady Jane was fuming about Clarissa's antics but was relieved that Lady Fiona cared for her son and remained with him.

Sitting back in her chair, she looked through the drawing-room windows at the beautiful landscape stretching into the valley. Her son may be long dead! She had no way of knowing. The countess checked the date of Lady Fiona's letter again and realised that another letter from her should arrive within the next few days.

The one thing that gave Lady Jane hope was that her son was alive at the time of Lady Fiona's writing. While there was life, there was hope.

Turner Household, High Street, Guildford ...
William entered the kitchen and asked Aggie where Ethel was.

"She is in her room, William."

"Thank you."

William rushed down the back hallway and knocked, entering Ethel's room. The housekeeper looked up in surprise and wiped her eyes. William stood there, realising he had disturbed Ethel at the wrong time and said, "I am sorry, Ethel, that I disturbed you. Are you crying?"

"Not really, just a sniffle."

"Anne always gave me a hug when I was crying. May I hug you?"

"That would be nice, William."

William rushed over and gave her a long hug. Ethel sobbed a few times and then released him, saying, "Thank you, William. I feel much better now."

"Why were you crying, Ethel?"

"I made a difficult decision, and I am not sure I made the correct choice. But do not worry about it. All these things work their way out over time. Now, what can I do for you?"

"We are leaving for Fintelton tomorrow, and Clemmie told me you are not coming. The Easter Egg dance will not be fun without you there. Please come, Ethel."

"That is kind of you, William, but the countess has not invited me. Also, someone must stay here with Clemmie, Marcia and Jeremy. I shall attend church with Rosalind and Marcia, so I will not be alone. I am sure Lady Anne knows the rules for the Easter egg dance."

"I could ask if Lady Fintelton would invite you."

"That is very sweet of you, William, but I could not come anyway, as I must remain here and care for Clemmie."

William was not convinced, but before he could protest, Simeon entered the room and said, "Quick, Ethel, Madeline and Clemmie are arguing again, and Clemmie threw something that hit Maddie. She is crying!"

Ethel stood up. "William, it will all work out. But now, we must first rescue Maddie. Come with me, boys!"

Belfast Port Area …

The crew piped the captain aboard as the marines jumped from the wagons. Lieutenant White followed Robert, and they both entered the captain's cabin finding a cheery Major Coombes sitting at Robert's desk scribbling out a letter.

"Ah, Robert! How did your mission go?"

"Well, thanks, Horace. The twenty marines you lent me with Lieutenant White did the trick. The magistrate attended, though he was a bit put out by the early rise, poor chap. He witnessed the eviction so that everything was legal. Now my father's attorneys must appoint new land agents for the estate. I will return in a few months and start changing the tenant agreements for the better. We have a far fairer system in England."

"Stanley, did you enjoy your quick sortie with Captain South?"

Lieutenant White put down some of the captain's equipment and gave a laugh, "Transporting the marines by coach was far faster than any movement I have ever done before, Sir. Captain South has given me ideas for future troop movements. Before dawn, we were in place, moved in, took the manor house, and had them booted out with their belongings before morning tea. A well-timed operation indeed, sir."

"Excellent work, Stanley. You may now attend your men. Get them onboard and settled in. Colonel Scott has advised we are excused from tonight's banquet. Evidently, with the reduced size of the mission now, they can handle the security with their garrison here. So, we may rest tonight. Thank you, White."

"Yes, Major!" Lieutenant White saluted both officers.

"Thank you, Lieutenant White. A splendid exercise."

After White left, Robert sat down and asked, "How is the shoulder, Horace?"

"Extremely painful, but I shall cope. Now there is a special dispatch for you, Robert. A government man called Stubbington delivered it this morning. He claims it is urgent and will call back tonight. I left it on your bunk over there. While you read it, I will finish this letter. I must give my sister some news about my shoulder. It is not every day that someone has a go at assassinating you!"

"How is Chloe?"

"I am not sure; that is why I am writing! I have not heard in months, so I thought I would write a letter. Thankfully it was not my right shoulder, or you would be wrestling with my dictation."

Robert grinned and called Swanton, who was settling into the servant's quarters after the early morning operation at 'Finteldown'.

"Some coffee, please, Swanton!"

"It is on the boil already, Sir."

"Good man. Horace, White is a good officer! He performed well today."

Horace grunted his agreement as he struggled with his letter and the pain in his shoulder. Robert frowned and picked up the package on his bunk, noticing the Admiralty seal. The captain was suddenly alert as this must be highly important.

"Horace, did you notice that this package came from the Admiralty? Who was this man Stubbington who delivered it?"

"No, sorry, I was writing this letter. Ouch!" He flinched as he turned. "I took little notice, but the chap was a well-built young fellow around his mid-twenties. The type you would want on your side if you were in a fight."

"I see. Horace, when did that navy frigate arrive?"

"Not sure. I have not been out on the deck today. I will after I write this letter."

On opening the package, Robert found three letters inside. One was from Admiral Crouch, one from Mrs Janet Stubbington, and another from Mr Aiden Reid. He read the letter from Aiden Reid first as it had his home address of 'Porting'.

Sir Robert South
Captain, HMS Shadow
Royal Navy
C/- 'Porting'
Guildford

Captain South
We have not met, yet I intimately know of some of your exploits. I believe you are an honourable gentleman and intelligent. So, I have taken a chance here to confide in you.

My name is Aiden Reid, and I am a commander in the Irish movement for a free state. I commanded the Port Charlotte action, where you retook the English frigate. I have considered this action and other operations over the last few years where many Irishmen have died for no reason.

I believe that someone in the ascendency and well-placed in your government is manipulating the Irish nationalist for their gain. The wealthy landholders (I am not sure whom) have infiltrated the Irish movement and convinced the Irish that high-profile actions that gain publicity and support must be carried out. Unfortunately, the reverse has happened, these actions have all failed, and many in our movement have died.

By communicating with you, I put my life at risk. I am sure you must also question why your men needlessly die. I suspect that certain members of the ascendency are behind these politically motivated events.

The Irish people desire the achievement of a free Ireland by peaceful means. However, the continual heavy-handed actions of the ascendency and the British government have forced Irish citizens into poverty and hopelessness. This policy encourages our men to take up arms. For the welfare of both British and Irish people, we must stop these underhand actions.

I propose a joint mission to flush out the traitors manipulating your government and our movement. I will send a message through the secret network between London and Dublin. The agent will be at a designated position at nine in the evening on Thursday, the twelfth of April, waiting for a courier delivery. By observing this meeting, we will discover the identity of the courier. I have attached instructions.

I believe the traitor is Mr Iain Murphy, an Irish commander in Dublin who receives and sends messages for the ascendency. I have discovered the navy contact in Portsmouth as Lieutenant Martin Russell. This information may assist you in finding who is manipulating your government.

Captain South, I cannot guarantee your safety if we meet in Dublin, but we will work together that night. I hope you will treat this letter with honour and act in a manner deserving of the British government and the Irish people.

Regards
Aiden Reid

Robert was stunned, understanding this man held the same suspicions as he did. Yet how did he know who to contact, and was he genuine? Perhaps he is desperate and taking a chance or a detailed plot luring our people into a trap. But the mention of actual names gave the message credibility.

He glanced at the other letters. Admiral Crouch's letter contained immediate sailing orders. He should dock at Dublin and rendezvous at the meeting place noted in Reid's instructions. The admiralty took the note seriously, and the frigate *Persistence* would replace Shadow from the parliamentary mission.

The other letter was from a government department he had never heard of before:

Captain Robert South
HMS Shadow

Dear Captain South
Re: Letter from Irish Republican, Mr Aiden Reid.

If possible, Captain South, you should contact Aiden Reid and work with him to expose the infiltrators.

Aiden Reid is a cold-blooded murderer and a commander in the Irish National movement, yet this letter shows a side of the man we have not observed before. He is articulate and logical in his arguments. It appears there is an internal power struggle for control of the Irish movement, and any information we might glean from him will be valuable for your King and country.

Aiden Reid may become the leader of a united Irish resistance. A direct link with him may prove invaluable in saving British lives and negotiating a future peace deal.

Be warned, the man is known as highly dangerous, cunning, and often invisible. You must take extreme care when dealing with him and ensure you have a backup. We have sent our man Mr Ross Stubbington who will assist you with this mission. He will arrive on HMS Persistence and deliver the package of letters.

Regards
Janet Stubbington
Director

PS: Please burn this letter once you have read it.

Once again, Robert was astonished. He remembered Janet Stubbington from the Irish Charity Ball, where she had shown great interest in Anne. He now realised these issues were all connected, and Admiral Crouch was involved but had not advised him. It appeared Aiden Reid had dragged Robert into the middle of an espionage situation. Still, there was no time for pondering.

He walked across the cabin and entered his servant's quarters, "Is your stove operating, Swanton?"

"Yes, sir." Swanton watched as the captain lifted the burner plate and dropped the note into the fire.

Swanton lifted his eyebrows and asked, "I take it something has come up?"

"Yes, Michael. If you would fetch Mr Fenton, please. Then go along the dock and find this man Stubbington on HMS Persistence. Bring him and his gear back here. We depart for Dublin within the hour."

Turner Household, Guildford ...

"Clemmie, Miss Victoria Sopwith, is here. Shall I show her in?"

"Oh, yes, please, Ethel! Some company at last!"

The housekeeper straightened the bedclothes, covered Clemmie with a shawl, and then went downstairs for Miss Sopwith.

"Clementine, how are you? I am sorry I have not been here sooner, but Anne and I have been planning the London shop for Hursts, and it has taken much time."

"Thank you for coming, Victoria. How was London?"

"It was amazing. It was far bigger than I had imagined, and the shopping was unlimited. Anne was so good, exploring and shopping with me, but I think I even exhausted her, and at times she needed a break and returned to 'Harting' for a rest. We had a lot of fun."

"I heard the court found the arsonists guilty. Perhaps that will stop others from attempting the same action."

"The leader of the gang received the death penalty. Anne wrote, asking for a more lenient sentence. I have not heard yet if that came about. Well, enough of that. What have you been doing with your time?"

"Slowly exercising and getting my strength back. I can walk easily up and down the stairs now but soon need rest. I hope I am not becoming lazy as Ethel takes such good care of me. I feel guilty about how much of her time I take up."

"I think she is fond of all the Turner children. Not that you are a child any longer as you are working at the bakery."

"I am not sure I should return there. I become so bored doing figures all day. Anne keeps telling me that the figures tell a story, but all I see are figures. I appreciate Father giving me employment, but I want more out of life."

"Most women find a husband and have children. I am sure there will be young men in your future. Would that be preferable?"

"Perhaps, I feel I am too young for marriage. Father will not let me marry until I am at least twenty. He has said so. Travel would be interesting – but again, he says I am too young. So, I have started drawing pictures of the places I might visit."

"Really! May I see some of them?"

Clementine pulled out a large folder of charcoal drawings. She passed a couple to Victoria.

"That is London, and this one is Paris. I copied some tapestries I found. It is amazing what you think about when you are drawing."

"These are very good. What plays on your mind when you are drawing?"

Ethel knocked and entered the room, "Excuse me, Miss Victoria and Clementine, but Mr Hotspur has arrived and asked if he may visit."

Clementine raised her eyebrows and said, "Not him again!"

"Clemmie, you must be polite. I am sure the Reverend Hotspur is a busy man, and it is an honour that he visits you."

"I am sorry, Ethel. Please bring him up."

"Miss Victoria, might I ask that you remain with Clementine while Mr Hotspur is here? I am sure it will be a short visit."

Victoria nodded in agreement and readied herself for the arrival of the young gentleman whose reputation had dived since the incident with Edward Blake.

The door opened, and the young curate burst in, "Miss Clementine, you look so much happier. Your recovery must be advancing. Miss Victoria Sopwith, fancy finding you here!"

"Perhaps you saw my carriage outside, Mr Hotspur?"

Clementine smiled, thinking how obvious it must have been that Victoria was visiting.

"Yes, I did. A fine carriage, indeed! I have always asked myself, and excuse me if I inquire too deeply, but how might a single lady of limited means afford so fine a carriage? Why, as a clergyman on a generous stipend, I would find financing such an equipage difficult."

Victoria was offended at first that he would make such an assumption about her means and would pry into her details. However, she saw the question for what it was. He was asking if she had wealth or not.

"My brother is a kind soul and maintains the carriage for me. He cannot afford it, but I would be housebound without it. You will understand, Mr Hotspur, that a lady requires safety when she calls on her friends."

"I agree indeed, Miss Victoria. Now, I will make this small presentation of flowers for Miss Clementine. Perhaps I might join you in your carriage as far as my lodgings, Miss Victoria."

"Mr Hotspur, I am afraid that would be inappropriate. One day when Miss Clementine fully recovers and will join us, please ask again. At present, I must be considerate of my good name."

Philip Hotspur was most put out but continued making polite conversation.

HMS Shadow, approaching Dublin …

"You realise that this might be a trap? Reid and his Irish republicans may have some other plan afoot."

"I have thought of that, Horace, but you read the letter. There is more there than a murderer luring his victim into place. The man loves his country. You have seen the look on the Irish when they know they will die. They are proud men, despite their lack of education. They have a feeling for their country that is the same as ours for England. It is part of them.

I suspect that Aiden Reid has decided that the old ways are not working, and he will change the direction of their fight for freedom. A peaceful struggle. I would welcome that."

"I doubt it, Robert, but I will not dispute your orders. I cannot be with you on this mission, so who will you take with you? Someone must watch your back."

"Stubbington, Peters and Swanton. They will be sufficient. This operation will be quick. All we must do is confirm the traitor's identity and then hand over the parcel. Once that is done, we are out of there."

"If I were you, I would surround the library with marines. Some substantial backup will give you a bargaining chip."

"No, Horace! This mission will be undercover work, and many students will be in the library, so we must take care. The last thing we want is several students shot for no reason. Stubbington will go individually and be in the library disguised as a student. Trust me. This will work."

"As long as Reid is a man of honour!"

Fintelton Manor, Harting near Petersfield, Sussex …

Pike, the old butler, knocked on the open door of Lady Fintelton's study.

"Excuse me, your Ladyship! A rider delivered this letter."

"Thank you, Pike."

Lady Jane took the letter and saw it was from Lady Fiona Green in Jamaica. She had eagerly expected this letter and prayed it contained good news.

Opening the letter, she read:

The Grand Hotel
Kingston, Jamaica

The Right Honourable
The Countess of Fintelton
'Harting'
St James's Square
St James, London

1 March 1827

Madam

I hope this letter finds you and your family well.

Further to my last letter, I have good news. Sir Hugh has shown re-markable fortitude and survived the severe illness that nearly killed him. He is frail, but we take each day at a time, and his strength continues to improve. He is not at the point of managing writing, but I am encour-aging his attempts, and he may soon address you, the Earl, and his other family members in a letter.

I am so glad I can advise you that all our prayers have been answered. Please continue your prayers for Sir Hugh's full recovery. Doctor Cowper attends daily and encourages your son in his quest. Sir Hugh shows fine courage and entertains us with humour and antics.

Once he has regained enough strength for the journey home, I am sure he will quickly book a passage as he has many tails from his adventure.

Your friend
Lady Fiona Green

Tears rolled down Lady Jane's cheeks, and she commenced sobbing. Her son was alive and gaining strength. A mother's prayer that she would see him again might yet be fulfilled. Thank the Lord for this wonderful woman Fiona Green. From her letters, Lady Jane could feel the love for Hugh emanating from her words. She must be an exceptional person. Oh, if only Hugh had found someone like her long ago. Perhaps things would be different.

Pike entered the room with a tray and a drink, "My Ladyship, I thought you might require a gin and tonic. There is a mite more gin involved than your regular."

"Oh! Thank you, Pike. You are so good. I have news. Sir Hugh is alive and is coming home."

"That is fine news indeed, your Ladyship."

As Pike returned downstairs, he wondered if Sir Hugh's manners had improved since he left for Jamaica.

University College, Dublin ...

A slight rain fell as Captain South and his men stepped down from the carriage, clothed in their dark capes. Earlier, they had agreed that Mr Stub-bington would be dropped off and disappear into the city crowd. He would remain undercover but be seated in the library if Robert needed help. Several other coaches were passing, and there was a lot of foot traffic despite being eight forty-five in the evening. Robert felt slightly relaxed, knowing they would be well concealed amid the bustle of Aston Quay.

Using the shadows, they went down Westmoreland Street towards the college. At the front entrance, the crowds were thinning out, and once through the gates, Robert led them aside into a dark shadow beside a building in Library Square.

"You chaps cover me from the shadows. I will make for the campanile[32]; hopefully, he will be there. Swanton, take my hat and cape, please. The hat stands out like a sore thumb!"

Robert strode towards the campanile as if on his evening exercise walk. Several students passed by, obviously heading towards their lodgings. As he approached, he slowed, glancing around for a gentleman waiting. There was no one there.

Sheltering from the misty rain, he stood underneath the bell tower and waited. Nine o'clock came and went, and South worried Reid had fooled him. He would allow five minutes more, and then if no one appeared, he would exit. A young couple walking closely together passed, sharing confidences, and Robert remembered his time of education in the Navy. Midshipmen were at the mercy of the worst bully in their group. He thought of Hugh at Oxford and wondered if the freedom there had led him astray.

From the dark, a deep voice said, "Turn around slowly, South. I do not want any scenes."

"You are late, Reid."

"I was checking if you had any more men positioned beside the two in the shadows. I would say one is an army sergeant as he is particularly skilled at camouflage."

"You are correct. You have a sharp eye."

"Are there any other men?"

"No!"

"Well, nice meeting you, Captain. We are friends for tonight." Reid held out his hand in friendship.

Robert shook his hand and said, "You are not who I expected. You sound like an officer."

"What did you expect? I have been commanding men for the last twenty years on missions."

Robert did not reply.

"Here, put this academic gown on over your coat. I thought you might have

---

[32] The Campanile of Trinity College Dublin is a bell tower and one of its most iconic landmarks. Donated by then Archbishop of Armagh, Lord John Beresford, it was designed by Sir Charles Lanyon, sculpted by Thomas Kirk and finished in 1853. Wikipedia. The author has used the landmark for dramatic purposes and is aware that the Campanile was not in existence in April 1827. JS

come in a less formal dress, but the gown will hide the uniform long enough. You will find him sitting alone at the end of the table in the fifteenth row. I will escort you in. Then you are on your own. I suggest you walk normally down the aisle and sit directly opposite. Use the code, "I am studying the importing of pigs." Then give him the package.

I doubt he will say anything but see if you can get his name if he does. Once you ask for his name, he will be suspicious and leave quickly. I will be waiting for him as he exits the library."

"I thought I was only observing?"

"That is correct but observing closely! You are the courier tonight. I will always be close and intercept him at the exit."

"What if he uses another exit?"

"I have checked the exits. Only the main exit is open. He will come out that way. He will have backup outside, but I am prepared for that. Keep in the shadows when you come out."

"What will you do out here?"

"It is all planned, so stay in the shadows. My men already know where your men are. They will be safe as well. If you need me as a bargaining chip, that is fine. Tell him I am above on the library balcony. He will see me there. I will make sure of that."

"If it is Murphy, what will you do with him?"

"What will you do with Russell in Portsmouth? I suggest you quickly leave once we have dealt with the courier here."

Robert wanted more, "I must know who his instructions are coming from!"

"You will not find that out here, Captain South. I have given you the name of the contact in Portsmouth. I am sure your security people are working on that already."

"How did you find him?"

"There are ways and means. But tonight, we end these stupid actions that have wasted so many lives on both sides. After tonight I am your enemy, and hopefully, we will never meet again."

"Reid, there may be benefits from us staying in contact. How should I contact you if there is a need?"

Aiden Reid smiled and took a hard look at South. Perhaps there was wisdom in what South was suggesting.

"You contact me the same way any general contacts his opponent. But you will not find me in the next five years, but perhaps after that, try around Cobh. Now, it is time. Our friend will be becoming restless."

They walked together from the campanile and approached the library, where several students were leaving. As they entered the study area, one of the library staff pointed at his timepiece and said, "Masters, we are closing in thirty minutes. Please be quick."

Robert smiled and then noticed that Reid was also wearing an academic gown with a short beard. He looked like a university professor.

"Remember fifteen down." Aiden quickly moved up the stairs towards the balcony.

Robert swallowed and started walking alongside the tables and counting as he went. He could see many students packing the central section of the study area, but the numbers decreased towards the last row. As the count approached fifteen, Robert saw the man watching him. He sat on the opposite chair and placed the package on the table.

"I am studying the importing of pigs!"

The man relaxed. "You are late. I must be off quickly as my men are waiting. Are the orders in there?"

Robert replied, "Yes. A new mission."

Robert could see that the man was in his late fifties and had a long narrow face with eyes that would look through you if they could. He suddenly glanced down at Robert's chest. His academic gown had slightly sagged open, revealing part of his uniform.

"What is a navy man doing delivering these orders?"

"It is an important mission. There is little time after the success at the castle."

The man sat there thinking and slowly moved his right hand into his coat, but Robert quickly reached across and clasped the concealed hand that now held the pistol. "No antisocial activities here, Mr Murphy. Too many innocent students are present, and we do not want a scene. Take the orders and get your job done."

Murphy glared into Robert's eyes, questioning if this navy man was a legitimate courier. Robert did not flinch and continued a stern gaze back into the man's eyes. After ten seconds, he relaxed and returned his hand to the tabletop.

The library staff moved around the tables, advising students it was closing time.

"How did you know my name?"

"I am far higher up the chain than you. Remember, I said it was an important mission. There is no time to be lost." Robert smiled and tapped the package.

Murphy spat on the floor, grabbed the package, and nearly knocked a staff member over as he rushed past her. Robert quietly stood and asked, "Are you alright, Ma'am?"

"Yes, Master, but that man was somewhat clumsy. He nearly knocked me over."

"I saw that. I believe it has been a difficult day. Failed an exam!"

"Oh, I see. I have not seen you here before, Master. What faculty are you from?"

"Humanities, Ma'am. Please, excuse me! I must make sure my friend does not injure anyone else."

Robert walked off quickly, wondering what was happening outside. Exiting the building, he saw two men walking closely together towards the campanile. They walked in beneath the bell tower and disappeared. Knowing the man had a pistol, Robert feared for Reid's safety. He strode out towards the building and peered around the corner. Confronted by a pistol in his face, he was dragged forward by Murphy and found Aiden Reid held by two other men.

Murphy pushed the pistol into Robert's cheek and said, "Now, who are you, Mr Navy man?"

"Captain Robert South of his Majesties Royal Navy, Mr Murphy, and you are under arrest."

Murphy started laughing as he cocked the pistol. Then he suddenly stopped and froze as Braydon Kelly appeared, shoving his pistol barrel into Murphy's ear.

"Drop your guns, you men and stand aside from Reid!" Braydon Kelly stood like a rock taking command of the situation. "Of you go, Aiden and thanks for your help." Robert, who had been watching Braydon, turned but found Reid was gone.

Murphy said, "What are you doing, Braydon?"

"Something I should have done some time ago. Now Captain South if you would move across here, please."

Robert followed his directions, and as he walked, Braydon fired his pistol into Murphy's ear and blew the other side of his head off. The lifeless body fell to the ground, spreading blood across the tiles. Within seconds Peters and Swanton were under the bell tower with guns drawn.

"It is all safe, men. We are among friends. Now young man, who are you?"

"It is best if you don't know Captain South. We have the evidence we need."

Braydon pointed his pistol at the two other men, now restrained by Dan O'Leary and two of Braydon Kelly's followers. Robert noticed that Braydon took the package from Murphy's now limp hand and passed it to another man.

Braydon said, "Gentlemen, we must go. Best if it were quickly."

Robert and his men retreated the way they had entered the college and could see a crowd gathering behind them around the campanile. They heard two more shots in the distance as they neared the entry gates. Robert quickly thought, 'Perhaps Reid's friends did not want any witnesses.'

Discarding the academic gown, Robert took on the identity of a Navy officer again.

"Well, Swanton, it got a bit exciting inside the library for a while."

"You were in no danger, Sir. I was behind a bookcase right beside you. If he had drawn that pistol, I would have blown his brains out."

"Thank you, Swanton. You are always one step ahead of me! There was me thinking I was brave on my lonesome!"

"You were not alone. Stubbington was watching from another table. He knew I was there and gave me a wink. Quite a shrewd operator, that one. Will we see him again, Sir?"

"Probably not! He was intent on following Aiden Reid. Good luck with that. The man can disappear in an instant."

Peters entered the conversation, "Are we sailing tonight, Captain?"

"Yes, we will surprise Mr Fenton again. As soon as we are aboard, we cast off. No time for the harbourmaster as after tonight's escapade, there may be some difficulty explaining our presence here in Dublin harbour. Gentlemen, we sail for Portsmouth."

On the far side of the road, Aiden Reid watched as South, and his men returned up Westmoreland Street. He smiled as he thought, 'Amateurs!' Then, as the smile subsided, Reid considered South's request. 'Perhaps there was a benefit in what the Englishman had suggested!'

'Porting', Guildford …

Anne watched as the porters loaded her luggage into the carriage. The weather was closing in, and the hood had been raised over the carriage, offering protection from the weather.

"I hope we do not have a rainy week as that will spoil the children's riding lessons. This weather at present is so unpredictable. Still, it will soon be summer, and we shall visit the seaside."

Mrs Kirby peeked at the sky and said, "The clear summer skies will be welcome, Lady South. Soon, Sir Robert will be home."

"I do hope so. Come, Mary! You may ride with me and join Judith in the maid's coach when we reach the Turner's house. Please, Mrs Kirby, if any letters come, have a rider bring them directly. Now we must be off."

She tapped the carriage's ceiling and felt the motion as it commenced along the drive.

As Victoria Sopwith arrived at the Turner's house, Simeon and William were waiting with their luggage. They ran down the stairs and waved madly. Victoria enjoyed the boys' excitement.

"You two may travel with me, and Katherine and Madeline may go in Anne's carriage. So, bring your luggage down, and the driver will store it for you."

William asked, "Victoria, can you ride a horse?"

"Yes, William, I had my own horse on our estate in Ireland. It was a beautiful little pony."

"Then you will ride with us and help us learn?"

"We will see. Now you two, we need your luggage down here."

As Anne's carriage arrived, the boys were almost finished stowing their cases. Ethel came down and welcomed the ladies and asked, "Might you have time for a few minutes with Clemmie? She is downcast about not attending Fintelton. A quick talk upstairs might cheer her up."

"Certainly."

As Victoria and Anne entered Clementine's room, she sat there with a disappointed face and a handkerchief held against one of her eyes.

Victoria said, "As soon as you are up and about, Clementine, you must come and have morning tea. I will have a new rented house by then, and you might assist me with the decorations."

"Now, there is a fair offer, Clemmie. While we are away, you could consider decorating and the colours for the walls. See if you can gather a palate together for Victoria."

Clementine was unhappy with the suggestion, "But I am left at home while you all go off. It is all William's fault – he should stay at home and chop wood." She blew her nose and continued, "Why is it always me who misses out? If it weren't for that clumsy William, I would be coming with you."

Anne was sympathetic, "I promise you, Clementine, you shall come next time we go. Now we must be off, or we will not make Fintelton by dark. We will return the week after Easter."

Victoria slipped a small book from her bag and put it in Clemmie's hand. It was a beautifully covered book of Irish poetry. "Might I lend you that, Clemmie, while we are away? I will come and see you as soon as we are back."

Clemmie made a half-smile and sullenly said, "Thank you."

As Victoria reached the bottom of the staircase, she pulled Ethel aside and said in a low voice, "If Reverend Hotspur comes visiting, make sure someone is with Clemmie. For that matter, with any of the children. There is something wrong with that man. I fear the good Reverend has an agenda!"

Chapter 25

Fintelton Manor, Outside Petersfield, Sussex ...

"The first thing you should understand is that a horse is a living animal, and he or she will be frightened of you." Mr Stem had the children standing in a group as he led their first lesson.

Madeline asked, "But the horses are so big, and we are so small. Surely, we should be afraid of them?"

"You would think so, Madeline, but you must not be afraid. They will sense your fear and take advantage of you. These horses are not dumb, but they are gentle. I picked them out, especially for you. Now, you will each have a horse for the week. The sooner you make friends with them, the sooner they will trust you. Watch as I show you how you should introduce yourself. Please stand a little closer."

Malcolm Stem approached his horse slowly. The horse was eating grass and continued eating. He moved within a step or two of the horse and then stopped. Mr Stem put his arm out so the horse could smell the back of his hand. At first, the horse ignored him, but as he reached lower, it immediately moved its head around and smelt his hand. Then, it continued eating grass.

"That is how you say hello. The horse will now allow you closer."

Malcolm then moved in beside the horse and patted its side.

"We have allocated each of you a horse for the week. You will look after that horse for the week. So, it will be far more than riding. I will explain that later. Make sure you offer the back of your hand before patting the horse."

Then, one by one, Malcolm took each child over, and they made their introductions.

"Lady Jane, this is wonderful. Thank you so much for allowing them this experience. They will never forget it."

"It is my pleasure, Anne. It has been so long since there were children here.

It may even bring the Earl out of the rose garden soon. Since the children arrived, he has already shown signs of being more active. We must keep this up, as he will sleep better at night."

"How is his health?"

"Slowly fading. But we all grow old, so we must bear it as best we can. Now, Anne! There is something I must explain. The children will be safe with Mr Stem and his men. They will only ride near the stables this morning. Come with me for a walk. Perhaps we should follow the path out past the estate office."

Anne agreed and was curious about Lady Jane's need for privacy.

As soon as they were out of hearing distance, Lady Jane commenced.

"We received a letter from our attorneys in London. I understand you have a copy of the letter from Mrs Constance?"

"Yes. I have a copy and was waiting for an appropriate time when we could discuss it."

Anne was surprised that Lady Jane was aware of Mrs Constance's existence. She became fearful that the countess would believe she was withholding information from her.

"I must admit, Anne, I am relieved you now know. Mr Finchley advised me that you were hot on the trail. I admire your skills of inquiry and understanding of finance. You have some special skills and are also perceptive of people's feelings. I am sure you thought I would be dreadfully surprised about Mrs Constance, but I have known about her for over twenty years. It is a complex story that I must explain, but now you know this is necessary for several reasons."

"Lady Jane, I was not aware you knew."

"Of course, Anne."

"I felt the news would make you extremely sad and even destroy your relationship with your husband. So, I was waiting for Robert's return before discussing the information with anyone."

"You are so good and thoughtful, Anne. I am so fortunate you are my daughter-in-law. I thank God every night for the blessing He has bestowed on our family. But I must explain what happened more than twenty-three years ago. First, please promise me that Emma will never hear certain parts of this story?"

"You have my word."

"Good. You understand that the aristocracy mostly arranges marriages in the upper class."

"Yes, I most certainly do!"

"Well. I was late being married. No suitable fellow had presented by the time I was twenty-five, and my parents were worried, so they commenced a search for an advantageous match. Sir David came on the scene when I was twenty-seven, and we were married that year."

"Are you saying that you did not love him?"

"That is a difficult question, but he was the best option then, and my mother wanted me married. He offered a solid future, seemed competent in farming, and would inherit a title and a fine Estate." Lady Jane waved at the estate grounds surrounding them. "I was unaware of what I was taking on then, which was probably for the best. I will tell you about that some other time."

She became silent and stood there looking down the valley, hearing the happy cries of the children in the distance.

She smiled at Anne and continued, "Sir David tended to fancy women. I am sure Hugh inherited the same characteristic from his father. The difference was that Sir David kept it quiet, as did most other men in his class. He found someone he could safely stay with when in town on business. Usually, it involved an upper-class lady of the night."

Anne was unsettled and felt she had heard enough, "Lady Jane, there is no need. I have heard enough. I am…."

"There is Anne. There is every reason, as this woman is most dangerous. She has knowledge that could destroy this family, and we must be most cautious. Let me continue, please."

Anne was surprised by the outburst and remained quiet, nodding in agreement.

"I was not aware at first, but over time, mixing with the other wives in our class, little slips of the tongue alerted me that Sir David had other interests. By the time Robert was two, I was fully aware and most disillusioned. The problem was that I was lonely and needed love. There was no problem with our physical union as he was always keen on that. I knew he would be with her each time he was away."

She stopped and looked for a pump. The water poured out as she moved the pump handle up and down. She washed her hands and then sipped the water.

"That is better. I find my throat dries out with too much talking. I do not often have the opportunity these days of intelligent conversation." She smiled and continued. "There was another man of our class, a close friend of David with a similar-sized estate. Sometimes, he would stay over. Unfortunately, he did not have a happy marriage, and with David away, the opportunity arose one night, and we made love. It was only once and never happened again. We both felt guilty afterwards and agreed that our mistake would remain a secret. But somehow, David found out.

It was difficult as he threatened me with a divorce and would have thrown me out. When I made him aware that I knew of his affairs, he was beside himself, took me that night, and had his pleasure with me. He apologised in the morning, but the damage was done. To be short and not delay you too long - we agreed that we would never raise the subject again, and he would end his relationship in Portsmouth.

For a man of means, casting a woman aside is relatively easy. He put in place specific financial arrangements, and the woman willingly agreed with the conditions. The problem was that there were two babies conceived at that time. The first was Emma, and the second was a boy in Portsmouth."

Anne breathed in deeply, in shock.

"You mean Emma is not Sir David's daughter?"

With tears running down her face, Lady Jane said, "I don't know, Anne! The timing was right, and either might have been the father. Their physical attributes are similar, so it is impossible to tell. I may never know, but I know one thing: Emma is my daughter. I will never allow the destruction of my relationship with her."

She pulled out a handkerchief and started sobbing. Anne moved over and embraced her mother-in-law and comforted her. After some minutes, Lady Jane regained her countenance.

"I made one simple mistake and have lived under that curse ever since. David sits in his garden smelling his roses and has no care in the world. Men create the problem, and women must pick up the pieces."

Anne could see the resentment that Lady Jayne held for her husband but marvelled at the considerate way in which she treated him.

"How is it then that your marriage appears so committed and loving?"

"Anne, in this life, there will be events that you must set aside and then make the best of what you have. After Sir David and I made our agreement, we never raised the issue again. It was as if nothing had ever happened. When I received the attorney's letter, I knew this woman could publicly reveal the most sensitive details of my life. I could not bear that. Somehow, we must appease this lady and let sleeping dogs lie. Emma must never know of this! It would destroy her. I will not let that happen. I cannot!"

Anne held Lady Jane's hands and said, "Your secret is safe with me, Mother."

Lady Jane began crying again and hugged Anne hard. They stood there together for a long time, watching out over the fields and gaining comfort from the happy shouts and screams of the children.

Turner Household, Guildford …

On Thursday afternoon, a coach pulled up outside carrying Jonathan Turner. As he surveyed the house, it seemed strangely quiet. He did not expect a welcoming committee as he arrived a few days early. However, he did expect the boys on the porch, or some windows open above.

Climbing the stairs onto the entrance, he tried the door and found it locked. The footman from the coach brought his bags up, and he was ready for an afternoon cup of tea. Sighing, he gave a loud knock and continued waiting. There was no answer, and he wondered why not. Becoming impatient, he decided to try the back door. The front door opened as he was halfway down the steps, and Jess, the scullery maid, peered out.

"Mr Turner, please wait! Welcome back, Sir!"

"Thank you, Jess. Your friendly face is welcome. Where is the family?"

"They are upstairs. Mr Petherton and Clare are here visiting Clementine. Ethel and Aggie are also there, as Nany Smithers needed a few hours off. Aggie is looking after Jeremy. He has grown since you were here, sir!"

Jonathan smiled, "I am glad he is flourishing. Tell me, why are they upstairs and not in the drawing room?"

"Clementine tripped over William and broke two bones in her shoulder. Doctor Bassington has plastered her shoulder, but she remains in her bedroom. She is recovering well."

"William!"

"I believe it was an unfortunate accident, Sir. How was your trip?"

"It was wonderful, Jess. I am a new man, and now I must see the family."

"Do not worry about the bags, Sir. I will take care of them."

"Thank you, Jess." Jonathan took off his coat and hung it near the door. He slowly climbed the stairs and found Ethel emerging from Clemmie's room with Jeremy in her arms. She was laughing and hugging the baby. The picture entranced Jonathan.

"Why, Mr Turner, welcome back. We did not expect you until Sunday."

"Hamish gave me passage on one of his ships, and we had fair winds that brought me home quickly." Jonathan walked along and kissed Jeremy, then, putting a hand on Ethel's shoulders, kissed her on the cheek. "Thank you for your care of the children, Ethel."

Mrs Nibley was surprised by the warm welcome and smiled into his eyes. There was something different about this complex man who had been her employer for over a year. Standing near the half-open door, Benjamin Petherton had a good view of the hallway and noticed Jonathan kissing Ethel on the cheek.

Ethel blushed and asked, "Would you like a cup of tea, Mr Turner?"

"Now, that would be an ideal welcome home. But I must greet Clementine first. Is Marcia in there?"

"Yes, she will be so happy you are here. She expected you in a kilt."

Jonathan laughed, "Actually, I purchased a kilt for her. We shall have some fun at dinner when she opens her present."

"I will have Ivy prepare some tea and rolls and set them in the dining room. Mr Petherton and Clare are here visiting Clemmie, and I am sure he will welcome your company. He is the only man in the room!"

"Why Ivy? Why not Mrs Jennings?"

"Mrs Jennings has a heavy cold, and I asked that she remain in her room until she recovers. I prefer the children are safely separated from her as the cold is probably infectious. Mrs Jennings has trained Ivy well. She is now an excellent cook."

"I see."

Jonathan held out his arms towards Jeremy. Ethel held the baby close and said, "Perhaps a little later, Mr Turner. Jeremy has a dirty nappy, and I will change him now."

Quickly withdrawing his hands, Jonathan said, "Oh! Of course."

He then entered Clementine's room, "Hello, everyone!"

Ethel smiled as she heard Marcia squealing at the surprise of her father's return.

Fintelton Manor, Outside Petersfield, Sussex …

The sun finally set, and darkness swept across the valley, engulfing the landscape as it rushed on. Pike, descending the stairs, noticed a light on the western horizon slowly moving towards the manor. He realised it must be the candle lights from a coach and wondered who it could be. He was not aware of any further guests.

Descending the steps, he called two footmen, and they readied themselves for the arrival of the coach. As the twilight was nearly gone, the footmen lit several outside lanterns.

"They can see us coming, Horace! The lanterns are being lit. There will be a reception committee. I bet it will be Pike. He never misses a thing."

"Good! It will be a relief to escape this infernal coach. My shoulder is hurting like hell from all the movement. Peter's, you must carry my bags! I am sorry, but it will be all I can do mounting the steps."

"My pleasure, Major."

As the coach pulled up, Pike stepped forward and opened the door. Robert jumped out and hugged the butler. Pike never changed his expression as he partially welcomed the hug, stepped back, and said, "Welcome home, Sir Robert. I see you brought some friends. Lady Anne will be most surprised that you have arrived."

"Is Anne here? I thought she was in Guildford. This is wonderful." He sprinted off up the stairs.

Yelling from inside the coach, Horace demanded, "Peters and Pike, get me out of this infernal thing, please!"

Pike raised his eyebrows and hastily called the footmen.

Robert burst into the drawing room and found the Earl and Countess sitting beside the fire reading. He noticed that one of the verandah doors was only half shut.

Without saying a welcome, he pointed and said, "Anne!"

Lady Jane stood, and, with emotion in her voice, said. "Yes! Yes. Robert."

He was through the door in a second, and there, not ten yards from him, stood the most beautiful girl in the world, his wife, Anne. She turned, hearing someone and saw Robert walking towards her with his wide smile looking larger than life. As tears formed in her eyes, she ran and jumped into his arms, kissing him over and over again.

"I am home at last. "

"Thank the Lord!"

Turner Household, High Street, Guildford …

The dinner was most enjoyable, Bethany and Neville had returned home, and the children were in bed. Ethel said, "The staff have finished, and everything is done, Mr Turner. I will say goodnight."

"Ethel, if you would spare me a moment. I would value a few moments talking with you."

She entered the room hesitantly, uncertain of what Mr Turner required.

"Certainly, Sir."

"Please have a seat, Ethel. Here, in the chair beside me."

Ethel quietly sat down and waited for whatever was on his mind.

"Thank you again for your care of the children. I am sure the burden is somewhat lessened having four of them away at Fintelton?"

"It makes things slightly easier, Sir."

"Yes, it does."

Jonathan sat there as he thought through exactly what he would say. In a business situation, he would talk concisely and quickly. But Jonathan Turner knew this was far from business. This issue had troubled his mind for the last two weeks. Whatever he said must be clear and said with feeling.

"Ethel, I went away on the trip determined that I would overcome the loss for Eleanora. I remember you saying that time is a great healer. Your words proved correct, and time does help, yet I think we never forget a relationship even after it ends. I am sure you still have fond memories of your husband."

"Oh, yes, Sir! When he was first dead, I thought of him every day and lamented what I would do. But now, as you say, they are fond memories. I shall never lose them, but we must move on."

"Precisely! While away, I realised I would always hold fond memories of Eleanora. My grief and the need to hold her memories confused my thinking.

I understand now that she is gone and will never return. I must now build a new life – whatever that may be."

Ethel nodded in agreement.

"Yet, while I was away, there was this great longing in my heart, and I thought it was for Eleanora. I was lonely and sad. Despite being with most entertaining friends, I still felt melancholy."

"It is a common experience for those who have lost a partner."

"You will be interested in what I discovered. My melancholy came not from the loss of Eleanora but loneliness for you, Ethel. I missed you greatly. You have been there with me through this entire experience and have guided the children and me.

Nearly two weeks ago, I realised I had fallen in love with you. Since that day of realisation, I have longed for your company desperately. I love you dearly, Ethel."

Jonathan lowered himself off the chair, kneeled on one knee, took Ethel's hand, and asked, "Ethel Nibley, would you do me the honour of becoming my wife?"

The housekeeper sat there in astonishment, receiving a second proposal within three weeks. She looked into his eyes and was sure she could see genuine love. This proposal was different. Benjamin's proposal was more like a business arrangement, and the financial incentives had been most enticing.

In Jonathan's case, it was true romance, which Ethel felt was more important. Since Eleanora Turner's death, she had found another side of Jonathan Turner that was profoundly loving and an unswerving devotion to his family. The man was complex, overcoming his behaviour problems and could achieve more change with her help. This proposal was genuine and from a man who cherished her as a person. But could she trust him, given his past?

Then she thought of Benjamin. She had accepted him, giving the man great pleasure. He had already confided in her, showing his trust in her integrity. But that was not what she wanted. She wanted a lover, and she could hear the love in his voice.

The tears started as she gazed lovingly into his eyes. She struggled with her voice, "Oh, Jonathan, I would give anything to marry you. I would accept, but I received a proposal from Benjamin Petherton while you were away. I accepted him as I thought you had no feelings for me. What can I do, Jonathan?"

She fell into his arms and kissed him passionately. He found himself loving her more and more as they embraced. He became aroused as he smelt her familiar scent and soft touch. Her lips on his were like sparkling honey, and he wanted all of her now, yet he knew he must control himself, or he might lose everything.

As she drew back, tears running down her face, he quietly whispered, "We will find a way through this, Ethel. We will find a way."

Jonathan looked aside and thought he saw William's little face peering from the bottom of the stairs. He said, "Oh, no! William is watching."

Ethel said, "No, Jonathan! It is Marcia. William is at Fintelton."

Jonathan rubbed his eyes and peered again.

Ethel softly said, "I will handle it, Jonathan. You go and check the mail in your study. Leave Marcia with me. We will talk again in the morning."

Jonathan left and Ethel walked across and sat beside Marcia on the step.

"Why were you down here, little one, when you should have been in bed?"

"I wanted to say goodnight, so I came down and could not find you in your room. I was lonely."

Ethel gave Marcia a long hug, "Now we are both better. It is time for bed. Have you said your prayers?"

"Yes! Ethel, why were you kissing Father?"

"Your father was lonely, too. He needed a kiss goodnight. I think he is happier now."

Marcia thought about that and said, "Oh! Marcia would be happier with a kiss."

"Goodnight, Marcia."

Ethel kissed her on the cheek, and she returned the kiss. Then she ran away up the stairs, giggling.

Ethel sat on the step for some time, thinking about the situation that had now developed. How would this be resolved?

In his study, Jonathan picked up a letter from his brother Richard. He opened the envelope and read:

'Ewell Station'
Rathbury Road
Via Grahamstown
Eastern Cape Province
South Africa

Mr Jonathan Turner
High Street
Guildford, Surrey
England

Dear Jonathan

We have arrived in Grahamstown and settled on our land some five miles out in the country. Sarah already longs for home, but that probably is because we have not built the house yet, and the neighbours live quite a distance away. The house materials are en route from Port Elizabeth, and I expect the house to be built by the end of the year.

I am encouraged by how the sheep and cattle graze happily on the land. Hiring shepherds from the local tribespeople is complex because of the languages. The native people seem friendly, and they are keen to work. Their willingness gives me great confidence in the success of this project.

Grahamstown is small and has very few inhabitants. The farmers here are primarily ex-soldiers with no idea of farming. They grow crops in soil that is only suitable for grazing. I am unsure, but the rainfall will be light, so water is scarce. The riverbed beside my land is dry most of the year, but I am told the summer rains are plentiful. There is an urgent need for a dam. I will hire many natives for the job and have it done before the rainy season. The local farmers advised me that there is an underground water table, which should see us through the winter.

My life is busy with so much manual work. The boys would have loved this adventure, but they should watch over our assets in England. I will employ more of the natives for the many jobs around the station.

Would you please pass on my regards to Katherine and your children? Sarah asks if you have married again. She is keen on news from home. Katherine often writes and says she has settled in well. Thank you for taking her in. We are glad she has been safely deposited with your family at Guildford.

I must go now, as much is still awaiting my attention today!

Your brother
Richard Turner

Jonathan set aside the letter. He was still fuming at the thought of William's disturbing influence on the family. The boy was a continual nuisance. As soon as he returned, there was the news of William tripping Clemmie and causing her much harm. Then, his mistake of thinking William was there disturbing his conversation with Ethel. He had not been home a day before the irritation had grown again.

He sat back and examined his feelings. Remembering a proverb that advised 'not to act in haste,' he considered his motivations. The rage was still there, but he found he could control it. The problem was not with William; it was with himself. He had restrained himself from lashing out, thank goodness. Marcia would have been terrified. But what if he had lashed out at William? The child would be afraid of him forever.

The question for Jonathan was how he would solve this problem. Jonathan was afraid if there was no space between them and William, he might lose control, lash out and seriously injure the child Jonathan must protect his son from himself. He decided once and for all that he should act on his proposed solution.

He pulled out paper, quill and ink bottle and scribbled a reply to Richard.

High Street
Guildford, England

Mr Richard Turner
'Ewell Station'
Rathbury Road
Via Grahamstown
Eastern Cape Province
South Africa

April 1827

Dear Richard

Thank you for your letter and all the news you sent. I am glad you are progressing well, and I pray your labour will result in great earnings. I shudder when you talk about the natives. It makes me think of the darkest Africa and the many dangers that may occur there.

Katherine is with Madeline, Simeon, and William at Fintelton, where the estate manager instructs them on horse riding. Anne has been kind and taken them there for the week from Easter. I would be interested in learning how you celebrate Easter in Africa. I am sure there must be missionaries near Grahamstown and perhaps some clergy.

I spent the last month with Hamish McPherson in Scotland. The highlands are a vast place. I found it a raw, untouched wilderness with its own beauty. During my vacation, I contemplated my future. Tell Sarah her suggestions remain with me, and I will consider marrying again. The difficulty will be finding someone who will put up with me.

I have long considered my relationship with William. My vacation with Hamish gave me several opportunities to ponder upon our relationship. I now realise that the problem is not William's but mine. Yet, I am unsure if I can overcome this rage that still haunts me, and I must protect him. I am sure he and I would benefit from spending time with you in Africa. I will dispatch William by ship in our spring next year and your autumn. An experienced lady will accompany him and remain with him until they reach your station. By then, he will be eight, and I am sure he will enjoy the experience of working with you.

I will write nearer the time to advise you of the arrangements. Be assured you will remain in my prayers.

Your loving brother
Jonathan Turner

www.ingramcontent.com/pod-product-compliance
Lightning Source LLC
Chambersburg PA
CBHW020243030726

47499CB00001B/35